CHARLES DICKENS

SKETCHES BY BOZ

Edited with an introduction and notes by
DENNIS WALDER

and original illustrations by
GEORGE CRUIKSHANK

PENGUIN BOOKS

PENGUIN BOOKS

Published by the Penguin Group
Penguin Books Ltd, 80 Strand, London, WC2R 0RL, England
Penguin Books USA Inc., 375 Hudson Street, New York, New York 10014, USA
Penguin Books Australia Ltd, Ringwood, Victoria, Australia
Penguin Books Canada Ltd, 10 Alcorn Avenue, Toronto, Ontario, Canada M4V 3B2
Penguin Books (NZ) Ltd, 182–190 Wairau Road, Auckland 10, New Zealand

Penguin Books Ltd, Registered Offices: 80 Strand, London, WC2R 0RL, England

First published 1839
Published in Penguin Classics 1995
16

Introduction and Notes copyright © Dennis Walder, 1995
A Dickens Chronology copyright © Stephen Wall, 1995
All rights reserved

The moral right of the editor has been asserted

Set in 11/12.5 pt Monotype Fournier
Typeset by Datix International Limited, Bungay, Suffolk
Printed by CIP Antony Rowe Ltd, Chippenham, Wiltshire

ISBN 978-0-14-043345-6

CONTENTS

LIST OF ILLUSTRATIONS

Sketches by Boz was the first of Dickens's published books. The first of his novels was, of course, *Pickwick Papers*, which appeared in monthly instalments between April 1836 and November 1837. But it was the impression made by the short essays and stories that had been appearing in newspapers and magazines since December 1833 that led the publishers of *Pickwick* to approach Dickens. And even before they made their offer there had appeared, in two volumes, *Sketches by 'Boz', Illustrative of Every-day Life and Every-day People*, published by John Macrone on 8 February 1836. This was a substantial selection of Dickens's previously published pieces (with three new items), later known as the First Series. Its reception was everything the 24-year-old newspaper reporter could have wished – a reaction summed up by the *Examiner*, a radical weekly whose reviewer noted that 'a second perusal' of these sketches 'strengthened the favourable impression' already made of a new field of imaginative literature being opened up, focusing on urban and suburban London.[1] As far afield as America, where the book appeared in a pirated edition as *Watkins Tottle, and Other Sketches*, the arrival of a unique literary phenomenon with 'lofty powers' was registered by Edgar Allan Poe.[2] To the reading public of 1836, Dickens's *Sketches* were of much more significance than the early numbers of *Pickwick*, which was in any case classified as a magazine rather than a novel by its first reviewers. To the author, the *Sketches* carried 'all his hopes of future fame, and all his chances of future success' (see Dickens's Preface to the First Edition of the First Series, p. 7).

1. *Examiner* (28 February 1836), pp. 132–3.
2. *Southern Literary Messenger*, vol. 2 (June 1836), reprinted in *Edgar Allan Poe: Essays and Reviews* (New York: Library of America, 1984), pp. 204–7; and see Walter Dexter's survey of the book's reception in the *Dickensian*, vol. 32 (Winter 1935–6), pp. 43–50; (Summer 1936), pp. 193–5.

Nevertheless, when a second edition of the *Sketches* was published, only six months after the first, it was already being overshadowed by the monthly numbers of *Pickwick*. The appearance of the all-knowing Cockney Sam Weller in the fourth number of *Pickwick*, in July 1836, signalled the take-off of Dickens's gigantic career as a novelist. Even the appearance within the year of a Second Series of sketches and tales, while confirming public interest in the *Sketches*, failed to capture the extraordinary attention that had by then switched to the adventures of Mr Pickwick and his faithful servant – sales of the monthly instalments had by then increased forty times, to over 20,000. So it is perhaps not surprising that critics and publishers alike have since then tended to overlook the importance of *Sketches by Boz*, which for too long has been one of the least known, reprinted or appreciated works in the Dickens canon.

Dickens himself did not help. Most editions of *Sketches by Boz* reprint the Preface he added for the Cheap Edition of 1850. There, from the dizzy heights of thirty-eight, he observed that the sketches were written and published when 'I was a very young man', they were 'collected and re-published while I was still a very young man; and sent into the world with all their imperfections (a good many) on their heads'. They comprised, he added, his 'first attempts at authorship – with the exception of certain tragedies achieved at the mature age of eight or ten, and represented with great applause to overflowing nurseries'. As if that were not enough (the Preface is reprinted below, p. 11), he went on to describe the sketches as 'crude and ill-considered, and bearing obvious marks of haste and inexperience', which he had done little to correct, 'beyond a few words and phrases here and there'.

This is far from the truth. Not surprisingly, some crudeness and inexperience may be observed in Dickens's writings in their initial, journalistic form. But, as Kathleen Tillotson was the first to show, when Dickens collected his various pieces together for the First Series of 1836, he 'made extensive cuts, rewrote whole paragraphs, and made innumerable minute changes both of substance and style'; and he 'continued to revise in successive editions including the very one for which this Preface was written'.[3] The 'most minute and careful revision'[4] was applied to the edition I have chosen as the basis of this text, the 1839 edition, and the first combined edition of all the sketches. I call it the 1839 edition, yet it was in fact first published in monthly parts from November 1837 to June 1839, to cash in on the unprecedented success of the monthly parts of *Pickwick Papers*, before coming out (unrevised) as a single volume, uniform with *Pickwick*, in May 1839. By then Dickens was an established author, with a sense of his position and his relationship to his audience; and it was then that he decided to reorganize all fifty-six items into four clear groups with a fairly consistent logic, moving from personal memory and observation towards an increasingly fictive narrative – that is to say, from Seven Sketches from Our Parish (shortened to Our Parish in references below and in the Notes) Scenes and Characters, to the Tales; a structure kept for all later editions.

By then, too, Dickens had the advice of his close friend and confidant John Forster to rely on. Forster wrote that early commendation in the *Examiner*, and over thirty years later offered, in his biography of Dickens, the most informed and judicious account of the importance of *Sketches by Boz* in its time.

The *Sketches* were much more talked about than the first two or three numbers of *Pickwick* . . . Richly did it merit all the praise it had, and more, I will add, than he was ever disposed to give it himself. He decidedly underrated it. He gave, in subsequent writings, so much more perfect form and fullness to everything it contained, that he did not care to credit himself with the marvel of having yet so early anticipated so much. But the first sprightly runnings of his genius are undoubtedly here. Mr Bumble is in the parish sketches, and Mr Dawkins the dodger in the Old-bailey scenes. There is laughter and fun to excess, never misapplied; there are the minute points and shades of character, with all the discrimination and nicety of detail, afterwards so famous; there is everywhere the most perfect ease and skill of handling. The observation shown throughout is nothing short of

3. In John Butt and Kathleen Tillotson, *Dickens at Work* (London: Methuen, 1957; reissued 1968), p. 39.
4. Ibid., p. 56.

wonderful. Things are painted literally as they are; and, whatever the picture, whether of every-day vulgar, shabby genteel, or downright low, with neither the condescending air which is affectation, nor the too familiar one which is slang . . . Of course there are inequalities in it, and some things that would have been better away: but it is a book that might have stood its ground, even if it had stood alone, as containing unusually truthful observation of a sort of life between the middle class and the low, which, having few attractions for bookish observers, was quite unhacknied ground . . . It was a picture of every-day London at its best and worst . . .[5]

The 'first sprightly runnings' of Dickens's 'genius' are certainly apparent in the *Sketches*. There is, as Forster noticed, the pompous beadle of Our Parish, who surveys the urchins in church 'with a glare of the eye peculiar to beadles ('The Beadle', p. 18). And there is the anonymous young boy who appears before the Court: '*Court*: Have you any witnesses to speak to your character, boy? *Boy*: Yes, my Lord; fifteen gen'lm'n is a vaten outside, and vos a vaten all day yesterday, vich they told me the night afore my trial vos a comin' on' ('Criminal Courts', p. 233). But it is not only the Artful Dodger who is foreshadowed – there is that 'stout, broad-shouldered, sturdy-chested man' in Monmouth Street, who 'seldom walked forth without a dog at his heels' – unmistakable as an early version of Bill Sikes, whose girlfriend Nancy is anticipated in the beaten young woman who refuses to testify against her 'powerful, ill-looking young fellow' in 'The Hospital Patient' (p. 279).

It is not too surprising to find anticipations of *Oliver Twist* among the *Sketches*, since Dickens probably had that novel in mind well before he actually began to write it, which was before he had finished *Pickwick*.[6] But many hints and suggestions of characters, motifs and novels to come in the longer perspective of his career are

5. John Forster, *The Life of Charles Dickens*, ed. and intro. J.W.T. Ley (London: Cecil Palmer, 1928), pp. 76–7.

6. See *The Letters of Charles Dickens*, eds. Madeline House and Graham Storey, the Pilgrim Edition (Oxford: Clarendon Press, 1965–?), vol. 1, pp. 33–4. Kathleen Tillotson was the first to argue on the basis of this and other evidence that Dickens already had *Oliver Twist* in mind in 1833: see *Essays and Studies*, New Series, vol. 12 (1959), pp. 88–90.

INTRODUCTION

already there. As A.W. Ward observed shortly after Dickens's death: 'Even before *Pickwick* was written, the *Sketches by Boz* had shown that the life of our middle and lower classes, and more especially the middle and lower classes of that great city where it displays itself in the most multitudinous variety, of London, was the chosen sphere for his inimitably faithful observation and inimitably faithful reproduction.'[7] A mere glance at the headings of the chapters reminds us of how much Dickens went on to write about: London streets, pawnshops, theatres, shows, inns, coaching, law courts, prisons and the river Thames. The satirical portraits of politicians, the animus against religious excesses, the pathos of debt and imprisonment, the laughter to be drawn from snobbery – all, and more, indicate the prophetic quality of this book. It is as if Dickens were laying out his territory before starting on those deeper operations that were to bring to the world the mature offerings of his genius. The sheer range and variety of tone are astonishing: from the sudden deepening of his prose as we enter into the mind of the man in the condemned cell – 'The feeble light is wasting gradually, and the deathlike stillness of the street without, broken only by the rumbling of some passing vehicle which echoes mournfully through the empty yards, warns him that the night is waning fast away' ('A Visit to Newgate', p. 247); to the characteristic fun of the 'carnivorous' Mrs Bloss, in quest of rooms at Mrs Tibbs's boarding-house:

'Money isn't no object whatever to me,' said the *lady*, 'so much as living in a state of retirement and obtrusion.'

Mrs Tibbs, as a matter of course, acquiesced in such an exceedingly natural desire.

'I am constantly attended by a medical man,' resumed the pelisse wearer; 'I have been a shocking unitarian for some time – I, indeed, have had very little peace since the death of Mr Bloss.'

Mrs Tibbs looked at the relict of the departed Bloss, and thought he must have had very little peace in his time. ('The Boarding-house', p. 341)

---

7. A.W. Ward, *Charles Dickens: A Lecture* (1870), reprinted in *Dickens: The Critical Heritage*, ed. Philip Collins (London: Routledge & Kegan Paul, 1971), pp. 537–41 (p. 539).

Mrs Nickleby, Mrs Gamp, Flora Finching and other deluded, voluble matrons continue this line of humour – based in part, no doubt, on Dickens's exploitation of the stock comic figure of women like Fielding's Mrs Slipslop or Sheridan's Mrs Malaprop – but a figure who, when she exerts power,-like Mrs Joe Gargery in *Great Expectations*, has to be brought down.

Men are also, if not equally, subject to the satiric vision of the *Sketches*, from the young clerks who 'exhibit their lamentable ignorance and boobyism' in the 'Private Theatres' of the metropolis (p. 145), to the repressed and often misanthropic, Scrooge-like bachelors such as Nicodemus Dumps or Watkins Tottle, whose limitations are almost savagely exposed, and who remind us of one of Dickens's favourite devices: exploiting the sound and shape of names to suggest, if not subvert, a character or institution – Gobler, Bung, Kitterbell, Wisbottle, Minns, Sludberry, Tuggs – the stream of comic invention seems endless; including the redoubtable Mrs Johnson Parker, president of the ladies' bible and prayer-book distribution society, who imports from Exeter Hall (the Strand meeting-house whose Evangelical endeavours Dickens was to attack time and again) a 'celebrated orator . . . (an Irishman)', to outface the other benevolent old ladies in the parish, by making a speech on 'green isles – other shores – vast Atlantic – bosom of the deep – Christian charity – blood and extermination – mercy in hearts . . . He wiped his eyes, he blew his nose, and he quoted Latin. The effect was tremendous – the Latin was a decided hit' ('The Ladies' Societies', p. 57). Overseas missions and their supporters were always anathema to Dickens: even the recent abolition of slavery throughout the Empire, to which 'The Parlour Orator' enthusiastically refers, is questioned: by the 'little greengrocer' who remarks that he at least had 'got no good out of the twenty million that was paid' by the British taxpayer in compensation to the slave-owners (p. 275).

Dickens was not alone in criticizing those who seemed more sensitive to the condition of black slaves abroad than to the condition of the poor at home – many of whom in London were in fact former slaves. The Empire is accepted as a fact throughout; the

place for a 'fine, handsome fellow' to go to after breaking the heart
of his old mother ('The Old Lady', p. 27); or for a violent,
thieving omnibus cad to spend a term of seven years, 'like another
Cincinnatus, in clearing and cultivating the soil' ('The First Omnibus Cad', p. 178). Dickens's position is closest to that of the
newspaper that employed him from 1834 to 1836, and for which
many of these sketches were written, the *Morning Chronicle* − that
is to say, reformist-radical. Like Thomas Carlyle, Dickens's thinking was profoundly affected by the social and political upheavals
that marked the period immediately preceding Victoria's arrival on
the throne. Legislators and commentators alike were struggling to
come to terms with the problems caused by rapid industrialization,
one result of which was the First Reform Bill of 1832, which
Dickens as a parliamentary reporter witnessed going through the
Commons. This was the most striking of the sequence of reforms
achieved in the 1830s, including legislation to improve religious
toleration, the police, local government − and provision for the
poor. When the Liberal politician Sir John Easthope took over the
Morning Chronicle early in 1834 it became a mouthpiece for reform.

Where Dickens parted from the reformers was in relation to
such Benthamite measures as the New Poor Law of 1834, which
was to become the permanent object of his disapproval; and, as the
'parochial convulsion' in Chapter 4 of Our Parish ('The Election
for Beadle') amusingly demonstrates, he was already unimpressed
by politicians of any stripe. Further anticipation of his attitude to
parliamentarians is provided by 'A Parliamentary Sketch', a sketch
replete with topical portraits and allusions, many of which would
have been libellous today, since the originals of the characters −
even after extensive revision between its first appearance in the
Evening Chronicle in 1835 and book publication − could not fail to
have recognized themselves. Sir Andrew Agnew, for example,
referred to here as the 'Lord's-Day-Bill Baronet', whose several
attempts to introduce a bill for the Better Observance of Sunday
became in June 1836 the subject of an even more explicit attack by
Dickens, under the pseudonym 'Timothy Sparks', in *Sunday under
Three Heads*, a pamphlet published by Chapman and Hall, with

illustrations by Cruikshank. This anti-sabbatarianism became a permanent feature of Dickens's work, an aspect of his complex relationship with contemporary puritan views on society and morals.

But if it is striking how much of the future Dickens is anticipated in the *Sketches*, we should also consider it on its own terms, in so far as that is possible. Was it, or is it, 'a book', as Forster said, 'that might have stood its ground, even if it had stood alone'? The terms on which Forster's judgement was based – 'Things are painted literally as they are' – were the terms of what is now a familiar realist aesthetic, which at the time was just emerging (coinciding with the invention of photography). It is sometimes easy to forget, after the great achievements of realist fiction of the Victorian era – the achievements of Thackeray, Trollope, George Eliot and Elizabeth Gaskell – how uncertain or unstable the novel genre was still in the 1830s, and how much the impact of Dickens's early work contributed towards the establishment of realist criteria as the norm. To many, the death of Scott in 1832 seemed to signal the end of an era as far as serious fiction in English was concerned, and nobody appeared to replace him. Instead, as Bulwer Lytton remarked in *England and the English* (1833), literary production was in a state of transition, in which 'novels of all sorts' rather than 'as in former times, the great novel alone', were being read. There was a profusion of sub-genres, including 'silver-fork', social-problem, Irish, marine, Newgate and historical novels (the latter a genre Lytton himself helped popularize). The 'great literary works' of the time, according to Lytton, were to be found 'not in detached and avowed and standard publications, but in periodical miscellanies'. He had in mind the writings of Hazlitt, Lamb and Leigh Hunt, who had been inspired by their eighteenth-century predecessors, Defoe, Goldsmith, Addison and Steele, to open up a new field of literary endeavour, and, he said, to give weight to periodical publication.[8]

8. Edward Lytton Bulwer, *England and the English*, ed. and intro. Standish Meacham (Chicago and London: University of Chicago Press, 1970), pp. 287, 261;

Certainly Dickens belonged to this tradition: not only was he familiar with the eighteenth-century essayists from childhood, but he went on to make one particular form of earlier publication – the novel in monthly parts – the staple form of literary production for his career as a novelist. The name 'Tibbs', which he used for the husband and wife of 'The Boarding House', and then borrowed as a pseudonym for some of the sketches, came from Goldsmith's essays; and 'Boz' itself was 'the nickname of a pet child, a younger brother, whom I had dubbed Moses, in honour of the Vicar of Wakefield; which being facetiously pronounced through the nose, became Boses, and being shortened, became Boz'.[9] But 'Boz' quickly became identified with a kind of writing that went beyond the eighteenth-century essayists like Goldsmith and Romantic successors like Leigh Hunt in range and variety of style and subject. In particular, it was his penetration of the metropolitan milieu, his startling ability 'to excite our sympathy in behalf of the aggrieved and suffering in all classes; and especially in those who are most removed from observation',[10] that led the more percipient to recognize in his form of realism a new and lasting vision, born of the disturbed times they were living through, and contributing a unique insight to the modern world.

As Walter Bagehot once remarked, Dickens wrote about London 'like a special correspondent for posterity'.[11] It is not only in the centrality of London as the subject of the *Sketches* that the book's singular strength lies, but in the way it bears witness to the everyday experience of the largest concentration of newly

---

see also J.S. Mill, 'Civilization', *Westminster Review* (April 1836): 'literature is becoming more and more ephemeral: books, of any solidity, are almost gone by . . .', reprinted in *Mill's Essays on Literature and Society*, ed. and intro. J.B. Schneewind (New York and London: Collier-Macmillan, 1965), p. 168.

9. Preface to the Cheap Edition (1847), *Pickwick Papers*, ed. and intro. Robert Patten (Harmondsworth, Middlesex: Penguin, 1972), p. 45.

10. [Thomas Lister] *'Sketches* (First and Second Series) . . .', *Edinburgh Review*, vol. 68 (October 1838), reprinted in Collins (1971), pp. 71–7 (p. 73).

11. [Walter Bagehot] 'Charles Dickens', *National Review*, vol. 7 (October 1858), reprinted in Collins (1971), pp. 390–401 (p. 394).

urbanized people in the world. The London 'sketch' or anecdote was not entirely new, as the writings of Pierce Egan, John Poole, Theodore Hook and Thomas Hood at the time testify; but nobody approached the startling accuracy and wealth of detail, much less the mix of humour and pathos, with which the everyday life and language of ordinary people in the city, from shop assistants to omnibus cads, from debt-collectors to bank clerks, was here displayed. I have already referred to one of the most celebrated of the sketches, 'A Visit to Newgate', written specially to conclude the First Series volume: in it, the narrator remarks how many 'pass and repass this gloomy depository of the guilt and misery of London ... unmindful of the throng of wretched creatures pent up within it' (p. 234), before he goes on to reveal the lives of those 'wretched creatures', finally leading up to the powerful rendering of the mind of the condemned man. Similarly motivated is the sketch of 'Shabby-genteel People' who appear to Boz 'as purely local as the statue at Charing-cross, or the pump at Aldgate' (p. 304), and are then individualized as the man who 'once haunted' him after first attracting attention in the reading room of the British Museum, and whose fortunes he observes to decline and revive with his clothes – 'Whether our readers have noticed these men in their walks as often as we have, we know not; this we know – that the miserably poor man ... who feels his poverty and vainly strives to conceal it, is one of the most pitiable objects in human nature' (p. 307).

Yet it is in moments less overtly directed at extending the reader's sympathies that the *Sketches* most persuasively register the unseen or unknown life of the metropolis – from the poor governess 'stuck behind the pillar' to allow her small charges to see the show at Astley's Equestrian Amphitheatre (p. 130), to the old pensioners in Greenwich Park 'who, for the moderate charge of a penny, exhibit the mast-house, the Thames and shipping, the place where the men used to hang in chains, and other interesting sights, through a telescope' (p. 139). It is in these repeated, fragmentary glimpses of things witnessed in passing that the obscure life of the metropolis is most tellingly suggested: things which, as contemporary reviewers put it, everyone had seen, but nobody had consciously noted.[12] When the young law student Percy Noakes sallies forth at 5 a.m. to organize 'The Steam Excursion' on the river, he passes a 'street breakfast' at the corner of a by-street near Temple Bar:

The coffee was boiling over a charcoal fire, and large slices of bread and butter were piled one upon the other, like deals in a timber-yard. The company were seated on a form, which, with a view both to security and comfort, was placed against a neighbouring wall. Two young men, whose uproarious mirth and disordered dress bespoke the conviviality of the preceding evening, were treating three 'ladies' and an Irish labourer. A little sweep was standing at a short distance, casting a longing eye at the tempting delicacies; and a policeman was watching the group from the opposite side of the street. The wan looks, and gaudy finery of the wretched thinly-clad females, contrasted as strangely with the gay sunlight, as did their forced merriment with the boisterous hilarity of the two young men, who now and then varied their amusements by 'bonneting' the proprietor of this itinerant coffee-house. (pp. 447–8)

Noakes walks briskly on, we're told; but this image of the street-life of the city, caught with humour and precision, remains; an indelible instance of Dickens's observation as a youthful Londoner – he was a young lawyer's clerk himself – but who here observes the passing scene with that depth of understanding which typifies the best sketches. He misses nothing: neither the drunken aggression of the young men towards their 'thinly-clad' prostitutes, nor the longing eye of the 'little sweep', nor the watchful policeman. In the close-packed metropolis everyone is watching everyone else; as if on some level trying to work out who they are, what they are up to – in short, to make sense of its unprecedentedly large, growing and various population.

London had doubled in size since 1800, to over one and a half million people, and it grew by a million more by the mid century, when the railways running to and from the city made it ever more

---

12. For example, see *Chambers's Edinburgh Journal*, vol. 5 (9 April 1836).

accessible.[13] Like so many others before and since, the young Dickens had first arrived from the provincial peace of an earlier age: as a ten-year-old alone in the Chatham coach, 'packed — like game — and forwarded, carriage paid, to the Cross Keys, Wood-street, Cheapside, London',[14] to join his family in their rented terrace house in Camden Town, then a recently developed, respectable suburb not yet fully part of the city. The image of himself arriving in London friendless and alone, at the mercy of those around him, helps us to understand the sympathetic power of his insight into the lives of the lonely and neglected; equally, however, the humorous detachment with which he views himself, and documents his direction in London, suggests his durability and appetite for experience — qualities that enabled him to observe his environment, and to survive blows such as his father's imprisonment for debt, and his spell as 'a common labouring hind' of twelve. This was at Warren's Blacking warehouse at Hungerford Stairs in the Strand, on the north bank of the river Thames, where he worked at sticking labels on jars. While employed at the warehouse, he began to develop an intimate and extensive knowledge of the people and places of London, especially, as Peter Ackroyd has noted, the area around Warren's — the Strand and Covent Garden, Blackfriars Bridge and the old London Bridge, but also the streets he walked to and from work between the house in Camden and the factory on the river, streets 'fitfully illuminated' by the new gas, and all sites that 'emerge again and again in his fiction. If there is such a thing as a landscape of the imagination,' Ackroyd adds, 'then it lies for Dickens within these few square miles of early nineteenth-century London'.[15]

13. For a useful account, see Donald J. Olson, *The Growth of Victorian London* (London: Batsford, 1976; Peregrine, 1979).

14. As recalled in the essay 'Dullborough Town' in 1860: reprinted in *The Uncommercial Traveller and Reprinted Pieces*, New Oxford Illustrated Dickens (London: Oxford University Press, 1968), p. 116.

15. Peter Ackroyd, *Dickens* (London: Minerva, 1991), pp. 58–9, 63, 93–4. Ackroyd's biography is by far the most detailed and evocative account available of this period in Dickens's life, although it is far from easy to follow his sources.

Dickens's knowledge of the expanding city was never quite that confined, and the far-flung suburbs of Norwood and Clapham in the south, Barnet and Hampstead in the north – villages yet, with tracts of open land or forest surrounding them – were a part of his subject, too, since they were reachable by coach and omnibus, if not by foot, from the centre. The three sketches on public transport ('Early Coaches', 'Omnibuses', 'The Last Cab-driver, and the First Omnibus Cad') are grouped together, and mark the introduction of new and faster modes of travel for ordinary people. But Dickens, as he presents himself here, is above all 'the speculative pedestrian' (p. 223), the metropolitan wanderer, and wonderer. 'We are very fond of speculating as we walk through a street, on the character and pursuits of the people who inhabit it,' the narrator remarks near the beginning of the book (p. 58); and in a passage in the periodical version of 'The Prisoners' Van', but cut from the collected *Sketches*, he says:

We have a most extraordinary partiality for lounging about the streets. Whenever we have an hour or two to spare, there is nothing we enjoy more than a little amateur vagrancy – walking up one street and down another, and staring into shop windows, and gazing about as if, instead of being on intimate terms with every shop and house in Holborn, the Strand, Fleet-street and Cheapside, the whole were an unknown region to our wandering mind.[16]

'We will be bold to say,' he opens the last chapter of the book, 'that there is scarcely a man in the constant habit of walking, day after day, through any of the crowded thoroughfares of London, who cannot recollect among the people whom he "knows by sight," to use a familiar phrase, some being of abject and wretched appearance whom he remembers to have seen in a very different condition . . .' (p. 554).

'Knowing by sight' suggests both the familiarity that Dickens calls on, and the way in which he 'speculates' or opens up what he

---

16. Cited in Butt and Tillotson (1968), p. 44, where it is suggested that the whole passage (considerably longer than this) was omitted for considerations of space.

sees. It is a quality of vision that renders the very visibility of the surface of everyday urban life its secret, since it is so various and evanescent. Dickens's point of view includes an awareness of the instability of people's lives, of the possibility that they, too, will succumb, as the Dickens family succumbed, to the pressures of debt or mischance. The door of the pawnbroker's shop 'stands always doubtfully, a little way open, half inviting, half repelling'; but for the 'speculative pedestrian' its ambivalences evaporate, and he enters to describe the scene within, including the customers and their conversations with the pawn clerks. The different classes seem as distinct as they are depicted in Cruikshank's illustration: there, on the left, is the 'old sallow-looking woman' with her bundles; the 'unshaven, dirty, sottish-looking fellow' who has come to redeem some tools, after 'kicking his wife up the court'; and the ragged urchin 'unable to bring his face on a level with the counter'; in the box on the right, there is the 'miserably poor but extremely gaudy' female whose appearance 'too plainly bespeaks her station' as a prostitute; between them, in the 'darkest and most obscure corner of the shop', there is the 'delicate', genteel young woman and her mother. 'Who shall say,' he asks, 'how soon these women may change places?' (p. 229) The faceless clerk's indifference to the answer is superbly caught by the artist's representation of his posture – a good example of what Cruikshank added to the impact and, as the publisher doubtless hoped, the saleability of the *Sketches*.

Yet the class insecurity that lies behind this sombre depiction of some of the people of the streets also provides some of the book's most entertaining comedy. The transitoriness of social position is forcefully suggested by showing how the pretensions of London's new suburbanites are punctured – the Maldertons of Oak Lodge, Camberwell, for instance, who search among the 'eligible bachelors of Camberwell, and even of Wandsworth and Brixton; to say nothing of those who "dropped in" from town', for a suitable match for their daughter; only to be caught out by the genteel airs of 'the junior partner in a slippery firm of some three weeks' existence' in Tottenham Court Road, whose imposture is finally exposed by one of those chance encounters which typify urban experience ('Horatio Sparkins', pp. 411, 425). A more whimsical, ironic tone plays over the London sweeps, whose sense of their own importance has grown to the degree that — 'Why, the master sweeps, influenced by a restless spirit of innovation,' have abandoned their traditional springtime celebrations of dancing in the street on May Day, 'and substituted a dinner — an anniversary dinner at White Conduit House — where clean faces appeared in lieu of black ones smeared with rose pink; and knee cords and tops, superseded nankeen drawers and rosetted shoes' ('The First of May', p. 205).

The metonymic substitution of the sweeps' faces and articles of clothing to express their changing status is a notable feature of the narrator's imagination in the *Sketches*. The book bristles with lists and catalogues of things seen — artefacts, clothes, vehicles, buildings, food, streets — which frequently take on a life of their own, as if they were independent of the observer, a life both surprising and grotesque. One of the best examples is a well-known passage in 'Meditations in Monmouth-street', which the critic J. Hillis Miller took as the basis of a brilliant deconstructive reading of the *Sketches*, referring *en passant* to Nietzsche, Heidegger, Derrida, Lacan and other policemen of the postmodern, to argue the fictive, self-referential, endlessly deferred play of meaning as the mode of existence of this work.[17] The passage is extraordinary, but it is debatable how far it supports his case. 'We love to walk among these extensive groves of the illustrious dead,' Boz begins in musing vein, as he peers in at a window full of second-hand clothes:

and to indulge in the speculations to which they give rise; now fitting a deceased coat, then a dead pair of trousers, and anon the mortal remains of a gaudy waistcoat, upon some being of our own conjuring up, and

17. J. Hillis Miller, 'The Fiction of Realism: *Sketches by Boz*, *Oliver Twist*, and Cruikshank's Illustrations', in *Charles Dickens and George Cruikshank*, ed. Ada B. Nisbet (Los Angeles: William Andrews Clark Memorial Library, University of California, 1971), p. 12.

endeavouring, from the shape and fashion of the garment itself, to bring its former owner before our mind's eye. We have gone on speculating in this way, until whole rows of coats have started from their pegs, and buttoned up, of their own accord, round the waists of imaginary wearers; lines of trousers have jumped down to meet them; waistcoats have almost burst with anxiety to put themselves on; and half an acre of shoes have suddenly found feet to fit them, and gone stumping down the street with a noise which has fairly awakened us from our pleasant revery, and driven us slowly away, with a bewildered stare, an object of astonishment to the good people of Monmouth-street, and of no slight suspicion to the policemen at the opposite street corner. (p. 98)

The reverie gives rise to an imaginary narrative, the tale of an idle apprentice who comes to no good, 'a story with many antecedents in eighteenth-century fiction, drama and graphic representation', as Miller points out. Hence, according to Miller, it can be understood that the fundamental motif of the *Sketches* does not after all reside in their representation of urban life, it is 'not "truth" but literary fiction, perhaps no more than a sentimental lie . . . The movement from Scene to Character to Tale is not the metonymic process authenticating realistic representation but a movement deeper and deeper into the conventional, the concocted, the schematic'.[18]

One's suspicion is of a critic moving deeper and deeper into the conventional, the concocted, the schematic. If, as I believe he does, Hillis Miller offers a healthy antidote against the naïve presumption of any direct correspondence between the language of the text and the world out there, his approach also drains the book of significance by turning it into any text circulating among other texts, all of them equally fictional and unhistorical. His interpretation of the *Sketches* depends upon the structure devised in 1837–9, when it made sense to place the most conventional or derivative pieces at the end. But there remains a central paradox: that in the *Sketches* the writer's imaginative fancy is often most persuasive when it is not attempting a consciously fictional tale, but when it is engaged with the surface of the city.

18. Ibid., pp. 31–2, 35.

What this suggests is not so much a postmodern perspective upon Dickens as the need for a more historically informed approach. If we ask, for example, who else but Dickens could have written that Monmouth Street passage, there start up a number of contemporary candidates – E.T.A. Hoffmann for one. The German Romantic fantasy-writing of the 1820s anticipated that visionary excess of metonymy that makes the everyday objects of the streets take on a life of their own in Dickens's writings. Hoffmann may be best known nowadays for the doll Coppelia who comes to life (in 'The Sandman'), but in 'The Golden Pot', for example, there is a door-knocker just like those in 'Our Next-door Neighbour', which express their owners' personalities (pp. 58–61). And the shoes that go noisily 'stumping down' Monmouth Street, driving away the observer whose reverie has supplied them with feet, bear a very close affinity with all those grotesquely animated everyday objects that feature in the Grimms' *German Popular Stories* (translated by Edgar Taylor, 1823; also illustrated by Cruikshank) – a copy of which Dickens owned, as he did Roscoe's four-volume collection *German Novelists* (1826), including work by Fouqué and Tieck, Hoffmann and the Grimms. Dickens could not read German, but this was no disqualification for reading these books and the many others that had been translated and made widely available. Their influence upon Dickens's Christmas Books is familiar, but the *Sketches* register a much earlier effect. While the *Morning Chronicle* was publishing some of the *Sketches*, there appeared on 18 December 1834 a clever little parody of Carové's *Das Märchen Ohne Ende* (*The Story without an End*, translated by Sarah Austin, 1833), under the title 'The Story without a Beginning', supposedly 'Translated from the German by Boz'. A topical satire upon the instability of government, in which Whigs and Tories are symbolized by bees and insects respectively, and 'burrows' refer to the 'rotten boroughs' that the Reform Bill swept away, the piece demonstrates Dickens's close knowledge of political events, his radicalism, and his interest in the generic mixing of the German romances.[19]

19. See my *Dickens and Religion* (London: Allen & Unwin, 1981), pp. 88–90;

So, although there is no question that the dominant mode of the *Sketches* lies towards the realist end of the fictional spectrum, as most contemporaries and many later readers have acknowledged, the contrary pull towards what was called 'fancy' involves more than merely the occasional, fanciful elaboration of style or verbal conceit, but a vision of a kind of reciprocal attraction between the human and the non-human. At the same time, if the loitering, 'vagrant' observer finds the boundary between the real and the unreal occasionally shifting and uncertain, this does not mean it is non-existent. This has moral overtones, too; as the Monmouth Street 'meditation' reveals when the narrator returns to himself, aware of being stared at, aware of the watching police, as if guilty about transgressing a certain borderline of order and social norms. It is this sense of the urban life of London becoming at once available for scrutiny, and yet remaining ultimately inscrutable, even threatening – its 'reality' escaping, only to haunt the observer, subject to the constraints of the everyday, and so unable ever fully to capture it – that not only characterizes the effect of such passages, but which also suggests how they offer a route to the modern urban imagination.

Walter Benjamin refers to the 'profane illumination' of the French surrealists, who transformed the great city of Paris by their vision of a 'world of things' seemingly unconnected, yet brought together 'by virtue of a dialectical optic that perceives the everyday as impenetrable, the impenetrable as everyday'. The 'loiterer, the *flaneur*', he says, is a type of 'illuminati' just as much as the opium taker. 'Not to mention that most terrible drug – ourselves – which we take in solitude.'[20] The solitude of many of the characters witnessed in the city of London, the many lonely, isolated figures

also W.J. Carlton, '"The Story without a Beginning": An Unrecorded Contribution by Boz to the *Morning Chronicle*', *Dickensian*, vol. 47 (Spring 1951), pp. 67–70; and Michael Hollington, *Dickens and the Grotesque* (London and Sydney: Croom Helm, 1984), pp. 17–25.

20. Walter Benjamin, 'Surrealism', in *One Way Street, and Other Writings*, intro. Susan Sontag (London: Verso, 1985), pp. 228–30, 237.

in the pages of the *Sketches*, the bitter widows and despairing bachelors, confirm this sense of modernity in the text's perception of urban life, running counter to the celebration of contemporary domesticity in set-pieces like 'A Christmas Dinner'; or at least implying how fragile and idealized those communal get-togethers are. It appears as more than merely a function of structural contrast – although some deliberate patterning of that kind was looked for in collecting the pieces together. After the shy and reserved bachelor Watkins Tottle learns he has completely misunderstood how the situation stands between himself and the preposterous Miss Lillerton, we are informed that:

the body of a gentleman unknown, was found in the Regent's canal. In the trousers-pockets were four shillings and threepence-halfpenny; a matrimonial advertisement from a lady, which appeared to have been cut out of a Sunday paper; a toothpick, and a card-case, which it is confidently believed would have led to the identification of the unfortunate gentleman, but for the circumstance of there being none but blank cards in it. ('Passage in the Life of Mr Watkins Tottle', p. 535)

Here is not the progressive heightening of effect typified by the second-hand clothes that become alive as they are observed; at such moments, Dickens's realism is more akin to surrealism, in that it offers both the kind of literal-minded reflection of urban reality that contemporaries noted, and the more modern apprehension of the strange, even grotesquely comic effect produced by cataloguing that reality.

A sense of estrangement, of alienation, leads to the self-destructive urge that hovers behind several characters. One of the more overtly moralistic Tales, and the last in the book, 'The Drunkard's Death', is a largely predictable account of the descent into isolation and despair of a drunkard whose misspent life destroys both family and fortune. But then he arrives at the river below Waterloo Bridge:

The tide was in, and the water flowed at his feet. The rain had ceased, the wind was lulled, and all was, for the moment, still and quiet – so quiet that the slightest sound on the opposite bank, even the rippling of the water against the barges that were moored there, was distinctly audible to his ear. The stream stole languidly and sluggishly on. Strange and fantastic forms rose to the surface, and beckoned him to approach; dark gleaming eyes peered from the water, and seemed to mock his hesitation, while hollow murmurs from behind, urged him onwards. He retreated a few paces, took a short run, desperate leap, and plunged into the river. (p. 565)

This suggests the writing of Gothic novelists like Mrs Radcliffe, and would draw on the contemporary popularity of the form, but Dickens distances himself from it elsewhere, for instance in 'Criminal Courts', where the revelations of conditions by a prison reformer such as Elizabeth Fry are invoked in preference to the kind of account offered in Radcliffe's novels (p. 230). One contemporary reviewer struggled revealingly to define the hallucinatory quality that makes the city in Dickens's early writings more than merely spectacle, that makes it at once absurd and threatening: this was George Henry Lewes. 'If asked by what peculiar talent is Boz characterized,' he remarked, 'we find ourselves at a dead fault'; and went on to propose that it was precisely the singular blend of different literary modes that brought Dickens his 'surprising popularity' with 'all classes' from the moment of the *Sketches*' appearance onwards.[21]

That popularity was perhaps less inspired by the sombre scenes that call on the reader's feelings of compassion towards the lonely and unhappy than by the abiding awareness of incongruity, which not only rescues the dullest or least fashionable Londoner from obscurity, but promotes a sympathetic enjoyment of their aspirations as well as failings. There is the pathetically credulous Mr Kitterbell, for instance, who 'looked like a faded giant, with the head and face partially restored' – a comparison that simultaneously brings the character before us with comically arresting, indeed grotesque clarity (and alludes in passing to Mary Shelley's *Frankenstein*),

21. '*Sketches, Pickwick, Oliver Twist . . .*', *National Magazine*, vol. 1 (December 1837), reprinted in Collins (1971), pp. 64–8 (pp. 64–5).

while allowing commiseration for his weakness towards his uncle, the morose, child-hating Nicodemus Dumps. Kitterbell's letter (which is given to us in its entirety) inviting Dumps to attend the christening of his firstborn reinforces this sympathetic impression. 'Dear Uncle,' it begins,

You will be delighted to hear that my dear Jemima has left her room, and that your future godson is getting on capitally. He was very thin at first, but he is getting much larger, and nurse says he is filling out every day. He cries a good deal, and is a very singular colour, which made Jemima and me rather uncomfortable; but as nurse says it's natural, and as of course we know nothing about these things yet, we are quite satisfied with what nurse says. We think he will be a sharp child; and nurse says she's sure he will, because he never goes to sleep. You will readily believe that we are all very happy, only we're a little worn out for want of rest, as he keeps us awake all night; but this we must expect, nurse says, for the first six or eight months. He has been vaccinated, but in consequence of the operation being rather awkwardly performed, some small particles of glass were introduced into the arm with the matter. Perhaps this may in some degree account for his being rather fractious; at least, so nurse says . . . ('The Bloomsbury Christening', p. 540)

Dickens's sense of the absurd here encourages rather than prevents identification with Kitterbell; and indeed the more humorous sketches often manage to be touching and comic at once, while the consciously 'serious' pieces ('The Black Veil' is another example) tend to sound the same melodramatic note throughout.

The vision of the city in the *Sketches* as a source of both melodrama and farce suggests not only the literary fantasies of European Romanticism but the more popular, sub- or non-literary origins of the various pieces brought together at this stage of Dickens's literary career. This is confirmed by the focus of a high proportion of the sketches upon popular recreations, especially but not exclusively the theatre. Dickens was at the time deeply involved in the theatre as an amateur actor and playwright: 'Mrs Joseph Porter' is probably based upon a domestic production of Bishop's opera-drama *Clari* (best known for its central song, 'Home Sweet

Home') in the Dickens lodgings nine months before the sketch's first appearance in the *Monthly Magazine*; and while revising the *Sketches* Dickens was working on a burlesque, *O'Thello* (an intimate knowledge of Shakespeare is evident in the *Sketches*), and on a farce, *The Strange Gentleman*, based on one of the Tales, 'The Great Winglebury Duel'. Dickens was an outstanding mimic, and singer of comic songs; and if it had not been for a bad cold, which prevented him auditioning before the stage manager of the Lyceum and the leading actor Charles Kemble a few years before, he might well have performed on the professional stage. His hero when working as a lawyer's clerk in Holborn was Charles Mathews (1803–78), whose most famous act was to perform a short play in which, using different voices and dialects, he would take all the parts. Dickens's taste for the popular theatre went deep. Years later, he recalled being lost in the city of London as a young lad fresh from Kent; terrified to begin with, the boy soon becomes enthralled by what he sees as he wanders about, and he ends the day by going to a cheap theatre before deciding to find someone to take charge of him.[22] What his innocent eye beheld there, the tears and laughter inspired by the wonderful absurdity of the proceedings, all help explain the fascination that the popular amusements of an earlier age held for Dickens.

The importance of the everyday as a spectacle to be imaginatively rehearsed is nowhere more evident than in the depiction of the private and public theatre, the circus, the fairs, the wild-beast shows, the gardens, the 'harmonic meetings', the exhibitions and dioramas, the dancing, music and games with which the book is stuffed. The people of London are so conditioned by the appeal of these popular cultural activities that they appear to perform themselves, in their characteristic attitudes, dress and gesture. The neighbourhood of Drury Lane and Covent Garden is

essentially a theatrical neighbourhood. There is not a potboy in the vicinity who is not, to a greater or less extent, a dramatic character. The

22. 'Gone Astray', *Household Words* (13 August 1853), reprinted in *Miscellaneous Papers*, ed. B.W. Matz (London: Chapman and Hall, 1914), pp. 395–405.

errand-boys and chandler's-shop-keepers' sons are all stage-struck: they
'get up' plays in back kitchens hired for the purpose, and will stand before
a shop-window for hours, contemplating a great staring portrait of
Mr Somebody or other, of the Royal Coburg Theatre, 'as he appeared
in the character of Tongo the Denounced.' The consequence is, that there
is not a marine-store shop in the neighbourhood, which does not exhibit
for sale some faded articles of dramatic finery, such as three or four
pairs of soiled buff boots with turn-over red tops, heretofore worn by
a 'fourth robber,' or 'fifth mob,' . . . ('Brokers' and Marine-store Shops',
p. 212)

The infection to perform reaches the more well off, such as the
nouveaux riches Tuggses and their pseudo-aristocratic acquaintances,
Captain and Mrs Waters and the Captain's friend Lieutenant
Slaughter. The confrontation of the two 'lovers', Mrs Waters and
the foolish Simon ('Cymon') Tuggs, by the supposedly jealous
Captain, is a standard farcical situation, heightened by the role-
playing of the fraudsters and their victims. Soon after Cymon
conceals himself behind the curtain with 'pantomimic suddenness',
the lieutenant draws it to reveal Cymon 'pallid with apprehension,
and blue with wanting to cough'.

'Ah!' exclaimed the captain, furiously, 'What do I see? Slaughter, your sabre!'
'Cymon!' screamed the Tuggs's.
'Mercy,' said Belinda.
'Platonic,' gasped Cymon. ('The Tuggs's at Ramsgate', p. 408)

The idea of impersonation as a dimension of everyday urban
experience is confirmed by those sketches devoted specifically to
giving an account of popular recreations: one of the most entertaining, 'Astley's', opens once again with the viewpoint of a wandering
observer of the streets − an observer who finds the 'very large,
staring, black Roman capitals' of placards bring recollections of
'when we were first initiated in the mysteries of the alphabet',
which in turn reminds him that 'there is no place which recalls so
strongly our recollections of childhood as Astley's. It was not a
"Royal Amphitheatre" in those days, nor had Ducrow arisen to

shed the light of classic taste and portable gas over the sawdust of the circus . . .' (p. 129). Dickens here pretends to an age he could not claim: Andrew Ducrow (1793–1848), the most famous equestrian entertainer of the time, joined Astley's eight years before the novelist was born. But this only serves to emphasize the importance of nostalgia for this aspect of the *Sketches*.

Descriptions of the entertainments are characteristically offered as if they exist in a kind of eternal present. Ducrow, we're told, used to star in a duet with the ethereal equestrienne Miss Woolford, introduced by a riding-master

who always wears a military uniform with a table-cloth inside the breast of the coat, in which costume he forcibly reminds one of a fowl trussed for roasting. He is – but why should we attempt to describe that of which no description can convey an adequate idea? Every body knows the man, and every body remembers his polished boots, his graceful demeanour, stiff, as some misjudging persons have in their jealousy considered it, and the splendid head of black hair, parted high on the forehead, to impart to the countenance an appearance of deep thought and poetic melancholy. His soft and pleasing voice, too, is in perfect unison with his noble bearing, as he humours the clown by indulging in a little badinage; and the striking recollection of his own dignity, with which he exclaims, 'Now, sir, if you please, inquire for Miss Woolford, sir,' can never be forgotten. The graceful air, too, with which he introduces Miss Woolford into the arena, and, after assisting her to the saddle, follows her fairy courser round the circle, can never fail to create a deep impression in the bosom of every female servant present. ('Astley's', p. 132)

The text's subtle manipulation of tone ensures that we enjoy the nostalgic illusion, and appreciate its audience appeal, while recognizing its patent unreality. There is nothing patronizing in the depiction of the pleasures to be found at Astley's, any more than at Greenwich Fair, which Boz recalls constantly frequenting, in 'our earlier days' (p. 135). One of the central features of the fair was John Richardson's travelling theatre, which consists of an immense booth, with a large stage in front, illuminated with pots of burning fat, 'where you have a melo-drama (with three murders and a ghost), a pantomime, a comic song, an overture, and some incidental music, all done in five-and-twenty minutes'. There follows an hilarious, page-long account of the standard action of the melodrama. Underlying the comedy there is a longing to break through the dullness of the everyday, into a world where the improbable has become conventional, and ordinary people can transcend themselves at least briefly. In 'The Great Winglebury Duel', the farce of mistaken identities leads not as we might expect to the aristocratic lover and his intended departing in triumph, but to the cowardly Mr Trott accepting his enforced elopement with the lady who, after all, is not too particular about whom she marries (p. 482).

This is of a piece with the mixed status of the *Sketches* as fiction. With it, Dickens established something new: an intermingling of reportage, fantasy and social concern that transforms ordinary people, events and landscape into something rich and strange, without losing a grip on reality. The ragged boys crouch in little knots under the cheesemonger's blind, where they 'amuse themselves with theatrical converse, arising out of their last half-price visit to the Victoria gallery'; the 'wretched woman' with an infant in her arms who attempts to sing 'some popular ballad' receives only a 'brutal laugh at her weak voice' ('The Streets – Night', p. 77); the irreverent Cockney cab-driver 'who must make war upon society in his own way [since] society made war upon him', ends up in solitary confinement, singing comic songs all day ('The Last Cab-driver', pp. 173–5); the Cursitor Street lock-up factotum, staying to recount at length but without completing 'one of the rummiest rigs you ever heard on', the story of the delicate-looking young couple who inspire the curiosity of the other debtors ('Passage in the Life of Mr Watkins Tottle', pp. 517–19): all these, and more, witness to a multitude struggling to survive in a changing world and, at times, succeeding.

It is impossible to say whether or not the book might have stood its ground alone, as Forster speculates, since it is impossible to ignore the novels that accompanied and succeeded it. Whatever it lacks in unity, complexity and insight, the *Sketches* prophetically signal the arrival of a new voice in English literature. What they also signal, with extraordinary imaginative force and observation, is the shape of a society caught in a crucial stage of its development, on the brink of modernity.

Dennis Walder
London, 1994

ACKNOWLEDGEMENTS

I would like here to acknowledge the assistance of the staff of the British Library and the Open University Library, especially Tony Coulson; and to thank Valerie Bishop of the Literature Department, for patiently xeroxing and keying-in material. Professors Graham Martin and Grahame Smith helped free the Introduction from solecism; and Professor Michael Slater offered friendly encouragement while promptly answering some queries. Anybody who works on Dickens's *Sketches* owes an immense debt to the scholarly labours of Professors Kathleen Tillotson and Virgil Grillo; and so do I. Sarah Coward's editorial assistance was invaluable.

1812   *7 February* Charles John Huffam Dickens born at Portsmouth, where his father is a clerk in the Navy Pay Office. The eldest son in a family of eight, two of whom die in childhood.

1817   Family move to Chatham.

1822   Family move to London.

1824   Dickens's father in Marshalsea Debtors' Prison for three months. Dickens employed in a blacking warehouse, labelling bottles. Attends Wellington House Academy, a private school, 1824–7.

1827   Becomes a solicitor's clerk.

1832   Becomes a parliamentary reporter after mastering shorthand. In love with Maria Beadnell, 1830–33.

1833   First published story, 'A Dinner at Poplar Walk', in the *Monthly Magazine*. Further stories and sketches in this and other periodicals, 1834–5.

1834   Becomes reporter on the *Morning Chronicle*.

1835   Engaged to Catherine Hogarth, daughter of editor of the *Evening Chronicle*.

1836   *Sketches by Boz*, First and Second Series, published. Marries Catherine Hogarth. Meets John Forster, his literary adviser and future biographer.

1837   *The Pickwick Papers* published in one volume (issued in monthly parts, 1836–7). Birth of a son, the first of ten children. Death of Mary Hogarth, Dickens's sister-in-law. Edits *Bentley's Miscellany*, 1837–9.

1838   *Oliver Twist* published in three volumes (serialized monthly in *Bentley's Miscellany*, 1837–9). Visits Yorkshire schools of the Dotheboys type.

1839   *Nicholas Nickleby* published in one volume (issued in monthly parts, 1838–9).

1841   Declines invitation to stand for Parliament. *The Old Curiosity Shop* and *Barnaby Rudge* published in separate volumes after appearing in weekly numbers in *Master Humphrey's Clock*, 1840–41. Public dinner in his honour at Edinburgh.

1842   *January–June* First visit to North America, described in *American Notes*, two volumes.

1843   *December* *A Christmas Carol* appears.

1844   *Martin Chuzzlewit* published in one volume (issued in monthly parts, 1843–4). Dickens and family leave for Italy, Switzerland and France. Dickens returns to London briefly to read *The Chimes* to friends before its publication in December.

1845   Dickens and family return from Italy. *The Cricket on the Hearth* published at Christmas. Writes autobiographical fragment, ?1845–6, not published until included in Forster's *Life* (three volumes, 1872–4).

1846   Becomes first editor of the *Daily News* but resigns after seventeen issues. *Pictures from Italy* published. Dickens and family in Switzerland and Paris. *The Battle of Life* published at Christmas.

1847   Returns to London. Helps Miss Burdett Coutts to set up, and later to run, a 'Home for Homeless Women'.

1848   *Dombey and Son* published in one volume (issued in monthly parts, 1846–8). Organizes and acts in charity performances of *The Merry Wives of Windsor* and *Every Man in His Humour* in London and elsewhere. *The Haunted Man* published at Christmas.

1850   *Household Words*, a weekly journal 'Conducted by Charles Dickens', begins in March and continues until 1859. Dickens makes speech at first meeting of Metropolitan Sanitary Association. *David Copperfield* published in one volume (issued in monthly parts, 1849–50).

1851   Death of Dickens's father. Further theatrical activities in aid of the Guild of Literature and Art, including a performance before Queen Victoria. *A Child's History of England* appears at intervals in *Household Words*, published in three volumes (1852, 1853, 1854).

1853 *Bleak House* published in one volume (issued in monthly parts, 1852–3). Dickens gives first public readings (from *The Christmas Carol*).

1854 Visits Preston, Lancashire, to observe industrial unrest. *Hard Times* appears weekly in *Household Words* and is published in book form.

1855 Speech in support of the Administrative Reform Association.

1856 Dickens buys Gad's Hill Place, near Rochester.

1857 *Little Dorrit* published in one volume (issued in monthly parts, 1855–7). Dickens acts in Wilkie Collins's melodrama *The Frozen Deep* and falls in love with the young actress Ellen Ternan. *The Lazy Tour of Two Idle Apprentices*, written jointly with Wilkie Collins about a holiday in Cumberland, appears in *Household Words*.

1858 Publishes *Reprinted Pieces* (articles from *Household Words*). Separation from his wife followed by statement in *Household Words*. Dickens's household now largely run by his sister-in-law Georgina.

1859 *All the Year Round*, a weekly journal again 'Conducted by Charles Dickens', begins. *A Tale of Two Cities*, serialized both in *All the Year Round* and in monthly parts, appears in one volume.

1860 Dickens sells London house and moves family to Gad's Hill.

1861 *Great Expectations* published in three volumes after appearing weekly in *All the Year Round* (1860–61). *The Uncommercial Traveller* (papers from *All the Year Round*) appears; expanded edition, 1868. Further public readings, 1861–3.

1863 Death of Dickens's mother, and of his son Walter (in India). Reconciled with Thackeray, with whom he had quarrelled, shortly before the latter's death. Publishes 'Mrs Lirriper's Lodgings' in Christmas number of *All the Year Round*.

1865   *Our Mutual Friend* published in two volumes (issued in monthly parts, 1864–5). Dickens severely shocked after a train accident when returning from France with Ellen Ternan and her mother.

1866   Begins another series of readings. Takes a house for Ellen at Slough. 'Mugby Junction' appears in Christmas number of *All the Year Round*.

1867   Moves Ellen to Peckham. Second journey to America. Gives readings in Boston, New York, Washington and elsewhere, despite increasing ill-health. 'George Silverman's Explanation' appears in *Atlantic Monthly* (then in *All the Year Round*, 1868).

1868   Returns to England. Readings now include the sensational 'Sikes and Nancy' from *Oliver Twist*; Dickens's health further undermined.

1870   Farewell readings in London. *The Mystery of Edwin Drood* issued in six monthly parts, intended to be completed in twelve.

9 June Dies, after collapse at Gad's Hill, aged fifty-eight. Buried in Westminster Abbey.

Stephen Wall, 1995

No manuscripts or proof sheets for the *Sketches by Boz* survive, although the periodicals in which they first appeared do. So the history of the text begins with the publication on 1 December 1833 of 'A Dinner at Poplar Walk' (subsequently retitled 'Mr Minns and His Cousin'), in the *Monthly Magazine*. It was Dickens's first attempt at writing fiction. Neither his name nor any payment appeared, but he was happy to supply the *Monthly Magazine* with six more tales, although still unpaid, over the next year. Soon he was contributing to other periodicals, such as the *Morning Chronicle*, which took five 'Street Sketches' under the 'Boz' signature (which he first used for the second half of 'The Boarding-house', in the *Monthly Magazine*, in August 1834). He wrote twenty 'Sketches of London', including the Parish series, as Boz, for his future father-in-law George Hogarth's *Evening Chronicle*, followed almost immediately by another group of twelve papers, for *Bell's Life in London*, entitled 'Scenes and Characters', for which he adopted the new and jokey pseudonym 'Tibbs', borrowed from one of the characters in 'The Boarding-house'.

The plan of collecting the sketches together into volume form began in October 1834, at the suggestion of the publisher John Macrone (1809–37), who offered Dickens £100 for the copyright, and secured the services of the most popular illustrator of the time, George Cruikshank. Cruikshank and Dickens collaborated well, and after various delays, *Sketches by 'Boz', Illustrative of Every-day Life and Every-day People*, with forty illustrations, appeared in two duodecimo volumes for one guinea on 8 February 1836, the day after the author's twenty-fourth birthday. As Kathleen Tillotson demonstrated in *Dickens at Work* (1957), Dickens carefully revised the sketches for inclusion in this, the First Series, as it later became known; removing topicalities and sharpening up the style, especially (for reasons of space and continuity) modifying the opening and concluding paragraphs of several sketches. Three new pieces were included: 'A Visit to Newgate', 'The Black Veil' and 'The Great Winglebury Duel'.

Sales and reviews of the First Series were good enough for a second edition before the end of July 1836, while Dickens continued to write sketches and tales for various periodicals, although his energies were increasingly taken up with the monthly instalments of *Pickwick Papers*, which began to appear at the end of March. However, planning for a two-volume sequel, *Sketches by Boz: Second Series*, had begun. This involved carefully revising the new pieces in time for publication by Macrone on 17 December 1836 (title-page dated 1837), with more illustrations by Cruikshank. Four of the periodical pieces were amalgamated into two, and 'The Drunkard's Death' was written specially to conclude the volume, which in the event was not followed by a second. The selection continued to look as random as for the First Series. Meanwhile, the success of *Pickwick* led Macrone to try reissuing both series in monthly numbers resembling those in which the novel was appearing, but he was forestalled by Chapman and Hall, who bought him out and reissued the work in shilling monthly numbers – with pink covers, to distinguish it from *Pickwick*'s green – from 1 November 1837 to 1 June 1839. For this combined edition, which was reprinted by Chapman and Hall complete in a single octavo volume in May 1839, uniform with *Pickwick*, Dickens carried out further revisions; Cruikshank provided some new etchings and redrew most of the old ones; and, for the first and last time, all the items were divided into four clear groups: Seven Sketches from Our Parish, Scenes, Characters and Tales.

The next edition was for the first collected edition of Dickens's works, the so-called Cheap Edition, which began to appear in 1850. In October of that year the *Sketches* appeared with a new and apologetic Preface, and some small revisions – modifying religious and sexual overtones to suit the sensitivities, real or imagined, of the mid-Victorian audience – so that, for example, oaths became milder, and the waitress of Bellamy's, who is chucked under the chin by the 'Lord's-Day-Bill Baronet' (Sir Andrew Agnew), and whose 'pastoral friskings and rompings (Jane's only recreations) which occasionally take place in the passage' ('A Parliamentary Sketch', p. 191), has her character improved by the insertion within the parenthesis, after 'recreations', the words 'and they are very innocent too'. Dickens added descriptive headlines for the right-hand side of each leaf for the last edition of the work to appear in his lifetime, the 1868 Charles Dickens Edition, which otherwise simply reprinted the text of the Cheap Edition, including its Preface. It is the basis of all modern texts.

Except this one. I have chosen the 1839 text of *Sketches* as my copy-text on the following grounds: (1) it is the first complete text the author, in collaboration with publisher, printer and illustrator, wished to present to the public as a book; (2) it is the text the author revised most closely, and the one for which he provided the first and only structural revision; (3) although the author's responsibility for the 1850 text is higher than his Preface suggests, numerous errors crept in unnoticed, and his responsibility for it is less certain than for the earlier text; finally (4), the 1839 text retains the uncensored rawness and vitality of the time of its writing. Important or interesting variants are referred to in the Notes, but I have not included the (often lengthy) passages deleted from the original periodical publication. I have silently corrected only those errors that are obvious and interfere with sense, otherwise I have retained the spelling, punctuation and inconsistencies of the original. In accordance with Penguin house style, I have used single quotation marks first, Arabic numerals for the chapters in the text, en rules for dashes (instead of the longer em rule), em rules where Dickens uses double dashes, and deleted the point after contractions like Mr, Mrs and Dr. Section titles are used as left-hand running heads, instead of *Sketches by Boz*, for the benefit of the reader. The illustrations, with their original captions, are those of the 1839 edition, as near as possible to their original position in the text.

I have provided a more detailed outline of the first publication of the *Sketches* in Appendix A. Appendix B lists the descriptive headlines or running heads provided for the 1868 edition.

SUGGESTED FURTHER READING

Peter Ackroyd, *Dickens* (London: Sinclair-Stevenson, 1990). Reprinted as Minerva paperback, 1991. Contains the most up-to-date and insightful account of the genesis of *Sketches* in relation to Dickens's early life.

Robert Browning, '*Sketches by Boz*', in *Dickens and the Twentieth Century*, eds. John Gross and Gabriel Pearson (London: Routledge & Kegan Paul, 1962), pp. 19–34.

John Butt and Kathleen Tillotson, *Dickens at Work* (London: Methuen, 1957; reissued 1968). Tillotson's chapter provided the first really thorough, scholarly account of the detailed revisions of *Sketches*.

Kathryn Chittick, *Dickens and the 1830s* (Cambridge: Cambridge University Press, 1990). The early journalism set in its contemporary literary context.

Philip Collins, ed., *Dickens: The Critical Heritage* (London: Routledge & Kegan Paul, 1971). Contains lengthy extracts from contemporary reviews, helpfully identified and introduced.

Edward Costigan, 'Drama and Everyday Life in *Sketches by Boz*', *Review of English Studies*, New Series, 27 (1976), pp. 403–21.

Duane DeVries, *Dickens' Apprentice Years: The Making of a Novelist* (Brighton, Sussex: Harvester Press, 1976).

Angus Easson, 'Who is Boz? Dickens and his Sketches', *Dickensian*, vol. 81 (March 1985), pp. 13–22.

John Forster, *The Life of Charles Dickens*, ed. and intro. J.W.T. Ley (London: Cecil Palmer, 1928). The classic contemporary biography by Dickens's friend, containing much sympathetic criticism as well.

Margaret Ganz, 'Humor's Alchemy: The Lesson of *Sketches by Boz*', in *Humor, Irony, and the Realm of Madness* (New York: AMS Press, 1990), pp. 1–24. A corrective to over-solemnity.

Virgil Grillo, *Charles Dickens' 'Sketches by Boz': End in the Beginning* (Boulder, Colorado: Colorado Associated University Press, 1974). Fullest account of the gathering together of the periodical pieces into *Sketches*, looking towards the connections between these and Dickens's later novels.

Michael Hollington, *Dickens and the Grotesque* (London and Sydney: Croom Helm, 1984). Contains a useful chapter treating *Sketches* as a 'romance of real life'.

J. Hillis Miller, 'The Fiction of Realism: *Sketches by Boz*, *Oliver Twist*, and Cruikshank's Illustrations', in *Charles Dickens and George Cruikshank*, ed. Ada B. Nisbet (Los Angeles: William Andrews Clark Memorial Library, University of California, 1971). Milestone in the analysis of *Sketches* according to recent literary theory.

F.S. Schwarzbach, *Dickens and the City* (London: Athlone Press, University of London, 1979), has an excellent chapter on the metropolitan outlook of the *Sketches*.

Michael Slater, ed. and intro., *Sketches by Boz and Other Early Papers* (London: J.M. Dent, 1994). The first of several volumes, which will eventually contain all the journalism Dickens published in collected form.

The Election for Beadle

SKETCHES BY BOZ

LONDON - CHAPMAN & HALL, LTD

ADVERTISEMENT

THE following pages contain the earliest productions of their Author, written from time to time to meet the exigencies of a Newspaper or a Magazine. They were originally published in two series; the first in two volumes, and the second in one. Several editions having been exhausted, both are now published together in one volume, uniform with the 'Pickwick Papers,' and 'Nicholas Nickleby.'

London, May 15, 1839.

Facsimile of the title-page of the 1839 edition

SKETCHES BY BOZ

ILLUSTRATIVE OF

EVERY-DAY LIFE AND EVERY-DAY PEOPLE.

———

WITH FORTY ILLUSTRATIONS

BY

GEORGE CRUIKSHANK.

———

NEW EDITION, COMPLETE.

———

LONDON:

CHAPMAN AND HALL, 186, STRAND.

1839.

PREFACE TO THE FIRST EDITION
OF THE FIRST SERIES

IN humble imitation of a prudent course, universally adopted by aeronauts, the Author of these volumes throws them up as his pilot balloon, trusting it may catch favourable current, and devoutly and earnestly hoping it may *go off well* — a sentiment in which his Publisher cordially concurs.

Unlike the generality of pilot balloons which carry no car, in this one it is very possible for a man to embark, not only himself, but all his hopes of future fame, and all his chances of future success. Entertaining no inconsiderable feeling of trepidation at the idea of making so perilous a voyage in so frail a machine, alone and unaccompanied, the Author was naturally desirous to secure the assistance and companionship of some well-known individual, who had frequently contributed to the success, though his well-earned reputation rendered it impossible for him ever to have shared the hazard, of similar undertakings. To whom, as possessing the requisite in an eminent degree, could he apply but to GEORGE CRUIKSHANK?[1] The application was readily heard, and at once acceded to: this is their first voyage in company, but it may not be the last.

If any further excuse be wanted for adding this book to the hundreds which every season produces, the Author may be permitted to plead the very favourable reception, which several of the following Sketches received, on their original appearance in different periodicals. In behalf of the remainder, he can only entreat the kindness and favour of the public: his object has been to present little pictures of life and manners as they really are; and should they be approved of, he hopes to repeat his experiment with increased confidence, and on a more extensive scale.

FURNIVAL'S INN,[2] *February*, 1836.

PREFACE TO THE SECOND EDITION
OF THE FIRST SERIES

THE Second Edition of a work, while it affords its author an opportunity of returning his warmest thanks to the Public, for their favourable reception of the first impression, furnishes in itself the best of all apologies for his again intruding upon their notice, with a few words in his individual capacity.

The words which the Author feels it necessary to say, in the present instance, are few indeed. He has to vindicate himself from no censure – to notice no illiberality – to complain of no attack. He has only in one single sentence, to acknowledge, with feelings of the deepest gratitude, the kindness and indulgence with which these volumes have been universally received, and the unlooked-for success with which his efforts have been crowned.

If the pen that designed these little outlines, should present its labours to the Public frequently hereafter; if it should produce fresh sketches, and even connected works of fiction of a higher grade, they have only themselves to blame. They have encouraged a young and unknown writer, by their patronage and approval; they have stimulated him to fresh efforts, by their liberality and praise; and if they *will* be guilty of such actions, they must be content to bear the consequences which naturally result from them.

FURNIVAL'S INN, *August* 1, 1836.

IF brevity be the soul of wit,[1] anywhere, it is most especially so in a preface; firstly, because those who do read such things as prefaces, prefer them, like grace before meat, in an epigrammatic form; and, secondly, because nine hundred and ninety-nine people out of every thousand, never read a preface at all.

Some of these sketches were written before the appearance of the former series, and the remainder have been added at different periods since that time. The Author ventures to hope that they may experience as favourable a reception as the first productions of his pen; and that the present volume will not be considered an unwelcome, or inappropriate sequel, to the two which preceded it.

With these few words, he gives a modest tap at the door of the Public with his Christmas Piece,[2] when, perhaps, he may imagine the following dialogue to ensue, founded on the well-known precedent of the charity boys and the housemaid.

Publisher (to Author). – *You* knock.

Author (to Publisher). – No – you. [Here the Publisher seizes knocker, and gives a loud rap at the door.]

Public (suspiciously, and with the door a-jar). – Well; what do *you* want?

Publisher. – Please, will you look at this Christmas Piece; me and the other boy goes partners in it.

Public. – Go away; we have so many knocks of the same kind, at this time of year, that we are tired of answering the door. Go away.

Publisher (pushing it). – No; but do look at it, please. It's all his own doing, except the pictures; and they're capital, let alone the writing. [Here the Public gradually softens, and takes the Christmas Piece in; upon which the Publisher makes a bow, and retires] –

while the Author lingers behind, for one instant, to repeat an old form with much sincerity; and to express his hearty wish that his best friend, the Public, may enjoy 'a merry Christmas, and a happy new year.'

FURNIVAL'S INN, *December* 17, 1836.

THE whole of these sketches were written and published, one by one, when I was a very young man. They were collected and re-published while I was still a very young man; and sent into the world with all their imperfections (a good many) on their heads.

They comprise my first attempts at authorship – with the exception of certain tragedies achieved at the mature age of eight or ten, and represented with great applause to overflowing nurseries. I am conscious of their often being extremely crude and ill-considered, and bearing obvious marks of haste and inexperience; particularly in that section of the present volume which is comprised under the general head of Tales.

But as this collection is not originated now, and was very leniently and favourably received when it was first made, I have not felt it right either to remodel or expunge, beyond a few words and phrases here and there.[2]

LONDON, *October*, 1850.

CONTENTS

SEVEN SKETCHES FROM OUR PARISH

SCENES

CONTENTS

CHARACTERS

TALES

SEVEN SKETCHES
FROM OUR PARISH

The Beadle — The Parish Engine — The Schoolmaster

How much is conveyed in those two short words — 'The Parish!'[1]
And with how many tales of distress and misery, of broken fortune and ruined hopes, too often of unrelieved wretchedness and
successful knavery, are they associated! A poor man, with small
earnings, and a large family, just manages to live on from hand
to mouth, and to procure food from day to day; he has barely
sufficient to satisfy the present cravings of nature, and can take no
heed of the future. His taxes are in arrear, quarter day passes
by, another quarter day arrives: he can procure no more quarter
for himself, and is summoned by — the parish. His goods are
distrained, his children are crying with cold and hunger, and the
very bed on which his sick wife is lying, is dragged from beneath
her. What can he do? To whom is he to apply for relief? To
private charity? To benevolent individuals? Certainly not — there
is his parish. There are the parish vestry, the parish infirmary,
the parish surgeon, the parish officers, the parish beadle. Excellent
institutions, and gentle, kind-hearted men. The woman dies — she
is buried by the parish. The children have no protector — they
are taken care of by the parish. The man first neglects, and
afterwards cannot obtain, work — he is relieved by the parish;
and when distress and drunkenness have done their work upon
him, he is maintained, a harmless babbling idiot, in the parish
asylum.

The parish beadle[2] is one of the most, perhaps *the* most,
important member of the local administration. He is not so well off
as the churchwardens, certainly, nor is he so learned as the vestry-
clerk, nor does he order things quite so much his own way as
either of them. But his power is very great, notwithstanding; and
the dignity of his office is never impaired by the absence of efforts
on his part to maintain it. The beadle of our parish is a splendid

fellow. It is quite delightful to hear him, as he explains the state of the existing poor laws to the deaf old women in the board-room-passage on business nights; and to hear what he said to the senior churchwarden, and what the senior churchwarden said to him; and what 'we' (the beadle and the other gentlemen), came to the determination of doing. A miserable looking woman is called into the board-room, and represents a case of extreme destitution, affecting herself – a widow, with six small children. 'Where do you live?' inquires one of the overseers. 'I rents a two-pair back, gentlemen, at Mrs Brown's, Number 3, Little King William's-alley, which has lived there this fifteen year, and knows me to be very hard-working and industrious, and when my poor husband was alive, gentlemen, as died in the hospital.' – 'Well, well,' interrupts the overseer, taking a note of the address, 'I'll send Simmons, the beadle, to-morrow morning, to ascertain whether your story is correct; and if so, I suppose you must have an order into the House³ – Simmons, go to this woman's the first thing to-morrow morning, will you?' Simmons bows assent, and ushers the woman out. Her previous admiration of 'the board' (who all sit behind great books, and with their hats on) fades into nothing before her respect for her lace-trimmed conductor; and her account of what has passed inside, increases – if that be possible – the marks of respect, shown by the assembled crowd, to that solemn functionary. As to taking out a summons, it's quite a hopeless case if Simmons attends it, on behalf of the parish. He knows all the titles of the Lord Mayor by heart; states the case without a single stammer: and it is even reported that on one occasion he ventured to make a joke, which the Lord Mayor's head footman (who happened to be present) afterwards told an intimate friend, confidentially, was almost equal to one of Mr Hobler's.⁴

See him again on Sunday in his state-coat and cocked-hat, with a large-headed staff for show in his left hand, and a small cane for use in his right. How pompously he marshals the children into their places! and how demurely the little urchins look at him askance as he surveys them when they are all seated, with a glare of the eye peculiar to beadles! The churchwardens and overseers being

The Parish Engine

duly installed in their curtained pews, he seats himself on a mahogany bracket, erected expressly for him at the top of the aisle, and divides his attention between his prayer-book and the boys. Suddenly, just at the commencement of the communion service, when the whole congregation is hushed into a profound silence, broken only by the voice of the officiating clergyman, a penny is heard to ring on the stone floor of the aisle with astounding clearness. Observe the generalship of the beadle. His involuntary look of horror is instantly changed into one of perfect indifference, as if he were the only person present who had not heard the noise. The artifice succeeds. After putting forth his right leg now and then, as a feeler, the victim who dropped the money ventures to make one or two distinct dives after it; and the beadle, gliding softly round, salutes his little round head, when it again appears above the seat, with divers double knocks, administered with the cane before noticed, to the intense delight of three young men in an adjacent pew, who cough violently at intervals until the conclusion of the sermon.

Such are a few traits of the importance and gravity of a parish-beadle – a gravity which has never been disturbed in any case that has come under our observation, except when the services of that particularly useful machine, a parish fire-engine, are required: then indeed all is bustle. Two little boys run to the beadle as fast as their legs will carry them, and report from their own personal observation that some neighbouring chimney is on fire; the engine is hastily got out, and a plentiful supply of boys being obtained, and harnessed to it with ropes, away they rattle over the pavement, the beadle, running – we do not exaggerate – running at the side, until they arrive at some house, smelling strongly of soot, at the door of which the beadle knocks with considerable gravity for half an hour. No attention being paid to these manual applications, and the turncock having turned on the water, the engine turns off amidst the shouts of the boys; it pulls up once more at the workhouse, and the beadle 'pulls up' the unfortunate householder next day, for the amount of his legal reward.[5] We never saw a parish engine at a regular fire but once. It came up in gallant style – three miles and a half an hour, at least; there was a capital supply of water, and it was first on the spot. Bang went the pumps — the people cheered — the beadle perspired profusely; but it was unfortunately discovered, just as they were going to put the fire out, that nobody understood the process by which the engine was filled with water; and that eighteen boys, and a man, had exhausted themselves in pumping for twenty minutes, without producing the slightest effect!

The personages next in importance to the beadle, are the master of the workhouse and the parish schoolmaster. The vestry-clerk, as every body knows, is a short, pudgy little man, in black, with a thick gold watch-chain of considerable length, terminating in two large seals and a key. He is an attorney, and generally in a bustle; at no time more so, than when he is hurrying to some parochial meeting, with his gloves crumpled up in one hand, and a large red book under the other arm. As to the churchwardens and overseers, we exclude them altogether, because all we know of them is, that they are usually respectable tradesmen, who wear hats with brims inclined to flatness, and who occasionally testify in gilt letters on a blue ground, in some conspicuous part of the church, to the important fact of a gallery having been enlarged and beautified, or an organ rebuilt.

The master of the workhouse is not, in our parish — nor is he usually in any other — one of that class of men the better part of whose existence has passed away, and who drag out the remainder in some inferior situation, with just enough thought of the past, to feel degraded by, and discontented with, the present. We are unable to guess precisely to our own satisfaction what station the man can have occupied before; we should think he had been an inferior sort of attorney's clerk, or else the master of a national school[6] — whatever he was, it is clear his present position is a change for the better. His income is small, certainly, as the rusty black coat and threadbare velvet collar demonstrate: but then he lives free of house-rent, has a limited allowance of coals and candles, and an almost unlimited allowance of authority in his petty kingdom. He is a tall, thin, bony man; always wears shoes and black cotton stockings with his surtout; and eyes you, as you pass his parlour window, as if he wished you were a pauper, just to give you a specimen of his power. He is an admirable specimen of a small tyrant: morose, brutish, and ill-tempered; bullying to his inferiors, cringing to his superiors, and jealous of the influence and authority of the beadle.

Our schoolmaster is just the very reverse of this amiable official. He has been one of those men one occasionally hears of, on whom misfortune seems to have set her mark; nothing he ever did, or was concerned in, appears to have prospered. A rich old relation who had brought him up, and openly announced his intention of providing for him, left him 10,000*l.* in his will, and revoked the bequest in a codicil. Thus unexpectedly reduced to the necessity of providing for himself, he procured a situation in a public office. The young clerks below him, died off as if there were a plague among them; but the old fellows over his head, for the reversion of whose places he was anxiously waiting, lived on and on, as if they were immortal. He speculated and lost. He speculated again, and won – but never got his money. His talents were great; his disposition, easy, generous and liberal. His friends profited by the one, and abused the other. Loss succeeded loss; misfortune crowded on misfortune; each successive day brought him nearer the verge of hopeless penury, and the quondam friends who had been warmest in their professions, grew strangely cold and indifferent. He had children whom he loved, and a wife on whom he doted. The former turned their backs on him; the latter died broken-hearted. He went with the stream – it had ever been his failing, and he had not courage sufficient to bear up against so many shocks – he had never cared for himself, and the only being who had cared for him, in his poverty and distress, was spared to him no longer. It was at this period that he applied for parochial relief. Some kind-hearted man who had known him in happier times, chanced to be church-warden that year, and through his interest he was appointed to his present situation.

He is an old man now. Of the many who once crowded round him in all the hollow friendship of boon-companionship, some have died, some have fallen like himself, some have prospered – all have

forgotten him. Time and misfortune have mercifully been permitted
to impair his memory, and use has habituated him to his present
condition. Meek, uncomplaining, and zealous in the discharge of his
duties, he has been allowed to hold his situation long beyond the
usual period; and he will no doubt continue to hold it, until
infirmity renders him incapable, or death releases him. As the gray-
headed old man feebly paces up and down the sunny side of the
little court-yard between school hours, it would be difficult, indeed,
for the most intimate of his former friends to recognise their once
gay and happy associate, in the person of the Pauper Schoolmaster.

CHAPTER 2

The Curate — The Old Lady —
The Half-pay Captain

WE commenced our last chapter with the beadle of our parish,
because we are deeply sensible of the importance and dignity of his
office. We will begin the present, with the clergyman. Our curate
is a young gentleman of such prepossessing appearance, and fascinating manners, that within one month after his first appearance in the
parish, half the young-lady inhabitants were melancholy with
religion, and the other half, desponding with love. Never were so
many young ladies seen in our parish-church on Sunday before;
and never had the little round angels' faces on Mr Tomkins's
monument in the side aisle, beheld such devotion on earth as they
all exhibited. He was about five-and-twenty when he first came to
astonish the parishioners. He parted his hair on the centre of his
forehead in the form of a Norman arch, wore a brilliant of the first
water on the fourth finger of his left hand (which he always applied
to his left cheek when he read prayers), and had a deep sepulchral
voice of unusual solemnity. Innumerable were the calls made by

prudent mammas on our new curate, and innumerable the invitations with which he was assailed, and which, to do him justice, he readily accepted. If his manner in the pulpit had created an impression in his favour, the sensation was increased tenfold, by his appearance in private circles. Pews in the immediate vicinity of the pulpit or reading-desk rose in value; sittings in the centre aisle were at a premium: an inch of room in the front row of the gallery could not be procured for love or money; and some people even went so far as to assert, that the three Miss Browns,[1] who had an obscure family pew just behind the churchwardens', were detected, one Sunday, in the free seats[2] by the communion-table, actually lying in wait for the curate as he passed to the vestry! He began to preach extempore sermons, and even grave papas caught the infection. He got out of bed at half-past twelve o'clock one winter's night, to half-baptize[3] a washerwoman's child in a slop-basin, and the gratitude of the parishioners knew no bounds – the very churchwardens grew generous, and insisted on the parish defraying the expense of the watch-box on wheels,[4] which the new curate had ordered for himself, to perform the funeral service in, in wet weather. He sent three pints of gruel and a quarter of a pound of tea to a poor woman who had been brought to bed of four small children, all at once – the parish were charmed. He got up a subscription for her – the woman's fortune was made. He spoke for one hour and twenty-five minutes, at an anti-slavery meeting at the Goat and Boots – the enthusiasm was at its height. A proposal was set on foot for presenting the curate with a piece of plate, as a mark of esteem for his valuable services rendered to the parish. The list of subscriptions was filled up in no time; the contest was, not who should escape the contribution, but who should be the foremost to subscribe. A splendid silver inkstand was made, and engraved with an appropriate inscription; the curate was invited to a public breakfast, at the before-mentioned Goat and Boots; the inkstand was presented in a neat speech by Mr Gubbins, the ex-churchwarden, and acknowledged by the curate in terms which drew tears into the eyes of all present – the very waiters were melted.

One would have supposed that, by this time, the theme of

universal admiration was lifted to the very pinnacle of popularity.
No such thing. The curate began to cough; four fits of coughing
one morning between the Litany and the Epistle, and five in the
afternoon service. Here was a discovery — the curate was consumptive. How interestingly melancholy! If the young ladies were
energetic before, their sympathy and solicitude now knew no
bounds. Such a man as the curate — such a dear — such a perfect
love — to be consumptive! It was too much. Anonymous presents
of black-currant jam, and lozenges, elastic waistcoats, bosom
friends,[5] and warm stockings, poured in upon the curate until he
was as completely fitted out, with winter clothing, as if he were on
the verge of an expedition to the North Pole: verbal bulletins of the
state of his health were circulated throughout the parish half-a-
dozen times a day; and the curate was in the very zenith of his
popularity.

About this period, a change came over the spirit of the parish. A
very quiet, respectable, dozing old gentleman, who had officiated in
our chapel of ease for twelve years previously, died one fine
morning, without having given any notice whatever of his intention.
This circumstance gave rise to counter-sensation the first; and the
arrival of his successor occasioned counter-sensation the second. He
was a pale, thin, cadaverous man, with large black eyes, and long
straggling black hair: his dress was slovenly in the extreme, his
manner ungainly, his doctrines startling; in short, he was in every
respect the antipodes of the curate.[6] Crowds of our female parishioners flocked to hear him: at first, because he was *so* odd-looking,
then because his face was *so* expressive, then because he preached *so*
well; and at last, because they really thought that, after all, there
was something about him which it was quite impossible to describe.
As to the curate, he was all very well; but certainly, after all, there
was no denying that — that — in short, the curate wasn't a novelty,
and the other clergyman was. The inconstancy of public opinion is
proverbial: the congregation migrated one by one. The curate
coughed till he was black in the face — it was in vain. He respired
with difficulty — it was equally ineffectual in awakening sympathy.
Seats are once again to be had in any part of our parish church, and

the chapel-of-ease is going to be enlarged as it is crowded to suffocation every Sunday!

The best known and most respected among our parishioners, is an old lady, who resided in our parish long before our name was registered in the list of baptisms.[7] Our parish is a suburban one, and the old lady lives in a neat row of houses in the most airy and pleasant part of it. The house is her own; and it, and every thing about it, except the old lady herself, who looks a little older than she did ten years ago, is in just the same state as when the old gentleman was living. The little front parlour, which is the old lady's ordinary sitting-room, is a perfect picture of quiet neatness: the carpet is covered with brown Holland, the glass and picture-frames are carefully enveloped in yellow muslin; the table-covers are never taken off, except when the leaves are turpentined and bees'waxed, an operation which is regularly commenced every other morning at half-past nine o'clock — and the little nicnacs are always arranged in precisely the same manner. The greater part of these are presents from little girls whose parents live in the same row; but some of them, such as the two old fashioned watches (which never keep the same time, one being always a quarter of an hour too slow, and the other a quarter of an hour too fast), the little picture of the Princess Charlotte and Prince Leopold as they appeared in the Royal Box at Drury-lane Theatre,[8] and others of the same class, have been in the old lady's possession for many years. Here the old lady sits with her spectacles on, busily engaged in needle-work — near the window in summer time; and if she sees you coming up the steps, and you happen to be a favourite, she trots out to open the street door for you before you knock, and as you must be fatigued after that hot walk, insists on your swallowing two glasses of sherry before you exert yourself by talking. If you call in the evening you will find her cheerful, but rather more serious[9] than usual, with an open Bible on the table, before her, of which 'Sarah,' who is just as neat and methodical as her mistress, regularly reads two or three chapters in the parlour aloud.

The old lady sees scarcely any company, except the little girls before noticed, each of whom has always a regular fixed day for a

periodical tea-drinking with her, to which the child looks forward
as the greatest treat of its existence. She seldom visits at a greater
distance than the next door but one on either side; and when she
drinks tea here, Sarah runs out first and knocks a double-knock, to
prevent the possibility of her 'Missis's' catching cold by having to
wait at the door. She is very scrupulous in returning these little
invitations, and when she asks Mr and Mrs So-and-so, to meet Mr
and Mrs Somebody-else, Sarah and she dust the urn, and the best
china tea service, and the Pope Joan board;[10] and the visiters are
received in the drawing-room in great state. She has but few
relations, and they are scattered about in different parts of the
country, and she seldom sees them. She has a son in India, whom
she always describes to you as a fine, handsome fellow – so like the
profile of his poor dear father over the sideboard, but the old lady
adds, with a mournful shake of the head, that he has always been
one of her greatest trials, and that indeed he once almost broke her
heart; but it pleased God to enable her to get the better of it, and
she would prefer your never mentioning the subject to her, again.
She has a great number of pensioners: and on Saturday, after she
comes back from market, there is a regular levee of old men and
women in the passage, waiting for their weekly gratuity. Her name
always heads the list of any benevolent subscriptions, and hers are
always the most liberal donations to the Winter Coal and Soup
Distribution Society. She subscribed twenty pounds towards the
erection of an organ in our parish church, and was so overcome the
first Sunday the children sang to it, that she was obliged to be
carried out by the pew-opener.[11] Her entrance into church on
Sunday is always the signal for a little bustle in the side aisle,
occasioned by a general rise among the poor people, who bow and
curtsy until the pew-opener has ushered the old lady into her
accustomed seat, dropped a respectful curtsy, and shut the door:
and the same ceremony is repeated on her leaving church, when she
walks home with the family next door but one, and talks about the
sermon all the way, invariably opening the conversation by asking
the youngest boy where the text was.

Thus, with the annual variation of a trip to some quiet place on the sea-coast, passes the old lady's life. It has rolled on in the same unvarying and benevolent course for many years now, and must at no distant period be brought to its final close. She looks forward to its termination, with calmness and without apprehension. She has every thing to hope and nothing to fear.

A very different personage, but one who has rendered himself very conspicuous in our parish, is one of the old lady's next door neighbours. He is an old naval officer on half-pay,[12] and his bluff and unceremonious behaviour, disturbs the old lady's domestic economy, not a little. In the first place he *will* smoke cigars in the front court, and when he wants something to drink with them – which is by no means an uncommon circumstance – he lifts up the old lady's knocker with his walking-stick, and demands to have a glass of table ale, handed over the rails. In addition to this cool proceeding, he is a bit of a Jack of all trades, or to use his own words, 'A regular Robinson Crusoe;'[13] and nothing delights him better, than to experimentalize on the old lady's property. One morning he got up early, and planted three or four roots of full-grown marigolds in every bed of her front garden, to the inconceivable astonishment of the old lady, who actually thought when she got up and looked out of the window, that it was some strange eruption which had come out in the night. Another time he took to pieces the eight-day clock on the front landing, under pretence of cleaning the works, which he put together again, by some undiscovered process, in so wonderful a manner, that the large hand has done nothing but trip up the little one ever since. Then he took to breeding silk-worms, which he *would* bring in two or three times a day, in little paper boxes, to show the old lady, generally dropping a worm or two at every visit. The consequence was, that one morning a very stout silk-worm was discovered in the act of walking up stairs – probably with the view of inquiring after his friends, for, on further inspection, it appeared that some of his companions had already found their way to every room in the house. The old lady went to the sea-side in despair, and during her absence he completely effaced the name from her brass door-plate, in his attempts to polish it with aqua-fortis.

But all this, is nothing to his seditious conduct in public life. He attends every vestry meeting that is held; always opposes the constituted authorities of the parish, denounces the profligacy of the churchwardens, contests legal points against the vestry-clerk, *will* make the tax-gatherer call for his money till he won't call any longer, and then he sends it: finds fault with the sermon every Sunday, says that the organist ought to be ashamed of himself, offers to back himself for any amount to sing the psalms better than all the children put together, male and female; and, in short, conducts himself in the most turbulent and uproarious manner. The worst of it is, that having a high regard for the old lady, he wants to make her a convert to his views, and therefore walks into her little parlour with his newspaper in his hand, and talks violent politics by the hour. He is a charitable, open-hearted old fellow at bottom, after all; so, although he puts the old lady a little out occasionally, they agree very well in the main, and she laughs as much at each feat of his handiwork when it is all over, as anybody else.

CHAPTER 3

The Four Sisters

THE row of houses in which the old lady and her troublesome neighbour reside, comprises, beyond all doubt, a greater number of characters within its circumscribed limits, than all the rest of the parish put together. As we cannot, consistently with our present plan, however, extend the number of our parochial sketches beyond six, it will be better, perhaps, to select the most peculiar, and to introduce them at once without further preface.

The four Miss Willises, then, settled in our parish thirteen years ago. It is a melancholy reflection that the old adage, 'time and tide wait for no man,'[1] applies with equal force to the fairer portion of the creation; and willingly would we conceal the fact, that even thirteen years ago, the Miss Willises were far from juvenile. Our duty as faithful parochial chroniclers, however, is paramount to every other consideration, and we are bound to state, that thirteen years since, the authorities in matrimonial cases considered the youngest Miss Willis in a very precarious state, while the eldest sister was positively given over, as being far beyond all human hope. Well, the Miss Willises took a lease of the house; it was fresh painted and papered from top to bottom: the paint inside was all wainscoted, the marble all cleaned, the old grates taken down, and register-stoves,[2] you could see to dress by, put up; four trees were planted in the back garden, several small baskets of gravel sprinkled over the front one, vans of elegant furniture arrived, spring blinds were fitted to the windows, carpenters who had been employed in the various preparations, alterations, and repairs, made confidential statements to the different maid-servants in the row, relative to the magnificent scale on which the Miss Willises were commencing; the maid-servants told their 'Missises,' the Missises told their friends, and vague rumours were circulated throughout the parish, that No. 25, in Gordon-place, had been taken by four maiden ladies of immense property.

At last, the Miss Willises moved in; and then the 'calling' began. The house was the perfection of neatness – so were the four Miss Willises. Every thing was formal, stiff, and cold – so were the four Miss Willises. Not a single chair of the whole set was ever seen out of its place – not a single Miss Willis of the whole four was ever seen out of hers. There they always sat, in the same places, doing precisely the same things at the same hour. The eldest Miss Willis used to knit, the second to draw, the two others to play duets on the piano. They seemed to have no separate existence, but to have made up their minds just to winter through life together. They were three long graces in drapery, with the addition, like a school-dinner, of another long grace afterwards – the three fates with another sister – the Siamese twins multiplied by two.[3] The eldest Miss Willis grew bilious – the four Miss Willises grew bilious immediately. The eldest Miss Willis grew ill-tempered and religious – the four Miss Willises were ill-tempered and religious directly. Whatever the eldest did, the others did, and whatever any body else did, they all disapproved of; and thus they vegetated – living in Polar harmony among themselves, and, as they sometimes went out, or saw company 'in a quiet-way' at home, occasionally iceing the neighbours. Three years passed over in this way, when an unlooked-for and extraordinary phenomenon occurred. The Miss Willises showed symptoms of summer, the frost gradually broke up; a complete thaw took place. Was it possible? one of the four Miss Willises was going to be married!

Now, where on earth the husband came from, by what feelings the poor man could have been actuated, or by what process of reasoning the four Miss Willises succeeded in persuading themselves that it was possible for a man to marry one of them, without marrying them all, are questions too profound for us to resolve: certain it is, however, that the visits of Mr Robinson (a gentleman in a public office, with a good salary and a little property of his own, beside) were received – that the four Miss Willises were courted in due form by the said Mr Robinson – that the neighbours were perfectly frantic in their anxiety to discover which of the four Miss Willises was the fortunate fair, and that the difficulty they experienced in solving the problem was not at all lessened by the announcement of the eldest Miss Willis, – '*We* are going to marry Mr Robinson.'

It was very extraordinary. They were so completely identified, the one with the other, that the curiosity of the whole row – even of the old lady herself – was roused almost beyond endurance. The subject was discussed at every little card-table and tea-drinking. The old gentleman of silk-worm notoriety did not hesitate to express his decided opinion that Mr Robinson was of Eastern descent,[4] and contemplated marrying the whole family at once; and the row, generally, shook their heads with considerable gravity, and declared the business to be very mysterious. They hoped it might all end well; – it certainly had a very singular appearance, but still it would be uncharitable to express any opinion without good grounds to go upon, and certainly the Miss Willises were *quite* old enough to judge for themselves, and to be sure people ought to know their own business best, and so forth.

At last, one fine morning, at a quarter before eight o'clock, A.M., two glass-coaches[5] drove up to the Miss Willises' door, at which Mr Robinson had arrived in a cab ten minutes before, dressed in a light blue coat and double-milled kersey[6] pantaloons, white neckerchief, pumps, and dress-gloves, his manner denoting, as appeared from the evidence of the housemaid at No. 23, who was sweeping the door-steps at the time, a considerable degree of nervous excitement. It was also hastily reported on the same testimony, that the cook who opened the door, wore a large white bow of unusual dimensions, in a much smarter head-dress than the regulation cap to which the Miss Willises invariably restricted the somewhat excursive tastes of female servants in general.

The intelligence spread rapidly from house to house. It was quite clear that the eventful morning had at length arrived; the whole row stationed themselves behind their first and second floor blinds, and waited the result in breathless expectation.

At last the Miss Willises' door opened; the door of the first glass-coach did the same. Two gentlemen, and a pair of ladies to correspond — friends of the family, no doubt; up went the steps, bang went the door, off went the first glass-coach, and up came the second.

The street-door opened again; the excitement of the whole row increased — Mr Robinson and the eldest Miss Willis. 'I thought so,' said the lady at No. 19; 'I always said it was *Miss* Willis!' — 'Well, I never!' ejaculated the young lady at No. 18 to the young lady at No. 17 — 'Did you ever, dear!' responded the young lady at No. 17 to the young lady at No. 18. 'It's too ridiculous!' exclaimed a spinster of an *un*certain age, at No. 16, joining in the conversation. But who shall portray the astonishment of Gordon-place, when Mr Robinson handed in *all* the Miss Willises, one after the other, and then squeezed himself into an acute angle of the glass-coach, which forthwith proceeded at a brisk pace, after the other glass-coach, which other glass-coach had itself proceeded, at a brisk pace, in the direction of the parish church. Who shall depict the perplexity of the clergyman, when *all* the Miss Willises knelt down at the communion-table, and repeated the responses incidental to the marriage service in an audible voice – or who shall describe the confusion which prevailed, when – even after the difficulties thus occasioned had been adjusted – *all* the Miss Willises went into hysterics at the conclusion of the ceremony, until the sacred edifice resounded with their united wailings!

As the four sisters and Mr Robinson continued to occupy the same house after this memorable occasion, and as the married sister, whoever she was, never appeared in public without the other three, we are not quite clear that the neighbours ever would have discovered the real Mrs Robinson, but for a circumstance of the most gratifying description, which *will* happen occasionally in the best regulated families.[7] Three quarter-days elapsed, and the row, on whom a new light appeared to have been bursting for some time, began to speak with a sort of implied confidence on the subject, and to wonder how Mrs Robinson – the youngest Miss Willis that was – got on; and servants might be seen running up the steps, about nine or ten o'clock every morning, with 'Mississ's compliments, and wishes to know how Mrs Robinson find herself this morning?' And the answer always was, 'Mrs Robinson's compliments, and she's in very good spirits, and doesn't find herself any worse.' The piano was heard no longer, the knitting-needles were laid aside, drawing was neglected, and mantua-making and millinery, on the smallest scale imaginable, appeared to have become the favourite amusement of the whole family. The parlour wasn't quite as tidy as it used to be, and if you called in the morning, you would see lying on a table, with an old newspaper carelessly thrown over them, two or three particularly small caps, rather larger than if they had been made for a moderate-sized doll, with a small piece of lace, in the shape of a horse-shoe, let in behind: or perhaps a white robe, not very large in circumference, but very much out of proportion in point of length, with a little tucker round the top, and a frill round the bottom; and once when we called, we saw a long white roller, with a kind of blue margin down each side, the probable use of which, we were at a loss to conjecture.[8] Then we fancied that Mr Dawson, the surgeon, &c., who displays a large lamp with a different colour in every pane of glass, at the corner of the row, began to be knocked up at night oftener than he used to be; and once we were very much alarmed by hearing a hackney-coach stop at Mrs Robinson's door, at half-past two o'clock in the morning, out of which there emerged a fat old woman, in a cloak and nightcap, with a bundle in one hand, and a pair of pattens in the other, who looked as if she had been suddenly knocked up out of bed for some very special purpose.

When we got up in the morning we saw that the knocker was tied up in an old white kid glove; and we, in our innocence (we were in a state of bachelorship then), wondered what on earth it all meant, until we heard the eldest Miss Willis, *in propriá personá*,[9] say, with great dignity, in answer to the next inquiry, '*My* compliments, and Mrs Robinson's doing as well as can be expected, and the little girl thrives wonderfully.' And then, in common with the rest of the row, our curiosity was satisfied, and we began to wonder it had never occurred to us what the matter was, before.

CHAPTER 4

The Election for Beadle

A GREAT event has recently occurred in our parish. A contest of paramount interest has just terminated; a parochial convulsion has taken place. It has been succeeded by a glorious triumph, which the country – or at least the parish – it is all the same – will long remember. We have had an election; an election for beadle. The supporters of the old beadle system have been defeated in their strong hold, and the advocates of the great new beadle principles have achieved a proud victory.

Our parish, which, like all other parishes, is a little world of its own, has long been divided into two parties, whose contentions, slumbering for a while, have never failed to burst forth with unabated vigour, on any occasion on which they could by possibility be renewed. Watching-rates,[1] lighting-rates, paying-rates, sewer's-rates, church-rates, poor's-rates — all sorts of rates, have been in their turns the subjects of a grand struggle; and as to questions of patronage, the asperity and determination with which they have been contested is scarcely credible.

The leader of the official party — the steady advocate of the churchwardens, and the unflinching supporter of the overseers — is an old gentleman who lives in our row. He owns some half-dozen houses in it, and always walks on the opposite side of the way, so that he may be able to take in a view of the whole of his property at once. He is a tall, thin, bony man, with an interrogative nose, and little restless perking eyes, which appear to have been given him for the sole purpose of peeping into other people's affairs with. He is deeply impressed with the importance of our parish business, and prides himself, not a little, on his style of addressing the parishioners in vestry assembled. His views are rather confined than extensive; his principles more narrow than liberal. He has been heard to declaim very loudly in favour of the liberty of the press, and advocates the repeal of the stamp duty on newspapers,[2] because the daily journals who now have a monopoly of the public, never give *verbatim* reports of vestry meetings. He would not appear egotistical for the world, but at the same time he must say, that there *are* speeches — that celebrated speech of his own, on the emoluments of the sexton, and the duties of the office, for instance — which might be communicated to the public, greatly to their improvement and advantage.

His great opponent in public life is Captain Purday, the old naval officer on half-pay, to whom we have already introduced our readers. The captain being a determined opponent of the constituted authorities, whoever they may chance to be, and our other friend being their steady supporter, with an equal disregard of their individual merits, it will readily be supposed, that occasions for their coming into direct collision are neither few nor far between. They divided the vestry fourteen times on a motion for heating the church with warm water instead of coals: and made speeches about liberty and expenditure, and prodigality and hot water, which threw the whole parish into a state of excitement. Then the captain, when he was on the visiting committee, and his opponent overseer, brought forward certain distinct and specific charges relative to the management of the workhouse, boldly expressed his total want of confidence in the existing authorities, and moved for 'a copy of the recipe by which the paupers' soup³ was prepared, together with 'any documents relating thereto.' This the overseer steadily resisted; he fortified himself by precedent, appealed to the established usage, and declined to produce the papers, on the ground of the injury that would be done to the public service, if documents of a strictly private nature, passing between the master of the workhouse and the cook, were to be thus dragged to light on the motion of any individual member of the vestry. The motion was lost by a majority of two; and then the captain, who never allows himself to be defeated, moved for a committee of inquiry into the whole subject. The affair grew serious: the question was discussed at meeting after meeting, and vestry after vestry; speeches were made, attacks repudiated, personal defiances exchanged, explanations received, and the greatest excitement prevailed, until at last, just as the question was going to be finally decided, the vestry found that somehow or other, they had become entangled in a point of form, from which it was impossible to escape with propriety. So, the motion was dropped, and every body looked extremely important, and seemed quite satisfied with the meritorious nature of the whole proceeding.

This was the state of affairs in our parish a week or two since, when Simmons, the beadle, suddenly died. The lamented deceased had over-exerted himself, a day or two previously, in conveying an aged female, highly intoxicated, to the strong room of the workhouse. The excitement thus occasioned, added to a severe cold, which this indefatigable officer had caught in his capacity of director of the parish engine, by inadvertently playing over himself instead of a fire, proved too much for a constitution already enfeebled by age; and the intelligence was conveyed to the Board one evening, that Simmons had died, and left his respects.

The breath was scarcely out of the body of the deceased functionary, when the field was filled with competitors for the vacant office, each of whom rested his claims to public support, entirely on the number and extent of his family, as if the office of beadle were originally instituted as an encouragement for the propagation of the human species. 'Bung for Beadle. Five small children!' — 'Hopkins for Beadle. Seven small children!!' — 'Timkins for Beadle. Nine small children!!!' Such were the placards in large black letters on a white ground, which were plentifully pasted on the walls, and posted in the windows of the principal shops. Timkins's success was considered certain: several mothers of families half promised their votes, and the nine small children would have run over the course, but for the production of another placard, announcing the appearance of a still more meritorious candidate. 'Spruggins for Beadle. Ten small children (two of them twins), and a wife!!!' There was no resisting this; ten small children would have been almost irresistible in themselves, without the twins, but the touching parenthesis about that interesting production of nature, and the still more touching allusion to Mrs Spruggins, must ensure success. Spruggins was the favourite at once, and the appearance of his lady, as she went about to solicit votes (which encouraged confident hopes of a still further addition to the house of Spruggins at no remote period), increased the general prepossession in his favour. The other candidates, Bung alone excepted, resigned in despair. The day of election was fixed; and the canvass proceeded with briskness and perseverance on both sides.

The members of the vestry could not be supposed to escape the contagious excitement inseparable from the occasion. The majority of the lady inhabitants of the parish declared at once for Spruggins; and the *quondam* overseer took the same side, on the ground that men with large families always had been elected to the office, and that although he must admit, that, in other respects, Spruggins was the least qualified candidate of the two, still it was an old practice, and he saw no reason why an old practice should be departed from. This was enough for the captain. He immediately sided with Bung, canvassed for him personally in all directions, wrote squibs on Spruggins, and got his butcher to skewer them up on conspicuous joints in his shop-front; frightened his neighbour, the old lady, into a palpitation of the heart, by his awful denunciations of Spruggins's party; and bounced in and out, and up and down, and backwards and forwards, until all the sober inhabitants of the parish thought it inevitable that he must die of a brain fever, long before the election began.

The day of election arrived. It was no longer an individual struggle, but a party contest between the ins and outs. The question was, whether the withering influence of the overseers, the domination of the churchwardens, and the blighting despotism of the vestry-clerk, should be allowed to render the election of beadle a form − a nullity: whether they should impose a vestry-elected beadle on the parish, to do their bidding and forward their views, or whether the parishioners, fearlessly asserting their undoubted rights, should elect an independent beadle of their own.

The nomination was fixed to take place in the vestry, but so great was the throng of anxious spectators, that it was found necessary to adjourn to the church, where the ceremony commenced with due solemnity. The appearance of the churchwardens and overseers, and the ex-churchwardens and ex-overseers, with Spruggins in the rear, excited general attention. Spruggins was a little thin man, in rusty black, with a long pale face, and a countenance expressive of care and fatigue, which might either be attributed to the extent of his family or the anxiety of his feelings. His opponent appeared in a cast-off coat of the captain's − a blue coat with bright buttons: white trousers, and that description of shoes familiarly known by the appellation of 'high-lows.'[4] There was a serenity in the open countenance of Bung − a kind of moral dignity in his confident air − an 'I wish you may get it' sort of expression in his eye − which infused animation into his supporters, and evidently dispirited his opponents.

The ex-churchwarden rose to propose Thomas Spruggins for

beadle. He had known him long. He had had his eye upon him closely for years; he had watched him with twofold vigilance for months. (A parishioner here suggested that this might be termed 'taking a double sight,'[5] but the observation was drowned in loud cries of 'Order!') He would repeat that he had had his eye upon him for years, and this he would say, that a more well-conducted, a more well-behaved, a more sober, a more quiet man, with a more well-regulated mind he had never met with. A man with a larger family he had never known (cheers). The parish required a man who could be depended on ('Hear!' from the Spruggins side answered by ironical cheers from the Bung party). Such a man he now proposed ('No,' 'Yes'). He would not allude to individuals (the ex-churchwarden continued, in the celebrated negative style adopted by great speakers). He would not advert to a gentleman who had once held a high rank in the service of his majesty; he would not say, that that gentleman was no gentleman; he would not assert that that man was no man; he would not say, that he was a turbulent parishioner; he would not say, that he had grossly misbehaved himself, not only on this, but on all former occasions; he would not say, that he was one of those discontented and treasonable spirits, who carried confusion and disorder wherever they went; he would not say, that he harboured in his heart envy, and hatred, and malice, and all uncharitableness.[6] No! He wished to have everything comfortable and pleasant, and therefore, he would say – nothing about him (cheers).

The captain replied in a similar parliamentary style. He would not say, he was astonished at the speech they had just heard; he would not say, he was disgusted (cheers). He would not retort the epithets which had been hurled against him (renewed cheering); he would not allude to men once in office, but now happily out of it, who had mismanaged the workhouse, ground the paupers, diluted the beer, slack-baked the bread, boned the meat, heightened the work, and lowered the soup (tremendous cheers). He would not ask what such men deserved (a voice, 'Nothing a-day, and find themselves!'). He would not say, that one burst of general indignation should drive them from the parish they polluted with their presence ('Give it him!'). He would not allude to the unfortunate man who had been proposed – he would not say, as the vestry's tool, but as Beadle. He would not advert to that individual's family; he would not say, that nine children, twins, and a wife, were very bad examples for pauper imitation (loud cheers). He would not advert in detail to the qualifications of Bung. The man stood before him, and he would not say in his presence, what he might be disposed to say of him, if he were absent. (Here Mr Bung telegraphed to a friend near him, under cover of his hat, by contracting his left eye, and applying his right thumb to the tip of his nose.) It had been objected to Bung that he had only five children ('Hear, hear!' from the opposition). Well; he had yet to learn that the legislature had affixed any precise amount of infantine qualification to the office of beadle; but taking it for granted that an extensive family were a great requisite, he entreated them to look to facts, and compare *data*, about which there could be no mistake. Bung was 35 years of age. Spruggins – of whom he wished to speak with all possible respect – was 50. Was it not more than possible – was it not very probable – that by the time Bung attained the latter age, he might see around him a family, even exceeding in number and extent, that to which Spruggins at present laid claim (deafening cheers and waving of handkerchiefs)? The captain concluded, amidst loud applause, by calling upon the parishioners to sound the tocsin, rush to the poll, free themselves from dictation, or be slaves for ever.

On the following day the polling began, and we never have had such a bustle in our parish since we got up our famous anti-slavery petition,[7] which was such an important one, that the House of Commons ordered it to be printed, on the motion of the member for the district. The captain engaged two hackney-coaches and a cab for Bung's people – the cab for the drunken voters, and the two coaches for the old ladies, the greater portion of whom, owing to the captain's impetuosity, were driven up to the poll and home again, before they recovered from their flurry sufficiently to know, with any degree of clearness, what they had been doing. The opposite party wholly neglected these precautions, and the consequence was, that a great many ladies who were walking leisurely up to the church – for it was a very hot day – to vote for Spruggins, were artfully decoyed into the coaches, and voted for Bung. The captain's arguments, too, had produced considerable effect: the attempted influence of the vestry produced a greater. A threat of exclusive dealing was clearly established against the vestry-clerk – a case of heartless and profligate atrocity. It appeared that the delinquent had been in the habit of purchasing six penn'orth of muffins, weekly, from an old woman who rents a small house in the parish, and resides among the original settlers; on her last weekly visit, a message was conveyed to her through the medium of the cook, couched in mysterious terms, but indicating with sufficient clearness, that the vestry-clerk's appetite for muffins, in future, depended entirely on her vote on the beadleship. This was sufficient: the stream had been turning previously, and the impulse thus administered directed its final course. The Bung party ordered one shilling's-worth of muffins weekly for the remainder of the old woman's natural life; the parishioners were loud in their exclamations; and the fate of Spruggins was sealed.

It was in vain that the twins were exhibited in dresses of the same pattern, and night caps to match, at the church door: the boy in Mrs Spruggins's right arm, and the girl in her left – even Mrs Spruggins herself failed to be an object of sympathy any longer. The majority attained by Bung on the gross poll was four hundred and twenty-eight, and the cause of the parishioners triumphed.

CHAPTER 5

The Broker's Man

THE excitement of the late election has subsided, and our parish being once again restored to a state of comparative tranquillity, we are enabled to devote our attention to those parishioners who take

The Broker's Man

little share in our party contests or in the turmoil and bustle of public life. And we feel sincere pleasure in acknowledging here, that in collecting materials for this task we have been greatly assisted by Mr Bung himself, who has imposed on us a debt of obligation which we fear we can never repay. The life of this gentleman has been one of a very chequered description: he has undergone transitions — not from grave to gay, for he never was grave — not from lively to severe, for severity forms no part of his disposition; his fluctuations have been between poverty in the extreme, and poverty modified, or, to use his own emphatic language, 'between nothing to eat and just half enough.' He is not, as he forcibly remarks, 'One of those fortunate men who, if they were to dive under one side of a barge stark-naked, would come up on the other with a new suit of clothes on, and a ticket for soup in the waistcoat-pocket:' neither is he one of those, whose spirit has been broken beyond redemption by misfortune and want. He is just one of the careless, good-for-nothing, happy fellows, who float, cork-like, on the surface, for the world to play at hockey with: knocked here, and there, and every where: now to the right, then to the left, again up in the air, and anon to the bottom, but always reappearing and bounding with the stream buoyantly and merrily along. Some few months before he was prevailed upon to stand a contested election for the office of beadle, necessity attached him to the service of a broker;[1] and on the opportunities he here acquired of ascertaining the condition of most of the poorer inhabitants of the parish, his patron, the captain, first grounded his claims to public support. Chance threw the man in our way a short time since. We were, in the first instance, attracted by his prepossessing impudence at the election; we were not surprised, on further acquaintance, to find him a shrewd knowing fellow, with no inconsiderable power of observation; and, after conversing with him a little, were somewhat struck (as we dare say our readers have frequently been in other cases) with the power some men seem to have, not only of sympathising with, but to all appearance of understanding feelings to which they themselves are entire strangers. We had been expressing to the new functionary our surprise that

he should ever have served in the capacity to which we have just
adverted, when we gradually led him into one or two professional
anecdotes. As we are induced to think, on reflection, that they will
tell better in nearly his own words, than with any attempted
embellishments of ours, we will at once entitle them

Mr Bung's Narrative

'It's very true, as you say, sir,' Mr Bung commenced, 'that a
broker's man's is not a life to be envied; and in course you know as
well as I do, though you don't say it, that people hate and scout'em
because they're the ministers of wretchedness, like, to poor people.
But what could I do, sir? The thing was no worse because I did it,
instead of somebody else; and if putting me in possession of a
house would put me in possession of three and sixpence a day, and
levying a distress[2] on another man's goods would relieve my
distress and that of my family, it can't be expected but what I'd
take the job and go through with it. I never liked it, God knows; I
always looked out for something else, and the moment I got other
work to do, I left it. If there is any thing wrong in being the agent
in such matters — not the principal, mind you — I'm sure the
business, to a beginner like I was, at all events, carries its own
punishment along with it. I wished again and again that the people
would only blow me up, or pitch into me — that I wouldn't have
minded, it's all in my way; but it's the being shut up by yourself in
one room for five days, without so much as an old newspaper to
look at, or any thing to see out o' the winder but the roofs and
chimneys at the back of the house, or any thing to listen to, but the
ticking, perhaps, of an old Dutch clock,[3] the sobbing of the missis,
now and then, the low talking of friends in the next room, who
speak in whispers, lest "the man" should overhear them, or
perhaps the occasional opening of the door, as a child peeps in to
look at you, and then runs half-frightened away — It's all this, that
makes you feel sneaking somehow, and ashamed of yourself; and
then, if it's winter time, they just give you fire enough to make you
think you'd like more, and bring in your grub as if they wished it

'ud choke you — as I dare say they do, for the matter of that, most heartily. If they're very civil, they make you up a bed in the room at night, and if they don't, your master sends one in for you; but there you are, without being washed or shaved all the time, shunned by everybody, and spoken to by no one, unless some one comes in at dinner time, and asks you whether you want any more, in a tone as much as to say "I hope you don't," or, in the evening, to inquire whether you wouldn't rather have a candle, after you've been sitting in the dark half the night. When I was left in this way, I used to sit, think, think, thinking, till I felt as lonesome as a kitten in a wash-house copper with the lid on;[4] but I believe the old broker's men who are regularly trained to it, never think at all. I have heard some on 'em say, indeed, that they don't know how!

'I put in a good many distresses in my time (continued Mr Bung), and in course I wasn't long in finding that some people are not as much to be pitied as others are, and that people with good incomes who get into difficulties, which they keep patching up day after day, and week after week, get so used to these sort of things in time, that at last they come scarcely to feel them at all. I remember the very first place I was put in possession of, was a gentleman's house in this parish here, that everybody would suppose couldn't help having money if he tried. I went with old Fixem, my old master, 'bout half arter eight in the morning; rang the area-bell; servant in livery opened the door: "Governor at home?" — "Yes, he is," says the man; "but he's breakfasting just now." "Never mind," says Fixem, "just you tell him there's a gentleman here, as wants to speak to him partickler." So the servant he opens his eyes, and stares about him all ways — looking for the gentleman as it struck me, for I don't think anybody but a man as was stone-blind would mistake Fixem for one; and as for me, I was as seedy as a cheap cowcumber.[5] Hows'ever, he turns round, and goes to the breakfast-parlour, which was a little snug sort of room at the end of the passage, and Fixem (as we always did in that profession), without waiting to be announced, walks in arter him, and before the servant could get out — "Please, sir, here's a man as wants to speak to you," looks in at the door as familiar and pleasant as may be. "Who the devil are you, and how dare you walk into a gentleman's house without leave?" says the master, as fierce as a bull in fits. "My name," says Fixem, winking to the master to send the servant away, and putting the warrant into his hands folded up like a note, "My name's Smith," says he, "and I called from Johnson's about that business of Thompson's" — "Oh," says the other, quite down on him directly, "How *is* Thompson?" says he; "Pray sit down, Mr Smith: John, leave the room." Out went the servant; and the gentleman and Fixem looked at one another till they couldn't look any longer, and then they varied the amusements by looking at me, who had been standing on the mat all this time. "Hundred and fifty pounds, I see," said the gentleman at last. "Hundred and fifty pound," said Fixem, "besides cost of levy, sheriff's poundage,[6] and all other incidental expenses." — "Um" says the gentleman, "I sha'n't be able to settle this before to-morrow afternoon." — "Very sorry; but I shall be obliged to leave my man here till then," replies Fixem, pretending to look very miserable over it. "That's very unfort'nate," says the gentleman, "for I have got a large party here to-night, and I'm ruined if those fellows of mine get an inkling of the matter — just step here, Mr Smith," says he, after a short pause. So Fixem walks with him up to the window, and after a good deal of whispering, and a little chinking of suverins, and looking at me, he comes back and says, "Bung, you're a handy fellow, and very honest I know. This gentleman wants an assistant to clean the plate and wait at table to-day, and if you're not particularly engaged," says old Fixem, grinning like mad, and shoving a couple of suverins into my hand, "he'll be very glad to avail himself of your services." Well, I laughed, and the gentleman laughed, and we all laughed; and I went home and cleaned myself, leaving Fixem there, and when I went back, Fixem went away, and I polished up the plate, and waited at table, and gammoned the servants, and nobody had the least idea I was in possession, though it very nearly came out after all; for one of the last gentlemen who remained, came down stairs into the hall where I was sitting pretty late at night, and putting half-a-crown into my hand, says, "Here my man," says he, "run and get me a coach, will you?" I thought it was a do, to get me out of the house, and was just going to say so, sulkily enough, when the gentleman (who was up to every thing) came running down stairs, as if he was in great anxiety. "Bung," says he, pretending to be in a consuming passion. "Sir," says I. "Why the devil an't you looking after that plate?" — "I was just going to send him for a coach for me," says the other gentleman. "And I was just a-going to say," says I — "Any body else, my dear fellow," interrupts the master of the house, pushing me down the passage to get me out of the way — "any body else; but I have put this man in possession of all the plate and valuables, and I cannot allow him on any consideration whatever, to leave the house. Bung, you scoundrel, go and count those forks in the breakfast-parlour instantly." You may be sure I went laughing pretty hearty when I found it was all right. The money was paid next day, with the addition of something else for myself, and that was the best job that I (and I suspect old Fixem too) ever got in that line.

'But this is the bright side of the picture, sir, after all,' resumed Mr Bung, laying aside the knowing look, and flash air, with which he had repeated the previous anecdote — 'and I'm sorry to say, it's the side one sees very, very, seldom, in comparison with the dark one. The civility which money will purchase, is rarely extended to those who have none; and there's a consolation even in being able to patch up one difficulty, to make way for another, to which very poor people are strangers. I was once put into a house down George's-yard — that little dirty court at the back of the gas-works; and I never shall forget the misery of them people, dear me! It was a distress for half a year's rent — two pound ten I think. There was only two rooms in the house, and as there was no passage, the lodgers up stairs always went through the room of the people of the house, as they passed in and out; and every time they did so — which, on the average, was about four times every quarter of an hour — they blowed up quite frightful: for their things had been seized too, and included in the inventory. There was a little piece of enclosed dust in front of the house, with a cinder-path leading up to the door, and an open rain-water butt on one side. A dirty striped curtain, on a very slack string, hung in the window, and a little triangular bit of broken looking-glass rested on the sill inside. I suppose it was meant for the people's use, but their appearance was so wretched, and so miserable, that I'm certain they never could have plucked up courage to look themselves in the face a second time, if they survived the fright of doing so once. There was two or three chairs, that might have been worth, in their best days, from eightpence to a shilling a-piece; a small deal table, an old corner cupboard with nothing in it, and one of those bedsteads which turn up half way, and leave the bottom legs sticking out for you to knock your head against, or hang your hat upon; no bed, no bedding. There was an old sack, by way of rug, before the fire-place, and four or five children were grovelling about, among the sand on the floor. The execution was only put in, to get 'em out of the house, for there was nothing to take to pay the expenses; and here I stopped for three days, though that was a mere form too: for, in course, I knew, and we all knew, they could never pay the money. In one of the chairs, by the side of the place where the fire ought to have been, was an old 'ooman – the ugliest and dirtiest I ever see – who sat rocking herself backwards and forwards, backwards and forwards, without once stopping, except for an instant now and then, to clasp together the withered hands which, with these exceptions, she kept constantly rubbing upon her knees, just raising and depressing her fingers convulsively, in time to the rocking of the chair. On the other side sat the mother with an infant in her arms, which cried till it cried itself to sleep, and when it 'woke, cried till it cried itself off again. The old 'ooman's voice I never heard: she seemed completely stupified; and as to the mother's, it would have been better if she had been so too, for misery had changed her to a devil. If you had heard how she cursed the little naked children as was rolling on the floor, and seen how savagely she struck the infant when it cried with hunger, you'd have shuddered as much as I did. There they remained all the time: the children ate a morsel of bread once or twice, and I gave 'em best part of the dinners my missis brought me, but the woman ate nothing; they never even laid on the bedstead, nor was the room swept or cleaned all the time. The neighbours were all too poor themselves to take any notice of 'em, but from what I could make out from the abuse of the woman up stairs, it seemed the husband had been transported a few weeks before. When the time was up, the landlord and old Fixem too, got rather frightened about the family, and so they made a stir about it, and had 'em taken to the workhouse. They sent the sick couch for the old 'ooman, and Simmons took the children away at night. The old 'ooman went into the infirmary, and very soon died. The children are all in the house[7] to this day, and very comfortable they are in comparison. As to the mother, there was no taming her at all. She had been a quiet, hard-working woman, I believe, but her misery had actually drove her wild; so after she had been sent to the house of correction half-a-dozen times, for throwing inkstands at the overseers, blaspheming the churchwardens, and smashing every body as come near her, she burst a bloodvessel one mornin', and died too; and a happy release it was, both for herself and the old paupers, male and female, which she used to tip over in all directions, as if they were so many skittles, and she the ball.

'Now this was bad enough,' resumed Mr Bung, taking a half-step towards the door, as if to intimate that he had nearly concluded. 'This was bad enough, but there was a sort of quiet misery – if you understand what I mean by that, sir – about a lady at one house I was put into, as touched me a good deal more. It doesn't matter where it was exactly: indeed, I'd rather not say, but it was the same sort o' job. I went with Fixem in the usual way – there was a year's rent in arrear; a very small servant-girl opened the door, and three or four fine-looking little children was in the front parlour we were shown into, which was very clean, but very scantily furnished, much like the children themselves. "Bung," says Fixem to me, in a low voice, when we were left alone for a minute, "I know something about this here family, and my opinion is, it's no go." "Do you think they can't settle?" says I, quite anxiously; for I liked the looks of them children. Fixem shook his head, and was just about to reply, when the door opened, and in came a lady, as white as ever I see any one in my days, except about the eyes, which were red with crying. She walked in, as firm as I could have done; shut the door carefully after her, and sat herself down with a face as composed as if it was made of stone. "What is the matter, gentlemen?" says she, in a surprisin' steady voice. "*Is* this an execution?"[8] – "It is, mum," says Fixem. The lady looked at him as steady as ever: she didn't seem to have understood him. "It is, mum," says Fixem again; "this is my warrant of distress, mum," says he, handing it over as polite as if it was a newspaper which had been bespoke arter the next gentleman.

'The lady's lip trembled as she took the printed paper. She cast her eye over it, and old Fixem began to explain the form, but I saw she wasn't reading it, plain enough, poor thing. "Oh, my God!" says she, suddenly a-bursting out crying, letting the warrant fall, and hiding her face in her hands. "Oh, my God! what will become of us!" The noise she made, brought in a young lady of about nineteen or twenty, who, I suppose, had been a-listening at the door, and who had got a little boy in her arms: she sat him down in the lady's lap, without speaking, and she hugged the poor little fellow to her bosom, and cried over him, 'till even old Fixem put on his blue spectacles to hide the two tears, that was a-trickling down, one on each side of his dirty face. "Now, dear ma," says the young lady, "you know how much you have borne. For all our sakes – for pa's sake," says she, "don't give way to this!" – "No, no, I won't!" says the lady, gathering herself up hastily, and drying her eyes; "I am very foolish, but I'm better now – much better." And then she roused herself up, went with us into every room while we took the inventory, opened all the drawers of her own accord, sorted the children's little clothes to make the work easier; and, except doing every thing in a strange sort of hurry, seemed as calm and composed as if nothing had happened. When we came down stairs again, she hesitated a minute or two, and at last says, "Gentlemen," says she, "I am afraid I have done wrong, and perhaps it may bring you into trouble. I secreted just now," she says, "the only trinket I have left in the world – here it is." So she lays down on the table, a little miniature mounted in gold. "It's a miniature," she says, "of my poor dear father! I little thought once, that I should ever thank God for depriving me of the original, but I do, and have done for years back, most fervently. Take it away, sir," she says, "it's a face that never turned from me in sickness or distress, and I can hardly bear to turn from it now, when, God knows, I suffer both in no ordinary degree." I couldn't say nothing, but I raised my head from the inventory which I was filling up, and looked at Fixem; the old fellow nodded to me significantly, so I ran my pen through the "*Mini*" I had just written, and left the miniature on the table.

'Well, sir, to make short of a long story, I was left in possession, and in possession I remained; and though I was an ignorant man, and the master of the house a clever one, I saw what he never did, but what he would give worlds now (if he had 'em) to have seen in time. I saw, sir, that his wife was wasting away, beneath cares of which she never complained, and griefs she never told. I saw that she was dying before his eyes; I knew that one exertion from him might have saved her, but he never made it. I don't blame him: I don't think he *could* rouse himself. She had so long anticipated all his wishes, and acted for him, that he was a lost man when left to himself. I used to think when I caught sight of her, in the clothes she used to wear, which looked shabby even upon her, and would have been scarcely decent on any one else, that if I was a gentleman it would wring my very heart to see the woman that was a smart and merry girl when I courted her, so altered through her love for me. Bitter cold and damp weather it was, yet, though her dress was thin, and her shoes none of the best, during the whole three days, from morning to night, she was out of doors running about to try and raise the money. The money *was* raised, and the execution was paid out. The whole family crowded into the room where I was, when the money arrived. The father was quite happy as the inconvenience was removed – I dare say he didn't know how; the children looked merry and cheerful again; the eldest girl was bustling about, making preparations for the first comfortable meal they had had since the distress was put in; and the mother looked pleased to see them all so. But if ever I saw death in a woman's face, I saw it in hers that night.

'I was right, sir,' continued Mr Bung, hurriedly passing his coat-sleeve over his face, 'the family grew more prosperous, and good fortune arrived. But it was too late. Those children are motherless now, and their father would give up all he has since gained – house, home, goods, money: all that he has, or ever can have, to restore the wife he has lost.'

CHAPTER 6

The Ladies' Societies

OUR Parish is very prolific in ladies' charitable institutions. In winter, when wet feet are common, and colds not scarce, we have the ladies' soup distribution society, the ladies' coal distribution society, and the ladies' blanket distribution society; in summer, when stone fruits flourish and stomach aches prevail, we have the ladies' dispensary, and the ladies' sick visitation committee; and all the year round we have the ladies' child's examination society, the ladies' bible and prayer-book circulation society, and the ladies' childbed-linen monthly loan society. The two latter are decidedly the most important; whether they are productive of more benefit than the rest, is not for us to say, but we can take upon ourselves to affirm, with the utmost solemnity, that they create a greater stir and more bustle, than all the others put together.

We should be disposed to affirm, on the first blush of the matter, that the bible and prayer-book society is not so popular as the childbed-linen society; the bible and prayer-book society has, however, considerably increased in importance within the last year or two, having derived some adventitious aid from the factious opposition of the child's examination society; which factious opposition originated in manner following:– When the young curate was popular, and all the unmarried ladies in the parish took a serious turn, the charity children all at once became objects of peculiar and especial interest. The three Miss Browns (enthusiastic admirers of the curate) taught, and exercised, and examined, and re-examined the unfortunate children, until the boys grew pale, and the girls consumptive, with study and fatigue. The three Miss Browns stood it out very well, because they relieved each other; but the children, having no relief at all, exhibited decided symptoms of weariness and care. The unthinking part of the parishioners laughed at all this, but the more reflective portion of the inhabitants abstained from expressing any opinion on the subject until that of the curate had been clearly ascertained.

The opportunity was not long wanting. The curate preached a charity sermon on behalf of the charity school, and in the charity sermon aforesaid, expatiated in glowing terms on the praiseworthy and indefatigable exertions of certain estimable individuals. Sobs were heard to issue from the three Miss Browns' pew; the pew-opener of the division was seen to hurry down the centre aisle to the vestry door, and to return immediately, bearing a glass of water in her hand. A low moaning ensued; two more pew-openers rushed to the spot, and the three Miss Browns, each supported by a pew-opener, were led out of the church, and led in again after the lapse of five minutes with white pocket-handkerchiefs to their eyes, as if they had been attending a funeral in the churchyard adjoining. If any doubt had for a moment existed, as to whom the allusion was intended to apply, it was at once removed. The wish to enlighten the charity children became universal, and the three Miss Browns were unanimously besought to divide the school into classes, and to assign each class to the superintendence of two young ladies.

A little learning is a dangerous thing,[1] but a little patronage is more so: the three Miss Browns appointed all the old maids, and carefully excluded the young ones. Maiden aunts triumphed, mammas were reduced to the lowest depth of despair, and there is no telling in what act of violence the general indignation against the three Miss Browns might have vented itself, had not a perfectly providential occurrence changed the tide of public feeling. Mrs Johnson Parker, the mother of seven extremely fine girls – all unmarried – hastily reported to several other mammas of several other unmarried families, that five old men, six old women, and children innumerable, in the free seats[2] near her pew, were in the habit of coming to church every Sunday, without either bible or prayer-book. Was this to be borne in a civilized country? Could such things be tolerated in a Christian land? Never! A ladies' bible and prayer-book distribution society was instantly formed: president, Mrs Johnson Parker; treasurers, auditors, and secretary, the Misses Johnson Parker: subscriptions were entered into, books were bought, all the free-seat people provided therewith, and when the first lesson was given out, on the first Sunday succeeding these events, there was such a dropping of books, and rustling of leaves, that it was morally impossible to hear one word of the service for five minutes afterwards.

The three Miss Browns, and their party, saw the approaching danger, and endeavoured to avert it by ridicule and sarcasm. Neither the old men nor the old women could read their books, now they had got them, said the three Miss Browns. Never mind; they could learn, replied Mrs Johnson Parker. The children couldn't read either, suggested the three Miss Browns. No matter; they could be taught, retorted Mrs Johnson Parker. A balance of parties took place. The Miss Browns publicly examined – popular feeling inclined to the child's examination society. The Miss Johnson Parkers publicly distributed – a reaction took place in favour of the prayer-book distribution. A feather would have turned the scale, and a feather did turn it. A missionary returned from the West Indies;[3] he was to be presented to the Dissenters' Missionary Society on his marriage with a wealthy widow. Overtures were made to the Dissenters by the Johnson Parkers. Their object was the same, and why not have a joint meeting of the two societies? The proposition was accepted. The meeting was duly heralded by public announcement, and the room was crowded to suffocation. The missionary appeared on the platform; he was hailed with enthusiasm. He repeated a dialogue he had heard between two negroes, behind a hedge, on the subject of distribution societies; the approbation was tumultuous. He gave an imitation of the two negroes in broken English; the roof was rent with applause. From that period we date (with one trifling exception) a daily increase in the popularity of the distribution society, and an increase of popularity, which the feeble and impotent opposition of the examination party, has only tended to augment.

Now, the great points about the childbed-linen monthly loan society are, that it is less dependent on the fluctuations of public opinion than either the distribution or the child's examination; and that, come what may, there is never any lack of objects on which to exercise its benevolence. Our parish is a very populous one, and, if any thing, contributes, we should be disposed to say, rather more than its due share to the aggregate amount of births in the metropolis and its environs. The consequence is, that the monthly loan society flourishes, and invests its members with a most enviable amount of bustling patronage. The society (whose only notion of dividing time, would appear to be its allotment into months) holds monthly tea-drinkings, at which the monthly report is received, a secretary elected for the month ensuing, and such of the monthly boxes as may not happen to be out on loan for the month, carefully examined.

We were never present at one of these meetings, from all of which it is scarcely necessary to say, gentlemen are carefully excluded; but Mr Bung has been called before the board once or twice, and we have his authority for stating, that its proceedings are conducted with great order and regularity: not more than four members being allowed to speak at one time on any pretence whatever. The regular committee is composed exclusively of married ladies, but a vast number of young unmarried ladies of from eighteen to twenty-five years of age, respectively, are admitted as honorary members, partly because they are very useful in replenishing the boxes, and visiting the confined; partly because it is highly desirable that they be initiated, at an early period, into the more serious and matronly duties of after-life; and partly, because prudent mammas have not unfrequently been known to turn this circumstance to wonderfully good account in matrimonial speculations.

In addition to the loan of the monthly boxes (which are always painted blue, with the name of the society in large white letters on the lid), the society dispense occasional grants of beef-tea, and a composition of warm beer, spice, eggs, and sugar, commonly known by the name of 'caudle,' to its patients. And here again the services of the honorary members are called into requisition, and most cheerfully conceded. Deputations of twos or threes are sent out to visit the patients, and on these occasions there is such a tasting of caudle and beef-tea, such a stirring about of little messes in tiny saucepans on the hob, such a dressing and undressing of infants, such a tying, and folding, and pinning; such a nursing and warming of little legs and feet before the fire, such a delightful confusion of talking and cooking, bustle, importance, and officious-ness, as never can be enjoyed in its full extent but on similar occasions.

In rivalry of these two institutions, and as a last expiring effort to acquire parochial popularity, the child's examination people determined, the other day, on having a grand public examination of the pupils; and the large school-room of the national seminary was, by and with the consent of the parish authorities, devoted to the purpose. Invitation circulars were forwarded to all the principal parishioners, including, of course, the heads of the other two societies, for whose especial behoof and edification the display was intended; and a large audience was confidently anticipated on the occasion. The floor was carefully scrubbed the day before, under the immediate superintendence of the three Miss Browns; forms were placed across the room for the accommodation of the visiters, specimens of writing were carefully selected, and as carefully patched and touched up, until they astonished the children who had written them, rather more than the company who read them; sums in compound addition were rehearsed and re-rehearsed until all the children had the totals by heart; and the preparations altogether were on the most laborious and most comprehensive scale. The morning arrived: the children were yellow-soaped and flannelled, and towelled, till their faces shone again; every pupil's hair was carefully combed into his or her eyes, as the case might be; the girls were adorned with snow-white tippets, and caps bound round the head by a single purple ribbon: the necks of the elder boys were fixed into collars of startling dimensions.

The doors were thrown open, and the Misses Brown and Co. were discovered in plain white muslin dresses, and caps of the same – the child's examination uniform. The room filled: the greetings of the company were loud and cordial. The distributionists trembled, for their popularity was at stake. The eldest boy fell forward, and delivered a propitiatory address from behind his collar. It was from the pen of Mr Henry Brown; the applause was universal, and the Johnson Parkers were aghast. The examination proceeded with success, and terminated in triumph. The child's examination society gained a momentary victory, and the Johnson Parkers retreated in despair.

A secret council of the distributionists was held that night, with Mrs Johnson Parker in the chair, to consider of the best means of recovering the ground they had lost in the favour of the parish. What could be done? Another meeting! Alas! who was to attend it? The Missionary would not do twice; and the slaves were emancipated. A bold step must be taken. The parish must be astonished in some way or other; but no one was able to suggest what the step should be. At length, a very old lady was heard to mumble, in indistinct tones, 'Exeter Hall.'[4] A sudden light broke in upon the meeting. It was unanimously resolved, that a deputation of old ladies should wait upon a celebrated orator imploring his assistance, and the favour of a speech; and that the deputation should also wait on two or three other imbecile old women, not resident in the parish, and entreat their attendance. The application was successful, the meeting was held; the orator (an Irishman) came.[5] He talked of green isles – other shores – vast Atlantic – bosom of the deep – Christian charity – blood and extermination – mercy in hearts – arms in hands – altars and homes – household gods. He wiped his eyes, he blew his nose, and he quoted Latin. The effect was tremendous – the Latin was a decided hit. Nobody knew exactly what it was about, but every body knew it must be affecting, because even the orator was overcome. The popularity of the distribution society among the ladies of our parish is unprecedented; and the child's examination is going fast to decay.

CHAPTER 7

Our Next-door Neighbour

WE are very fond of speculating as we walk through a street, on the character and pursuits of the people who inhabit it; and nothing so materially assists us in these speculations as the appearance of the house doors. The various expressions of the human countenance afford a beautiful and interesting study; but there is something in the physiognomy of street-door knockers, almost as characteristic, and nearly as infallible. Whenever we visit a man for the first time, we contemplate the features of his knocker with the greatest curiosity, for we well know, that between the man and his knocker, there will inevitably be a greater or less degree of resemblance and sympathy.

For instance, there is one description of knocker that used to be common enough, but which is fast passing away — a large round one, with the jolly face of a convivial lion smiling blandly at you, as you twist the sides of your hair into a curl, or pull up your shirt-collar while you are waiting for the door to be opened; we never saw that knocker on the door of a churlish man — so far as our experience is concerned, it invariably bespoke hospitality and another bottle.

No man ever saw this knocker on the door of a small attorney or bill-broker; they always patronize the other lion; a heavy ferocious-looking fellow, with a countenance expressive of savage stupidity — a sort of grand master among the knockers, and a great favourite with the selfish and brutal.

Then there is a little pert Egyptian knocker, with a long thin

George Cruikshank

Our Next-door Neighbours

face, a pinched up nose, and a very sharp chin; he is most in vogue with your government-office people, in light drabs and starched cravats; little spare priggish men, who are perfectly satisfied with their own opinions, and consider themselves of paramount importance.

We were greatly troubled a few years ago, by the innovation of a new kind of knocker, without any face at all, composed of a wreath, depending from a hand or small truncheon. A little trouble and attention, however, enabled us to overcome this difficulty, and to reconcile the new system to our favourite theory. You will invariably find this knocker on the doors of cold and formal people, who always ask you why you *don't* come, and never say *do*.

Every body knows the brass knocker is common to suburban villas, and extensive boarding-schools; and having noticed this genus we have recapitulated all the most prominent and strongly-defined species.

Some phrenologists affirm, that the agitation of a man's brain by different passions, produces corresponding developments in the form of his skull. Do not let us be understood as pushing our theory to the length of asserting, that any alteration in a man's disposition would produce a visible effect on the feature of his knocker. Our position merely is, that in such a case, the magnetism which must exist between a man and his knocker, would induce the man to remove, and seek some knocker more congenial to his altered feelings. If you ever find a man changing his habitation without any reasonable pretext, depend upon it, that, although he may not be aware of the fact himself, it is because he and his knocker are at variance. This is a new theory, but we venture to launch it, nevertheless, as being quite as ingenious and infallible as many thousand of the learned speculations which are daily broached for public good and private fortune-making.

Entertaining these feelings on the subject of knockers, it will be readily imagined with what consternation we viewed the entire removal of the knocker from the door of the next house to the one we lived in, some time ago, and the substitution of a bell. This was a calamity we had never anticipated. The bare idea of any body being able to exist without a knocker, appeared so wild and visionary, that it had never for one instant entered our imagination.

We sauntered moodily from the spot, and bent our steps towards Eaton Square, then just building.[1] What was our astonishment and indignation to find that bells were fast becoming the rule, and knockers the exception! Our theory trembled beneath the shock. We hastened home; and fancying we foresaw in the swift progress of events, its entire abolition, resolved from that day forward to vent our speculations on our next-door neighbours in person. The house adjoining ours on the left hand was uninhabited, and we had, therefore, plenty of leisure to observe our next-door neighbours on the other side.

The house without the knocker was in the occupation of a city clerk, and there was a neatly-written bill in the parlour window intimating that lodgings for a single gentleman were to be let within.

It was a neat, dull little house, on the shady side of the way, with new, narrow floorcloth in the passage, and new, narrow stair-carpets up to the first floor. The paper was new, and the paint was new, and the furniture was new; and all three, paper, paint, and furniture, bespoke the limited means of the tenant. There was a little red and black carpet in the drawing-room, with a border of flooring all the way round; a few stained chairs and a pembroke table. A pink shell was displayed on each of the little sideboards, which, with the addition of a tea-tray and caddy, a few more shells on the mantelpiece, and three peacock's feathers tastefully arranged above them, completed the decorative furniture of the apartment.

This was the room destined for the reception of the single gentleman during the day, and a little back room on the same floor was assigned as his sleeping apartment by night.

The bill had not been long in the window, when a stout good-humoured looking gentleman, of about five-and-thirty, appeared as a candidate for the tenancy. Terms were soon arranged, for the bill was taken down immediately after his first visit. In a day or two the single gentleman came in, and shortly afterwards his real character came out.

First of all, he displayed a most extraordinary partiality for sitting up till three or four o'clock in the morning, drinking whiskey-and-water, and smoking cigars; then he invited friends home, who used to come at ten o'clock, and begin to get happy about the small hours, when they evinced their perfect contentment by singing songs with half-a-dozen verses of two lines each, and a chorus of ten, which chorus used to be shouted forth by the whole strength of the company, in the most enthusiastic and vociferous manner, to the great annoyance of the neighbours, and the special discomfort of another single gentleman overhead.

Now, this was bad enough, occurring as it did three times a week on the average, but this was not all; for when the company *did* go away, instead of walking quietly down the street, as any body else's company would have done, they amused themselves by making alarming and frightful noises, and counterfeiting the shrieks of females in distress; and one night, a red-faced gentleman in a white hat knocked in a most urgent manner at the door of the powdered-headed old gentleman at No. 3, and when the powdered-headed old gentleman who thought one of his married daughters must have been taken ill prematurely, had groped down stairs, and after a great deal of unbolting and key-turning, opened the street door, the red-faced man in the white hat said he hoped he'd excuse his giving him so much trouble, but he'd feel obliged if he'd favour him with a glass of cold spring water, and the loan of a shilling for a cab to take him home, on which the old gentleman slammed the door and went up stairs, and threw the contents of his water jug out of window – very straight, only it went over the wrong man; and the whole street was involved in confusion.

A joke's a joke; and even practical jests are very capital in their way, if you can only get the other party to see the fun of them; but the population of our street were so dull of apprehension, as to be quite lost to a sense of the drollery of this proceeding: and the consequence was, that our next-door neighbour was obliged to tell the single gentleman, that unless he gave up entertaining his friends at home, he really must be compelled to part with him. The single gentleman received the remonstrance with great good-humour, and promised from that time forward, to spend his evenings at a coffee-house — a determination which afforded general and unmixed satisfaction.

The next night passed off very well, every body being delighted with the change; but on the next, the noises were renewed with greater spirit than ever. The single gentleman's friends being unable to see him in his own house every alternate night, had come to the determination of seeing him home every night; and what with the discordant greetings of the friends at parting, and the noise created by the single gentleman in his passage up stairs, and his subsequent struggles to get his boots off, the evil was not to be borne. So, our next-door neighbour gave the single gentleman, who was a very good lodger in other respects, notice to quit; and the single gentleman went away, and entertained his friends in other lodgings.

The next applicant for the vacant first floor, was of a very different character from the troublesome single gentleman who had just quitted it. He was a tall, thin, young gentleman, with a profusion of brown hair, reddish whiskers, and very slightly developed mustaches. He wore a braided surtout, with frogs behind,[2] light gray trousers, and wash-leather gloves, and had altogether rather a military appearance. So unlike the roystering single gentleman. Such insinuating manners, and such a delightful address! So seriously disposed, too! When he first came to look at the lodgings, he inquired most particularly whether he was sure to be able to get a seat in the parish church, and when he had agreed to take them, he requested to have a list of the different local charities, as he intended to subscribe his mite to the most deserving among them.

Our next-door neighbour was now perfectly happy. He had got a lodger at last, of just his own way of thinking — a serious, well-disposed man, who abhorred gaiety, and loved retirement. He took down the bill with a light heart, and pictured in imagination a long series of quiet Sundays, on which he and his lodger would exchange mutual civilities and Sunday papers.

The serious man arrived, and his luggage was to arrive from the country next morning. He borrowed a clean shirt, and a prayer-book, from our next-door neighbour, and retired to rest at an early hour, requesting that he might be called punctually at ten o'clock next morning – not before, as he was much fatigued.

He *was* called, and did not answer: he was called again, but there was no reply. Our next-door neighbour became alarmed and burst the door open. The serious man had left the house mysteriously; carrying with him the shirt, the prayer-book, a tea-spoon, and the bedclothes.

Whether this occurrence, coupled with the irregularities of his former lodger, gave our next-door neighbour an aversion to single gentlemen, we know not; we only know that the next bill which made its appearance in the parlour window intimated generally, that there were furnished apartments to let on the first floor. The bill was soon removed. The new lodgers at first attracted our curiosity, and afterwards excited our interest.

They were a young lad of eighteen or nineteen, and his mother, a lady of about fifty, or it might be less. The mother wore a widow's weeds, and the boy was also clothed in deep mourning. They were poor – very poor; for their only means of support, arose from the pittance the boy earned, by copying writings, and translating for booksellers.

They had removed from some country place and settled in London; partly because it afforded better chances of employment for the boy, and partly, perhaps, with the natural desire to leave a place where they had been in better circumstances, and where their poverty was known. They were proud under their reverses, and above revealing their wants and privations to strangers. How bitter those privations were, and how hard the boy worked to remove them, no one ever knew but themselves. Night after night, two, three, four hours after midnight, could we hear the occasional raking up of the scanty fire, or the hollow and half-stifled cough, which indicated his being still at work; and day after day, could we see more plainly, that nature had set that unearthly light in his plaintive face, which is the beacon of her worst disease.

Actuated, we hope, by a higher feeling than mere curiosity, we contrived to establish, first an acquaintance, and then a close intimacy, with the poor strangers. Our worst fears were realized; the boy was sinking fast. Through a part of the winter, and the whole of the following spring and summer, his labours were unceasingly prolonged: and the mother attempted to procure needle-work embroidery — any thing for bread.

A few shillings now and then, were all she could earn. The boy worked steadily on; dying by minutes, but never once giving utterance to complaint or murmur.

One beautiful autumn evening we went to pay our customary visit to the invalid. His little remaining strength had been decreasing rapidly for two or three days preceding, and he was lying on the sofa at the open window, gazing at the setting sun. His mother had been reading the Bible to him, for she closed the book as we entered, and advanced to meet us.

'I was telling William,' she said, 'that we must manage to take him into the country somewhere, so that he may get quite well. He is not ill, you know, but he is not very strong, and has exerted himself too much lately.' Poor thing! The tears that streamed through her fingers, as she turned aside, as if to adjust her close widow's cap, too plainly showed how fruitless was the attempt to deceive herself.

We sat down by the head of the sofa but said nothing, for we saw the breath of life was passing gently but rapidly from the young form before us. At every respiration, his heart beat more slowly.

The boy placed one hand in ours, grasped his mother's arm with the other, drew her hastily towards him, and fervently kissed her cheek. There was a pause. He sunk back upon his pillow, and looked long and earnestly in his mother's face.

'William, William!' murmured the mother after a long interval, 'don't look at me so — speak to me, dear!'

The boy smiled languidly, but an instant afterwards his features resolved into the same cold, solemn gaze.

'William, dear William! rouse yourself, dear; don't look at me so, love — pray don't! Oh, my God! what shall I do!' cried the widow, clasping her hands in agony — 'my dear boy! he is dying!'

The boy raised himself by a violent effort, and folded his hands together — 'Mother! dear, dear mother, bury me in the open fields — any where but in these dreadful streets. I should like to be where you can see my grave, but not in these close crowded streets; they have killed me; kiss me again mother; put your arm round my neck —'

He fell back, and a strange expression stole upon his features; not of pain or suffering, but an indescribable fixing of every line and muscle.

The boy was dead.

SCENES

The Streets. Morning

The Streets — Morning

THE appearance presented by the streets of London an hour before sunrise, on a summer's morning, is most striking even to the few whose unfortunate pursuits of pleasure, or scarcely less unfortunate pursuits of business, cause them to be well acquainted with the scene. There is an air of cold, solitary desolation about the noiseless streets which we are accustomed to see thronged at other times by a busy, eager crowd, and over the quiet, closely-shut buildings, which throughout the day are swarming with life and bustle, that is very impressive.

The last drunken man, who shall find his way home before sunlight, has just staggered heavily along, roaring out the burden of the drinking song of the previous night: the last houseless vagrant whom penury and police have left in the streets, has coiled up his chilly limbs in some paved corner, to dream of food and warmth. The drunken, the dissipated, and the wretched have disappeared; the more sober and orderly part of the population have not yet awakened to the labours of the day, and the stillness of death is over the streets; its very hue seems to be imparted to them, cold and lifeless as they look in the gray, sombre light of daybreak. The coach-stands in the larger thoroughfares are deserted: the nighthouses are closed; and the chosen promenades of profligate misery are empty.

An occasional policeman may alone be seen at the street-corners, listlessly gazing on the deserted prospect before him; and now and then a rakish-looking cat runs stealthily across the road and descends his own area with as much caution and sliness – bounding first on the water-butt, then on the dust-hole,[1] and then alighting on the flag-stones – as if he were conscious that his character depended on his gallantry of the preceding night escaping public observation. A partially opened bedroom window here and there, bespeaks the heat of the weather, and the uneasy slumbers of its occupant; and the dim scanty flicker of the rushlight, through the window-blind, denotes the chamber of watching or sickness. With these few exceptions, the streets present no signs of life, nor the houses of habitation.

An hour wears away; the spires of the churches and roofs of the principal buildings are faintly tinged with the light of the rising sun; and the streets, by almost imperceptible degrees, begin to resume their bustle and animation. Market-carts roll slowly along: the sleepy waggoner impatiently urging on his tired horses, or vainly endeavouring to awaken the boy, who, luxuriously stretched on the top of the fruit-baskets, forgets, in happy oblivion, his long-cherished curiosity to behold the wonders of London.

Rough, sleepy-looking animals of strange appearance, something between ostlers and hackney-coachmen, begin to take down the shutters of early public-houses; and little deal tables, with the ordinary preparations for a street breakfast, make their appearance at the customary stations. Numbers of men and women (principally the latter), carrying upon their heads heavy baskets of fruit, toil down the park side of Piccadilly, on their way to Covent Garden,[2] and, following each other in rapid succession, form a long straggling line from thence to the turn of the road at Knightsbridge.

Here and there, a bricklayer's labourer, with the day's dinner tied up in a handkerchief, walks briskly to his work, and occasionally a little knot of three or four schoolboys on a stolen bathing expedition rattle merrily over the pavement, their boisterous mirth contrasting forcibly with the demeanour of the little sweep, who, having knocked and rung till his arm aches, and being interdicted by a merciful legislature from endangering his lungs by calling out, sits patiently down on the door-step until the housemaid may happen to awake.

Covent Garden market, and the avenues leading to it, are thronged with carts of all sorts, sizes, and descriptions, from the heavy lumbering waggon, with its four stout horses, to the jingling costermonger's cart with its consumptive donkey. The pavement is already strewed with decayed cabbage-leaves, broken haybands, and all the indescribable litter of a vegetable market; men are shouting, carts backing, horses neighing, boys fighting, basket-women talking, piemen expatiating on the excellence of their pastry, and donkeys braying. These and a hundred other sounds form a compound discordant enough to a Londoner's ears, and remarkably disagreeable to those of country gentlemen who are sleeping at the Hummums[3] for the first time.

Another hour passes away, and the day begins in good earnest. The servant of all work, who, under the plea of sleeping very soundly, has utterly disregarded 'Missis's' ringing for half an hour previously, is warned by Master (whom Missis has sent up in his drapery to the landing-place for that purpose), that it's half-past six, whereupon she awakes all of a sudden, with well-feigned astonishment, and goes down stairs very sulkily, wishing, while she strikes a light, that the principle of spontaneous combustion[4] would extend itself to coals and kitchen range. When the fire is lighted, she opens the street-door to take in the milk, when, by the most singular coincidence in the world, she discovers that the servant next-door has just taken in her milk too, and that Mr Todd's young man over the way, is, by an equally extraordinary chance, taking down his master's shutters. The inevitable consequence is, that she just steps, milk-jug in hand, as far as next-door, just to say 'good morning,' to Betsy Clark, and that Mr Todd's young man just steps over the way to say 'good morning' to both of 'em; and as the aforesaid Mr Todd's young man is almost as good-looking and fascinating as the baker himself, the conversation quickly becomes very interesting, and probably would become more so, if Betsy Clark's Missis, who always will be a followin' her about, didn't give an angry tap at her bedroom window, on which Mr Todd's young man tries to whistle coolly, as he goes back to his shop much faster than he came from it; and the two girls run back to their respective places, and shut their street-doors with surprising softness, each of them poking their heads out of the front parlour-window, a minute afterwards, however, ostensibly with the view of looking at the mail which just then passes by, but really for the purpose of catching another glimpse of Mr Todd's young man,

who being fond of mails, but more of females, takes a short look at
the mails, and a long look at the girls, much to the satisfaction of
all parties concerned.

The mail itself goes on to the coach-office in due course, and
the passengers who are going out by the early coach, stare with
astonishment at the passengers who are coming in by the early
coach, who look blue and dismal, and are evidently under the
influence of that odd feeling produced by travelling, which makes
the events of yesterday morning seem as if they had happened at
least six months ago, and induces people to wonder with considerable gravity whether the friends and relations they took leave of a
fortnight before, have altered much since they left them. The
coach-office is all alive, and the coaches which are just going out,
are surrounded by the usual crowd of Jews and nondescripts, who
seem to consider, Heaven knows why, that it is quite impossible
any man can mount a coach without requiring at least six penny-
worth of oranges, a pen-knife, a pocket-book, a last-year's annual,
a pencil-case, a piece of sponge, and a small series of caricatures.

Half an hour more, and the sun darts his bright rays cheerfully
down the still half-empty streets, and shines with sufficient force to
rouse the dismal laziness of the apprentice, who pauses every other
minute from his task of sweeping out the shop and watering the
pavement in front of it, to tell another apprentice similarly employed, how hot it will be to-day, or to stand with his right hand
shading his eyes, and his left resting on the broom, gazing at
the 'Wonder,' or the 'Tally-ho,' or the 'Nimrod,' or some other fast
coach, till it is out of sight, when he re-enters the shop, envying
the passengers on the outside of the fast coach, and thinking of the
old red brick house 'down in the country,' where he went to
school: the miseries of the milk and water, and thick bread
and scrapings, fading into nothing before the pleasant recollection
of the green field the boys used to play in, and the green pond he
was caned for presuming to fall into, and other schoolboy
associations.

Cabs, with trunks and band-boxes between the drivers' legs and
outside the apron, rattle briskly up and down the streets on their

way to the coach-offices or steam-packet wharfs; and the cab-drivers and hackney-coachmen who are on the stand polish up the ornamental part of their dingy vehicles – the former wondering how people can prefer 'them wild beast cariwans of homnibuses, to a riglar cab with a fast trotter,' and the latter admiring how people can trust their necks into one of 'them crazy cabs, when they can have a 'spectable 'ackney cotche with a pair of 'orses as von't run away with no vun;' a consolation unquestionably founded on fact, seeing that a hackney coach-horse never was known to run at all, 'except' as the smart cabman in front of the rank observes, 'except one, and *he* run back'ards.'

The shops are now completely opened, and apprentices and shop-men are busily engaged in cleaning and decking the windows for the day. The bakers' shops in town are filled with servants and children waiting for the drawing of the first batch of rolls – an operation which was performed a full hour ago in the suburbs, for the early clerk population of Somers and Camden towns, Islington, and Pentonville,[5] are fast pouring into the city; or directing their steps towards Chancery-lane and the Inns of Court. Middle-aged men, whose salaries have by no means increased in the same proportion as their families, plod steadily along, apparently with no object in view but the counting-house; knowing by sight almost every body they meet or overtake, for they have seen them every morning (Sundays excepted) during the last twenty years, but speaking to no one. If they do happen to overtake a personal acquaintance, they just exchange a hurried salutation, and keep walking on, either by his side, or in front of him, as his rate of walking may chance to be. As to stopping to shake hands, or to take the friend's arm, they seem to think that as it is not included in their salary, they have no right to do it. Small office lads in large hats, who are made men before they are boys, hurry along in pairs with their first coat carefully brushed, and the white trousers of last Sunday plentifully besmeared with dust and ink. It evidently requires a considerable mental struggle to avoid investing part of the day's dinner-money in the purchase of the stale tarts so temptingly exposed in dusty tins at the pastry-cooks' doors;[6] but a consciousness of their own importance and the receipt of seven shillings a week, with the prospect of an early rise to eight, comes to their aid, and they accordingly put their hats a little more on one side, and look under the bonnets of all the milliners' and stay-makers' apprentices they meet — poor girls! — the hardest worked, the worst paid, and too often, the worst used class of the community.

Eleven o'clock, and a new set of people fill the streets. The goods in the shop-windows are invitingly arranged; the shop-men in their white neckerchiefs and spruce coats, look as if they couldn't clean a window if their lives depended on it; the carts have disappeared from Covent Garden; the waggoners have returned, and the costermongers repaired to their ordinary 'beats' in the suburbs; clerks are at their offices, and gigs, cabs, omnibuses, and saddle-horses, are conveying their masters to the same destination. The streets are thronged with a vast concourse of people, gay and shabby, rich and poor, idle and industrious; and we come to the heat, bustle, and activity of NOON.

CHAPTER 2

The Streets — Night

BUT the streets of London, to be beheld in the very height of their glory, should be seen on a dark, dull, murky winter's night, when there is just enough damp gently stealing down to make the pavement greasy, without cleansing it of any of its impurities; and when the heavy lazy mist, which hangs over every object, makes the gas-lamps look brighter, and the brilliantly-lighted shops more splendid, from the contrast they present to the darkness around. All the people who are at home on such a night as this, seem disposed to make themselves as snug and comfortable as possible; and the passengers in the streets have excellent reason to envy the fortunate individuals who are seated by their own firesides.

In the larger and better kind of streets, dining-parlour curtains are closely drawn, kitchen fires blaze brightly up, and savoury steams of hot dinners salute the nostrils of the hungry wayfarer, as he plods wearily by the area railings. In the suburbs, the muffin-boy rings his way down the little street, much more slowly than he is wont to do; for Mrs Macklin, at No. 4, has no sooner opened her little street-door, and screamed out 'Muffins!' with all her might, than Mrs Walker, at No. 5, puts her head out of the parlour-window, and screams 'Muffins!' too; and Mrs Walker has scarcely got the words out of her lips, than Mrs Peplow, over the way, lets loose Master Peplow, who darts down the street, with a velocity which nothing but buttered muffins in perspective could possibly inspire, and drags the boy back by main force, whereupon Mrs Macklin and Mrs Walker, just to save the boy trouble, and to say a few neighbourly words to Mrs Peplow at the same time, run over the way and buy their muffins at Mrs Peplow's door, when it appears from the voluntary statement of Mrs Walker, that her 'kittle's jist a-biling, and the cups and sarsers ready laid,' and that, as it was such a wretched night out o' doors, she's made up her mind to have a nice hot comfortable cup o' tea – a determination at which, by the most singular coincidence, the other two ladies had simultaneously arrived.

After a little conversation about the wretchedness of the weather and the merits of tea, with a digression relative to the viciousness of boys as a rule, and the amiability of Master Peplow as an exception, Mrs Walker sees her husband coming down the street; and as he must want his tea, poor man, after his dirty walk from the Docks, she instantly runs across, muffins in hand, and Mrs Macklin does the same, and after a few words to Mrs Walker, they all pop into their little houses, and slam their little street-doors, which are not opened again for the remainder of the evening, except to the nine o'clock 'beer,'[1] who comes round with a lantern in front of his tray, and says as he lends Mrs Walker 'Yesterday's 'Tiser,'[2] that he's blessed if he can hardly hold the pot, much less feel the paper, for it's one of the bitterest nights he ever felt, 'cept the night when the man was frozen to death in the Brick-field.

After a little prophetic conversation with the policeman at the street-corner, touching a probable change in the weather, and the setting-in of a hard frost, the nine o'clock beer returns to his master's house, and employs himself for the remainder of the evening, in assiduously stirring the tap-room fire, and deferentially taking part in the conversation of the worthies assembled round it.

The streets in the vicinity of the Marsh-gate[3] and Victoria Theatre present an appearance of dirt and discomfort on such a night, which the groups who lounge about them in no degree tend to diminish. Even the little block-tin temple sacred to baked potatoes, surmounted by a splendid design in variegated lamps, looks less gay than usual; and as to the kidney-pie stand, its glory has quite departed. The candle in the transparent lamp, manufactured of oil-paper, embellished with 'characters,' has been blown out fifty times, so the kidney-pie merchant, tired with running backwards and forwards to the next wine-vaults, to get a light, has given up the idea of illumination in despair, and the only signs of his 'whereabout,' are the bright sparks, of which a long irregular train is whirled down the street every time he opens his portable oven to hand a hot kidney-pie to a customer.

Flat fish, oyster, and fruit venders linger hopelessly in the kennel, in vain endeavouring to attract customers; and the ragged boys who usually disport themselves about the streets, stand crouched in little knots in some projecting doorway, or under the canvass blind of the cheesemonger's, where great flaring gas-lights, unshaded by any glass, display huge piles of bright red, and pale yellow cheeses, mingled with little five-penny dabs of dingy bacon, various tubs of weekly Dorset,[4] and cloudy rolls of 'best fresh.'[5]

Here they amuse themselves with theatrical converse, arising out of their last half-price visit to the Victoria gallery, admire the terrific combat, which is nightly encored, and expatiate on the inimitable manner in which Bill Thompson can 'come the double monkey,'[6] or go through the mysterious involutions of the sailor's hornpipe.

It is nearly eleven o'clock, and the cold thin rain which has been drizzling so long, is beginning to pour down in good earnest; the baked-potato man has departed — the kidney-pie man has just walked away with his warehouse on his arm — the cheesemonger has drawn in his blind, and the boys have dispersed. The constant clicking of pattens on the slippy and uneven pavement, and the rustling of umbrellas, as the wind blows against the shop-windows, bear testimony to the inclemency of the night; and the policeman, with his oilskin cape buttoned closely round him, seems as he holds his hat on his head, and turns round to avoid the gust of wind and rain which drives against him at the street-corner, to be very far from congratulating himself on the prospect before him.

The little chandler's shop with the cracked bell behind the door, whose melancholy tinkling has been regulated by the demand for quarterns of sugar and half-ounces of coffee, is shutting up. The crowds which have been passing to and fro during the whole day, are rapidly dwindling away; and the noise of shouting and quarrelling which issues from the public-houses, is almost the only sound that breaks the melancholy stillness of the night.

There was another, but it has ceased. That wretched woman with the infant in her arms, round whose meagre form the remnant of her own scanty shawl is carefully wrapped, has been attempting to sing some popular ballad, in the hope of wringing a few pence from the compassionate passer-by. A brutal laugh at her weak voice is all she has gained. The tears fall thick and fast down her own pale face; the child is cold and hungry, and its low half-stifled wailing adds to the misery of its wretched mother, as she moans aloud, and sinks despairingly down, on a cold damp door-step.

Singing! How few of those who pass such a miserable creature as this, think of the anguish of heart, the sinking of soul and spirit, which the very effort of singing produces. Bitter mockery! Disease, neglect, and starvation, faintly articulating the words of the joyous ditty, that has enlivened your hours of feasting and merriment, God knows how often! It is no subject of jeering. The weak tremulous voice tells a fearful tale of want and famishing; and the feeble singer of this roaring song may turn away, only to die of cold and hunger.

One o'clock! Parties returning from the different theatres foot it through the muddy streets; cabs, hackney-coaches, carriages, and theatre-omnibuses, roll swiftly by; watermen with dim dirty lanterns in their hands, and large brass plates[7] upon their breasts, who have been shouting and rushing about, for the last two hours retire to their watering-houses, to solace themselves with the creature comforts of pipes and purl;[8] the half-price pit and box frequenters of the theatres throng to the different houses of refreshment; and chops, kidneys, rabbits, oysters, stout, cigars, and 'goes' innumerable, are served up amidst a noise and confusion of smoking, running, knife-clattering, and waiter-chattering, perfectly indescribable.

The more musical portion of the play-going community betake themselves to some harmonic meeting.[9] As a matter of curiosity let us follow them thither for a few moments.

In a lofty room of spacious dimensions, are seated some eighty or a hundred guests knocking little pewter measures on the tables, and hammering away, with the handles of their knives, as if they were so many trunk-makers. They are applauding a glee, which has just been executed by the three 'professional gentlemen' at the top of the centre table, one of whom is in the chair – the little pompous man with the bald head just emerging from the collar of his green coat. The others are seated on either side of him – the stout man with the small voice, and the thin-faced dark man in black. The little man in the chair is a most amusing personage, – *such* condescending grandeur, and *such* a voice!

'Bass!' as the young gentleman near us with the blue stock forcibly remarks to his companion, 'bass! I b'lieve you; he can go down lower than any man: so low sometimes that you can't hear him.' And so he does. To hear him growling away, gradually lower and lower down, till he can't get back again, is the most delightful thing in the world, and it is quite impossible to witness unmoved the impressive solemnity with which he pours forth his soul in 'My 'art's in the 'ighlands,'[10] or 'The brave old Hoak.'[11] The stout man is also addicted to sentimentality, and warbles 'Fly, fly from the world, my Bessy with me,'[12] or some such song, with lady-like sweetness, and in the most seductive tones imaginable.

'Pray give your orders, gen'l'm'n — pray give your orders,' — says the pale-faced man with the red head; and demands for 'goes' of gin and 'goes' of brandy, and pints of stout, and cigars of peculiar mildness, are vociferously made from all parts of the room. The 'professional' gentlemen are in the very height of their glory, and bestow condescending nods, or even a word or two of recognition, on the better known frequenters of the room, in the most bland and patronizing manner possible.

That little round-faced man, with the small brown surtout, white stockings and shoes, is in the comic line; the mixed air of self-denial, and mental consciousness of his own powers, with which he acknowledges the call of the chair, is particularly gratifying. 'Gen'l'men,' says the little pompous man, accompanying the word with a knock of the president's hammer on the table — 'Gen'l'men, allow me to claim your attention — our friend, Mr Smuggins will oblige.' — 'Bravo!' shout the company; and Smuggins, after a considerable quantity of coughing by way of symphony, and a most facetious sniff or two, which afford general delight, sings a comic song, with a fal-de-ral — tol-de-rol chorus at the end of every verse, much longer than the verse itself. It is received with unbounded applause, and after some aspiring genius has volunteered a recitation, and failed dismally therein, the little pompous man gives another knock, and says, 'Gen'l'men, we will attempt a glee, if you please.' This announcement calls forth tumultuous applause, and the more energetic spirits express the unqualified approbation it affords them, by knocking one or two stout glasses off their legs[13] — a humorous device; but one which frequently occasions some slight altercation when the form of paying the damage is proposed to be gone through by the waiter.

Scenes like these are continued until three or four o'clock in the morning; and even when they close, fresh ones open to the inquisitive novice. But as a description of all of them, however slight, would require a volume, the contents of which, however instructive, would be by no means pleasing, we make our bow, and drop the curtain.

CHAPTER 3

Shops and Their Tenants

WHAT inexhaustible food for speculation, do the streets of London afford! We never were able to agree with Sterne in pitying the man who could travel from Dan to Beersheba, and say that all was barren;[1] we have not the slightest commiseration for the man who can take up his hat and stick, and walk from Covent-garden to St Paul's churchyard, and back into the bargain, without deriving some amusement — we had almost said instruction — from his perambulation. And yet there are such beings: we meet them every day. Large black stocks and light waistcoats, jet canes and discontented countenances, are the characteristics of the race; other people brush quickly by you, steadily plodding on to business, or cheerfully running after pleasure. These men linger listlessly past, looking as happy and animated as a policeman on duty. Nothing seems to make an impression on their minds: nothing short of being knocked down by a porter, or run over by a cab, will disturb their equanimity. You will meet them on a fine day in any of the leading thoroughfares: peep through the window of a west-end cigar-shop in the evening, if you can manage to get a glimpse between the blue curtains which intercept the vulgar gaze, and you see them in their only enjoyment of existence. There they are lounging about, on round tubs and pipe-boxes, in all the dignity of whiskers, and gilt watch-guards; whispering soft nothings to the young lady in amber, with the large earrings, who, as she sits behind the counter in a blaze of adoration and gas-light, is the admiration of all the female servants in the neighbourhood, and the envy of every milliner's apprentice within two miles round.

One of our principal amusements is to watch the gradual progress – the rise or fall – of particular shops. We have formed an intimate acquaintance with several, in different parts of town, and are perfectly acquainted with their whole history. We could name off-hand, twenty at least, which we are quite sure have paid no taxes for the last six years. They are never inhabited for more than two months consecutively, and, we verily believe, have witnessed every retail trade in the directory.

There is one, whose history is a sample of the rest, in whose fate we have taken especial interest, having had the pleasure of knowing it ever since it has been a shop. It is on the Surrey side of the water – a little distance beyond the Marsh-gate. It was originally a substantial, good-looking private house enough; the landlord got into difficulties, the house got into Chancery, the tenant went away, and the house went to ruin. At this period our acquaintance with it commenced: the paint was all worn off; the windows were broken, the area was green with neglect and the overflowings of the water-butt; the butt itself was without a lid, and the street-door was the very picture of misery. The chief pastime of the children in the vicinity had been to assemble in a body on the steps, and take it in turn to knock loud double knocks at the door, to the great satisfaction of the neighbours generally, and especially of the nervous old lady next door but one. Numerous complaints were made, and several small basins of water discharged over the offenders, but without effect. In this state of things, the marine-store dealer at the corner of the street, in the most obliging manner took the knocker off, and sold it: and the unfortunate house looked more wretched than ever.

We deserted our friend for a few weeks. What was our surprise, on our return, to find no trace of its existence! In its place was a handsome shop, fast approaching to a state of completion, and on the shutters were large bills, informing the public that it would shortly be opened with 'an extensive stock of linen-drapery and haberdashery.' It opened in due course; there was the name of the proprietor 'and Co.' in gilt letters, almost too dazzling to look at. Such ribbons and shawls! and two such elegant young men behind the counter, each in a clean collar and white neckcloth, like the lover in a farce. As to the proprietor, he did nothing but walk up and down the shop, and hand seats to the ladies, and hold important conversations with the handsomest of the young men, who was shrewdly suspected by the neighbours to be the 'Co.' We saw all this with sorrow; we felt a fatal presentiment that the shop was doomed – and so it was. Its decay was slow, but sure. Tickets gradually appeared in the windows; then rolls of flannel, with labels on them, were stuck outside the door; then a bill was pasted on the street-door, intimating that the first floor was to let *un*furnished; then one of the young men disappeared altogether, and the other took to a black neckerchief, and the proprietor took to drinking. The shop became dirty, broken panes of glass remained unmended, and the stock disappeared piecemeal. At last the company's man came to cut off the water, and then the linen-draper cut off himself, leaving the landlord his compliments and the key.

The next occupant was a fancy stationer. The shop was more modestly painted than before, still it was neat; but somehow we always thought, as we passed, that it looked like a poor and struggling concern. We wished the man well, but we trembled for his success. He was a widower evidently, and had employment elsewhere, for he passed us every morning on his road to the city. The business was carried on by his eldest daughter. Poor girl! she needed no assistance. We occasionally caught a glimpse of two or three children, in mourning like herself, as they sat in the little parlour behind the shop; and we never passed at night without seeing the eldest girl at work, either for them, or in making some elegant little trifle for sale. We often thought, as her pale face looked more sad and pensive in the dim candle-light, that if those thoughtless females who interfere with the miserable market of poor creatures such as these, knew but one half of the misery they suffer, and the bitter privations they endure, in their honourable attempts to earn a scanty subsistence, they would, perhaps, resign even opportunities for the gratification of vanity, and an immodest love of self-display, rather than drive them to a last dreadful resource, which it would shock the delicate feelings of these *charitable* ladies to hear named.

But we are forgetting the shop. Well, we continued to watch it, and every day showed too clearly, the increasing poverty of its inmates. The children were clean, it is true, but their clothes were threadbare and shabby; no tenant had been procured for the upper part of the house, from the letting of which, a portion of the means of paying the rent was to have been derived, and a slow, wasting consumption prevented the eldest girl from continuing her exertions. Quarter-day arrived. The landlord had suffered from the extravagance of his last tenant, and he had no compassion for the struggles of his successor; he put in an execution. As we passed one morning, the broker's men were removing the little furniture there was in the house, and a newly-posted bill informed us it was again 'To Let.' What became of the last tenant we never could learn; we believe the girl is past all suffering, and beyond all sorrow. God help her! We hope she is.

We were somewhat curious to ascertain what would be the next stage — for that the place had no chance of succeeding now, was perfectly clear. The bill was soon taken down, and some alterations were being made in the interior of the shop. We were in a fever of expectation; we exhausted conjecture — we imagined all possible trades, none of which were perfectly reconcilable with our idea of the gradual decay of the tenement. It opened, and we wondered why we had not guessed at the real state of the case before. The shop — not a large one at the best of times — had been converted into two: one was a bonnet-shape maker's, the other was opened by a tobacconist, who also dealt in walking-sticks and Sunday newspapers; the two were separated by a thin partition, covered with tawdry striped paper.

The tobacconist remained in possession longer than any tenant within our recollection. He was a red-faced, impudent, good-for-nothing dog, evidently accustomed to take things as they came, and to make the best of a bad job. He sold as many cigars as he could, and smoked the rest. He occupied the shop as long as he could make peace with the landlord, and when he could no longer live in quiet, he very coolly locked the door, and bolted himself. From this period, the two little dens have undergone innumerable changes. The tobacconist was succeeded by a theatrical hair-dresser, who ornamented the window with a great variety of 'characters,' and terrific combats. The bonnet-shape maker gave place to a green-grocer, and the histrionic barber was succeeded, in his turn, by a tailor. So numerous have been the changes, that we have of late done little more than mark the peculiar but certain indications of a house being poorly inhabited. It has been progressing by almost imperceptible degrees. The occupiers of the shops have gradually given up room after room, until they have only reserved the little parlour for themselves. First there appeared a brass plate on the private door, with 'Ladies' School' legibly engraved thereon; shortly afterwards we observed a second brass plate, then a bell, and then another bell.

When we paused in front of our old friend, and observed these signs of poverty, which are not to be mistaken, we thought, as we turned away, that the house had attained its lowest pitch of degradation. We were wrong. When we last passed it, a 'dairy' was established in the area, and a party of melancholy-looking fowls were amusing themselves by running in at the front door, and out at the back one.

CHAPTER 4

Scotland-yard

SCOTLAND-YARD[1] is a small — a very small — tract of land, bounded on one side by the river Thames, on the other by the gardens of Northumberland House: abutting at one end on the bottom of Northumberland-street, at the other on the back of

Whitehall-place. When this territory was first accidentally discovered by a country gentleman who lost his way in the Strand, some years ago, the original settlers were found to be a tailor, a publican, two eating-house keepers, and a fruit-pie maker; and it was also found to contain a race of strong and bulky men, who repaired to the wharfs in Scotland-yard regularly every morning, about five or six o'clock, to fill heavy waggons with coal, with which they proceeded to distant places up the country, and supplied the inhabitants with fuel. When they had emptied their waggons, they again returned for a fresh supply; and this trade was continued throughout the year.

As the settlers derived their subsistence from ministering to the wants of these primitive traders, the articles exposed for sale, and the places where they were sold, bore strong outward marks of being expressly adapted to their tastes and wishes. The tailor displayed in his window a Lilliputian pair of leather gaiters, and a diminutive round frock, while each doorpost was appropriately garnished with a model of a coal-sack. The two eating-house keepers exhibited joints of a magnitude, and puddings of a solidity, which coalheavers alone could appreciate; and the fruit-pie maker displayed on his well-scrubbed window-board large white compositions of flour and dripping, ornamented with pink stains, giving rich promise of the fruit within, which made their huge mouths water, as they lingered past.

But the choicest spot in all Scotland-yard was the old public-house in the corner. Here, in a dark wainscotted-room of ancient appearance, cheered by the glow of a mighty fire, and decorated with an enormous clock, whereof the face was white, and the figures black, sat the lusty coalheavers, quaffing large draughts of Barclay's best,[2] and puffing forth volumes of smoke, which wreathed heavily above their heads, and involved the room in a thick dark cloud. From this apartment might their voices be heard on a winter's night, penetrating to the very bank of the river, as they shouted out some sturdy chorus, or roared forth the burden of a popular song; dwelling upon the last few words with a strength and length of emphasis which made the very roof tremble above them.

Scotland Yard

Here, too, would they tell old legends of what the Thames was in ancient times, when the Patent Shot Manufactory[3] wasn't built, and Waterloo-bridge[4] had never been thought of; and then they would shake their heads with portentous looks, to the deep edification of the rising generation of heavers, who crowded round them, and wondered where all this would end; whereat the tailor would take his pipe solemnly from his mouth, and say, how that he hoped it might end well, but he very much doubted whether it would or not, and couldn't rightly tell what to make of it — a mysterious expression of opinion, delivered with a semi-prophetic air, which never failed to elicit the fullest concurrence of the assembled company; and so they would go on drinking and wondering till ten o'clock came, and with it the tailor's wife to fetch him home, when the little party broke up, to meet again in the same room, and say and do precisely the same things on the following evening at the same hour.

About this time the barges that came up the river began to bring vague rumours to Scotland-yard of somebody in the city having been heard to say, that the Lord Mayor had threatened in so many words to pull down the old London-bridge,[5] and build up a new one. At first these rumours were disregarded as idle tales, wholly destitute of foundation, for nobody in Scotland-yard doubted that if the Lord Mayor contemplated any such dark design, he would just be clapped up in the Tower for a week or two, and then killed off for high treason.

By degrees, however, the reports grew stronger, and more frequent, and at last a barge, laden with numerous chaldrons of the best Wallsend,[6] brought up the positive intelligence that several of the arches of the old bridge were stopped, and that preparations were actually in progress for constructing the new one. What an excitement was visible in the old tap-room on that memorable night! Each man looked into his neighbour's face, pale with alarm and astonishment, and read therein an echo of the sentiments which filled his own breast. The oldest heaver present proved to demonstration, that the moment the piers were removed, all the water in the Thames would run clean off, and leave a dry gulley in its place.

What was to become of the coal-barges — of the trade of Scotland-yard — of the very existence of its population? The tailor shook his head more sagely than usual, and grimly pointing to a knife on the table, bid them wait and see what happened. He said nothing — not he; but if the Lord Mayor didn't fall a victim to popular indignation, why he would be rather astonished; that was all.

They did wait; barge after barge arrived, and still no tidings of the assassination of the Lord Mayor. The first stone was laid; it was done by a Duke — the King's brother.[7] Years passed away, and the bridge was opened by the King himself. In course of time, the piers were removed; and when the people in Scotland-yard got up next morning in the confident expectation of being able to step over to Pedlar's Acre[8] without wetting the soles of their shoes, they found to their unspeakable astonishment that the water was just where it used to be.

A result so different from that which they had anticipated from this first improvement, produced its full effect upon the inhabitants of Scotland-yard. One of the eating-house keepers began to court public opinion, and to look for customers among a new class of people. He covered his little dining-tables with white cloths, and got a painter's apprentice to inscribe something about hot joints from twelve to two, in one of the little panes of his shop-window. Improvement began to march with rapid strides to the very threshold of Scotland-yard. A new market sprung up at Hunger-ford,[9] and the Police Commissioners established their office in Whitehall-place. The traffic in Scotland-yard increased; fresh Members were added to the House of Commons, the Metropolitan Representatives found it a near cut, and many other foot passengers followed their example.

We marked the advance of civilization, and beheld it with a sigh. The eating-house keeper who manfully resisted the innovation of table-cloths, was losing ground every day, as his opponent gained it, and a deadly feud sprung up between them. The genteel one no longer took his evening's pint in Scotland-yard, but drank gin and water at a 'parlour' in Parliament-street. The fruit-pie maker still continued to visit the old room, but he took to smoking cigars, and began to call himself a pastrycook, and to read the papers. The old heavers still assembled round the ancient fireplace, but their talk was mournful: and the loud song and the joyous shout were heard no more.

And what is Scotland-yard now? How have its old customs changed; and how has the ancient simplicity of its inhabitants faded away! The old tottering public-house is converted into a spacious and lofty 'wine-vaults;' gold leaf has been used in the construction of the letters which emblazon its exterior, and the poet's art has been called into requisition, to intimate that if you drink a certain description of ale, you must hold fast by the rail. The tailor exhibits in his window the pattern of a foreign-looking brown surtout, with silk buttons, a fur collar and fur cuffs. He wears a stripe down the outside of each leg of his trousers: and we have detected his assistants (for he has assistants now) in the act of sitting on the shop-board in the same uniform.

At the other end of the little row of houses a boot-maker has established himself in a brick box, with the additional innovation of a first floor; and here he exposes for sale, boots – real Wellington boots – an article which a few years ago, none of the original inhabitants had ever seen or heard of. It was but the other day, that a dress-maker opened another little box in the middle of the row; and, when we thought that the spirit of change could produce no alteration beyond that, a jeweller appeared, and not content with exposing gilt rings and copper bracelets out of number, put up an announcement, which still sticks in his window, that 'ladies' ears may be pierced within.' The dress-maker employs a young lady who wears pockets in her apron; and the tailor informs the public that gentlemen may have their own materials made up.

Amidst all this change, and restlessness, and innovation, there remains but one old man, who seems to mourn the downfall of this ancient place. He holds no converse with human kind, but, seated on a wooden bench at the angle of the wall which fronts the crossing from Whitehall-place, watches in silence the gambols of his sleek and well-fed dogs. He is the presiding genius of Scotland-yard. Years and years have rolled over his head; but, in fine weather or in foul, hot or cold, wet or dry, hail, rain, or snow, he is still in his accustomed spot. Misery and want are depicted in his countenance; his form is bent by age, his head is gray with length of trial, but there he sits from day to day, brooding over the past; and thither he will continue to drag his feeble limbs, until his eyes have closed upon Scotland-yard, and upon the world together.

A few years hence, and the antiquary of another generation looking into some mouldy record of the strife and passions that agitated the world in these times, may glance his eye over the pages we have just filled: and on all his knowledge of the history of the past, not all his black-letter lore, or his skill in book-collecting, not all the dry studies of a long life, or the dusty volumes that have cost him a fortune, may help him to the whereabout, either of Scotland-yard, or of any one of the landmarks we have mentioned in describing it.

CHAPTER 5

Seven Dials

WE have always been of opinion that if Tom King and the Frenchman[1] had not immortalized Seven Dials,[2] Seven Dials would have immortalized itself. Seven Dials! the region of song and poetry — first effusions, and last dying speeches: hallowed by the names of Catnach and of Pitts[3] — names that will entwine themselves with costermongers, and barrel organs, when penny magazines shall have superseded penny yards of song,[4] and capital punishment be unknown!

Look at the construction of the place. The gordian knot[5] was all very well in its way: so was the maze of Hampton Court:[6] so is the maze at the Beulah Spa:[7] so were the ties of stiff white neckcloths, when the difficulty of getting one on, was only to be equalled by

Seven Dials

the apparent impossibility of ever getting it off again. But what involutions can compare with those of Seven Dials? Where is there such another maze of streets, courts, lanes, and alleys? Where such a pure mixture of Englishmen and Irishmen, as in this complicated part of London? We boldly aver that we doubt the veracity of the legend to which we have adverted. We *can* suppose a man rash enough to inquire at random – at a house with lodgers too – for a Mr Thompson, with all but the certainty before his eyes, of finding at least two or three Thompsons in any house of moderate dimensions; but a Frenchman – a Frenchman in Seven Dials! Pooh! He was an Irishman. Tom King's education had been neglected in his infancy, and as he couldn't understand half the man said, he took it for granted he was talking French.

The stranger who finds himself in 'The Dials' for the first time, and stands Belzoni-like,[8] at the entrance of seven obscure passages, uncertain which to take, will see enough around him to keep his curiosity and attention awake for no inconsiderable time. From the irregular square into which he has plunged, the streets and courts dart in all directions, until they are lost in the unwholesome vapour which hangs over the house-tops, and renders the dirty perspective uncertain and confined; and lounging at every corner, as if they came there to take a few gasps of such fresh air as has found its way so far, but is too much exhausted already, to be enabled to force itself into the narrow alleys around, are groups of people, whose appearance and dwellings would fill any mind but a regular Londoner's with astonishment.

On one side, a little crowd has collected round a couple of ladies, who having imbibed the contents of various 'three-outs'[9] of gin and bitters in the course of the morning, have at length differed on some point of domestic arrangement, and are on the eve of settling the quarrel satisfactorily, by an appeal to blows, greatly to the interest of other ladies who live in the same house, and tenements adjoining, and who are all partisans on one side or other.

'Vy don't you pitch into her, Sarah?' exclaims one half-dressed matron, by way of encouragement. 'Vy don't you? if *my* 'usband had treated her with a drain last night, unbeknown to me, I'd tear her precious eyes out – a wixen!'

'What's the matter, ma'am?' inquires another old woman, who has just bustled up to the spot.

'Matter!' replies the first speaker, talking *at* the obnoxious combatant, 'matter! Here's poor dear Mrs Sulliwin, as has five blessed children of her own, can't go out a-charing for one arternoon, but what hussies must be a-comin', and 'ticing avay her oun' 'usband, as she's been married to twelve year come next Easter Monday, for I see the certificate ven I vas a drinkin' a cup o' tea vith her, only the werry last blessed Ven'sday as ever was sent. I 'appen'd to say promiscuously "Mrs Sulliwin, says I —" '

'What do you mean by hussies?' interrupts a champion of the other party, who has evinced a strong inclination throughout to get up a branch fight on her own account ('Hoo-roar,' ejaculates a pot-boy in parenthesis, 'put the kye-bosk on her,[10] Mary!'), 'What do you mean by hussies?' reiterates the champion.

'Niver mind,' replies the opposition expressively, 'niver mind; *you* go home, and, ven you're quite sober, mend your stockings.'

This somewhat personal allusion, not only to the lady's habits of intemperance, but also to the state of her wardrobe, rouses her utmost ire, and she accordingly complies with the urgent request of the bystanders to 'pitch in,' with considerable alacrity. The scuffle becomes general, and terminates, in minor play-bill phraseology, with 'arrival of the policemen, interior of the station-house, and impressive *dénouement*.'

In addition to the numerous groups who are idling about the gin-shops, and squabbling in the centre of the road, every post in the open space has its occupant, who leans against it for hours, with listless perseverance. It is odd enough that one class of men in London appear to have no enjoyment beyond leaning against posts. We never saw a regular bricklayer's labourer take any other recreation, fighting excepted. Pass through St Giles's[11] in the evening of a week-day, there they are in their fustian dresses, spotted with brick-dust and whitewash, leaning against posts. Walk through Seven Dials on Sunday morning: there they are again, drab, or light corduroy trousers, Blucher boots,[12] blue coats, and great yellow waistcoats, leaning against posts. The idea of a man dressing himself in his best clothes, to lean against a post all day!

The peculiar character of these streets, and the close resemblance each one bears to its neighbour, by no means tends to decrease the bewilderment in which the unexperienced wayfarer through 'the Dials' finds himself involved. He traverses streets of dirty, straggling houses, with now and then an unexpected court composed of buildings as ill-proportioned and deformed as the half-naked children that wallow in the kennels. Here and there, a little dark chandler's shop, with a cracked bell hung up behind the door to announce the entrance of a customer, or betray the presence of some young gentleman in whom a passion for shop tills has developed itself at an early age: others, as if for support, against some handsome lofty building, which usurps the place of a low dingy public-house; long rows of broken and patched windows expose plants that may have flourished when 'The Dials' were built, in vessels as dirty as 'The Dials' themselves; and shops for the purchase of rags, bones, old iron, and kitchen-stuff, vie in cleanliness with the bird-fanciers and rabbit-dealers, which one might fancy so many arks, but for the irresistible conviction that no bird in its proper senses, who was permitted to leave one of them, would ever come back again. Brokers' shops, which would seem to have been established by humane individuals, as refuges for destitute bugs, interspersed with announcements of day-schools, penny theatres, petition-writers, mangles, and music for balls or routs, complete the 'still life' of the subject; and dirty men, filthy women, squalid children, fluttering shuttlecocks, noisy battledores, reeking pipes, bad fruit, more than doubtful oysters, attenuated cats, depressed dogs, and anatomical fowls, are its cheerful accompaniments.

If the external appearance of the houses, or a glance at their inhabitants, present but few attractions, a closer acquaintance with either is little calculated to alter one's first impression. Every room has its separate tenant, and every tenant is, by the same mysterious dispensation which causes a country curate to 'increase and multiply'[13] most marvellously, generally the head of a numerous family.

The man in the shop, perhaps, is in the baked 'jemmy'[14] line, or the firewood and hearthstone line, or any other line which requires a floating capital of eighteen pence or thereabouts; and he and his family live in the shop, and the small back parlour behind it. Then there is an Irish labourer and *his* family in the back kitchen, and a jobbing-man – carpet-beater and so forth – with *his* family in the front one. In the front one-pair, there's another man with another wife and family, and in the back one-pair there's 'a young 'oman as takes in tambour-work, and dresses quite genteel,' who talks a good deal about 'my friend,' and can't 'abear any thing low.' The second floor front, and the rest of the lodgers, are just a second edition of the people below, except a shabby-genteel man in the back attic, who has his half-pint of coffee every morning from the coffee-shop next door but one, which boasts a little front den called a coffee-room, with a fireplace, over which is an inscription, politely requesting that, 'to prevent mistakes,' customers will 'please to pay on delivery.' The shabby-genteel man is an object of some mystery, but as he leads a life of seclusion, and never was known to buy any thing beyond an occasional pen, except half-pints of coffee, penny loaves, and ha'porths of ink, his fellow-lodgers very naturally suppose him to be an author; and rumours are current in the Dials, that he writes poems for Mr Warren.[15]

Now any body who passed through the Dials on a hot summer's evening, and saw the different women of the house gossiping on the steps, would be apt to think that all was harmony among them, and that a more primitive set of people than the native Diallers could not be imagined. Alas! the man in the shop illtreats his family; the carpet-beater extends his professional pursuits to his wife; the one-pair front has an undying feud with the two-pair front, in consequence of the two-pair front persisting in dancing over his (the one-pair front's) head, when he and his family have retired for the night; the two-pair back *will* interfere with the front kitchen's children; the Irishman comes home drunk every other night, and attacks every body; and the one-pair back screams at every thing. Animosities spring up between floor and floor; the very cellar asserts his equality. Mrs A. 'smacks' Mrs B.'s child, for 'making faces.' Mrs B. forthwith throws cold water over Mrs A.'s child for 'calling names.' The husbands are embroiled – the quarrel becomes general – an assault is the consequence, and a police-officer the result.

CHAPTER 6

Meditations in Monmouth-street

WE have always entertained a particular attachment towards Monmouth-street,[1] as the only true and real emporium for second-hand wearing apparel. Monmouth-street is venerable from its antiquity, and respectable from its usefulness. Holywell-street[2] we despise; the red-headed and red-whiskered Jews who forcibly haul you into their squalid houses, and thrust you into a suit of clothes, whether you will or not, we detest.

The inhabitants of Monmouth-street are a distinct class; a peaceable and retiring race, who immure themselves for the most part in deep cellars, or small back parlours, and who seldom come forth into the world, except in the dusk and coolness of evening, when they may be seen seated, in chairs on the pavement, smoking their pipes, or watching the gambols of their engaging children as they revel in the gutter, a happy troop of infantine scavengers. Their countenances bear a thoughtful and a dirty cast, certain indications of their love of traffic; and their habitations are distinguished by that disregard of outward appearance, and neglect of personal comfort, so common among people who are constantly immersed in profound speculations, and deeply engaged in sedentary pursuits.

We have hinted at the antiquity of our favourite spot. 'A

George Cruikshank

Monmouth Street

Monmouth-street laced coat' was a by-word a century ago; and still we find Monmouth-street the same. Pilot great-coats with wooden buttons, have usurped the place of the ponderous laced coats with full skirts; embroidered waistcoats with large flaps, have yielded to double-breasted checks with roll-collars; and three-cornered hats of quaint appearance, have given place to the low crowns and broad brims of the coachman school; but it is the times that have changed, not Monmouth-street. Through every alteration and every change, Monmouth-street has still remained the burial-place of the fashions; and such, to judge from all present appearances, it will remain until there are no more fashions to bury.

We love to walk among these extensive groves of the illustrious dead, and to indulge in the speculations to which they give rise; now fitting a deceased coat, then a dead pair of trousers, and anon the mortal remains of a gaudy waistcoat, upon some being of our own conjuring up, and endeavouring, from the shape and fashion of the garment itself, to bring its former owner before our mind's eye. We have gone on speculating in this way, until whole rows of coats have started from their pegs, and buttoned up, of their own accord, round the waists of imaginary wearers; lines of trousers have jumped down to meet them; waistcoats have almost burst with anxiety to put themselves on; and half an acre of shoes have suddenly found feet to fit them, and gone stumping down the street with a noise which has fairly awakened us from our pleasant revery, and driven us slowly away, with a bewildered stare, an object of astonishment to the good people of Monmouth-street, and of no slight suspicion to the policemen at the opposite street corner.

We were occupied in this manner the other day, endeavouring to fit a pair of lace-up half-boots[3] on an ideal personage, for whom, to say the truth, they were full a couple of sizes too small, when our eyes happened to alight on a few suits of clothes ranged outside a shop-window, which it immediately struck us, must at different periods have all belonged to, and been worn by, the same individual, and had now by one of those strange conjunctions of circumstances which will occur sometimes, come to be exposed together for sale in the same shop. The idea seemed a fantastic one, and we looked at the clothes again, with a firm determination not to be easily led away. No, we were right; the more we looked, the more we were convinced of the accuracy of our previous impression. There was the man's whole life written as legibly on those clothes, as if we had his autobiography engrossed on parchment before us.

The first was a patched and much-soiled skeleton suit; one of those straight blue cloth cases in which small boys used to be confined, before belts and tunics had come in, and old notions had gone out: an ingenious contrivance for displaying the full symmetry of a boy's figure, by fastening him into a very tight jacket, with an ornamental row of buttons over each shoulder, and then buttoning his trousers over it, so as to give his legs the appearance of being hooked on, just under the armpits. This was the boy's dress. It had belonged to a town boy, we could see; there was a shortness about the legs and arms of the suit; and a bagging at the knees, peculiar to the rising youth of London streets. A small day-school he had been at, evidently. If it had been a regular boys' school they wouldn't have let him play on the floor so much, and rub his knees so white. He had an indulgent mother too, and plenty of halfpence, as the numerous smears of some sticky substance about the pockets, and just below the chin, which even the salesman's skill could not succeed in disguising, sufficiently betokened. They were decent people, but not overburdened with riches, or he would not have so far outgrown the suit when he passed into those corduroys with the round jacket; in which he went to a boys' school, however, learnt to write — and in ink of pretty tolerable blackness too, if the place where he used to wipe his pen might be taken as evidence.

A black suit and the jacket changed into a diminutive coat. His father had died, and the mother had got the boy a message-lad's place in some office. A long-worn suit that one; rusty and thread-bare before it was laid aside, but clean and free from soil to the last. Poor woman! We could imagine her assumed cheerfulness over the scanty meal, and the refusal of her own small portion, that her hungry boy might have enough. Her constant anxiety for his welfare, her pride in his growth mingled sometimes with the thought, almost too acute to bear, that as he grew to be a man his old affection might cool, old kindnesses fade from his mind, and old promises be forgotten — the sharp pain that even then a careless word or a cold look would give her — all crowded on our thoughts as vividly as if the very scene were passing before us.

These things happen every hour, and we all know it; and yet we felt as much sorrow when we saw, or fancied we saw — it makes no difference which — the change that began to take place now, as if we had just conceived the bare possibility of such a thing for the first time. The next suit, smart but slovenly; meant to be gay, and yet not half so decent as the threadbare apparel; redolent of the idle lounge, and the blackguard companions, told us, we thought, that the widow's comfort had rapidly faded away. We could imagine that coat — imagine! we could see it; we *had* seen it a hundred times — sauntering in company with three or four other coats of the same cut, about some place of profligate resort at night.

We dressed, from the same shop-window in an instant, half a dozen boys of from fifteen to twenty; and putting cigars into their mouths, and their hands into their pockets, watched them as they sauntered down the street, and lingered at the corner, with the obscene jest, and the oft-repeated oath. We never lost sight of them, till they had cocked their hats a little more on one side, and swaggered into the public-house; and then we entered the desolate home, where the mother sat late in the night, alone; we watched her, as she paced the room in feverish anxiety, and every now and then opened the door, looked wistfully into the dark and empty street, and again returned, to be again and again disappointed. We beheld the look of patience with which she bore the brutish threat, nay, even the drunken blow; and we heard the agony of tears that gushed from her very heart, as she sank upon her knees in her solitary and wretched apartment.

A long period had elapsed, and a greater change had taken place, by the time of casting off the suit that hung above. It was that of a stout, broad-shouldered, sturdy-chested man; and we knew at once, as any body would, who glanced at that broad-skirted green coat, with the large metal buttons, that its wearer seldom walked forth without a dog at his heels, and some idle ruffian, the very counterpart of himself, at his side. The vices of the boy had grown with the man, and we fancied his home then − if such a place deserved the name.

We saw the bare and miserable room, destitute of furniture, crowded with his wife and children, pale, hungry, and emaciated; the man cursing their lamentations, staggering to the tap-room, from whence he had just returned, followed by his wife and a sickly infant, clamouring for bread; and heard the street-wrangle and noisy recrimination that his striking her occasioned. And then imagination led us to some metropolitan workhouse, situated in the midst of crowded streets and alleys, filled with noxious vapours, and ringing with boisterous cries, where an old and feeble woman, imploring pardon for her son, lay dying in a close dark room, with no child to clasp her hand, and no pure air from heaven to fan her brow. A stranger closed the eyes that settled into a cold unmeaning glare, and strange ears received the words that murmured from the white and half-closed lips.

A coarse round frock, with a worn cotton neckerchief, and other articles of clothing of the commonest description, completed the history. A prison, and the sentence − banishment or the gallows. What would the man have given then, to be once again the contented humble drudge of his boyish years; to have restored to life, but for a week, a day, an hour, a minute, only for so long a time as would enable him to say one word of passionate regret to, and hear one sound of heartfelt forgiveness from, the cold and ghastly form that lay rotting in the pauper's grave! The children wild in the streets, the mother a destitute widow; both deeply tainted with the deep disgrace of the husband and father's name, and impelled by sheer necessity, down the precipice that had led him to a lingering death, possibly of many years' duration, thousands of miles away. We had no clue to the end of the tale; but it was easy to guess its termination.

We took a step or two further on, and by way of restoring the naturally cheerful tone of our thoughts, began fitting visionary feet and legs into a cellar-board full of boots and shoes, with a speed and accuracy that would have astonished the most expert artist in leather, living. There was one pair of boots in particular – a jolly, good-tempered, hearty-looking pair of tops,[4] that excited our warmest regard; and we had got a fine, red-faced, jovial fellow of a market-gardener into them, before we had made their acquaintance half a minute. They were just the very thing for him. There were his huge fat legs bulging over the tops, and fitting them too tight to admit of his tucking in the loops he had pulled them on by; and his knee-cords[5] with an interval of stocking; and his blue apron tucked up round his waist; and his red neckerchief and blue coat, and a white hat stuck on one side of his head; and there he stood with a broad grin on his great red face, whistling away, as if any other idea but that of being happy and comfortable had never entered his brain.

This was the very man after our own heart; we knew all about him; we had seen him coming up to Covent-garden in his green chaise-cart, with the fat tubby little horse, half a thousand times; and even while we cast an affectionate look upon his boots, at that instant, the form of a coquettish servant-maid suddenly sprung into a pair of Denmark satin[6] shoes that stood beside them, and we at once recognised the very girl who accepted his offer of a ride, just on this side the Hammersmith suspension-bridge,[7] the very last Tuesday morning we rode into town from Richmond.

A very smart female, in a showy bonnet, stepped into a pair of gray cloth boots, with black fringe and binding, that were studiously pointing out their toes on the other side of the top-boots, and seemed very anxious to engage his attention, but we didn't observe that our friend the market-gardener appeared at all captivated with these blandishments; for beyond giving a knowing wink when they first began, as if to imply that he quite understood their end and object, he took no further notice of them. His indifference, however, was amply recompensed by the excessive gallantry of a very old gentleman with a silver-headed stick, who tottered into a pair of large list shoes, that were standing in one corner of the board, and indulged in a variety of gestures expressive of his admiration of the lady in the cloth boots, to the immeasurable amusement of a young fellow we put into a pair of long-quartered pumps, who we thought would have split the coat that slid down to meet him, with laughing.

We had been looking on at this little pantomime with great satisfaction for some time, when, to our unspeakable astonishment, we perceived that the whole of the characters, including a numerous *corps de ballet* of boots and shoes in the back-ground, into which we had been hastily thrusting as many feet as we could press into the service, were arranging themselves in order for dancing; and some music striking up at the moment, to it they went without delay. It was perfectly delightful to witness the agility of the market-gardener. Out went the boots, first on one side, then on the other, then cutting, then shuffling, then setting to the Denmark satins, then advancing, then retreating, then going round, and then repeating the whole of the evolutions again, without appearing to suffer in the least from the violence of the exercise.

Nor were the Denmark satins a bit behindhand, for they jumped and bounded about, in all directions; and though they were neither so regular, nor so true to the time as the cloth boots, still, as they seemed to do it from the heart, and to enjoy it more, we candidly confess that we preferred their style of dancing to the other. But the old gentleman in the list shoes was the most amusing object in the whole party; for, besides his grotesque attempts to appear youthful, and amorous, which were sufficiently entertaining in themselves, the young fellow in the pumps managed so artfully that every time the old gentleman advanced to salute the lady in the cloth boots, he trod with his whole weight on the old fellow's toes, which made him roar with anguish, and rendered all the others like to die of laughing.

We were in the full enjoyment of these festivities when we heard a shrill, and by no means musical voice, exclaim, 'Hope you'll know me agin, imperence!'[8] and on looking intently forward to see from whence the sound came, we found that it proceeded, not from the young lady in the cloth boots, as we had at first been inclined to suppose, but from a bulky lady of elderly appearance, who was seated in a chair at the head of the cellar-steps, apparently for the purpose of superintending the sale of the articles arranged there.

A barrel organ, which had been in full force close behind us, ceased playing; the people we had been fitting into the shoes and boots took to flight at the interruption; and as we were conscious that in the depth of our meditations we might have been rudely staring at the old lady for half an hour without knowing it, we took to flight too, and were soon immersed in the deepest obscurity of the adjacent 'Dials.'

CHAPTER 7

Hackney-coach Stands

WE maintain that hackney-coaches, properly so called, belong solely to the metropolis. We may be told, that there are hackney-coach stands in Edinburgh; and not to go quite so far for a contradiction to our position, we may be reminded that Liverpool, Manchester, 'and other large towns' (as the Parliamentary phrase goes), have *their* hackney-coach stands. We readily concede to these places, the possession of certain vehicles, which may look almost as dirty, and even go almost as slowly, as London hackney-coaches: but that they have the slightest claim to compete with the metropolis, either in point of stands, drivers, or cattle, we indignantly deny.

Take a regular, ponderous, rickety, London hackney-coach of the old school, and let any man have the boldness to assert, if he can, that he ever beheld any object on the face of the earth which at all resembled it, unless, indeed, it were another hackney-coach of the same date. We have recently observed on certain stands, and we say it with deep regret, rather dapper green chariots, and coaches of polished yellow, with four wheels of the same colour as the coach, whereas it is perfectly notorious to every one who has studied the

Hackney Coach Stands

subject, that every wheel ought to be of a different colour, and a different size. These are innovations, and, like other mis-called improvements, awful signs of the restlessness of the public mind, and the little respect paid to our time-honoured institutions. Why should hackney-coaches be clean? Our ancestors found them dirty, and left them so. Why should we, with a feverish wish to 'keep moving,' desire to roll along at the rate of six miles an hour, while they were content to rumble over the stones at four? These are solemn considerations. Hackney-coaches are part and parcel of the law of the land; they were settled by the Legislature; plated and numbered by the wisdom of Parliament.[1]

Then why have they been swamped by cabs and omnibuses?[2] Or why should people be allowed to ride quickly for eightpence a mile, after Parliament had come to the solemn decision that they should pay a shilling a mile for riding slowly? We pause for a reply; – and, having no chance of getting one, begin a fresh paragraph.

Our acquaintance with hackney-coach stands is of long standing. We are a walking book of fares, feeling ourselves half-bound, as it were, to be always in the right on contested points. We know all the regular watermen[3] within three miles of Covent-garden by sight, and should be almost tempted to believe that all the hackney-coach horses in that district knew us by sight too, if one-half of them were not blind. We take great interest in hackney-coaches, but we seldom drive, having a knack of turning ourselves over, when we attempt to do so. We are as great friends to horses, hackney-coach and otherwise, as the renowned Mr Martin, of costermonger notoriety,[4] and yet we never ride. We keep no horse, but a clothes-horse; enjoy no saddle so much as a saddle of mutton; and, following our own inclinations, have never followed the hounds. Leaving these fleeter means of getting over the ground, or of depositing oneself upon it, to those who like them, by hackney-coach stands we take our stand.

There is a hackney-coach stand under the very window at which we are writing;[5] there is only one coach on it now, but it is a fair specimen of the class of vehicles to which we have alluded – a great, lumbering, square concern of a dingy yellow colour (like a bilious brunette), with very small glasses, but very large frames; the panels are

ornamented with a faded coat of arms,[6] in shape something like a
dissected bat, the axletree is red, and the majority of the wheels are
green. The box is partially covered by an old great-coat, with a
multiplicity of capes, and some extraordinary-looking clothes; and the
straw, with which the canvass cushion is stuffed, is sticking up in
several places, as if in rivalry of the hay, which is peeping through the
chinks in the boot. The horses, with drooping heads, and each with a
mane and tail as scanty and straggling as those of a worn-out rocking-
horse, are standing patiently on some damp straw, occasionally
wincing, and rattling the harness; and, now and then, one of them lifts
his mouth to the ear of his companion, as if he were saying, in a
whisper, that he should like to assassinate the coachman. The
coachman himself is in the watering-house; and the waterman, with his
hands forced into his pockets as far as they can possibly go, is dancing
the 'double shuffle,' in front of the pump, to keep his feet warm.

The servant-girl, with the pink ribbons, at No. 5, opposite,
suddenly opens the street-door, and four small children forthwith
rush out, and scream 'Coach!' with all their might and main. The
waterman darts from the pump, seizes the horses by their respective
bridles, and drags them, and the coach too, round to the house,
shouting all the time for the coachman at the very top, or rather
very bottom of his voice, for it is a deep bass growl. A response is
heard from the tap-room; the coachman, in his wooden-soled
shoes, makes the street echo again as he runs across it; and then
there is such a struggling, and backing, and grating of the kennel,
to get the coach-door opposite the house-door, that the children are
in perfect ecstasies of delight. What a commotion! The old lady,
who has been stopping there for the last month, is going back to
the country. Out comes box after box, and one side of the vehicle
is filled with luggage in no time; the children get into every body's
way, and the youngest, who has upset himself in his attempts to
carry an umbrella, is borne off wounded and kicking. The young-
sters disappear, and a short pause ensues, during which the old lady
is, no doubt, kissing them all round in the back parlour. She
appears at last, followed by her married daughter, all the children,
and both the servants, who, with the joint assistance of the

coachman and waterman, manage to get her safely into the coach. A cloak is handed in, and a little basket, which we could almost swear contains a small black bottle, and a paper of sandwiches. Up go the steps, bang goes the door, 'Golden-cross, Charing-cross,[7] Tom,' says the waterman; 'Good bye, grandma,' cry the children, off jingles the coach at the rate of three miles an hour, and the mamma and children retire into the house, with the exception of one little villain, who runs up the street at the top of his speed, pursued by the servant; not ill pleased to have such an opportunity of displaying her attractions. She brings him back, and, after casting two or three gracious glances across the way, which are either intended for us or the potboy (we are not quite certain which) shuts the door, and the hackney-coach stand is again at a stand still.

We have been frequently amused with the intense delight with which 'a servant of all work,' who is sent for a coach, deposits herself inside; and the unspeakable gratification which boys, who have been despatched on a similar errand, appear to derive from mounting the box. But we never recollect to have been more amused with a hackney-coach party, than one we saw early the other morning in Tottenham-court-road.[8] It was a wedding-party, and emerged from one of the inferior streets near Fitzroy-square. There were the bride, with a thin white dress, and a great red face; and the bridesmaid, a little, dumpy, good-humoured young woman, dressed, of course, in the same appropriate costume; and the bridegroom and his chosen friend, in blue coats, yellow waistcoats, white trousers, and Berlin gloves[9] to match. They stopped at the corner of the street, and called a coach with an air of indescribable dignity. The moment they were in, the bridesmaid threw a red shawl, which she had, no doubt, brought on purpose, negligently over the number on the door, evidently to delude pedestrians into the belief that the hackney-coach was a private carriage; and away they went, perfectly satisfied that the imposition was successful, and quite unconscious that there was a great staring number stuck up behind, on a plate as large as a schoolboy's slate. A shilling a mile! – the ride was worth five, at least, to them.

What an interesting book a hackney-coach might produce, if it could carry as much in its head as it does in its body! The autobiography of a broken-down hackney-coach, would surely be as amusing as the autobiography of a broken-down hackneyed dramatist; and it might tell as much of its travels *with* the pole, as others have of their expeditions *to* it. How many stories might be related of the different people it had conveyed on matters of business or profit — pleasure or pain! And how many melancholy tales of the same people at different periods! The country-girl — the showy, over-dressed woman — the drunken prostitute! The raw apprentice — the dissipated spendthrift — the thief!

Talk of cabs! Cabs are all very well in cases of expedition, when it's a matter of neck or nothing, life or death, your temporary home or your long one. But, beside a cab's lacking that gravity of deportment which so peculiarly distinguishes a hackney-coach, let it never be forgotten that a cab is a thing of yesterday, and that he never was any thing better. A hackney-cab has always been a hackney-cab, from his first entry into public life; whereas a hackney-coach is a remnant of past gentility, a victim to fashion, a hanger-on of an old English family, wearing their arms, and, in days of yore, escorted by men wearing their livery, stripped of his finery, and thrown upon the world, like a once-smart footman when he is no longer sufficiently juvenile for his office, progressing lower and lower in the scale of four-wheeled degradation, until at last it comes to — *a stand!*

CHAPTER 8

Doctors' Commons

WALKING, without any definite object, through St Paul's Church-yard, a little while ago, we happened to turn down a street entitled 'Paul's-chain,'[1] and keeping straight forward for a few hundred yards, found ourself, as a natural consequence, in Doctors' Commons.[2] Now Doctors' Commons being familiar by name to every body, as the place where they grant marriage-licences to love-sick couples, and divorces to unfaithful ones; register the wills of people who have any property to leave, and punish hasty gentlemen who call ladies by unpleasant names, we no sooner discovered that we were really within its precincts, than we felt a laudable desire to become better acquainted therewith; and as the first object of our curiosity was the Court, whose decrees can even unloose the bonds of matrimony, we procured a direction to it; and bent our steps thither without delay.

Crossing a quiet and shady courtyard, paved with stone, and frowned upon by old red brick houses, on the doors of which were painted the names of sundry learned civilians, we paused before a small, green-baized, brass-headed-nailed door, which yielding to our gentle push, at once admitted us into an old quaint-looking apartment, with sunken windows, and black carved wainscotting, at the upper end of which, seated on a raised platform, of semicircular shape, were about a dozen solemn-looking gentlemen, in crimson gowns and wigs.

At a more elevated desk in the centre, sat a very fat and red-faced gentleman, in tortoise-shell spectacles, whose dignified appearance announced the judge; and round a long green-baized table below, something like a billiard-table without the cushions and pockets, were a number of very self-important-looking personages, in stiff neckcloths, and black gowns with white fur collars, whom we at once set down as proctors. At the lower end of the billiard-table was an individual in an arm-chair, and a wig, whom we afterwards discovered to be the registrar; and seated behind a little desk, near the door, were a respectable-looking man in black, of about twenty stone weight or thereabouts, and a fat-faced, smirking, civil-looking body, in a black gown, black kid gloves, knee shorts, and silks, with a shirt-frill in his bosom, curls on his head, and a silver staff in his hand, whom we had no difficulty in recognising as the officer of the Court. The latter, indeed, speedily set our mind at rest upon this point, for, advancing to our elbow, and opening a conversation forthwith, he had communicated to us, in less than five minutes, that he was the apparitor,[3] and the other the

110

court-keeper; that this was the Arches Court,[4] and therefore the counsel wore red gowns, and the proctors fur collars; and that when the other Courts sat there, they didn't wear red gowns or fur collars either; with many other scraps of intelligence equally interesting. Besides these two officers, there was a little thin old man, with long grizzly hair, crouched in a remote corner, whose duty, our communicative friend informed us, was to ring a large hand-bell when the Court opened in the morning, and who, for aught his appearance betokened to the contrary, might have been similarly employed for the last two centuries at least.

The red-faced gentleman in the tortoise-shell spectacles had got all the talk to himself just then, and very well he was doing it, too, only he spoke very fast, but that was habit; and rather thick, but that was good living. So we had plenty of time to look about us. There was one individual who amused us mightily. This was one of the bewigged gentlemen in the red robes, who was straddling before the fire in the centre of the Court, in the attitude of the brazen Colossus,[5] to the complete exclusion of every body else. He had gathered up his robe behind, in much the same manner as a slovenly woman would her petticoats on a very dirty day, in order that he might feel the full warmth of the fire. His wig was put on all awry, with the tail straggling about his neck, his scanty gray trousers and short black gaiters, made in the worst possible style, imparted an additionally inelegant appearance to his uncouth person; and his limp, badly-starched shirt-collar almost obscured his eyes. We shall never be able to claim any credit as a physiognomist again, for, after a careful scrutiny of this gentleman's countenance, we had come to the conclusion that it bespoke nothing but conceit and silliness, when our friend with the silver staff whispered in our ear that he was no other than a doctor of civil law, and heaven knows what besides. So of course we were mistaken, and he must be a very talented man. He conceals it so well though – perhaps with the merciful view of not astonishing ordinary people too much – that you would suppose him to be one of the stupidest dogs alive.

The gentleman in the spectacles having concluded his judgment, and a few minutes having been allowed to elapse, to afford time for the buzz in the Court to subside, the registrar called on the next cause, which was 'the office of the Judge promoted by Bumple against Sludberry.' A general movement was visible in the Court, at this announcement, and the obliging functionary with silver staff whispered us that 'there would be some fun now, for this was a brawling case.'

We were not rendered much the wiser by this piece of information, till we found by the opening speech of the counsel for the promoter, that, under a half-obsolete statute of one of the Edwards, the court was empowered to visit with the penalty of excommunication, any person who should be proved guilty of the crime of 'brawling,' or 'smiting,' in any church, or vestry adjoining thereto; and it appeared, by some eight-and-twenty affidavits, which were duly referred to, that on a certain night, at a certain vestry-meeting, in a certain parish particularly set forth, Thomas Sludberry, the party appeared against in that suit, had made use of, and applied to Michael Bumple, the promoter, the words 'You be blowed;' and that, on the said Michael Bumple and others remonstrating with the said Thomas Sludberry, on the impropriety of his conduct, the said Thomas Sludberry repeated the aforesaid expression, 'You be blowed;' and furthermore desired and requested to know, whether the said Michael Bumple 'wanted any thing for himself;' adding, 'that if the said Michael Bumple did want any thing for himself, he, the said Thomas Sludberry, was the man to give it him;' at the same time making use of other heinous and sinful expressions, all of which, Bumple submitted, came within the intent and meaning of the Act; and therefore he, for the soul's health and chastening of Sludberry, prayed for sentence of excommunication against him accordingly.

Upon these facts a long argument was entered into, on both sides, to the great edification of a number of persons interested in the parochial squabbles, who crowded the court; and when some very long and grave speeches had been made *pro* and *con*, the red-faced gentleman in the tortoiseshell spectacles took a review of the case, which occupied half an hour more, and then pronounced upon

Sludberry the awful sentence of excommunication for a fortnight, and payment of the costs of the suit. Upon this, Sludberry, who was a little, red-faced, sly-looking, ginger-beer-seller, addressed the court, and said, if they'd be good enough to take off the costs, and excommunicate him for the term of his natural life instead, it would be much more convenient to him, for he never went to church at all. To this appeal the gentleman in the spectacles made no other reply than a look of virtuous indignation; and Sludberry and his friends retired. As the man with the silver staff informed us that the court was on the point of rising, we retired too – pondering, as we walked away, upon the beautiful spirit of these ancient ecclesiastical laws, the kind and neighbourly feelings they are calculated to awaken, and the strong attachment to religious institutions which they cannot fail to engender.

We were so lost in these meditations, that we had turned into the street, and run up against a door-post, before we recollected where we were walking. On looking upwards to see what house we had stumbled upon, the words 'Prerogative-Office,'[6] written in large characters, met our eye; and as we were in a sight-seeing humour and the place was a public one, we walked in.

The room into which we walked, was a long, busy-looking place, partitioned off, on either side, into a variety of little boxes, in which a few clerks were engaged in copying or examining deeds. Down the centre of the room were several desks, nearly breast high, at each of which, three or four people were standing, poring over large volumes. As we knew that they were searching for wills, they attracted our attention at once.

It was curious to contrast the lazy indifference of the attorneys' clerks who were making a search for some legal purpose, with the air of earnestness and interest which distinguished the strangers to the place, who were looking up the will of some deceased relative; the former pausing every now and then with an impatient yawn, or raising their heads to look at the people who passed up and down the room; the latter stooping over the book, and running down column after column of names in the deepest abstraction.

There was one little dirty-faced man in a blue apron, who after a whole morning's search, extending some fifty years back, had just found the will to which he wished to refer, which one of the officials was reading to him in a low hurried voice from a thick vellum book with large clasps. It was perfectly evident that the more the clerk read, the less the man with the blue apron understood about the matter. When the volume was first brought down, he took off his hat, smoothed down his hair, smiled with great self-satisfaction, and looked up in the reader's face with the air of a man who had made up his mind to recollect every word he heard. The first two or three lines were intelligible enough; but then the technicalities began, and the little man began to look rather dubious. Then came a whole string of complicated trusts, and he was regularly at sea. As the reader proceeded, it was quite apparent that it was a hopeless case, and the little man, with his mouth open and his eyes fixed upon his face, looked on with an expression of bewilderment and perplexity irresistibly ludicrous.

A little further on, a hard-featured old man with a deeply wrinkled face, was intently perusing a lengthy will with the aid of a pair of horn spectacles: occasionally pausing from his task, and slily noting down some brief memorandum of the bequests contained in it. Every wrinkle about his toothless mouth, and sharp keen eyes, told of avarice and cunning. His clothes were nearly threadbare, but it was easy to see that he wore them from choice and not from necessity; all his looks and gestures down to the very small pinches of snuff which he every now and then took from a little tin canister, told of wealth, and penury, and avarice.

As he leisurely closed the register, put up his spectacles, and folded his scraps of paper in a large leathern pocket-book, we thought what a nice hard bargain he was driving with some poverty-stricken legatee, who, tired of waiting year after year, until some life-interest should fall in, was selling his chance, just as it began to grow most valuable, for a twelfth part of its worth. It was a good speculation – a very safe one. The old man stowed his pocket-book carefully in the breast of his great-coat, and hobbled away with a leer of triumph. That will had made him ten years younger at the lowest computation.

Having commenced our observations, we should certainly have extended them to another dozen of people at least, had not a sudden shutting up and putting away of the wormeaten old books, warned us that the time for closing the office had arrived; and thus deprived us of a pleasure, and spared our readers an infliction.

We naturally fell into a train of reflection as we walked homewards, upon the curious old records of likings and dislikings; of jealousies and revenges; of affection defying the power of death, and hatred pursued beyond the grave, which these depositories contain; silent but striking tokens, some of them, of excellence of heart, and nobleness of soul; melancholy examples, others, of the worst passions of human nature. How many men as they lay speechless and helpless on the bed of death, would have given worlds but for the strength and power to blot out the silent evidence of animosity and bitterness, which now stands registered against them in Doctors' Commons!

CHAPTER 9

London Recreations

THE wish of persons in the humbler classes of life, to ape the manners and customs of those whom fortune has placed above them, is often the subject of remark, and not unfrequently of complaint. The inclination may, and no doubt does, exist to a great extent, among the small gentility – the would-be aristocrats – of the middle classes. Tradesmen and clerks, with fashionable novel-reading families, and circulating-library-subscribing daughters, get up small assemblies in humble imitation of Almack's,[1] and promenade the dingy 'large room' of some second-rate hotel with as much complacency as the enviable few who are privileged to exhibit their magnificence in that exclusive haunt of fashion and

London Recreations

foolery. Aspiring young ladies, who read flaming accounts of some 'fancy fair[2] in high life,' suddenly grow desperately charitable; visions of admiration and matrimony float before their eyes; some wonderfully meritorious institution, which, by the strangest accident in the world, has never been heard of before, is discovered to be in a languishing condition: Thomson's great room, or Johnson's nursery-ground is forthwith engaged, and the aforesaid young ladies, from mere charity, exhibit themselves for three days, from twelve to four, for the small charge of one shilling per head! With the exception of these classes of society, however, and a few weak and insignificant persons, we do not think the attempt at imitation to which we have alluded, prevails in any great degree. The different character of the recreations of different classes, has often afforded us amusement; and we have chosen it for the subject of our present sketch, in the hope that it may possess some amusement for our readers.

If the regular City man, who leaves Lloyd's at five o'clock, and drives home to Hackney, Clapton, Stamford-hill,[3] or elsewhere, can be said to have any daily recreation beyond his dinner, it is his garden. He never does any thing to it with his own hands; but he takes great pride in it notwithstanding; and if you are desirous of paying your addresses to the youngest daughter, be sure to be in raptures with every flower and shrub it contains. If your poverty of expression compel you to make any distinction between the two, we would certainly recommend your bestowing more admiration on his garden than his wine. He always takes a walk round it, before he starts for town in the morning, and is particularly anxious that the fish-pond should be kept specially neat. If you call on him on Sunday in summer-time, about an hour before dinner, you will find him sitting in an arm-chair, on the lawn behind the house, with a straw hat on, reading a Sunday paper. A short distance from him you will most likely observe a handsome paroquet[4] in a large brass-wire cage; ten to one but the two eldest girls are loitering in one of the side walks accompanied by a couple of young gentlemen, who are holding parasols over them – of course only to keep the sun off – while the younger children, with the under nursery-maid, are strolling listlessly about, in the shade. Beyond these occasions, his delight in his garden appears to arise more from the consciousness of possession than actual enjoyment of it. When he drives you down to dinner on a week-day, he is rather fatigued with the occupations of the morning, and tolerably cross into the bargain; but when the cloth is removed, and he has drank three or four glasses of his favourite port, he orders the French windows of his dining-room (which of course look into the garden) to be opened, and throwing a silk handkerchief over his head, and leaning back in his arm-chair, descants at considerable length upon its beauty, and the cost of maintaining it. This is to impress you – who are a young friend of the family – with a due sense of the excellence of the garden, and the wealth of its owner; and when he has exhausted the subject, he goes to sleep.

There is another and a very different class of men, whose recreation is their garden. An individual of this class, resides some short distance from town – say in the Hampstead-road, or the Kilburn-road,[5] or any other road where the houses are small and neat, and have little slips of back garden. He and his wife – who is as clean and compact a little body as himself – have occupied the same house ever since he retired from business twenty years ago. They have no family. They once had a son, who died at about five years old. The child's portrait hangs over the mantelpiece in the best sitting-room, and a little cart he used to draw about, is carefully preserved as a relic.

In fine weather the old gentleman is almost constantly in the garden; and when it is too wet to go into it, he will look out of the window at it, by the hour together. He has always something to do there, and you will see him digging, and sweeping, and cutting, and planting, with manifest delight. In spring time, there is no end to the sowing of seeds, and sticking little bits of wood over them, with labels, which look like epitaphs to their memory; and in the evening, when the sun has gone down, the perseverance with which he lugs a great watering-pot about is perfectly astonishing. The only other recreation he has, is the newspaper, which he peruses every day, from beginning to end, generally reading the most interesting pieces of intelligence to his wife, during breakfast. The old lady is very fond of flowers, as the hyacinth-glasses in the parlour window, and geranium-pots in the little front court, testify. She takes a great pride in the garden too: and when one of the four fruit-trees produces rather a larger gooseberry than usual, it is carefully preserved under a wine-glass on the sideboard, for the edification of visiters, who are duly informed that Mr So-and-so planted the tree which produced it, with his own hands. On a summer's evening, when the large watering-pot has been filled and emptied some fourteen times, and the old couple have quite exhausted themselves by trotting about, you will see them sitting happily together in the little summer-house, enjoying the calm and peace of the twilight, and watching the shadows as they fall upon the garden, and gradually growing thicker and more sombre, obscure the tints of their gayest flowers – no bad emblem of the years that have silently rolled over their heads, deadening in their course the brightest hues of early hopes and feelings which have long since faded away. These are their only recreations, and they require no more. They have within themselves, the materials of comfort and content; and the only anxiety of each, is to die before the other.

This is no ideal sketch. There *used* to be many old people of this description; their numbers may have diminished, and may decrease still more. Whether the course female education has taken of late days – whether the pursuit of giddy frivolities, and empty nothings, has tended to unfit women for that quiet domestic life, in which they show far more beautifully than in the most crowded assembly, is a question we should feel little gratification in discussing: we hope not.

Let us turn now, to another portion of the London population, whose recreations present about as strong a contrast as can well be conceived – we mean the Sunday pleasurers; and let us beg our readers to imagine themselves stationed by our side in some well-known rural 'Tea-gardens.'

The heat is intense this afternoon, and the people, of whom there are additional parties arriving every moment, look as warm as the tables which have been recently painted, and have the appearance of being red-hot. What a dust and noise! Men and women — boys and girls — sweethearts and married people — babies in arms, and children in chaises — pipes and shrimps — cigars and periwinkles — tea and tobacco. Gentlemen, in alarming waistcoats, and steel watch-guards, promenading about, three abreast, with surprising dignity (or as the gentleman in the next box facetiously observes, 'cutting it uncommon fat!') — ladies, with great, long, white pocket-handkerchiefs like small table-cloths, in their hands, chasing one another on the grass in the most playful and interesting manner, with the view of attracting the attention of the aforesaid gentlemen — husbands in perspective ordering bottles of ginger-beer for the objects of their affections, with a lavish disregard of expense; and the said objects washing down huge quantities of 'shrimps' and 'winkles,' with an equal disregard of their own bodily health and subsequent comfort — boys, with great silk hats just balanced on the top of their heads, smoking cigars, and trying to look as if they liked them — gentlemen in pink shirts and blue waistcoats, occasionally upsetting either themselves, or somebody else, with their own canes.

Some of the finery of these people provokes a smile, but they are all clean, and happy, and disposed to be good-natured and sociable. Those two motherly-looking women in the smart pelisses, who are chatting so confidentially, inserting a 'ma'am' at every fourth word, scraped an acquaintance about a quarter of an hour ago: it originated in admiration of the little boy who belongs to one of them — that diminutive specimen of mortality in the three-cornered pink satin hat with black feathers. The two men in the blue coats and drab trousers, who are walking up and down, smoking their pipes, are their husbands. The party in the opposite box are a pretty fair specimen of the generality of the visiters. These are the father and mother, and old grandmother: a young man and woman, and an individual addressed by the euphonius title of 'Uncle Bill,' who is evidently the wit of the party. They have some half-dozen children with them, but it is scarcely necessary to notice the fact, for that is a matter of course here. Every woman in 'the gardens,' who has been married for any length of time, must have had twins on two or three occasions; it is impossible to account for the extent of juvenile population in any other way.

Observe the inexpressible delight of the old grandmother, at Uncle Bill's splendid joke of 'tea for four: bread and butter for forty;' and the loud explosion of mirth which follows his wafering a paper 'pigtail' on the waiter's collar. The young man is evidently 'keeping company' with Uncle Bill's niece: and Uncle Bill's hints – such as 'Don't forget me at the dinner, you know,' 'I shall look out for the cake, Sally,' 'I'll be godfather to your first – wager it's a boy,' and so forth, are equally embarrassing to the young people, and delightful to the elder ones. As to the old grandmother, she is in perfect ecstasies, and does nothing but laugh herself into fits of coughing, until they have finished the 'gin-and-water warm with,'[6] of which Uncle Bill ordered 'glasses round' after tea, 'just to keep the night air out, and do it up comfortable and riglar arter sitch an as-tonishing hot day!'

It is getting dark, and the people begin to move. The field leading to town is quite full of them; the little hand-chaises[7] are dragged wearily along, the children are tired, and amuse themselves and the company generally by crying, or resort to the much more pleasant expedient of going to sleep – the mothers begin to wish they were at home again – sweethearts grow more sentimental than ever, as the time for parting arrives – the gardens look mournful enough, by the light of the two lanterns which hang against the trees for the convenience of smokers – and the waiters, who have been running about incessantly for the last six hours, think they feel a little tired, as they count their glasses and their gains.

CHAPTER 10

The River

'ARE you fond of the water?' is a question very frequently asked, in hot summer weather, by amphibious-looking young men. 'Very,' is the general reply. 'An't you?' – 'Hardly ever off it,' is the response, accompanied by sundry adjectives, expressive of the speaker's heartfelt admiration of that element. Now, with all respect for the opinion of society in general, and cutter clubs in particular, we humbly suggest that some of the most painful reminiscences in the mind of every individual who has occasionally disported himself on the Thames, must be connected with his aquatic recreations. Who ever heard of a successful water-party? – or to put the question in a still more intelligible form, who ever saw one? We have been on water excursions out of number, but we solemnly declare that we cannot call to mind one single occasion of the kind, which was not marked by more miseries than any one would suppose could reasonably be crowded into the space of some eight or nine hours. Something has always gone wrong. Either the cork of the salad-dressing has come out, or the most anxiously expected member of the party has not come out, or the most disagreeable man in company would come out, or a child or two have fallen into the water, or the gentleman who undertook to steer has endangered every body's life all the way, or the gentlemen who volunteered to row have been 'out of practice,' and performed very alarming evolutions, putting their oars down into the water and not being able to get them up again, or taking terrific pulls without putting them in at all; in either case, pitching over on the backs of their heads with startling violence, and exhibiting the soles of their pumps to the 'sitters' in the boat, in a very humiliating manner.

We grant that the banks of the Thames are very beautiful at Richmond and Twickenham, and other distant havens, often sought though seldom reached: but from the 'Red-us'[1] back to Black-friar's-bridge, the scene is wonderfully changed. The Penitentiary[2] is a noble building, no doubt, and the sportive youths who 'go in' at that particular part of the river, on a summer's evening, may be all very well in perspective; but when you are obliged to keep in shore coming home, and the young ladies will colour up, and look perseveringly the other way, while the married dittoes cough slightly, and stare very hard at the water, you feel awkward – especially if you happen to have been attempting the most distant approach to sentimentality, for an hour or two previously.

Although experience and suffering have produced in our minds the result we have just stated, we are by no means blind to a proper sense of the fun which a looker-on may extract from the amateurs of boating. What can be more amusing than Searle's yard[3] on a fine Sunday morning? It's a Richmond tide, and some dozen boats are preparing for the reception of the parties who have engaged them. Two or three fellows in great rough trousers and Guernsey shirts,[4] are getting them ready by easy stages; now coming down the yard with a pair of sculls and a cushion – then having a chat with the 'jack,'[5] who, like all his tribe, seems to be wholly incapable of doing any thing but lounging about – then going back again, and returning with a rudder-line and a stretcher – then solacing themselves with another chat – and then wondering, with their hands in their capacious pockets, 'where them gentlemen's got to as ordered the six.' One of these, the head man, with the legs of his trousers carefully tucked up at the bottom, to admit the water, we presume – for it is an element in which he is infinitely more at home than on land – is quite a character, and shares with the defunct oyster-swallower the celebrated name of 'Dando.'[6] Watch him, as taking a few minutes respite from his toils, he negligently seats himself on the edge of a boat, and fans his broad bushy chest with a cap scarcely half so furry. Look at his magnificent, though reddish whiskers, and mark the somewhat native humour with which he 'chaffs' the boys and prentices, or cunningly gammons the gen'lm'n into the gift of a glass of gin, of which we verily believe he swallows in one day as much as any six ordinary men, without ever being one atom the worse for it.

But the party arrives, and Dando relieved from his state of uncertainty, starts up into activity. They approach in full aquatic costume, with round blue jackets, striped shirts, and caps of all sizes and patterns, from the velvet skull-cap of French manufacture, to the easy head-dress familiar to the students of the old spelling-books, as having, on the authority of the portrait, formed part of the costume of the Reverend Mr Dilworth.[7]

This is the most amusing time to observe a regular Sunday water-party. There has evidently been up to this period no inconsiderable degree of boasting on every body's part relative to his knowledge of navigation; the sight of the water rapidly cools their courage, and the air of self-denial with which each of them insists on somebody else's taking an oar, is perfectly delightful. At length, after a great deal of changing and fidgeting, consequent upon the election of a stroke-oar: the inability of one gentleman to pull on this side, of another to pull on that, and of a third to pull at all, the boat's crew are seated. 'Shove her off!' cries the cockswain, who looks as easy and comfortable as if he were steering in the Bay of Biscay. The order is obeyed; the boat is immediately turned completely round, and proceeds towards Westminster-bridge, amidst such a splashing and struggling as never was seen before, except when the Royal George went down.[8] 'Back wa'ater, sir,' shouts Dando, 'Back wa'ater, you sir, aft;' upon which every body thinking he must be the individual referred to, they all back water, and back comes the boat, stern first, to the spot whence it started. 'Back water, you sir, aft; pull round, you sir, for'ad, can't you?' shouts Dando, in a frenzy of excitement. 'Pull round, Tom, can't you?' re-echoes one of the party. 'Tom an't for'ad,' replies another. 'Yes, he is,' cries a third; and the unfortunate young man, at the imminent risk of breaking a blood-vessel, pulls and pulls, until the head of the boat fairly lies in the direction of Vauxhall-bridge. 'That's right – now pull all on you!' shouts Dando again, adding, in an under tone, to somebody by him, 'Blowed if hever I see sich a set of muffs!' and away jogs the boat in a zigzag direction, every one of the six oars dipping into the water at a different time; and the yard is once more clear, until the arrival of the next party.

A well-contested rowing-match on the Thames, is a very lively and interesting scene. The water is studded with boats of all sorts, kinds, and descriptions; places in the coal-barges at the different wharfs are let to crowds of spectators, beer and tobacco flow freely about; men, women, and children wait for the start in breathless expectation, cutters of six and eight oars glide gently up and down, waiting to accompany their *proteges* during the race; bands of music add to the animation, if not to the harmony of the scene, groups of watermen are assembled at the different stairs, discussing the merits of the respective candidates: and the prize wherry which is rowed slowly about by a pair of sculls, is an object of general interest.

Two o'clock strikes, and every body looks anxiously in the direction of the bridge through which the candidates for the prize will come – half-past two, and the general attention which has been preserved so long begins to flag, when suddenly a gun is heard, and the noise of distant hurra'ing along each bank of the river – every head is bent forward – the noise draws nearer and nearer – the boats which have been waiting at the bridge start briskly up the river, and a well-manned galley shoots through the arch, the sitters cheering on the boats behind them, which are not yet visible.

'Here they are,' is the general cry – and through darts the first boat, the men in her, stripped to the skin, and exerting every muscle to preserve the advantage they have gained – four other boats follow close astern; there are not two boats' length between them – the shouting is tremendous, and the interest intense. 'Go on, Pink' – 'Give it her, Red' – 'Sulliwin for ever' – 'Bravo! George' – 'Now, Tom, now – now – now – why don't your partner stretch out?' – 'Two pots to a pint⁹ on Yellow,' &c. &c. Every little public-house fires its gun, and hoists its flag; and the men who win the heat, come in, amidst a splashing and shouting, and banging and confusion, which no one can imagine who has not witnessed it, and of which any description would convey a very faint idea.

One of the most amusing places we know, is the steam-wharf of the London-bridge, or St Katharine's Dock Company,¹⁰ on a Saturday morning in summer, when the Gravesend and Margate steamers are usually crowded to excess; and as we have just taken a glance at the river above bridge, we hope our readers will not object to accompany us on board a Gravesend packet.

Coaches are every moment setting down at the entrance to the wharf, and the stare of bewildered astonishment with which the 'fares' resign themselves and their luggage into the hands of the porters, who seize all the packages at once as a matter of course, and run away with them, heaven knows where, is laughable in the extreme. A Margate boat lies alongside the wharf, the Gravesend boat (which starts first) lies alongside that again; and as a temporary communication is formed between the two, by means of a plank and hand-rail, the natural confusion of the scene is by no means diminished.

'Gravesend?' inquires a stout father of a stout family, who follow him, under the guidance of their mother, and a servant, at the no small risk of two or three of them being left behind in the confusion. 'Gravesend?'

'Pass on, if you please, sir,' replies the attendant – 'other boat, sir.'

Hereupon the stout father, being rather mystified, and the stout mother rather distracted by maternal anxiety, the whole party deposit themselves in the Margate boat, and after having congratulated himself on having secured very comfortable seats, the stout father sallies to the chimney to look for his luggage, which he has a faint recollection of having given some man, something, to take somewhere. No luggage, however, bearing the most remote resemblance to his own, in shape or form, is to be discovered; on which the stout father calls very loudly for an officer, to whom he states the case, in the presence of another father of another family – a little thin man – who entirely concurs with him (the stout father) in thinking that it's high time something was done with these steam companies, and that as the Corporation Bill[11] failed to do it, something else must; for really people's property is not to be sacrificed in this way; and that if the luggage isn't restored without delay, he will take care it shall be put in the papers, for the public is not to be the victim of these great monopolies. To this, the officer, in his turn, replies, that that company, ever since it has been St Kat'rine's Dock Company, has protected life and property; that if it had been the London Bridge Wharf Company, indeed, he shouldn't have wondered, seeing that the morality of that company (they being the opposition) can't be answered for, by no one; but as it is, he's convinced there must be some mistake, and he wouldn't mind taking a solemn oath afore a magistrate that the gentleman 'll find his luggage afore he gets to Margate.

Here the stout father, thinking he is making a capital point, replies, that as it happens he is not going to Margate at all, and that 'Passenger to Gravesend' was on the luggage, in letters of full two inches long; on which the officer rapidly explains the mistake, and the stout mother, and the stout children, and the servant, are hurried with all possible despatch on board the Gravesend boat, which they reach just in time to discover that their luggage is there, and that their comfortable seats are not. Then the bell, which is the signal for the Gravesend boat starting, begins to ring most furiously: and people keep time to the bell, by running in and out of our boat at a double-quick pace. The bell stops; the boat starts: people who have been taking leave of their friends on board, are carried away against their will; and people who have been taking leave of their friends on shore, find that they have performed a very needless ceremony, in consequence of their not being carried away at all. The regular passengers, who have season-tickets, go below to breakfast; people who have purchased morning papers, compose themselves to read them; and people who have not been down the river before, think that both the shipping and the water, look a great deal better at a distance.

When we get down about as far as Blackwall,[12] and begin to move at a quicker rate, the spirits of the passengers appear to rise in proportion. Old women who have brought large wicker hand-baskets with them, set seriously to work at the demolition of heavy sandwiches, and pass round a wine-glass, which is frequently replenished from a flat bottle like a stomach-warmer, with consider-able glee: handing it first to the gentleman in the foraging-cap, who plays the harp – partly as an expression of satisfaction with his previous exertions, and partly to induce him to play 'Dumbledum-deary,'[13] for 'Alick' to dance to; which being done, Alick, who is a damp earthy child in red worsted socks, takes certain small jumps upon the deck, to the unspeakable satisfaction of his family circle. Girls who have brought the first volume of some new novel in their reticule, become extremely plaintive, and expatiate to Mr Brown, or young Mr O'Brien, who has been looking over them, on the blueness of the sky, and brightness of the water; on which Mr Brown or Mr O'Brien, as the case may be, remarks in a low voice that he has been quite insensible of late to the beauties of nature — that his whole thoughts and wishes have centred in one object alone — whereupon the young lady looks up, and failing in her attempt to appear unconscious, looks down again; and turns over the next leaf with great difficulty, in order to afford opportunity for a lengthened pressure of the hand.

Telescopes, sandwiches, and glasses of brandy-and-water cold without, begin to be in great requisition; and bashful men who have been looking down the hatchway at the engine, find, to their great relief, a subject on which they can converse with one another — and a copious one too — Steam.

'Wonderful thing steam, sir.' 'Ah! (a deep-drawn sigh) it is indeed, sir.' 'Great power, sir.' 'Immense — immense!' 'Great deal done by steam, sir.' 'Ah! (another sigh at the immensity of the subject, and a knowing shake of the head) you may say that, sir.' 'Still in its infancy they say, sir.' Novel remarks of this kind, are generally the commencement of a conversation which is prolonged until the conclusion of the trip, and, perhaps, lays the foundation of a speaking acquaintance between half a dozen gentlemen, who, having their families at Gravesend, take season-tickets for the boat, and dine on board regularly every afternoon.

CHAPTER I I

Astley's

WE never see any very large, staring, black Roman capitals, in a book, or shop-window, or placarded on a wall, without their immediately recalling to our mind an indistinct and confused recollection of the time when we were first initiated in the mysteries of the alphabet. We almost fancy we see the pin's point following the letter, to impress its form more strongly on our bewildered imagination; and wince involuntarily, as we remember the hard knuckles with which the reverend old lady who instilled into our mind the first principles of education for ninepence per week, or ten and sixpence per quarter, was wont to poke our juvenile head occasionally, by way of adjusting the confusion of ideas in which we were generally involved. The same kind of feeling pursues us in many other instances, but there is no place which recalls so strongly our recollections of childhood as Astley's.[1] It was not a 'Royal Amphitheatre'[2] in those days, nor had Ducrow[3] arisen to shed the light of classic taste and portable gas over the sawdust of the circus; but the whole character of the place was the same, the pieces were the same, the clown's jokes were the same, the riding-masters were equally grand, the comic performers equally witty, the tragedians equally hoarse, and the 'highly-trained chargers' equally spirited. Astley's has altered for the better – we have changed for the worse. Our histrionic taste is gone, and with shame we confess, that we are far more delighted and amused with the audience, than with the pageantry we once so highly appreciated.

We like to watch a regular Astley's party in the Easter or Midsummer holidays – pa and ma, and nine or ten children, varying from five foot six to two foot eleven: from fourteen years of age to four. We had just taken our seat in one of the boxes, in the centre of the house, the other night, when the next was occupied by just such a party as we should have attempted to describe, had we depicted our *beau idéal* of a group of Astley's visiters.

First of all, there came three little boys and a little girl, who, in pursuance of pa's directions, issued in a very audible voice from the box-door, occupied the front-row; then two more little girls were ushered in by a young lady, evidently the governess. Then came three more little boys, dressed like the first, in blue jackets and trousers, with lay-down shirt-collars: then a child in a braided frock and high state of astonishment, with very large round eyes, opened to their utmost width, was lifted over the seats – a process which occasioned a considerable display of little pink legs – then came ma and pa, and then the eldest son, a boy of fourteen years old, who was evidently trying to look as if he did not belong to the family.

The first five minutes were occupied in taking the shawls off the little girls, and adjusting the bows which ornamented their hair; then it was providentially discovered that one of the little boys was seated behind a pillar and could not see, so the governess was stuck behind the pillar, and the boy lifted into her place. Then pa drilled the boys, and directed the stowing away of their pocket-handker-chiefs; and ma having first nodded and winked to the governess to pull the girls' frocks a little more off their shoulders, stood up to review the little troop – an inspection which appeared to terminate much to her own satisfaction, for she looked with a complacent air at pa, who was standing up at the further end of the seat. Pa returned the glance, and blew his nose very emphatically; and the poor governess peeped out from behind the pillar, and timidly tried to catch ma's eye, with a look expressive of her high admiration of the whole family. Then two of the little boys who had been discussing the point whether Astley's was more than twice as large as Drury-lane,[4] agreed to refer it to 'George' for his decision; at which 'George,' who was no other than the young gentleman before noticed, waxed indignant, and remonstrated in no very gentle terms on the gross impropriety of having his name repeated in so loud a voice at a public place, on which all the children laughed very heartily, and one of the little boys wound up by expressing his opinion that 'George began to think himself quite a man now,' whereupon both pa and ma laughed too; and George (who carried a dress cane, and was cultivating whiskers) muttered that 'William always was encouraged in his impertinence;' and assumed a look of profound contempt, which lasted the whole evening.

The play began, and the interest of the little boys knew no bounds. Pa was clearly interested too, although he very unsuccess-fully endeavoured to look as if he wasn't. As for ma, she was perfectly overcome by the drollery of the principal comedian, and laughed till every one of the immense bows on her ample cap trembled, at which the governess peeped out from behind the pillar again, and whenever she could catch ma's eye, put her handkerchief to her mouth, and appeared, as in duty bound, to be in convulsions of laughter also. Then when the man in the splendid armour vowed to rescue the lady or perish in the attempt, the little boys applauded vehemently, especially one little fellow who was apparently on a visit to the family, and had been carrying on a child's flirtation, the whole evening, with a small coquette of twelve years old, who looked like a model of her mamma on a reduced scale; and who in common with the other little girls (who generally speaking have even more coquettishness about them than much older ones) looked very properly shocked, when the knight's squire kissed the princess's confidential chambermaid.

When the scenes in the circle commenced, the children were more delighted than ever; and the wish to see what was going forward, completely conquering pa's dignity, he stood up in the box, and applauded as loudly as any of them. Between each feat of horsemanship, the governess leant across to ma, and retailed the clever remarks of the children on that which had preceded: and ma, in the openness of her heart, offered the governess an acidulated drop, and the governess, gratified to be taken notice of, retired behind her pillar again with a brighter countenance: and the whole party seemed quite happy, except the exquisite in the back of the box, who, being too grand to take any interest in the children, and too insignificant to be taken notice of by any body else, occupied himself, from time to time, in rubbing the place where the whiskers ought to be, and was completely alone in his glory.

We defy any one who has been to Astley's two or three times, and is consequently capable of appreciating the perseverance with which precisely the same jokes are repeated night after night, and season after season, not to be amused with one part of the performances at least – we mean the scenes in the circle. For ourself, we know that when the hoop, composed of jets of gas, is let down, the curtain drawn up for the convenience of the half-price on their ejectment from the ring, the orange-peel cleared away, and the sawdust shaken, with mathematical precision, into a complete circle, we feel as much enlivened as the youngest child present; and actually join in the laugh which follows the clown's shrill shout of 'Here we are!' just for old acquaintance' sake. Nor can we quite divest ourself of our old feeling of reverence for the riding-master, who follows the clown with a long whip in his hand, and bows to the audience with graceful dignity. He is none of your second-rate riding-masters in nankeen dressing-gowns, with brown frogs,[5] but the regular gentleman-attendant on the principal riders, who always wears a military uniform with a table-cloth inside the breast of the coat, in which costume he forcibly reminds one of a fowl trussed for roasting. He is – but why should we attempt to describe that of which no description can convey an adequate idea? Every body knows the man, and every body remembers his polished boots, his graceful demeanour, stiff, as some misjudging persons have in their jealousy considered it, and the splendid head of black hair, parted high on the forehead, to impart to the countenance an appearance of deep thought and poetic melancholy. His soft and pleasing voice, too, is in perfect unison with his noble bearing, as he humours the clown by indulging in a little badinage; and the striking recollection of his own dignity, with which he exclaims, 'Now, sir, if you please, inquire for Miss Woolford, sir,' can never be forgotten. The graceful air, too, with which he introduces Miss Woolford into the arena, and, after assisting her to the saddle, follows her fairy courser round the circle, can never fail to create a deep impression in the bosom of every female servant present.

When Miss Woolford, and the horse, and the orchestra, all stop together to take breath, he urbanely takes part in some such dialogue as the following (commenced by the clown): 'I say, sir!' – 'Well, sir?' (it's always conducted in the politest manner.) 'Did you ever happen to hear I was in the army, sir?' – 'No sir.' – 'Oh, yes, sir – I can go through my exercise, sir.' – 'Indeed, sir!' – 'Shall I do it now, sir?' – 'If you please, sir; come, sir – make haste' (a cut with the long whip, and 'Ha' done now – I don't like it,' from the clown). Here the clown throws himself on the ground, and goes through a variety of gymnastic convulsions, doubling himself up, and untying himself again, and making himself look very like a

man in the most hopeless extreme of human agony, to the vociferous delight of the gallery, until he is interrupted by a second cut
from the long whip, and a request to see 'what Miss Woolford's
stopping for?' On which, to the inexpressible mirth of the gallery,
he exclaims, 'Now, Miss Woolford, what can I come for to go, for
to fetch, for to bring, for to carry, for to do, for you, ma'am?' On
the lady's announcing with a sweet smile that she wants the two
flags, they are with sundry grimaces, procured and handed up; the
clown facetiously observing after the performance of the latter
ceremony – 'He, he, oh! I say, sir, Miss Woolford knows me; she
smiled at me.' Another cut from the whip, a burst from the
orchestra, a start from the horse, and round goes Miss Woolford
again on her graceful performance, to the delight of every member
of the audience, young or old. The next pause affords an opportunity for similar witticisms, the only additional fun being that of
the clown making ludicrous grimaces at the riding-master every
time his back is turned; and finally quitting the circle by jumping
over his head, having previously directed his attention another
way.

Did any of our readers ever notice the class of people, who hang
about the stage-doors of our minor theatres in the daytime? You
will rarely pass one of these entrances without seeing a group of
three or four men conversing on the pavement, with an indescribable public-house-parlour swagger, and a kind of conscious air,
peculiar to people of this description. They always seem to think
they are exhibiting; the lamps are ever before them. That young
fellow in the faded brown coat, and very full light green trousers,
pulls down the wristbands of his check shirt, as ostentatiously as if
it were of the finest linen, and cocks the white hat of the summer-
before-last as knowingly over his right eye, as if it were a purchase
of yesterday. Look at the dirty white Berlin gloves,[6] and the cheap
silk-handkerchief stuck in the bosom of his threadbare coat. Is it
possible to see him for an instant, and not come to the conclusion
that he is the walking gentleman who wears a blue surtout, clean
collar, and white trousers, for half an hour, and then shrinks into
his worn-out scanty clothes: who has to boast night after night of

his splendid fortune, with the painful consciousness of a pound a-week and his boots to find; to talk of his father's mansion in the country, with a dreary recollection of his own two-pair back, in the New Cut;[7] and to be envied and flattered as the favoured lover of a rich heiress, remembering all the while that the ex-dancer at home, is in the family way, and out of an engagement?

Next to him, perhaps, you will see a thin pale man, with a very long face, in a suit of shining black, thoughtfully knocking that part of his boot which once had a heel, with an ash stick. He is the man who does the heavy business, such as prosy fathers, virtuous servants, curates, landlords, and so forth.

By the way, talking of fathers, we should very much like to see some piece in which all the dramatis personæ were orphans. Fathers are invariably great nuisances on the stage, and always have to give the hero or heroine a long explanation of what was done before the curtain rose, usually commencing with 'It is now nineteen years, my dear child, since your blessed mother (here the old villain's voice falters) confided you to my charge. You were then an infant,' &c. &c. Or else they have to discover, all of a sudden, that somebody whom they have been in constant communication with, during three long acts, without the slightest suspicion, is their own child: in which case they exclaim, 'Ah! what do I see? This bracelet! That smile! These documents! Those eyes! Can I believe my senses? — It must be! — Yes — it is, it is my child!' — 'My father!' exclaims the child; and they fall into each other's arms, and look over each other's shoulders, and the audience give three rounds of applause.

To return from this digression, we were about to say, that these are the sort of people whom you see talking, and attitudinizing, outside the stage-doors of our minor theatres. At Astley's they are always more numerous than at any other place. There is generally a groom or two, sitting on the window-sill, and two or three dirty shabby-genteel men in checked neckerchiefs, and sallow linen, lounging about, and carrying, perhaps, under one arm, a pair of stage shoes badly wrapped up in a piece of old newspaper. Some years ago we used to stand looking, open-mouthed, at these men, with a feeling of mysterious curiosity, the very recollection of which provokes a smile at the moment we are writing. We could not believe, that the beings of light and elegance, in milk-white tunics, salmon-coloured legs, and blue scarfs, who flitted on sleek cream-coloured horses before our eyes at night, with all the aid of lights, music, and artificial flowers, could be the pale, dissipated-looking creatures we beheld by day.

We can hardly believe it now. Of the lower class of actors we have seen something, and it requires no great exercise of imagination to identify the walking gentleman with the 'dirty swell,'[8] the comic singer with the public-house chairman, or the leading tragedian with drunkenness and distress; but these other men are mysterious beings, never seen out of the ring, never beheld but in the costume of gods and sylphs. With the exception of Ducrow, who can scarcely be classed among them, who ever knew a rider at Astley's, or saw him but on horseback? Can our friend in the military uniform, ever appear in threadbare attire, or descend to the comparatively un-wadded costume of every-day life? Impossible! We cannot — we will not — believe it.

CHAPTER 12

Greenwich Fair

IF the Parks be 'the lungs of London,'[1] we wonder what Greenwich Fair[2] is — a periodical breaking out, we suppose, a sort of spring-rash: a three day's fever, which cools the blood for six months afterwards, and at the expiration of which, London is restored to its old habits of plodding industry, as suddenly and completely as if nothing had ever happened to disturb them.

In our earlier days, we were a constant frequenter of Greenwich Fair, for years. We have proceeded to, and returned from it, in

Greenwich Fair

almost every description of vehicle. We cannot conscientiously deny the charge of having once made the passage in a spring-van, accompanied by thirteen gentlemen, fourteen ladies, an unlimited number of children, and a barrel of beer; and we have a vague recollection of having, in later days, found ourself the eighth outside, on the top of a hackney-coach, at something past four o'clock in the morning, with a rather confused idea of our own name, or place of residence. We have grown older since then, and quiet, and steady: liking nothing better than to spend our Easter, and all our other holidays, in some quiet nook, with people of whom we shall never tire; but we think we still remember something of Greenwich Fair, and of those who resort to it. At all events we will try.

The road to Greenwich during the whole of Easter Monday, is in a state of perpetual bustle and noise. Cabs, hackney-coaches, 'shay' carts, coal-waggons, stages, omnibuses, sociables, gigs, donkey-chaises — all crammed with people (for the question never is, what the horse can draw, but what the vehicle will hold), roll along at their utmost speed; the dust flies in clouds, ginger-beer corks go off in volleys, the balcony of every public-house is crowded with people, smoking and drinking, half the private houses are turned into tea-shops, fiddles are in great request, every little fruit-shop displays its stall of gilt gingerbread and penny toys; turnpike men are in despair; horses won't go on, and wheels will come off; ladies in 'carawans' scream with fright at every fresh concussion, and their admirers find it necessary to sit remarkably close to them, by way of encouragement; servants-of-all-work, who are not allowed to have followers, and have got a holiday for the day, make the most of their time with the faithful admirer who waits for a stolen interview at the corner of the street every night, when they go to fetch the beer — apprentices grow sentimental, and straw-bonnet makers kind. Every body is anxious to get on, and actuated by the common wish to be at the fair, or in the park, as soon as possible.

Pedestrians linger in groups at the roadside, unable to resist the allurements of the stout proprietress of the 'Jack-in-the-box — three shies a penny,' or the more splendid offers of the man with three thimbles and a pea on a little round board, who astonishes the bewildered crowd with some such address as, 'Here's the sort o'game to make you laugh seven years arter you're dead, and turn ev'ry air on your ed gray vith delight! Three thimbles and vun little pea – with a vun, two, three, and a two, three, vun: catch him who can, look on, keep your eyes open, and niver say die! niver mind the change, and the expense; all fair and above board: them as don't play can't vin, and luck attend the ryal sportsman! Bet any gen'lm'n any sum of money, from harf-a-crown up to a suverin, as he doesn't name the thimble as kivers the pea!' Here some greenhorn whispers his friend, that he distinctly saw the pea roll under the middle thimble – an impression which is immediately confirmed by a gentleman in top-boots, who is standing by, and who, in a low tone, regrets his own inability to bet in consequence of having unfortunately left his purse at home, but strongly urges the stranger not to neglect such a golden opportunity. The 'plant' is successful, the bet is made, the stranger of course loses: and the gentleman with the thimbles consoles him, as he pockets the money, with an assurance that it's 'all the fortin of war! this time I vin, next time you vin: niver mind the loss of two bob and a bender![3] Do it up in a small parcel, and break out in a fresh place. Here's the sort o' game,' &c. – and the eloquent harangue, with such variations as the speaker's exuberant fancy suggests, is again repeated to the gaping crowd, reinforced by the accession of several new comers.

The chief place of resort in the day-time, after the public-houses, is the park, in which the principal amusement is to drag young ladies up the steep hill which leads to the observatory,[4] and then drag them down again, at the very top of their speed, greatly to the derangement of their curls and bonnet-caps, and much to the edification of lookers-on from below. 'Kiss in the Ring,' and 'Threading my Grandmother's Needle,' too, are sports which receive their full share of patronage. Love-sick swains, under the influence of gin-and-water, and the tender passion, become violently affectionate: and the fair objects of their regard, enhance the value of stolen kisses, by a vast deal of struggling, and holding down of heads, and cries of 'Oh! Ha' done, then, George – Oh, do tickle him for me, Mary – Well, I never!' and similar Lucretian ejaculations.[5] Little old men and women, with a small basket under one arm, and a wine-glass, without a foot, in the other hand, tender 'a drop o' the right sort' to the different groups; and young ladies, who are persuaded to indulge in a drop of the aforesaid right sort, display a pleasing degree of reluctance to taste it, and cough afterwards with great propriety.

The old pensioners, who, for the moderate charge of a penny, exhibit the mast-house, the Thames and shipping, the place where the men used to hang in chains, and other interesting sights, through a telescope, are asked questions about objects within the range of the glass, which it would puzzle a Solomon[6] to answer; and requested to find out particular houses in particular streets, which it would have been a task of some difficulty for Mr Horner (not the young gentleman who ate mince-pies with his thumb, but the man of Colosseum notoriety)[7] to discover. Here and there, where some three or four couple are sitting on the grass together, you will see a sunburnt woman in a red cloak 'telling fortunes' and prophesying husbands, which it requires no extraordinary observation to describe, for the originals are before her. Thereupon, the lady concerned, laughs and blushes, and ultimately buries her face in an imitation-cambric handkerchief, and the gentleman described, looks extremely foolish, and squeezes her hand, and fees the gipsy liberally; and the gipsy goes away, perfectly satisfied herself, and leaving those behind her perfectly satisfied also: and the prophecy, like many other prophecies of greater importance, fulfils itself in time.

But it grows dark: the crowd has gradually dispersed, and only a few stragglers are left behind. The light in the direction of the church, shows that the fair is illuminated; and the distant noise proves it to be filling fast. The spot which half an hour ago, was ringing with the shouts of boisterous mirth, is as calm and quiet as if nothing could ever disturb its serenity; the fine old trees, the majestic building[8] at their feet, with the noble river beyond, glistening in the moonlight, appear in all their beauty, and under their most favourable aspect; the voices of the boys,[9] singing their evening hymn, are borne gently on the air; and the humblest mechanic who has been lingering on the grass so pleasant to the feet that beat the same dull round from week to week in the paved streets of London, feels proud to think as he surveys the scene before him, that he belongs to the country which has selected such a spot as a retreat for its oldest and best defenders in the decline of their lives.

Five minutes' walking brings you to the fair; a scene calculated to awaken very different feelings. The entrance is occupied on either side by the vendors of gingerbread and toys: the stalls are gaily lighted up, the most attractive goods profusely disposed, and unbonneted young ladies, in their zeal for the interest of their employers, seize you by the coat, and use all the blandishments of 'Do dear' — 'There's a love' — 'Don't be cross, now,' &c., to induce you to purchase half a pound of the real spice nuts, of which the majority of the regular fair-goers carry a pound or two as a present supply, tied up in a cotton pocket-handkerchief. Occasionally you pass a deal table, on which are exposed pen'orths of pickled salmon (fennel included), in little white saucers: oysters, with shells as large as cheese-plates, and divers specimens of a species of snail (*wilks*,[10] we think they are called), floating in a somewhat bilious-looking green liquid. Cigars, too, are in great demand; gentlemen must smoke, of course, and here they are, two a penny, in a regular authentic cigar-box, with a lighted tallow candle in the centre.

Imagine yourself in an extremely dense crowd, which swings you to and fro, and in and out, and every way but the right one; add to this the screams of women, the shouts of boys, the clanging of gongs, the firing of pistols, the ringing of bells, the bellowings of speaking-trumpets, the squeaking of penny dittos, the noise of a dozen bands, with three drums in each, all playing different tunes at the same time, the hallooing of showmen, and an occasional roar from the wild-beast shows; and you are in the very centre and heart of the fair.

This immense booth, with the large stage in front, so brightly illuminated with variegated lamps, and pots of burning fat, is 'Richardson's,'[11] where you have a melo-drama (with three murders and a ghost), a pantomime, a comic song, an overture, and some incidental music, all done in five-and-twenty minutes.

The company are now promenading outside in all the dignity of wigs, spangles, red-ochre, and whitening. See with what a ferocious air the gentleman who personates the Mexican chief, paces up and down, and with what an eye of calm dignity the principal tragedian gazes on the crowd below, or converses confidentially with the harlequin! The four clowns, who are engaged in a mock broad-sword combat, may be all very well for the low-minded holiday-makers; but these are the people for the reflective portion of the community. They look so noble in those Roman dresses, with their yellow legs and arms, long black curly heads, bushy eyebrows, and scowl expressive of assassination, and vengeance, and every thing else that is grand and solemn. Then, the ladies – were there ever such innocent and awful-looking beings; as they walk up and down the platforms in twos and threes; with their arms round each other's waists, or leaning for support on one of those majestic men! Their spangled muslin dresses and blue satin shoes and sandals (a *leetle* the worse for wear) are the admiration of all beholders; and the playful manner in which they check the advances of the clown is perfectly enchanting.

'Just a-going to begin! Pray come for'erd, come for'erd,' exclaims the man in the countryman's dress, for the seventieth time: and people force their way up the steps in crowds. The band suddenly strikes up, the harlequin and columbine[12] set the example, reels are formed in less than no time, the Roman heroes place their arms a-kimbo, and dance with considerable agility; and the leading tragic actress, and the gentleman who enacts the 'swell' in the pantomime, foot it to perfection. 'All in to begin,' shouts the manager, when no more people can be induced to 'come for'erd,' and away rush the leading members of the company to do the dreadful in the first piece.

A change of performance takes place every day during the fair, but the story of the tragedy is always pretty much the same.

There is a rightful heir, who loves a young lady, and is beloved by her; and a wrongful heir, who loves her too, and isn't beloved by her; and the wrongful heir gets hold of the rightful heir, and throws him into a dungeon, just to kill him off when convenient, for which purpose he hires a couple of assassins — a good one and a bad one — who, the moment they are left alone, get up a little murder on their own account, the good one killing the bad one, and the bad one wounding the good one. Then the rightful heir is discovered in prison, carefully holding a long chain in his hands, and seated despondingly in a large arm-chair; and the young lady comes in to two bars of soft music, and embraces the rightful heir; and then the wrongful heir comes in to two bars of quick music, (technically called 'a hurry') and goes on in the most shocking manner, throwing the young lady about, as if she was nobody, and calling the rightful heir 'Ar-recreant — ar-wretch!' in a very loud voice, which answers the double purpose of displaying his passion, and preventing the sound being deadened by the sawdust. The interest becomes intense; the wrongful heir draws his sword, and rushes on the rightful heir; a blue smoke is seen, a gong is heard, and a tall white figure (who has been all this time, behind the arm-chair, covered over with a table-cloth), slowly rises to the tune of 'Oft in the stilly night.'[13] This is no other than the ghost of the rightful heir's father, who was killed by the wrongful heir's father, at sight of which the wrongful heir becomes apoplectic, and is literally 'struck all of a heap,' the stage not being large enough to admit of his falling down at full length. Then the good assassin staggers in, and says he was hired in conjunction with the bad assassin, by the wrongful heir, to kill the rightful heir; and he's killed a good many people in his time, but he's very sorry for it, and won't do so any more — a promise which he immediately redeems, by dying off hand, without any nonsense about it. Then the rightful heir throws down his chain; and then two men, a sailor, and a young woman (the tenantry of the rightful heir) come in, and the ghost makes dumb motions to them, which they, by supernatural interference, understand — for no one else can; and the ghost (who can't do any thing without blue fire) blesses the rightful heir and the young lady, by half suffocating them with smoke: and then a muffin-bell rings, and the curtain drops.

The exhibitions next in popularity to these itinerant theatres, are the travelling menageries, or, to speak more intelligibly, the 'Wild-beast shows,' where a military band in beef-eater's costume, with leopard-skin caps, play incessantly; and where large highly-coloured representations of tigers tearing men's heads open, and a lion being burnt with red-hot irons to induce him to drop his victim, are hung up outside, by way of attracting visiters.

The principal officer at these places, is generally a very tall, hoarse man, in a scarlet coat, with a cane in his hand, with which he occasionally raps the pictures we have just noticed, by way of illustrating his description – something in this way. 'Here, here, here; the lion, the lion (tap), exactly as he is represented on the canvass outside (three taps): no waiting, remember; no deception. The fe-ro-cious lion (tap, tap) who bit off the gentleman's head last Cambervel vos a twelvemonth, and has killed on the awerage three keepers a-year ever since he arrived at matoority. No extra charge on this account recollect; the price of admission is only sixpence.' This address never fails to produce a considerable sensation, and sixpences flow into the treasury with wonderful rapidity.

The dwarfs are also objects of great curiosity, and as a dwarf, a giantess, a living skeleton, a wild Indian, 'a young lady of singular beauty, with perfectly white hair and pink eyes,' and two or three other natural curiosities, are usually exhibited together for the small charge of a penny, they attract very numerous audiences. The best thing about a dwarf is, that he has always a little box, about two feet six inches high, into which, by long practice, he can just manage to get, by doubling himself up like a boot-jack; this box is painted outside like a six-roomed house, and as the crowd see him ring a bell, or fire a pistol out of the first-floor window, they verily believe that it is his ordinary town residence, divided like other mansions into drawing-rooms, dining-parlour, and bedchambers. Shut up in this case, the unfortunate little object is brought out to delight the throng by holding a facetious dialogue with the propri-etor: in the course of which, the dwarf (who is always particularly drunk) pledges himself to sing a comic song inside, and pays various compliments to the ladies, which induce them to 'come for'erd' with great alacrity. As a giant is not so easily moved, a pair of indescribables[14] of most capacious dimensions, and a huge shoe, are usually brought out, into which two or three stout men get all at once, to the enthusiastic delight of the crowd, who are quite satisfied with the solemn assurance that these habiliments form part of the giant's every-day costume.

The grandest and most numerously-frequented booth in the whole fair, however, is 'The Crown and Anchor' – a temporary ball-room – we forget how many hundred feet long, the price of admission to which is one shilling. Immediately on your right hand as you enter, after paying your money, is a refreshment place, at which cold beef, roast and boiled, French rolls, stout, wine, tongue, ham, even fowls, if we recollect right, are displayed in tempting array. There is a raised orchestra, and the place is boarded all the way down, in patches, just wide enough for a country dance.

There is no master of the ceremonies in this artificial Eden – all is primitive, unreserved, and unstudied. The dust is blinding, the heat insupportable, the company somewhat noisy, and in the highest spirits possible: the ladies, in the height of their innocent animation, dancing in the gentlemen's hats, and the gentlemen promenading 'the gay and festive scene' in the ladies' bonnets, or with the more expensive ornaments of false noses, and low-crowned, tinder-box-looking hats: playing children's drums, and accompanied by ladies on the penny trumpet.

The noise of these various instruments, the orchestra, the shouting, the 'scratchers,' and the dancing, is perfectly bewildering. The dancing, itself, beggars description – every figure lasts about an hour, and the ladies bounce up and down the middle; with a degree of spirit which is quite indescribable. As to the gentlemen, they stamp their feet against the ground, every time 'hands four round' begins, go down the middle and up again, with cigars in their mouths, and silk handkerchiefs in their hands, and whirl their partners round, nothing loth, scrambling and falling, and embracing, and knocking up against the other couples, until they are fairly tired out, and can move no longer. The same scene is repeated again and again (slightly varied by an occasional 'row') until a late hour at night: and a great many clerks and 'prentices find themselves next morning with aching heads, empty pockets, damaged hats, and a very imperfect recollection of how it was, they did *not* get home.

CHAPTER 13

Private Theatres

'RICHARD THE THIRD. — DUKE OF GLOSTER, 2*l.*;
EARL OF RICHMOND, 1*l.*; DUKE OF BUCKINGHAM,
15*s.*; CATESBY, 12*s.*; TRESSELL, 10*s.* 6*d.*; LORD
STANLEY, 5*s.*; LORD MAYOR OF LONDON, 2*s.* 6*d.*'[1]

SUCH are the written placards wafered up in the gentlemen's dressing-room, or the green-room (where there is any), at a private theatre;[2] and such are the sums extracted from the shop till, or overcharged in the office expenditure, by the donkeys who are prevailed upon to pay for permission to exhibit their lamentable ignorance and boobyism on the stage of a private theatre. This they do, in proportion to the scope afforded by the character for the display of their imbecility. For instance, the Duke of Glo'ster is well worth two pounds, because he has it all to himself; he must wear a real sword, and what is better still, he must draw it, several times in the course of the piece. The soliloquies alone are well worth fifteen shillings; then there is the stabbing King Henry — decidedly cheap at three-and-sixpence, that's eighteen-and-sixpence; bullying the coffin-bearers — say eighteen-pence, though it's worth much more — that's a pound. Then the love scene with Lady Ann, and the bustle of the fourth act, can't be dear at ten shillings more — that's only one pound ten, including the 'off with his head!' —

George Cruikshank

Private Theatres

which is sure to bring down the applause, and it is very easy to do
– 'Orf with his ed' (very quick and loud; – then slow and
sneeringly) – 'So much for Bu-u-u-uckingham!'³ Lay the emphasis
on the 'uck;' get yourself gradually into a corner, and work with
your right hand, while you're saying it, as if you were feeling your
way, and it's sure to do. The tent scene is confessedly worth half-a-
sovereign, and so you have the fight in, gratis, and every body
knows what an effect may be produced by a good combat. One –
two – three – four – over; then, one – two – three – four – under;
then thrust; then dodge and slide about; then fall down on one
knee; then fight upon it, and then get up again and stagger. You
may keep on doing this, as long as it seems to take – say ten
minutes – and then fall down (backwards, if you can manage it
without hurting yourself), and die game: nothing like it for
producing an effect. They always do it at Astley's and Sadler's
Wells,⁴ and if they don't know how to do this sort of thing, who
in the world does? A small child, or a female in white, increases the
interest of a combat materially – indeed, we are not aware that a
regular legitimate terrific broadsword combat could be done without; but it would be rather difficult, and somewhat unusual, to
introduce this effect in the last scene of Richard the Third, so the
only thing to be done, is, just to make the best of a bad bargain,
and be as long as possible fighting it out.

The principal patrons of private theatres are dirty boys, low
copying-clerks in attorneys' offices, capacious-headed youths from
city counting-houses, Jews whose business, as lenders of fancy
dresses, is a sure passport to the amateur stage, shop-boys who
now and then mistake their master's money for their own; and a
choice miscellany of idle vagabonds. The proprietor of a private
theatre, may be an ex-scene-painter, a low coffee-house-keeper, a
disappointed eighth-rate actor, a retired smuggler, or an uncertifi-
cated bankrupt. The theatre itself, may be in Catherine-street,
Strand, the purlieus of the city, the neighbourhood of Gray's-inn-
lane, or the vicinity of Sadler's Wells; or it may, perhaps, form the
chief nuisance of some shabby street, on the Surrey side of
Waterloo bridge.

The lady performers pay nothing for their characters, and it is needless to add, are usually selected from one class of society; the audiences are necessarily of much the same character as the performers, who receive, in return for their contributions to the management, tickets to the amount of the money they pay.

All the minor theatres in London, especially the lowest, constitute the centre of a little stage-struck neighbourhood. Each of them has an audience exclusively its own; and at any you will see dropping into the pit at half-price, or swaggering into the back of a box, if the price of admission be a reduced one, divers boys of from fifteen to twenty-one years of age, who throw back their coat and turn up their wristbands, after the portraits of Count D'Orsay,[5] hum tunes and whistle when the curtain is down, by way of persuading the people near them, that they are not at all anxious to have it up again, and speak familiarly of the inferior performers as Bill Such-a-one, and Ned So-and-so, or tell each other how a new piece called *The Unknown Bandit of the Invisible Cavern*, is in rehearsal; how Mister Palmer is to play *The Unknown Bandit*; how Charley Scarton is to take the part of an English sailor, and fight a broadsword combat with six unknown bandits, at one and the same time (one theatrical sailor is always equal to half a dozen men at least); how Mister Palmer and Charley Scarton are to go through a double hornpipe in fetters in the second act; how the interior of the invisible cavern is to occupy the whole extent of the stage; and other town-surprising theatrical announcements. These gentlemen are the amateurs – the *Richards*, *Shylocks*, *Beverleys*, and *Othellos* – the *Young Dorntons*, *Rovers*, *Captain Absolutes*, and *Charles Surfaces*[6] – of a private theatre.

See them at the neighbouring public-house or the theatrical coffee-shop! They are the kings of the place, supposing no real performers to be present; and roll about, hats on one side, and arms a-kimbo, as if they had actually come into possession of eighteen shillings a-week, and a share of a ticket night. If one of them does but know an Astley's supernumerary he is a happy fellow. The mingled air of envy and admiration with which his companions will regard him, as he converses familiarly with some mouldy-looking man in a fancy neckerchief, whose partially corked eyebrows, and half-rouged face, testify to the act of his having just left the stage or the circle, sufficiently shows in what high admiration these public characters are held.

With the double view of guarding against the discovery of friends or employers, and enhancing the interest of an assumed character, by attaching a high-sounding name to its representative, these geniuses assume fictitious names, which are not the least amusing part of the play-bill of a private theatre. Belville, Melville, Treville, Berkeley, Randolph, Byron, St Clair, and so forth, are among the humblest; and the less imposing titles of Jenkins, Walker, Thomson, Barker, Solomons, &c., are completely laid aside. There is something imposing in this, and it is an excellent apology for shabbiness into the bargain. A shrunken, faded coat, a decayed hat, a patched and soiled pair of trousers – nay even a very dirty shirt (and none of these appearances are very uncommon among the members of the *corps dramatique*), may be worn for the purpose of disguise, and to prevent the remotest chance of recognition. Then it prevents any troublesome inquiries or explanations about employment and pursuits; every body is a gentleman at large, for the occasion, and there are none of those unpleasant and unnecessary distinctions to which even genius must occasionally succumb elsewhere. As to the ladies (God bless them), they are quite above any formal absurdities; the mere circumstance of your being behind the scenes is a sufficient introduction to their society – for of course they know that none but strictly respectable persons would be admitted into that close fellowship with them, which acting engenders. They place implicit reliance on the manager, no doubt; and as to the manager, he is all affability when he knows you well, – or, in other words, when he has pocketed your money once, and entertains confident hopes of doing so again.

A quarter before eight – there will be a full house to-night – six parties in the boxes, already; four little boys and a woman in the pit; and two fiddles and a flute in the orchestra, who have got through five overtures since seven o'clock (the hour fixed for the commencement of the performances), and have just begun the sixth. There will be plenty of it, though, when it does begin, for there is enough in the bill to last six hours at least.

That gentleman in the white hat and checked shirt, brown coat and brass buttons, lounging behind the stage-box on the O.P. side,[7] is Mr Horatio St Julien, alias Jem Larkins. His line is genteel comedy – his father's, coal and potato. He *does* Alfred Highflier in the last piece, and very well he'll do it – at the price. The party of gentlemen in the opposite box, to whom he has just nodded, are friends and supporters of Mr Beverley (otherwise Loggins), the *Macbeth* of the night. You observe their attempts to appear easy and gentlemanly, each member of the party, with his feet cocked upon the cushion in front of the box! They let them do these things here, upon the same humane principle which permits poor people's children to knock double knocks at the door of an empty house – because they can't do it any where else. The two stout men in the centre box, with an opera-glass ostentatiously placed before them, are friends of the proprietor – opulent country managers, as he confidentially informs every individual among the crew behind the curtain – opulent country managers looking out for recruits; a representation which Mr Nathan, the dresser, who is in the manager's interest, and has just arrived with the costumes, offers to confirm upon oath if required – corroborative evidence, however, is quite unnecessary, for the gulls believe it at once.

The stout Jewess, who has just entered, is the mother of the pale bony little girl, with the necklace of blue glass beads, sitting by her; she is being brought up to 'the profession.' Pantomime is to be her line, and she is coming out to-night, in a hornpipe after the tragedy. The short thin man beside Mr St Julien, whose white face is so deeply seared with the smallpox, and whose dirty shirt-front is inlaid with open-work, and embossed with coral studs like ladybirds, is the low comedian and comic singer of the establishment. The remainder of the audience – a tolerably numerous one by this time – are a motley group of dupes and blackguards.

The foot-lights have just made their appearance: the wicks of the six little oil lamps round the only tier of boxes, are being turned up, and the additional light thus afforded, serves to show the presence of dirt, and absence of paint, which forms a prominent feature in the audience part of the house. As these preparations, however, announce the speedy commencement of the play, let us take a peep 'behind,' previous to the ringing-up.

The little narrow passages beneath the stage are neither especially clean nor too brilliantly lighted; and the absence of any flooring, together with the damp mildewy smell which pervades the place, does not conduce in any great degree to their comfortable appearance. Don't fall over this plate-basket – it's one of the 'properties' – the caldron for the witches' cave; and the three uncouth-looking figures, with broken clothes-props in their hands, who are drinking gin-and-water out of a pint pot, are the weird sisters. This miserable room, lighted by candles in sconces placed at lengthened intervals round the wall, is the dressing-room, common to the gentlemen performers, and the square hole in the ceiling is *the* trap-door of the stage above. You will observe that the ceiling is ornamented with the beams that support the boards, and tastefully hung with cobwebs.

The characters in the tragedy are all dressed, and their own clothes are scattered in hurried confusion over the wooden dresser which surrounds the room. That snuff-shop-looking figure, in front of the glass, is *Banquo*: and the young lady with the liberal display of legs, who is kindly painting his face with a hare's foot, is dressed for *Fleance*. The large woman, who is consulting the stage directions in Cumberland's edition of *Macbeth*, is the *Lady Macbeth* of the night; she is always selected to play the part, because she is tall and stout, and *looks* a little like Mrs Siddons[8] – at a considerable distance. That stupid-looking milksop, with light hair and bow legs – a kind of man whom you can warrant town-made – is fresh caught; he plays *Malcolm* to-night, just to accustom himself to an audience. He will get on better by degrees; he will play *Othello* in a month, and in a month more, will very probably be apprehended on a charge of embezzlement. The black-eyed female with whom

he is talking so earnestly, is dressed for the 'gentlewoman.' It is *her*
first appearance, too – in that character. The boy of fourteen, who
is having his eyebrows smeared with soap and whitening, is
Duncan, King of Scotland; and the two dirty men with the corked
countenances, in very old green tunics, and dirty drab boots, are
the 'army.'

'Look sharp below there, gents,' exclaims the dresser, a red-
headed and red-whiskered Jew, calling through the trap, 'they're
a-going to ring up. The flute says he'll be blowed if he plays
any more, and they're getting precious noisy in front.' A general
rush immediately takes place to the half-dozen little steep steps
leading to the stage, and the heterogeneous group are soon
assembled at the side scenes, in breathless anxiety and motley
confusion.

'Now,' cries the manager, consulting the written list which
hangs behind the first P.S. wing, 'Scene 1, open country – lamps
down – thunder and lightning – all ready, White?' [This is
addressed to one of the army.] 'All ready.' – 'Very well. Scene 2,
front chamber. Is the front chamber down?' – 'Yes.' – 'Very well.'
– 'Jones' [to the other army who is up in the flies]. 'Hallo!' –
'Wind up the open country when we ring up.' – 'I'll take care.'–
'Scene 3, back perspective with practical bridge. Bridge ready,
White? Got the tressels there?' – 'All right.'

'Very well. Clear the stage,' cries the manager, hastily packing
every member of the company into the little space there is between
the wings and the wall, and one wing and another. 'Places, places.
Now then, Witches – Duncan – Malcolm – bleeding officer –
where's the bleeding officer?' – 'Here!' replies the officer, who
has been rose-pinking for the character. 'Get ready, then; now,
White, ring the second music-bell.' The actors who are to be
discovered, are hastily arranged, and the actors who are not to be
discovered place themselves, in their anxiety to peep at the house,
just where the whole audience can see them. The bell rings, and
the orchestra, in acknowledgement of the call, play three distinct
chords. The bell rings – the tragedy (!) opens – and our description closes.

CHAPTER 14

Vauxhall-gardens by Day

THERE was a time when if a man ventured to wonder how Vauxhall-gardens[1] would look by day, he was hailed with a shout of derision at the absurdity of the idea. Vauxhall by daylight! A porter-pot without porter, the House of Commons without the Speaker, a gas-lamp without the gas – pooh, nonsense, the thing was not to be thought of. It was rumoured, too, in those times, that Vauxhall-gardens by day, were the scene of secret and hidden experiments; that there, carvers were exercised in the mystic art of cutting a moderate-sized ham into slices thin enough to pave the whole of the grounds; that beneath the shade of the tall trees, studious men were constantly engaged in chemical experiments, with the view of discovering how much water a bowl of negus could possibly bear; and that in some retired nooks, appropriated to the study of ornithology, other sage and learned men were, by a process known only to themselves, incessantly employed in reducing fowls to a mere combination of skin and bone.

Vague rumours of this kind, together with many others of a similar nature, cast over Vauxhall-gardens an air of deep mystery; and as there is a great deal in the mysterious, there is no doubt that to a good many people, at all events, the pleasure they afforded was not a little enhanced by this very circumstance.

Of this class of people we confess to having made one. We loved to wander among these illuminated groves, thinking of the patient and laborious researches which had been carried on there during the day, and witnessing their results in the suppers which were served up beneath the light of lamps, and to the sound of music, at night. The temples and saloons and cosmoramas[2] and fountains glittered and sparkled before our eyes; the beauty of the lady singers and the elegant deportment of the gentlemen, captivated our hearts; a few hundred thousand of additional lamps dazzled our

Vauxhall Gardens by Day

senses; a bowl or two of reeking punch bewildered our brains; and we were happy.

In an evil hour, the proprietors of Vauxhall-gardens took to opening them by day. We regretted this, as rudely and harshly disturbing that veil of mystery which had hung about the property for many years, and which none but the noonday sun, and the late Mr Simpson,[3] had ever penetrated. We shrunk from going; at this moment we scarcely know why. Perhaps a morbid consciousness of approaching disappointment – perhaps a fatal presentiment – perhaps the weather; whatever it was, we did *not* go until the second or third announcement of a race between two balloons tempted us, and we went.

We paid our shilling at the gate, and then we saw for the first time, that the entrance, if there had ever been any magic about it at all, was now decidedly disenchanted, being, in fact, nothing more nor less than a combination of very roughly-painted boards and sawdust. We glanced at the orchestra and supper-room as we hurried past – we just recognised them, and that was all. We bent our steps to the firework-ground; there, at least, we should not be disappointed. We reached it, and stood rooted to the spot with mortification and astonishment. *That* the moorish tower – that wooden shed with a door in the centre, and daubs of crimson and yellow all round, like a gigantic watch-case! *That* the place where night after night we had beheld the undaunted Mr Blackmore[4] make his terrific ascent, surrounded by flames of fire, and peals of artillery, and where the white garments of Madame Somebody[5] (we forget even her name now), who nobly devoted her life to the manufacture of fireworks, had so often been seen fluttering in the wind, as she called up a red, blue, or party-coloured light to illumine her temple! *That* the —— but at this moment the bell rung; the people scampered away, pell-mell, to the spot from whence the sound proceeded; and we, from the mere force of habit, found ourself running among the first, as if for very life.

It was for the concert in the orchestra. A small party of dismal men in cocked hats were 'executing' the overture to *Tancredi*,[6] and a numerous assemblage of ladies and gentlemen, with their families, had rushed from their half-emptied stout mugs in the supper boxes, and crowded to the spot. Intense was the low murmur of admiration when a particularly small gentleman, in a dress coat, led on a particularly tall lady in a blue sarcenet pelisse and bonnet of the same, ornamented with large white feathers, and forthwith commenced a plaintive duet.

We knew the small gentleman well; we had seen a lithographed semblance of him, on many a piece of music, with his mouth wide open as if in the act of singing; a wine-glass in his hand; and a table with two decanters and four pine-apples on it in the back-ground. The tall lady, too, we had gazed on, lost in raptures of admiration, many and many a time – how different, people *do* look by daylight, and without punch, to be sure! It was a beautiful duet: first the small gentleman asked a question, and then the tall lady answered it; then the small gentleman and the tall lady sang together most melodiously; then the small gentleman went through a little piece of vehemence by himself, and got very tenor indeed, in the excitement of his feelings, to which the tall lady responded in a similar manner; then the small gentleman had a shake or two, after which the tall lady had the same, and then they both merged imperceptibly into the original air: and the band wound themselves up to a pitch of fury, and the small gentleman handed the tall lady out, and the applause was rapturous.

The comic singer, however, was the especial favourite; we really thought that a gentleman, with his dinner in a pocket-handkerchief, who stood near us, would have fainted with excess of joy. A marvellously facetious gentleman that comic singer is; his distinguishing characteristics are, a wig approaching to the flaxen, and an aged countenance, and he bears the name of one of the English counties,[7] if we recollect right. He sang a very good song about the seven ages, the first half-hour of which afforded the assembly the purest delight; of the rest we can make no report, as we did not stay to hear any more.

We walked about, and met with a disappointment at every turn; our favourite views were mere patches of paint; the fountain that had sparkled so showily by lamp-light, presented very much the appearance of a water-pipe that had burst; all the ornaments were dingy, and all the walks gloomy. There was a spectral attempt at rope-dancing in the little open theatre. The sun shone upon the spangled dresses of the performers, and their evolutions were about as inspiriting and appropriate as a country-dance in a family-vault. So we retraced our steps to the firework-ground, and mingled with the little crowd of people who were contemplating Mr Green.[8]

Some half-dozen men were restraining the impetuosity of one of the balloons, which was completely filled, and had the car already attached; and as rumours had gone abroad that a Lord was 'going up,' the crowd were more than usually anxious and talkative. There was one little man in faded black, with a dirty face and a rusty black neckerchief with a red border, tied in a narrow wisp round his neck, who entered into conversation with every body, and had something to say upon every remark that was made within his hearing. He was standing with his arms folded, staring up at the balloon, and every now and then vented his feelings of reverence for the aëronaut, by saying, as he looked round to catch somebody's eye, 'He's a rum 'un is Green; think o' this here being up'ards of his two hundredth ascent; ecod the man as is ekal to Green never had the toothache yet, nor won't have within this hundred year, and that's all about it. When you meets with real talent, and native, too, encourage it, that's what I say;' and when he had delivered himself to this effect, he would fold his arms with more determination than ever, and stare at the balloon with a sort of admiring defiance of any other man alive, beyond himself and Green, that impressed the crowd with the opinion that he was an oracle.

'Ah, you're very right, sir,' said another gentleman, with his wife, and children, and mother, and wife's sister, and a host of female friends, in all the gentility of white pocket-handkerchiefs, frills, and spencers, 'Mr Green is a steady hand, sir, and there's no fear about him.'

'Fear!' said the little man: 'isn't it a lovely thing to see him and his wife a-going up in one balloon, and his own son and *his* wife a-jostling up against them in another, and all of them going twenty or thirty mile in three hours or so, and then coming back in pochayses?⁹ I don't know where this here science is to stop, mind you; that's what bothers me.'

Here there was a considerable talking among the females in the spencers.

'What's the ladies a-laughing at, sir?' inquired the little man, condescendingly.

'It's only my sister Mary,' said one of the girls, 'as says she hopes his lordship won't be frightened when he's in the car, and want to come out again.'

'Make yourself easy about that there, my dear,' replied the little man. 'If he was so much as to move a inch without leave, Green would jist fetch him a crack over the head with the telescope, as would send him into the bottom of the basket in no time, and stun him till they come down again.'

'Would he, though?' inquired the other man.

'Yes, would he,' replied the little one, 'and think nothing of it, neither, if he was the king himself. Green's presence of mind is wonderful.'

Just at this moment all eyes were directed to the preparations which were being made for starting. The car was attached to the second balloon, the two were brought pretty close together, and a military band commenced playing, with a zeal and fervour which would render the most timid man in existence but too happy to accept any means of quitting that particular spot of earth on which they were stationed. Then Mr Green, sen., and his noble companion entered one car, and Mr Green, jun., and *his* companion the other; and then the balloons went up, and the aërial travellers stood up, and the crowd outside roared with delight, and the two gentlemen who had never ascended before, tried to wave their flags, as if they were not nervous, but held on very fast all the while; and the balloons were wafted gently away, our little friend solemnly protesting, long after they were reduced to mere specks in the air, that he could still distinguish the white hat of Mr Green. The gardens disgorged their multitudes, boys ran up and down screaming 'balloon!' and in all the crowded thoroughfares people rushed out of their shops into the middle of the road, and having stared up in the air at two little black objects till they almost dislocated their necks, walked slowly in again, perfectly satisfied.

The next day there was a grand account of the ascent in the morning papers, and the public were informed how it was the finest day but four in Mr Green's remembrance; how they retained sight of the earth till they lost it behind the clouds; and how the reflection of the balloon on the undulating masses of vapour was gorgeously picturesque; together with a little science about the refraction of the sun's rays, and some mysterious hints respecting atmospheric heat and eddying currents of air.

There was also an interesting account how a man in a boat was distinctly heard by Mr Green, jun., to exclaim, 'My eye!' which Mr Green, jun., attributed to his voice rising to the balloon, and the sound being thrown back from its surface into the car; and the whole concluded with a slight allusion to another ascent next Wednesday, all of which was very instructive and very amusing, as our readers will see if they look to the papers. If we have forgotten to mention the date, they have only to wait till next summer, and take the account of the first ascent, and it will answer the purpose equally well.

CHAPTER 15

Early Coaches

WE have often wondered how many months' incessant travelling in a post-chaise, it would take to kill a man; and wondering by analogy, we should very much like to know how many months of constant travelling in a succession of early coaches, an unfortunate mortal could endure.[1] Breaking a man alive upon the wheel, would be nothing to breaking his rest, his peace, his heart — every thing but his fast — upon four; and the punishment of Ixion[2] (the only

Early Coaches

practical person, by the by, who has discovered the secret of the perpetual motion) would sink into utter insignificance before the one we have suggested. If we had been a powerful churchman in those good times when blood was shed as freely as water and men were mowed down like grass, in the sacred cause of religion,[3] we would have lain by very quietly till we got hold of some especially obstinate miscreant, who positively refused to be converted to our faith, and then we would have booked him for an inside place in a small coach, which travelled day and night: and securing the remainder of the places for stout men with a slight tendency to coughing and spitting, we would have started him forth on his last travels: leaving him mercilessly to all the tortures which the waiters, landlords, coachmen, guards, boots, chambermaids, and other familiars on his line of road, might think proper to inflict.

Who has not experienced the miseries inevitably consequent upon a summons to undertake a hasty journey? You receive an intimation from your place of business – wherever that may be, or whatever you may be – that it will be necessary to leave town without delay. You and your family are forthwith thrown into a state of tremendous excitement; an express is immediately despatched to the washerwoman's; every body is in a bustle; and you, yourself, with a feeling of dignity which you cannot altogether conceal, sally forth to the booking-office to secure your place. Here a painful consciousness of your own unimportance first rushes on your mind – the people are as cool and collected as if nobody were going out of town, or as if a journey of a hundred odd miles were a mere nothing. You enter a mouldy-looking room, ornamented with large posting-bills:[4] the greater part of the place enclosed behind a huge lumbering rough counter, and fitted up with recesses that look like the dens of the smaller animals in a travelling menagerie, without the bars. Some half-dozen people are 'booking' brown-paper parcels, which one of the clerks fling into the aforesaid recesses with an air of recklessness which you, remembering the new carpet-bag you bought in the morning, feel considerably annoyed at; porters, looking like so many Atlases,[5] keep rushing in and out, with large packages on their shoulders;

and while you are waiting to make the necessary inquiries, you wonder what on earth the booking-office clerks can have been before they were booking-office clerks; one of them with his pen behind his ear, and his hands behind him, is standing in front of the fire, like a full-length portrait of Napoleon; the other with his hat half off his head, enters the passengers' names in the books with a coolness which is inexpressibly provoking; and the villain whistles – actually whistles – while a man asks him what the fare is outside, all the way to Holyhead! – in frosty weather too! They are clearly an isolated race, evidently possessing no sympathies or feelings in common with the rest of mankind. Your turn comes at last, and having paid the fare, you tremblingly inquire – 'What time will it be necessary for me to be here in the morning?' – 'Six o'clock,' replies the whistler, carelessly pitching the sovereign you have just parted with, into a wooden bowl on the desk. 'Rather before than arter,' adds the man with the semi-roasted unmentionables,[6] with just as much ease and complacency as if the whole world got out of bed at five. You turn into the street, ruminating as you bend your steps homewards on the extent to which men become hardened in cruelty, by custom.

If there be one thing in existence more miserable than another, it most unquestionably is the being compelled to rise by candle-light. If you ever doubted the fact, you are painfully convinced of your error, on the morning of your departure. You left strict orders, overnight, to be called at half-past four, and you have done nothing all night but doze for five minutes at a time, and start up suddenly from a terrific dream of a large church-clock with the small hand running round, with astonishing rapidity, to every figure on the dial-plate. At last, completely exhausted, you fall gradually into a refreshing sleep – your thoughts grow confused – the stage-coaches, which have been 'going off' before your eyes all night, become less and less distinct, until they go off altogether; one moment you are driving with all the skill and smartness of an experienced whip – the next you are exhibiting, à la Ducrow,[7] on the off-leader; anon you are closely muffled up, inside, and have just recognised in the person of the guard an old schoolfellow, whose funeral, even in your dream, you remember to have attended eighteen years ago. At last you fall into a state of complete oblivion, from which you are aroused, as if into a new state of existence, by a singular illusion. You are apprenticed to a trunk-maker; how, or why, or when, or wherefore, you don't take the trouble to inquire; but there you are, pasting the lining in the lid of a portmanteau. Confound that other apprentice in the back shop, how he is hammering! – rap, rap, rap – what an industrious fellow he must be! you have heard him at work for half an hour past, and he has been hammering incessantly the whole time. Rap, rap, rap, again – he's talking now – what's that he said? Five o'clock! You make a violent exertion, and start up in bed. The vision is at once dispelled; the trunk-maker's shop is your own bedroom, and the other apprentice your shivering servant, who has been vainly endeavouring to wake you for the last quarter of an hour, at the imminent risk of breaking either his own knuckles, or the panels of the door.

You proceed to dress yourself, with all possible despatch. The flaring flat candle with the long snuff, gives light enough to show that the things you want, are not where they ought to be, and you undergo a trifling delay in consequence of having carefully packed up one of your boots in your over anxiety of the preceding night. You soon complete your toilet, however, for you are not particular on such an occasion, and you shaved yesterday evening; so mounting your Petersham great-coat,[8] and green travelling-shawl, and grasping your carpet-bag in your right hand, you walk lightly down stairs, lest you should awaken any of the family, and after pausing in the common sitting-room for one moment, just to have a cup of coffee (the said common sitting-room looking remarkably comfortable, with every thing out of its place, and strewed with the crumbs of last night's supper), you undo the chain and bolts of the street-door, and find yourself fairly in the street.

A thaw, by all that is miserable! The frost is completely broken up. You look down the long perspective of Oxford-street, the gas-lights mournfully reflected on the wet pavement, and can discern no speck in the road to encourage the belief that there is a cab or a coach to be had — the very coachmen have gone home in despair. The cold sleet is drizzling down with that gentle regularity, which betokens a duration of four-and-twenty hours at least; the damp hangs upon the house-tops, and lamp-posts, and clings to you like an invisible cloak. The water is 'coming in' in every area, the pipes have burst, the water-butts are running over; the kennels seem to be doing matches against time, pump-handles descend of their own accord, horses in market-carts fall down, and there's no one to help them up again, policemen look as if they had been carefully sprinkled with powdered glass; here and there a milk-woman trudges slowly along, with a bit of list round each foot to keep her from slipping; boys who 'don't sleep in the house,' and are not allowed much sleep out of it, can't wake their masters by thundering at the shop-door, and cry with the cold — the compound of ice, snow, and water on the pavement, is a couple of inches thick — nobody ventures to walk fast to keep himself warm, and nobody could succeed in keeping himself warm if he did.

It strikes a quarter past five as you trudge down Waterloo-place on your way to the Golden-cross,[9] and you discover, for the first time, that you were called about an hour too early. You have not time to go back; there is no place open to go into, and you have, therefore, no resource but to go forward, which you do, feeling remarkably satisfied with yourself, and every thing about you. You arrive at the office, and look wistfully up the yard for the Birmingham High-flier, which, for aught you can see, may have flown away altogether, for no preparations appear to be on foot for the departure of any vehicle in the shape of a coach. You wander into the booking-office, which with the gas-lights and blazing fire, looks quite comfortable by contrast — that is to say, if any place *can* look comfortable at half-past five on a winter's morning. There stands the identical book-keeper in the same position as if he had not moved since you saw him yesterday. As he informs you, that the coach is up the yard, and will be brought round in about a quarter of an hour, you leave your bag, and repair to 'The Tap' — not with any absurd idea of warming yourself, because you feel such a result to be utterly hopeless, but for the purpose of procuring some hot brandy-and-water, which you do, – when the kettle boils! an event which occurs exactly two minutes and a half before the time fixed for the starting of the coach.

The first stroke of six, peals from St Martin's[10] church steeple, just as you take the first sip of the boiling liquid. You find yourself at the booking-office in two seconds, and the tap-waiter finds himself much comforted by your brandy-and-water, in about the same period. The coach is out; the horses are in, and the guard and two or three porters, are stowing the luggage away, and running up the steps of the booking-office, and down the steps of the booking-office, with breathless rapidity. The place, which a few minutes ago was so still and quiet, is now all bustle; the early venders of the morning papers have arrived, and you are assailed on all sides with shouts of '*Times*, gen'lm'n, *Times*,' 'Here's *Chron* – *Chron* – *Chron*,' '*Herald*,[11] ma'am,' 'Highly interesting murder, gen'lm'n,' 'Curious case o' breach o' promise, ladies.' The inside passengers are already in their dens, and the outsides with the exception of yourself, are pacing up and down the pavement to keep themselves warm; they consist of two young men with very long hair, to which the sleet has communicated the appearance of crystallized rats' tails; one thin young woman cold and peevish, one old gentleman ditto ditto, and something in a cloak and cap, intended to represent a military officer; every member of the party, with a large stiff shawl over his chin, looking exactly as if he were playing a set of Pan's pipes.[12]

'Take off the cloths, Bob,' says the coachman, who now appears for the first time, in a rough blue great-coat, of which the buttons behind are so far apart, that you can't see them both at the same time. 'Now, gen'lm'n,' cries the guard, with the way-bill in his hand. 'Five minutes behind time already!' Up jump the passengers – the two young men smoking like lime-kilns, and the old gentleman grumbling audibly. The thin young woman is got upon the roof, by dint of a great deal of pulling, and pushing, and helping and trouble, and she repays it by expressing her solemn conviction that she will never be able to get down again.

'All right,' sings out the guard at last, jumping up as the coach starts, and blowing his horn directly afterwards, in proof of the soundness of his wind. 'Let 'em go, Harry, give 'em their heads,' cries the coachman – and off we start as briskly as if the morning were 'all right,' as well as the coach: and looking forward as anxiously to the termination of our journey, as we fear our readers will have done, long since, to the conclusion of our paper.

CHAPTER 16

Omnibuses

IT is very generally allowed that public conveyances afford an extensive field for amusement and observation. Of all the public conveyances that have been constructed since the days of the Ark – we think that is the earliest on record – to the present time, commend us to an omnibus.[1] A long stage is not to be despised, but there you have only six insides, and the chances are, that the same people go all the way with you – there is no change, no variety. Besides, after the first twelve hours or so, people get cross and sleepy, and when you have seen a man in his nightcap, you lose all respect for him; at least, that is the case with us. Then on smooth roads people frequently get prosy, and tell long stories, and even those who don't talk, may have very unpleasant predilections. We once travelled four hundred miles, inside a stage-coach, with a stout man, who had a glass of rum-and-water, warm, handed in at the window at every place where we changed horses. This was decidedly unpleasant. We have also travelled occasionally, with a small boy of a pale aspect, with light hair, and no perceptible neck, coming up to town from school under the protection of the guard, and directed to be left at the Cross Keys[2] till called for. This is, perhaps, even worse than rum-and-water in a close atmosphere. Then there is the whole train of evils consequent on a change of the coachman; and the misery of the discovery – which the guard is sure to make the moment you begin to doze – that he wants a brown-paper parcel, which he distinctly remembers to have deposited under the seat on which you are reposing. A great deal of bustle and groping takes place, and when you are thoroughly awakened, and severely cramped, by holding your legs up by an almost supernatural exertion, while he is looking behind them, it suddenly occurs to him that he put it in the fore-boot. Bang goes the door, the parcel is immediately found: off starts the coach again, and the guard plays the key-bugle as loud as he can play it, as if in mockery of your wretchedness.

Now you meet with none of these afflictions in an omnibus; sameness there can never be. The passengers change as often in the course of one journey as the figures in a kaleidoscope, and though not so glittering, are far more amusing. We believe there is no instance upon record, of a man's having gone to sleep in one of these vehicles. As to long stories, would any man venture to tell a long story in an omnibus? and even if he did, where would be the harm? nobody could possibly hear what he was talking about. Again; children, though occasionally, are not often to be found in an omnibus; and even when they are, if the vehicle be full, as is generally the case, somebody sits upon them, and we are unconscious of their presence. Yes, after mature reflection, and considerable experience, we are decidedly of opinion, that of all known vehicles, from the glass-coach[3] in which we were taken to be christened, to that sombre caravan in which we must one day make our last earthly journey, there is nothing like an omnibus.

We will back the machine in which we make our daily peregrination from the top of Oxford-street to the city, against any 'buss'[4] on the road, whether it be for the gaudiness of its exterior, the perfect simplicity of its interior, or the native coolness of its cad.[5] This young gentleman is a singular instance of self-devotion; his somewhat intemperate zeal on behalf of his employers, is constantly getting him into trouble, and occasionally into the house of correction. He is no sooner emancipated, however, than he resumes the duties of his profession with unabated ardour. His principal distinction is his activity. His great boast is, 'that he can chuck an old gen'lm'n into the buss, shut him in, and rattle off, afore he knows where it's a-going to' – a feat which he frequently performs, to the infinite amusement of every one but the old gentleman concerned, who, somehow or other, never can see the joke of the thing.

We are not aware that it has ever been precisely ascertained, how many passengers our omnibus will contain. The impression on the cad's mind, evidently is, that it is amply sufficient for the accommodation of any number of persons that can be enticed into it. 'Any room?' cries a very hot pedestrian. 'Plenty o' room, sir,' replies the conductor, gradually opening the door, and not disclosing the real state of the case, till the wretched man is on the steps. 'Where?' inquires the entrapped individual, with an attempt to back out again. 'Either side, sir,' rejoins the cad, shoving him in, and slamming the door. 'All right, Bill.' Retreat is impossible; the newcomer rolls about, till he falls down somewhere, and there he stops.

As we get into the city a little before ten, four or five of our party are regular passengers. We always take them up at the same places, and they generally occupy the same seats; they are always dressed in the same manner, and invariably discuss the same topics – the increasing rapidity of cabs, and the disregard of moral obligations evinced by omnibus men. There is a little testy old man, with a powdered head, who always sits on the right-hand side of the door as you enter, with his hands folded on the top of his umbrella. He is extremely impatient, and sits there for the purpose of keeping a sharp eye on the cad, with whom he generally holds a running dialogue. He is very officious in helping people in and out, and always volunteers to give the cad a poke with his umbrella, when any one wants to alight. He usually recommends ladies to have sixpence ready to prevent delay; and if any body puts a window down, that he can reach, he immediately puts it up again.

'Now, what are you stopping for?' says the little old man every morning, the moment there is the slightest indication of 'pulling up' at the corner of Regent-street, when some such dialogue as the following takes place between him and the cad:

'What are you stopping for?'

Here the cad whistles, and affects not to hear the question.

'I say [a poke], what are you stopping for?'

'For passengers, sir. Ba–nk. –Ty.'⁶

'I know you're stopping for passengers; but you've no business to do so. *Why* are you stopping?'

'Vy, sir, that's a difficult question. I think it is because we perfer stopping here to going on.'

'Now mind,' exclaims the little old man, with great vehemence, 'I'll pull you up to-morrow; I've often threatened to do it; now I will.'

'Thankee, sir,' replies the cad, touching his hat with a mock expression of gratitude; – 'werry much obliged to you indeed, sir.' Here the young men in the omnibus laugh very heartily, and the old gentleman gets very red in the face, and seems highly exasperated.

The stout gentleman in the white neckcloth, at the other end of the vehicle, looks very prophetic, and says that something must shortly be done with these fellows, or there's no saying where all this will end; and the shabby-genteel man with the green bag, expresses his entire concurrence in the opinion, as he has done regularly every morning for the last six months.

A second omnibus now comes up, and stops immediately behind us. Another old gentleman elevates his cane in the air, and runs with all his might towards our omnibus; we watch his progress with great interest; the door is opened to receive him, he suddenly disappears – he has been spirited away by the opposition. Hereupon the driver of the opposition taunts our people with his having 'regularly done 'em out of that old swell' and the voice of the 'old swell' is heard, vainly protesting against this unlawful detention. We rattle off, the other omnibus rattles after us, and every time we stop to take up a passenger, they stop to take him too; sometimes we get him; sometimes they get him; but whoever don't get him, say they ought to have had him, and the cads of the respective vehicles abuse one another accordingly.

As we arrive in the vicinity of Lincoln's-inn-fields, Bedford-row, and other legal haunts, we drop a great many of our original passengers, and take up fresh ones, who meet with a very sulky reception. It is rather remarkable, that the people already in an omnibus, always look at new-comers, as if they entertained some undefined idea that they have no business to come in at all. We are quite persuaded the little old man has some notion of this kind and that he considers their entry as a sort of negative impertinence.

Conversation is now entirely dropped; each person gazes vacantly through the window in front of him, and every body thinks that his opposite neighbour is staring at him. If one man gets out at Shoe-lane, and another at the corner of Farringdon-street,[7] the little old gentleman grumbles, and suggests to the latter, that if he had got out at Shoe-lane too, he would have saved them the delay of another stoppage; whereupon the young men laugh again, and the old gentleman looks very solemn, and says nothing more till he gets to the Bank, when he trots off as fast as he can, leaving us to do the same, and to wish, as we walk away, that we could impart to others any portion of the amusement we have gained for ourselves.

CHAPTER 17

The Last Cab-driver, and the First Omnibus Cad

OF all the cabriolet-drivers whom we ever had the honour and gratification of knowing by sight – and our acquaintance in this way has been most extensive – there is one who made an impression on our mind which can never be effaced, and who awakened in our bosom a feeling of admiration and respect, which we entertain a fatal presentiment will never be called forth again by any human being. He was a man of most simple and prepossessing appearance. He was a brown-whiskered, white-hatted, no-coated cabman; his nose was generally red, and his bright blue eye not unfrequently stood out in bold relief against a black border of artificial workmanship; his boots were of the Wellington form, pulled up to meet his corduroy knee-smalls,[1] or at least to approach as near them as their dimensions would admit of; and his neck was usually garnished with a bright yellow handkerchief. In summer he carried in his mouth a flower; in winter, a straw – slight, but to a comtemplative mind, certain indications of a love of nature, and a taste for botany.

His cabriolet was gorgeously painted – a bright red; and wherever we went, City or West End, Paddington or Holloway,[2] North, East, West, or South, there was the red cab, bumping up against the posts at the street corners, and turning in and out, among hackney-coaches, and drays, and carts, and waggons, and omnibuses, and contriving by some strange means or other, to get out of places which no other vehicle but the red cab could ever by any possibility have contrived to get into at all. Our fondness for that red cab was unbounded. How we should have liked to see it in the circle at Astley's![3] Our life upon it, that it should have performed such evolutions as would have put the whole company to shame – Indians, chiefs, knights, Swiss peasants, and all.

Some people object to the exertion of getting into cabs, and others object to the difficulty of getting out of them; we think both these are objections which take their rise in perverse and ill-conditioned minds. The getting into a cab is a very pretty and graceful process, which, when well performed, is essentially melo-dramatic. First, there is the expressive pantomime of every one of the eighteen cabmen on the stand, the moment you raise your eyes from the ground. Then there is your own pantomime in reply – quite a little ballet. Four cabs immediately leave the stand, for your especial accommodation; and the evolutions of the animals who draw them, are beautiful in the extreme, as they grate the wheels of the cabs against the curb-stones, and sport playfully in the kennel. You single out a particular cab, and dart swiftly towards it. One bound, and you are on the first step; turn your body lightly round to the right, and you are on the second; bend gracefully beneath the reins, working round to the left at the same time, and you are in the cab. There is no difficulty in finding a seat: the apron knocks you comfortably into it at once, and off you go.

The getting out of a cab, is, perhaps, rather more complicated in its theory, and a shade more difficult in its execution. We have studied the subject a great deal, and we think the best way is, to throw yourself out, and trust to chance for alighting on your feet. If you make the driver alight first, and then throw yourself upon him, you will find that he breaks your fall materially. In the event of your comtemplating an offer of eightpence, on no account make the tender, or show the money, until you are safely on the pavement. It is very bad policy attempting to save the fourpence.[4] You are very much in the power of a cabman, and he considers it a kind of fee not to do you any wilful damage. Any instruction, however, in the art of getting out of a cab, is wholly unnecessary if you are going any distance, because the probability is, that you will be shot lightly out before you have completed the third mile.

We are not aware of any instance on record in which a cab-horse has performed three consecutive miles without going down once. What of that? It is all excitement. And in these days of derangement of the nervous system and universal lassitude, people are content to pay handsomely for excitement; where can it be procured at a cheaper rate?

But to return to the red cab; it was omnipresent. You had but to walk down Holborn, or Fleet-street,[5] or any of the principal thoroughfares in which there is a great deal of traffic, and judge for yourself. You had hardly turned into the street, when you saw a trunk or two, lying on the ground: an uprooted post, a hat-box, a portmanteau, and a carpet-bag, strewed about in a very picturesque manner: a horse in a cab standing by, looking about him with great unconcern; and a crowd, shouting and screaming with delight, cooling their flushed faces against the glass windows of a chemist's shop.[6] − 'What's the matter here, can you tell me?' − 'O'ny a cab, sir.' − 'Any body hurt, do you know?' − 'O'ny the fare, sir. I see him a turnin' the corner, and I ses to another gen'lm'n, "that's a reg'lar little oss that, and he's a comin' along rayther sweet, an't he?" − "He just is," ses the other gen'lm'n, ven bump they cums agin the post, and out flies the fare like bricks.' Need we say it was the red cab; or that the gentleman with the straw in his mouth, who emerged so coolly from the chemist's shop and philosophically climbing into the little dickey, started off at full gallop, was the red cab's licensed driver?

The ubiquity of this red cab, and the influence it exercised over the risible muscles of justice itself, was perfectly astonishing. You walked into the justice-room of the Mansion-house; the whole court resounded with merriment. The Lord Mayor threw himself back in his chair, in a state of frantic delight at his own joke, every vein in Mr Hobler's[7] countenance was swollen with laughter, partly at the Lord Mayor's facetiousness, but more at his own, the constables and police-officers were (as in duty bound) in ecstasies at Mr Hobler and the Lord Mayor combined; and the very paupers, glancing respectfully at the beadle's countenance, tried to smile, as even he relaxed. A tall, weazen-faced man, with an impediment in his speech, would be endeavouring to state a case of imposition against the red cab's driver; and the red cab's driver, and the Lord Mayor and Mr Hobler, would be having a little fun among themselves to the inordinate delight of every body but the complainant. In the end, justice would be so tickled with the red-cab-driver's native humour, that the fine would be mitigated, and he would go away full gallop, in the red cab, to impose on somebody else without loss of time.

The driver of the red cab, confident in the strength of his own moral principles, like many other philosophers, was wont to set the feelings and opinions of society at complete defiance. Generally speaking, perhaps, he would as soon carry a fare safely to his destination, as he would upset him – sooner, perhaps, because in that case he not only got the money, but had the additional amusement of running a longer heat against some smart rival. But society made war upon him in the shape of penalties, and he must make war upon society in his own way. This was the reasoning of the red-cab-driver. So, he bestowed a searching look upon the fare, as he put his hand in his waistcoat pocket, when he had gone half the mile, to get the money ready; and if he brought forth eightpence, out he went.

The last time we saw our friend was one wet evening in

Tottenham-court-road, when he was engaged in a very warm and somewhat personal altercation with a loquacious little gentleman in a green coat. Poor fellow! there were great excuses to be made for him: he had not received above eighteen-pence more than his fare, and consequently laboured under a great deal of very natural indignation. The dispute had attained a pretty considerable height, when at last the loquacious little gentleman, making a mental calculation of the distance, and finding that he had already paid more than he ought, avowed his unalterable determination to 'pull up' the cabman in the morning.

'Now, just mark this, young man,' said the little gentleman, 'I'll pull you up to-morrow morning.'

'No! will you though?' said our friend, with a sneer.

'I will,' replied the little gentleman, 'mark my words, that's all. If I live till to-morrow morning, you shall repent this.'

There was a steadiness of purpose, and indignation of speech, about the little gentleman, as he took an angry pinch of snuff, after this last declaration, which made a visible impression on the mind of the red-cab-driver. He appeared to hesitate for an instant. It was only for an instant; his resolve was soon taken.

'You'll pull me up, will you?' said our friend.

'I will,' rejoined the little gentleman, with even greater vehemence than before.

'Very well,' said our friend, tucking up his shirt sleeves very calmly. 'There'll be three veeks for that. Wery good; that'll bring me up to the middle o' next month. Three veeks more would carry me on to my birthday, and then I've got ten pound to draw. I may as well get board, lodgin', and washin', till then, out of the county, as pay for it myself; consequently here goes!'

So, without more ado, the red-cab-driver knocked the little gentleman down, and then called the police to take himself into custody, with all the civility in the world.

A story is nothing without the sequel; and therefore, we may state, that to our certain knowledge, the board, lodging, and washing, were all provided in due course. We happen to know the fact, for it came to our knowledge thus: We went over the House of Correction for the county of Middlesex shortly after, to witness the operation of the silent system;[8] and looked on all the 'wheels'[9] with the greatest anxiety, in search of our long-lost friend. He was nowhere to be seen, however, and we began to think that the little gentleman in the green coat must have relented, when, as we were traversing the kitchen-garden, which lies in a sequestered part of the prison, we were startled by hearing a voice, which apparently proceeded from the wall, pouring forth its soul in the plaintive air of 'All round my hat,'[10] which was then just beginning to form a recognised portion of our national music.

We started. – 'What voice is that?' said we.

The Governor shook his head.

'Sad fellow,' he replied, 'very sad. He positively refused to work on the wheel; so, after many trials, I was compelled to order him into solitary confinement. He says he likes it very much though, and I am afraid he does, for he lies on his back on the floor, and sings comic songs all day!'

Shall we add, that our heart had not deceived us; and that the comic singer was no other than our eagerly-sought friend, the red-cab-driver?

We have never seen him since, but we have strong reason to suspect that this noble individual was a distant relative of a waterman of our acquaintance, who, on one occasion, when we were passing the coach-stand over which he presides, after standing very quietly to see a tall man struggle into a cab, ran up very briskly when it was all over (as his brethren invariably do), and, touching his hat, asked, as a matter of course, for 'a copper for the waterman.' Now, the fare was by no means a handsome man; and, waxing very indignant at the demand, he replied – 'Money! What for? Coming up and looking at me, I suppose?' – 'Vell, sir,' rejoined the waterman, with a smile of immoveable complacency, '*That's* worth twopence, at least.'

This identical waterman afterwards attained a very prominent station in society; and as we know something of his life, and have often thought of telling what we *do* know, perhaps we shall never have a better opportunity than the present.

The Last Cabdriver

Mr William Barker, then, for that was the gentleman's name. Mr William Barker was born — but why need we relate where Mr William Barker was born, or when? Why scrutinize the entries in parochial ledgers, or seek to penetrate the Lucinian mysteries[11] of lying-in hospitals? Mr William Barker *was* born, or he had never been. There is a son – there was a father. There is an effect – there was a cause. Surely this is sufficient information for the most Fatima-like[12] curiosity; and, if it be not, we regret our inability to supply any further evidence on the point. Can there be a more satisfactory, or more strictly parliamentary course? Impossible.

We at once avow a similar inability to record at what precise period, or by what particular process, this gentleman's patronymic, of William Barker, became corrupted into 'Bill Boorker.' Mr Barker acquired a high standing, and no inconsiderable reputation, among the members of that profession to which he more peculiarly devoted his energies; and to them he was generally known, either by the familiar appellation of 'Bill Boorker,' or the flattering designation of 'Aggerawatin Bill,' the latter being a playful and expressive *sobriquet*, illustrative of Mr Barker's great talent in 'aggerawatin' and rendering wild such subjects of her Majesty as are conveyed from place to place, through the instrumentality of omnibuses. Of the early life of Mr Barker little is known, and even that little is involved in considerable doubt and obscurity. A want of application, a restlessness of purpose, a thirsting after porter, a love of all that is roving and cadger-like in nature, shared in common with many other great geniuses, appear to have been his leading characteristics. The busy hum of a parochial free-school, and the shady repose of a county gaol, were alike inefficacious in producing the slightest alteration in Mr Barker's disposition. His feverish attachment to change and variety, nothing could repress; his native daring no punishment could subdue.

If Mr Barker can be fairly said to have had any weakness in his earlier years, it was an amiable one – love; love in its most comprehensive form – a love of ladies, liquids, and pocket-handkerchiefs. It was no selfish feeling; it was not confined to his own possessions, which but too many men regard with exclusive complacency. No;

it was a nobler love – a general principle. It extended itself with equal force to the property of other people.

There is something very affecting in this. It is still more affecting to know, that such philanthropy is but imperfectly rewarded. Bow-street, Newgate, and Millbank,[13] are a poor return for general benevolence, evincing itself in an irrepressible love for all created objects. Mr Barker felt it so. After a lengthened interview with the highest legal authorities, he quitted his ungrateful country, with the consent, and at the expense, of its Government;[14] proceeded to a distant shore, and there employed himself, like another Cincinnatus,[15] in clearing and cultivating the soil – a peaceful pursuit, in which a term of seven years glided almost imperceptibly away.

Whether, at the expiration of the period we have just mentioned, the British Government required Mr Barker's presence here, or did not require his residence abroad, we have no distinct means of ascertaining. We should be inclined, however, to favour the latter position, inasmuch as we do not find that he was advanced to any other public post on his return, than the post at the corner of the Haymarket, where he officiated as assistant-waterman to the hackney-coach-stand. Seated, in this capacity, on a couple of tubs near the curb-stone, with a brass-plate and number suspended round his neck by a massive chain, and his ankles curiously enveloped in haybands, he is supposed to have made those observations on human nature which exercised so material an influence over all his proceedings in later life.

Mr Barker had not officiated for many months in this capacity, when the appearance of the first omnibus[16] caused the public mind to go in a new direction, and prevented a great many hackney-coaches from going in any direction at all. The genius of Mr Barker at once perceived the whole extent of the injury that would be eventually inflicted on cab and coach stands, and, by consequence, on watermen also, by the progress of the system of which the first omnibus was a part. He saw, too, the necessity of adopting some more profitable profession; and his active mind at once perceived how much might be done in the way of enticing the youthful and unwary, and shoving the old and helpless, into the wrong buss, and carrying them off, until, reduced to despair, they ransomed themselves by the payment of sixpence a-head, or, to adopt his own figurative expression in all its native beauty, 'till they was rig'larly done over, and forked out the stumpy.'

An opportunity for realizing his fondest anticipations, soon presented itself. Rumours were rife on the hackney-coach-stands, that a buss was building, to run from Lisson-grove to the Bank, down Oxford-street and Holborn; and the rapid increase of buses on the Paddington-road, encouraged the idea. Mr Barker secretly and cautiously inquired in the proper quarters. The report was correct; the 'Royal William'[17] was to make its first journey on the following Monday. It was a crack affair altogether. An enterprising young cabman, of established reputation as a dashing whip – for he had compromised with the parents of three scrunched children, and just 'worked out' his fine, for knocking down an old lady – was the driver; and the spirited proprietor, knowing Mr Barker's qualifications, appointed him to the vacant office of cad on the very first application. The bus began to run, and Mr Barker entered into a new suit of clothes, and on a new sphere of action.

To recapitulate all the improvements introduced by this extraordinary man, into the omnibus system – gradually, indeed, but surely – would occupy a far greater space than we are enabled to devote to this imperfect memoir. To him is universally assigned the original suggestion of the practice which afterwards became so general – of the driver of a second buss keeping constantly behind the first one, and driving the pole of his vehicle either into the door of the other, every time it was opened, or through the body of any lady or gentleman who might make an attempt to get into it; a humorous and pleasant invention, exhibiting all that originality of idea, and fine bold flow of spirits, so conspicuous in every action of this great man.

Mr Barker had opponents of course; what man in public life has not? But even his worst enemies cannot deny that he has taken more old ladies and gentlemen to Paddington who wanted to go to the Bank, and more old ladies and gentlemen to the Bank who

wanted to go to Paddington, than any six men on the road; and
however much malevolent spirits may pretend to doubt the accuracy
of the statement, they well know it to be an established fact, that he
has forcibly conveyed a variety of ancient persons of either sex, to
both places, who had not the slightest or most distant intention of
going any where at all.

Mr Barker was the identical cad who nobly distinguished himself,
sometime since, by keeping a tradesman on the step – the omnibus
going at full speed all the time – till he had thrashed him to his
entire satisfaction, and finally throwing him away, when he had
quite done with him. Mr Barker it *ought* to have been, who, honestly
indignant at being ignominiously ejected from a house of public
entertainment, kicked the landlord in the knee, and thereby caused
his death. We say it *ought* to have been Mr Barker, because the
action was not a common one, and could have emanated from no
ordinary mind.

It has now become matter of history; it is recorded in the
Newgate Calendar;[18] and we wish we could attribute this piece of
daring heroism to Mr Barker. We regret being compelled to state
that it was not performed by him. Would, for the family credit we
could add, that it was achieved by his brother!

It was in the exercise of the nicer details of his profession, that
Mr Barker's knowledge of human nature was beautifully displayed.
He could tell at a glance where a passenger wanted to go to, and
would shout the name of the place accordingly, without the
slightest reference to the real destination of the vehicle. He knew
exactly the kind of old lady that would be too much flurried by the
process of pushing in, and pulling out of the caravan, to discover
where she had been put down, until too late; had an intuitive
perception of what was passing in a passenger's mind when he
inwardly resolved to 'pull that cad up to-morrow morning;' and
never failed to make himself agreeable to female servants, whom he
would place next the door, and talk to all the way.

Human judgment is never infallible, and it would occasionally
happen that Mr Barker experimentalised with the timidity or
forbearance of the wrong person, in which case a summons to a

Police-office, was, on more than one occasion, followed by a committal to prison. It was not in the power of trifles such as these, however, to subdue the freedom of his spirit. As soon as they passed away, he resumed the duties of his profession with unabated ardour.

We have spoken of Mr Barker and of the red-cab-driver, in the past tense. Alas! Mr Barker has again become an absentee; and the class of men to which they both belonged are fast disappearing. Improvement has peered beneath the aprons of our cabs, and penetrated to the very innermost recesses of our omnibuses. Dirt and fustian will vanish before cleanliness and livery. Slang will be forgotten when civility becomes general: and that enlightened, eloquent, sage, and profound body, the Magistracy of London, will be deprived of half their amusement, and half their occupation.

CHAPTER 18

A Parliamentary Sketch

WE hope our readers will not be alarmed at this rather ominous title. We assure them that we are not about to become political, neither have we the slightest intention of being more prosy than usual – if we can help it. It has occurred to us that a slight sketch of the general aspect of 'the House,'[1] and the crowds that resort to it on the night of an important debate, would be productive of some amusement; and as we have made some few calls at the aforesaid house in our time – have visited it quite often enough for our purpose, and a great deal too often for our own personal peace and comfort – we have determined to attempt the description. Dismissing from our minds, therefore, all that feeling of awe, which vague ideas of breaches of privilege, Serjeant-at-Arms,[2] heavy denunciations, and still heavier fees, are calculated to awaken, we enter at once into the building, and upon our subject.

Half-past four o'clock – and at five the mover of the Address will be 'on his legs,' as the newspapers announce sometimes by way of novelty, as if speakers were occasionally in the habit of standing on their heads. The members are pouring in, one after the other, in shoals. The few spectators who can obtain standing-room in the passages, scrutinize them as they pass, with the utmost interest, and the man who can identify a member occasionally, becomes a person of great importance. Every now and then you hear earnest whispers of 'That's Sir John Thomson.' 'Which? him with the gilt order round his neck?' 'No, no; that's one of the messengers – that other with the yellow gloves, is Sir John Thomson.' 'Here's Mr Smith.' 'Lor!' 'Yes, how d'ye do, sir? – (He is our new member) – How do you do, sir?' Mr Smith stops: turns round with an air of enchanting urbanity (for the rumour of an intended dissolution has been very extensively circulated this morning), seizes both the hands of his gratified constituent, and, after greeting him with the most enthusiastic warmth, darts into the lobby with an extraordinary display of ardour in the public cause, leaving an immense impression in his favour on the mind of his 'fellow-townsman.'

The arrivals increase in number, and the heat and noise increase in very unpleasant proportion. The livery servants form a complete lane on either side of the passage, and you reduce yourself into the smallest possible space to avoid being turned out. You see that stout man with the hoarse voice, in the blue coat, queer-crowned, broad-brimmed hat, white corduroy breeches, and great boots, who has been talking incessantly for half an hour past, and whose importance has occasioned no small quantity of mirth among the strangers. That is the great conservator of the peace of Westminster. You cannot fail to have remarked the grace with which he saluted the noble Lord who passed just now, or the excessive dignity of his air, as he expostulates with the crowd. He is rather out of temper now, in consequence of the very irreverent behaviour of those two young fellows behind him, who have done nothing but laugh all the time they have been here.

'Will they divide to-night, do you think, Mr — ?' timidly inquires a little thin man in the crowd, hoping to conciliate the man of office.

'How *can* you ask such questions, sir?' replies the functionary, in an incredibly loud key, and pettishly grasping the thick stick he carries in his right hand. 'Pray do not, sir, I beg of you; pray do not, sir.' The little man looks remarkably out of his element, and the uninitiated part of the throng are in positive convulsions of laughter.

Just at this moment some unfortunate individual appears, with a very smirking air, at the bottom of the long passage. He has managed to elude the vigilance of the special constable down stairs, and is evidently congratulating himself on having made his way so far.

'Go back, sir — you must *not* come here,' shouts the hoarse one, with tremendous emphasis of voice and gesture, the moment the offender catches his eye.

The stranger pauses.

'Do you hear, sir — will you go back?' continues the official dignitary, gently pushing the intruder some half-dozen yards.

'Come, don't push me,' replies the stranger, turning angrily round.

'I will, sir.'

'You won't, sir.'

'Go out, sir.'

'Take your hands off me, sir.'

'Go out of the passage, sir.'

'You're a Jack-in-office, sir.'

'A what?' ejaculates he of the boots.

'A Jack-in-office, sir, and a very insolent fellow,' reiterates the stranger, now completely in a passion.

'Pray do not force me to put you out, sir,' retorts the other — 'pray do not — my instructions are to keep this passage clear — it's the Speaker's orders, sir.'

'D—n the Speaker, sir!' shouts the intruder.

'Here, Wilson! — Collins!' gasps the officer, actually paralyzed at this insulting expression, which in his mind is all but high treason;

'take this man out — take him out, I say! How dare you, sir?' and down goes the unfortunate man five stairs at a time, turning round at every stoppage, to come back again, and denouncing bitter vengeance against the commander-in-chief, and all his supernumeraries.

'Make way, gentlemen, — pray make way for the Members, I beg of you;' shouts the zealous officer, turning back, and preceding a whole string of the liberal and independent.

You see this ferocious-looking gentleman,[3] with a complexion almost as sallow as his linen, and whose large black mustaches would give him the appearance of a figure in a hair-dresser's window, if his countenance possessed the thought which is communicated to those waxen caricatures of the human face divine. He is a militia-officer, and the most amusing person in the House. Can any thing be more exquisitely absurd than the burlesque grandeur of his air, as he strides up to the lobby, his eyes rolling like those of a Turk's head in a cheap Dutch clock?[4] He never appears without that bundle of dirty papers which he carries under his left arm, and which are generally supposed to be the miscellaneous estimates for 1804, or some equally important documents. He is very punctual in his attendance at the House, and his self-satisfied 'He-ar-He-ar,' is not unfrequently the signal for a general titter.

This is the gentleman who once actually sent a messenger up to the Strangers' gallery in the old House of Commons, to inquire the name of an individual who was using an eye-glass, in order that he might complain to the Speaker that the person in question was quizzing him! On another occasion, he is reported to have repaired to Bellamy's kitchen — a refreshment-room,[5] where persons who are not Members are admitted on sufferance, as it were — and perceiving two or three gentlemen at supper, who he was aware were not Members, and could not, in that place, very well resent his behaviour, he indulged in the pleasantry of sitting with his booted leg on the table at which they were supping! He is generally harmless, though, and always exceedingly amusing.

By dint of patience, and some little interest with our friend the constable, we have contrived to make our way to the Lobby, and you can just manage to catch an occasional glimpse of the House, as the door is opened for the admission of Members. It is tolerably full already, and little groups of Members are congregated together here, discussing the interesting topics of the day.

That smart-looking fellow in the black coat with velvet facings and cuffs, who wears his *D'Orsay* hat[6] so rakishly, is 'Honest Tom,' a metropolitan representative;[7] and the large man in the cloak with the white lining — not the man by the pillar; the other with the light hair hanging over his coat collar behind — is his colleague. The quiet gentlemanly-looking man in the blue surtout, gray trousers, white neckerchief, and gloves, whose closely-buttoned coat displays his manly figure and broad chest to great advantage, is a very well-known character.[8] He has fought a great many battles in his time, and conquered like the heroes of old, with no other arms than those the gods gave him. The old hard-featured man[9] who is standing near him, is really a good specimen of a class of men, now nearly extinct. He is a county Member, and has been from time whereof the memory of man is not to the contrary.[10] Look at his loose, wide, brown coat, with capacious pockets on each side; the knee-breeches and boots, the immensely long waistcoat, and silver watch-chain dangling below it, the wide-brimmed brown hat, and the white handkerchief tied in a great bow, with straggling ends sticking out beyond his shirt frill. It is a costume one seldom sees nowadays, and when the few who wear it have died off, it will be quite extinct. He can tell you long stories of Fox, Pitt, Sheridan, and Canning,[11] and how much better the House was managed in those times, when they used to get up at eight or nine o'clock, except on regular field-days, of which every body was apprized beforehand. He has a great contempt for all young Members of Parliament, and thinks it quite impossible that a man can say any thing worth hearing, unless he has sat in the House for fifteen years at least, without saying anything at all. He is of opinion that 'that young Macaulay'[12] was a regular impostor; he allows, that Lord Stanley[13] may do something one of these days, but 'he's too young, sir — too young.' He is an excellent authority on points of precedent, and when he grows talkative, after his wine, will tell you how Sir Somebody Something, when he was whipper-in[14] for the Government, brought four men out of their beds to vote in the majority, three of whom died on their way home again; how the House once divided on the question, that fresh candles be now brought in; how the Speaker was once upon a time left in the chair by accident, at the conclusion of business, and was obliged to sit in the House by himself for three hours, till some Member could be knocked up and brought back again, to move the adjournment; and a great many other anecdotes of a similar description.

There he stands, leaning on his stick; looking at the throng of Exquisites[15] around him with most profound contempt; and conjuring up, before his mind's eye, the scenes he beheld in the old House in days gone by, when his own feelings were fresher and brighter, and when, as he imagines, wit, talent, and patriotism flourished more brightly too.

You are curious to know who that young man in the rough great-coat is, who has accosted every Member who has entered the House since we have been standing here. He is not a Member; he is only an 'hereditary bondsman,'[16] or, in other words, an Irish correspondent of an Irish newspaper, who has just procured his forty-second frank[17] from a Member whom he never saw in his life before. There he goes again – another! Bless the man, he has his hat and pockets full already.

We will try our fortune at the Strangers' gallery, though the nature of the debate encourages very little hope of success. What on earth are you about? Holding up your order as if it were a talisman at whose command the wicket would fly open? Nonsense. Just preserve the order for an autograph, if it be worth keeping at all, and make your appearance at the door with your thumb and forefinger expressively inserted in your waistcoat-pocket. This tall stout man in black is the door-keeper. 'Any room?' 'Not an inch – two or three dozen gentlemen waiting down stairs on the chance of somebody's going out.' Pull out your purse – 'Are you *quite* sure there's no room?' – 'I'll go and look,' replies the door-keeper, with a wistful glance at your purse, 'but I'm afraid there's not.' He returns, and with real feeling assures you that it is morally impossible to get near the gallery. It is of no use waiting. When you are refused admission into the Strangers' gallery at the House of Commons, under such circumstances, you may return home thoroughly satisfied that the place must be remarkably full indeed.*

Retracing our steps through the long passage, descending the stairs, and crossing Palace-yard, we halt at a small temporary doorway adjoining the King's entrance to the House of Lords. The order of the serjeant-at-arms will admit you into the Reporters' gallery, from whence you can obtain a tolerably good view of the House. Take care of the stairs, they are none of the best; through this little wicket − there. As soon as your eyes become a little used to the mist of the place, and the glare of the chandeliers below you, you will see that some unimportant personage on the Ministerial side of the House (to your right hand) is speaking, amidst a hum of voices and confusion which would rival Babel,[18] but for the circumstance of its being all in one language.

The 'hear, hear,' which occasioned that laugh, proceeded from our warlike friend in the mustaches; he is sitting on the back seat against the wall, behind the Member who is speaking, looking as ferocious and intellectual as usual. Take one look around you, and retire! The body of the House and the side galleries are full of Members, some with their legs on the back of the opposite seat; some with theirs stretched out to their utmost length on the floor; some going out, others coming in; all of them talking, laughing, lounging, coughing, oh-ing, questioning, or groaning; presenting a conglomeration of noise and confusion, to be met with in no other place in existence, not even excepting Smithfield on a market-day,[19] or a cockpit in its glory.

But let us not omit to notice Bellamy's kitchen, or, in other words, the refreshment-room, common to both Houses of Parliament, where Ministerialists and Oppositionists, Whigs and Tories, Radicals, Peers, and Destructives, strangers from the gallery, and the more favoured strangers from below the bar, are alike at

---

* This paper was written before the practice of exhibiting Members of Parliament, like other curiosities, for the small charge of half-a-crown, was abolished.

liberty to resort; where divers honourable members prove their perfect independence by remaining during the whole of a heavy debate, solacing themselves with the creature comforts; and whence they are summoned by whippers-in, when the House is on the point of dividing; either to give their 'conscientious votes' on questions of which they are conscientiously innocent of knowing any thing whatever, or to find a vent for the playful exuberance of their wine-inspired fancies, in boisterous shouts of 'Divide,' occasionally varied with a little howling, barking, and crowing, or other ebullitions of senatorial pleasantry.

When you have ascended the narrow staircase which, in the present temporary House of Commons, leads to the place we are describing, you will probably observe a couple of rooms on your right hand, with tables spread for dining. Neither of these is the kitchen, although they are both devoted to the same purpose; the kitchen is further on to our left, up these half-dozen stairs. Before we ascend the staircase, however, we must request you to pause in front of this little bar-place with the sash-windows; and beg your particular attention to the steady honest-looking old fellow in black, who is its sole occupant. Nicholas (we do not mind mentioning the old fellow's name, for if Nicholas be not a public man, who is? – and public men's names are public property) – Nicholas is the butler of Bellamy's, and has held the same place, dressed exactly in the same manner, and said precisely the same things, ever since the oldest of its present visiters can remember. An excellent servant Nicholas is – an unrivalled compounder of salad-dressing – an admirable preparer of soda-water and lemon – a special mixer of cold grog and punch, and, above all, an unequalled judge of cheese. If the old man have such a thing as vanity in his composition, this is certainly his pride; and if it be possible to imagine that any thing in this world could disturb his impenetrable calmness, we should say it would be the doubting his judgment on this important point.

We needn't tell you all this, however, for if you have an atom of observation, one glance at his sleek knowing-looking head and face – his prim white neckerchief, with the wooden tie into which it has been regularly folded for twenty years past, merging by imperceptible degrees into a small-plaited shirt-frill; and his comfortable-looking form encased in a well-brushed suit of black – would give you a better idea of his real character than a column of our poor description could convey.

Nicholas is rather out of his element now; he cannot see the kitchen as he used to in the old House; there, one window of his glass-case opened into the room, and then for the edification and behoof of more juvenile questioners, he would stand for an hour together, answering deferential questions about Sheridan, and Perceval, and Castlereagh,[20] and Heaven knows who beside, with manifest delight, always inserting a 'Mister' before every commoner's name.

Nicholas, like all men of his age and standing, has a great idea of the degeneracy of the times. He seldom expresses any political opinions, but we managed to ascertain, just before the passing of the Reform Bill,[21] that Nicholas was a thorough Reformer. What was our astonishment to discover shortly after the meeting of the first reformed Parliament, that he was a most inveterate and decided Tory! It was very odd: some men change their opinions from necessity, others from expediency, others from inspiration; but that Nicholas should undergo any change in any respect, was an event we had never contemplated, and should have considered impossible. His strong opinion against the clause which empowered the metropolitan districts to return Members to Parliament, too, was perfectly unaccountable.

We discovered the secret at last; the metropolitan Members always dined at home. The rascals! As for giving additional Members to Ireland, it was even worse – decidedly unconstitutional. Why, sir, an Irish Member would go up there, and eat more dinner than three English Members put together. He took no wine; drank table-beer by the half-gallon; and went home to Manchester-buildings, or Milbank-street,[22] for his whiskey-and-water, and what was the consequence? Why the concern lost – actually lost – by their patronage.

A queer old fellow is Nicholas, and as completely a part of the building as the house itself. We wonder he ever left the old place, and fully expected to see in the papers, the morning after the fire, a pathetic account of an old gentleman in black, of decent appearance, who was seen at one of the upper windows when the flames were at their height, and declared his resolute intention of falling with the floor. He must have been got out by force. However, he was got out – here he is again, looking as he always does, as if he had been in a bandbox ever since the last session. There he is, at his old post every night, just as we have described him: and, as characters are scarce, and faithful servants scarcer, long may he be there, say we!

Now, when you have taken your seat in the kitchen, and duly noticed the large fire and roasting-jack at one end of the room – the little table for washing glasses and draining jugs at the other – the clock over the window opposite St Margaret's church[23] – the deal tables and wax candles – the damask table-cloths and bare floor – the plate and china on the tables, and the gridiron on the fire; and a few other anomalies peculiar to the place – we will point out to your notice two or three of the people present, whose station or absurdities render them the most worthy of remark.

It is half-past twelve o'clock, and as the division is not expected for an hour or two, a few Members are lounging away the time here, in preference to standing at the bar of the House, or sleeping in one of the side galleries. That singularly awkward and ungainly-looking man, in the brownish-white hat, with the straggling black trousers, which reach about half-way down the leg of his boots, who is leaning against the meat-screen, apparently deluding himself into the belief that he is thinking about something, is a splendid sample of a Member of the House of Commons concentrating in his own person the wisdom of a constituency. Observe the wig, of a dark hue but indescribable colour, for if it be naturally brown, it has acquired a black tint by long service, and if it be naturally black, the same cause has imparted to it a tinge of rusty brown; and remark how very materially the great blinker-like spectacles assist the expression of that most intelligent face. Seriously speaking, did you ever see a countenance so expressive of the most hopeless extreme of heavy dulness, or behold a form so strangely put together? He is no great speaker: but when he *does* address the House the effect is absolutely irresistible.

The small gentleman with the sharp nose, who has just saluted him, is a Member of Parliament, an ex-Alderman, and a sort of amateur fireman. He, and the celebrated fireman's dog, were observed to be remarkably active at the conflagration of the two Houses of Parliament – they both ran up and down, and in and out, getting under people's feet, and into every body's way, fully impressed with the belief, that they were doing a great deal of good, and barking tremendously. The dog went quietly back to his kennel with the engine, but the other gentleman kept up such an incessant noise for some weeks after the occurrence, that he became a positive nuisance. As no more parliamentary fires have occurred, however, and he has consequently had no more opportunities of writing to the newspapers to relate how by way of preserving pictures he cut them out of their frames, and performed other great national services, he has gradually relapsed into his old state of calmness.

That female in black – not the one whom the Lord's-Day-Bill Baronet[24] has just chucked under the chin; the shorter of the two – is 'Jane:' the Hebe[25] of Bellamy's. Jane is as great a character as Nicholas in her way. Her leading features are a thorough contempt for the great majority of her visiters; her predominant quality, love of admiration, as you cannot fail to observe, if you mark the glee with which she listens to something the young Member near her mutters somewhat unintelligibly in her ear (for his speech is rather thick from some cause or other), and how playfully she digs the handle of a fork into the arm with which he detains her, by way of reply.

Jane is no bad hand at repartees, and showers them about, with a degree of liberality and total absence of reserve or constraint, which occasionally excites no small amazement in the minds of strangers. She cuts jokes with Nicholas too, but evidently looks up to him with a great deal of respect; and the immoveable solidity with which Nicholas receives the aforesaid jokes, and looks on, at certain pastoral friskings and rompings (Jane's only recreations[26]) which occasionally take place in the passage, is not the least amusing part of his character.

The two persons who are seated at the table in the corner, at the further end of the room, have been constant guests here, for many years past; and one of them has feasted within these walls, many a time, with the most brilliant characters of a brilliant period. He has gone up to the other House since then; the greater part of his boon companions have shared Yorick's fate,[27] and his visits to Bellamy's are comparatively few.

If he really be eating his supper now, at what hour can he possibly have dined! A second solid mass of rump-steak has disappeared, and he eat the first in four minutes and three-quarters, by the clock over the window. Was there ever such a personification of Falstaff![28] Mark the air with which he gloats over that Stilton as he removes the napkin which has been placed beneath his chin to catch the superfluous gravy of the steak, and with what gusto he imbibes the porter which has been fetched expressly for him in the pewter pot. Listen to the hoarse sound of that voice, kept down as it is by layers of solids, and deep draughts of rich wine, and tell us if you ever saw such a perfect picture of a regular *gourmand*; and whether he is not exactly the man whom you would pitch upon, as having been the partner of Sheridan's parliamentary carouses, the volunteer driver of the hackney-coach that took him home, and the involuntary upsetter of the whole party?

What an amusing contrast between his voice and appearance, and that of the spare, squeaking old man, who sits at the same table, and who elevating a little cracked bantam sort of voice to its highest pitch, invokes damnation upon his own eyes or somebody else's at the commencement of every sentence he utters. 'The Captain,' as they call him, is a very old frequenter of Bellamy's; much addicted to stopping 'after the House is up' (an inexpiable crime in Jane's eyes), and a complete walking reservoir of spirits and water.

The old Peer – or rather, the old man – for his peerage is of comparatively recent date – has a huge tumbler of hot punch brought him; and the other damns and drinks, and drinks and damns, and smokes. Members arrive every moment in a great bustle to report that 'The Chancellor of the Exchequer's up,' and to get glasses of brandy-and-water to sustain them during the division; people who have ordered supper, countermand it, and prepare to go down stairs, when suddenly a bell is heard to ring with tremendous violence, and a cry of 'Di-vi-sion' is heard in the passage. This is enough; away rush the members pell-mell. The room is cleared in an instant; the noise rapidly dies away; you hear the creaking of the last boot on the last stair, and are left alone with the leviathan of rump-steaks.

CHAPTER 19

Public Dinners

ALL public dinners in London, from the Lord Mayor's annual banquet at Guildhall, to the Chimney-sweepers' anniversary at White Conduit House;[1] from the Goldsmiths' to the Butchers', from the Sheriffs' to the Licensed Victuallers', are amusing scenes. Of all entertainments of this description, however, we think the annual dinner of some public charity is the most amusing. At a Company's dinner, the people are nearly all alike – regular old stagers who make it a matter of business, and a thing not to be laughed at. At a political dinner, every body is disagreeable, and inclined to speechify – much the same thing, by the by; but at a charity dinner you see people of all sorts, kinds, and descriptions. The wine may not be remarkably special, to be sure, and we have heard some hard-hearted monsters grumble at the collection; but we really think the amusement to be derived from the occasion, sufficient to counterbalance, even these disadvantages.

Let us suppose you are induced to attend a dinner of this description – 'Indigent Orphans' Friends' Benevolent Institution,' we think it is. The name of the charity is a line or two longer, but never mind the rest. You have a distinct recollection, however, that you purchased a ticket at the solicitation of some charitable friend: and you deposit yourself in a hackney-coach, the driver of which – no doubt that you may do the thing in style – turns a deaf ear to

Public Dinners

your earnest entreaties to be set down at the corner of Great Queen-street, and persists in carrying you to the very door of the Freemasons',[2] round which a crowd of people are assembled to witness the entrance of the indigent orphans' friends. You hear great speculations as you pay the fare, on the possibility of your being the noble Lord who is announced to fill the chair on the occasion, and are highly gratified to hear it eventually decided that you are only a 'wocalist.'

The first thing that strikes you, on your entrance, is the astonishing importance of the committee. You observe a door on the first landing, carefully guarded by two waiters, in and out of which stout gentlemen with very red faces keep running, with a degree of speed highly unbecoming the gravity of persons of their years and corpulency. You pause, quite alarmed at the bustle, and thinking, in your innocence, that two or three people must have been carried out of the dining-room in fits, at the very least. You are immediately undeceived by the waiter – 'Up stairs, if you please, sir; this is the committee-room.' Up stairs, you go, accordingly; wondering as you mount, what the duties of the committee can be, and whether they ever do any thing beyond confusing each other, and running over the waiters.

Having deposited your hat and cloak, and received a remarkably small scrap of pasteboard in exchange (which, as a matter of course, you lose, before you require it again), you enter the hall, down which there are three long tables for the less distinguished guests, with a cross-table on a raised platform at the upper end for the reception of the very particular friends of the indigent orphans. Being fortunate enough to find a plate without any body's card in it, you wisely seat yourself at once, and have a little leisure to look about you. Waiters, with wine-baskets in their hands, are placing decanters of sherry down the tables, at very respectable distances; melancholy-looking saltcellars, and decayed vinegar-cruets, which might have belonged to the parents of the indigent orphans in their time, are scattered at distant intervals on the cloth; and the knives and forks look as if they had done duty at every public dinner in London since the accession of George the First.[3] The musicians are scraping and grating and screwing tremendously – playing no notes but notes of preparation; and several gentlemen are gliding along the sides of the tables, looking into plate after plate with frantic eagerness, the expression of their countenances growing more and more dismal as they meet with every body's card but their own.

You turn round to take a look at the table behind you, and – not being in the habit of attending public dinners – are somewhat struck by the appearance of the party on which your eyes rest. One of its principal members appears to be a little man, with a long and rather inflamed face, and gray hair brushed bolt upright in front; he wears a wisp of black silk round his neck, without any stiffener, as an apology for a neckerchief, and is addressed by his companions by the familiar appellation of 'Fitz.' Near him is a stout man in a white neckerchief and buff waistcoat, with shining dark hair cut very short in front, and a great round healthy-looking face, on which he studiously preserves a half-sentimental simper. Next him again, is a large-headed man, with black hair and bushy whiskers; and opposite them are two or three others, one of whom is a little round-faced person, in a dress-stock and blue under-waistcoat. There is something peculiar in their air and manner, though you could hardly describe what it is; and you cannot divest yourself of the idea that they have come for some other purpose than mere eating and drinking. You have no time to debate the matter, however, for the waiters (who have been arranged in lines down the room, placing the dishes on table) retire to the lower end; the dark man in the blue coat and bright buttons, who has the direction of the music, looks up to the gallery, and calls out 'band' in a very loud voice; out burst the orchestra, up rise the visiters, in march fourteen stewards, each with a long wand in his hand like the evil genius in a pantomime; then the chairman, then the titled visiters; they all make their way up the room, as fast as they can, bowing, and smiling, and smirking, and looking remarkably amiable. The applause ceases, grace is said, the clatter of plates and dishes begins; and every one appears highly gratified, either with the presence of the distinguished visiters, or the commencement of the anxiously-expected dinner.

As to the dinner itself — the mere dinner — it goes off much the same every where. Tureens of soup are emptied with awful rapidity — waiters take plates of turbot away, to get lobster-sauce, and bring back plates of lobster-sauce, without turbot; people who can carve poultry, are great fools if they own it, and people who can't, have no wish to learn. — The knives and forks form a pleasing accompaniment to Auber's music,[4] and Auber's music would form a pleasing accompaniment to the dinner, if you could hear any thing besides the cymbals. The substantials disappear — moulds of jelly vanish like lightning — hearty eaters wipe their foreheads, and appear rather overcome with their recent exertions — people who have looked very cross hitherto, become remarkably bland, and ask you to take wine in the most friendly manner possible — old gentlemen direct your attention to the ladies' gallery,[5] and take great pains to impress you with the fact that the charity is always peculiarly favoured in this respect — every one appears disposed to become talkative — and the hum of conversation is loud and general.

'Pray, silence, gentlemen, if you please, for *Non nobis*,'[6] shouts the toast-master with stentorian lungs — a toast-master's shirt-front, waistcoat, and neckerchief, by the by, always exhibit three distinct shades of cloudy-white. — 'Pray, silence, gentlemen, for *Non nobis*.' The singers, whom you discover to be no other than the very party that excited your curiosity at first, after 'pitching' their voices immediately begin *too-too*ing most dismally, on which the regular old stagers burst into occasional cries of — 'Sh — Sh — waiters! — Silence, waiters — stand still, waiters — keep back, waiters,' and other exorcisms, delivered in a tone of indignant remonstrance. The grace is soon concluded, and the company resume their seats. The uninitiated portion of the guests applaud *Non nobis* as vehemently as if it were a capital comic song, greatly to the scandal and indignation of the regular diners, who immediately attempt to quell this sacrilegious approbation, by cries of 'Hush, hush!' whereupon the others, mistaking these sounds for hisses, applaud more tumultuously than before, and, by way of placing their approval beyond the possibility of doubt, shout '*Encore!*' most vociferously.

The moment the noise ceases, up starts the toast-master:—

'Gentlemen, charge your glasses, if you please.' Decanters having been handed about, and glasses filled, the toast-master proceeds, in a regular ascending scale; — 'Gentlemen — *air* — you — all charged? Pray — silence — gentlemen — for — the cha—i—r.' The chairman rises, and, after stating that he feels it quite unnecessary to preface the toast he is about to propose, with any observations whatever, wanders into a maze of sentences, and flounders about in the most extraordinary manner, presenting a lamentable spectacle of mystified humanity, until he arrives at the words, 'constitutional sovereign of these realms,' at which elderly gentlemen exclaim, 'Bravo!' and hammer the table tremendously with their knife-handles. 'Under any circumstances, it would give him the greatest pride, it would give him the greatest pleasure — he might almost say, it would afford him satisfaction [cheers] to propose that toast. What must be his feelings, then, when he has the gratification of announcing, that he has received her Majesty's commands to apply to the Treasurer of her Majesty's Household, for her Majesty's annual donation of 25*l*. in aid of the funds of this charity!' This announcement (which has been regularly made by every chairman, since the first foundation of the charity, forty-two years ago) calls forth the most vociferous applause; the toast is drunk with a great deal of cheering and knocking, and 'God save the Queen' is sung by the 'professional gentlemen;' the unprofessional gentlemen joining in the chorus, and giving the national anthem an effect which the newspapers, with great justice, describe as 'perfectly electrical.'

The other 'loyal and patriotic' toasts having been drunk with all due enthusiasm, a comic song having been well sung by the gentleman with the small neckerchief, and a sentimental one by the second of the party, we come to the most important toast of the evening — 'Prosperity to the charity.' Here again we are compelled to adopt newspaper phraseology, and to express our regret at being 'precluded from giving even the substance of the noble lord's observations.' Suffice it to say, that the speech, which is somewhat of the longest, is rapturously received; and the toast having been drunk, the stewards (looking more important than ever) leave the room, and presently return, heading a procession of

indigent orphans, boys and girls, who walk round the room,
curtseying, and bowing, and treading on each other's heels, and
looking very much as if they should like a glass of wine apiece, to
the high gratification of the company generally, and especially of
the lady patronesses in the gallery. *Exeunt* children, and re-enter
stewards, each with a blue plate in his hand. The band plays a
lively air; the majority of the company put their hands in their
pockets and look rather serious; and the noise of sovereigns,
rattling on crockery, is heard from all parts of the room.

After a short interval, occupied in singing and toasting, the
secretary puts on his spectacles, and proceeds to read the report and
list of subscriptions, the latter being listened to with great attention.
'Mr Smith, one guinea − Mr Tompkins, one guinea − Mr Wilson,
one guinea − Mr Hickson, one guinea − Mr Nixon, one guinea −
Mr Charles Nixon, one guinea − [hear, hear!] − Mr James Nixon,
one guinea − Mr Thomas Nixon, one pound one [tremendous
applause]. Lord Fitz Binkle, the chairman of the day, in addition to
an annual donation of fifteen pounds − thirty guineas [prolonged
knocking: several gentlemen knock the stems off their wine-glasses,
in the vehemence of their approbation]. Lady Fitz Binkle, in
addition to an annual donation of ten pound − twenty pound'
[protracted knocking and shouts of 'Bravo!']. The list being at
length concluded, the chairman rises and proposes the health of the
secretary, than whom he knows no more zealous or estimable
individual. The secretary, in returning thanks, observes that *he*
knows no more excellent individual than the chairman − except the
senior officer of the charity, whose health *he* begs to propose. The
senior officer, in returning thanks, observes that *he* knows no more
worthy man than the secretary − except Mr Walker, the auditor,
whose health *he* begs to propose. Mr Walker, in returning thanks,
discovers some other estimable individual, to whom alone the
senior officer is inferior − and so they go on toasting and lauding
and thanking: the only other toast of importance being 'The Lady
Patronesses now present,' on which all the gentlemen turn their
faces towards the ladies' gallery, shouting tremendously; and little
priggish men, who have imbibed more wine than usual, kiss their

hands and exhibit very distressing contortions of visage supposed to be intended for ogling.

We have protracted our dinner to so great a length, that we have hardly time to add one word by way of grace. We can only entreat our readers not to imagine, because we have attempted to extract some amusement from a charity dinner, that we are at all disposed to underrate, either the excellence of the benevolent institutions with which London abounds, or the estimable motives of those who support them.

CHAPTER 20

The First of May

'Now ladies, up in the sky-parlour: only once a year, if you please!'
YOUNG LADY WITH BRASS LADLE[1]

'Sweep — sweep — sw-e-ep!'
ILLEGAL WATCHWORD[2]

THE first of May![3] There is a merry freshness in the sound, calling to our minds a thousand thoughts of all that is pleasant and beautiful in nature, in her sweetest and most delightful form. What man is there, over whose mind a bright spring morning does not exercise a magic influence — carrying him back to the days of his childish sports, and conjuring up before him the old green field with its gently-waving trees, where the birds sang as he has never heard them since — where the butterfly fluttered far more gaily than he ever sees him now, in all his ramblings — where the sky seemed bluer, and the sun shone more brightly — where the air blew more freshly over greener grass, and sweeter-smelling flowers — where every thing wore a richer and more brilliant hue

George Cruikshank

The First of May

than it is ever dressed in now! Such are the deep feelings of childhood, and such are the impressions which every lovely object stamps upon its heart. The hardy traveller wanders through the maze of thick and pathless woods, where the sun's rays never shone, and heaven's pure air never played: he stands on the brink of the roaring waterfall, and, giddy and bewildered, watches the foaming mass as it leaps from stone to stone, and from crag to crag; he lingers in the fertile plains of a land of perpetual sunshine, and revels in the luxury of their balmy breath. But what are the deep forests, or the thundering waters, or the richest landscapes that bounteous nature ever spread, to charm the eyes, and captivate the senses of man, compared with the recollection of the old scenes of his early youth? – Magic scenes indeed; for the fairy thoughts of infancy dressed them in colours brighter than the rainbow, and almost as fleeting; colours which are the reflection only of the sparkling sunbeams of childhood, and can never be called into existence in the dark and cloudy days of after-life![4]

In former times, spring brought with it not only such associations as these, connected with the past, but sports and games for the present – merry dances round rustic pillars, adorned with emblems of the season, and reared in honour of its coming. Where are they now! Pillars we have, but they are no longer rustic ones; and as to dancers, they are used to rooms, and lights, and would not show well in the open air. Think of the immorality, too! What would your sabbath enthusiasts say, to an aristocratic ring encircling the Duke of York's column in Carlton-terrace[5] – a grand *poussette*[6] of the middle classes, round Alderman Waithman's monument in Fleet-street,[7] – or a general hands-four-round of ten-pound householders,[8] at the foot of the Obelisk in St George's-fields?[9] Alas! romance can make no head against the riot act; and pastoral simplicity is not understood by the police.

Well; many years ago we began to be a steady and matter-of-fact sort of people, and dancing in spring being beneath our dignity, we gave it up, and in course of time it descended to the sweeps – a fall certainly, because, though sweeps are very good fellows in their way, and moreover very useful in a civilized community, they are not exactly the sort of people to give the tone to the little elegances of society. The sweeps, however, got the dancing to themselves, and they kept it up, and handed it down. This was a severe blow to the romance of spring-time, but it did not entirely destroy it either; for a portion of it descended to the sweeps with the dancing, and rendered them objects of great interest. A mystery hung over the sweeps in those days. Legends were in existence of wealthy gentlemen who had lost children, and who, after many years of sorrow and suffering, had found them in the character of sweeps. Stories were related of a young boy who, having been stolen from his parents in his infancy, and devoted to the occupation of chimney-sweeping, was sent, in the course of his professional career, to sweep the chimney of his mother's bedroom; and how, being hot and tired when he came out of the chimney, he got into the bed he had so often slept in as an infant, and was discovered and recognised therein by his mother, who once every year of her life, thereafter, requested the pleasure of the company of every London sweep, at half-past one o'clock, to roast beef, plum-pudding, porter, and sixpence.

Such stories as these, and there were many such, threw an air of mystery round the sweeps, and produced for them some of those good effects which animals derive from the doctrine of the trans-migration of souls. No one, except the masters, thought of ill-treating a sweep, because no one knew who he might be, or what nobleman's or gentleman's son he might turn out. Chimney-sweeping was, by many believers in the marvellous, considered as a sort of probationary term, at an earlier or later period of which, divers young noblemen were to come into possession of their rank and titles: and the profession was held by them in great respect accordingly.

We remember, in our young days, a little sweep about our own age, with curly hair and white teeth, whom we devoutly and sincerely believed to be the lost son and heir of some illustrious personage – an impression which was resolved into an unchangeable conviction on our infant mind, by the subject of our speculations informing us, one day, in reply to our question, propounded a few moments before his ascent to the summit of the kitchen chimney, 'that he believed he'd been born in the vurkis, but he'd never know'd his father.' We felt certain from that time forth that he would one day be owned by a lord, at least; and we never heard the church-bells ring, or saw a flag hoisted in the neighbourhood, without thinking that the happy event had at last occurred, and that his long-lost parent had arrived in a coach and six, to take him home to Grosvenor-square.[10] He never came, however; and, at the present moment, the young gentleman in question is settled down as a master sweep in the neighbourhood of Battle Bridge,[11] his distinguishing characteristics being a decided antipathy to washing himself, and the possession of a pair of legs very inadequate to the support of his somewhat unwieldy and corpulent body.

The romance of spring having gone out before our time, we were fain to console ourselves as we best could with the uncertainty that enveloped the birth and parentage of its attendant dancers, the sweeps; and we *did* console ourselves with it, for many years. But even this wretched source of comfort received a shock, from which it has never recovered – a shock, which has been, in reality, its death-blow. We could not disguise from ourselves the fact that whole families of sweeps were regularly born of sweeps, in the rural districts of Somers Town and Camden Town[12] – that the eldest son succeeded to the father's business, that the other branches assisted him therein, and commenced on their own account; that their children again, were educated to the profession; and that about their identity there could be no mistake whatever. We could not be blind, we say, to this melancholy truth, but we could not bring ourselves to admit it, nevertheless, and we lived on for some years in a state of voluntary ignorance. We were roused from our pleasant slumber by certain dark insinuations thrown out by a friend of ours, to the effect that children in the lower ranks of life were beginning to *choose* chimney-sweeping as their particular walk; that applications had been made by various boys to the constituted authorities, to allow them to pursue the object of their ambition with the full concurrence and sanction of the law; that the affair, in short, was becoming one of mere legal contract. We turned a deaf ear to these rumours at first, but slowly and surely they stole upon us. Month after month, week after week, nay, day after day, at last, did we meet with accounts of similar applications. The veil was removed, all mystery was at an end, and chimney-sweeping had become a favourite and chosen pursuit. There is no longer any occasion to steal boys; for boys flock in crowds to bind themselves. The romance of the trade has fled, and the chimney-sweeper of the present day, is no more like unto him of thirty years ago, than is a Fleet-street pickpocket to a Spanish brigand, or Paul Pry to Caleb Williams.[13]

This gradual decay and disuse of the practice of leading noble youths into captivity, and compelling them to ascend chimneys, was a severe blow, if we may so speak, to the romance of chimney-sweeping, and to the romance of spring at the same time. But even this was not all, for some few years ago the dancing on May-day began to decline; small sweeps were observed to congregate in twos or threes, unsupported by a 'green,'[14] with no 'My Lord' to act as master of the ceremonies, and no 'My Lady' to preside over the exchequer. Even in companies where there was a 'green' it was an absolute nothing – a mere sprout; and the instrumental accompaniments rarely extended beyond the shovels and a set of Pan-pipes, better known to the many, as a 'mouth-organ.'[15]

These were signs of the times, portentous omens of a coming-change; and what was the result which they shadowed forth? Why, the master sweeps, influenced by a restless spirit of innovation, actually interposed their authority, in opposition to the dancing, and substituted a dinner – an anniversary dinner at White Conduit House[16] – where clean faces appeared in lieu of black ones smeared with rose pink; and knee cords and tops, superseded nankeen drawers and rosetted shoes.

Gentlemen who were in the habit of riding shy horses; and steady-going people, who have no vagrancy in their souls, lauded this alteration to the skies, and the conduct of the master sweeps was described as beyond the reach of praise. But how stands the real fact? Let any man deny, if he can, that when the cloth had been removed, fresh pots and pipes laid upon the table, and the customary loyal and patriotic toasts proposed, the celebrated Mr Sluffen, of

Adam-and-Eve-court,[17] whose authority not the most malignant of
our opponents can call in question, expressed himself in a manner
following: 'That now he'd cotcht the cheerman's hi, he vished he
might be jolly vell blessed, if he worn't a goin' to have his innins,
vich he voud say these here obserwashuns — that how some
mischeevus coves as know'd nuffin about the con-sarn, had tried to
sit people agin the mas'r swips, and take the shine out o' their
bis'nes, and the bread out o' the traps o' their preshus kids, by a
makin' o' this here remark, as chimblies could be as vell svept by
'sheenery as by boys; and that the makin' use o' boys for that there
purpuss vos babareous; vereas, he'ad been a chummy[18] — he begged
the cheerman's parding for usin' such a wulgar hexpression — more
nor thirty year — he might say he'd been born in a chimbley, and
he know'd uncommon vell as 'sheenery vos vus nor o' no use: and
as to ker-hewelty to the boys, every body in the chimbley line
know'd as vell as he did, that they liked the climbin' better nor
nuffin as vos.' From this day, we date the total fall of the last
lingering remnant of May-day dancing, among the *élite* of the
profession: and from this period we commence a new era in that
portion of our spring associations, which relates to the 1st of May.

We are aware that the unthinking part of the population will meet
us here, with the assertion, that dancing on May-day still continues —
that 'greens' are annually seen to roll along the streets — that youths
in the garb of clowns, precede them, giving vent to the ebullitions of
their sportive fancies; and that lords and ladies follow in their wake.

Granted. We are ready to acknowledge that in outward show,
these processions have greatly improved: we do not deny the
introduction of solos on the drum; we will even go so far as to
admit an occasional fantasia on the triangle, but here our admissions
end. We positively deny that the sweeps have art or part in these
proceedings. We distinctly charge the dustmen with throwing what
they ought to clear away, into the eyes of the public. We accuse
scavengers, brickmakers, and gentlemen who devote their energies
to the costermongering line, with obtaining money once a-year,
under false pretences. We cling with peculiar fondness to the custom
of days gone by, and have shut out conviction as long as we could,

but it has forced itself upon us; and we now proclaim to a deluded public, that the May-day dancers are *not* sweeps. The size of them, alone, is sufficient to repudiate the idea. It is a notorious fact that the widely-spread taste for register-stoves[19] has materially increased the demand for small boys; whereas the men, who, under a fictitious character, dance about the streets on the first of May nowadays, would be a tight fit in a kitchen flue, to say nothing of the parlour. This is strong presumptive evidence, but we have positive proof – the evidence of our own senses. And here is our testimony.

Upon the morning of the second[20] of the merry month of May, in the year of our Lord one thousand eight hundred and thirty-six, we went out for a stroll, with a kind of forlorn hope of seeing something or other which might induce us to believe that it was really spring, and not Christmas: and after wandering as far as Copenhagen House,[21] without meeting any thing calculated to dispel our impression that there was a mistake in the almanacks, we turned back down Maiden-lane,[22] with the intention of passing through the extensive colony lying between it and Battle-bridge, which is inhabited by proprietors of donkey-carts, boilers of horseflesh, makers of tiles, and sifters of cinders; and through this colony we should have passed, without stoppage or interruption, if a little crowd gathered round a shed had not attracted our attention, and induced us to pause.

When we say a 'shed,' we do not mean the conservatory sort of building, which, according to the old song, Love tenanted when he was a young man,[23] but a wooden house with windows stuffed with rags and paper, and a small yard at the side, with one dust-cart, two baskets, a few shovels, and little heaps of cinders, and fragments of china and tiles scattered about it. Before this inviting spot we paused; and the longer we looked, the more we wondered what exciting circumstance it could be, that induced the foremost members of the crowd to flatten their noses against the parlour window, in the vain hope of catching a glimpse of what was going on inside. After staring vacantly about us for some minutes, we appealed, touching the cause of this assemblage, to a gentleman in a suit of tarpauling, who was smoking his pipe on our right hand; but as the only answer we obtained was a playful inquiry whether our maternal parent had disposed of her mangle, we determined to await the issue in silence.

Judge of our virtuous indignation, when the street-door of the shed opened, and a party emerged therefrom, clad in the costume and emulating the appearance of May-day sweeps!

The first person who appeared was 'my lord,' habited in a blue coat and bright-buttons, with gilt paper tacked over the seams, yellow knee-breeches, pink cotton stockings, and shoes; a cocked hat, ornamented with shreds of various-coloured paper, on his head, a *bouquet* the size of a prize cauliflower in his button-hole, a long Belcher handkerchief[24] in his right hand, and a thin cane in his left. A murmur of applause ran through the crowd (which was chiefly composed of his lordship's personal friends), when this graceful figure made his appearance, which swelled into a burst of applause as his fair partner in the dance bounded forth to join him. Her ladyship was attired in pink crape over bed-furniture,[25] with a low body and short sleeves. The symmetry of her ankles was partially concealed by a very perceptible pair of frilled trousers; and the inconvenience which might have resulted from the circumstance of her white satin shoes being a few sizes too large, was obviated by their being firmly attached to her legs with strong tape sandals.[26]

Her head was ornamented with a profusion of artificial flowers; and in her hand she bore a large brass ladle, wherein to receive what she figuratively denominated 'the tin.' The other characters were a young gentleman in girl's clothes and a widow's cap: two clowns who walked upon their hands in the mud, to the immeasurable delight of all the spectators; a man with a drum; another man with a flageolet; a dirty woman in a large shawl, with a box under her arm for the money, – and last, though not least, the 'green,' animated by no less a personage than our identical friend in the tarpauling suit.

The man hammered away at the drum, the flageolet squeaked, the shovels rattled, the 'green' rolled about, pitching first on one side and then on the other – my lady threw her right foot over her left ankle, and her left foot over her right ankle, alternately; and my lord ran a few paces forward, and butted at the 'green,' and then a few paces backward upon the toes of the crowd, and then went to the right, and then to the left, and then dodged my lady round the 'green;' and finally drew her arm through his, and called upon the boys to shout, which they did lustily — for this was the dancing.

We passed the same group accidentally in the evening. We never saw a 'green' so drunk, a lord so quarrelsome (no: not even in the house of peers after dinner), a pair of clowns so melancholy, a lady so muddy, or a party so miserable.

How has May-day decayed![27] How many merry sports, such as dancing round the Maypole, have fallen into desuetude! And, apparently trifling as their loss may appear, with how many profligate and vicious customs have they been replaced! How much of cheerfulness, and simplicity of character, have they carried away with them, and how much of degradation and discontent have they left behind!

CHAPTER 21

Brokers' and Marine-store Shops

WHEN we affirm that brokers' shops are strange places, and that if an authentic history of their contents could be procured, it would furnish many a page of amusement, and many a melancholy tale, it is necessary to explain the class of shops to which we allude. — Perhaps when we make use of the term 'Brokers' Shop,' the minds of our readers will at once picture large, handsome warehouses, exhibiting a long perspective of French-polished dining-tables, rosewood chiffoniers, and mahogany washhand-stands, with an occasional vista of a four-post bedstead and hangings, and an appropriate foreground of dining-room chairs. Perhaps they will imagine that we mean an humble class of second-hand furniture repositories. Their imagination will then naturally lead them to that street at the back of Long-acre,[1] which is composed almost entirely of brokers' shops: where you walk through groves of deceitful, showy-looking furniture, and where the prospect is occasionally enlivened by a bright red, blue, and yellow hearth-rug, embellished with the pleasing device of a mail-coach at full speed, or a strange animal, supposed to have been originally intended for a dog, with a mass of worsted-work in his mouth, which conjecture has likened to a basket of flowers.

This, by the by, is a tempting article to young wives in the humbler ranks of life, who have got a first-floor front to furnish – they are lost in admiration, and hardly know which to admire most. The dog is very beautiful, but they have got a dog already on the best tea-tray, and two more on the mantelpiece. Then there is something so genteel about that mail-coach; and the passengers outside (who are all hat) give it such an air of reality!

The goods here are adapted to the taste, or rather to the means, of cheap purchasers. There are some of the most beautiful *looking* Pembroke tables that were ever beheld: the wood as green as the trees in the Park, and the leaves almost as certain to fall off in the course of a year. There is also a most extensive assortment of tent and turn-up bedsteads, made of stained wood, and innumerable specimens of that base imposition on society – a sofa bedstead. A turn-up bedstead, is a blunt, honest piece of furniture; it may be slightly disguised with a sham drawer, and sometimes a mad attempt is even made to pass it off for a bookcase: ornament it as you will, however, the turn-up bedstead seems to defy disguise, and to insist on having it distinctly understood that he is a turn-up bedstead, and nothing else; that he is indispensably necessary, and that being so useful, he disdains to be ornamental.

How different is the demeanour of a sofa bedstead! Ashamed of its real use, it strives to appear an article of luxury and gentility – an attempt in which it miserably fails. It has neither the respectability of a sofa, nor the virtues of a bed; every man who keeps a sofa bedstead in his house, becomes a party to a wilful and designing fraud – we question whether you could insult him more, than by insinuating that you entertain the least suspicion of its real use.

To return from this digression, we beg to say, that neither of these classes of brokers' shops forms the subject of this sketch. The shops to which we advert, are immeasurably inferior to those on whose outward appearance we have slightly touched. Our readers must often have observed in some by-street, in a poor neighbourhood, a small dirty shop exposing for sale the most extraordinary and confused jumble of old, worn-out, wretched articles, that can well be imagined. Our wonder at their ever having been bought, is only to be equalled by our astonishment at the idea of their ever being sold again. On a board, at the side of the door, are placed about twenty books — all odd volumes, and as many wine-glasses — all different patterns; several locks, an old earthenware pan, full of rusty keys; two or three gaudy chimney-ornaments — cracked of course; the remains of a lustre, without any drops; a round frame like a capital O, which has once held a mirror; a flute, complete with the exception of the middle joint; a pair of curling-irons; and a tinder-box. In front of the shop-window, are ranged some half-dozen high-backed chairs, with spinal complaints and wasted legs; a corner cupboard; two or three very dark mahogany tables with flaps like mathematical problems; some pickle-jars, some surgeons' ditto, with gilt labels and without stoppers; an unframed portrait of some lady who flourished about the beginning of the thirteenth century, by an artist who never flourished at all; an incalculable host of etceteras of every description, including bottles and cabinets, rags and bones, fenders and street-door knockers, fire-irons, wearing-apparel, and bedding, a hall-lamp, and a room-door. Imagine, in addition to this incongruous mass, a black doll in a white frock, with two faces — one looking up the street, and the other looking down, swinging over the door: a board with the squeezed-up inscription 'Dealer in marine stores,'[2] in lanky white letters, whose height is strangely out of proportion to their width; and you have before you precisely the kind of shop to which we wish to direct your attention.

Although the heterogeneous mixture of things which we have attempted to describe, will be found at all these places, it is curious to observe how truly and accurately some of the minor articles which are exposed for sale — articles of wearing-apparel, for instance — mark the character of the neighbourhood. Take Drury-lane and Covent-garden for example.

This is essentially a theatrical neighbourhood. There is not a potboy in the vicinity who is not, to a greater or less extent, a dramatic character. The errand-boys and chandler's-shop-keepers' sons, are all stage-struck: they 'get up' plays in back kitchens hired for the purpose, and will stand before a shop-window for hours, contemplating a great staring portrait of Mr Somebody or other, of the Royal Coburg Theatre, 'as he appeared in the character of Tongo the Denounced.'³ The consequence is, that there is not a marine-store shop in the neighbourhood, which does not exhibit for sale some faded articles of dramatic finery, such as three or four pairs of soiled buff boots with turn-over red tops, heretofore worn by a 'fourth robber,' or 'fifth mob;' a pair of rusty broadswords, a few gauntlets, and certain resplendent ornaments, which, if they were yellow instead of white, might be taken for insurance plates of the Sun Fire-office.⁴ There are several of these shops in the narrow streets and dirty courts, of which there are so many near the national theatres, and they all have tempting goods of this description, with the addition, perhaps, of a lady's pink dress covered with spangles, white wreaths, stage shoes, and a tiara like a tin lamp reflector. They have been purchased of some wretched supernumeraries, or sixth-rate actors, and are now offered for the benefit of the rising generation, who, on condition of their making certain weekly payments, amounting in the whole to about ten times their value, may avail themselves of such desirable bargains.

Let us take a very different quarter, and apply it to the same test. Look at a marine-store dealer's, in that reservoir of dirt, drunkenness, and drabs: thieves, oysters, baked potatoes, and pickled salmon – Ratcliff-highway.⁵ Here the wearing-apparel is all nautical. Rough blue jackets, with mother-of-pearl buttons, oilskin hats, coarse checked shirts, and large canvass trousers, that look as if they were made for a pair of bodies, instead of a pair of legs, are the staple commodities. Then, there are large bunches of cotton pocket-handkerchiefs, in colour and pattern unlike any, one ever saw before, with the exception of those on the backs of the three young ladies without bonnets who passed us just now. The furniture is much the same as elsewhere, with the addition of one or two models of ships, and some old prints of naval engagements in still older frames. In the window are a few compasses, a small tray containing silver watches, in clumsy thick cases; and tobacco-boxes, the lid of each ornamented with a ship or an anchor, or some such trophy. A sailor generally pawns or sells all he has before he has been long ashore, and if he does not, some favoured companion kindly saves him the trouble. In either case, it is an even chance that he afterwards unconsciously repurchases the same things at a higher price than he gave for them at first.

Again: pay a visit with a similar object, to a part of London, as unlike both of these as they are to each other. Cross over to the Surrey side, and look at such shops of this description as are to be found near the King's Bench prison, and in 'the Rules.'[6] How different, and how strikingly illustrative of the decay of some of the unfortunate residents in this part of the metropolis! Imprison-ment and neglect have done their work. There is contamination in the profligate denizens of a debtor's prison; old friends have fallen off; the recollection of former prosperity has passed away, and with it all thoughts for the past, all care for the future. First, watches and rings, then cloaks, coats, and all the more expensive articles of dress have found their way to the pawnbroker's. That miserable resource has failed at last, and the sale of some trifling article at one of these shops, has been the only mode left of raising a shilling or two, to meet the urgent demands of the moment. – Dressing-cases and writing-desks, too old to pawn but too good to keep: guns, fishing-rods, musical instruments, all in the same condition, have first been sold, and the sacrifice has been but slightly felt. But hunger must be allayed, and what has already become a habit, is easily resorted to, when an emergency arises. Light articles of clothing, first of the ruined man, then of his wife, and at last of their children, even of the youngest, have been parted with piece-meal. There they are, thrown carelessly together until a purchaser presents himself – old, and patched and repaired, it is true, but the make and materials tell of better days and the older they are, the greater the misery and destitution of those whom they once adorned.

CHAPTER 22

Gin-shops

IT is a very remarkable circumstance, that different trades appear to partake of the disease to which elephants and dogs are especially liable, and to run stark, staring, raving mad, periodically. The great distinction between the animals and the trades, is, that the former run mad with a certain degree of propriety — they are very regular in their irregularities. We know the period at which the emergency will arise, and provide against it accordingly. If an elephant run mad, we are all ready for him — kill or cure — pills or bullets — calomel in conserve of roses, or lead in a musket-barrel. If a dog happen to look unpleasantly warm in the summer months, and to trot about the shady side of the streets with a quarter of a yard of tongue hanging out of his mouth, a thick leather muzzle, which has been previously prepared in compliance with the thoughtful injunctions of the Legislature, is instantly clapped over his head by way of making him cooler, and he either looks remarkably unhappy for the next six weeks, or becomes legally insane, and goes mad, as it were, by act of Parliament. But these trades are as eccentric as comets; nay, worse, for no one can calculate on the recurrence of the strange appearances which betoken the disease. Moreover, the contagion is general, and the quickness with which it diffuses itself, almost incredible.

We will cite two or three cases in illustration of our meaning. Six or eight years ago, the epidemic began to display itself among the linendrapers and haberdashers. The primary symptoms, were an inordinate love of plate-glass, and a passion for gas-lights and gilding. The disease gradually progressed, and at last attained a fearful height. Quiet dusty old shops in different parts of town were pulled down; spacious premises with stuccoed fronts and gold letters, were erected instead; floors were covered with Turkey carpets; roofs supported by massive pillars; doors knocked into

OLD TOM 5|49
CREAM OF THE VALLEY 360
44
OUT and OUT 696
George Cruikshank

The Gin Shop

windows, a dozen squares of glass into one; one shopman into a dozen; and there is no knowing what would have been done, if it had not been fortunately discovered, just in time, that the Commissioners of Bankrupts were as competent to decide such cases as the Commissioners of Lunacy,[1] and that a little confinement and gentle examination did wonders. The disease abated. It died away; and a year or two of comparative tranquillity ensued. Suddenly it burst out again among the chemists; the symptoms were the same, with the addition of a strong desire to stick the royal arms over the shop-door, and a great rage for mahogany, varnish, and expensive floor-cloth. Then the hosiers were infected, and began to pull down their shop-fronts, with frantic recklessness. The mania again died away, and the public began to congratulate themselves upon its entire disappearance, when it burst forth with tenfold violence among the publicans and keepers of 'wine-vaults.' From that moment it has spread among them with unprecedented rapidity, exhibiting a concatenation of all the previous symptoms; and onward it has rushed to every part of town, knocking down all the old public-houses, and depositing splendid mansions, stone balustrades, rose-wood fittings, immense lamps, and illuminated clocks, at the corner of every street.

The extensive scale on which these places are established, and the ostentatious manner in which the business of even the smallest among them, is divided into branches, is most amusing. A handsome plate of ground glass in one door directs you 'To the Counting-house,' another to the 'Bottle Department;' a third to the 'Wholesale Department;' a fourth, to 'The Wine Promenade;' and so forth, until we are in daily expectation of meeting with a 'Brandy Bell,' or a 'Whiskey Entrance.' Then, ingenuity is exhausted in devising attractive titles for the different descriptions of gin; and the dram-drinking portion of the community as they gaze upon the gigantic black and white announcements, which are only to be equalled in size by the figures beneath them, are left in a state of pleasing hesitation between 'The Cream of the Valley,' 'The Out and Out,' 'The No Mistake,' 'The Good for Mixing,' 'The real Knock-me-down,' 'The celebrated Butter Gin,' 'The regular Flare-up,' and a dozen other, equally inviting and wholesome *liqueurs*. Although places of this description are to be met with in every second street, they are invariably numerous and splendid, in precise proportion to the dirt and poverty of the surrounding neighbourhood. The gin-shops in and near Drury-lane, Holborn, St Giles's, Covent-garden, and Clare-market,[2] are the handsomest in London. There is more of filth and squalid misery near those great thoroughfares than in any part of this mighty city.

We will endeavour to sketch the bar of a large gin-shop, and its ordinary customers, for the edification of such of our readers as may not have had opportunities of observing such scenes; and on the chance of finding one, well suited to our purpose, we will make for Drury-lane, through the narrow streets and dirty courts which divide it from Oxford-street, and that classical spot adjoining the brewery at the bottom of Tottenham-court-road, best known to the initiated as the 'Rookery.'

The filthy and miserable appearance of this part of London can hardly be imagined by those (and there are many such) who have not witnessed it. Wretched houses with broken windows patched with rags and paper: every room let out to a different family and in many instances to two or even three; fruit and 'sweet-stuff' manufacturers in the cellars, barbers and red-herring venders in the front parlours, and cobblers in the back; a bird-fancier in the first floor, three families on the second, starvation in the attics, Irishmen in the passage; a 'musician' in the front kitchen, and a charwoman and five hungry children in the back one — filth every where — a gutter before the houses and a drain behind them — clothes drying and slops emptying from the windows: girls of fourteen or fifteen with matted hair walking about barefooted, and in white great-coats, almost their only covering; boys of all ages, in coats of all sizes and no coats at all; men and women, in every variety of scanty and dirty apparel, lounging, scolding, drinking, smoking, squabling, fighting, and swearing.

You turn the corner, what a change! All is light and brilliancy. The hum of many voices, issues from that splendid gin-shop which forms the commencement of the two streets opposite, and the gay building with the fantastically ornamented parapet, the illuminated clock, the plate-glass windows surrounded by stucco rosettes, and its profusion of gas-lights in richly-gilt burners, is perfectly dazzling when contrasted with the darkness and dirt we have just left. The interior is even gayer than the exterior. A bar of French-polished mahogany, elegantly carved, extends the whole width of the place; and there are two side-aisles of great casks, painted green and gold, enclosed within a light brass rail, and bearing such inscriptions as 'Old Tom, 549;' 'Young Tom, 360;' 'Samson, 1421.' Beyond the bar is a lofty and spacious saloon, full of the same enticing vessels, with a gallery running round it, equally well furnished. On the counter, in addition to the usual spirit apparatus, are two or three little baskets of cakes and biscuits, which are carefully secured at the top with wicker-work, to prevent their contents being unlawfully abstracted. Behind it, are two showily-dressed damsels with large necklaces, dispensing the spirits and 'compounds.' They are assisted by the ostensible proprietor of the concern, a stout coarse fellow in a fur cap, put on very much on one side to give him a knowing air, and display his sandy whiskers to the best advantage.

The two old washerwomen, who are seated on the little bench to the left of the bar, are rather overcome by the head-dresses and haughty demeanour of the young ladies who officiate; and receive their half-quartern of gin and peppermint, with considerable defer- ence, prefacing a request for 'one of them soft biscuits,' with a 'Jist be good enough, ma'am,' &c. They are quite astonished at the impudent air of the young fellow in a brown coat and bright buttons, who, ushering in his two companions, and walking up to the bar in as careless a manner as if he had been used to green and gold ornaments all his life, winks at one of the young ladies with singular coolness, and calls for a 'kervorten and a three-out glass,'[3] just as if the place were his own, 'Gin for you, sir?' says the young lady when she has drawn it: carefully looking every way but the right one, to show that the wink had no effect upon her. 'For me, Mary my dear,' replies the gentleman in brown. 'My name an't Mary as it happens,' says the young girl, in a most insinuating manner as she delivers the change. 'Well, if it an't, it ought to be,' responds the irresistible one; 'all the Marys as ever I see, was handsome gals.' Here the young lady, not precisely remembering how blushes are managed in such cases, abruptly ends the flirtation by addressing the female in the faded feathers who has just entered, and who, after stating explicitly, to prevent any subsequent misunderstanding, that 'this gentleman pays,' calls for 'a glass of port wine and a bit of sugar,' the drinking which, and sipping another, accompanied by sundry whisperings to her companion, and no small quantity of giggling, occupies a considerable time.

Those two old men who came in 'just to have a drain,' finished their third quartern a few seconds ago; they have made themselves crying drunk, and the fat comfortable-looking elderly women, who had 'a glass of rum srub'[4] each, having chimed in with their complaints on the hardness of the times, one of the women has agreed to stand a glass round, jocularly observing that 'grief never mended no broken bones, and as good people's wery scarce, what I says is, make the most on 'em, and that's all about it;' a sentiment which appears to afford unlimited satisfaction to those who have nothing to pay.

It is growing late, and the throng of men, women, and children, who have been constantly going in and out, dwindles down to two or three occasional stragglers – cold, wretched-looking creatures, in the last stage of emaciation and disease. The knot of Irish labourers at the lower end of the place, who have been alternately shaking hands with, and threatening the life of, each other for the last hour, become furious in their disputes, and finding it impossible to silence one man, who is particularly anxious to adjust the difference, they resort to the infallible expedient of knocking him down and jumping on him afterwards. The man in the fur cap, and the potboy rush out: a scene of riot and confusion ensues; half the Irishmen get shut out, and the other half get shut in, the potboy is knocked among the tubs in no time; the landlord hits every body, and every body hits the landlord, the barmaids scream, the police come in; and the rest is a confused mixture of arms, legs, staves, torn coats, shouting, and struggling. Some of the party are borne off to the station-house, and the remainder slink home to beat their wives for complaining, and kick the children for daring to be hungry.

We have sketched this subject very slightly, not only because our limits compel us to do so, but because, if it were pursued further, it would be painful and repulsive. Well-disposed gentlemen, and charitable ladies, would alike turn with coldness and disgust from a description of the drunken besotted men, and wretched broken-down miserable women, who form no inconsiderable portion of the frequenters of these haunts; forgetting, in the pleasant consciousness of their own high rectitude, the poverty of the one, and the temptation of the other. Gin-drinking is a great vice in England, but poverty is a greater; and until you can cure it, or persuade a half-famished wretch not to seek relief in the temporary oblivion of his own misery, with the pittance which, divided among his family, would just furnish a morsel of bread for each, gin-shops will increase in number and splendour. If Temperance Societies could suggest an antidote against hunger and distress, or establish dispensaries for the gratuitous distribution of bottles of Lethe-water, gin-palaces would be numbered among the things that were. Until then, their decrease may be despaired of.

CHAPTER 23

The Pawnbroker's Shop

OF all the numerous receptacles for misery and distress with which the streets of London unhappily abound, there are, perhaps, none which present such striking scenes of vice and poverty[1] as the pawnbroker's shops. The very nature and description of these places occasions their being but little known, except to the unfortunate beings whose profligacy or misfortune drives them to seek the temporary relief they offer. The subject may appear, at first sight,

The Pawnbroker's Shop

SCENES

to be any thing but an inviting one, but we venture on it nevertheless, in the hope that, as far as the limits of our present paper are concerned, it will present, at all events, nothing to disgust even the most fastidious reader.

There are some pawnbrokers' shops of a very superior description. There are grades in pawning as in every thing else, and distinctions must be observed even in poverty. The aristocratic Spanish cloak and the plebeian calico shirt, the silver fork and the flat iron, the muslin cravat and the Belcher neckerchief,[2] would but ill assort together; so the better sort of pawnbroker calls himself a silversmith, and decorates his shop with handsome trinkets and expensive jewellery, while the more humble money-lender boldly advertises his calling, and invites observation. It is with pawn-brokers' shops of the latter class, that we have to do. We have selected one for our purpose, and will endeavour to describe it.

The pawnbroker's shop is situated near Drury-lane, at the corner of a court, which affords a side entrance for the accommoda-tion of such customers as may be desirous of avoiding the observa-tion of the passers-by, or the chance of recognition in the public street. It is a low, dirty-looking, dusty shop, the door of which stands always doubtfully, a little way open, half inviting, half repelling the hesitating visiter, who, if he be as yet uninitiated, examines one of the old garnet brooches in the window for a minute or two with affected eagerness, as if he contemplated making the purchase; and then looking cautiously round to ascertain that no one watches him, hastily slinks in: the door closing of itself after him, to just its former width. The shop front and the window-frames bear evident marks of having been once painted; but what the colour was originally, or at what date it was probably laid on, are at this remote period questions which may be asked, but cannot be answered. Tradition states that the transparency in the front door, which displays at night three red balls on a blue ground, once bore also, inscribed in graceful waves, the words 'Money advanced on plate, jewels, wearing apparel, and every description of property,' but a few illegible hieroglyphics are all that now remain to attest the fact. The plate and jewels would seem

222

to have disappeared together with the anouncement, for the articles of stock, which are displayed in some profusion in the window, do not include any very valuable luxuries of either kind. A few old china cups, some modern vases adorned with paltry paintings of three Spanish cavaliers playing three Spanish guitars, or a party of boors carousing: each boor with one leg painfully elevated in the air, by way of expressing his perfect freedom and gaiety; several sets of chessmen, two or three flutes, a few fiddles, a round-eyed portrait staring in astonishment from a very dark ground; some gaudily-bound prayer-books and testaments, two rows of silver watches quite as clumsy and almost as large as Ferguson's first;[3] numerous old-fashioned table and tea spoons displayed, fan-like, in half-dozens; strings of coral with great broad gilt snaps; cards of rings and brooches, fastened and labelled separately, like the insects in the British Museum; cheap silver penholders and snuff-boxes, with a masonic star, complete the jewellery department; while five or six beds in smeary clouded ticks, strings of blankets and sheets, silk and cotton handkerchiefs, and wearing apparel of every description, form the more useful, though even less ornamental, part of the articles exposed for sale. An extensive collection of planes, chisels, saws, and other carpenters' tools, which have been pledged, and never redeemed, form the foreground of the picture; while the large frames full of ticketed bundles which are dimly seen through the dirty casement up stairs – the squalid neighbourhood – the adjoining houses, straggling, shrunken, and rotten, with one or two filthy, unwholesome-looking heads, thrust out of every window, and old red pans and stunted plants exposed on the tottering parapets, to the manifest hazard of the heads of the passers-by – the noisy men loitering under the archway at the corner of the court, or about the gin-shop next door, and their wives patiently standing on the curb-stone, with large baskets of cheap vegetables slung round them for sale, are its immediate auxiliaries.

If the outside of the pawnbroker's shop be calculated to attract the attention, or excite the interest, of the speculative pedestrian, its interior cannot fail to produce the same effect in a very increased degree. The front door, which we have before noticed, opens into the common shop, which is the resort of all those customers whose habitual acquaintance with such scenes renders them indifferent to the observation of their companions in poverty. The side door opens into a small passage from which some half-dozen doors (which may be secured on the inside by bolts) open into a corresponding number of little dens, or closets, which face the counter. Here the more timid or respectable portion of the crowd shroud themselves from the notice of the remainder, and patiently wait until the gentleman behind the counter, with the curly black hair, diamond ring, and double silver watch-guard, shall feel disposed to favour them with his notice – a consummation which depends considerably on the temper of the aforesaid gentleman for the time being.

At the present moment this elegantly-attired individual, is in the act of entering the duplicate he has just made out, in a thick book, a process from which he is diverted occasionally, by a conversation he is carrying on with another young man similarly employed at a little distance from him, whose allusions to 'that last bottle of soda-water last night,' and 'how regularly round my hat⁴ he felt himself when the young 'ooman gave 'em in charge,' would appear to refer to the consequences of some stolen joviality of the preceding evening. The customers generally, however, seem rather unable to participate in the amusement derivable from this source, for an old sallow-looking woman, who has been leaning with both arms on the counter with a small bundle before her, for half an hour previously, suddenly interrupts the conversation by addressing the jewelled shop-man – 'Now, Mr Henry, do make haste, there's a good soul, for my two grandchildren's locked up at home, and I'm afeer'd of the fire.' The shopman slightly raises his head, with an air of deep abstraction, and resumes his entry with as much deliberation as if he were engraving. 'You're in a hurry, Mrs Tatham, this ev'nin', an't you?' is the only notice he deigns to take, after the lapse of five minutes or so. 'Yes, I am indeed, Mr Henry; now, do serve me next, there's a good creetur. I wouldn't worry you, only it's all along o' them botherin' children.' – 'What have you got here?' inquires the shopman, unpinning the bundle – 'old concern, I suppose – pair o' stays and a petticoat. You must look up somethin' else, old 'ooman; I can't lend you any thing more upon them, they're completely worn out by this time, if it's only by putting in, and taking out again, three times a week.' – 'Oh! you're a rum un, you are,' replies the old woman, laughing extremely, as in duty bound; 'I wish I'd got the gift of the gab like you; see if I'd be up the spout⁵ so often then. No, no; it an't the petticut; it's a child's frock and a beautiful silk-ankecher, as belongs to my husband. He gave four shillin' for it, the werry same blessed day as he broke his arm.' – 'What do you want upon these?' inquires Mr Henry slightly glancing at the articles, which in all probability are old acquaintances. 'What do you want upon these?' – 'Eighteenpence.' – 'Lend you ninepence.' – 'Oh, make it a shillin'; there's a dear – do now.' – 'Not another farden.' – 'Well, I suppose I must take it.' The duplicate is made out, one ticket pinned on the parcel, the other given to the old woman: the parcel is flung carelessly down into a corner, and some other customer prefers his claim to be served without further delay.

The choice falls on an unshaven, dirty, sottish-looking fellow, whose tarnished paper-cap, stuck negligently over one eye, communicates an additionally repulsive expression to his very uninviting countenance. He was enjoying a little relaxation from his sedentary pursuits a quarter of an hour ago, in kicking his wife up the court. He has come to redeem some tools:– probably to complete a job with, on account of which he has already received some money, if his inflamed countenance and drunken stagger, may be taken as evidence of the fact. Having waited some little time, he makes his presence known by venting his ill-humour on a ragged urchin, who, being unable to bring his face on a level with the counter by any other process, has employed himself in climbing up, and then hooking himself on with his elbows – an uneasy perch, from which he has fallen at intervals, generally alighting on the toes of the person in his immediate vicinity. In the present case, the unfortunate little wretch has received a cuff which sends him reeling to the door; and the donor of the blow is immediately the object of general indignation.

'What do you strike the boy for, you brute?' exclaims a slipshod woman, with two flat irons in a little basket. 'Do you think he's your wife, you willin?' – 'Go and hang yourself!' replies the gentleman addressed, with a drunken look of savage stupidity, aiming at the same time a blow at the woman which fortunately misses its object. 'Go and hang yourself; and wait till I come and cut you down.' – 'Cut you down,' rejoins the woman, 'I wish I had the cutting of you up, you wagabond! (loud.) Oh! you precious wagabond! (rather louder.) Where's your wife, you willin? (louder still; women of this class are always sympathetic, and work themselves into a tremendous passion on the shortest notice.) Your poor dear wife as you uses worser nor a dog – strike a woman – you a man! (very shrill;) I wish I had you – I'd murder you, I would, if I died for it.' – 'Now be civil,' retorts the man fiercely. 'Be civil, you wiper!' ejaculates the woman contemptuously, 'An't it shocking?' she continues, turning round, and appealing to an old woman who is peeping out of one of the little closets we have before described, and who has not the slightest objection to join in the attack, possessing, as she does, the comfortable conviction that she is bolted in. 'An't it shocking ma'am? (Dreadful! says the old woman in a parenthesis, not exactly knowing what the question refers to.) He's got a wife, ma'am, as takes in mangling, and is as 'dustrious and hard-working a young 'ooman as can be, (very fast) as lives in the back parlour of our 'ous, which my husband and me lives in the front one (with great rapidity) – and we hears him a beaten' on her sometimes when he comes home drunk, the whole night through, and not only a beaten' her, but beaten' his own child too, to make her more miserable – ugh, you beast! – and she, poor creater, won't swear the peace agin him, nor do nothin', because she likes the wretch arter all – worse luck!' Here, as the woman has completely run herself out of breath, the pawnbroker himself, who has just appeared behind the counter in a gray dressing-gown, embraces the favourable opportunity of putting in a word:– 'Now I won't have none of this sort of thing on my premises,' he interposes with an air of authority; 'Mrs Mackin, keep yourself to yourself, or you don't get fourpence for a flat iron here; and Jinkins, you leave your ticket here till you're sober, and send your wife for them two planes, for I won't have you in my shop at no price; so make yourself scarce, before I make you scarcer.'

This eloquent address produces any thing but the effect desired; the women rail in concert; the man hits about him in all directions, and is in the act of establishing an indisputable claim to gratuitous lodgings for the night, when the entrance of his wife, a wretched worn-out woman, apparently in the last stage of consumption, whose face bears evident marks of recent ill-usage, and whose strength seems hardly equal to the burden – light enough, God knows – of the thin sickly child she carries in her arms, turns his cowardly rage in a safer direction. 'Come home, dear,' cries the miserable creature, in an imploring tone; '*do* come home, there's a good fellow, and go to bed.' – 'Go home yourself,' rejoins the furious ruffian, accompanying an epithet we will not repeat, with a kick we will not describe. 'Do come home quietly,' repeats the wife, bursting into tears. 'Go home yourself,' retorts the husband again, enforcing his argument, by the application we have before hinted at. The poor creature flies out of the shop, with the impetus thus administered, and her 'natural protector' follows her up the court, alternately venting his rage in accelerating her progress, and in knocking the little scanty blue bonnet of the unfortunate child over its still more scanty and faded-looking face.

In the last box, which is situated in the darkest and most obscure corner of the shop, considerably removed from either of the gas-lights, are a young delicate girl of about twenty, and an elderly female, evidently her mother from the resemblance between them, who stand at some distance back, as if to avoid the observation even of the shopman. It is not their first visit to a pawnbroker's shop, for they answer without a moment's hesitation the usual questions, put in a rather respectful manner, and in a much lower tone than usual, of 'What name shall I say? – Your own property of course? – Where do you live, ma'am? – Housekeeper or lodger?' They bargain, too, for a higher loan than the shopman is at first inclined to offer, which a perfect stranger would be little disposed to do; and the elder female urges her daughter on, in scarcely audible whispers, to exert her utmost powers of persuasion to obtain an advance of the sum, and expatiate on the value of the articles they have brought to raise a present supply upon. They are a small gold chain and a 'Forget me not' ring, the girl's property, for they are both too small for the mother; given her in better times, prized perhaps once for the giver's sake, but parted with now without a struggle, for want has hardened the mother, and her example has hardened the girl, and the prospect of receiving money coupled with a recollection of the misery they have both endured from the want of it – the coldness of old friends – the stern refusal of some, and the still more galling compassion of others – appears to have obliterated the consciousness of self-humiliation, which the bare idea of their present situation would once have aroused.

In the next box, is a young female, whose attire, miserably poor, but extremely gaudy, wretchedly cold but extravagantly fine, too plainly bespeaks her station in life. The rich satin gown with its faded trimmings, the worn-out thin shoes, and pink silk stockings, the summer bonnet in winter, and the sunken face, where a daub of rouge only serves as an index to the ravages of squandered health never to be regained, and lost happiness never to be restored, and where the practised smile is a wretched mockery of the misery of the heart, cannot be mistaken. There is something in the glimpse she has just caught of her young neighbour, and in the sight of the little trinkets she has offered in pawn, that seems to have awakened in the woman's mind some long slumbering recollection, and to have changed, for an instant, her whole demeanour. Her first hasty impulse was to bend forward as if to scan more minutely the appearance of her half-concealed companions; her next, on seeing them involuntarily shrink from her, to retreat to the back of the box, cover her face with her hands, and burst into an agony of tears.

There are strange chords in the human heart, which will lie dormant through years of depravity and wickedness, but which will vibrate at last to some slight circumstance apparently trivial in itself, but connected by some undefined and indistinct association, with past days that can never be recalled, and with bitter recollections from which the most degraded creature in existence cannot escape.

There has been another spectator, in the person of a woman in the common shop; the lowest of the low; dirty, unbonneted, flaunting, and slovenly. Her curiosity was at first attracted by the little she could see of the group; then her attention. The half intoxicated leer changed to an expression of something like interest, and a feeling similar to that we have described, appeared for a moment, and only a moment, to extend itself even to her bosom.

Who shall say how soon these women may change places? The last has but two more stages — the hospital and the grave. How many females situated as her two companions are, and as she may have been once, have terminated the same wretched course, in the same wretched manner. One is already tracing her footsteps with frightful rapidity. How soon may the other follow her example! How many have done the same!

CHAPTER 24

Criminal Courts

WE shall never forget the mingled feelings of awe and respect with which we used to gaze on the exterior of Newgate in our schoolboy days. How dreadful its rough heavy walls, and low massive doors, appeared to us — the latter looking as if they were made for the express purpose of letting people in, and never letting them out again. Then the fetters over the debtors' door,[1] which we used to think were a *bonâ fide* set of irons, just hung up there, for convenience sake, ready to be taken down at a moment's notice, and riveted on the limbs of some refractory felon! We were never tired of wondering how the hackney-coachmen on the opposite stand could cut jokes in the presence of such horrors, and drink pots of half-and-half[2] so near the last drop.

Often have we strayed here in sessions time, just to catch a glimpse of the whipping-place, and that dark building on one side of the yard, in which is kept the gibbet with all its dreadful apparatus, and on the door of which we half expected to see a brass plate, with the inscription 'Mr Ketch;'[3] for we never imagined that the distinguished functionary could by possibility live any where else. The days of these childish dreams have passed away, and with them many other boyish ideas of a gayer nature. But we still retain so much of our original feeling, that to this hour we never pass the building without something like a shudder.

What London pedestrian is there who has not, at some time or other, cast a hurried glance through the wicket at which prisoners are admitted into this gloomy mansion, and surveyed the few objects he could discern, with an indescribable feeling of curiosity? The thick door, plated with iron and mounted with spikes, just low enough to enable you to see, leaning over them, an ill-looking fellow in a broad-brimmed hat, belcher handkerchief and top-boots, with a brown coat, something between a great-coat and a 'sporting' jacket, on his back, and an immense key in his left hand. Perhaps you are lucky enough to pass, just as the gate is being opened; then you see on the other side of the lodge, another gate, the very image of its predecessor, and two or three more turnkeys, who look like multiplications of the first one, seated round a fire which just lights up the whitewashed apartment sufficiently to enable you to catch a hasty glimpse of these different objects. We have a great respect for Mrs Fry, but she certainly ought to have written more romances than Mrs Radcliffe.[4]

We were walking leisurely down the Old Bailey,[5] sometime ago, when, just as we passed this identical gate, it was opened by the officiating turnkey. We turned quickly round, as a matter of course, and saw two persons descending the steps. We could not help stopping and observing them.

They were an elderly woman, of decent appearance, though evidently poor, and a boy of about fourteen or fifteen. The woman was crying bitterly; she carried a small bundle in her hand, and the boy followed at a short distance behind her. Their little history was obvious. The boy was her son, to whose early comfort she had perhaps sacrificed her own – for whose sake she had borne misery without repining, and poverty without a murmur: looking steadily forward to the time, when he who had so long witnessed her struggles for himself, might be enabled to make some exertions for their joint support. He had formed dissolute connexions; idleness had led to crime, and he had been committed to take his trial for some petty theft. He had been long in prison, and, after receiving some trifling additional punishment, had been ordered to be discharged that morning. It was his first offence, and his poor old mother, still hoping to reclaim him, had been waiting at the gate to implore him to return home.

We cannot forget the boy; he descended the steps with a dogged look, shaking his head with an air of bravado and obstinate determination. They walked a few paces, and paused. The woman put her hand upon his shoulder in an agony of entreaty, and the boy sullenly raised his head as if in refusal. It was a brilliant morning, and every object looked fresh and happy in the broad, gay sun-light; he gazed round him for a few moments, bewildered with the brightness of the scene, for it was long since he had beheld any thing save the gloomy walls of a prison. Perhaps the wretchedness of his mother made some impression on the boy's heart; perhaps some undefined recollection of the time when he was a happy child, and she his only friend, and best companion, crowded on him – he burst into tears; and covering his face with one hand, and hurriedly placing the other in his mother's, they walked away together.

Curiosity has occasionally led us into both Courts at the Old Bailey. Nothing is so likely to strike the person who enters them for the first time, as the calm indifference with which the proceedings are conducted; every trial seems a mere matter of business. There is a great deal of form, but no compassion; considerable interest, but no sympathy. Take the Old Court for example. There sit the Judges, with whose great dignity every body is acquainted, and of whom therefore we need say no more. Then there is the Lord Mayor in the centre, looking as cool as a Lord Mayor *can* look, with an immense *bouquet*[6] before him, and habited in all the splendour of his office. Then there are the Sheriffs, who are almost as dignified as the Lord Mayor himself, and the Barristers, who are quite dignified enough in their own opinion, and the spectators, who having paid for their admission, look upon the whole scene as if it were got up especially for their amusement. Look upon the whole group in the body of the Court – some wholly engrossed in the morning papers, others carelessly conversing in low whispers, and others, again, quietly dozing away an hour – and you can scarcely believe that the result of the trial is a matter of life or death to one wretched being present.

Turn your eyes to the dock; watch the prisoner attentively for a few moments, and the fact is before you, in all its painful reality. Mark how restlessly he has been engaged for the last ten minutes, in forming all sorts of fantastic figures with the herbs which are strewed upon the ledge before him;[7] observe the ashy paleness of his face when a particular witness appears, and how he changes his position and wipes his clammy forehead, and feverish hands, when the case for the prosecution is closed, as if it were a relief to him to feel that the jury knew the worst.

The defence is concluded; the judge proceeds to sum up the evidence, and the prisoner watches the countenances of the jury, as a dying man, clinging to life to the very last, vainly looks in the face of his physician for one slight ray of hope. They turn round to consult; you can almost hear the man's heart beat, as he bites the stalk of rosemary, with a desperate effort to appear composed. They resume their places – a dead silence prevails as the foreman delivers in the verdict – 'Guilty!' A shriek bursts from a female in the gallery; the prisoner casts one look at the quarter from whence the noise proceeded, and is immediately hurried from the dock by the gaoler. The clerk directs one of the officers of the court to 'take the woman out,' and fresh business is proceeded with, as if nothing had occurred.

No imaginary contrast to a case like this, could be as complete as that which is constantly presented in the New Court, the gravity of which is frequently disturbed in no small degree, by the cunning and pertinacity of juvenile offenders. A boy of thirteen is tried, say for picking the pocket of some subject of her Majesty, and the offence is about as clearly proved as an offence can be. He is called upon for his defence, and contents himself with a little declamation about the jurymen and his country — asserts that all the witnesses have committed perjury, and hints that the police force generally, have entered into a conspiracy 'again' him.[8] However probable this statement may be, it fails to convince the Court, and some such scene as the following then takes place:—

Court: Have you any witnesses to speak to your character, boy?

Boy: Yes, my Lord; fifteen gen'lm'n is a vaten outside, and vos a vaten all day yesterday, vich they told me the night afore my trial vos a comin' on.

Court: Inquire for these witnesses.

Here a very stout beadle runs out, and vociferates for the witnesses at the very top of his voice; for you hear his cry grow fainter and fainter as he descends the steps into the court-yard below. After an absence of five minutes, he returns very warm and hoarse, and informs the Court of what it was perfectly well aware before — namely, that there are no such witnesses in attendance. Hereupon the boy sets up the most awful howling ever heard within or without the walls of a court; screws the lower part of the palms of his hands into the corners of his eyes, and endeavours to look the very picture of injured innocence. The jury at once find him 'guilty,' and his endeavours to squeeze out a tear or two are redoubled. The governor of the gaol then states, in reply to an inquiry from the bench, that the prisoner has been under his care twice before. This the urchin resolutely denies in some such terms as — 'S'elp me God, gen'lm'n, I never vos in trouble afore — indeed, my Lord, I never vos. It's all a howen to my having a twin brother, vich has wrongfully taken to prigging,[9] and vich is so exactly like me, that no vun ever knows the difference atween us.'

This representation, like the defence, fails in producing the desired effect, and the boy is sentenced, perhaps, to seven years' transportation. Finding it impossible to excite compassion, he gives vent to his feelings in an imprecation bearing reference to the eyes of 'old big vig!' and as he declines to take the trouble of walking from the dock, he is forthwith carried out by two men, congratulating himself on having succeeded in giving every body as much trouble as possible.

CHAPTER 25

A Visit to Newgate

'THE force of habit' is a trite phrase in every body's mouth; and it is not a little remarkable that those who use it most as applied to others, unconsciously afford in their own persons singular examples of the power which habit and custom exercise over the minds of men, and of the little reflection they are apt to bestow on subjects with which every day's experience has rendered them familiar. If Bedlam could be suddenly removed like another Aladdin's palace,[1] and set down on the space now occupied by Newgate,[2] scarcely one man out of a hundred, whose road to business every morning lies through Newgate-street or the Old Bailey,[3] would pass the building without bestowing a hasty glance on its small, grated windows, and a transient thought at least upon the condition of the unhappy beings immured in its dismal cells; and yet these same men, day by day, and hour by hour, pass and repass this gloomy depository of the guilt and misery of London, in one perpetual stream of life and bustle, utterly unmindful of the throng of wretched creatures pent up within it – may not even knowing, or if they do, not heeding the fact, that as they pass one particular angle of the massive wall with a light laugh or a merry whistle, they stand within one yard of a fellow-creature, bound and helpless, whose hours are numbered, from whom the last feeble ray of hope has fled for ever, and whose miserable career will shortly terminate in a violent and shameful death. Contact with death even in its least terrible shape is solemn and appalling. How much more awful is it to reflect on this near vicinity to the dying — to men in full health and vigour, in the flower of youth or the prime of life, with all their faculties and perceptions as acute and perfect as your own; but dying, nevertheless — dying as surely — with the hand of death imprinted upon them as indelibly — as if mortal disease had wasted their frames to shadows, and loathsome corruption had already begun!

It was with some such thoughts as these that we determined not many weeks since to visit the interior of Newgate[4] — in an amateur capacity, of course; and, having carried our intention into effect, we proceed to lay its results before our readers, in the hope — founded more upon the nature of the subject, than on any presumptuous confidence in our own descriptive powers — that this paper may not be found wholly devoid of interest. We have only to premise, that we do not intend to fatigue the reader with any statistical accounts of the prison: they will be found at length in numerous reports of numerous committees, and a variety of authorities of equal weight. We took no notes, made no memoranda, measured none of the yards, ascertained the exact number of inches in no particular room; are unable even to report of how many apartments the jail is composed.

We saw the prison, and saw the prisoners; and what we did see, and what we thought, we will tell at once in our own way.

Having delivered our credentials to the servant who answered our knock at the door of the governor's house, we were ushered into the 'office;' a little room, on the right-hand side as you enter, with two windows looking into the Old Bailey, fitted up like an ordinary attorney's office, or merchant's counting-house, with the usual fixtures — a wainscoted partition, a shelf or two, a desk, a couple of stools, a pair of clerks, an almanack, a clock, and a few maps. After a little delay, occasioned by sending into the interior of the prison for the officer whose duty it was to chaperon us, that functionary arrived; a respectable-looking man of about two or three and fifty, in a broad-brimmed hat, and full suit of black, who, but for his keys, would have looked quite as much like a clergyman as a turnkey: we were quite disappointed; he had not even top-boots on. Following our conductor by a door opposite to that at which we had entered, we arrived at a small room, without any

other furniture than a little desk, with a book for visiters' auto-
graphs, and a shelf, on which were a few boxes for papers, and
casts of the heads and faces of the two notorious murderers, Bishop
and Williams;[5] the former, in particular, exhibiting a style of head
and set of features, which would have afforded sufficient moral
grounds for his instant execution at any time, even had there been
no other evidence against him. Leaving this room also, by an
opposite door, we found ourself in the lodge which opens on the
Old Bailey; one side of which is plentifully garnished with a choice
collection of heavy sets of irons, including those worn by the
redoubtable Jack Sheppard – genuine; and those *said* to have been
graced by the sturdy limbs of the no less celebrated Dick Turpin[6]
– doubtful. From this lodge, a heavy oaken gate, bound with iron,
studded with nails of the same material, and guarded by another
turnkey, opens on a few steps, if we remember right, which
terminate in a narrow and dismal stone passage, running parallel
with the Old Bailey, and leading to the different yards, through a
number of tortuous and intricate windings, guarded in their turn
by huge gates and gratings, whose appearance is sufficient to dispel
at once the slightest hope of escape that any new comer may have
entertained: and the very recollection of which, on eventually
traversing the place again, involves one in a maze of confusion.

It is necessary to explain here, that the buildings in the prison,
or in other words the different wards – form a square, of which the
four sides abut respectively on the Old Bailey, the old College of
Physicians (now forming a part of Newgate-market), the Sessions-
house,[7] and Newgate-street. The intermediate space is divided into
several paved yards, in which the prisoners take such air and
exercise as can be had in such a place. These yards, with the
exception of that in which prisoners under sentence of death are
confined (of which we shall presently give a more detailed description), run parallel with Newgate-street, and consequently from the
Old Bailey, as it were, to Newgate-market. The women's side is in
the right wing of the prison nearest the Sessions-house; and as we
were introduced into this part of the building first, we will adopt
the same order, and introduce our readers to it also.

Turning to the right, then, down the passage to which we just now adverted, omitting any mention of intervening gates – for if we noticed every gate that was unlocked for us to pass through, and locked again as soon as we had passed, we should require a gate at every comma – we came to a door composed of thick bars of wood, through which were discernible, passing to and fro in a narrow yard, some twenty women, the majority of whom, however, as soon as they were aware of the presence of strangers, retreated to their wards. One side of this yard is railed off at a considerable distance, and formed into a kind of iron cage, about five feet ten inches in height, roofed at the top, and defended in front by iron bars, from which the friends of the female prisoners communicate with them. In one corner of this singular-looking den was a yellow, haggard, decrepit old woman, in a tattered gown that had once been black, and the remains of an old straw bonnet, with faded ribbon of the same hue, in earnest conversation with a young girl – a prisoner of course – of about two-and-twenty. It is impossible to imagine a more poverty-stricken object, or a creature so borne down in soul and body, by excess of misery and destitution. The girl was a good-looking robust female, with a profusion of hair streaming about in the wind – for she had no bonnet on – and a man's silk pocket-handkerchief was loosely thrown over a most ample pair of shoulders. The old woman was talking in that low, stifled tone of voice which tells so forcibly of mental anguish; and every now and then burst into an irrepressible sharp, abrupt cry of grief, the most distressing sound that human ears can hear. The girl was perfectly unmoved. Hardened beyond all hope of redemption, she listened doggedly to her mother's entreaties, whatever they were: and, beyond inquiring after 'Jem,' and eagerly catching at the few halfpence her miserable parent had brought her, took no more apparent interest in the conversation than the most unconcerned spectators. God knows there were enough of them in the persons of the other prisoners in the yard, who were no more concerned by what was passing before their eyes, and within their hearing, than if they were blind and deaf. Why should they be? Inside the prison, and out, such scenes were too familiar to them, to excite even a passing thought, unless of ridicule or contempt, for the display of feelings which they had long since forgotten, and lost all sympathy for.

A little further on, a squalid-looking woman in a slovenly, thick-bordered cap, with her arms muffled up in a large red shawl, the fringed ends of which straggled nearly to the bottom of a dirty white apron, was communicating some instructions to *her* visiter – her daughter evidently. The girl was thinly clad, and shaking with the cold. Some ordinary word of recognition passed between her and her mother when she appeared at the grating, but neither hope, condolence, regret, nor affection was expressed on either side. The mother whispered her instructions, and the girl received them with her pinched-up half-starved features twisted into an expression of careful cunning. It was some scheme for the woman's defence that she was disclosing; and a sullen smile came over the girl's face for an instant, as if she were pleased, not so much at the probability of her mother's liberation, as at the chance of her 'getting off' in spite of her prosecutors. The dialogue was soon concluded; and with the same careless indifference with which they had approached each other, the mother turned towards the inner end of the yard, and the girl to the gate at which she had entered.

The girl belonged to a class – unhappily but too extensive – the very existence of which should make men's hearts bleed. Barely past her childhood, it required but a glance to discover that she was one of those children born and bred in poverty and vice, who have never known what childhood is; who have never been taught to love and court a parent's smile, or to dread a parent's frown. The thousand nameless endearments of childhood, its gaiety and its innocence, are alike unknown to them. They have entered at once upon the stern realities and miseries of life, and to their better nature it is almost hopeless to appeal in aftertimes, by any of the references which will awaken, if it be only for a moment, some good feeling in ordinary bosoms, however corrupt they may have become. Talk to *them* of parental solicitude, the happy days of childhood, and the merry games of infancy! Tell them of hunger and the streets, beggary and stripes, the gin-shop, the station-house, and the pawnbrokers, and they will understand you.

Two or three women were standing at different parts of the grating conversing with their friends, but a very large proportion of the prisoners appeared to have no friends at all, beyond such of their old companions as might happen to be within the walls. So, passing hastily down the yard, and pausing only for an instant to notice the little incidents we have just recorded, we were conducted up a clean and well-lighted flight of stone stairs to one of the wards. There are several in this part of the building, but a description of one is a description of the whole.

It was a spacious, bare, whitewashed apartment, lighted of course, by windows looking into the interior of the prison, but far more light and airy than one could reasonably expect to find in such a situation. There was a large fire with a deal table before it, round which ten or a dozen women were seated on wooden forms at dinner. Along both sides of the room ran a shelf; and below it, at regular intervals, a row of large hooks were fixed in the wall, on each of which was hung the sleeping-mat of a prisoner; her rug and blanket being folded up, and placed on the shelf above. At night these mats are placed upon the floor, each beneath the hook on which it hangs during the day; and the ward is thus made to answer the purposes both of a day-room and sleeping apartment. Over the fireplace was a large sheet of pasteboard, on which were displayed a variety of texts from Scripture, which were also scattered about the room in scraps about the size and shape of the copy-slips which are used in schools. On the table was a sufficient provision of a kind of stewed beef, and brown bread, in pewter dishes, which are kept perfectly bright, and displayed on shelves in great order and regularity when they are not in use.

The women rose hastily on our entrance, and retired in a hurried manner to either side of the fireplace. They were all cleanly – many of them decently – attired, and there was nothing peculiar either in their appearance or demeanour. One or two resumed the needlework which they had probably laid aside at the commencement of their meal, others gazed at the visitors with listless curiosity, and a few retired behind their companions to the very end of the room, as if desirous to avoid even the casual observation of the strangers. Some old Irish women, both in this and other wards, to whom the thing was no novelty, appeared perfectly indifferent to our presence, and remained standing close to the seats from which they had just risen; but the general feeling among the females seemed to be one of uneasiness during the period of our stay among them, which was very brief. Not a word was uttered during the time of our remaining, unless indeed by the wardswoman in reply to some question which we put to the turnkey who accompanied us. In every ward on the female side a wardswoman is appointed to preserve order, and a similar regulation is adopted among the males. The wardsmen and wardswomen are all prisoners, selected for good conduct. They alone are allowed the privilege of sleeping on bedsteads; a small stump bedstead⁸ being placed in every ward for that purpose. On both sides of the jail is a small receiving-room to which prisoners are conducted on their first reception, and whence they cannot be removed until they have been examined by the surgeon of the prison.*

Retracing our steps to the dismal passage in which we found ourselves at first (and which, by the by, contains three or four dark cells for the accommodation of refractory prisoners) we were led through a narrow yard to the 'school' – a portion of the prison set apart for boys under fourteen years of age. In a tolerable-sized room, in which were writing-materials and some copy-books, was the schoolmaster, with a couple of his pupils; and the remainder having been fetched from an adjoining apartment, the whole were drawn up in line for our inspection. There were fourteen of them in all, some with shoes, some without; some in pinafores without jackets, others in jackets without pinafores, and one in scarce any thing at all. The whole number, without an exception we believe, had been committed for trial on charges of pocket-picking; and

* The regulations of the prison relative to the confinement of prisoners during the day, their sleeping at night, their taking their meals, and other matters of gaol economy have been all altered – greatly for the better – since this sketch was written three years ago.

fourteen such villainous little faces we never beheld. – There was
not one redeeming feature among them – not a glance of honesty –
not a wink expressive of any thing but the gallows and the hulks,
in the whole collection. As to any thing like shame or contrition,
that was entirely out of the question. They were evidently quite
gratified at being thought worth the trouble of looking at; their
idea appeared to be that we had come to see Newgate as a grand
affair, and that they were an indispensable part of the show: and
every boy as he 'fell in' to the line, actually seemed as pleased and
important as if he had done something excessively meritorious in
getting there at all. We never looked upon a more disagreeable
sight, because we never saw fourteen such hopeless and irreclaimable
wretches[9] before.

On either side of the school-yard is a yard for men, in one of
which – that towards Newgate-street – prisoners of the more
respectable class are confined. Of the other we have little description
to offer, as the different wards necessarily partake of the same
character. They are provided, like the wards on the women's side,
with mats and rugs, which are disposed of in the same manner
during the day; and the only very striking difference between their
appearance and that of the wards inhabited by the females, is the
utter absence of any employment whatever. Huddled together upon
two opposite forms, by the fireside, sit twenty men perhaps; here a
boy in livery, there a man in a rough great-coat and top-boots;
further on, a desperate-looking fellow in his shirt sleeves, with an
old Scotch cap[10] upon his shaggy head; near him again, a tall
ruffian, in a smock-frock, and next to him a miserable being of
distressed appearance, with his head resting on his hand; – but all
alike in one respect, all idle and listless: when they do leave the fire,
sauntering moodily about, lounging in the window, or leaning
against the wall, vacantly swinging their bodies to and fro. With
the exception of a man reading an old newspaper in two or three
instances, this was the case in every ward we entered.

The only communication these men have with their friends is
through two close iron gratings, with an intermediate space of
about a yard in width between the two, so that nothing can be

handed across, nor can the prisoner have any communication by touch with the person who visits him. The married men have a separate grating, at which to see their wives, but its construction is the same.

The prison chapel is situated at the back of the governor's house, the latter having no windows looking into the interior of the prison. Whether the associations connected with the place – the knowledge that here a portion of the burial service is, on some dreadful occasions, performed over the quick and not upon the dead – cast over it a still more gloomy and sombre air than art has imparted to it, we know not, but its appearance is very striking. There is something in a silent and deserted place of worship highly solemn and impressive at any time; and the very dissimilarity of this one from any we have been accustomed to, only enhances the impression. The meanness of its appointments – the bare and scanty pulpit, with the paltry painted pillars on either side – the women's gallery with its great heavy curtain, the men's with its unpainted benches and dingy front – the tottering little table at the altar, with the commandments on the wall above it, scarcely legible through lack of paint and dust and damp – so unlike the rich velvet and gilding, the stately marble and polished wood of a modern church – are the more striking from their powerful contrast. There is one subject, too, which rivets the attention and fascinates the gaze, and from which we may turn disgusted and horror-stricken in vain, for the recollection of it will haunt us, waking and sleeping, for months afterwards. Immediately below the reading-desk, on the floor of the chapel, and forming the most conspicuous object in its little area, is *the condemned pew*; a huge black pen, in which the wretched men who are singled out for death, are placed, on the Sunday preceding their execution, in sight of all their fellow-prisoners, from many of whom they may have been separated but a week before; to hear prayers for their own souls, to join in the responses of their own burial service, and to listen to an address, warning their recent companions to take example by their fate, and urging themselves, while there is yet time – nearly four-and-twenty hours – to 'turn, and flee from the wrath to come!'[11] Imagine what have been the feelings of the men whom that fearful pew has enclosed, and of whom, between the gallows and the knife, no mortal remnant may now remain; think of the hopeless clinging to life to the last, and the wild despair, far exceeding in anguish the felon's death itself by which they have heard the certainty of their speedy transmission to another world, with all their crimes upon their heads, rung into their ears by the officiating clergyman!

At one time – and at no distant period either – the coffins of the men about to be executed, were placed in that pew, upon the seat by their side, during the whole service. It may seem incredible, but it is strictly true. Let us hope that the increased spirit of civilization and humanity which abolished this frightful and degrading custom, may extend itself to other usages equally barbarous; usages which have not even the plea of utility in their defence, as every year's experience has shown them to be more and more inefficacious.

Leaving the chapel, descending to the passage so frequently alluded to, and crossing the yard before noticed as being allotted to prisoners of a more respectable description than the generality of men confined here, the visiter arrives at a thick iron gate of great size and strength. Having been admitted through it by the turnkey on duty, he turns sharp round to the left, and pauses before another gate; and having passed this last barrier, he stands in the most terrible part of this gloomy building – the condemned ward.

The press-yard, well known by name to newspaper readers, from its frequent mention (formerly, thank God!) in accounts of executions, is at the corner of the building, and next to the ordinary's[12] house, in Newgate-street: running from Newgate-street, towards the centre of the prison, parallel with Newgate-market. It is a long, narrow court of which a portion of the wall in Newgate-street forms one end, and the gate the other. At the upper end, on the left-hand – that is, adjoining the wall in Newgate-street – is a cistern of water, and at the bottom a double grating (of which the gate itself forms a part) similar to that before described. Through these grates the prisoners are allowed to see their friends, a turnkey always remaining in the vacant space between, during the whole interview. Immediately on the right as you enter, is a building containing the press-room, day-room, and cells; the yard is on every side surrounded by lofty walls guarded by *chevaux de frise*; and the whole is under the constant inspection of vigilant and experienced turnkeys.

In the first apartment into which we were conducted – which was at the top of a staircase, and immediately over the press-room – were five-and-twenty or thirty prisoners, all under sentence of death, awaiting the result of the recorder's report[13] – men of all ages and appearances, from a hardened old offender with swarthy face and grizzly beard of three day's growth, to a handsome boy, not fourteen years old, of singularly youthful appearance even for that age, who had been condemned for burglary. There was nothing remarkable in the appearance of these prisoners. One or two decently-dressed men were brooding with a dejected air over the fire; several little groups of two or three had been engaged in conversation at the upper end of the room, or in the windows; and the remainder were crowded round a young man seated at the table, who appeared to be engaged in teaching the younger ones to write. The room was large, airy, and clean. There was very little anxiety or mental suffering depicted in the countenance of any of the men; – they had all been sentenced to death, it is true, and the recorder's report had not yet been made; but we question whether there was one man among them, notwithstanding, who did not *know* that although he had undergone the ceremony, it never was intended that his life should be sacrificed. On the table lay a testament, but there were no signs of its having been in recent use.

In the press-room below, were three men,[14] the nature of whose offence rendered it necessary to separate them, even from their companions in guilt. It is a long, sombre room, with two windows sunk into the stone wall, and here the wretched men are pinioned on the morning of their execution, before moving towards the scaffold. The fate of one of these men was uncertain; some mitigatory circumstances having come to light since his trial, which had been humanely represented in the proper quarter. The other two had nothing to expect from the mercy of the crown; their doom was sealed; no plea could be urged in extenuation of their crime, and they well knew that for them there was no hope in this world. 'The two short ones,' the turnkey whispered, 'were dead men.'

The man to whom we have alluded as entertaining some hopes of escape, was lounging at the greatest distance he could place between himself and his companions, in the window nearest the door. He was probably aware of our approach, and had assumed an air of courageous indifference; his face was purposely averted towards the window, and he stirred not an inch while we were present. The other two men were at the upper end of the room. One of them, who was imperfectly seen in the dim light, had his back towards us, and was stooping over the fire with his right arm on the mantelpiece, and his head sunk upon it. The other leaning on the sill of the furthest window. The light fell full upon him, and communicated to his pale, haggard face, and disordered hair, an appearance which, at that distance, was perfectly ghastly. His cheek rested upon his hand; and, with his face a little raised, and his eyes widely staring before him, he seemed to be unconsciously intent on counting the chinks in the opposite wall. We passed this room again afterwards. The first man was pacing up and down the court with a firm military step – he had been a soldier in the foot-guards – and a cloth cap jauntily thrown on one side of the head. He bowed respectfully to our conductor, and the salute was returned. The other two still remained in the positions we have described, and were motionless as statues.*

A few paces up the yard, and forming a continuation of the building, in which are the two rooms we have just quitted, lie the condemned cells. The entrance is by a narrow and obscure staircase leading to a dark passage, in which a charcoal stove casts a lurid tint over the objects in its immediate vicinity, and diffuses something like warmth around. From the left-hand side of this passage, the massive door of every cell on the story opens, and from it alone can they be approached. There are three of these passages, and

---

* These two men were executed shortly afterwards. The other was respited during his majesty's pleasure.

three of these ranges of cells one above the other, but in size, furniture and appearance, they are all precisely alike. Prior to the recorder's report being made, all the prisoners under sentence of death are removed from the day-room at five o'clock in the afternoon, and locked up in these cells, where they are allowed a candle until ten o'clock; and here they remain until seven next morning. When the warrant for a prisoner's execution arrives, he is immediately removed to the cells and confined in one of them until he leaves it for the scaffold. He is at liberty to walk in the yard, but both in his walks and in his cell, he is constantly attended by a turnkey who never leaves him on any pretence whatever.

We entered the first cell! It was a stone dungeon, eight feet long by six wide, with a bench at the further end, under which were a common horse-rug, a bible, and prayer-book. An iron candlestick was fixed into the wall at the side; and a small high window in the back admitted as much air and light as could struggle in between a double row of heavy, crossed iron bars. It contained no other furniture of any description.

Conceive the situation of a man, spending his last night on earth in this cell. Buoyed up with some vague and undefined hope of reprieve, he knew not why – indulging in some wild and visionary idea of escaping, he knew not how – hour after hour of the three preceding days allowed him for preparation, has fled with a speed which no man living would deem possible, for none but this dying man can know. He had wearied his friends with entreaties, exhausted the attendants with importunities, neglected in his feverish restlessness the timely warnings of his spiritual consoler; and now that the illusion is at last dispelled, now that eternity is before him and guilt behind, now that his fears of death amount almost to madness, and an overwhelming sense of his helpless, hopeless state rushes upon him, he is lost and stupified, and has neither thoughts to turn to, nor power to call upon the Almighty Being, from whom alone he can seek mercy and forgiveness, and before whom his repentance can alone avail.

Hours have glided by, and still he sits upon the same stone bench with folded arms, heedless alike of the fast decreasing time before him, and the urgent entreaties of the good man at his side. The feeble light is wasting gradually, and the deathlike stillness of the street without, broken only by the rumbling of some passing vehicle which echoes mournfully through the empty yards, warns him that the night is waning fast away. The deep bell of St Paul's strikes — one! He heard it; it has roused him. Seven hours left! He paces the narrow limits of his cell with rapid strides, cold drops of terror starting on his forehead, and every muscle of his frame quivering with agony. Seven hours! He suffers himself to be led to his seat, mechanically takes the bible which is placed in his hand, and tries to read and listen. No: his thoughts will wander. The book is torn and soiled by use — how like the book he read his lessons in at school just forty years ago! He has never bestowed a thought upon it since he left it as a child: and yet the place, the time, the room — nay, the very boys he played with, crowd as vividly before him as if they were scenes of yesterday; and some forgotten phrase, some childish word of kindness, rings in his ears like the echo of one uttered but a minute since. The deep voice of the clergyman recalls him to himself. He is reading from the sacred book its solemn promises of pardon for repentance, and its awful denunciation of obdurate men. He falls upon his knees and clasps his hands to pray. Hush! what sound was that? He starts upon his feet. It cannot be two yet. Hark! Two quarters have struck; — the third — the fourth. It is! Six hours left. Tell him not of repentance. Six hours' repentance for eight times six years of guilt and sin! He buries his face in his hands, and throws himself on the bench.

Worn with watching and excitement, he sleeps, and the same unsettled state of mind pursues him in his dreams. An insupportable load is taken from his breast; he is walking with his wife in a pleasant field, with the bright blue sky above them, and a fresh and boundless prospect on every side — how different from the stone walls of Newgate! She is looking — not as she did when he saw her for the last time in that dreadful place, but as she used when he loved her — long, long ago, before misery and ill-treatment had altered her looks, and vice had changed his nature, and she is leaning upon his arm, and looking up into his face with tenderness and affection – and he does *not* strike her now, nor rudely shake her from him. And oh! how glad he is to tell her all he had forgotten in that last hurried interview, and to fall on his knees before her and fervently beseech her pardon for all the unkindness and cruelty that wasted her form and broke her heart! The scene suddenly changes. He is on his trial again: there are the judge and jury, and prosecutors, and witnesses, just as they were before. How full the court is – what a sea of heads – with a gallows, too, and a scaffold – and how all those people stare at *him*! Verdict, 'Guilty.' No matter; he will escape.

The night is dark and cold, the gates have been left open, and in an instant he is in the street, flying from the scene of his imprisonment like the wind. The streets are cleared, the open fields are gained and the broad wide country lies before him. Onward he dashes in the midst of darkness, over hedge and ditch, through mud and pool, bounding from spot to spot with a speed and lightness, astonishing even to himself. At length he pauses: he must be safe from pursuit now; he will stretch himself on that bank and sleep till sunrise.

A period of unconsciousness succeeds. He wakes cold and wretched; the dull gray light of morning is stealing into the cell, and falls upon the form of the attendant turnkey. Confused by his dreams, he starts from his uneasy bed in momentary uncertainty. It is but momentary. Every object in that narrow cell is too frightfully real to admit of doubt or mistake. He is the condemned felon again, guilty and despairing; and in two hours more he is a corpse.

CHARACTERS

Thoughts about People

CHAPTER I

Thoughts about People

'TIS strange, with how little notice, good, bad, or indifferent, a man may live and die in London. He awakens no sympathy in the breast of any single person; his existence is a matter of interest to no one save himself, and he cannot be said to be forgotten when he dies, for no one remembered him when he was alive. There is a very numerous class of people in this great metropolis who seem not to possess a single friend, and whom nobody appears to care for. Urged by imperative necessity in the first instance, they have resorted to London in search of employment, and the means of subsistence. It is hard, we know, to break the ties which bind us to our homes and friends, and harder still to efface the thousand recollections of happy days and old times, which have been slumbering in our bosoms for years, and only rush upon the mind to bring before it, with startling reality, associations connected with the friends we have left, the scenes we have beheld too probably for the last time, and the hopes we once cherished, but may entertain no more. These men, however, happily for themselves, have long since forgotten such thoughts. Old country friends have died or emigrated; former correspondents have become lost, like themselves, in the crowd and turmoil of some busy city, and they have gradually settled down into mere passive creatures of habit and endurance.

We were seated in the enclosure of St James's Park[1] the other day, when our attention was attracted by a man whom we immediately put down in our own mind as one of this class. He was a tall, thin, pale person, in a black coat, scanty gray trousers, little pinched-up gaiters, and brown beaver gloves. He had an umbrella in his hand – not for use, for the day was fine – but evidently because he always carried one to the office in the morning; and he walked up and down before the little patch of grass on which the chairs are placed for hire, not as if he were doing it for pleasure or recreation, but as if it were a matter of compulsion, just as he would walk to the office every morning from the back settlements of Islington. It was Monday: he had escaped for four-and-twenty hours from the thraldom of the desk, and was walking here for exercise and amusement — perhaps for the first time in his life. We were inclined to think he had never had a holiday before, and that even now he did not know what to do with himself. Children were playing on the grass; groups of people were loitering about, chatting and laughing, but the man walked steadily up and down, unheeding and unheeded, his spare pale face looking as if it were incapable of bearing the expression of curiosity or interest.

There was something in the man's manner and appearance which told us, we fancied, his whole life, or rather his whole day, for a man of this sort has no variety. We almost saw the dingy little back office into which he walks every morning, hanging his hat on the same peg, and placing his legs beneath the same desk: first taking off that black coat which lasts the year through, and putting on the one which did duty last year, and which he keeps in his desk to save the other. There he sits till five o'clock, working on all day as regularly as the dial over the mantelpiece, whose loud ticking is as monotonous as his whole existence, only raising his head when some one enters the counting-house, or when, in the midst of some difficult calculation, he looks up to the ceiling as if there were inspiration in the dusty skylight with a green knot in the centre of every pane of glass. About five, or half-past, he slowly dismounts from his accustomed stool, and again changing his coat, proceeds to his usual dining-place, somewhere near Bucklersbury.[2] The waiter recites the bill of fare in a rather confidential manner — for he is a regular customer — and after inquiring 'What's in the best cut?' and 'What was up last?' he orders a small plate of roast beef, with greens, and half-a-pint of porter. He has a small plate to-day, because greens are a penny more than potatoes, and he had 'two breads' yesterday, with the additional enormity of 'a cheese' the day before. This important point being settled, he hangs up his hat — he took it off the moment he sat down — and bespeaks the paper after the next gentleman. If he can get it while he is at dinner, he appears to eat with much greater zest; balancing it against the water-bottle, and eating a bit of beef, and reading a line or two, alternately. Exactly at five minutes before the hour is up, he produces a shilling, pays the reckoning, carefully deposits the change in his waistcoat-pocket (first deducting a penny for the waiter), and returns to the office, from which, if it is not foreign post night, he again sallies forth in about half an hour. He then walks home, at his usual pace, to his little back room at Islington, where he has his tea; perhaps solacing himself during the meal with the conversation of his landlady's little boy, whom he occasionally rewards with a penny, for solving problems in simple addition. Sometimes there is a letter or two to take up to his employer's, in Russell-square;[3] and then the wealthy man of business, hearing his voice calls out from the dining-parlour, – 'Come in, Mr Smith:' and Mr Smith, putting his hat at the feet of one of the hall chairs, walks timidly in, and being condescendingly desired to sit down, carefully tucks his legs under his chair, and sits at a considerable distance from the table while he drinks the glass of sherry which is poured out for him by the eldest boy, and after drinking which, he backs and slides out of the room, in a state of nervous agitation from which he does not perfectly recover, until he finds himself once more in the Islington-road. Poor, harmless creatures these men are; contented but not happy; broken-spirited and humbled, they may feel no pain, but they never know pleasure.

Compare these men with another class of beings who, like them have neither friend nor companion, but whose position in society is the result of their own choice. These are generally old fellows with white heads and red faces, addicted to port wine and Hessian boots,[4] who from some cause, real or imaginary – generally the former, the excellent reason being that they are rich, and their relations poor – grow suspicious of every body, and do the misanthropical in chambers, taking great delight in thinking themselves unhappy, and making every body they come near, miserable. You may see such men as these any where; you will know them at coffee-houses by their discontented exclamations and the luxury of their dinners; at theatres, by their always sitting in the same place and looking with a jaundiced eye on all the young people near them; at church by the pomposity with which they enter, and the loud tone in which they repeat the responses; at parties, by their getting cross at whist and hating music. An old fellow of this kind will have his chambers splendidly furnished, and collect books, plate, and pictures about him in profusion; not so much for his own gratification as to annoy those who have the desire, but not the means, to compete with him. He belongs to two or three clubs, and is envied, and flattered, and hated by the members of them all. Sometimes he will be appealed to by a poor relation – a married nephew perhaps – for some little assistance and relief: and then he will declaim with honest indignation on the improvidence of young married people, the worthlessness of a wife, the insolence of having a family, the atrocity of getting into debt with a hundred and twenty-five pounds a-year, and other unpardonable crimes; winding up his exhortations with a complacent review of his own conduct, and a delicate allusion to parochial relief. He dies some day after dinner of apoplexy, having bequeathed his property to a Bible Society, and the Institution erects a tablet to his memory expressive of their admiration of his Christian conduct in this world, and their comfortable conviction of his happiness in the next.

But next to our very particular friends, hackney-coachmen, cabmen, and cads, whom we admire in proportion to the extent of their cool impudence and perfect self-possession, there is no class of people who amuse us more than London apprentices. They are no longer an organized body, bound down by solemn compact to terrify his majesty's subjects whenever it pleases them to take offence in their heads and staves in their hands. They are only bound now by indentures; and as to their valour, it is easily restrained by the wholesome dread of the New Police,[5] and a perspective view of a damp station-house, terminating in a police-office and a reprimand. They are still, however, a peculiar class, and not the less pleasant for being inoffensive. Can any one fail to have noticed them in the streets on Sunday? And were there ever such beautiful attempts at the grand and magnificent as they display in their own proper persons! We walked down the Strand a Sunday or two ago behind a little group; and they furnished food for our amusement the whole way. They had come out of some part of the city; it was between three and four o'clock in the afternoon, and they were on their way to the Park. There were four of them, all arm-in-arm, with white kid gloves like so many bridegrooms, light trousers of unprecedented patterns, and coats for which the English language has yet no name — a kind of cross between a great-coat and a surtout, with the collar of the one, the skirts of the other, and pockets peculiar to themselves.

Each of the gentlemen carried a thick stick with a large tassel at the top, which he occasionally twirled gracefully round, and the whole four, by way of looking easy and unconcerned, were walking with a sort of paralytic swagger irresistibly ludicrous. One of the party had got a watch about the size and shape of a Ribstone pippin,[6] jammed into his ˙waistcoat-pocket, which he carefully compared with the clocks at St Clement's and the New Church, the illuminated clock at Exeter 'Change, St Martin's Church, and the Horse Guards,[7] and when they at last arrived in Saint James's Park, the member of the party who had the best-made boots on, hired a second chair expressly for his feet, and flung himself on this two-pennyworth of sylvan luxury with an air which levelled all distinctions between Brookes's and Snooks's, Crockford's and Bagnigge Wells.[8]

We may smile at such people as these, but they can never excite our anger. They are usually on the best terms with themselves, and it follows almost as a matter of course, in good humour with every one about them. And if they do display a little occasional foolery in their own proper persons, it is surely more tolerable than the precocious puppyism of the Quadrant,[9] the whiskered dandyism of Regent-street and Pall-mall, or gallantry in its dotage any where.

CHAPTER 2

A Christmas Dinner

CHRISTMAS time! The man must be a misanthrope indeed, in whose breast something like a jovial feeling is not roused — in whose mind some pleasant associations are not awakened — by the recurrence of Christmas. There are people who will tell you that Christmas is not to them what it used to be: that each succeeding Christmas has found some cherished hope, or happy prospect, of the year before, dimmed or passed away, and that the present only serves to remind them of reduced circumstances and straitened incomes — of the feasts they once bestowed on hollow friends, and of the cold looks that meet them now, in adversity and misfortune. Never heed such dismal reminiscences. There are few men who have lived long enough in the world, who cannot call up such thoughts any day in the year. Then do not select the merriest of the three hundred and sixty-five, for your doleful recollections, but draw your chair nearer the blazing fire — fill the glass and send round the song — and if your room be smaller than it was a dozen years ago, or if your glass be filled with reeking punch, instead of sparkling wine, put a good face on the matter, and empty it off-hand, and fill another, and troll off the old ditty you used to sing, and thank God it's no worse. Look on the merry faces of your children as they sit round the fire. One little seat may be empty; one slight form that gladdened the father's heart, and roused the mother's pride to look upon, may not be there. Dwell not upon the past; think not that one short year ago, the fair child now resolving into dust, sat before you, with the bloom of health upon its cheek, and the gay unconsciousness of infancy in its joyous eye. Reflect upon your present blessings — of which every man has many — not on your past misfortunes, of which all men have some. Fill your glass again, with a merry face and contented heart. Our life on it, but your Christmas shall be merry, and your new year a happy one!

Who can be insensible to the outpourings of good feeling, and the honest interchange of affectionate attachment, which abound at this season of the year? A Christmas family-party! We know nothing in nature more delightful! There seems a magic in the very name of Christmas. Petty jealousies and discords are forgotten: social feelings are awakened in bosoms to which they have long been strangers: father and son, or brother and sister, who have met and passed with averted gaze, or a look of cold recognition, for months before, proffer and return the cordial embrace, and bury their past animosities in their present happiness. Kindly hearts that have yearned towards each other, but have been withheld by false notions of pride and self-dignity, are again reunited, and all is kindness and benevolence! Would that Christmas lasted the whole year through, and that the prejudices and passions which deform our better nature, were never called into action among those to whom they should ever be strangers!

The Christmas family-party that we mean, is not a mere assemblage of relations, got up at a week or two's notice, originating this year, having no family precedent in the last, and not likely to be repeated in the next. It is an annual gathering of all the accessible members of the family, young or old, rich or poor; and all the children look forward to it, for two months beforehand, in a fever of anticipation. Formerly it was held at grandpapa's; but grandpapa getting old, and grandmamma getting old too, and rather infirm, they have given up housekeeping, and domesticated themselves with uncle George; so the party always takes place at uncle George's house, but grandmamma sends in most of the good things, and grandpapa always *will* toddle down, all the way to Newgate-market, to buy the turkey, which he engages a porter to bring home behind him in triumph, always insisting on the man's being rewarded with a glass of spirits, over and above his hire, to drink 'a merry Christmas and a happy new year' to aunt George. As to grandmamma she is very secret and mysterious for two or three days beforehand, but not sufficiently so to prevent rumours getting afloat that she has purchased a beautiful new cap with pink ribbons for each of the servants, together with sundry books, and penknives, and pencil-cases for the younger branches; to say nothing of divers secret additions to the order originally given by aunt George at the pastry-cook's, such as another dozen of mince-pies for the dinner, and a large plum-cake for the children.

On Christmas-eve, grandmamma is always in excellent spirits, and after employing all the children, during the day, in stoning the plums and all that, insists regularly every year on uncle George coming down into the kitchen, taking off his coat, and stirring the pudding for half an hour or so, which uncle George good-humouredly does to the vociferous delight of the children and servants; and the evening concludes with a glorious game of blind-man's-buff, in an early stage of which grandpapa takes great care to be caught, in order that he may have an opportunity of displaying his dexterity.

On the following morning, the old couple, with as many of the children as the pew will hold, go to church in great state, leaving aunt George at home dusting decanters and filling castors, and uncle George carrying bottles into the dining-parlour, and calling for cork-screws, and getting into every body's way.

When the church-party return to lunch, grandpapa produces a small sprig of misletoe from his pocket, and tempts the boys to kiss their little cousins under it − a proceeding which affords both the boys and the old gentleman unlimited satisfaction, but which rather outrages grandmamma's ideas of decorum, until grandpapa says, that when he was just thirteen years and three months old, *he* kissed grandmamma under a misletoe too, on which the children clap their hands, and laugh very heartily, as do aunt George and uncle George; and grandmamma looks pleased, and says, with a benevolent smile, that grandpapa always was an impudent dog, on which the children laugh very heartily again, and grandpapa more heartily than any of them.

But all these diversions are nothing to the subsequent excitement when grandmamma in a high cap, and slate-coloured silk gown, and grandpapa with a beautifully plaited shirt-frill, and white neckerchief, seat themselves on one side of the drawing-room fire, with uncle George's children and little cousins innumerable, seated in the front, waiting the arrival of the anxiously-expected visiters. Suddenly a hackney-coach is heard to stop, and uncle George, who has been looking out of the window, exclaims 'Here's Jane!' on which the children rush to the door, and helter-skelter down stairs; and uncle Robert and aunt Jane, and the dear little baby, and the nurse, and the whole party, are ushered up stairs amidst tumultuous shouts of 'Oh, my!' from the children, and frequently-repeated warnings not to hurt baby from the nurse: and grandpapa takes the child, and grandmamma kisses her daughter, and the confusion of this first entry has scarcely subsided, when some other aunts and uncles with more cousins arrive, and the grown-up cousins flirt with each other, and so do the little cousins too, for that matter, and nothing is to be heard but a confused din of talking, laughing, and merriment.

A hesitating double knock at the street-door, heard during a momentary pause in the conversation, excites a general inquiry of 'Who's that?' and two or three children, who have been standing at the window, announce in a low voice, that it's 'poor aunt Margaret.' Upon which aunt George leaves the room to welcome the new comer, and grandmamma draws herself up rather stiff and stately, for Margaret married a poor man without her consent, and poverty not being a sufficiently weighty punishment for her offence, has been discarded by her friends, and debarred the society of her dearest relatives. But Christmas has come round, and the unkind feelings that have struggled against better dispositions during the year, have melted away before its genial influence, like half-formed ice beneath the morning sun. It is not difficult in a moment of angry feeling for a parent to denounce a disobedient child; but to banish her at a period of general good-will and hilarity, from the hearth round which she has sat on so many anniversaries of the same day, expanding by slow degrees from infancy to girlhood, and then bursting, almost imperceptibly, into the high-spirited and beautiful woman, is widely different. The air of conscious rectitude, and cold forgiveness, which the old lady has assumed, sits ill upon her; and when the poor girl is led in by her sister, pale in looks and broken in spirit – not from poverty, for that she could bear, but from the consciousness of undeserved neglect, and unmerited unkindness — it is easy to see how much of it is assumed. A momentary pause succeeds; the girl breaks suddenly from her sister and throws herself, sobbing, on her mother's neck. The father steps hastily forward, and grasps her husband's hand. Friends crowd round to offer their hearty congratulations, and happiness and harmony again prevail.

As to the dinner, it's perfectly delightful — nothing goes wrong, and every body is in the very best of spirits, and disposed to please and be pleased. Grandpapa relates a circumstantial account of the purchase of the turkey, with a slight digression relative to the purchase of previous turkeys, on former Christmas-days, which grandmamma corroborates in the minutest particular. Uncle George tells stories, and carves poultry, and takes wine, and jokes with the children at the side-table, and winks at the cousins that are making love, or being made love to, and exhilarates every body with his good humour and hospitality; and when at last a stout servant, staggers in with a gigantic pudding with a sprig of holly in the top, there is such a laughing, and shouting, and clapping of little chubby hands, and kicking up of fat dumpy legs, as can only be equalled by the applause with which the astonishing feat of pouring lighted brandy into mince pies, is received by the younger visiters. Then the dessert! — and the wine! — and the fun! Such beautiful speeches, and *such* songs, from aunt Margaret's husband, who turns out to be such a nice man, and *so* attentive to grandmamma! Even grandpapa not only sings his annual song with unprecedented vigour, but on being honoured with an unanimous *encore*, according to annual custom, actually comes out with a new one which nobody but grandmamma ever heard before: and a young scape-grace of a cousin, who has been in some disgrace with the old people, for certain heinous sins of omission and commission — neglecting to call, and persisting in drinking Burton ale[1] — astonishes every body into convulsions of laughter by volunteering the most extraordinary comic songs that were ever heard. And thus the evening passes, in a strain of rational good-will and cheerfulness, doing more to awaken the sympathies of every member of the party in behalf of his neighbour, and to perpetuate their good feeling during the ensuing year, than all the homilies that have ever been written, by all the Divines[2] that have ever lived.

CHAPTER 3

The New Year

NEXT to Christmas-day, the most pleasant annual epoch in existence is the advent of the New Year. There are a lachrymose set of people who usher in the New Year with watching and fasting, as if they were bound to attend as chief mourners at the obsequies of the old one. Now, we cannot but think it a great deal more complimentary, both to the old year that has rolled away, and to the New Year that is just beginning to dawn upon us, to see the old fellow out, and the new one in, with gaiety and glee.

There must have been some few occurrences in the past year to which we can look back with a smile of cheerful recollection, if not with a feeling of heartfelt thankfulness. And we are bound by every rule of justice and equity to give the New Year credit for being a good one, until he proves himself unworthy the confidence we repose in him.

This is our view of the matter; and entertaining it, notwithstanding our respect for the old year, one of the few remaining moments of whose existence passes away with every word we write, here we are, seated by our fireside on this last night of the old year, one thousand eight hundred and thirty-six,[1] penning this article with as jolly a face as if nothing extraordinary had happened, or was about to happen, to disturb our equanimity.

Hackney-coaches and carriages keep rattling up the street and down the street in rapid succession, conveying, doubtless, smartly-dressed coachfuls to crowded parties; loud and repeated double knocks at the house with green blinds, opposite, announce to the whole neighbourhood that there's one large party in the street at all events; and we saw through the window, and through the fog too, till it grew so thick that we rung for candles, and drew our curtains, pastrycooks' men with green boxes on their heads, and rout-furniture-warehouse-carts,[2] with cane seats and French lamps,[3] hurrying to the numerous houses where an annual festival is held in honour of the occasion.

We can fancy one of these parties, we think as well as if we were duly dress-coated and pumped, and had just been announced at the drawing-room door.

Take the house with green blinds for instance. We know it is a quadrille party,[4] because we saw a man taking up the front drawing-room carpet while we sat at breakfast this morning, and if further evidence be required, and we must tell the truth, we just now saw one of the young ladies 'doing' another of the young ladies' hair, near one of the bedroom windows, in an unusual style of splendour, which nothing else but a quadrille party could possibly justify.

The master of the house with the green blinds is in a public office; we know the fact by the cut of his coat, the tie of his neck-cloth, and the self-satisfaction of his gait – the very green blinds themselves have a Somerset-House[5] air about them.

Hark! – a cab! That's a junior clerk in the same office; a tidy sort of young man, with a tendency to cold and corns, who comes in a pair of boots with black cloth fronts, and brings his shoes in his coat-pocket, which shoes he is at this very moment putting on in the hall. Now he is announced by the man in the passage to another man in a blue coat, who is a disguised messenger from the office.

The man on the first landing precedes him to the drawing-room door. 'Mr Tupple!' shouts the messenger. 'How *are* you, Tupple?' says the master of the house, advancing from the fire, before which he has been talking politics and airing himself. 'My dear, this is Mr Tupple (a courteous salute from the lady of the house); Tupple, my eldest daughter; Julia, my dear, Mr Tupple; Tupple, my other daughters, my son, sir;' Tupple rubs his hands very hard, and smiles as if it were all capital fun, and keeps constantly bowing and turning himself round till the whole family have been introduced, when he glides into a chair at the corner of the sofa, and opens a miscellaneous conversation with the young ladies upon the weather, and the theatres, and the old year, and the last new murder, and the balloon, and the ladies' sleeves, and the festivities of the season, and a great many other topics of small talk beside.

More double knocks! what an extensive party; what an incessant hum of conversation and general sipping of coffee! We see Tupple now, in our mind's eye, in the very height of his glory. He has just handed that stout old lady's cup to the servant, and now he dives among the crowd of young men by the door, to intercept the other servant, and secure the muffin-plate for the old lady's daughter, before he leaves the room; and as he passes the sofa on his way back, he bestows a glance of recognition and patronage upon the young ladies, as condescending and familiar as if he had known them from their infancy.

Charming person that Mr Tupple – perfect ladies' man – such a delightful companion, too. Laugh! – nobody ever understood papa's jokes half so well as Mr Tupple, who laughs himself into convulsions at every fresh burst of facetiousness. Most delightful partner! talks through the whole set; and although he does seem at first rather gay and frivolous, so romantic and with so *much* feeling! Quite a love. No great favourite with the young men, certainly, who sneer at, and affect to despise him; but every body knows that's only envy, and they needn't give themselves the trouble to depreciate his merits at any rate, for Ma says he shall be asked to every future dinner-party, if it's only to talk to people between the courses, and to distract their attention when there's any unexpected delay in the kitchen.

At supper, Mr Tupple shows to still greater advantage than he has done throughout the evening, and when Pa requests every one to fill their glasses for the purpose of drinking happiness throughout the year, Mr Tupple is *so* droll, insisting on all the young ladies having their glasses filled, notwithstanding their repeated assurances that they never can, by any possibility, think of emptying them:

and subsequently begging permission to say a few words on the sentiment which has just been uttered by Pa, when he makes one of the most brilliant and poetical speeches that can possibly be imagined, about the old year and the new one. After the toast has been drunk, and when the ladies have retired, Mr Tupple requests that every gentleman will do him the favour of filling his glass, for he has a toast to propose: on which all the gentlemen cry 'Hear! hear!' and pass the decanters accordingly: and Mr Tupple being informed by the master of the house that they are all charged, and waiting for his toast, rises, and begs to remind the gentlemen present, how much they have been delighted by the dazzling array of elegance and beauty which the drawing-room has exhibited that night, and how their senses have been charmed, and their hearts captivated, by the bewitching concentration of female loveliness which that very room has so recently displayed. (Loud cries of 'Hear!') Much as he (Tupple) would be disposed to deplore the absence of the ladies, on other grounds, he cannot but derive some consolation from the reflection that the very circumstance of their not being present, enables him to propose a toast, which he would have otherwise been prevented from giving – that toast he begs to say is – 'The Ladies!' (Great applause). The Ladies! among whom the fascinating daughters of their excellent host, are alike conspicuous for their beauty, their accomplishments, and their elegance. He begs them to drain a bumper to 'The Ladies, and a happy new year to them!' (Prolonged approbation; above which the noise of the ladies dancing the Spanish dance among themselves, over head, is distinctly audible.)

The applause consequent on this toast has scarcely subsided, when a young gentleman in a pink under-waistcoat, sitting towards the bottom of the table, is observed to grow very restless and fidgety, and to evince strong indications of some latent desire to give vent to his feelings in a speech, which the wary Tupple at once perceiving, determines to forestal by speaking himself. He, therefore, rises again with an air of solemn importance, and trusts he may be permitted to propose another toast (unqualified approbation, and Mr Tupple proceeds); he is sure they must all be deeply impressed with the hospitality – he may say the splendour – with which they have been that night received by their worthy host and hostess. (Unbounded applause.) Although this is the first occasion on which he has had the pleasure and delight of sitting at that board, he has known his friend Dobble long and intimately; he has been connected with him in business – he wishes every body present knew Dobble as well as he does. (A cough from the host.) He (Tupple) can lay his hand upon his (Tupple's) heart, and declare his confident belief that a better man, a better husband, a better father, a better brother, a better son, a better relation in any relation of life, than Dobble, never existed. (Loud cries of 'Hear!') They have seen him to night in the peaceful bosom of his family: they should see him in the morning, in the trying duties of his office. Calm in the perusal of the morning papers, uncompromising in the signature of his name, dignified in his replies to the inquiries of stranger applicants, deferential in his behaviour to his superiors, majestic in his deportment to the messengers. (Cheers.) When he bears this merited testimony to the excellent qualities of his friend Dobble, what can he say in approaching such a subject as Mrs Dobble? Is it requisite for him to expatiate on the qualities of that amiable woman? No; he will spare his friend Dobble's feelings; he will spare the feelings of his friend – if he will allow him to have the honour of calling him so – Mr Dobble, junior. (Here Mr Dobble, junior, who has been previously distending his mouth to a considerable width, by thrusting a particularly fine orange into that feature, suspends operations, and assumes a proper appearance of intense melancholy.) He will simply say – and he is quite certain it is a sentiment in which all who hear him will readily concur – that his friend Dobble is as superior to any man he ever knew, as Mrs Dobble is far beyond any woman he ever saw (except her daughters), and he will conclude by proposing their worthy 'Host and Hostess, and may they live to enjoy many more new years!'

The toast is drunk with acclamation; Dobble returns thanks, and the whole party rejoin the ladies in the drawing-room. Young men who were too bashful to dance before supper, find tongues and partners; the musicians exhibit unequivocal symptoms of having drunk the new year in, while the company were out; and dancing is kept up until far in the first morning of the new year.

We have scarcely written the last word of the previous sentence, when the first stroke of twelve, peals from the neighbouring churches. There is something awful in the sound. Strictly speaking it may not be more impressive now, than at any other time, for the hours steal as swiftly on at other periods, and their flight is little heeded. But we measure man's life by years, and it is a solemn knell that warns us we have passed another of the landmarks which stand between us and the grave; disguise it as we may, the reflection will force itself on our minds, that when the next bell announces the arrival of a new year, we may be insensible alike of the timely warning we have so often neglected, and of all the warm feelings that glow within us now.

CHAPTER 4

Miss Evans and the Eagle

MR SAMUEL WILKINS was a carpenter, a journeyman carpenter of small dimensions; decidedly below the middle size – bordering, perhaps, upon the dwarfish. His face was round and shining and his hair carefully twisted into the outer corner of each eye, till it formed a variety of that description of semi-curls, usually known as 'haggerawators.' His earnings were all-sufficient for his wants, varying from eighteen shillings to one pound five, weekly: his manner undeniable – his sabbath waistcoats dazzling. No wonder that, with these qualifications, Samuel Wilkins found favour in the eyes of the other sex: many women have been captivated by far less substantial qualifications. But Samuel was proof against their blandishments, until at length his eyes rested on those of a Being for whom, from that time forth, he felt fate had destined him. He

George Cruikshank

Jemima Evans

came, and conquered[1] – proposed, and was accepted – loved, and was beloved. Mr Wilkins 'kept company' with Jemima Evans.

Miss Evans (or Ivins, to adopt the pronunciation most in vogue with her circle of acquaintance) had adopted in early life the harmless pursuit of shoe-binding, to which she had afterwards supperadded the occupation of a straw-bonnet maker. Herself, her maternal parent, and two sisters, formed an harmonious quartett in the most secluded portion of Camden-town; and here it was that Mr Wilkins presented himself one Monday afternoon in his best attire, with his face more shining and his waistcoat more bright than either had ever appeared before. The family were just going to tea, and were *so* glad to see him. It was quite a little feast; two ounces of seven-and-sixpenny green, and a quarter of a pound of the best fresh;[2] and Mr Wilkins had brought a pint of shrimps, neatly folded up in a clean belcher, to give a zest to the meal, and propitiate Mrs Ivins. Jemima was 'cleaning herself' up stairs; so Mr Samuel Wilkins sat down and talked domestic economy with Mrs Ivins, whilst the two youngest Miss Ivinses poked bits of lighted brown paper between the bars under the kettle, to make the water boil for tea.

'I vos a thinking,' said Mr Samuel Wilkins, during a pause in the conversation – 'I vos a thinking of taking J'mima to the Eagle[3] to night.' – 'O my!' exclaimed Mrs Ivins. 'Lor! how nice!' said the youngest Miss Ivins. 'Well, I declare!' added the youngest Miss Ivins but one. 'Tell J'mima to put on her white muslin, Tilly,' screamed Mrs Ivins, with motherly anxiety; and down came J'mima herself soon afterwards in a white muslin gown carefully hooked and eyed, and little red shawl, plentifully pinned, and white straw bonnet trimmed with red ribbons, and a small necklace, and large pair of bracelets, and Denmark satin shoes, and open-worked stockings, white cotton gloves on her fingers, and a cambric pocket-handkerchief, carefully folded up, in her hand – all quite genteel and ladylike. And away went Miss Jemima Ivins and Mr Samuel Wilkins, and a dress cane, with a gilt knob at the top, to the admiration and envy of the street in general, and to the high gratification of Mrs Ivins, and the two youngest Miss Ivinses in particular. They had no sooner turned into the Pancras road,[4] than who should Miss J'mima Ivins stumble upon by the most fortunate accident in the world but a young lady as she knew, with *her* young man; and it is so strange how things do turn out sometimes – they were actually going to the Eagle too. So Mr Samuel Wilkins was introduced to Miss J'mima Ivins's friend's young man, and they all walked on together, talking, and laughing, and joking away like any thing; and when they got as far as Pentonville, Miss Ivins's friend's young man *would* have the ladies go into the Crown, to taste some shrub, which, after a great blushing and giggling, and hiding of faces in elaborate pocket-handkerchiefs, they consented to do. Having tasted it once, they were easily prevailed upon to taste it again; and they sat out in the garden tasting shrub and looking at the Busses alternately, till it was just the proper time to go to the Eagle; and then they resumed their journey, and walked very fast, for fear they should lose the beginning of the concert in the rotunda.[5]

'How ev'nly!' said Miss Jemima Ivins, and Miss Jemima Ivins's friend, both at once, when they had passed the gate and were fairly inside the gardens. There were the walks beautifully gravelled and planted, and the refreshment-boxes painted and ornamented like so many snuff-boxes, and the variegated lamps shedding their rich light upon the company's heads, and the place for dancing ready chalked for the company's feet, and a Moorish band playing at one end of the gardens, and an opposition military band playing away at the other. Then the waiters were rushing to and fro with glasses of negus, and glasses of brandy-and-water, and bottles of ale, and bottles of stout; and ginger-beer was going off in one place, and practical jokes going on in another; and people were crowding to the door of the Rotunda; and in short the whole scene was, as Miss J'mima Ivins, inspired by the novelty, or the shrub, or both, observed – 'one of dazzling excitement.' As to the concert-room, never was any thing half so splendid. There was an orchestra for the singers, all paint, gilding, and plate-glass; and such an organ! Miss J'mima Ivins's friend's young man whispered it had cost 'four hundred pound,' which Mr Samuel Wilkins said was 'not dear neither;' an opinion in which the ladies perfectly coincided. The audience were seated on elevated benches round the room, and crowded into every part of it, and every body was eating and drinking as comfortably as possible. Just before the concert commenced, Mr Samuel Wilkins ordered two glasses of rum-and-water 'warm with —' and two slices of lemon, for himself and the other young man, together with 'a pint o' sherry wine for the ladies, and some sweet carrawayseed biscuits;' and they would have been quite comfortable and happy, only one gentleman with large whiskers *would* stare at Miss J'mima Ivins, and another gentleman in a plaid waistcoat *would* wink at Miss J'mima Ivins's friend on which Miss J'mima Ivins's friend's young man exhibited symptoms of boiling over, and began to mutter about 'people's imperence,' and 'swells out o.' luck;' and to intimate, in oblique terms, a vague intention of knocking somebody's head off; which he was only prevented from announcing more emphatically, by both Miss J'mima Ivins and her friend threatening to faint away on the spot if he said another word.

The concert commenced — overture on the organ. 'How solemn!' exclaimed Miss J'mima Ivins, glancing, perhaps unconsciously, at the gentleman with the whiskers. Mr Samuel Wilkins, who had been muttering apart for some time past, as if he were holding a confidential conversation with the gilt knob of the dress cane, breathed very hard — breathing vengeance, perhaps, — but said nothing. 'The soldier tired,' Miss Somebody in white satin.[6] 'Ancore!' cried Miss J'mima Ivins's friend. 'Ancore!' shouted the gentleman in the plaid waistcoat immediately, hammering the table with a stout-bottle. Miss J'mima Ivins's friend's young man eyed the man behind the waistcoat from head to foot, and cast a look of interrogative contempt towards Mr Samuel Wilkins. Comic song, accompanied on the organ. Miss J'mima Ivins was convulsed with laughter — so was the man with the whiskers. Every thing the ladies did, the plaid waistcoast and whiskers did, by way of expressing a unity of sentiment and congeniality of soul; and Miss J'mima Ivins, and Miss J'mima Ivins's friend, grew lively and talkative, as Mr Samuel Wilkins, and Miss J'mima Ivins's friend's young man, grew morose and surly in inverse proportion.

Now, if the matter had ended here, the little party might soon have recovered their former equanimity, but Mr Samuel Wilkins and his friend began to throw looks of defiance upon the waistcoat and whiskers. And the waistcoat and whiskers, by way of intimating the slight degree in which they were affected by the looks aforesaid, bestowed glances of increased admiration upon Miss J'mima Ivins and friend. The concert and vaudeville concluded, they promenaded the gardens. The waistcoat and whiskers did the same; and made divers remarks complimentary to the ankles of Miss J'mima Ivins and friend in an audible tone. At length, not satisfied with these numerous atrocities, they actually came up and asked Miss J'mima Ivins, and Miss J'mima Ivins's friend to dance, without taking no more notice of Mr Samuel Wilkins, and Miss J'mima Ivins's friend's young man, than if they was nobody!

'What do you mean by that, scoundrel?' exclaimed Mr Samuel Wilkins, grasping the gilt-knobbed dress cane firmly in his right hand. 'What's the matter with *you*, you little humbug?' replied the whiskers. 'How dare you insult me and my friend?' inquired the friend's young man. 'You and your friend be hanged,' responded the waistcoat. 'Take that,' exclaimed Mr Samuel Wilkins. The ferrule of the gilt-knobbed dress-cane was visible for an instant, and then the light of the variegated lamps shone brightly upon it as it whirled into the air, cane and all. 'Give it him,' said the waistcoast. 'Horficer!' screamed the ladies. It was too late. Miss J'mima Ivins's beau and the friend's young man, lay gasping on the gravel, and the waistcoat and whiskers were seen no more.

Miss J'mima Ivins and friend being conscious that the affray was in no slight degree attributable to themselves, of course went into hysterics forthwith; declared themselves the most injured of women, exclaimed, in incoherent ravings, that they had been suspected — wrongfully suspected — oh! that they should ever have lived to see the day, and so forth; suffered a relapse every time they opened their eyes and saw their unfortunate little admirers; and were carried to their respective abodes in a hackney-coach, and a state of insensibility, compounded of shrub, sherry, and excitement.

CHAPTER 5

The Parlour Orator

WE had been lounging one evening, down Oxford-street, Holborn, Cheapside, Coleman-street, Finsbury-square, and so on, with the intention of returning by Pentonville and the New-road,[1] when we began to feel rather thirsty, and disposed to rest for five or ten minutes. So, we turned back towards an old, quiet, decent public-house, which we remembered to have passed but a moment before (it was not far from the City-road), for the purpose of solacing ourself with a glass of ale. The house was none of your stuccoed, French-polished, illuminated palaces, but a modest public-house of the old school, with a little old bar, and a little old landlord, who, with a wife and daughter of the same pattern, was comfortably seated in the bar aforesaid – a snug little room with a cheerful fire, protected by a large screen, from behind which the young lady emerged on our representing our inclination for a glass of ale.

'Won't you walk into the parlour, sir?' said the young lady, in seductive tones.

'You had better walk into the parlour, sir,' said the little old landlord, throwing his chair back, and looking round one side of the screen, to survey our appearance.

'You had much better step into the parlour, sir,' said the little old lady, popping out her head, on the other side of the screen.

We cast a slight glance around, as if to express our ignorance of the locality so much recommended. The little old landlord observed it; bustled out of the small door of the small bar; and forthwith ushered us into the parlour itself.

It was an ancient, dark-looking room, with oaken wainscoting, a sanded floor, and a high mantelpiece. The walls were ornamented with three or four old coloured prints in black frames, each print representing a naval engagement, with a couple of men-of-war banging away at each other most vigorously, while another vessel or two were blowing up in the distance, and the foreground presented a miscellaneous collection of broken masts and blue legs sticking up out of the water. Depending from the ceiling in the centre of the room, were a gas-light and bell-pull; and on each side were three or four long narrow tables, behind which was a thickly-planted row of those slippy, shiny-looking wooden chairs, peculiar to places of this description. The monotonous appearance of the sanded boards was relieved by an occasional spittoon; and a triangular pile of those useful articles adorned the two upper corners of the apartment.

At the furthest table, nearest the fire, with his face towards the door at the bottom of the room, sat a stoutish man of about forty, whose short, stiff, black hair curled closely round a broad high forehead, and a face to which something besides water and exercise had communicated a rather inflamed appearance. He was smoking a cigar, with his eyes fixed on the ceiling, and had that confident oracular air which marked him as the leading politician, general authority, and universal anecdote-relater of the place. He had evidently just delivered himself of something very weighty; for the remainder of the company were puffing at their respective pipes and cigars in a kind of solemn abstraction, as if quite overwhelmed with the magnitude of the subject recently under discussion.

On his right hand sat an elderly gentleman with a white head, and broad-brimmed brown hat; and on his left, a sharp-nosed light-haired man in a brown surtout reaching nearly to his heels, who took a whiff at his pipe, and an admiring glance at the red-faced man, alternately.

'Very extraordinary!' said the light-haired man after a pause of five minutes. A murmur of assent ran through the company.

'Not at all extraordinary — not at all,' said the red-faced man, awakening suddenly from his reverie, and turning upon the light-haired man, the moment he had spoken.

'Why should it be extraordinary? — why is it extraordinary? prove it to be extraordinary!'

'Oh, if you come to that —' said the light-haired man.

'Come to that!' ejaculated the man with the red face; 'but we *must* come to that. We stand, in these times, upon a calm elevation of intellectual attainment, and not in the dark recess of mental deprivation. Proof is what I require — proof, and not assertions, in these stirring times. Every gen'lem'n that knows me, knows what was the nature and effect of my observations, when it was in the contemplation of the Old-street Suburban Representative Discovery Society, to recommend a candidate for that place in Cornwall there — I forget the name of it. "Mr Snobee," said Mr Wilson, "is a fit and proper person to represent the borough in Parliament." "Prove it," says I. "He is a friend to Reform," says Mr Wilson. "Prove it," says I. "The abolitionist of the national debt, the unflinching opponent of pensions, the uncompromising advocate of the negro, the reducer of sinecures and the duration of Parliaments; the extender of nothing but the suffrages of the people," says Mr Wilson. "Prove it," says I. "His acts prove it," says he. "Prove *them*," says I.

'And he could not prove them,' said the red-faced man, looking round triumphantly; 'and the borough didn't have him; and if you carried this principle to the full extent, you'd have no debt, no pensions, no sinecures, no negroes, no nothing. And then, standing upon an elevation of intellectual attainment, and having reached the summit of popular prosperity, you might bid defiance to the nations of the earth, and erect yourselves in the proud confidence of wisdom and superiority. This is my argument — this always has been my argument — and if I was a Member of the House of Commons to-morrow I'd make 'em shake in their shoes with it.' And the red-faced man having struck the table very hard with his clenched fist, by way of adding weight to the declaration, smoked away like a brewery.

'Well!' said the sharp-nosed man, in a very slow and soft voice, addressing the company in general, 'I always do say, that of all the gentlemen I have the pleasure of meeting in this room, there is not one whose conversation I like to hear so much as Mr Rogers's or who is such improving company.'

'Improving company!' said Mr Rogers, for that was the name of the red-faced man. 'You may say I am improving company, for I've improved you all to some purpose, though as to my conversation being as my friend Mr Ellis here describes it, that is not for me to say any thing about. You, gentlemen, are the best judges on that point; but this I will say, when I came into this parish, and first used this room, ten years ago, I don't believe there was one man in it; who knew he was a slave, and now you all know it, and writhe under it. Inscribe that upon my tomb, and I am satisfied.'

'Why, as to inscribing it on your tomb,' said a little greengrocer with a rather chubby face, 'of course you can have any thing chalked up, as you likes to pay for, so far as it relates to yourself and your affairs, but when you come to talk about slaves, and that there abuse, you'd better keep it in the family, 'cos I for one don't like to be called them names night after night.'

'You *are* a slave,' said the red-faced man, 'and the most pitiable of all slaves.'

'Werry hard if I am,' interrupted the greengrocer, 'for I got no good out of the twenty million that was paid for 'mancipation,[2] any how.'

'A willing slave,' ejaculated the red-faced man, getting more red with eloquence, and contradiction – 'resigning the dearest birthright of your children – neglecting the sacred call of Liberty – who, standing imploringly before you, appeals to the warmest feelings of your heart, and points to your helpless infants but in vain.'

'Prove it,' said the greengrocer.

'Prove it!' sneered the man with the red-face. 'What! bending beneath the yoke of an insolent and factious oligarchy; bowed down by the domination of cruel laws; groaning beneath tyranny and oppression on every hand, at every side, and in every corner. Prove it! –' The red-faced man abruptly broke off, sneered melodramatically, and buried his countenance and his indignation together, in a pint pot.

'Ah, to be sure, Mr Rogers,' said a stout broker in a large

waistcoat, who had kept his eyes fixed on this luminary all the time he was speaking. 'Ah, to be sure,' said the broker with a sigh, 'that's the point.'

'Of course, of course,' said divers members of the company who understood almost as much about the matter as the broker himself.

'You had better let him alone, Tommy,' said the broker, by way of advice to the little greengrocer, 'he can tell what's o'clock by an eight-day,[3] without looking at the minute hand, he can. Try it on, on some other suit; it won't do with him, Tommy.'

'What is a man?' continued the red-faced specimen of the species, jerking his hat indignantly, from its peg on the wall. 'What is an Englishman? Is he to be trampled upon by every oppressor? Is he to be knocked down at every body's bidding? What's freedom? Not a standing army. What's a standing army? Not freedom. What's general happiness? Not universal misery. Liberty ain't the window-tax,[4] is it? The Lords ain't the Commons, are they?' And the red-faced man, gradually bursting into a radiating sentence, in which such adjectives as 'dastardly,' 'oppressive,' 'violent,' and 'sanguinary,' formed the most conspicuous words, knocked his hat indignantly over his eyes, left the room, and slammed the door after him.

'Wonderful man!' said he of the sharp nose.

'Splendid speaker!' added the broker.

'Great power!' said every body but the greengrocer. And as they said it, the whole party shook their heads mysteriously, and one by one retired, leaving us alone in the old parlour.

If we had followed the established precedent in all such instances, we should have fallen into a fit of musing, without delay. The ancient appearance of the room – the old panelling of the wall – the chimney blackened with smoke and age – would have carried us back a hundred years at least, and we should have gone dreaming on, until the pewter-pot on the table, or the little beer-chiller[5] on the fire, had started into life, and addressed to us a long story of days gone by. But by some means or other, we were not in a romantic humour; and although we tried very hard to invest the furniture with vitality, it remained perfectly unmoved, obstinate and sullen. Being thus reduced to the unpleasant necessity of musing about ordinary matters, our thoughts reverted to the red-faced man, and his oratorical display.

A numerous race are these red-faced men; there is not a parlour, or club-room, or benefit society, or humble party of any kind, without its red-faced man. Weak-pated dolts they are, and a great deal of mischief they do to their cause, however good. So, just to hold a pattern one up, to know the others by, we took his likeness at once, and put him in here. And that is the reason why we have written this paper.

CHAPTER 6

The Hospital Patient

IN our rambles through the streets of London after evening has set in, we often pause beneath the windows of some public hospital, and picture to ourself the gloomy and mournful scenes that are passing within. The sudden moving of a taper as its feeble ray shoots from window after window, until its light gradually disappears, as if it were carried further back into the room to the bedside of some suffering patient, is enough to awaken a whole crowd of reflections; the mere glimmering of the low-burning lamps, which, when all other habitations are wrapped in darkness and slumber, denote the chamber where so many forms are writhing with pain, or wasting with disease, is sufficient to check the most boisterous merriment.

Who can tell the anguish of those weary hours, when the only sound the sick man hears, is the disjointed wanderings of some feverish slumberer near him, the low moan of pain, or perhaps the muttered, long-forgotten prayer of a dying man? Who but those who have felt it, can imagine the sense of loneliness and desolation

A Pickpocket in Custody

which must be the portion of those who in the hour of dangerous illness are left to be tended by strangers; for what hands, be they ever so gentle, can wipe the clammy brow, or smooth the restless bed, like those of mother, wife, or child?

Impressed with these thoughts, we have turned away, through the nearly-deserted streets; and the sight of the few miserable creatures still hovering about them, has not tended to lessen the pain which such meditations awaken. The hospital is a refuge and resting-place for hundreds, who but for such institutions must die in the streets and doorways; but what can be the feelings of outcasts like these, when they are stretched on the bed of sickness with scarcely a hope of recovery? The wretched woman who lingers about the pavement, hours after midnight, and the miserable shadow of a man — the ghastly remnant that want and drunkenness have left — which crouches beneath a window-ledge, to sleep where there is some shelter from the rain, have little to bind them to life, but what have they to look back upon, in death? What are the unwonted comforts of a roof and a bed to them, when the recollections of a whole life of debasement stalk before them; when repentance seems a mockery, and sorrow comes too late?

About a twelvemonth ago, as we were strolling through Covent-garden (we had been thinking about these things overnight) we were attracted by the very prepossessing appearance of a pickpocket, who having declined to take the trouble of walking to the Police-office, on the ground that he hadn't the slightest wish to go there at all, was being conveyed thither in a wheelbarrow, to the huge delight of a crowd, but apparently not very much to his own gratification.

Somehow we never can resist joining a crowd, so we turned back with the mob, and entered the office, in company with our friend the pickpocket, a couple of policemen, and as many dirty-faced spectators as could squeeze their way in.

There was a powerful, ill-looking young fellow at the bar, who was undergoing an examination, on the very common charge of having, on the previous night, ill-treated a woman, with whom he lived in some court hard by. Several witnesses bore testimony to acts of the grossest brutality; and a certificate was read from the house-surgeon of a neighbouring hospital, describing the nature of the injuries the woman had received, and intimating that her recovery was extremely doubtful.

Some question appeared to have been raised about the identity of the prisoner; for when it was agreed that the two magistrates should visit the hospital at eight o'clock that evening, to take her deposition, it was settled that the man should be taken there also. He turned deadly pale at this, and we saw him clench the bar very hard when the order was given. He was removed directly afterwards, and he spoke not a word.

We felt an irrepressible curiosity to witness this interview, although it is hard to tell why, at this instant, for we knew it must be a painful one. It was no very difficult matter for us to gain permission, and we obtained it.

The prisoner, and the officer who had him in custody, were already at the hospital when we reached it, and waiting the arrival of the magistrates in a small room below stairs. The man was handcuffed, and his hat was pulled forward over his eyes. It was easy to see, though, by the livid whiteness of his countenance, and the constant twitching of the muscles of his face, that he dreaded what was to come. After a short interval, the magistrates and clerk were bowed in by the house-surgeon and a couple of young men who smelt very strong of tobacco-smoke – they were introduced as 'dressers' – and after one magistrate had complained bitterly of the cold, and the other of the absence of any news in the evening paper, it was announced that the patient was prepared: and we were conducted to the 'casualty ward' in which she was lying.

The dim light which burnt in the spacious room, increased rather than diminished the ghastly appearance of the hapless creatures in the beds, which were ranged in two long rows on either side. In one bed lay a child enveloped in bandages, with its body half consumed by fire; in another, a female, rendered hideous by some dreadful accident, was wildly beating her clenched fists on the coverlet, in an agony of pain; on a third, there lay stretched a young girl, apparently in that heavy stupor so often the immediate precursor of death: her face was stained with blood, and her breast and arms were bound up in folds of linen. Two or three of the beds were empty, and their recent occupants were sitting beside them, but with faces so wan, and eyes so bright and glassy, that it was fearful to meet their gaze. On every face was stamped the expression of anguish and suffering.

The object of the visit was lying at the upper end of the room. She was a fine young woman of about two or three and twenty. Her long black hair had been hastily cut from about the wounds on her head, and streamed over the pillow in jagged and matted locks. Her face bore frightful marks of the ill-usage she had received: her hand was pressed upon her side, as if her chief pain were there; her breathing was short and heavy; and it was plain to see that she was dying fast. She murmured a few words in reply to the magistrate's inquiry whether she was in great pain; and having been raised on the pillow by the nurse, looked vacantly upon the strange countenances that surrounded her bed. The magistrate nodded to the officer, to bring the man forward. He did so, and stationed him at the bedside. The girl looked on, with a wild and troubled expression of face; but her sight was dim, and she did not know him.

'Take off his hat,' said the magistrate. The officer did as he was desired, and the man's features were fully disclosed.

The girl started up, with an energy quite preternatural; the fire gleamed in her heavy eyes, and the blood rushed to her pale and sunken cheeks. It was a convulsive effort. She fell back upon her pillow, and covering her scarred and bruised face with her hands, burst into tears. The man cast an anxious look towards her, but otherwise appeared wholly unmoved. After a brief pause the nature of their errand was explained, and the oath tendered.

'Oh, no, gentlemen,' said the girl, raising herself once more, and folding her hands together; 'no, gentlemen, for God's sake! I did it myself – it was nobody's fault – it was an accident. He didn't hurt me; he wouldn't for all the world. Jack, dear Jack, you know you wouldn't.'

Her sight was fast failing her, and her hand groped over the bedclothes in search of his. Brute as the man was, he was not prepared for this. He turned his face from the bed, and sobbed aloud. The girl's colour changed, and her breathing grew more difficult. She was evidently dying.

'We respect the feelings which prompt you to this,' said the gentleman who had spoken first, 'but let me warn you, not to persist in what you know to be untrue, until it is too late. It cannot save him.'

'Jack,' murmured the girl, laying her hand upon his arm, 'they shall not persuade me to swear your life away.' He didn't do it, gentlemen. He never hurt me.' She grasped his arm tightly, and added, in a broken whisper, 'I hope God Almighty will forgive me all the wrong I have done, and the life I have led. God bless you, Jack. Some kind gentleman take my love to my poor old father. Five years ago, he said he wished I had died a child. Oh, I wish I had! I wish I had!'

The nurse bent over the girl for a few seconds, and then drew the sheet over her face. It covered a corpse.

CHAPTER 7

Misplaced Attachment of Mr John Dounce

IF we had to make a classification of society, there are a particular kind of men whom we should immediately set down under the head of 'Old Boys;' and a column of most extensive dimensions the old boys would require. To what precise causes the rapid advance of old boy population is to be traced we are unable to determine; it would be an interesting and curious speculation, but as we have not sufficient space to devote to it here, we simply state the fact that the numbers of the old boys have been gradually augmenting within the last few years, and that they are at this moment alarmingly on the increase.

Mr John Dounce

Upon a general review of the subject, and without considering it minutely in detail, we should be disposed to subdivide the old boys into two distinct classes — the gay old boys and the steady old boys. The gay old boys, are paunchy old men in the disguise of young ones, who frequent the Quadrant and Regent-street in the day-time; the theatres (especially theatres under lady management) at night, and who assume all the foppishness and levity of boys, without the excuse of youth or inexperience. The steady old boys are certain stout old gentlemen of clean appearance, who are always to be seen in the same taverns, at the same hours every evening, smoking and drinking in the same company.

There was once a fine collection of old boys to be seen round the circular table at Offley's[1] every night, between the hours of half-past eight and half-past eleven. We have lost sight of them for some time. There were, and may be still for aught we know, two splendid specimens in full blossom at the Rainbow Tavern in Fleet-street,[2] who always used to sit in the box nearest the fireplace, and smoked long cherry-stick pipes which went under the table, with the bowls resting upon the floor. Grand old boys they were — fat, red-faced, white-headed old fellows; always there — one on one side the table, and the other opposite — puffing and drinking away in great state; every body knew them, and it was supposed by some people that they were both immortal.

Mr John Dounce was an old boy of the latter class (we don't mean immortal, but steady) — a retired glove and braces maker, a widower, resident with three daughters — all grown up, and all unmarried — in Cursitor-street,[3] Chancery-lane. He was a short, round, large-faced, tubbish sort of man, with a broad-brimmed hat, and a square coat; and had that grave, but confident, kind of roll, peculiar to old boys in general. Regular as clock-work — breakfast at nine — dress and tittivate a little — down to the Sir Somebody's Head — glass of ale and the paper — come back again, and take the daughters out for a walk — dinner at three — glass of grog and a pipe — nap — tea — little walk — Sir Somebody's Head again — capital house! — delightful evenings! There were Mr Harris the law-stationer, and Mr Jennings, the robe-maker (two jolly young fellows like himself), and Jones, the barrister's clerk – rum fellow that Jones – capital company – full of anecdote! and there they sat every night till just ten minutes before twelve, drinking their brandy-and-water, and smoking their pipes, and telling stories, and enjoying themselves, with a kind of solemn joviality particularly edifying.

Sometimes Jones would propose a half-price visit to Drury Lane or Covent Garden, to see two acts of a five-act play, and a new farce, perhaps, or a ballet, on which occasions the whole four of them went together; none of your hurrying and nonsense, but having their brandy-and-water first, comfortably, and ordering a steak and some oysters for their supper against they came back, and then walking coolly into the pit, when the 'rush' had gone in, as all sensible people do, and did when Mr Dounce was a young man, except when the celebrated Master Betty⁴ was at the height of his popularity, and then, sir, – then Mr Dounce perfectly well remembered getting a holiday from business, and going to the pit doors at eleven o'clock in the forenoon, and waiting there till six in the afternoon, with some sandwiches in a pocket-handkerchief and some wine in a phial, and fainting after all, with the heat and fatigue before the play began; in which situation he was lifted out of the pit into one of the dress boxes, sir, by five of the finest women of that day, sir, who compassionated his situation and administered restoratives, and sent a black servant, six foot high, in blue and silver livery, next morning with their compliments, and to know how he found himself, sir – by G—! Between the acts Mr Dounce and Mr Harris, and Mr Jennings used to stand up, and look round the house, and Jones – knowing fellow that Jones – knew every body – pointed out the fashionable and celebrated lady So-and-So in the boxes, at the mention of whose name Mr Dounce, after brushing up his hair, and adjusting his neckhandkerchief, would inspect the aforesaid lady So-and-So through an immense glass, and remark either that she was a 'fine woman – very fine woman, indeed,' or that 'there might be a little more of her, – eh, Jones?' just as the case might happen to be. When the dancing began, John Dounce, and the other old boys, were particularly anxious to see what was going forward on the stage, and Jones – wicked dog that Jones – whispered little critical remarks into the ears of John Dounce, which John Dounce retailed to Mr Harris and Mr Harris to Mr Jennings, and then they all four laughed till the tears ran down, out of their eyes.

When the curtain fell, they walked back together, two and two, to the steaks and oysters, and when they came to the second glass of brandy-and-water, Jones – hoaxing scamp, that Jones – used to recount how he had observed a lady in white feathers in one of the pit boxes, gazing intently on Mr Dounce all the evening, and how he had caught Mr Dounce, whenever he thought no one was looking at him, bestowing ardent looks of intense devotion on the lady in return; on which Mr Harris and Mr Jennings used to laugh very heartily, and John Dounce more heartily than either of them, acknowledging, however, that the time *had* been when he *might* have done such things; upon which Mr Jones used to poke him in the ribs, and tell him he had been a sad dog in his time, which John Dounce, with chuckles confessed. And after Mr Harris and Mr Jennings had preferred their claims to the character of having been sad dogs too, they separated harmoniously, and trotted home.

The decrees of Fate, and the means by which they are brought about, are mysterious and inscrutable. John Dounce had led this life for twenty years and upwards, without wish for change, or care for variety, when his whole social system was suddenly upset, and turned completely topsy-turvy – not by an earthquake, or some other dreadful convulsion of nature, as the reader would be inclined to suppose, but by the simple agency of an oyster; and thus it happened:

Mr John Dounce was returning one night from the Sir Some-body's Head, to his residence in Cursitor-street – not tipsy, but rather excited, for it was Mr Jennings's birthday, and they had had a brace of partridges for supper, and a brace of extra glasses afterwards, and Jones had been more than ordinarily amusing – when his eyes rested on a newly-opened oyster-shop, on a magnificent scale, with natives laid one deep in circular marble basins in the windows, together with little round barrels of oysters directed to Lords and Baronets, and Colonels and Captains, in every part of the habitable globe.

Behind the natives were the barrels, and behind the barrels was a young lady of about five-and-twenty, all in blue, and all alone – splendid creature, charming face, and lovely figure! It is difficult to say whether Mr John Dounce's red countenance, illuminated as it was by the flickering gas-light in the window before which he paused, excited the lady's risibility, or whether a natural exuberance of animal spirits proved too much for that staidness of demeanour which the forms of society rather dictatorially prescribe. But certain it is, that the lady smiled, then put her finger upon her lip, with a striking recollection of what was due to herself: and finally retired, in oyster-like bashfulness, to the very back of the counter. The sad-dog sort of feeling came strongly upon John Dounce: he lingered – the lady in blue made no sign. He coughed – still she came not. He entered the shop.

'Can you open me an oyster, my dear?' said Mr John Dounce.

'Dare say I can, sir,' replied the lady in blue, with enchanting playfulness. And Mr John Dounce eat one oyster, and then looked at the young lady, and then eat another, and then squeezed the young lady's hand as she was opening the third, and so forth, until he had devoured a dozen of those at eightpence in less than no time.

'Can you open me half-a-dozen more, my dear?' inquired Mr John Dounce.

'I'll see what I can do for you, sir,' replied the young lady in blue, even more bewitchingly than before; and Mr John Dounce eat half-a-dozen more of those at eightpence, and his gallantry increased.

'You couldn't manage to get me a glass of brandy-and-water, my dear, I suppose?' said Mr John Dounce, when he had finished the oysters, in a tone which clearly implied his supposition that she could.

'I'll see, sir,' said the young lady: and away she ran out of the shop, and down the street, her long auburn ringlets shaking in the wind in the most enchanting manner; and back she came again, tripping over the coal-cellar lids like a whipping-top, with a tumbler of brandy-and-water, which Mr John Dounce insisted on her taking a share of, as it was regular ladies' grog — hot, strong, sweet, and plenty of it.

So the young lady sat down with Mr John Dounce in a little red box with a green curtain, and took a small sip of the brandy-and-water, and a small look at Mr John Dounce, and then turned her head away, and went through various other serio-pantomimic fascinations, which forcibly reminded Mr John Dounce of the first time he courted his first wife, and which made him feel more affectionate than ever; in pursuance of which affection, and actuated by which feeling, Mr John Dounce sounded the young lady on her matrimonial engagements, when the young lady denied having formed any such engagements at all — she couldn't abear the men, they were such deceivers; thereupon Mr John Dounce inquired whether this sweeping condemnation was meant to include other than very young men; on which the young lady blushed deeply — at least she turned away her head, and said Mr John Dounce had made her blush, so of course she *did* blush — and Mr John Dounce was a long time drinking the brandy-and-water; and the young lady said 'Ha' done, sir,' very often;[5] and at last John Dounce went home to bed, and dreamt of his first wife, and his second wife, and the young lady, and partridges, and oysters, and brandy-and-water, and disinterested attachments.

The next morning, John Dounce was rather feverish with the extra brandy-and-water of the previous night; and partly in the hope of cooling himself with an oyster, and partly with the view of ascertaining whether he owed the young lady any thing, or not, went back to the oyster-shop. If the young lady had appeared beautiful by night, she was perfectly irresistible by day; and from this time forward a change came over the spirit of John Dounce's dream. He bought shirt-pins; wore a ring on his third finger; read poetry; bribed a cheap miniature-painter to perpetrate a faint resemblance to a youthful face, with a curtain over his head, six large books in the background, and an open country in the distance (this he called his portrait): 'went on' altogether in such an uproarious manner, that the three Miss Dounces went off on small pensions, he having made the tenement in Cursitor-street too warm to contain them; and in short, comported and demeaned himself in every respect like an unmitigated old Saracen, as he was.

As to his ancient friends, the other old boys, at the Sir Somebody's Head, he dropped off from them by gradual degrees; for even when he did go there, Jones — vulgar fellow that Jones — persisted in asking 'when it was to be?' and 'whether he was to have any gloves?'[6] together with other inquiries of an equally offensive nature, at which not only Harris laughed, but Jennings also; so he cut the two altogether, and attached himself solely to the blue young lady at the smart oyster-shop.

Now comes the moral of the story — for it has a moral after all. The lastmentioned young lady, having derived sufficient profit and emolument from John Dounce's attachment, not only refused when matters came to a crisis to take him for better for worse, but expressly declared, to use her own forcible words, that she 'wouldn't have him at no price;' and John Dounce, having lost his old friends, alienated his relations, and rendered himself ridiculous to every body, made offers successively to a schoolmistress, a landlady, a feminine tobacconist, and a housekeeper; and being directly rejected by each and every of them, was accepted by his cook, with whom he now lives, a henpecked husband, a melancholy monument of antiquated misery, and a living warning to all uxorious old boys.

CHAPTER 8

The Mistaken Milliner

A Tale of Ambition

MISS AMELIA MARTIN was pale, tallish, thin, and two-and-thirty
– what ill-natured people would call plain, and police reports
interesting. She was a milliner and dressmaker, living on her
business and not above it. If you had been a young lady in service,
and wanted Miss Martin, as a great many young ladies in service
did, you would just have stepped up, in the evening, to number
forty-seven, Drummond-street, George-street, Euston-square,[1] and
after casting your eye on a brass door-plate one foot ten by one
and a half, ornamented with a great brass knob at each of the four
corners, and bearing the inscription – 'Miss Martin; millinery and
dressmaking, in all its branches;' you'd just have knocked two loud
knocks at the street-door; and down would have come Miss Martin
herself, in a merino gown of the newest fashion, black velvet
bracelets on the genteelest principle, and other little elegances of
the most approved description.

If Miss Martin knew the young lady who called, or if the young
lady who called, had been recommended by any other young lady
whom Miss Martin knew, Miss Martin would forthwith show her
upstairs into the two-pair front, and chat she would – *so* kind, and
so comfortable – it really wasn't like a matter of business, she was
so friendly; and then Miss Martin, after contemplating the figure
and general appearance of the young lady in service with great
apparent admiration, would say how well she would look, to-be-
sure, in a low dress with short sleeves, made very full in the skirts,
with four tucks in the bottom, to which the young lady in service
would reply in terms expressive of her entire concurrence in the
notion, and the virtuous indignation with which she reflected on
the tyranny of 'Missis,' who wouldn't allow a young girl to wear a
short sleeve of an arternoon – no, nor nothing smart, not even a

pair of earrings; let alone hiding people's heads of hair under them frightful caps; at the termination of which complaint, Miss Amelia Martin would distantly suggest certain dark suspicions that some people were jealous on account of their own daughters, and were obliged to keep their servants' charms under, for fear they should get married first, which was no uncommon circumstance – least-ways she had known two or three young ladies in service, who had married a great deal better than their missises, and *they* were not very good-looking either; and then the young lady would inform Miss Martin, in confidence, that how one of their young ladies was engaged to a young man and was a-going to be married, and Missis was so proud about it there was no bearing her; but she needn't hold her head quite so high neither, for, after all, he was only a clerk. And, after expressing a due contempt for clerks in general, and the engaged clerk in particular, and the highest opinion possible of themselves and each other, Miss Martin and the young lady in service would bid each other good night in a friendly but perfectly genteel manner: and the one went back to her 'place,' and the other, to her room on the second-floor front.

There is no saying how long Miss Amelia Martin might have continued this course of life; how extensive a connexion she might have established among young ladies in service; or what amount her demands upon their quarterly receipts might have ultimately attained, had not an unforeseen train of circumstances directed her thoughts to a sphere of action very different from dressmaking or millinery.

A friend of Miss Martin's who had long been keeping company with an ornamental painter and decorator's journeyman, at last consented (on being at last asked to do so) to name the day which would make the aforesaid journeyman a happy husband. It was a Monday that was appointed for the celebration of the nuptials, and Miss Amelia Martin was invited, among others, to honour the wedding-dinner with her presence. It was a charming party; Somers-town² the locality, and a front parlour the apartment. The ornamental painter and decorator's journeyman, had taken a house – no lodgings nor vulgarity of that kind, but a house – four beautiful rooms, and a delightful little washhouse at the end of the passage, which was the most convenient thing in the world, for the bridesmaids could sit in the front parlour and receive the company, and then run into the little washhouse and see how the pudding and boiled pork were getting on in the copper, and then pop back into the parlour again, as snug and comfortable as possible. And such a parlour as it was too! beautiful Kidderminster! carpet[3] – six brannew cane-bottomed stained chairs – three wine-glasses and a tumbler on each sideboard – a farmer's girl and a farmer's boy on the mantelpiece: one tumbling over a stile, and the other spitting himself, on the handle of a pitchfork – long white dimity curtains in the window – and, in short, every thing on the most genteel scale imaginable.

Then the dinner. There was baked leg of mutton at the top, a boiled leg of mutton at the bottom, a pair of fowls and leg of pork in the middle; porter pots at the corners; pepper, mustard, and vinegar in the centre; vegetables on the floor; and plum-pudding and apple-pie and tartlets without number; to say nothing of cheese, and celery, and water-cresses, and all that sort of thing. As to the company! Miss Amelia Martin herself declared, on a subsequent occasion, that much as she had heard of the ornamental painter's journeyman's connexion, she never could have supposed it was half so genteel. There was his father, such a funny old gentleman – and his mother, such a dear old lady – and his sister, such a charming girl – and his brother, such a manly-looking young man – with such a eye! But even all these were as nothing when compared with his musical friends Mr and Mrs Jennings Rodolph, from White Conduit,[4] with whom the ornamental painter's journeyman had been fortunate enough to contract an intimacy while engaged in decorating the concert-room of that noble institution. To hear them sing separately, was perfectly divine, but when they went through the tragic duet of 'Red Ruffian, retire!'[5] it was, as Miss Martin afterwards remarked, 'thrilling.' And why (as Mr Jennings Rodolph observed) – why were they not engaged at one of the patent theatres?[6] If he was to be told that their voices were not powerful enough to fill the

House, his only reply was, that he would back himself for any amount to fill Russell-square – a statement in which the company, after hearing the duet, expressed their full belief; so they all said it was shameful treatment; and both Mr and Mrs Jennings Rodolph said it was shameful too, and Mr Jennings Rodolph looked very serious, and said he knew who his malignant opponents were, but they had better take care how far they went, for if they irritated him too much he had not quite made up his mind whether he wouldn't bring the subject before Parliament; and they all agreed that it "ud serve 'em quite right, and it was very proper that such people should be made an example of.' So Mr Jennings Rodolph said he'd think of it.

When the conversation resumed its former tone, Mr Jennings Rodolph claimed his right to call upon a lady, and the right being conceded, trusted Miss Martin would favour the company – a proposal which met with unanimous approbation, whereupon Miss Martin after sundry hesitatings and coughings with a preparatory choke or two, and an introductory declaration that she was frightened to death to attempt it before such great judges of the art, commenced a species of treble chirruping containing constant allusions to some young gentleman of the name of Hen-e-ry, with an occasional reference to madness and damaged hearts. Mr Jennings Rodolph, frequently interrupted the progress of the song, by ejaculating 'Beautiful!' – 'Charming!' – 'Brilliant!' – 'Oh! splendid,' &c.; and at its close the admiration of himself, and his lady, knew no bounds.

'Did you ever hear so sweet a voice, my dear?' inquired Mr Jennings Rodolph of Mrs Jennings Rodolph.

'Never; indeed I never did, love;' replied Mrs Jennings Rodolph.

'Don't you think Miss Martin with a little cultivation, would be very like Signora Marro Boni,[7] my dear?' asked Mr Jennings Rodolph.

'Just exactly the very thing that struck me, my love,' answered Mrs Jennings Rodolph.

And thus the time passed away; Mr Jennings Rodolph played tunes on a walkingstick, and then went behind the parlour-door and gave his celebrated imitations of actors, edge-tools, and animals; Miss Martin sang several other songs with increased admiration every time, and even the funny old gentleman began singing; his song had properly seven verses, but as he couldn't recollect more than the first one he sang that over seven times, apparently very much to his own personal gratification. And then all the company sang the national anthem with national independence – each for himself, without reference to the other – and finally separated, all declaring that they never had spent so pleasant an evening, and Miss Martin inwardly resolving to adopt the advice of Mr Jennings Rodolph, and to 'come out' without delay.

Now, 'coming out,' either in acting, or singing, or society, or facetiousness, or any thing else, is all very well, and remarkably pleasant to the individual principally concerned, if he or she can but manage to come out with a burst, and being out, to keep out, and not go in again; but it does unfortunately happen that both consummations are extremely difficult to accomplish, and that the difficulties of getting out at all in the first instance, and if you surmount them, of keeping out in the second, are pretty much on a par, and no slight ones either – and so Miss Amelia Martin shortly discovered. It is a singular fact (there being ladies in the case) that Miss Amelia Martin's principal foible was vanity, and the leading characteristic of Mrs Jennings Rodolph an attachment to dress. Dismal wailings were heard to issue from the second-floor front, of number forty-seven, Drummond-street, George-street, Euston-square; it was Miss Martin practising. Half-suppressed murmurs disturbed the calm dignity of the White Conduit orchestra at the commencement of the season. It was the appearance of Mrs Jennings Rodolph in full dress, that occasioned them. Miss Martin studied incessantly – the practising was the consequence. Mrs Jennings Rodolph taught gratuitously now and then – the dresses were the result.

Weeks passed away; the White Conduit season had begun, had progressed, and was more than half over. The dressmaking business had fallen off from neglect; and its profits had dwindled away almost imperceptibly. A benefit-night approached; Mr Jennings

Rodolph yielded to the earnest solicitations of Miss Amelia Martin, and introduced her personally to the 'comic gentleman' whose benefit it was. The comic gentleman was all smiles and blandness — he had composed a duet expressly for the occasion, and Miss Martin should sing it with him. The night arrived; there was an immense room — ninety-seven sixpenn'orths of gin-and-water, thirty-two small glasses of brandy-and-water, five-and-twenty bottled ales, and forty-one neguses; and the ornamental painter's journeyman with his wife and a select circle of acquaintance were seated at one of the side-tables near the orchestra. The concert began. Song — sentimental — by a light-haired young gentleman in a blue coat, and bright basket buttons [applause]. Another song, doubtful, by another gentleman in another blue coat and more bright basket buttons — [increased applause]. Duet, Mr Jennings Rodolph, and Mrs Jennings Rodolph, 'Red Ruffian, retire!' — [great applause.] Solo, Miss Julia Montague (positively on this occasion only) — 'I am a Friar'[8] — [enthusiasm]. Original duet, comic — Mr H. Taplin (the comic gentleman) and Miss Martin — 'The Time of Day.'[9] — 'Brayvo! — Brayvo!' cried the ornamental painter's journeyman's party as Miss Martin was gracefully led in by the comic gentleman. 'Go to work, Harry,' cried the comic gentleman's personal friends. 'Tap — tap — tap,' went the leader's bow on the music-desk. The symphony began, and was soon afterwards followed by a faint kind of ventriloquial chirping, proceeding apparently from the deepest recesses of the interior of Miss Amelia Martin — 'Sing out' — shouted one gentleman in a white great-coat. 'Don't be afraid to put the steam on, old gal,' exclaimed another. 'S — s — s — s — s — s — s' — went the five-and-twenty bottled ales. 'Shame, shame!' remonstrated the ornamental painter's journeyman's party — 'S — s — s — s' went the bottled ales again, accompanied by all the gins and a majority of the brandies.

'Turn them geese out,' cried the ornamental painter's journeyman's party, with great indignation.

'Sing out,' whispered Mr Jennings Rodolph.

'So I do,' responded Miss Amelia Martin.

'Sing louder,' said Mrs Jennings Rodolph.

'I can't,' replied Miss Amelia Martin.

'Off, off, off,' cried the rest of the audience.

'Bray-vo!' shouted the painter's party. It wouldn't do – Miss Amelia Martin left the orchestra with much less ceremony than she had entered it; and as she couldn't sing out, never came out. The general goodhumour was not restored until Mr Jennings Rodolph had become purple in the face, by imitating divers quadrupeds for half an hour without being able to render himself audible; and to this day, neither has Miss Amelia Martin's good humour been restored, nor the dresses made for and presented to Mrs Jennings Rodolph, nor the vocal abilities which Mr Jennings Rodolph once staked his professional reputation that Miss Martin possessed.

CHAPTER 9

The Dancing Academy

OF all the dancing academies that ever were established, there never was one more popular in its immediate vicinity than Signor Billsmethi's, of the 'King's Theatre.'¹ It was not in Spring-gardens, or Newman-street, or Berners-street, or Gower-street, or Charlotte-street, or Percy-street, or any other of the numerous streets which have been devoted time out of mind to professional people, dispensaries, and boarding-houses; it was not in the West-end at all – it rather approximated to the eastern portion of London, being situated in the populous and improving neighbourhood of Gray's-inn-lane. It was not a dear dancing-academy – four-and-sixpence a quarter is decidedly cheap upon the whole. It was *very* select, the number of pupils being strictly limited to seventy-five, and a quarter's payment in advance being rigidly exacted. There was public tuition and private tuition – an assembly-room and a parlour. Signor Billsmethi's family were

SIGNOR
BILLSMETHI'S
GRAND
BALL
will take place
on
The first of March

george Cruikshank

The Dancing Academy

always thrown in with the parlour, and included in parlour price; that is to say a private pupil had Signor Billsmethi's parlour to dance *in*, and Signor Billsmethi's family to dance *with*; and when he had been sufficiently broken in in the parlour he began to run in couples in the Assembly-room.

Such was the dancing academy of Signor Billsmethi when Mr Augustus Cooper, of Fetter-lane, first saw an unstamped advertisement[2] walking leisurely down Holborn-hill, announcing to the world that Signor Billsmethi, of the King's Theatre, intended opening for the season with a Grand Ball.

Now, Mr Augustus Cooper was in the oil and colour line — just of age, with a little money, a little business, and a little mother, who, having managed her husband and *his* business in his lifetime took to managing her son and *his* business after his decease; and so, somehow or other, he had been cooped up in the little back parlour behind the shop on week-days, and in a little deal box without a lid (called by courtesy a pew) at Bethel Chapel,[3] on Sundays, and had seen no more of the world than if he had been an infant all his days; whereas Young White, at the Gas-fitter's over the way, three years younger than him, had been flaring away like winkin' — going to the theatre — supping at harmonic meetings — eating oysters by the barrel — drinking stout by the gallon — even stopping out all night, and coming home as cool in the morning as if nothing had happened. So Mr Augustus Cooper made up his mind that he would not stand it any longer, and had that very morning expressed to his mother a firm determination to be 'blowed,' in the event of his not being instantly provided with a street-door key. And he was walking down Holborn-hill thinking about all these things, and wondering how he could manage to get introduced into genteel society for the first time, when his eyes rested on Signor Billsmethi's announcement, which it immediately struck him was just the very thing he wanted; for he should not only be able to select a genteel circle of acquaintance at once out of the five-and-seventy pupils at four-and-sixpence a quarter, but should qualify himself at the same time to go through a hornpipe in private society, with perfect ease to himself, and great delight to his friends. So he stopped the unstamped advertisement – an animated sandwich, composed of a boy between two boards – and having procured a very small card with the Signor's address indented thereon, walked straight at once to the Signor's house – and very fast he walked too, for fear the list should be filled up, and the five-and-seventy completed before he got there. The Signor was at home, and, what was still more gratifying, he was an Englishman! Such a nice man – and so polite! The list was not full, but it was a most extraordinary circumstance that there was only just one vacancy, and even that one would have been filled up that very morning, only Signor Billsmethi was dissatisfied with the reference, and being very much afraid that the lady wasn't select, wouldn't take her.

'And very much delighted I am, Mr Cooper,' said Signor Billsmethi, 'that I did *not* take her. I assure you, Mr Cooper – I don't say it to flatter you, for I know you're above it – that I consider myself extremely fortunate in having a gentleman of your manners and appearance, sir.'

'I am very glad of it too, sir,' said Augustus Cooper.

'And I hope we shall be better acquainted, sir,' said Signor Billsmethi.

'And I'm sure I hope we shall too, sir,' responded Augustus Cooper. Just then the door opened, and in came a young lady with her hair curled in a crop all over her head, and her shoes tied in sandals all over her legs.

'Don't run away, my dear,' said Signor Billsmethi; for the young lady didn't know Mr Cooper was there when she ran in, and was going to run out again in her modesty, all in confusion-like. 'Don't run away, my dear,' said Signor Billsmethi, 'this is Mr Cooper – Mr Cooper, of Fetter-lane. Mr Cooper, my daughter, sir – Miss Billsmethi, sir, who I hope will have the pleasure of dancing many a quadrille, minuet, gavotte, country-dance, fandango, double-hornpipe, and faringolkajingo with you, sir. She dances them all, sir; and so shall you sir before you're a quarter older sir.'

And Signor Billsmethi slapped Mr Augustus Cooper on the back as if he had known him a dozen years, – so friendly; and Mr Cooper bowed to the young lady, and the young lady curtseyed to him, and Signor Billsmethi said they were as handsome a pair as ever he'd wish to see; upon which the young lady exclaimed, 'Lor, pa!' and blushed as red as Mr Cooper himself – you might have thought they were both standing under a red lamp at a chemist's shop; and before Mr Cooper went away it was settled that he should join the family circle that very night – taking them just as they were – no ceremony nor nonsense of that kind – and learn his positions, in order that he might lose no time and be able to come out at the forthcoming ball.

Well; Mr Augustus Cooper went away to one of the cheap shoemakers' shops in Holborn, where gentlemen's dress-pumps are seven-and-sixpence, and men's strong walking, just nothing at all, and bought a pair of the regular seven-and-sixpenny, long-quartered, town-mades, in which he astonished himself quite as much as his mother, and sallied forth to Signor Billsmethi's. There were four other private pupils in the parlour: two ladies and two gentlemen. Such nice people! Not a bit of pride about them. One of the ladies in particular, who was in training for a Columbine,[4] was remarkably affable, and she and Miss Billsmethi took such an interest in Mr Augustus Cooper, and joked and smiled, and looked so bewitching, that he got quite at home and learnt his steps in no time. After the practising was over, Signor Billsmethi, and Miss Billsmethi, and Master Billsmethi, and a young lady, and the two ladies, and the two gentlemen, danced a quadrille – none of your slipping and sliding about but regular warm work, flying into corners, and diving among chairs, and shooting out at the door, – something like dancing! Signor Billsmethi in particular, notwithstanding his having a little fiddle to play all the time, was out on the landing every figure, and Master Billsmethi, when every body else was breathless, danced a hornpipe with a cane in his hand, and a cheese-plate on his head, to the unqualified admiration of the whole company. Then Signor Billsmethi insisted as they were so happy, that they should all stay to supper, and proposed sending Master Billsmethi for the beer and spirits, whereupon the two gentlemen swore, 'strike 'em wulgar if they'd stand that;' and they were just going to quarrel who should pay for it, when Mr Augustus Cooper said he would, if they'd have the kindness to allow him – and they *had* the kindness to allow him; and Master

Billsmethi brought the beer in a can, and the rum in a quart-pot. They had a regular night of it; and Miss Billsmethi squeezed Mr Augustus Cooper's hand under the table; and Mr Augustus Cooper returned the squeeze and returned home too, at something to six o'clock in the morning when he was put to bed by main force by the apprentice, after repeatedly expressing an uncontrollable desire to pitch his reverend parent out of the second-floor window, and to throttle the apprentice with his own neck-handkerchief.

Weeks had worn on, and the seven-and-sixpenny town-mades had nearly worn out, when the night arrived for the grand dress-ball at which the whole of the five-and-seventy pupils were to meet together for the first time that season, and to take out some portion of their respective four-and-sixpences in lamp-oil and fiddlers. Mr Augustus Cooper had ordered a new coat for the occasion – a two-pound-tenner from Turnstile.[5] It was his first appearance in public; and after a grand Sicilian shawl-dance by fourteen young ladies in character, he was to open the quadrille department with Miss Billsmethi herself, with whom he had become quite intimate since his first introduction. It *was* a night! Every thing was admirably arranged. The sandwich-boy took the hats and bonnets at the street-door; there was a turn-up bedstead in the back parlour, on which Miss Billsmethi made tea and coffee for such of the gentlemen as chose to pay for it, and such of the ladies as the gentlemen treated; red port-wine negus and lemonade were handed round at eighteen-pence a head, and, in pursuance of a previous engagement with the public-house at the corner of the street, an extra potboy was laid on for the occasion. In short, nothing could exceed the arrangements, except the company. Such ladies! Such pink silk stockings! Such artificial flowers! Such a number of cabs! No sooner had one cab set down a couple of ladies, than another cab drove up and set down another couple of ladies, and they all knew, not only one another, but the majority of the gentlemen into the bargain, which made it all as pleasant and lively as could be. Signor Billsmethi in black tights, with a large blue bow in his buttonhole, introduced the ladies to such of the gentlemen as were strangers: and the ladies talked away – and laughed they did – it was delightful to see them.

As to the shawl-dance, it was the most exciting thing that ever was beheld; there was such a whisking, and rustling, and fanning, and getting ladies into a tangle with artificial flowers, and then disentangling them again; and as to Mr Augustus Cooper's share in the quadrille, he got through it admirably. He was missing from his partner now and then certainly, and discovered on such occasions to be either dancing with laudable perseverance in another set, or sliding about in perspective, apparently without any definite object; but, generally speaking, they managed to shove him through the figure, until he turned up in the right place. Be this as it may, when he had finished, a great many ladies and gentlemen came up and complimented him very much, and said they had never seen a beginner do any thing like it before; and Mr Augustus Cooper was perfectly satisfied with himself, and every body else into the bargain, and 'stood' considerable quantities of spirits and water, negus, and compounds, for the use and behoof of two or three dozen very particular friends, selected from the select circle of five-and-seventy pupils.

Now, whether it was the strength of the compounds, or the beauty of the ladies, or what not, it did so happen that Mr Augustus Cooper encouraged, rather than repelled, the very flattering attentions of a young lady in brown gauze over white calico who had appeared particularly struck with him from the first; and when the encouragements had been prolonged for some time, Miss Billsmethi betrayed her spite and jealousy thereat by calling the young lady in brown gauze a 'creeter,' which induced the young lady in brown gauze to retort in certain sentences containing a taunt founded on the payment of four-and-sixpence a quarter, and some indistinct reference to a 'fancy man;' which reference Mr Augustus Cooper, being then and there in a state of considerable bewilderment, expressed his entire concurrence in. Miss Billsmethi, thus renounced, forthwith began screaming in the loudest key of her voice at the rate of fourteen screams a minute; and being unsucessful, in an onslaught on the eyes and face, first of the lady in gauze and then of Mr Augustus Cooper, called distractedly on the other three-and-seventy pupils to furnish her with oxalic acid[6] for her own private drinking, and the call not being honoured, made another rush at Mr Cooper, and then had her stay-lace cut and was carried off to bed. Mr Augustus Cooper, not being remarkable for quickness of apprehension, was at a loss to understand what all this meant, till Signor Billsmethi explained it in a most satisfactory manner by stating to the pupils that Mr Augustus Cooper had made and confirmed divers promises of marriage to his daughter on divers occasions, and had now basely deserted her; on which the indignation of the pupils became universal and as several chivalrous gentlemen inquired rather pressingly of Mr Augustus Cooper, whether he required any thing for his own use, or, in other words, whether he 'wanted any thing for himself,' he deemed it prudent to make a precipitate retreat. And the upshot of the matter was, that a lawyer's letter came the next day, and an action was commenced next week; and that Mr Augustus Cooper, after walking twice to the Serpentine[7] for the purpose of drowning himself, and coming twice back without doing it, made a confidant of his mother who compromised the matter with twenty pounds from the till, which made twenty pounds four shillings and sixpence paid to Signor Billsmethi, exclusive of treats and pumps; and Mr Augustus Cooper went back and lived with his mother, and there he lives to this day; and as he has lost his ambition for society, and never goes into the world, he will never see this account of himself and will never be any the wiser.

CHAPTER 10

Shabby-genteel People

THERE are certain descriptions of people who, oddly enough, appear to appertain exclusively to this metropolis. You meet them every day in the streets of London, but no one ever encounters them elsewhere; they seem to be indigenous to the soil, and to belong as exclusively to London as its own smoke, or the dingy bricks and mortar. We could illustrate the remark by a variety of examples, but in our present sketch we will only advert to one class as a specimen — that class which is so aptly and expressively designated as 'shabby-genteel.'

Now shabby people, God knows, may be found any where, and genteel people are not articles of greater scarcity out of London than in it, but this compound of the two — this shabby-gentility — is as purely local as the statue at Charing-cross, or the pump at Aldgate.[1] It is worthy of remark too, that only men are shabby-genteel; a woman is always either dirty and slovenly in the extreme, or neat and respectable, however poverty-stricken in appearance. A very poor man, 'who has seen better days,' as the phrase goes, is a strange compound of dirty-slovenliness, and wretched attempts at a kind of faded smartness.

We will endeavour to explain our conception of the term which forms the title of this paper. If you meet a man lounging up Drury-lane, or leaning with his back against a post in Long-acre, with his hands in the pockets of a pair of drab trousers plentifully besprinkled with grease-spots: the trousers made very full over the boots, and ornamented with two cords down the outside of each leg — wearing also what has been a brown coat with bright buttons, and a hat very much pinched up at the sides, cocked over his right eye — don't pity him. He is not shabby-genteel. The 'harmonic meetings' at some fourth-rate public-house, or the purlieus of a private theatre, are his chosen haunts; he entertains a rooted antipathy to any kind of work, and is on familiar terms with several pantomime men at the large houses. But if you see hurrying along a by street, keeping as close as he can to the area-railings, a man of about forty or fifty clad in an old rusty suit of threadbare black cloth which shines with constant wear as if it had been beeswaxed, the trousers tightly strapped down, partly for the look of the thing and partly to keep his old shoes from slipping off at the heels, — if you observe too that his yellowish-white neckerchief is carefully pinned up, to conceal the tattered garment underneath, and that his hands are encased in the remains of an old pair of beaver gloves, you may set him down as a shabby-genteel man. A glance at that depressed face, and timorous air of conscious poverty, will make your heart ache — always supposing that you are neither a philosopher, nor a political economist.[2].

We were once haunted by a shabby-genteel man; he was bodily present to our senses all day, and he was in our mind's eye all night. The man of whom Sir Walter Scott speaks in his Demono-logy,[3] did not suffer half the persecution from his imaginary gentlemen-usher in black velvet, that we sustained from our friend in quondam black cloth. He first attracted our notice by sitting opposite to us in the reading-room at the British Museum,[4] and what made the man more remarkable was, that he had always got before him a couple of shabby-genteel books — two old dogseared folios, in mouldy worm-eaten covers, which had once been smart. He was in his chair every morning just as the clock struck ten; he was always the last to leave the room in the afternoon; and when he did, he quitted it with the air of a man who knew not where else to go for warmth and quiet. There he used to sit all day, as close to the table as possible in order to conceal the lack of buttons on his coat, with his old hat carefully deposited at his feet, where he evidently flattered himself it escaped observation.

About two o'clock you would see him munching a French roll or a penny loaf; not taking it boldly out of his pocket at once, like a man who knew he was only making a lunch, but breaking off little bits in his pocket, and eating them by stealth. He knew too well it was his dinner.

When we first saw this poor object, we thought it quite impossible that his attire could ever become worse. We even went so far as to speculate on the possibility of his shortly appearing in a decent second-hand suit. We knew nothing about the matter; he grew more and more shabby-genteel every day. The buttons dropped off his waistcoat one by one; then he buttoned his coat, and when one side of the coat was reduced to the same condition as the waistcoat, he buttoned it over on the other side. He looked somewhat better at the beginning of the week than at the conclusion, because the neckerchief, though yellow, was not quite so dingy, and in the midst of all this wretchedness he never appeared without gloves and straps. He remained in this state for a week or two. At length one of the buttons on the back of the coat fell off, and then the man himself disappeared, and we thought he was dead.

We were sitting at the same table about a week after his disappearance, and as our eyes rested on his vacant chair, we insensibly fell into a train of meditation on the subject of his retirement from public life. We were wondering whether he had hung himself or thrown himself off a bridge, whether he really was dead or had only been arrested – when our conjectures were suddenly set at rest by the entry of the very man himself. He had undergone some strange metamorphosis and walked up the centre of the room with an air which showed he was fully conscious of the improvement in his appearance. It was very odd; his clothes were a fine, deep, glossy black, and yet they looked like the same suit; nay, there were the very darns with which old acquaintance had made us familiar. The hat, too – nobody could mistake the shape of that hat, with its high crown gradually increasing in circumference towards the top. Long service had imparted to it a reddish brown tint, but now it was as black as the coat. The truth flashed suddenly upon us – they had been 'revived.' 'Tis a deceitful liquid that black and blue reviver; we have watched its effects on many a shabby-genteel man. It betrays its victims into a temporary assumption of importance, possibly into the purchase of a new pair of gloves, or a cheap stock, or some other trifling article of dress. It elevates their spirits for a week, only to depress them, if possible, below their original level. It was so in this case; the transient dignity of the unhappy man decreased, in exact proportion as the 'reviver' wore off. The knees of the unmentionables, and the elbows of the coat, and the seams generally, soon began to get alarmingly white. The hat was once more deposited under the table, and its owner crept into his seat as quietly as ever.

There was a week of incessant small rain and mist. At its expiration the 'reviver' had entirely vanished, and the shabby-genteel man never afterwards attempted to effect any improvement in his outward appearance.

It would be difficult to name any particular part of town as the principal resort of shabby-genteel men. We have met a great many persons of this description in the neighbourhood of the inns of court. They may be met with in Holborn between eight and ten any morning, and whoever has the curiosity to enter the Insolvent Debtors' Court will observe, both among spectators and practitioners, a great variety of them. We never went on 'Change[5] by any chance without seeing some shabby-genteel men, and we have often wondered what earthly business they can have there. They will sit there for hours, leaning on great, dropsical, mildewed umbrellas, or eating Abernethy biscuits; nobody speaks to them, nor they to any one. On consideration, we remember to have occasionally seen two shabby-genteel men conversing together on 'Change, but our experience assures us that this is an uncommon circumstance, occasioned by the offer of a pinch of snuff, or some such ordinary civility.

It would be a task of equal difficulty either to assign any particular spot for the residence of these beings, or to endeavour to enumerate their general occupations. We were never engaged in business with more than one shabby-genteel man; he was a drunken engraver and lived in a damp back parlour in a new row of houses at Camden-town, half street, half brickfield, somewhere near the canal. A shabby-genteel man may have no occupation at all, or he may be a corn agent or a coal agent, or a wine agent, or a collector of debts, or a broker's assistant, or a broken-down attorney. He may be a clerk of the lowest description, or a contributor to the press of the same grade. Whether our readers have noticed these men in their walks as often as we have, we know not; this we know – that the miserably poor man (no matter whether he owes his distresses to his own conduct, or that of others) who feels his poverty and vainly strives to conceal it, is one of the most pitiable objects in human nature. Such objects, with few exceptions, are shabby-genteel people.

CHAPTER II

Making a Night of It

DAMON and Pythias[1] were undoubtedly very good fellows in their way: the former for his extreme readiness to put in special bail for a friend, and the latter for a certain trump-like punctuality in turning up just in the very nick of time, scarcely less remarkable. Many points in their character have however grown obsolete. Damons are rather hard to find in these days of imprisonment for debt (except the sham ones, and they cost half-a-crown); and, as to the Pythiases, the few that have existed in these degenerate times have had an unfortunate knack of making themselves scarce at the very moment when their appearance would have been strictly classical. If the actions of these heroes, however, can find no parallel in modern times, their friendship can. We have Damon and Pythias on the one hand — Potter and Smithers on the other; and lest the two lastmentioned names should never have reached the ears of our unenlightened readers, we can do no better than make them acquainted with the owners thereof.

Mr Thomas Potter,[2] then, was a clerk in the city, and Mr Robert Smithers was a ditto in the same; their incomes were limited, but their friendship was unbounded. They lived in the same street, walked into town every morning at the same hour, dined at the same slap-bang[3] every day, and revelled in each other's company every night. They were knit together by the closest ties of intimacy and friendship, or, as Mr Thomas Potter touchingly observed they were 'thick-and-thin pals, and nothing but it.' There was a spice of romance in Mr Smithers's disposition, a ray of poetry, a gleam of misery, a sort of consciousness of he didn't exactly know what, coming across him he didn't precisely know why — which stood out in fine relief against the offhand, dashing, amateur-pickpocket-sort-of-manner, which distinguished Mr Potter in an eminent degree.

Making a Night of it

The peculiarity of their respective dispositions, extended itself to their individual costume. Mr Smithers generally appeared in public in a surtout and shoes, with a narrow black neckerchief and a brown hat, very much turned up at the sides – peculiarities which Mr Potter wholly eschewed for it was his ambition to do something in the celebrated 'kiddy' or stage-coach way, and he had even gone so far as to invest capital in the purchase of a rough blue coat with wooden buttons, made upon the fireman's principle, in which, with the addition of a low-crowned, flowerpot-saucer-shaped hat, he had created no inconsiderable sensation at the Albion[4] in Little Russell-street, and divers other places of public and fashionable resort.

Mr Potter and Mr Smithers had mutually agreed that on the receipt of their quarter's salary, they would jointly and in company 'spend the evening' – an evident misnomer – the spending applying, as every body knows, not to the evening itself but to all the money the individual may chance to be possessed of on the occasion to which reference is made; and they had further agreed that, on the evening aforesaid, they would 'make a night of it' – an expressive term, implying the borrowing of several hours from to-morrow morning, adding them to the night before, and manufacturing a compound night of the whole.

The quarter-day arrived at last – we say at last, because quarter days are as eccentric as comets, moving wonderfully quick when you have a good deal to pay, and marvellously slow when you have a little to receive. Mr Thomas Potter and Mr Robert Smithers met by appointment to begin the evening with a dinner; and a nice, snug, comfortable dinner they had, consisting of a little procession of four chops and four kidneys following each other, supported on either side by a pot of the real draught stout, and attended by divers cushions of bread and wedges of cheese.

When the cloth was removed, Mr Thomas Potter ordered the waiter to bring in, two goes of his best Scotch whiskey, with warm water and sugar, and a couple of his 'very mildest' Havannahs, which the waiter did. Mr Thomas Potter mixed his grog, and lit his cigar; Mr Robert Smithers did the same; and then Mr Thomas Potter jocularly proposed as the first toast, 'the abolition of all offices whatever' (not sinecures, but counting-houses), which was immediately drunk by Mr Robert Smithers, with enthusiastic applause. So they went on talking politics, puffing cigars and sipping whiskey-and-water, till the 'goes' — most appropriately so called — were both gone, which Mr Robert Smithers perceiving, immediately ordered in two more goes of the best Scotch whiskey and two more of the very mildest Havannahs; and the goes kept coming in, and the mild Havannahs kept going out, until what with the drinking and lighting, and puffing, and the stale ashes on the table, and the tallow-grease on the cigars, Mr Robert Smithers began to doubt the mildness of the Havannahs, and to feel very much as if he had been sitting in a hackney-coach with his back to the horses.

As to Mr Thomas Potter, he *would* keep laughing out loud, and volunteering inarticulate declarations that he was 'all right,' in proof of which, he feebly bespoke the evening paper after the next gentleman, but finding it a matter of some difficulty to discover any news in its columns or to ascertain distinctly whether it had any columns at all, he walked slowly out to look for the moon, and after coming back quite pale with looking up at the sky so long, and attempting to express mirth at Mr Robert Smithers having fallen asleep, by various galvanic chuckles, he laid his head on his arm, and went to sleep also. When he woke again, Mr Robert Smithers woke too, and they both very gravely agreed that it was extremely unwise to eat so many pickled walnuts with the chops, as it was a notorious fact that they always made people queer and sleepy; indeed, if it had not been for the whiskey and cigars, there was no knowing what harm they mightn't have done 'em. So they took some coffee, and after paying the bill, — twelve and twopence the dinner, and the odd tenpence for the waiter — thirteen shillings in all — started out on their expedition to manufacture a night.

It was just half-past eight, so they thought they couldn't do better than go half-price to the slips at the City Theatre,[5] which they did accordingly. Mr Robert Smithers, who had become extremely poetical after the settlement of the bill, enlivening the walk by informing Mr Thomas Potter in confidence that he felt an inward presentiment of approaching dissolution, and subsequently embellishing the theatre, by falling asleep, with his head and both arms gracefully drooping over the front of the boxes.

Such was the quiet demeanour of the unassuming Smithers, and such were the happy effects of Scotch whiskey and Havannahs on that interesting person; but Mr Thomas Potter, whose great aim it was to be considered as a 'knowing card,' a 'fast goer' and so forth, conducted himself in a very different manner, and commenced going very fast indeed – rather too fast at last, for the patience of the audience to keep pace with him. On his first entry, he contented himself by earnestly calling upon the gentlemen in the gallery to 'flare up,' accompanying the demand with another request, expressive of his wish that they would instantaneously 'form a union,' both which requisitions were responded to, in the manner most in vogue on such occasions.

'Give that dog a bone!' cried one gentleman in his shirt-sleeves.

'Where have you been a having half a pint of intermediate beer?' cried a second. 'Tailor!' screamed a third. 'Barber's clerk!' shouted a fourth. 'Throw him o–ver!' roared a fifth; while numerous voices concurred in desiring Mr Thomas Potter to return to the arms of his maternal parent, or in common parlance to 'go home to his mother!' All these taunts Mr Thomas Potter received with supreme contempt, cocking the low-crowned hat a little more on one side whenever any reference was made to his personal appearance, and, standing up with his arms a-kimbo, expressing defiance most melo-dramatically.

The overture – to which these various sounds had been an *ad libitum* accompaniment – concluded, the second piece began, and Mr Thomas Potter, emboldened by impunity, proceeded to behave in a most unprecedented and outrageous manner. First of all, he imitated the shake of the principal female singer; then groaned at the blue fire, then affected to be frightened into convulsions of terror at the appearance of the ghost; and lastly not only made a running commentary in an audible voice, upon the dialogue on the stage, but actually awoke Mr Robert Smithers who, hearing his companion making a noise, and having a very indistinct notion of where he was, or what was required of him, immediately by way of imitating a good example, set up the most unearthly, unremitting, and appalling howling that ever audience heard. It was too much. 'Turn them out!' was the general cry. A noise as of shuffling of feet, and men being knocked up with violence against wainscotting was heard: a hurried dialogue of 'come out!' – 'I won't!' – 'You shall!' 'I shan't!' – 'Give me your card, Sir!' – 'You're a scoundrel, Sir!' and so forth, succeeded. A round of applause betokened the approbation of the audience, and Mr Robert Smithers and Mr Thomas Potter found themselves shot with astonishing swiftness into the road, without having had the trouble of once putting foot to ground during the whole progress of their rapid descent.

Mr Robert Smithers being constitutionally one of the slow-goers, and having had quite enough of fast-going, in the course of his recent expulsion to last till the quarter-day then next ensuing at the very least, had no sooner emerged with his companion from the precincts of Milton-street, than he proceeded to indulge in circuitous references to the beauties of sleep, mingled with distant allusions to the propriety of returning to Islington, and testing the influence of their patent Bramahs[6] over the street-door locks to which they respectively belonged. Mr Thomas Potter, however, was valorous and peremptory. They had come out to make a night of it: and a night must be made. So Mr Robert Smithers, who was three parts dull, and the other dismal, despairingly assented; and they went into a wine-vaults to get materials for assisting them in making a night, where they found a good many young ladies, and various old gentlemen, and a plentiful sprinkling of hackney-coachmen and cab-drivers, all drinking and talking together; and Mr Thomas Potter and Mr Robert Smithers drank small glasses of brandy, and large glasses of soda, till they began to have a very confused idea, either of things in general, or anything in particular; and when they had done treating themselves they began to treat everybody else: and the rest of the entertainment was a confused mixture of heads and heels, black eyes and blue uniforms, mud and gas-lights, thick doors, and a stone paving.

Then, as standard novelists expressively inform us – 'all was a blank!' and in the morning the blank was filled up with the words

'STATION HOUSE,' and the station house was filled up with Mr Thomas Potter, Mr Robert Smithers, and the major part of their wine-vault companions of the preceeding night, with a comparatively small portion of clothing of any kind. And it was disclosed at the Police-office to the indignation of the Bench, and the astonishment of the spectators, how one Robert Smithers aided and abetted by one Thomas Potter, had knocked down and beaten, in divers streets, at different times, five men, four boys, and three women; how the said Thomas Potter had feloniously obtained possession of five door-knockers, two bell-handles, and a bonnet: how Robert Smithers, his friend, had sworn at least forty pounds' worth of oaths, at the rate of five shillings apiece; terrified whole streets full of Her Majesty's subjects with awful shrieks and alarms of fire; destroyed the uniforms of five policemen, and committed various other atrocities, too numerous to recapitulate. And the magistrate, after an appropriate reprimand, fined Mr Thomas Potter and Mr Robert Smithers five shillings each, for being, what the law vulgarly terms, drunk, with the trifling addition of thirty-four pounds for seventeen assaults at forty shillings a-head, with liberty to speak to the prosecutors.

The prosecutors *were* spoken to and Messrs Potter and Smithers lived on credit for a quarter as best they might; and, although the prosecutors expressed their readiness to be assaulted twice a-week on the same terms, they have never since been detected in 'making a night of it.'

CHAPTER 12

The Prisoners' Van

WE were passing the corner of Bow-street, on our return from a lounging excursion the other afternoon, when a crowd, assembled round the door of the Police Office, attracted our attention and we turned up the street accordingly. There were thirty or forty people standing on the pavement and half across the road, and a few stragglers were patiently stationed on the opposite side of the way – all evidently waiting in expectation of some arrival. We waited too, a few minutes, but nothing occurred; so we turned round to an unshaved sallow-looking cobbler, who was standing next us with his hands under the bib of his apron, and put the usual question of 'What's the matter?' The cobbler eyed us from head to foot with superlative contempt, and laconically replied 'Nuffin.'

Now, we were perfectly aware that if two men stop in the street to look at any given object, or even to gaze in the air, two hundred men will be assembled in no time: but as we knew very well that no crowd of people could by possibility remain in a street for five minutes without getting up a little amusement among themselves, unless they had some absorbing object in view, the natural inquiry next in order was, 'What are all these people waiting here for?' – 'Her Majesty's carriage,' replied the cobbler. This was still more extraordinary. We could not imagine what earthly business Her Majesty's carriage could have at the Public Office, Bow-street, and we were beginning to ruminate upon the possible causes of such an uncommon appearance, when a general exclamation from all the boys in the crowd of 'Here's the wan!' caused us to raise our heads and look up the street.

The covered vehicle, in which prisoners are conveyed from the police offices to the different prisons, was coming along at full speed, and it then occurred to us for the first time that Her Majesty's carriage was merely another name for the prisoners' van, conferred upon it, not only by reason of the superior gentility of the term, but because the aforesaid van is maintained at Her Majesty's expense, having been originally started for the exclusive accommodation of ladies and gentlemen under the necessity of visiting the various houses of call known by the general denomination of 'Her Majesty's Gaols.'

The van drew up at the office-door, and the people thronged round the steps, just leaving a little alley for the prisoners to pass through. Our friend the cobbler and the other stragglers crossed over, and we followed their example. The driver, and another man who had been seated by his side in front of the vehicle, dismounted, and were admitted into the office. The office-door was closed after them, and the crowd were on the tiptoe of expectation.

After a few minutes delay the door again opened, and the two first prisoners appeared. They were a couple of girls, of whom the elder could not be more than sixteen, and the younger of whom had certainly not attained her fourteenth year. That they were sisters was evident from the resemblance which still subsisted between them, though two additional years of depravity had fixed their brand upon the elder girl's features as legibly as if a red-hot iron had seared them. They were both gaudily dressed, the younger one especially, and although there was a strong similarity between them in both respects, which was rendered the more obvious by their being handcuffed together, it is impossible to conceive a greater contrast than the demeanour of the two presented. The younger girl was weeping bitterly – not for display or in the hope of producing effect, but for very shame; her face was buried in her handkerchief, and her whole manner was but too expressive of bitter and unavailing sorrow.

'How long are you for, Emily?' screamed a red-faced woman in the crowd. 'Six weeks and labour,' replied the elder girl with a flaunting laugh; 'and that's better than the stone jug[1] any how; the mill's a deal better than the Sessions,[2] and here's Bella a-going too for the first time. Hold up your head, you chicken,' she continued, boisterously tearing the other girl's handkerchief away; 'Hold up your head, and show 'em your face, I an't jealous, but I'm blessed if I an't game.' – 'That's right, old gal,' exclaimed a man in a paper cap, who, in common with the greater part of the crowd, had been inexpressibly delighted with this little incident. – 'Right!' replied the girl; 'ah, to be sure; what's the odds, eh?' – 'Come, in with you,' interrupted the driver. – 'Don't you be in a hurry, coachman,' replied the girl, 'and recollect I want to be set down in Cold Bath Fields[3] – large house with a high garden-wall in front; you can't mistake it. Hallo. Bella, where are you going to – you'll pull my precious arm off?' This was addressed to the younger girl, who, in her anxiety to hide herself in the caravan, had ascended the steps first, and forgotten the strain upon the handcuff; 'Come down, and let's show you the way.' And after jerking the miserable girl down with a force which made her stagger on the pavement, she got into the vehicle, and was followed by her wretched companion.

These two girls had been thrown upon London streets, their vices and debauchery, by a sordid and rapacious mother. What the younger girl was then, the elder had been once; and what the elder then was, she must soon become. A melancholy prospect, but how surely to be realized: a tragic drama, but how often acted! Turn to the prisons and police offices of London — nay, look into the very streets themselves. These things pass before our eyes day after day, and hour after hour — they have become such matters of course, that they are utterly disregarded. The progress of these girls in crime will be as rapid as the flight of a pestilence, resembling it too in its baneful influence and wide-spreading infection. Step by step how many wretched females, within the sphere of every man's observation, have become involved in a career of vice frightful to contemplate; hopeless at its commencement, loathsome and repulsive in its course, friendless, forlorn, and unpitied, at its miserable conclusion!

There were other prisoners — boys of ten, as hardened in vice as men of fifty — a houseless vagrant going joyfully to prison as a place of food and shelter, handcuffed to a man whose prospects were ruined, character lost, and family rendered destitute by his first offence. — Our curiosity, however, was satisfied. The first group had left an impression on our mind we would gladly have avoided, and would willingly have effaced.

The crowd dispersed; the vehicle rolled away with its load of guilt and misfortune, and we saw no more of the Prisoners' Van.

TALES

The Boarding House

CHAPTER I

The Boarding-house

Chapter the First

MRS TIBBS was, beyond all dispute, the most tidy, fidgety, thrifty little personage that ever inhaled the smoke of London; and the house of Mrs Tibbs was decidedly the neatest in all Great Coram-street.[1] The area and the area steps, and the street-door and the street-door steps, and the brass handle, and the door-plate, and the knocker, and the fan-light, were all as clean and bright as indefatigable white-washing, and hearth-stoning, and scubbing and rubbing could make them. The wonder was, that the brass door-plate, with the interesting inscription 'MRS TIBBS,' had never caught fire from constant friction, so perseveringly was it polished. There were meat-safe-looking blinds in the parlour windows, blue and gold curtains in the drawing-room, and spring-roller blinds, as Mrs Tibbs was wont in the pride of her heart to boast, 'all the way up.' The bell-lamp in the passage looked as clear as a soap-bubble; you could see yourself in all the tables, and French-polish yourself on any one of the chairs. The banisters were bees'-waxed, and the very stair-wires[2] made your eyes wink, they were so glittering.

Mrs Tibbs was somewhat short of stature, and Mr Tibbs was by no means a large man. He had, moreover, very short legs, but, by way of indemnification, his face was peculiarly long. He was to his wife what the o is in 90 – he was of some importance *with* her – he was nothing without her. Mrs Tibbs was always talking. Mr Tibbs rarely spoke; but if it were at any time possible to put in a word, just when he should have said nothing at all, he did it. Mrs Tibbs detested long stories, and Mr Tibbs had one, the conclusion of which had never been heard by his most intimate friends. It always began, 'I recollect when I was in the volunteer corps, in eighteen hundred and six,' – but as he spoke very slowly and softly and his better half very quickly and loudly, he rarely got beyond the introductory sentence. He was a melancholy specimen of the story-teller. He was the wandering Jew of Joe Millerism.[3]

Mr Tibbs enjoyed a small independence from the pension-list – about 43*l.* 15*s.* 10*d.* a-year. His father, mother, and five interesting scions from the same stock drew a like sum from the revenue of a grateful country, though for what particular service was never distinctly known. But, as this said independence was not quite sufficient to furnish two people with *all* the luxuries of this life, it had occurred to the busy little spouse of Tibbs, that the best thing she could do with a legacy of 700*l.*, would be to take and furnish a tolerable house, some where in that partially-explored tract of country which lies between the British Museum, and a remote village called Somers Town, for the reception of boarders. Great Coram-street was the spot pitched upon. The house had been furnished accordingly; two female servants and a boy engaged, and an advertisement inserted in the morning papers, informing the public that 'Six individuals would meet with all the comforts of a cheerful musical home in a select private family, residing within ten minutes' walk of' – everywhere. Answers out of number were received, with all sorts of initials; all the letters of the alphabet seemed to be seized with a sudden wish to go out boarding and lodging; voluminous was the correspondence be-tween Mrs Tibbs and the applicants, and most profound was the secrecy which was to be observed. 'E.' didn't like this, and 'I.' couldn't think of putting up with that; 'I.O.U.' didn't think the terms would suit him; and 'G.R.' had never slept in a French bed.[4] The result, however, was, that three gentlemen became inmates of Mrs Tibbs's house, on terms which were 'agreeable to all parties.' In went the advertisement again, and a lady with her two daughters, proposed to increase – not their families, but Mrs Tibbs's.

'Charming woman, that Mrs Maplesone!' said Mrs Tibbs, as she and her spouse were sitting by the fire after breakfast; the gentlemen having gone out on their several avocations. 'Charming woman, indeed!' repeated little Mrs Tibbs, more by way of soliloquy than any thing else, for she never thought of consulting her husband.

'And the two daughters are delightful. We must have some fish to-day; they'll join us at dinner for the first time.'

Mr Tibbs placed the poker at right angles with the fire-shovel, and essayed to speak, but recollected he had nothing to say.

'The young ladies,' continued Mrs T., 'have kindly volunteered to bring their own piano.'

Tibbs thought of the volunteer story, but did not venture it. A bright thought struck him –

'It's very likely,' said he.

'Pray don't lean your head against the paper,' interrupted Mrs Tibbs – 'and don't put your feet on the steel fender; that's worse.'

Tibbs took his head from the paper, and his feet from the fender, and proceeded. 'It's very likely one of the young ladies may set her cap at young Mr Simpson, and you know a marriage' —

'A what!' shrieked Mrs Tibbs. Tibbs modestly repeated his former suggestion.

'I beg you won't mention such a thing,' said Mrs T. 'A marriage, indeed! – to rob me of my boarders – no, not for the world.'

Tibbs thought in his own mind that the event was by no means unlikely, but as he never argued with his wife, he put a stop to the dialogue, by observing it was 'time to go to business.' He always went out at ten o'clock in the morning, and returned at five in the afternoon, with an exceedingly dirty face, and smelling very mouldy. Nobody knew what he was, or where he went to; but Mrs Tibbs used to say with an air of great importance, that he was engaged in the City.

The Miss Maplesones and their accomplished parent arrived in the course of the afternoon in a hackney-coach, and accompanied by a most astonishing number of packages. Trunks, bonnet-boxes, muff-boxes and parasols, guitar-cases, and parcels of all imaginable shapes, done up in brown paper, and fastened with pins, filled the passage. Then, there was such a running up and down with the luggage, such scampering for warm water for the ladies to wash in, and such a bustle, and confusion, and heating of servants and curling-irons, as had never been known in Great Coram-street before. Little Mrs Tibbs was quite in her element, bustling about, talking incessantly, and distributing towels and soap, and all the *et ceteras*, like a head nurse in a hospital. The house was not restored to its usual state of quiet repose until the ladies were safely shut up in their respective bedrooms, engaged in the important occupation of dressing for dinner.

'Are these gals 'andsome?' inquired Mr Simpson of Mr Septimus Hicks, another of the boarders, as they were amusing themselves in the drawing-room before dinner, by lolling on sofas, and contemplating their pumps.

'Don't know,' replied Mr Septimus Hicks, who was a tallish, white-faced young man, with spectacles, and a black ribbon round his neck instead of a neckerchief – a most interesting person; a poetical walker of the hospitals, and a 'very talented young man.' He was fond of 'lugging' into conversation all sorts of quotations from Don Juan, without fettering himself by the propriety of their application, in which particular he was remarkably independent. The other, Mr Simpson, was one of those young men, who are in society what walking gentlemen are upon the stage, only infinitely worse skilled in his vocation than the most indifferent artist. He was as empty-headed as the great bell of St Paul's; always dressed according to the caricatures published in the monthly fashions, and spelt Character with a K.

'I saw a devilish number of parcels in the passage when I came home,' simpered Simpson.

'Materials for the toilet, no doubt,' rejoined the Don Juan reader.

> — 'Much linen, lace, and several pair
> Of stockings, slippers, brushes, combs, complete;
> With other articles of ladies' fair,
> To keep them beautiful, or leave them neat.'[5]

'Is that from Milton?' inquired Mr Simpson.

'No – from Byron,' returned Mr Hicks, with a look of profound contempt. He was quite sure of his author, because he had never read any other. – 'Hush!' said the sapient hospital walker, 'Here come the gals,' and they both commenced talking in a very loud key.

'Mrs Maplesone and the Miss Maplesones, Mr Hicks. Mr Hicks – Mrs Maplesone and the Miss Maplesones,' said Mrs Tibbs with a very red face, for she had been superintending the cooking operations below stairs, and looked like a wax doll on a sunny day. 'Mr Simpson, I beg your pardon – Mr Simpson – Mrs Maplesone and the Miss Maplesones' – and *vice versa*. The gentlemen immediately began to slide about with much politeness, and to look as if they wished their arms had been legs, so little did they know what to do with them. The ladies smiled, curtsied, and glided into chairs, and dived for dropped pocket-handkerchiefs: the gentlemen leant against two of the curtain-pegs; Mrs Tibbs went through an admirable bit of serious pantomime with a servant who had come up to ask some question about the fish-sauce, and then the two young ladies looked at each other; and every body else appeared to discover something very attractive in the pattern of the fender.

'Julia my love,' said Mrs Maplesone to her youngest daughter, in a tone just loud enough for the remainder of the company to hear, – 'Julia.'

'Yes, Ma.'

'Don't stoop.' – This was said for the purpose of directing general attention to Miss Julia's figure, which was undeniable. Every body looked at her, accordingly, and there was another pause.

'We had the most uncivil hackney-coachman to-day, you can imagine,' said Mrs Maplesone to Mrs Tibbs, in a confidential tone.

'Dear me!' replied the hostess, with an air of great commiseration. She couldn't say more, for the servant again appeared at the door, and commenced telegraphing most earnestly to her 'Misses.'

'I think hackney-coachmen generally are uncivil,' said Mr Hicks in his most insinuating tone.

'Positively I think they are,' replied Mrs Maplesone, as if the idea had never struck her before.

'And cabmen, too,' said Mr Simpson. This remark was a failure, for no one intimated by word or sign the slightest knowledge of the manners and customs of cabmen.

'Robinson, what *do* you want?' said Mrs Tibbs to the servant who, by way of making her presence known to her mistress, had been giving sundry hems and sniffs outside the door during the preceding five minutes.

'Please, ma'am, master wants his clean things,' replied the servant, completely taken off her guard. There was no resisting this: the two young men turned their faces to the window, and 'went off' like a couple of bottles of ginger beer; the ladies put their handkerchiefs to their mouths, and little Mrs Tibbs bustled out of the room to give Tibbs his clean linen, – and the servant warning.

Mr Calton, the remaining boarder, shortly afterwards made his appearance, and proved a surprising promoter of the conversation. Mr Calton was a superannuated beau – an old boy. He used to say of himself that although his features were not regularly handsome, they were striking. They certainly were: it was impossible to look at his face without being forcibly reminded of a chubby street-door knocker, half-lion half-monkey; and the comparison might be extended to his whole character and conversation. He had stood still while every thing else had been moving. He never originated a conversation, or started a new idea; but if any commonplace topic were broached, or, to pursue the comparison, if any body *lifted him up*, he would hammer away with surprising rapidity. He had the tic-douloureux occasionally, and then he might be said to be muffled, because he did not make quite as much noise as at other times, when he would go on prosing, rat-tat-tat the same thing over and over again. He had never been married; but he was still on the look-out for a wife with money. He had a life interest worth about 300*l*. a year – he was exceedingly vain, and inordinately selfish. He had acquired the reputation of being the very pink of politeness, and he walked round the park, and up Regent-street, every day.

This respectable personage had made up his mind to render himself exceedingly agreeable to Mrs Maplesone – indeed, the desire of being as amiable as possible extended itself to the whole party; Mrs Tibbs having considered it an admirable little bit of

management to represent to the gentlemen that she had *some* reason
to believe the ladies were fortunes, and to hint to the ladies, that all
the gentlemen were 'eligible.' A little flirtation, she thought, might
keep her house full, without leading to any other result.

Mrs Maplesone was an enterprising widow of about fifty: shrewd,
scheming, and good-looking. She was amiably anxious on behalf of
her daughters; in proof whereof she used to remark, that she would
have no objection to marry again, if it would benefit her dear
girls – she could have no other motive. The 'dear girls' themselves
were not at all insensible to the merits of 'a good establishment.'
One of them was twenty-five, the other three years younger. They
had been at different watering-places for four seasons; they had
gambled at libraries, read books in balconies, sold at fancy fairs,
danced at assemblies, talked sentiment – in short, they had done all
that industrious girls could do – and all to no purpose.

'What a magnificent dresser Mr Simpson is!' whispered Matilda
Maplesone to her sister Julia.

'Splendid!' returned the youngest. The magnificent individual
alluded to wore a sort of maroon-coloured dress-coat, with a velvet
collar and cuffs of the same tint – very like that which usually
invests the form of the distinguished unknown who condescends to
play the 'swell' in the pantomime at 'Richardson's Show.'[6]

'What whiskers!' said Miss Julia.

'Charming!' responded her sister; 'and what hair!' His hair was
like a wig, and distinguished by that insinuating wave which graces
the shining locks of those *chef-d'œuvres* of peruquerian art surmount-
ing the waxen images in Bartellot's window,[7] in Regent-street; his
whiskers meeting beneath his chin, seemed strings wherewith to tie
it on, ere science had rendered them unnecessary by her patent
invisible springs.

'Dinner's on the table, ma'am, if you please,' said the boy, who
now appeared for the first time, in a revived black coat of his
master's.

'Oh! Mr Calton, will you lead Mrs Maplesone? – Thank you.'
Mr Simpson offered his arm to Miss Julia; Mr Septimus Hicks
escorted the lovely Matilda; and the procession proceeded to the

dining-room. Mr Tibbs was introduced, and Mr Tibbs bobbed up and down to the three ladies like a figure in a Dutch clock with a powerful spring in the middle of his body, and then dived rapidly into his seat at the bottom of the table, delighted to screen himself behind a soup-tureen, which he could just see over, and that was all. The boarders were seated, a lady and gentleman alternately, like the layers of bread and meat in a plate of sandwiches; and then Mrs Tibbs directed James to take off the covers. Salmon, lobster-sauce, giblet-soup, and the usual accompaniments were *dis*-covered: potatoes like petrifactions, and bits of toasted bread, the shape and size of blank dice.

'Soup for Mrs Maplesone, my dear,' said the bustling Mrs Tibbs. She always called her husband 'my dear' before company. Tibbs, who had been eating his bread, and calculating how long it would be before he should get any fish, helped the soup in a hurry, made a small island on the tablecloth, and put his glass upon it, to hide it from his wife.

'Miss Julia, shall I assist you to some fish?'

'If you please – very little – oh! plenty, thank you' (a bit about the size of a walnut put upon the plate).

'Julia is a *very* little eater,' said Mrs Maplesone to Mr Calton.

The knocker gave a single rap. He was busy eating the fish with his eyes: so he only ejaculated, 'Ah!'

'My dear,' said Mrs Tibbs, to her spouse after every one else had been helped, 'What do *you* take?' The inquiry was accompanied with a look intimating that he mustn't say fish, because there was not much left. Tibbs thought the frown referred to the island on the tablecloth; he therefore coolly replied, 'Why – I'll take a little – fish, I think.'

'Did you say fish, my dear?' (another frown).

'Yes, dear,' replied the villain, with an expression of acute hunger depicted in his countenance. The tears almost started to Mrs Tibbs's eyes, as she helped her 'wretch of a husband,' as she inwardly called him, to the last eatable bit of salmon on the dish.

'James, take this to your master, and take away your master's knife.' This was deliberate revenge, as Tibbs never could eat fish without one. He was, however, constrained to chase small particles of salmon round and round his plate with a piece of bread and a fork, occasionally securing a bit; the number of successful attempts being about one in seventeen.

'Take away, James,' said Mrs Tibbs, just as Tibbs had swallowed the fourth mouthful – and away went the plates like lightning.

'I'll take a bit of bread, James,' said the poor '*master* of the house,' more hungry than ever.

'Never mind your master now, James,' said Mrs Tibbs, 'see about the meat.' – This was conveyed in the tone in which ladies usually give admonitions to servants in company, that is to say, a low one; but which, like a stage whisper, from its peculiar emphasis, is most distinctly heard by every body present.

A pause ensued before the table was replenished – a sort of parenthesis in which Mr Simpson, Mr Calton, and Mr Hicks produced respectively a bottle of sauterne, bucellas,[8] and sherry, and took wine with every body – except Tibbs: no one ever thought of him.

Between the fish and an intimated sirloin there was a prolonged interval.

Here was an opportunity for Mr Hicks. He could not resist the singularly appropriate quotation –

> 'But beef is rare within these oxless isles;
> Goats' flesh there is, no doubt, and kid, and mutton,
> And, when a holiday upon them smiles,
> A joint upon their barbarous spits they put on.'[9]

'Very ungentlemanly behaviour,' thought little Mrs Tibbs, 'to talk in that way.'

'Ah,' said Mr Calton, filling his glass. 'Tom Moore[10] is my poet.'

'And mine,' said Mrs Maplesone.

'And mine,' said Miss Julia.

'And mine,' added Mr Simpson.

'Look at his compositions,' resumed the knocker.

'To be sure,' said Simpson, with confidence.

'Look at Don Juan,' replied Mr Septimus Hicks.

'Julia's letter,'[11] suggested Miss Matilda.

'Can any thing be grander than the Fire Worshippers?'[12] inquired Miss Julia.

'To be sure,' said Simpson.

'Or Paradise and the Peri,'[13] said the old beau.

'Yes; or Paradise and the Peer,' repeated Simpson, who thought he was getting through it capitally.

'It's all very well,' replied Mr Septimus Hicks, who, as we have before hinted, never had read any thing but Don Juan. 'Where will you find any thing finer than the description of the siege, at the commencement of the seventh canto?'

'Talking of a siege,' said Tibbs, with a mouthful of bread — 'when I was in the volunteer corps, in eighteen hundred and six, our commanding officer was Sir Charles Rampart; and one day, when we were exercising on the ground on which the London University now stands,[14] he says, says he, "Tibbs (calling me from the ranks) Tibbs —"'

'Tell your master, James,' interrupted Mrs Tibbs, in an awfully distinct tone, 'tell your master if he *won't* carve those fowls, to send them to me.' The discomfited volunteer instantly set to work, and carved the fowls almost as expeditiously as his wife operated on the haunch of mutton. Whether he ever finished the story is not exactly known, but if he did nobody heard it.

As the ice was now broken, and the new inmates more at home, every member of the company felt more at ease. Tibbs himself most certainly did, because he went to sleep immediately after dinner. Mr Hicks and the ladies discoursed most eloquently about poetry, and the theatres, and Lord Chesterfield's Letters;[15] and Mr Calton followed up what every body said, with continuous double knocks. Mrs Tibbs highly approved of every observation that fell from Mrs Maplesone; and as Mr Simpson sat with a smile upon his face and said 'Yes,' or 'Certainly,' at intervals of about four minutes each, he received full credit for understanding what was going forward. The gentlemen rejoined the ladies in the drawing-room very shortly after they had left the dining-parlour. Mrs

Maplesone and Mr Calton played cribbage, and the 'young people' amused themselves with music and conversation. The Miss Maplesones sang the most fascinating duets, and accompanied themselves on guitars, ornamented with bits of ethereal blue ribbon. Mr Simpson put on a pink waistcoat, and said he was in raptures: and Mr Hicks felt in the seventh heaven of poetry, or the seventh canto of Don Juan – it was the same thing to him. Mrs Tibbs was quite charmed with the new comers, and Mr Tibbs spent the evening in his usual way – he went to sleep, and woke up, and went to sleep again, and woke at supper-time.

We are not about to adopt the licence of novel-writers and to let 'years roll on;' but we will take the liberty of requesting the reader to suppose that six months have elapsed since the dinner we have just described, and that Mrs Tibbs's boarders have, during that period, sang, and danced, and gone to theatres and exhibitions together, as ladies and gentlemen, wherever they board, often do; and we will beg them, the period we have mentioned having elapsed, to imagine further, that Mr Septimus Hicks received, in his own bedroom (a front attic), at an early hour one morning, a note from Mr Calton, requesting the favour of seeing him, as soon as convenient to himself, in his (Calton's) dressing-room on the second floor back.

'Tell Mr Calton I'll come down directly,' said Mr Septimus to the boy. 'Stop – is Mr Calton unwell?' inquired the excited walker of hospitals, as he put on a bed-furniture-looking dressing-gown.

'Not as I know on, sir,' replied the boy. 'Please, sir, he looked rather rum, as it might be.'

'Ah, that's no proof of his being ill,' returned Hicks, unconsciously. 'Very well: I'll be down directly.' Down stairs ran the boy with the message, and down went the excited Hicks himself, almost as soon as the message was delivered. 'Tap, tap.' 'Come in.' – Door opens, and discovers Mr Calton sitting in an easy chair, and looking more like a knocker than ever. Mutual shakes of the hand exchanged, and Mr Septimus Hicks motioned to a seat. A short pause. Mr Hicks coughed, and Mr Calton took a pinch of snuff. It was just one of those interviews where neither party knows what to say. Mr Septimus Hicks broke silence.

'I received a note —' he said, very tremulously, in a voice like a Punch[16] with a cold.

'Yes,' returned the other, 'you did.'

'Exactly.'

'Yes.'

Now, although this dialogue must have been satisfactory, both gentlemen felt there was something more important to be said; and so they did as many in such a situation would have done — they looked at the table with a most determined aspect. The conversation had been opened, however, and Mr Calton had made up his mind to continue it, with a regular double knock. He always spoke very pompously.

'Hicks,' said he, 'I have sent for you in consequence of certain arrangements which are pending in this house, connected with a marriage.'

'With a marriage!' gasped Hicks, compared with whose expression of countenance, Hamlet's, when he sees his father's ghost,[17] is pleasing and composed.

'With a marriage,' returned the knocker. 'I have sent for you to prove the great confidence I can repose in you.'

'And will you betray me?' eagerly inquired Hicks, who in his alarm had even forgotten to quote.

'*I* betray *you!* Won't *you* betray *me?*'

'Never: no one shall know to my dying day that you had a hand in the business,' responded the agitated Hicks, with an inflamed countenance, and his hair standing on end as if he were on the stool of an electrifying machine in full operation.

'People must know that, some time or other — within a year, I imagine,' said Mr Calton, with an air of great self-complacency — 'We *may* have a family, you know.'

'*We!* — That won't affect you, surely?'

'The devil it won't!'

'No! how can it?' said the bewildered Hicks. Calton was too much inwrapped in the contemplation of happiness to see the equivoque between Hicks and himself; and threw himself back in his chair. 'Oh, Matilda!' sighed the antique beau, in a lack-a-daysical voice, and applying his right hand a little to the left of the fourth button of his waistcoat, counting from the bottom. This was meant to be pathetic – 'Oh, Matilda!'

'What Matilda?' inquired Hicks, starting up.

'Matilda Maplesone,' responded the other, doing the same.

'I marry her to-morrow morning,' said Hicks, furiously.

'It's false,' rejoined his companion: 'I marry her!'

'You marry her!'

'I marry her!'

'You marry Matilda Maplesone?'

'Matilda Maplesone.'

'*Miss* Maplesone marry *you?*'

'Miss Maplesone! No: Mrs Maplesone.'

'Good God!'[18] said Hicks, falling into his chair: 'You marry the mother, and I the daughter!'

'Most extraordinary circumstance!' replied Mr Calton, 'and rather inconvenient too; for the fact is, that owing to Matilda's wishing to keep her intention secret from her daughters until the ceremony had taken place, she doesn't like applying to any of her friends to give her away. I entertain an objection to making the affair known to my acquaintance just now; and the consequence is, that I sent to you to know whether you'd oblige me by acting as father.'

'I should have been most happy, I assure you,' said Hicks, in a tone of condolence; 'but you see I shall be acting as bridegroom. One character is frequently a consequence of the other; but it is not usual to act in both at the same time. There's Simpson – I have no doubt he'll do it for you.'

'I don't like to ask him,' replied Calton; 'he's such a donkey.'

Mr Septimus Hicks looked up at the ceiling, and down at the floor; at last an idea struck him – 'Let the man of the house, Tibbs, be the father,' he suggested; and then he quoted, as peculiarly applicable to Tibbs and the pair –

'Oh Powers of Heaven! what dark eyes meets she there?
'Tis — 'tis her father's — fixed upon the pair.'[19]

'The idea has struck me already,' said Mr Calton: 'but, you see, Matilda, for what reason I know not, is very anxious that Mrs Tibbs should know nothing about it till it's all over. It's a natural delicacy, after all, you know.'

'He's the best-natured little man in existence, if you manage him properly,' said Mr Septimus Hicks. 'Tell him not to mention it to his wife, and assure him she won't mind it, and he'll do it directly. My marriage is to be a secret one, on account of the mother and *my* father: therefore he must be enjoined to secrecy.'

A small double knock, like a presumptuous single one, was that instant heard at the street-door. It was Tibbs; it could be no one else, for no one else occupied five minutes in rubbing their shoes. He had been out to pay the baker's bill.

'Mr Tibbs,' called Mr Calton in a very bland tone, looking over the banisters.

'Sir!' replied he of the dirty face.

'Will you have the kindness to step up stairs for a moment?'

'Certainly, sir,' said Tibbs, delighted to be taken notice of. The bedroom-door was carefully closed, and Tibbs, having put his hat on the floor (as all timid men do), and been accommodated with a seat, looked as astounded as if he were suddenly summoned before the familiars of the Inquisition.[20]

'A rather unpleasant occurrence, Mr Tibbs,' said Calton, in a very portentous manner, 'obliges me to consult you, and to beg you will not communicate what I am about to say to your wife.'

Tibbs acquiesced, wondering in his own mind what the deuce the other could have done, and imagining that at least he must have broken the best decanters.

Mr Calton resumed; 'I am placed, Mr Tibbs, in rather an unpleasant situation.'

Tibbs looked at Mr Septimus Hicks; as if he thought his being in the immediate vicinity of his fellow-boarder might constitute the unpleasantness of his situation; but as he did not exactly know what to say, he merely ejaculated the monosyllable 'Lor!'

'Now,' continued the knocker, 'let me beg you will exhibit no manifestations of surprise, which may be overheard by the domestics, when I tell you — command your feelings of astonishment — that two inmates of this house intend to be married to-morrow morning,' — and he drew back his chair several feet to perceive the effect of the unlooked-for announcement.

If Tibbs had rushed from the room, staggered down stairs, and fainted in the passage — if he had instantaneously jumped out of the window into the mews behind the house, in an agony of surprise — his behaviour would have been much less inexplicable to Mr Calton than it was, when he put his hands into his inexpressible-pockets, and said with a half-chuckle, 'Just so.'

'You are not surprised, Mr Tibbs?' inquired Mr Calton.

'Bless you, no, sir,' returned Tibbs; 'after all it's very natural. When two young people get together, you know —'

'Certainly, certainly,' said Calton, with an indescribable air of self-satisfaction.

'You don't think it's at all an out-of-the-way affair then?' asked Mr Septimus Hicks, who had watched the countenance of Tibbs in mute astonishment.

'No, sir,' replied Tibbs; 'I was just the same at his age.' He actually smiled when he said this.

'How devilish well I must carry my years!' thought the delighted old beau, knowing he was at least ten years older than Tibbs at that moment.

'Well, then, to come to the point at once,' he continued, 'I have to ask you whether you will object to act as father on the occasion?'

'Certainly not,' replied Tibbs; still without evincing an atom of surprise.

'You will not?'

'Decidedly not,' reiterated Tibbs, who appeared as calm as a pot of porter with the head off.

Mr Calton seized the hand of the petticoat-governed little man, and vowed eternal friendship from that hour. Hicks, who was all admiration and surprise, did the same.

'Now confess,' asked Mr Calton of Tibbs, as he picked up his hat, 'were you not a little surprised?'

'I b'lieve you!' replied that illustrious person, holding up one hand; 'I b'lieve you! when I first heard of it.'

'So sudden,' said Septimus Hicks.

'So strange to ask *me*, you know,' said Tibbs.

'So odd altogether,' said the superannuated love-maker; and then all three laughed.

'I say,' said Tibbs, shutting the door which he had previously opened, and giving full vent to a hitherto corked-up giggle, 'what bothers me is, what *will* his father say?'

Mr Septimus Hicks looked at Mr Calton.

'Yes; but the best of it is,' said the latter, giggling in his turn, 'I haven't got a father – he! he! he!'

'*You* haven't got a father. No; but *he* has,' said Tibbs.

'*Who* has?' inquired Septimus Hicks, almost rabid.

'Why *him*.'

'Him, who? Do you know my secret? Do you mean me?'

'You! No; you know who I mean,' returned Tibbs, with a knowing wink.

'For Heaven's sake whom *do* you mean?' inquired Mr Calton, who, like Septimus Hicks, was all but out of his senses at the strange confusion.

'Why, Mr Simpson, of course,' replied Tibbs; 'who else could I mean?'

'I see it all,' said the Byron-quoter; 'Simpson marries Julia Maplesone to-morrow morning!'

'Undoubtedly,' replied Tibbs, thoroughly satisfied; 'of course he does.'

It would require the pencil of Hogarth[21] to illustrate – our feeble pen is inadequate to describe – the expression which the countenances of Mr Calton and Mr Septimus Hicks respectively assumed at this unexpected announcement. Equally impossible is it to describe, although it is much easier for our lady readers to imagine, what arts the three ladies could have used, so completely to entangle their separate partners. Whatever they were, however, they were successful. The mother was perfectly aware of the intended marriage of both daughters; and the young ladies were equally acquainted with the intention of their estimable parent. They agreed, however, that it would have a much better appearance if each feigned ignorance of the other's engagement; and it was equally desirable that all the marriages should take place on the same day, to prevent the discovery of one clandestine alliance, operating prejudicially on the others. Hence the mystification of Mr Calton and Mr Septimus Hicks, and the pre-engagement of the unwary Tibbs.

On the following morning Mr Septimus Hicks was united to Miss Matilda Maplesone. Mr Simpson also entered into a 'holy alliance' with Miss Julia: Tibbs acting as father, 'his first appearance in that character.' Mr Calton, not being quite so eager as the two young men, was rather struck by the double discovery; and as he had found some difficulty in getting any one to give the lady away, it occurred to him that the best mode of obviating the inconvenience would be not to take her at all. The lady, however, 'appealed,' as her counsel said on the trial of the cause, *Maplesone* v. *Calton*, for a breach of promise, 'with a broken heart, to the outraged laws of her country.' She recovered damages to the amount of 1000*l.*, which the unfortunate knocker was compelled to pay. Mr Septimus Hicks having walked the hospitals, took it into his head to walk off altogether. His injured wife is at present residing with her mother at Boulogne. Mr Simpson, having the misfortune to lose his wife six weeks after marriage (by her eloping with an officer during his temporary sojourn in the Fleet Prison, in consequence of his inability to discharge her little mantua-maker's[22] bill), and being disinherited by his father, who died soon afterwards, was fortunate enough to obtain a permanent engagement at a fashionable hair-cutter's; hairdressing being a science to which he had frequently directed his attention. In this situation he had necessarily many opportunities of making himself acquainted with the habits and style of thinking of the exclusive portion of the nobility of this kingdom. To this fortunate circumstance are we indebted for the production of those brilliant efforts of genius, his fashionable novels, which so long as good taste, unsullied by exaggeration, cant, and maudlin quackery continues to exist, cannot fail to instruct and amuse the thinking portion of the community.

It only remains to add, that this complication of disorders completely deprived poor Mrs Tibbs of all her inmates, except the one whom it would have afforded her the greatest pleasure to lose – her husband. That wretched little man returned home on the day of the wedding in a state of partial intoxication; and under the influence of wine, excitement, and despair, actually dared to brave the anger of his wife. Since that ill-fated hour he has constantly taken his meals in the kitchen, to which apartment it is understood his witticisms will be in future confined: a turn-up bedstead having been conveyed there by Mrs Tibbs's order for his exclusive accommodation. It is very likely that he will be enabled to finish there his story of the volunteers.

The advertisement has again appeared in the morning papers. Results must be reserved for another chapter.

Chapter the Second

'WELL,' said little Mrs Tibbs to herself, as she sat in the front parlour of the Coram-street mansion one morning, mending a piece of stair-carpet off the first landing; – 'well! things have not turned out so badly either, and if I only get a favourable answer to the advertisement, we shall be full again.'

Mrs Tibbs resumed her occupation of making worsted lattice-work in the carpet, anxiously listening to the twopenny postman,[23] who was hammering his way down the street at the rate of a penny a knock. The house was as quiet as possible. There was only one low sound to be heard – it was the unhappy Tibbs cleaning the gentlemen's boots in the back kitchen, and accompanying himself with a buzzing noise, in wretched mockery of humming a tune.

The postman drew near the house. He paused – so did Mrs Tibbs – a knock – a bustle – a letter – post-paid.

The Boarding House
Chap. 2nd

'T.I. presents compt. to I.T. and T.I. begs To say that i see the advertisement And she will Do Herself the pleasure of calling On you at 12 o'clock to-morrow morning.

'T.I. as To apologise to I.T. for the shortness Of the notice But i hope it will not unconvenience you.

'I remain

'yours Truly

'Wednesday evening.'

Little Mrs Tibbs perused the document over and over again; and the more she read it, the more was she confused by the mixture of the first and third person; the substitution of the 'I' for the 'T.I.' and the transition from the 'I.T.' to the 'you.' The writing looked like a skein of thread in a tangle, and the note was ingeniously folded into a perfect square, with the direction squeezed up into the right-hand corner, as if it were ashamed of itself. The back of the epistle was pleasingly ornamented with a large red wafer,[24] which, with the addition of divers ink-stains, bore a marvellous resemblance to a black beetle trodden upon. One thing, however, was perfectly clear to the perplexed Mrs Tibbs. Somebody was to call at twelve. The drawing-room was forthwith dusted for the third time that morning; three or four chairs were pulled out of their places, and a corresponding number of books carefully upset, in order that there might be a due absence of formality. Down went the piece of stair-carpet before noticed, and up ran Mrs Tibbs 'to make herself tidy.'

The clock of New Saint Pancras Church[25] struck twelve, and the Foundling,[26] with laudable politeness, did the same ten minutes afterwards. Saint something else struck the quarter, and then there arrived a single lady with a double knock, in a pelisse the colour of the interior of a damson pie; a bonnet of the same, with a regular conservatory of artificial flowers; a white veil, and a green parasol, with a cobweb border.

The visiter (who was very fat and red-faced) was shown into the drawing-room; Mrs Tibbs presented herself, and the negotiation commenced.

'I called in consequence of an advertisement,' said the stranger, in a voice as if she had been playing a set of Pan's pipes[27] for a fortnight without leaving off.

'Yes!' said Mrs Tibbs, rubbing her hands very slowly, and looking the applicant full in the face — two things she always did on such occasions.

'Money isn't no object whatever to me,' said the *lady*, 'so much as living in a state of retirement and obtrusion.'

Mrs Tibbs, as a matter of course, acquiesced in such an exceedingly natural desire.

'I am constantly attended by a medical man,' resumed the pelisse wearer; 'I have been a shocking unitarian[28] for some time — I, indeed, have had very little peace since the death of Mr Bloss.'

Mrs Tibbs looked at the relict of the departed Bloss, and thought he must have had very little peace in his time. Of course she could not say so; so she looked very sympathizing.

'I shall be a good deal of trouble to you,' said Mrs Bloss; 'but for that trouble I am willing to pay. I am going through a course of treatment which renders attention necessary. I have one mutton chop in bed at half-past eight, and another at ten, every morning.'

Mrs Tibbs, as in duty bound, expressed the pity she felt for any body placed in such a distressing situation; and the carnivorous Mrs Bloss proceeded to arrange the various preliminaries with wonderful despatch. 'Now mind,' said that lady, after terms were arranged; 'I am to have the second-floor front for my bedroom?'

'Yes, ma'am.'

'And you'll find room for my little servant Agnes?'

'Oh! certainly.'

'And I can have one of the cellars in the area for my bottled porter.'

'With the greatest pleasure; — James shall get it ready for you by Saturday.'

'And I'll join the company at the breakfast-table on Sunday morning,' said Mrs Bloss. 'I shall get up on purpose.'

'Very well,' returned Mrs Tibbs, in her most amiable tone; for satisfactory references had been 'given and required,' and it was quite certain that the new comer had plenty of money. 'It's rather singular,' continued Mrs Tibbs, with what was meant for a most bewitching smile, 'that we have a gentleman now with us, who is in a very delicate state of health – a Mr Gobler. – His apartment is the back drawing-room.'

'The next room?' inquired Mrs Bloss.

'The next room,' repeated the hostess.

'How very promiscuous!' ejaculated the widow.

'He hardly ever gets up,' said Mrs Tibbs in a whisper.

'Lor!' cried Mrs Bloss, in an equally low tone.

'And when he is up,' said Mrs Tibbs, 'we never can persuade him to go to bed again.'

'Dear me!' said the astonished Mrs Bloss, drawing her chair nearer Mrs Tibbs. 'What is his complaint?'

'Why, the fact is,' replied Mrs Tibbs, with a most communicative air, 'he has no stomach whatever.'

'No what?' inquired Mrs Bloss, with a look of the most indescribable alarm.

'No stomach,' repeated Mrs Tibbs, with a shake of the head.

'Lord bless us! what an extraordinary case!' gasped Mrs Bloss, as if she understood the communication in its literal sense, and was astonished at a gentleman without a stomach finding it necessary to board any where.

'When I say he has no stomach,' explained the chatty little Mrs Tibbs, 'I mean that his digestion is so much impaired, and his interior so deranged, that his stomach is not of the least use to him; – in fact, it's rather an inconvenience than otherwise.'

'Never heard such a case in my life!' exclaimed Mrs Bloss. 'Why, he's worse than I am!'

'Oh, yes!' replied Mrs Tibbs; – 'certainly.' She said this with great confidence, for the damson pelisse satisfactorily proved that Mrs Bloss, at all events, was not suffering under Mr Gobler's complaint.

'You have quite incited my curiosity,' said Mrs Bloss, as she rose to depart. 'How I long to see him!'

'He generally comes down once a week,' replied Mrs Tibbs; 'I dare say you'll see him on Sunday.' With this consolatory promise Mrs Bloss was obliged to be contented. She accordingly walked slowly down the stairs, detailing her complaints all the way; and Mrs Tibbs followed her, uttering an exclamation of compassion at every step. James (who looked very gritty, for he was cleaning the knives) fell up the kitchen-stairs, and opened the street-door; and, after mutual farewells, Mrs Bloss slowly departed down the shady side of the street.

It is almost superfluous to say, that the lady whom we have just shown out at the street-door (and whom the two female servants are now inspecting from the second-floor windows) was exceedingly vulgar, ignorant, and selfish. Her deceased better-half had been an eminent cork-cutter, in which capacity he had amassed a decent fortune. He had no relative but his nephew, and no friend but his cook. The former had the insolence one morning to ask for the loan of fifteen pounds, and by way of retaliation he married the latter next day; he made a will immediately afterwards, containing a burst of honest indignation against his nephew (who supported himself and two sisters on 100*l.* a year), and a bequest of his whole property to his wife. He felt ill after breakfast, and died after dinner. There is a mantelpiece-looking tablet in a civic parish church, setting forth his virtues, and deploring his loss. He never dishonoured a bill, or gave away a halfpenny!

The relict and sole executrix of this noble-minded man was an odd mixture of shrewdness and simplicity, liberality and meanness. Bred up as she had been, she knew no mode of living so agreeable as a boarding-house; and having nothing to do, and nothing to wish for, she naturally imagined she must be very ill – an impression which was most assiduously promoted by her medical attendant, Dr Wosky, and her handmaid Agnes, both of whom, doubtless for excellent reasons, encouraged all her extravagant notions.

Since the catastrophe recorded in the last chapter, Mrs Tibbs had been very shy of young lady boarders. Her present inmates were all lords of the creation, and she availed herself of the opportunity of their assemblage at the dinner-table, to announce the expected arrival of Mrs Bloss. The gentlemen received the communication with stoical indifference, and Mrs Tibbs devoted all her energies to prepare for the reception of the valetudinarian. The second-floor front was scrubbed, and washed, and flannelled, till the wet went through to the drawing-room ceiling. Clean white counterpanes, and curtains, and napkins; water-bottles as clear as crystal, blue jugs, and mahogany furniture, added to the splendour and increased the comfort of the apartment. The warming-pan was in constant requisition, and a fire lighted in the room every day. The chattels of Mrs Bloss were forwarded by instalments. First there came a large hamper of Guinness's stout and an umbrella; then a train of trunks; then a pair of clogs and a bandbox; then an easy chair with an air-cushion, then a variety of suspicious-looking packages; and – 'though last not least' – Mrs Bloss and Agnes, the latter in a cherry-coloured merino dress, open-work stockings, and shoes with sandals; looking like a disguised Columbine.²⁹

The installation of the Duke of Wellington, as Chancellor of the University of Oxford,³⁰ was nothing in point of bustle and turmoil to the installation of Mrs Bloss in her new quarters. True, there was no bright doctor of civil law to deliver a classical address on the occasion; but there were several other old women present, who spoke quite as much to the purpose, and understood themselves equally well. The chop-eater was so fatigued with the process of removal that she declined leaving her room until the following morning; so a mutton-chop, pickle, a two grain calomel pill, a pint bottle of stout, and other medicines, were carried up stairs for her consumption.

'Why, what *do* you think, ma'am?' inquired the inquisitive Agnes of her mistress, after they had been in the house some three hours; 'what *do* you think, ma'am? the lady of the house is married.'

'Married!' said Mrs Bloss, taking the pill and a draught of Guinness – 'married! Unpossible!'

'She is indeed, ma'am,' returned the Columbine; 'and her husband, ma'am, lives – he – he – he – lives in the kitchen, ma'am.'

'In the kitchen!'

'Yes, ma'am: and he – he – he – the housemaid says, he never goes into the parlour except on Sundays; and that Mrs Tibbs makes him clean the gentlemen's boots; and that he cleans the windows, too, sometimes; and that one morning early, when he was in the front balcony cleaning the drawing-room windows, he called out to a gentleman on the opposite side of the way, who used to live here — "Ah! Mr Calton, sir, how are you?"' Here the attendant laughed till Mrs Bloss was in serious apprehension of her chuckling herself into a fit.

'Well, I never!' said Mrs Bloss.

'Yes, and please, ma'am, the servants give him gin-and-water sometimes; and then he cries and says he hates his wife and the boarders, and wants to tickle them.'

'Tickle the boarders!' exclaimed Mrs Bloss, seriously alarmed.

'No, ma'am, not the boarders, the servants.'

'Oh, is that all!' said Mrs Bloss, quite satisfied.

'He wanted to kiss me as I came up the kitchen-stairs, just now,' said Agnes, indignantly; 'but I gave it him — a little wretch!'

This intelligence was but too true. A long course of snubbing and neglect; his days spent in the kitchen, and his nights in the turn-up bedstead, had completely broken the little spirit that the unfortunate volunteer had ever possessed. He had no one to whom he could detail his injuries but the servants, and they were almost of necessity his chosen confidents. It is no less strange than true, however, that the little weaknesses which he had incurred, most probably during his military career, seemed to increase as his comforts diminished. He was actually a sort of journeyman Giovanni[31] in the basement story.

The next morning, being Sunday, breakfast was laid in the front parlour at ten o'clock. Nine was the usual time, but the family always breakfasted an hour later on sabbath. Tibbs enrobed himself in his Sunday costume — a black coat, and exceedingly short, thin trousers, with a very large white waistcoat, white stockings and cravat, and Blucher boots — and mounted to the parlour aforesaid. Nobody had come down, and he amused himself by drinking the contents of the milkpot with a teaspoon.

A pair of slippers were heard descending the stairs; Tibbs flew to a chair, and a stern-looking man, of about fifty, with very little hair on his head, and a Sunday paper in his hand, entered the room.

'Good morning, Mr Evenson,' said Tibbs, very humbly, with something between a nod and bow.

'How do you, Mr Tibbs?' replied he of the slippers, as he sat himself down, and began to read his paper without saying another word.

'Is Mr Wisbottle in town to-day, do you know, sir?' inquired Tibbs, just for the sake of saying something.

'I should think he was,' replied the stern gentleman. 'He was whistling "The Light Guitar,"[32] in the next room to mine, at five o'clock this morning.'

'He's very fond of whistling,' said Tibbs with a slight smirk.

'Yes – I ain't,' was the laconic reply.

Mr John Evenson was in the receipt of an independent income, arising chiefly from various houses he owned in the different suburbs. He was very morose and discontented. He was a thorough radical, and used to attend a great variety of public meetings, for the express purpose of finding fault with every thing that was proposed. Mr Wisbottle, on the other hand, was a high Tory. He was a clerk in the Woods and Forests Office,[33] which he considered rather an aristocratic employment; he knew the peerage by heart, and could tell you off-hand where any illustrious personage lived. He had a good set of teeth, and a capital tailor. Mr Evenson looked on all these qualifications with profound contempt; and the consequence was that the two were always disputing, much to the edification of the rest of the house. It should be added, that, in addition to his partiality for whistling, Mr Wisbottle had a great idea of his singing powers. There were two other boarders besides the gentleman in the back drawing-room – Mr Alfred Tomkins and Mr Frederick O'Bleary. Mr Tomkins was a clerk in a wine-house; he was a connoisseur in paintings, and had a wonderful eye for the picturesque. Mr O'Bleary was an Irishman, recently imported; he was in a perfectly wild state, and had come over to England to be an apothecary, a clerk in a government office, an actor, a reporter, or any thing else that turned up – he was not particular. He was on familiar terms with two small Irish members, and got franks for every body in the house.[34] He felt convinced that his intrinsic merits must procure him a high destiny. He wore shepherd's-plaid inexpressibles, and used to look under all the ladies' bonnets as he walked along the streets. His manners and appearance always forcibly reminded one of Orson.[35]

'Here comes Mr Wisbottle,' said Tibbs; and Mr Wisbottle forthwith appeared in blue slippers, and a shawl dressing-gown, whistling '*Di piacer*.'[36]

'Good morning, sir,' said Tibbs again. It was about the only thing he ever said to any body.

'How are you, Tibbs?' condescendingly replied the amateur; and he walked to the window, and whistled louder than ever.

'Pretty air, that!' said Evenson with a snarl, and without taking his eyes off the paper.

'Glad you like it,' replied Wisbottle, highly gratified.

'Don't you think it would sound better, if you whistled it a little louder?' inquired the mastiff.

'No; I don't think it would,' rejoined the unconscious Wisbottle.

'I'll tell you what, Wisbottle,' said Evenson, who had been bottling up his anger for some hours – 'the next time you feel disposed to whistle "The Light Guitar" at five o'clock in the morning, I'll trouble you to whistle it with your head out o'window. If you don't, I'll learn the triangle – I will by —.'

The entrance of Mrs Tibbs (with the keys in a little basket) interrupted the threat, and prevented its conclusion.

Mrs Tibbs apologized for being down rather late; the bell was rung; James brought up the urn, and received an unlimited order for dry toast and bacon. Tibbs sat down at the bottom of the table, and began eating water-cresses like a second Nebuchadnezzar.[37] Mr O'Bleary appeared, and Mr Alfred Tomkins. The compliments of the morning were exchanged, and the tea was made.

'God bless me!' exclaimed Tomkins, who had been looking out at the window. 'Here – Wisbottle – pray come here: make haste.'

Mr Wisbottle started from the table, and every one looked up.

'Do you see,' said the connoisseur, placing Wisbottle in the right position – 'a little more this way: there – do you see how splendidly the light falls upon the left side of that broken chimney-pot at No. 48?'

'Dear me! I see,' replied Wisbottle, in a tone of admiration.

'I never saw an object stand out so beautifully against the clear sky in my life,' ejaculated Alfred. Every body (except John Evenson) echoed the sentiment, for Mr Tomkins had a great character for finding out beauties which no one else could discover – he certainly deserved it.

'I have frequently observed a chimney-pot in College-green, Dublin, which has a much better effect,' said the patriotic O'Bleary who never allowed Ireland to be outdone on any point.

The assertion was received with obvious incredulity, for Mr Tomkins declared that no other chimney-pot in the United Kingdom, broken or unbroken, could be so beautiful as the one at No. 48.

The room-door was suddenly thrown open, and Agnes appeared leading in Mrs Bloss, who was dressed in a geranium-coloured muslin gown, and displayed a gold watch of huge dimensions; a chain to match, and a splendid assortment of rings, with enormous stones. A general rush was made for a chair, and a regular introduction took place. Mr John Evenson made a slight inclination of the head; Mr Frederick O'Bleary, Mr Alfred Tomkins, and Mr Wisbottle bowed like the mandarins in a grocer's shop;[38] Tibbs rubbed hands, and went round in circles. He was observed to close one eye, and to assume a clock-work sort of expression with the other; this has been considered as a wink, and it has been reported that Agnes was its object. We repel the calumny, and challenge contradiction.

Mrs Tibbs inquired after Mrs Bloss's health in a low tone. Mrs Bloss, with a supreme contempt for the memory of Lindley Murray,[39] answered the various questions in a most satisfactory manner; and a pause ensued, during which the eatables disappeared with awful rapidity.

'You must have been very much pleased with the appearance of the ladies going to the drawing-room the other day, Mr O'Bleary?' said Mrs Tibbs, hoping to start a topic.

'Yes,' replied Orson, with a mouthful of toast.

'Never saw any thing like it before, I suppose?' suggested Wisbottle.

'No – except the Lord Lieutenant's levees,'[40] replied O'Bleary.

'Are they at all equal to our drawing-rooms?'

'Oh, infinitely superior!'

'Gad! I don't know,' said the aristocratic Wisbottle, 'the Dowager Marchioness of Publiccash was most magnificently dressed and so was the Baron Slappenbachenhausen.'

'What was he presented on?' inquired Evenson.

'On his arrival in England.'

'I thought so,' growled the radical; 'you never hear of these fellows being presented on their going away again. They know better than that.'

'Unless somebody pervades them with an apintment,' said Mrs Bloss, joining in the conversation in a faint voice.

'Well,' said Wisbottle, evading the point, 'it's a splendid sight.'

'And did it never occur to you,' inquired the radical, who never would be quiet – 'did it never occur to you, that you pay for these precious ornaments of society?'

'It certainly *has* occurred to me,' said Wisbottle, who thought this answer was a poser; 'it *has* occurred to me, and I am willing to pay for them.'

'Well, and it has occurred to me too,' replied John Evenson, 'and I ain't willing to pay for 'em. Then why should I? – I say, why should I?' continued the politician, laying down the paper, and knocking his knuckles on the table. 'There are two great principles – demand –'

'A cup of tea if you please, dear,' interrupted Tibbs.

'And supply –'

'May I trouble you to hand this tea to Mr Tibbs?' said Mrs Tibbs, interrupting the argument, and unconsciously illustrating it.

The thread of the orator's discourse was broken. He drank his tea and resumed the paper.

'If it's very fine,' said Mr Alfred Tomkins, addressing the company in general, 'I shall ride down to Richmond to-day, and come back by the steamer. There are some splendid effects of light and shade on the Thames; the contrast between the blueness of the sky and the yellow water is frequently exceedingly beautiful.' Mr Wisbottle hummed, 'Flow on, thou shining river.'[41]

'We have some splendid steam-vessels in Ireland,' said O'Bleary.

'Certainly,' said Mrs Bloss, delighted to find a subject broached in which she could take part.

'The accommodations are extraordinary,' said O'Bleary.

'Extraordinary indeed,' returned Mrs Bloss. 'When Mr Bloss was alive he was promiscuously obligated to go to Ireland on business. I went with him, and raly the manner in which the ladies and gentlemen were accommodated with births, is not creditable.'

Tibbs, who had been listening to the dialogue, looked very aghast, and evinced a strong inclination to ask a question, but was checked by a look from his wife. Mr Wisbottle laughed, and said Tomkins had made a pun; and Tomkins laughed too, and said he had not.

The remainder of the meal passed off as breakfasts usually do. Conversation flagged, and people played with their teaspoons. The gentlemen looked out at the window; walked about the room, and when they got near the door, dropped off one by one. Tibbs retired to the back parlour by his wife's orders, to check the greengrocer's weekly account; and ultimately Mrs Tibbs and Mrs Bloss were left alone together.

'Oh dear!' said the latter, 'I feel alarmingly faint; it's very singular.' (It certainly was, for she had eaten four pounds of solids that morning.) 'By-the-by,' said Mrs Bloss, 'I have not seen Mr what's his name yet.'

'Mr Gobler?' suggested Mrs Tibbs.

'Yes.'

'Oh!' said Mrs Tibbs, 'he is a most mysterious person. He has his meals regularly sent up stairs, and sometimes don't leave his room for weeks together.'

'I haven't seen or heard nothing of him,' repeated Mrs Bloss.

'I dare say you'll hear him to-night,' replied Mrs Tibbs; 'he generally groans a good deal on Sunday evenings.'

'I never felt such an interest in any one in my life,' ejaculated Mrs Bloss. A finicking double-knock interrupted the conversation; Doctor Wosky was announced, and duly shown in. He was a little man with a red face, — dressed of course in black, with a stiff white neckerchief. He had a very good practice, and plenty of money, which he had amassed by invariably humouring the worst fancies of all the females of all the families he had ever been introduced into. Mrs Tibbs offered to retire, but was entreated to stay.

'Well, my dear ma'am, and how are we?' inquired Wosky in a soothing tone.

'Very ill, doctor — very ill,' said Mrs Bloss in a whisper.

'Ah! we must take care of ourselves; — we must, indeed,' said the obsequious Wosky, as he felt the pulse of his interesting patient.

'How is our appetite?'

Mrs Bloss shook her head.

'Our friend requires great care,' said Wosky, appealing to Mrs Tibbs, who of course assented. 'I hope, however, with the blessing of Providence,' continued the doctor, 'that we shall be enabled to make her quite stout again.' Mrs Tibbs wondered in her own mind what the patient would be when she had got quite stout.

'We must take stimulants,' said the cunning Wosky — 'plenty of nourishment, and, above all, we must keep our nerves quiet; we positively must not give way to our sensibilities. We must take all we can get,' concluded the doctor as he pocketed his fee, 'and we must keep quiet.'

'Dear man!' exclaimed Mrs Bloss as the doctor stepped into his carriage.

'Charming creature indeed — quite a lady's man,' said Mrs Tibbs, and Doctor Wosky rattled away to make fresh gulls of delicate females, and pocket fresh fees.

As we had occasion in a former paper to describe a dinner at Mrs Tibbs's, and as one meal went off very like another on all ordinary occasions, we will not fatigue our readers by entering into any other detailed account of the domestic economy of the establishment.

We will therefore proceed to events, merely premising that the mysterious tenant of the back drawing-room was a lazy, selfish, hypochondriac; always complaining and never ill. As his character in many respects closely assimilated to that of Mrs Bloss, a very warm friendship soon sprung up between them. He was tall, thin, and pale; he always fancied he had a severe pain somewhere or other, and his face invariably wore a pinched, screwed-up expression; he looked, indeed, like a man who had got his feet in a tub of exceedingly hot water against his will.

For two or three months after Mrs Bloss's first appearance in Coram-street, John Evenson was observed to become every day more sarcastic and more ill-natured, and there was a degree of additional importance in his manner, which clearly showed that he fancied he had discovered something, which he only wanted a proper opportunity of divulging. He found it at last.

One evening, the different inmates of the house were assembled in the drawing-room engaged in their ordinary occupations. Mr Gobler and Mrs Bloss were sitting at a small card-table near the centre window, playing cribbage; Mr Wisbottle was describing semicircles on the music-stool, turning over the leaves of a book on the piano, and humming most melodiously; Alfred Tomkins was sitting at the round table with his elbows duly squared, making a pencil sketch of a head considerably larger than his own; O'Bleary was reading Horace,[42] and trying to look as if he understood it; and John Evenson had drawn his chair close to Mrs Tibbs's work-table, and was talking to her very earnestly in a low tone.

'I can assure you, Mrs Tibbs,' said the radical, laying his forefinger on the muslin she was at work on; 'I can assure you, Mrs Tibbs, that nothing but the interest I take in your welfare would induce me to make this communication. I repeat that I fear Wisbottle is endeavouring to gain the affections of that young woman, Agnes, and that he is in the habit of meeting her in the storeroom on the first floor, over the leads. From my bedroom I distinctly heard voices there last night. I opened my door immediately, and crept very softly on to the landing; there I saw Mr

Tibbs, who, it seems, had been disturbed also. − Bless me, Mrs Tibbs, you change colour!'

'No, no − it's nothing,' returned Mrs T. in a hurried manner; 'it's only the heat of the room.'

'A flush!' ejaculated Mrs Bloss from the card-table; 'that's good for four.'

'If I thought it was Mr Wisbottle,' said Mrs Tibbs, after a pause, 'he should leave this house instantly.'

'Go!' said Mrs Bloss again.

'And if I thought,' continued the hostess with a most threatening air, 'if I thought he was assisted by Mr Tibbs' −

'One for his nob!' said Gobler.

'Oh,' said Evenson, in a most soothing tone − he liked to make mischief − 'I should hope Mr Tibbs was not in any way implicated. He always appeared to me very harmless.'

'I have generally found him so,' sobbed poor little Mrs Tibbs; crying like a watering-pot in full play.

'Hush! hush! pray − Mrs Tibbs − consider − we shall be observed − pray, don't!' said John Evenson, fearing his whole plan would be interrupted. 'We will set the matter at rest with the utmost care, and I shall be most happy to assist you in doing so.'

Mrs Tibbs murmured her thanks.

'When you think every one has retired to rest to-night,' said Evenson very pompously, 'if you'll meet me without a light, just outside my bedroom-door, by the staircase-window, I think we can ascertain who the parties really are, and you will afterwards be enabled to proceed as you think proper.'

Mrs Tibbs was easily persuaded; her curiosity was excited, her jealousy was roused, and the arrangement was forthwith made. She resumed her work, and John Evenson walked up and down the room with his hands in his pockets, looking as if nothing had happened. The game of cribbage was over, and conversation began again.

'Well, Mr O'Bleary,' said the humming top, turning round on his pivot, and facing the company, 'what did you think of Vauxhall the other night?'

'Oh, it's very fair,' replied Orson, who had been enthusiastically delighted with the whole exhibition.

'Never saw any thing like that Captain Ross's set-out[43] – eh?'

'No,' returned the patriot with his usual reservation – 'except in Dublin.'

'I saw the Count de Canky and Captain Fitzthompson in the Gardens,' said Wisbottle; 'they appeared much delighted.'

'Then it must be beautiful!' snarled Evenson.

'I think the white bears is partickerlerly well done,' suggested Mrs Bloss. 'In their shaggy white coats they look just like Polar bears – don't you think they do, Mr Evenson?'

'I think they look a great deal more like omnibus cads[44] on all fours,' replied the discontented one.

'Upon the whole, I should have liked our evening very well,' gasped Gobler; 'only I caught a desperate cold which increased my pain dreadfully; I was obliged to have several shower-baths, before I could leave my room.'

'Capital things those shower-baths!' ejaculated Wisbottle.

'Excellent!' said Tomkins.

'Delightful!' chimed in O'Bleary. (He had once seen one outside a tinman's.)

'Disgusting machines!' rejoined Evenson, who extended his dislike to almost every created object, masculine, feminine, or neuter.

'Disgusting, Mr Evenson!' said Gobler, in a tone of strong indignation. – 'Disgusting! Look at their utility – consider how many lives they have saved by promoting perspiration.'

'Promoting perspiration, indeed,' growled John Evenson, stopping short in his walk across the large squares in the pattern of the carpet – 'I was ass enough to be persuaded some time ago to have one in my bedroom. 'Gad, I was in it once, and it effectually cured *me* certainly, for the mere sight of it threw me into a profuse perspiration for six months afterwards.'

A general titter followed this anouncement, and before it had subsided James brought up 'the tray,' containing the remains of a leg of lamb which had made its *début* at dinner; bread, cheese; an atom of butter in a forest of parsley; one pickled walnut and the third of another, and so forth. The boy disappeared, and returned again with another tray, containing glasses and jugs of hot and cold water. The gentlemen brought in their spirit-bottles; the housemaid placed divers plated bedroom candlesticks under the card-table, and the servants retired for the night.

Chairs were drawn round the table, and the conversation proceeded in the customary manner. John Evenson, who never eat supper, lolled on the sofa, and amused himself by contradicting every body. O'Bleary eat as much as he could conveniently carry, and Mrs Tibbs felt a due degree of indignation thereat; Mr Gobler and Mrs Bloss conversed most affectionately on the subject of pill taking and other innocent amusements; and Tomkins and Wisbottle 'got into an argument;' that is to say, they both talked very loudly and vehemently, each flattering himself that he had got some advantage about something, and neither of them having more than a very indistinct idea of what they were talking about. An hour or two passed away; and the boarders and the brass candle-sticks retired in pairs to their respective bedrooms. John Evenson pulled off his boots, locked his door, and determined to sit up until Mr Gobler had retired. He always sat in the drawing-room about an hour after every body else had left it, taking medicine, and groaning.

Great Coram-street was hushed into a state of the most profound repose: it was nearly two o'clock. A hackney-coach now and then rumbled slowly by; and occasionally some stray lawyer's clerk on his way home to Somers-town struck his iron heel on the top of the coal-cellar with a noise resembling the click of a smoke-jack.[45] A low, monotonous, gushing sound was heard, which added considerably to the romantic dreariness of the scene. It was the water 'coming in' at No. 11.

'He must be asleep by this time,' said John Evenson to himself after waiting with exemplary patience for nearly an hour after Mr Gobler had left the drawing-room. He listened for a few moments; the house was perfectly quiet; he extinguished his rush-light, and opened his bedroom-door. The staircase was so dark that it was impossible to see any thing.

'S–s–s!' whispered the mischief-maker, making a noise like the first indication a catherine-wheel gives of the probability of its going off.

'Hush!' whispered somebody else.

'Is that you, Mrs Tibbs?'

'Yes, sir.'

'Where?'

'Here;' and the misty outline of Mrs Tibbs appeared at the staircase-window, like the ghost of Queen Anne in the tent scene in Richard.[46]

'This way, Mrs Tibbs,' whispered the delighted busybody: 'give me your hand – there. Whoever these people are, they are in the storeroom now, for I have been looking down from my window, and I could see that they accidentally upset their candlestick, and are now in darkness. You have no shoes on, have you?'

'No,' said little Mrs Tibbs, who could hardly speak for trembling.

'Well; I have taken my boots off, so we can go down close to the storeroom-door and listen over the banisters,' continued Evenson; and down stairs they both crept accordingly, every board creaking like a patent mangle on a Saturday afternoon.

'It's Wisbottle and somebody I'll swear,' exclaimed the radical in an energetic whisper, when they had listened for a few moments.

'Hush – pray let's hear what they say!' exclaimed Mrs Tibbs, the gratification of whose curiosity was now paramount to every other consideration.

'Ah! if I could but believe you,' said a female voice coquettishly, 'I'd be bound to settle my missis for life.'

'What does she say?' inquired Mr Evenson, who was not quite so well situated as his companion.

'She says she'll settle her missis's life,' replied Mrs Tibbs. 'The wretch! they're plotting murder.'

'I know you want money,' continued the voice, which belonged to Agnes; 'and if you'd secure me the five hundred pounds, I warrant she should take fire soon enough.'

'What's that?' inquired Evenson again. He could just hear enough to want to hear more.

'I think she says she'll set the house on fire,' replied the affrighted Mrs Tibbs. 'Thank God I'm insured in the Phœnix!'[47]

'The moment I have secured your mistress, my dear,' said a man's voice in a strong Irish brogue, 'you may depend on having the money.'

'Bless my soul, it's Mr O'Bleary!' exclaimed Mrs Tibbs in a parenthesis.

'The villain!' said the indignant Mr Evenson.

'The first thing to be done,' continued the Hibernian, 'is to poison Mr Gobler's mind.'

'Oh, certainly!' returned Agnes, with the utmost coolness.

'What's that?' inquired Evenson again, in an agony of curiosity and a whisper.

'He says she's to mind and poison Mr Gobler,' replied Mrs Tibbs, perfectly aghast at this awful sacrifice of human life.

'And in regard to Mrs Tibbs,' continued O'Bleary. – Mrs Tibbs shuddered.

'Hush!' exclaimed Agnes, in a tone of the greatest alarm, just as Mrs Tibbs was on the extreme verge of a fainting-fit. 'Hush!'

'Hush!' exclaimed Evenson, at the same moment to Mrs Tibbs.

'There's somebody coming *up* stairs,' said Agnes to O'Bleary.

'There's somebody coming *down* stairs,' whispered Evenson to Mrs Tibbs.

'Go into the parlour, sir,' said Agnes to her companion. 'You will get there, before whoever it is, gets to the top of the kitchen-stairs.'

'The drawing-room, Mrs Tibbs!' whispered the astonished Evenson to his equally astonished companion; and for the drawing-room they both made, plainly hearing the rustling of two persons, one coming down stairs, and one coming up.

'What can it be?' exclaimed Mrs Tibbs. 'It's like a dream. I wouldn't be found in this situation for the world!'

'Nor I,' returned Evenson, who could never bear a joke at his own expense. 'Hush! here they are at the door.'

'What fun!' whispered one of the new comers. – It was Wisbottle.

'Glorious!' replied his companion, in an equally low tone. – This was Alfred Tomkins. 'Who would have thought it?'

'I told you so,' said Wisbottle, in a most knowing whisper. 'Lord bless you, he has paid her most extraordinary attention for the last two months. I saw 'em when I was sitting at the piano to-night.'

'Well, do you know I didn't notice it?' interrupted Tomkins.

'Not notice it!' continued Wisbottle. 'Bless you; I saw him whispering to her, and she crying; and then I'll swear I heard him say something about to-night when we were all in bed.'

'They're talking of *us*!' exclaimed the agonized Mrs Tibbs, as the painful suspicion, and a sense of their situation, flashed upon her mind.

'I know it – I know it,' replied Evenson, with a melancholy consciousness that there was no mode of escape.

'What's to be done? we cannot both stop here!' ejaculated Mrs Tibbs, in a state of partial derangement.

'I'll get up the chimney,' replied Evenson, who really meant what he said.

'You can't,' said Mrs Tibbs, in despair. 'You can't – it's a register stove.'[48]

'Hush!' repeated John Evenson.

'Hush – hush!' cried somebody down stairs.

'What a d – d hushing!' said Alfred Tomkins, who began to get rather bewildered.

'There they are!' exclaimed the sapient Wisbottle, as a rustling noise was heard in the storeroom.

'Hark!' whispered both the young men.

'Hark!' repeated Mrs Tibbs and Evenson.

'Let me alone, sir,' said a female voice in the storeroom.

'Oh, Hagnes!' cried another voice, which clearly belonged to Tibbs, for nobody else ever owned one like it. 'Oh, Hagnes – lovely creature!'

'Be quiet, sir!' (A bounce.)

'Hag –'

'Be quiet, sir – I am ashamed of you. Think of your wife, Mr Tibbs. Be quiet, sir!'

'My wife!' exclaimed the valorous Tibbs, who was clearly under the influence of gin-and-water, and a misplaced attachment; 'I ate her! Oh, Hagnes! when I was in the volunteer corps, in eighteen hundred and –'

'I declare I'll scream. Be quiet, sir, will you?' (Another bounce, and a scuffle.)

'What's that?' exclaimed Tibbs, with a start.

'What's what?' said Agnes, stopping short.

'Why, that!'

'Ah! you have done it nicely now, sir,' sobbed the frightened Agnes, as a tapping was heard at Mrs Tibbs's bedroom-door, which would have beaten any twelve woodpeckers[49] hollow.

'Mrs Tibbs! Mrs Tibbs!' called out Mrs Bloss. 'Mrs Tibbs, pray get up.' (Here the imitation of a woodpecker was resumed with tenfold violence.)

'Oh, dear – dear!' exclaimed the wretched partner of the depraved Tibbs. 'She's knocking at my door. We must be discovered! What will they think?'

'Mrs Tibbs! Mrs Tibbs!' screamed the woodpecker again.

'What's the matter?' shouted Gobler, bursting out of the back drawing-room, like the dragon at Astley's[50] – only without the portable gas in his countenance.

'Oh, Mr Gobler!' cried Mrs Bloss, with a proper approximation to hysterics; 'I think the house is on fire, or else there's thieves in it. I have heard the most dreadful noises!'

'The devil you have!' shouted Gobler again, bouncing back into his den, in happy imitation of the aforesaid dragon, and returning immediately with a lighted candle. 'Why, what's this? Wisbottle! Tomkins! O'Bleary! Agnes! What the deuce! all up and dressed?'

'Astonishing!' said Mrs Bloss, who had run down stairs, and taken Mr Gobler's arm.

'Call Mrs Tibbs directly, somebody,' said Gobler, turning into the front drawing-room. – 'What! Mrs Tibbs and Mr Evenson!!'

'Mrs Tibbs and Mr Evenson!' repeated every body, as that unhappy pair were discovered, Mrs Tibbs seated in an arm-chair by the fireplace, and Mr Evenson standing by her side.

We must leave the scene that ensued to the reader's imagination. We could tell how Mrs Tibbs forthwith fainted away, and how it required the united strength of Mr Wisbottle and Mr Alfred Tomkins to hold her in her chair; how Mr Evenson explained, and how his explanation was evidently disbelieved; – how Agnes repelled the accusations of Mrs Tibbs, by proving that she was negotiating with Mr O'Bleary to influence her mistress's affections in his behalf; and how Mr Gobler threw a damp counterpane on the hopes of Mr O'Bleary by avowing that he (Gobler) had already proposed to, and been accepted by, Mrs Bloss; how Agnes was discharged from that lady's service; how Mr O'Bleary discharged himself from Mrs Tibbs's house, without going through the form of previously discharging his bill; and how that disappointed young gentleman rails against England and the English, and vows there is no virtue or fine feeling extant, 'except in Ireland.' We repeat that we *could* tell all this, but we love to exercise our self-denial, and we therefore prefer leaving it to be imagined.

The lady whom we have hitherto described as Mrs Bloss, is no more. Mrs Gobler exists: Mrs Bloss has left us for ever. In a secluded retreat in Newington Butts,[51] far – far removed from the noisy strife of that great boarding-house, the world, the enviable Gobler and his pleasing wife revel in retirement; happy in their complaints, their table, and their medicine; wafted through life by the grateful prayers of all the purveyors of animal food within three miles round.

We would willingly stop here, but we have a painful duty imposed upon us, which we must discharge. Mr and Mrs Tibbs have separated by mutual consent, Mrs Tibbs receiving one moiety of 43*l*. 15*s*. 10*d*., which we before stated to be the amount of her husband's annual income, and Mr Tibbs the other. He is spending the evening of his days in retirement, and he is spending also, annually, that small but honourable independence. He resides among the original settlers at Walworth,[52] and it has been stated, on unquestionable authority, that the conclusion of the volunteer story has been heard in a small tavern in that respectable neighbourhood.

The unfortunate Mrs Tibbs has determined to dispose of the whole of her furniture by public auction, and to retire from a residence in which she has suffered so much. Mr Robins[53] has been applied to, to conduct the sale, and the transcendent abilities of the literary gentleman connected with his establishment are now devoted to the task of drawing up the preliminary advertisement. It is to contain, among a variety of brilliant matter, seventy-eight words in large capitals, and six *original* quotations in inverted commas.

CHAPTER 2

Mr Minns and His Cousin

MR AUGUSTUS MINNS was a bachelor, of about forty as he said — of about eight-and-forty as his friends said. He was always exceedingly clean, precise, and tidy; perhaps somewhat priggish and the most retiring man in the world. He usually wore a brown frock-coat without a wrinkle, light inexplicables[1] without a spot, a neat neckerchief with a remarkably neat tie, and boots without a fault: moreover, he always carried a brown silk umbrella with an ivory handle. He was a clerk in Somerset-house,[2] or, as he said himself, he held 'a responsible situation under Government.' He had a good and increasing salary, in addition to some 10,000*l.* of his own (invested in the funds[3]), and he occupied a first floor in Tavistock-street, Covent-garden, where he had resided for twenty years, having been in the habit of quarrelling with his landlord the whole time, regularly giving notice of his intention to quit on the first day of every quarter, and as regularly countermanding it on the second. There were two classes of created objects which he held in the deepest and most unmingled horror: they were, dogs and

Mr Minns and his Cousin

children. He was not unamiable, but he could at any time have viewed the execution of a dog, or the assassination of an infant, with the liveliest satisfaction. Their habits were at variance with his love of order; and his love of order, was as powerful as his love of life. Mr Augustus Minns had no relations, in or near London, with the exception of his cousin Mr Octavius Budden, to whose son, whom he had never seen (for he disliked the father) he had consented to become godfather by proxy. Mr Budden having realized a moderate fortune by exercising the trade or calling of a corn-chandler, and having a great predilection for the country, had purchased a cottage in the vicinity of Stamford-hill,[4] whither he retired with the wife of his bosom, and his only son, Master Alexander Augustus Budden. One evening, as Mr and Mrs B. were admiring their son, discussing his various merits, talking over his education, and disputing whether the classics should be made an essential part thereof, the lady pressed so strongly upon her husband the propriety of cultivating the friendship of Mr Minns in behalf of their son, that Mr Budden at last made up his mind, that it should not be his fault if he and his cousin were not in future more intimate.

'I'll break the ice, my love,' said Mr Budden, stirring up the sugar at the bottom of his glass of brandy-and-water, and casting a sidelong look at his spouse to see the effect of the announcement of his determination, 'by asking Minns down to dine with us, on Sunday.'

'Then, pray Mr Budden, write to your cousin at once,' replied Mrs Budden. 'Who knows, if we could only get him down here, but that he might take a fancy to our Alexander, and leave him his property? – Alick, my dear, take your legs off the rail of the chair!'

'Very true,' said Mr Budden, musing, 'very true, indeed, my love!'

On the following morning, as Mr Minns was sitting at his breakfast-table, alternately biting his dry toast and casting a look upon the columns of his morning paper, which he always read from the title to the printer's name, he heard a loud knock at the street-door; which was shortly afterwards followed by the entrance of his servant, who put into his hand a particularly small card, on which was engraved in immense letters 'Mr Octavius Budden, Amelia Cottage (Mrs B.'s name was Amelia), Poplar-walk, Stamford-hill.'

'Budden,' ejaculated Minns, 'what the deuce⁵ can bring that vulgar fellow here! – say I'm asleep – say I'm out, and shall never be home again – any thing to keep him down stairs.'

'But please, sir, the gentleman's coming up,' replied the servant: and the fact was made perfectly evident, by an appalling creaking of boots on the staircase accompanied by a pattering noise, the cause of which Minns could not, for the life of him divine.

'Hem! – show the gentleman in,' said the unfortunate bachelor. Exit servant, and enter Octavius preceded by a large white dog, dressed in a suit of fleecy hosiery, with pink eyes, large ears, and no perceptible tail.

The cause of the pattering on the stairs was but too plain. Mr Augustus Minns staggered beneath the shock of the dog's appearance.

'My dear fellow, how are you?' said Budden as he entered.

He always spoke at the top of his voice, and always said the same thing half-a-dozen times.

'How are you, my hearty?'

'How do you do, Mr Budden? – pray take a chair!' politely stammered the discomfited Minns.

'Thank you – thank you – well – how are you, eh?'

'Uncommonly well, thank ye,' said Minns casting a diabolical look at the dog, who with his hind legs on the floor, and his fore paws resting on the table, was dragging a bit of bread-and-butter out of a plate, preparatory to devouring it, with the buttered side next the carpet.

'Ah, you rogue!' said Budden to his dog; 'you see, Minns, he's like me, always at home, eh, my boy? – Egad, I'm precious hot and hungry! I've walked all the way from Stamford-hill this morning.'

'Have you breakfasted?' inquired Minns.

'Oh, no! – came to breakfast with you; so ring the bell, my dear fellow, will you? and let's have another cup and saucer, and the cold ham. — Make myself at home you see!' continued Budden, dusting his boots with a table napkin. 'Ha! — ha! — ha! — 'pon my life, I'm hungry.'

Minns rang the bell, and tried to smile.

'I decidedly never was so hot in my life,' continued Octavius, wiping his forehead: 'well, but how are you, Minns. 'Pon my soul you wear capitally!'

'D'ye think so?' said Minns; and he tried another smile.

''Pon my life, I do!'

'Mrs B. and — what's his name – quite well?'

'Alick — my son, you mean, never better — never better. But at such a place as we've got at Poplar-walk, you know, he couldn't be ill if he tried. When I first saw it, by Jove! it looked so knowing, with the front garden, and the green railings, and the brass knocker, and all that — I really thought it was a cut above me.'

'Don't you think you'd like the ham better,' interrupted Minns 'if you cut it the other way?' He saw, with feelings which it is impossible to describe, that his visiter was cutting or rather maiming the ham, in utter violation of all established rules.

'No, thank ye,' returned Budden, with the most barbarous indifference to crime, 'I prefer it this way — it eats short. But I say, Minns, when will you come down and see us? You will be delighted with the place; I know you will. Amelia and I were talking about you the other night, and Amelia said — another lump of sugar, please; thank ye — she said, don't you think you could contrive, my dear, to say to Mr Minns, in a friendly way — come down, sir — damn the dog! he's spoiling your curtains, Minns — ha! — ha! — ha!' Minns leaped from his seat as though he had received the discharge from a galvanic battery.

'Come out, sir! — go out, hoo!' cried poor Augustus, keeping nevertheless, at a very respectful distance from the dog, having read of a case of hydrophobia in the paper of that morning. By dint of great exertion, much shouting, and a marvellous deal of poking under the tables with a stick and umbrella, the dog was at last dislodged, and placed on the landing, outside the door, where he immediately commenced a most appalling howling; at the same time vehemently scratching the paint off the two nicely-varnished bottom panels of the door, until they resembled the interior of a back-gammon-board.

'A good dog for the country that!' coolly observed Budden to the distracted Minns — 'he's not much used to confinement, though. But now, Minns, when will you come down? I'll take no denial, positively. Let's see, to-day's Thursday. — Will you come on Sunday? We dine at five, don't say no — do.'

After a great deal of pressing, Mr Augustus Minns, driven to despair, accepted the invitation and promised to be at Poplar-walk on the ensuing Sunday, at a quarter before five to the minute.

'Now mind the direction,' said Budden; 'the coach goes from the Flowerpot,⁶ in Bishopsgate-street, every half hour. When the coach stops at the Swan,⁷ you'll see, immediately opposite you a white house.'

'Which is your house — I understand,' said Minns, wishing to cut short the visit and the story at the same time.

'No, no, that's not mine; that's Grogus's, the great ironmonger's. I was going to say — you turn down by the side of the white house till you can't go another step further — mind that — and then you turn to your right, by some stables — well; close to you, you'll see a wall with "Beware of the Dog" written upon it in large letters — (Minns shuddered) — go along by the side of that wall for about a quarter of a mile, and any body will show you which is my place.'

'Very well — thank ye — good bye.'

'Be punctual.'

'Certainly: good morning.'

'I say, Minns, you've got a card?'

'Yes, I have: thank ye.' And Mr Octavius Budden departed leaving his cousin looking forward to his visit of the following Sunday, with the feelings of a penniless poet to the weekly visit of his Scotch landlady.

Sunday arrived; the sky was bright and clear; crowds of people were hurrying along the streets, intent on their different schemes of pleasure for the day; and every thing and every body looked cheerful and happy but Mr Augustus Minns.

The day was fine, but the heat was considerable; and by the time Mr Minns had fagged up the shady side of Fleet-street, Cheapside, and Threadneedle-street, he had become pretty warm, tolerably dusty, and it was getting late into the bargain. By the most extraordinary good fortune, however, a coach was waiting at the Flowerpot, into which Mr Augustus Minns got, on the solemn assurance of the cad that the vehicle would start in three minutes – that being the very utmost extremity of time it was allowed to wait by Act of Parliament. A quarter of an hour elapsed, and there were no signs of moving. Minns looked at his watch for the sixth time.

'Coachman, are you going or not?' bawled Mr Minns, with his head and half his body out of the coach-window.

'Di–rectly, sir,' said the coachman, with his hands in his pockets, looking as much unlike a man in a hurry as possible.

'Bill, take them cloths off.' Five minutes more elapsed; at the end of which time the coachman mounted the box, from whence he looked down the street and up the street, and hailed all the pedestrians for another five minutes.

'Coachman! if you don't go this moment, I shall get out,' said Mr Minns, rendered desperate by the lateness of the hour, and the impossibility of being in Poplar-walk at the appointed time.

'Going this minute, sir,' was the reply; – and, accordingly the machine trundled on for a couple of hundred yards, and then stopped again. Minns doubled himself up into a corner of the coach, and abandoned himself to fate, as a child, a mother, a bandbox, and a parasol became his fellow passengers.

The child was an affectionate and an amiable infant; the little dear mistook Minns for its other parent, and screamed to embrace him.

'Be quiet, dear,' said the mamma, restraining the impetuosity of the darling, whose little fat legs were kicking, and stamping, and twining themselves into the most complicated forms, in an ecstasy of impatience. 'Be quiet, dear, that's not your papa.'

'Thank Heaven I am not' – thought Minns, as the first gleam of pleasure he had experienced that morning shone like a meteor through his wretchedness.

Playfulness was agreeably mingled with affection in the disposition of the boy. When satisfied that Mr Minns was not his parent he endeavoured to attract his notice by scraping his drab trousers with his dirty shoes, poking his chest with his mamma's parasol, and other nameless endearments peculiar to infancy, with which he beguiled the tediousness of the ride, apparently very much to his own satisfaction.

When the unfortunate gentleman arrived at the Swan, he found to his great dismay, that it was a quarter past five. The white house, the stables, the 'Beware of the Dog,' – every landmark was passed, with a rapidity not unusual to a gentleman of a certain age when too late for dinner. After the lapse of a few minutes, Mr Minns found himself opposite a yellow brick house with a green door, brass knocker and door-plate, green window-frames and ditto railings, with 'a garden', in front, that is to say, a small loose bit of gravelled ground, with one round and two scalene triangular beds, containing a fir-tree, twenty or thirty bulbs, and an unlimited number of marigolds. The taste of Mr and Mrs Budden was further displayed by the appearance of a Cupid on each side of the door, perched upon a heap of large chalk flints, variegated with pink cone-shells. His knock at the door was answered by a stumpy boy, in drab livery, cotton stockings and high-lows,[8] who, after hanging his hat on one of the dozen brass pegs which ornamented the passage, denominated by courtesy 'The Hall,' ushered him into a front drawing-room commanding a very extensive view of the backs of the neighbouring houses. The usual ceremony of introduction, and so forth, over, Mr Minns took his seat, not a little agitated at finding that he was the last comer, and, somehow or other, the Lion of about a dozen people, sitting together in a small drawing-room, getting rid of that most tedious of all time, the time preceding dinner.

'Well Brogson,' said Budden, addressing an elderly gentleman in a black coat, drab knee-breeches, and long gaiters, who, under pretence of inspecting the prints in an Annual, had been engaged in satisfying himself upon the subject of Mr Minn's general appearance, by looking at him over the tops of the leaves – 'Well,

Brogson, what do Ministers mean to do? Will they go out, or what?'

'Oh – why – really, you know, I'm the last person in the world to ask for news. Your cousin, from his situation, is the most likely person to answer the question.'

Mr Minns assured the last speaker, that although he was in Somerset-house, he possessed no official communication relative to the projects of his Majesty's Ministers. But his remark was evidently received incredulously; and no further conjectures being hazarded on the subject, a long pause ensued, during which the company occupied themselves in coughing and blowing their noses, until the entrance of Mrs Budden caused a general rise.

The ceremony of introduction being over, dinner was announced, and down stairs the party proceeded accordingly – Mr Minns escorting Mrs Budden as far as the drawing-room door, but being prevented, by the narrowness of the staircase, from extending his gallantry any farther. The dinner passed off as such dinners usually do. Ever and anon amidst the clatter of knives and forks, and the hum of conversation, Mr B's voice might be heard, asking a friend to take wine, and assuring him he was glad to see him; and a great deal of by-play took place between Mrs B. and the servants, respecting the removal of the dishes, during which her countenance assumed all the variations of a weather-glass, from 'stormy' to 'set fair.'

Upon the dessert and wine being placed on the table, the servant, in compliance with a significant look from Mrs B., brought down 'Master Alexander,' habited in a sky-blue suit with silver buttons, and with hair of nearly the same colour as the metal. After sundry praises from his mother, and various admonitions as to his behaviour from his Pa, he was introduced to his godfather.

'Well my little fellow – you are a fine boy, ain't you?' said Mr Minns, as happy as a tomtit on birdlime.

'Yes.'

'How old are you?'

'Eight, next We'nsday. How old are *you*?'

'Alexander,' interrupted his mother, 'how dare you ask Mr Minns how old he is!'

'He asked me how old *I* was,' said the precocious child to whom Minns had from that moment internally resolved he never would bequeath one shilling. As soon as the titter occasioned by the observation had subsided, a little smirking man with red whiskers, sitting at the bottom of the table, who during the whole of dinner had been endeavouring to obtain a listener to some stories about Sheridan,[9] called out, with a very patronising air – 'Alick, what part of speech is *be*?'

'A verb.'

'That's a good boy,' said Mrs Budden with all a mother's pride. 'Now, you know what a verb is?'

'A verb is a word which signifies to be, to do, or to suffer;[10] as, I am – I rule – I am ruled. Give me an apple, Ma.'

'I'll give you an apple,' replied the man with the red whiskers, who was an established friend of the family, or in other words was always invited by Mrs Budden, whether Mr Budden liked it or not, 'if you'll tell me what is the meaning of *be*.'

'Be?' said the prodigy, after a little hesitation – 'an insect that gathers honey.'

'No, dear,' frowned Mrs Budden. – 'B double E is the substantive.'

'I don't think he knows much yet about *common* substantives,' said the smirking gentleman, who thought this an admirable opportunity for letting off a joke. 'It's clear he's not very well acquainted with *proper names*. He! he! he!'

'Gentlemen,' called out Mr Budden, from the end of the table, in a stentorian voice, and with a very important air, 'will you have the goodness to charge your glasses? I have a toast to propose.'

'Hear! hear!' cried the gentlemen, passing the decanters. After they had made the round of the table, Mr Budden proceeded – 'Gentlemen; there is an individual present –'

'Hear! hear!' said the little man with red whiskers.

'*Pray* be quiet, Jones,' remonstrated Budden.

'I say, gentlemen, there is an individual present,' resumed the host, 'in whose society, I am sure we must take great delight – and – and – the conversation of that individual must have afforded to every one present, the utmost pleasure.' 'Thank Heaven, he does not mean me!' thought Minns, conscious that his diffidence and exclusiveness had prevented his saying above a dozen words since he entered the house. 'Gentlemen, I am but a humble individual myself, and I perhaps ought to apologise for allowing any individual feelings of friendship and affection for the person I allude to, to induce me to venture to rise, to propose the health of that person – a person that, I am sure – that is to say, a person whose virtues must endear him to those who know him – and those who have not the pleasure of knowing him, cannot dislike him.'

'Hear! hear!' said the company, in a tone of encouragement and approval.

'Gentlemen,' continued Budden, 'my cousin is a man who – who is a relation of my own.' (Hear! hear!) Minns groaned audibly. 'Who I am most happy to see here, and who, if he were not here, would certainly have deprived us of the great pleasure we all feel in seeing him. (Loud cries of hear!) Gentlemen, I feel that I have already trespassed on your attention for too long a time. With every feeling — of — with every sentiment of — of —'

'Gratification' – suggested the friend of the family.

'— Of gratification, I beg to propose the health of Mr Minns.'

'Standing, gentlemen!' shouted the indefatigable little man with the whiskers – 'and with the honours. Take your time from me, if you please. Hip! hip! hip! – Za! – Hip! hip! hip! – Za! – Hip! hip! – Za–a–a!'

All eyes were now fixed on the subject of the toast, who by gulping down port-wine at the imminent hazard of suffocation, endeavoured to conceal his confusion. After as long a pause as decency would admit, he rose, but, as the newspapers sometimes say in their reports, 'we regret that we are quite unable to give even the substance of the honourable gentleman's observations.' The words 'present company – honour – present occasion,' and 'great happiness' – heard occasionally, and repeated at intervals, with a countenance expressive of the utmost confusion and misery, convinced the company that he was making an excellent speech; and accordingly, on his resuming his seat, they cried 'Bravo!' and manifested tumultuous applause. Jones, who had been long watching his opportunity, then darted up.

'Budden,' said he, 'will you allow *me* to propose a toast?'

'Certainly,' replied Budden, adding in an under tone to Minns right across the table – 'Devilish sharp fellow that: you'll be very much pleased with his speech. He talks equally well on any subject.' Minns bowed, and Mr Jones proceeded:

'It has on several occasions, in various instances, under many circumstances, and in different companies, fallen to my lot to propose a toast to those by whom, at the time, I have had the honour to be surrounded. I have sometimes, I will cheerfully own – for why should I deny it? – felt the overwhelming nature of the task I have undertaken, and my own utter incapability to do justice to the subject. If such have been my feelings, however, on former occasions, what must they be now – now – under the extraordinary circumstances in which I am placed. (Hear! hear!) – To describe my feelings accurately would be impossible; but I cannot give you a better idea of them, gentlemen, than by referring to a circumstance which happens, oddly enough, to occur to my mind at the moment. On one occasion, when that truly great and illustrious man, Sheridan, was —'

Now, there is no knowing what new villany in the form of a joke would have been heaped upon the memory of that very ill-used man, Mr Sheridan, if the boy in drab had not at that moment entered the room in a breathless state, to report that, as it was a very wet night, the nine o'clock stage had come round to know whether there was any body going to town, as, in that case, he (the nine o'clock) had room for one inside.

Mr Minns started up; and, despite countless exclamations of surprise, and entreaties to stay, persisted in his determination to accept the vacant place. But the brown silk umbrella was nowhere to be found; and as the coachman couldn't wait, he drove back to the Swan, leaving word for Mr Minns to 'run round' and catch him. But as it did not occur to Mr Minns for some ten minutes or so, that he had left the brown silk umbrella with the ivory handle in the other coach, coming down; and, moreover, as he was by no means remarkable for speed, it is no matter of surprise that when he accomplished the feat of 'running round' to the Swan, the coach – the last coach – had gone without him.

It was somewhere about three o'clock in the morning, when Mr Augustus Minns knocked feebly at the street-door of his lodgings in Tavistock-street, cold, wet, cross, and miserable. He made his will next morning, and his professional man informs us, in that strict confidence in which we inform the public, that neither the name of Mr Octavius Budden, nor of Mrs Amelia Budden, nor of Master Alexander Augustus Budden, appears therein.

CHAPTER 3

Sentiment

THE Miss Crumptons, or to quote the authority of the inscription on the garden-gate of Minerva House, Hammersmith[1] – 'The Misses Crumpton,' were two unusually tall, particularly thin, and exceedingly skinny personages: very upright, and very yellow. Miss Amelia Crumpton owned to thirty-eight, and Miss Maria Crumpton admitted she was forty; an admission which was rendered perfectly unnecessary by the self-evident fact of her being fifty at least. They dressed in the most interesting manner – like twins, and looked about as happy and comfortable as a couple of marigolds run to seed. They were very precise, had the strictest possible ideas of propriety, wore false hair, and always smelt very strongly of lavender.

Minerva House, conducted under the auspices of the two sisters, was a 'finishing establishment for young ladies,' where some twenty girls of the ages of from thirteen to nineteen inclusive,

George Cruikshank

Sentiment

acquired a smattering of every thing, and a knowledge of nothing; instruction in French and Italian, dancing lessons twice a-week, and other necessaries of life. The house was a white one, a little removed from the road-side, with close palings in front. The bedroom windows were always left partly open to afford a bird's-eye view of numerous little bedsteads with very white dimity furniture, and thereby impress the passer-by with a due sense of the luxuries of the establishment; and there was a front parlour hung round with highly-varnished maps which nobody ever looked at, and filled with books which no one ever read, appropriated exclusively to the reception of parents, who, whenever they called, could not fail to be struck with the very knowledge-imparting appearance of the place.

'Amelia, my dear,' said Miss Maria Crumpton, entering the school-room one morning, with her false hair in papers, as she occasionally did, in order to impress the young ladies with a conviction of its reality – 'Amelia, my dear, here's a most gratifying note I have just received. You needn't mind reading it aloud.'

Miss Amelia thus advised, proceeded to read the following note with an air of great triumph:–

'Cornelius Brook Dingwall, Esq., M.P., presents his compliments to Miss Crumpton, and will feel much obliged by Miss Crumpton's calling on him, if she conveniently can, to-morrow morning at one o'clock, as Cornelius Brook Dingwall, Esq., M.P., is anxious to see Miss Crumpton on the subject of placing Miss Brook Dingwall under her charge.

'Adelphi.

'Monday morning.'

'A Member of Parliament's daughter!' ejaculated Amelia, in an ecstatic tone.

'A Member of Parliament's daughter!' repeated Miss Maria, with a smile of delight, which of course elicited a concurrent titter of pleasure from all the young ladies.

'It's exceedingly delightful!' said Miss Amelia; whereupon all the young ladies murmured their admiration again. Courtiers are but schoolboys, and court-ladies schoolgirls.

So important an announcement at once superseded the business of the day. A holiday was declared in commemoration of the great event: the Miss Crumptons retired to their private apartment to talk it over; the smaller girls discussed the probable manners and customs of the daughter of a Member of Parliament; and the young ladies verging on eighteen wondered whether she was engaged, whether she was pretty, whether she wore much bustle, and many other *whethers* of equal importance.

The two Miss Crumptons proceeded to the Adelphi[2] at the appointed time next day, dressed, of course, in their best style, and looking as amiable as they possibly could – which, by the by, is not saying much for them. Having sent in their cards, through the medium of a red-hot looking footman in bright livery, they were ushered into the august presence of the profound Dingwall.

Cornelius Brook Dingwall, Esq., M.P., was very haughty, solemn, and portentous. He had naturally a somewhat spasmodic expression of countenance, which was not rendered the less remarkable by his wearing an extremely stiff cravat. He was wonderfully proud of the 'M.P.' attached to his name, and never lost an opportunity of reminding people of his dignity. He had a great idea of his own abilities, which must have been a great comfort to him, as no one else had; and in diplomacy, on a small scale in his own family arrangements, he considered himself unrivalled. He was a county magistrate, and discharged the duties of his station with all due justice and impartiality, frequently committing poachers, and occasionally committing himself. Miss Brook Dingwall was one of that numerous class of young ladies, who, like adverbs, may be known by their answering to a commonplace question, and doing nothing else.

On the present occasion this talented individual was seated in a small library at a table covered with papers, doing nothing, but trying to look busy – playing at shop. Acts of Parliament, and letters directed to 'Cornelius Brook Dingwall, Esq., M.P.,' were ostentatiously scattered over the table, at a little distance from which Mrs Brook Dingwall was seated at work. One of those public nuisances, a spoiled child, was playing about the room, dressed after the most approved fashion, in a blue tunic with a black belt a quarter of a yard wide, fastened with an immense buckle, and looking like a robber in a melodrama, seen through a diminishing-glass.

After a little pleasantry from the sweet child, who amused himself by running away with Miss Maria Crumpton's chair as fast as it was placed for her, the visiters were seated, and Cornelius Brook Dingwall, Esq. opened the conversation.

He had sent for Miss Crumpton, he said, in consequence of the high character he had received of her establishment from his friend, Sir Alfred Muggs.

Miss Crumpton murmured her acknowledgments to him (Muggs), and Cornelius proceeded.

'One of my principal reasons, Miss Crumpton, for parting with my daughter is, that she has lately acquired some sentimental ideas, which it is most desirable to eradicate from her young mind.' (Here the little innocent before noticed fell out of an arm-chair with an awful crash.)

'Naughty boy!' said his mamma, who appeared more surprised at his taking the liberty of falling down, than at any thing else; 'I'll ring the bell for James to take him away.'

'Pray don't check him, my love,' said the diplomatist, as soon as he could make himself heard amidst the unearthly howling consequent upon the threat and the tumble. 'It all arises from his great flow of spirits.' This last explanation was addressed to Miss Crumpton.

'Certainly, sir,' replied the antique Maria, not exactly seeing, however, the connexion between a flow of animal spirits and a fall from an arm-chair.

Silence was restored, and the M.P. resumed: 'Now, I know nothing so likely to effect this object, Miss Crumpton, as her mixing constantly in the society of girls of her own age; and as I know that in your establishment she will meet such as are not likely to contaminate her young mind, I propose to send her to you.'

The youngest Miss Crumpton expressed the acknowledgments

of the establishment generally. Maria was rendered perfectly speech-less by bodily pain – the dear little fellow, having recovered his spirits, was standing upon her most tender foot, by way of getting his face (which looked like a capital O in a red lettered play-bill) on a level with the writing-table.

'Of course, Lavinia will be a parlour boarder,' continued the enviable father; 'and on one point I wish my directions to be strictly observed. The fact is, that some ridiculous love affair with a person much her inferior in life has been the cause of her present state of mind. Knowing that of course, under your care, she can have no opportunity of meeting this person, I do not object to – indeed, I should rather prefer – her mixing with such society as you see yourself.'

The important statement was again interrupted by the high-spirited little creature, in the excess of his joyousness breaking a pane of glass, and nearly precipitating himself into an adjacent area. James was rung for; considerable confusion and screaming suc-ceeded, two little blue legs about the size of hoop-sticks were seen to kick violently in the air as the man left the room, and the child was gone.

'Mr Brook Dingwall would like Miss Brook Dingwall to learn every thing,' said Mrs Brook Dingwall, who hardly ever said any thing at all.

'Certainly,' said both the Miss Crumptons together.

'And as I trust the plan I have devised will be effectual in weaning my daughter from this absurd idea, Miss Crumpton,' continued the legislator, 'I hope you will have the goodness to comply in all respects with any request I may forward to you.'

The promise was of course made; and after a lengthened discus-sion, conducted on behalf of the Dingwalls with the most becoming diplomatic gravity, and on that of the Crumptons with profound respect, it was finally arranged that Miss Lavinia should be for-warded to Hammersmith on the next day but one, on which occasion the half-yearly ball given at the establishment was to take place. It might divert the dear girl's mind. This, by the way, was another bit of diplomacy.

Miss Lavinia was introduced to her future governess, and both the Miss Crumptons pronounced her 'a most charming girl;' an opinion which, by a singular coincidence, they always entertained of any new pupil.

Courtesies were made, acknowledgments expressed, condescension exhibited, and the interview terminated.

Preparations, to make use of theatrical phraseology, 'on a scale of magnitude never before attempted,' were incessantly made at Minerva House to give every effect to the forthcoming ball. The largest room in the house was pleasingly ornamented with blue calico roses, plaid tulips, and other equally natural-looking artificial flowers, the work of the young ladies themselves. The carpet was taken up, the folding-doors were taken down, the furniture was taken out, and rout-seats were taken in. The linendrapers of Hammersmith were astounded at the sudden demand for blue sarcenet ribbon, and long white gloves. Dozens of geraniums were purchased for bouquets, and a harp and two violins were bespoke from town, in addition to the grand piano already on the premises. The young ladies who were selected to show off on the occasion, and do credit to the establishment, practised incessantly, much to their own satisfaction, and greatly to the annoyance of the lame old gentleman over the way; and a constant correspondence was kept up between the Misses Crumpton and the Hammersmith pastrycook.

The evening came; and then there was such a lacing of stays, and tying of sandals, and dressing of hair, as never can take place with a proper degree of bustle out of a boarding-school. The smaller girls managed to be in every body's way, and were pushed about accordingly; and the elder ones dressed, and tied, and flattered and envied one another, as earnestly and sincerely as if they had actually *come out.*

'How do I look, dear?' inquired Miss Emily Smithers, the belle of the house, of Miss Caroline Wilson, who was her bosom friend, because she was the ugliest girl in Hammersmith, or out of it.

'Oh! charming, dear. How do I?'

'Delightful! you never looked so handsome,' returned the belle, adjusting her own dress, and not bestowing a glance on her poor companion.

'I hope young Hilton will come early,' said another young lady to Miss somebody else, in a fever of expectation.

'I'm sure he'd be highly flattered if he knew it,' returned the other, who was practising *l'été*[3] for effect.

'Oh! he's so handsome,' said the first.

'Such a charming person!' added a second.

'Such a *distingué* air!' said a third.

'Oh, what *do* you think?' said another girl, running into the room; 'Miss Crumpton says her cousin's coming.'

'What! Theodosius Butler?' said every body in raptures.

'Is *he* handsome?' inquired a novice.

'No, not particularly handsome,' was the general reply; 'but oh, so clever!'

Mr Theodosius Butler was one of those immortal geniuses who are to be met with in almost every circle. They have usually very deep monotonous voices. They always persuade themselves that they are wonderful persons, and that they ought to be very miserable, though they don't precisely know why. They are very conceited, and usually possess exactly half an idea; but with enthusiastic young ladies, and silly young gentlemen, they are very wonderful persons. The individual in question, Mr Theodosius, had written a pamphlet containing some very weighty considerations on the expediency of doing something or other; and as every sentence contained at least fifty words of four syllables, his admirers took it for granted that he meant a good deal.

'Perhaps that's he,' exclaimed several young ladies, as the first pull of the evening threatened destruction to the bell of the gate.

An awful pause ensued. Some boxes arrived, and a young lady – it was Miss Brook Dingwall, in full ball costume, with an immense gold chain round her neck, and her dress looped up with a single rose. An ivory fan in her hand, and a most interesting expression of despair in her face.

The Miss Crumptons inquired after the family with the most excruciating anxiety, and Miss Brook Dingwall was formally introduced to her future companions. The Miss Crumptons conversed with the young ladies in the most mellifluous tones, in order that Miss Brook Dingwall might be properly impressed with their amiable treatment.

Another pull at the bell. Mr Dadson, the writing-master, and his wife. The wife in green silk, with shoes and cap-trimmings to correspond, and the writing-master in a white waistcoat, black knee shorts, and ditto silk stockings, displaying a leg large enough for two writing-masters, at least. The young ladies whispered one another, and the writing-master and his wife flattered the Miss Crumptons, who were dressed in amber, with long sashes, like dolls.

Repeated pulls at the bell, and arrivals too numerous to particularize: papas and mammas, and aunts and uncles, the owners and guardians of the different pupils; the singing-master, Signor Lobskini, in a black wig; the pianoforte-player and the violins; the harp, in a state of intoxication; and some twenty young men, who stood near the door, and talked to one another, occasionally bursting into a giggle. A general hum of conversation. Coffee handed round and plentifully partaken of by fat mammas, looking like the stout people who come on in pantomimes for the sole purpose of being knocked down.

The popular Mr Hilton was the next arrival; and having, at the request of the Miss Crumptons, undertaken the office of Master of the Ceremonies, the quadrilles commenced with considerable spirit. The young men by the door gradually advanced into the middle of the room, and in time became sufficiently at ease to consent to be introduced to partners. The writing-master danced every set, springing about with the most fearful agility, and his wife played a rubber in the back parlour – a little room with five book-shelves, dignified by the name of the study. Setting her down to whist was a half-yearly piece of generalship on the part of the Miss Crumptons, as it was necessary to hide her somewhere on account of her being a fright.

The interesting Lavinia Brook Dingwall was the only girl present who appeared to take no interest in the proceedings of the evening. In vain was she solicited to dance; in vain was the universal homage paid to her as the daughter of a member of parliament. She was equally unmoved by the splendid tenor of the inimitable Lobskini, and the brilliant execution of Miss Lætitia Parsons, whose performance of 'The Recollections of Ireland'[4] was universally declared to be almost equal to that of Moschelles[5] himself. Not even the announcement of the arrival of Mr Theodosius Butler could induce her to leave the corner of the back drawing-room in which she was seated.

'Now, Theodosius,' said Miss Maria Crumpton, after that enlightened pamphleteer had nearly run the gauntlet of the whole company, 'I must introduce you to our new pupil.'

Theodosius looked as if he cared for nothing earthly.

'She's the daughter of a member of parliament,' said Maria. — Theodosius started.

'And her name is —?' he inquired.

'Miss Brook Dingwall.'

'Great Heaven!' poetically exclaimed Theodosius in a low tone.

Miss Crumpton commenced the introduction in due form. Miss Brook Dingwall languidly raised her head.

'Edward!' she exclaimed, with a half-shriek, on seeing the well-known nankeen legs.

Fortunately, as Miss Maria Crumpton possessed no remarkable share of penetration, and as it was one of the diplomatic arrangements that no attention was to be paid to Miss Lavinia's incoherent exclamations, she was perfectly unconscious of the mutual agitation of the parties; and therefore, seeing that the offer of his hand for the next quadrille was accepted, she left him by the side of Miss Brook Dingwall.

'Oh, Edward!' exclaimed that most romantic of all romantic young ladies, as the light of science seated himself beside her, 'Oh, Edward! is it you?'

Mr Theodosius assured the dear creature, in the most impassioned manner, that he was not conscious of being any body but himself.

'Then why — why — this disguise? Oh! Edward M'Neville Walter, what have I not suffered on your account!'

'Lavinia, hear me,' replied the hero, in his most poetic strain. 'Do not condemn me unheard. If any thing that emanates from the soul of such a wretch as I can occupy a place in your recollection — if any being, so vile, deserve your notice — you may remember that I once published a pamphlet (and paid for its publication) entitled "Considerations on the Policy of Removing the Duty on Bees'-wax."'

'I do — I do!' sobbed Lavinia.

'That,' continued the lover, 'was a subject to which your father was devoted heart and soul.'

'He was — he was!' reiterated the sentimentalist.

'I knew it,' continued Theodosius, tragically; 'I knew it — I forwarded him a copy. He wished to know me. Could I disclose my real name? Never! No, I assumed that name which you have so often pronounced in tones of endearment. As M'Neville Walter, I devoted myself to the stirring cause; as M'Neville Walter I gained your heart; in the same character I was ejected from your house by your father's domestics, and in no character at all have I since been enabled to see you. We now meet again and I proudly own that I am — Theodosius Butler.'

The young lady appeared perfectly satisfied with this very argumentative address, and bestowed a look of the most ardent affection on the immortal advocate of bees'-wax.

'May I hope,' said he, 'that the promise your father's violent behaviour interrupted, may be renewed?'

'Let us join this set,' replied Lavinia, coquettishly — for girls of nineteen can coquette.

'No,' ejaculated he of the nankeens; 'I stir not from this spot, writhing under this torture of suspense. May I — may I — hope?'

'You may.'

'The promise is renewed?'

'It is.'

'I have your permission?'

'You have.'

'To the fullest extent?'

'You know it,' returned the blushing Lavinia. The contortions of the interesting Butler's visage expressed his raptures.

We could dilate upon the occurrences that ensued. How Mr Theodosius and Miss Lavinia danced, and talked, and sighed for the remainder of the evening – how the Miss Crumptons were delighted thereat. How the writing-master continued to frisk about with one-horse power, and how his wife, from some unaccountable freak, left the whist-table in the little back parlour, and persisted in displaying her green head-dress in the most conspicuous part of the drawing-room. How the supper consisted of small triangular sand-wiches in trays, and a tart here and there by way of variety; and how the visiters consumed warm water disguised with lemon, and dotted with nutmeg, under the denomination of negus. These, and other matters of as much interest, however, we pass over, for the purpose of describing a scene of even more importance.

A fortnight after the date of the ball, Cornelius Brook Ding-wall, Esq, M.P., was seated at the same library-table, and in the same room as we have before described. He was alone, and his face bore an expression of deep thought and solemn gravity – he was drawing up 'A Bill for the better observance of Easter Monday.'

The footman tapped at the door – the legislator started from his revery, and 'Miss Crumpton' was announced. Permission was given for Miss Crumpton to enter the *sanctum*; Maria came sliding in, and having taken her seat with a due portion of affectation, the footman retired, and the governess was left alone with the M.P. Oh! how she longed for the presence of a third party! even the facetious young gentleman would have been a relief.

Miss Crumpton began the duet. She hoped Mrs Brook Dingwall and the handsome little boy were in good health.

They were. Mrs Brook Dingwall and little Frederick were at Brighton.

'Much obliged to you, Miss Crumpton,' said Cornelius, in his most dignified manner, 'for your attention in calling this morning. I should have driven down to Hammersmith to see Lavinia, but your account was so very satisfactory, and my duties in the House occupy me so much, that I determined to postpone it for a week. How has she gone on?'

'Very well indeed, sir,' returned Maria, dreading to inform the father that she had gone off.

'Ah, I thought the plan on which I proceeded would be a match for her.'

Here was a favourable opportunity to say that somebody else had been a match for her. The unfortunate governess was unequal to the task.

'You have persevered strictly in the line of conduct I prescribed, Miss Crumpton?'

'Strictly, sir.'

'You tell me in your note that her spirits gradually improved.'

'Very much indeed, sir.'

'To be sure. I was convinced they would.'

'But I fear, sir,' said Miss Crumpton, with visible emotion, 'I fear the plan has not succeeded quite so well as we could have wished.'

'No!' exclaimed the prophet. 'Bless me! Miss Crumpton, you look alarmed. What has happened?'

'Miss Brook Dingwall, sir —'

'Yes, ma'am?'

'Has gone, sir' — said Maria, exhibiting a strong inclination to faint.

'Gone!'

'Eloped, sir.'

'Eloped! — Who with — when — where — how?' almost shrieked the agitated diplomatist.

The natural yellow of the unfortunate Maria's face changed to all the hues of the rainbow, as she laid a small packet upon the member's table.

He hurriedly opened it. A letter from his daughter, and another from Theodosius. He glanced over their contents — 'Ere this reaches you, far distant — appeal to feelings — love to distraction — bees'-wax — slavery,' &c. &c. He dashed his hand to his forehead, and paced the room with fearfully long strides, to the great alarm of the precise Maria.

'Now mind; from this time forward,' said Mr Brook Dingwall,

suddenly stopping at the table, and beating time upon it with his hand – 'from this time forward, I never will, under any circumstances whatever, permit a man who writes pamphlets to enter any room of this house but the kitchen. – I'll allow my daughter and her husband one hundred and fifty pounds a-year, and never see their faces again; – and, dammee! ma'am, I'll bring in a bill for the abolition of finishing-schools!'

Some time has elapsed since this passionate declaration. Mr and Mrs Butler are at present rusticating in a small cottage at Ball's-pond,[6] pleasantly situated in the immediate vicinity of a brick-field. They have no family. Mr Theodosius looks very important, and writes incessantly; but, in consequence of some gross combination on the part of publishers, none of his productions appear in print. His young wife begins to think that ideal misery is preferable to real unhappiness; and that a marriage contracted in haste, and repented at leisure,[7] is the cause of more substantial wretchedness than she ever anticipated.

On cool reflection, Cornelius Brook Dingwall, Esq., M.P., was reluctantly compelled to admit that the untoward result of his admirable arrangements was attributable, not to the Miss Crumptons but his own diplomacy. He however consoles himself, like some other small diplomatists, by satisfactorily proving that if his plans did not succeed, they ought to have done so. Minerva House is in *statu quo*,[8] and 'The Misses Crumpton' remain in the peaceable and undisturbed enjoyment of all the advantages resulting from their Finishing-School.

CHAPTER 4

The Tuggs's at Ramsgate

ONCE upon a time there dwelt, in a narrow street on the Surrey side of the water within three minutes' walk of the old London Bridge,[1] Mr Joseph Tuggs – a little dark-faced man, with shiny

The Tuggs's at Ramsgate

hair, twinkling eyes, short legs, and a body of very considerable thickness, measuring from the centre button of his waistcoat in front, to the ornamental buttons of his coat behind. The figure of the amiable Mrs Tuggs, if not perfectly symmetrical, was decidedly comfortable; and the form of her only daughter, the accomplished Miss Charlotte Tuggs, was fast ripening into that state of luxuriant plumpness which had enchanted the eyes, and captivated the heart, of Mr Joseph Tuggs in his earlier days. Mr Simon Tuggs, his only son, and Miss Charlotte Tuggs's only brother, was as differently formed in body, as he was differently constituted in mind, from the remainder of his family. There was that elongation in his thoughtful face, and that tendency to weakness in his interesting legs, which tells so forcibly of a great mind and romantic disposition. The slightest traits of character in such a being, possess no mean interest to speculative minds. He usually appeared in public in capacious shoes with black cotton stockings; and was observed to be particularly attached to a black glazed stock, without tie or ornament of any description.

There is perhaps no profession, however useful; no pursuit, however meritorious, which can escape the petty attacks of vulgar minds. Mr Joseph Tuggs was a grocer. It might be supposed that a grocer was beyond the breath of calumny: but no – the neighbours stigmatized him as a chandler; and the poisonous voice of envy distinctly asserted that he dispensed tea and coffee by the quartern, retailed sugar by the ounce, cheese by the slice, tobacco by the screw, and butter by the pat. These taunts, however, were lost upon the Tuggs's. Mr Tuggs attended to the grocery department, Mrs Tuggs to the cheesemongery, and Miss Tuggs to her education. Mr Simon Tuggs kept his father's books, and his own counsel.

One fine spring afternoon, the latter gentleman was seated on a tub of weekly Dorset[2] behind the little red desk with a wooden rail, which ornamented a corner of the counter, when a stranger dismounted from a cab, and hastily entered the shop. He was habited in black cloth, and bore with him a green umbrella and a blue bag.

'Mr Tuggs?' said the stranger, inquiringly.

'*My* name is Tuggs,' replied Mr Simon.

'It's the other Mr Tuggs,' said the stranger, looking towards the glass door which led into the parlour behind the shop, and on the inside of which, the round face of Mr Tuggs, senior, was distinctly visible, peeping over the curtain.

Mr Simon gracefully waved his pen, as if in intimation of his wish that his father would advance, and Mr Joseph Tuggs, with considerable celerity, removed his face from the curtain, and placed it before the stranger.

'I come from the Temple,'³ said the man with the bag.

'From the Temple!' said Mrs Tuggs, flinging open the door of the little parlour, and disclosing Miss Tuggs in perspective.

'From the Temple!' said Miss Tuggs and Mr Simon Tuggs at the same moment.

'From the Temple!' said Mr Joseph Tuggs, turning as pale as a Dutch cheese.

'From the Temple,' repeated the man with the bag; 'from Mr Cower's, the solicitor's. Mr Tuggs, I congratulate you, sir. Ladies, I wish you joy of your prosperity! We have been successful.' And the man with the bag leisurely divested himself of his umbrella and glove, as a preliminary to shaking hands with Mr Joseph Tuggs.

Now the words 'we have been successful,' had no sooner issued from the mouth of the man with the bag, than Mr Simon Tuggs rose from the tub of weekly Dorset, opened his eyes very wide, gasped for breath, made figures of eight in the air with his pen, and finally fell into the arms of his anxious mother, and fainted away, without the slightest ostensible cause or pretence.

'Water!' screamed Mrs Tuggs.

'Look up, my son,' exclaimed Mr Tuggs.

'Simon! dear Simon!' shrieked Miss Tuggs.

'I'm better now,' said Mr Simon Tuggs. — 'What! successful!' And then, as corroborative evidence of his being better, he fainted away again, and was borne into the little parlour by the united efforts of the remainder of the family and the man with the bag.

To a casual spectator, or to any one unacquainted with the position of the family, this fainting would have been unaccountable.

To those who understood the mission of the man with the bag, and were moreover acquainted with the excitability of the nerves of Mr Simon Tuggs, it was quite comprehensible. A long-pending lawsuit respecting the validity of a will, had been unexpectedly decided; and Mr Joseph Tuggs was the possessor of twenty thousand pounds.

A prolonged consultation took place that night in the little parlour – a consultation that was to settle the future destinies of the Tuggs's. The shop was shut up at an unusually early hour; and many were the unavailing kicks bestowed upon the closed door by applicants for quarterns of sugar, or half-quarterns of bread, or penn'orths of pepper, which were to have been 'left till Saturday,' but which fortune had decreed were to be left alone altogether.

'We must certainly give up business,' said Miss Tuggs.

'Oh, decidedly,' said Mrs Tuggs.

'Simon shall go to the bar,' said Mr Joseph Tuggs.

'And I shall always sign myself "Cymon" in future,' said his son.

'And I shall call myself Charlotta,' said Miss Tuggs.

'And you must always call *me* "Ma," and father "Pa,"' said Mrs Tuggs.

'Yes, and Pa must leave off all his vulgar habits,' interposed Miss Tuggs.

'I'll take care of all that,' responded Mr Joseph Tuggs, complacently. – He was at that very moment eating pickled salmon with a pocket-knife.

'We must leave town immediately,' said Mr Cymon Tuggs.

Every body concurred that this was an indispensable preliminary to being genteel. The question then arose – Where should they go?

'Gravesend,' mildly suggested Mr Joseph Tuggs. The idea was unanimously scouted. Gravesend was *low*.

'Margate,' insinuated Mrs Tuggs. Worse and worse – nobody there but tradespeople.

'Brighton!' Mr Cymon Tuggs opposed an insurmountable objection. All the coaches had been upset in their turn within the last three weeks; each coach had averaged two passengers killed and six

wounded; and in every case the newspapers had distinctly understood that 'no blame whatever was attributable to the coachman.'

'Ramsgate!'[4] ejaculated Mr Cymon, thoughtfully. – To be sure:
how stupid they must have been not to have thought of that
before! Ramsgate was just the place of all others that they ought to
go to.

Two months after this conversation, the City of London
Ramsgate steamer was running gaily down the river. Her flag was
flying, her band was playing, her passengers were conversing;
every thing about her seemed gay and lively. – No wonder – the
Tuggs's were on board.

'Charming, ain't it?' said Mr Joseph Tuggs, in a bottle-green
great-coat, with a velvet collar of the same, and a blue travelling-
cap with a gold band.

'Soul-inspiring,' replied Mr Cymon Tuggs – he was entered at
the bar – 'Soul-inspiring!'

'Delightful morning sir,' said a stoutish, military-looking gentleman in a blue surtout buttoned up to his chin, and white trousers
chained down to the soles of his boots.

Mr Cymon Tuggs took upon himself the responsibility of
answering the observation. 'Heavenly!' he replied.

'You are an enthusiastic admirer of the beauties of Nature, sir?'
said the military gentleman, deferentially.

'I am, sir,' replied Mr Cymon Tuggs.

'Travelled much, sir?' inquired the military gentleman.

'Not much,' replied Mr Cymon Tuggs.

'You've been on the continent, of course?' inquired the military
gentleman.

'Not exactly,' replied Mr Cymon Tuggs, in a qualified tone, as if
he wished it to be implied that he had gone halfway and come back
again.

'You of course intend your son to make the grand tour,[5] sir?'
said the military gentleman, addressing Mr Joseph Tuggs.

As Mr Joseph Tuggs did not precisely understand what the
grand tour was, or how such an article was manufactured, he
replied, 'Of course.' Just as he said the word, there came tripping

up from her seat at the stern of the vessel, a young lady in a puce-coloured silk cloak and boots of the same, with long black ringlets, large black eyes, brief petticoats, and unexceptionable ankles.

'Walter, my dear,' said the young lady to the military gentleman.

'Yes, Belinda, my love,' responded the military gentleman to the black-eyed young lady.

'What have you left me alone so long for?' said the young lady. 'I have been stared out of countenance by those rude young men.'

'What! stared at?' exclaimed the military gentleman, with an emphasis which made Mr Cymon Tuggs withdraw his eyes from the young lady's face with inconceivable rapidity.

'Which young men – where?' and the military gentleman clenched his fist, and glared fearfully on the cigar-smokers around.

'Be calm, Walter, I entreat,' said the young lady.

'I won't,' said the military gentleman.

'Do, sir,' interposed Mr Cymon Tuggs. 'They ain't worth your notice.'

'No – no – they are not, indeed,' urged the young lady.

'I *will* be calm,' said the military gentleman. 'You speak truly, sir. I thank you for a timely remonstrance, which may have spared me the guilt of manslaughter.' Calming his wrath, the military gentleman wrung Mr Cymon Tuggs by the hand.

'My sister, sir,' said Mr Cymon Tuggs; seeing that the military gentleman was casting an admiring look towards Miss Charlotta.

'My wife, ma'am – Mrs Captain Waters,' said the military gentleman, presenting the black-eyed young lady.

'My mother, ma'am – Mrs Tuggs,' said Mr Cymon. The military gentleman and his wife murmured enchanting courtesies; and the Tuggs's looked as unembarrassed as they could.

'Walter, my dear,' said the black-eyed young lady, after they had sat chatting with the Tuggs's some half hour.

'Yes, my love,' said the military gentleman.

'Don't you think this gentleman (with an inclination of the head towards Mr Cymon Tuggs) is very much like the Marquis Carriwini?'

'God bless me, very!' said the military gentleman.

'It struck me, the moment I saw him,' said the young lady: gazing intently, and with a melancholy air, on the scarlet countenance of Mr Cymon Tuggs. Mr Cymon Tuggs looked at every body; and finding that every body was looking at him, appeared to feel some temporary difficulty in disposing of his eyesight.

'So exactly the air of the marquis,' said the military gentleman.

'Quite extraordinary!' sighed the military gentleman's lady.

'You don't know the marquis, sir?' inquired the military gentleman.

Mr Cymon Tuggs stammered a negative.

'If you did,' continued Captain Walter Waters, 'you would feel how much reason you have to be proud of the resemblance − a most elegant man; with a most prepossessing appearance.'

'He is − he is indeed!' exclaimed Belinda Waters energetically: and as her eye caught that of Mr Cymon Tuggs, she withdrew it from his features in bashful confusion.

All this was highly gratifying to the feelings of the Tuggs's: and when, in the course of further conversation, it was discovered that Miss Charlotta Tuggs was the *fac simile* of a titled relative of Mrs Belinda Waters, and that Mrs Tuggs herself was the very picture of the Dowager Duchess of Dobbleton, their delight in the acquisition of so genteel and friendly an acquaintance, knew no bounds. Even the dignity of Captain Walter Waters relaxed to that degree, that he suffered himself to be prevailed upon by Mr Joseph Tuggs, to partake of cold pigeon-pie and sherry on deck; and a most delightful conversation, aided by these agreeable stimulants, was prolonged until they ran alongside Ramsgate Pier.

'Good by'e, dear!' said Mrs Captain Waters to Miss Charlotta Tuggs, just before the bustle of landing commenced; 'we shall see you on the sands in the morning: and as we are sure to have found lodgings before then, I hope we shall be inseparables for many weeks to come.'

'Oh! I hope so,' said Miss Charlotta Tuggs, emphatically.

'Tickets, ladies and gen'lm'n,' said the man on the paddle-box.

'Want a porter, sir?' inquired a dozen men in smock-frocks.

'Now, my dear!' said Captain Waters.

'Good by'e!' said Mrs Captain Waters – 'good by'e, Mr Cymon!' and with a pressure of the hand that threw the amiable young man's nerves into a state of considerable derangement, Mrs Captain Waters disappeared among the crowd. A pair of puce-coloured boots were seen ascending the steps, a white handkerchief fluttered, a black eye gleamed. The Waters's were gone, and Mr Cymon Tuggs was alone in a heartless world.

Silently and abstractedly did that too sensitive youth follow his revered parents and a train of smock-frocks and wheelbarrows, along the pier, until the bustle of the scene around, recalled him to himself. The sun was shining brightly; the sea, dancing to its own music, rolled merrily in; crowds of people promenaded to and fro, young ladies tittered, old ladies talked, nursemaids displayed their charms to the greatest possible advantage, and their sweet little charges ran up and down, and to and fro, and in and out, under the feet, and between the legs of the assembled concourse, in the most playful and exhilarating manner possible. There were old gentlemen trying to make out objects through long telescopes, and young ones making objects of themselves in open shirt-collars; ladies carrying about portable chairs, and portable chairs carrying about invalids; parties waiting on the peer for parties who had come by the steam-boat; and nothing was to be heard but talking, laughing, welcoming, and merriment.

'Fly sir?'[6] exclaimed a chorus of fourteen men and six boys the moment that Mr Joseph Tuggs, at the head of his little party, had set foot in the street.

'Here's the gen'lm'n at last!' said one, touching his hat with mock politeness. 'Werry glad to see you, sir, – been watin' for you these six weeks. Jump in, if you please, sir.'

'Nice light fly and a fast trotter, sir,' said another: 'fourteen mile a hour, and surroundin' objects rendered inwisible by hextreme welocity!'

'Large fly for your luggage, sir,' cried a third. 'Werry large fly here, sir – reg'lar bluebottle!'

'Here's your fly, sir!' shouted another aspiring charioteer, mounting the box, and inducing an old gray horse to indulge in some imperfect reminiscences of a canter. 'Look at him, sir! – temper of a lamb and haction of a steam-ingein.'

Resisting even the temptation of securing the services of so valuable a quadruped as the last named, Mr Joseph Tuggs beckoned to the proprietor of a dingy conveyance of a greenish hue, lined with faded striped calico; and the luggage and the family having been deposited therein, the animal in the shafts, after describing circles in the road for a quarter of an hour, at last consented to depart in quest of lodgings.

'How many beds have you got?' screamed Mrs Tuggs out of the fly, to the woman who opened the door of the first house which displayed a bill intimating that apartments were to be let within.

'How many did you want, ma'am?' was of course the reply.

'Three.'

'Will you step in, ma'am?' Down got Mrs Tuggs. The family were delighted. Splendid view of the sea from the front windows – charming! A short pause. Back came Mrs Tuggs again. – One parlour, and a mattress.

'Why the devil didn't they say so at first?' inquired Mr Joseph Tuggs, rather pettishly.

'Don't know,' said Mrs Tuggs.

'Wretches!' exclaimed the nervous Cymon. Another bill – another stoppage. Same question – same answer – similar result.

'What do they mean by this?' inquired Mr Joseph Tuggs, thoroughly out of temper.

'Don't know,' said the placid Mrs Tuggs.

'Orvis the vay here, sir,' said the driver, by way of accounting for the circumstance in a satisfactory manner; and off they went again, to make fresh inquiries, and encounter fresh disappointments.

It had grown dusk when the 'fly' – the rate of whose progress greatly belied its name – after climbing up four or five perpendicular hills, stopped before the door of a dusty house, with a bay window, from which you could obtain a beautiful glimpse of the sea – if you thrust half your body out of it, at the imminent peril of falling into the area. Mrs Tuggs alighted. One ground-floor sitting-room, and three cells with beds in them up stairs – a double house – family on the opposite side – five children milk-and-watering in the parlour, and one little boy, expelled for bad behaviour, screaming on his back in the passage.

'What's the terms?' said Mrs Tuggs. The mistress of the house was deliberating on the expediency of putting on an extra guinea; so she coughed slightly, and affected not to hear the question.

'What's the terms?' said Mrs Tuggs, in a louder key.

'Five guineas a week, ma'am, *with* attendance,' replied the lodging-house keeper. (Attendance means the privilege of ringing the bell as often as you like, for your own amusement.)

'Rather dear,' said Mrs Tuggs.

'Oh dear, no, ma'am,' replied the mistress of the house, with a benign smile of pity at the ignorance of manners and customs, which the observation betrayed. 'Very cheap.

Such an authority was indisputable. Mrs Tuggs paid a week's rent in advance, and took the lodgings for a month. In an hour's time the family were seated at tea in their new abode.

'Capital srimps!' said Mr Joseph Tuggs.

Mr Cymon eyed his father with a rebellious scowl, as he emphatically said '*Shrimps*.'

'Well then, shrimps,' said Mr Joseph Tuggs. 'Srimps or shrimps, don't much matter.'

There was pity, blended with malignity, in Mr Cymon's eye, as he replied, 'Don't matter, father! What would Captain Waters say, if he heard such vulgarity?'

'Or what would dear Mrs Captain Waters says,' added Charlotta, 'if she saw mother – ma, I mean – eating them whole, heads and all?'

'It won't bear thinking of!' ejaculated Mr Cymon, with a shudder. 'How different,' he thought, 'from the Dowager Duchess of Dobbleton!'

'Very pretty woman, Mrs Captain Waters, is she not, Cymon?' inquired Miss Charlotta.

A glow of nervous excitement passed over the countenance of Mr Cymon Tuggs, as he replied, 'An angel of beauty!'

'Hallo!' said Mr Joseph Tuggs, 'Hallo, Cymon, my boy, take care — married lady you know;' and he winked one of his twinkling eyes knowingly.

'Why,' exclaimed Cymon, starting up with an ebullition of fury, as unexpected as alarming, 'Why am I to be reminded of that blight of my happiness, and ruin of my hopes? Why am I to be taunted with the miseries which are heaped upon my head? Is it not enough to — to — to' and the orator paused; but whether for want of words, or lack of breath, was never distinctly ascertained.

There was an impressive solemnity in the tone of this address, and in the air with which the romantic Cymon at its conclusion, rang the bell, and demanded a flat candlestick, which effectually forbade a reply. He stalked dramatically to bed, and the Tuggs's went to bed too, half an hour afterwards, in a state of considerable mystification and perplexity.

If the pier had presented a scene of life and bustle to the Tuggs's on their first landing at Ramsgate, it was far surpassed by the appearance of the sands on the morning after their arrival. It was a fine, bright, clear day, with a light breeze from the sea. There were the same ladies and gentlemen, the same children, the same nurse-maids, the same telescopes, the same portable chairs; the ladies were employed in needlework, or watch-guard making, or knitting, or reading novels; the gentlemen were reading newspapers and maga-zines, the children were digging holes in the sand with wooden spades, and collecting water therein: the nursemaids with their youngest charges in their arms, were running in after the waves, and then running back with the waves after them; and now and then a little sailing-boat either departed with a gay and talkative cargo of passengers, or returned with a very silent, and particularly uncomfortable-looking one.

'Well, I never!' exclaimed Mrs Tuggs, as she and Mr Joseph Tuggs, and Miss Charlotta Tuggs, and Mr Cymon Tuggs, with their eight feet in a corresponding number of yellow shoes, seated themselves on four rush-bottomed chairs, which, being placed in a soft part of the sand, forthwith sunk down some two feet and a half. — 'Well, I never!'

Mr Cymon, by an exertion of great personal strength, uprooted the chairs, and removed them further back.

'Why, I'm bless'd if there ain't some ladies a-going in!' exclaimed Mr Joseph Tuggs, with intense astonishment.

'Lor, pa!' exclaimed Miss Charlotta.

'There *is*, my dear,' said Mr Joseph Tuggs. And, sure enough, four young ladies, each furnished with a towel, tripped up the steps of a bathing-machine; in went the horse, floundering about in the water: round turned the machine, down sat the driver, and presently out burst the young ladies aforesaid, with four distinct splashes.

'Well, that's sing'ler, too!' ejaculated Mr Joseph Tuggs, after an awkward pause. Mr Cymon coughed slightly.

'Why, here's some gentlemen a-going in on this side,' exclaimed Mrs Tuggs, in a tone of horror.

Three machines — three horses — three flounderings — three turnings round — three splashes — three gentlemen, disporting themselves in the water like so many dolphins.

'Well, *that's* sing'ler!' said Mr Joseph Tuggs again. Miss Charlotta coughed this time, and another pause ensued. It was agreeably broken.

'How d'ye do, dear? We have been looking for you all the morning,' said a voice to Miss Charlotta Tuggs. Mrs Captain Waters was the owner of it.

'How d'ye do?' said Captain Walter Waters, all suavity; and a most cordial interchange of greetings ensued.

'Belinda, my love,' said Captain Walter Waters, applying his glass to his eye, and looking in the direction of the sea.

'Yes, my dear,' replied Mrs Captain Waters.

'There's Harry Thompson.'

'Where?' said Belinda, applying her glass to her eye.

'Bathing.'

'Lor, so it is! He don't see us, does he?'

'No, I don't think he does,' replied the captain. — 'Bless my soul, how very singular!'

'What?' inquired Belinda.

'There's Mary Golding, too.'

'Lor! – where?' (Up went the glass again.)

'There!' said the captain, pointing to one of the young ladies before noticed, who, in her bathing costume, looked as if she was enveloped in a patent Mackintosh,[7] of scanty dimensions.

'So it is, I declare!' exclaimed Mrs Captain Waters. – 'How very curious we should see them both!'

'Very,' said the captain, with perfect coolness.

'It's the reg'lar thing here, you see,' whispered Mr Cymon Tuggs to his father.

'I see it is,' whispered Mr Joseph Tuggs in reply. 'Queer though – ain't it?' Mr Cymon Tuggs nodded assent.

'What do you think of doing with yourself this morning?' inquired the captain. – 'Shall we lunch at Pegwell?'[8]

'I should like that very much indeed,' interposed Mrs Tuggs. She had never heard of Pegwell before; but the word 'lunch' had reached her ears, and it sounded very agreeably.

'How shall we go?' inquired the captain; 'it's too warm to walk.'

'A chay?' suggested Mr Joseph Tuggs.

'Chaise,' whispered Mr Cymon.

'I should think one would be enough,' said Mr Joseph Tuggs aloud, quite unconscious of the meaning of the correction. 'However, two chays if you like.'

'I should like a donkey *so* much,' said Belinda.

'Oh, so should I!' echoed Charlotta Tuggs.

'Well, we can have a fly,' suggested the captain, 'and you can have a couple of donkeys.'

A fresh difficulty arose. Mrs Captain Waters declared it would be decidedly improper for two ladies to ride alone. The remedy was obvious. Perhaps young Mr Tuggs would be gallant enough to accompany them.

Mr Cymon Tuggs blushed, smiled, looked vacant, and faintly protested he was no horseman. The objection was at once over-ruled. A fly was speedily found; and three donkeys – which the proprietor declared on his solemn asseveration to be 'three parts blood, and the other corn' – were engaged in the service.

'Kim up!' shouted one of the two boys who followed behind to propel the donkeys, when Belinda Waters and Charlotta Tuggs had been hoisted and pushed and pulled into their respective saddles.

'Hi–hi–hi!' groaned the other boy behind Mr Cymon Tuggs. Away went the donkey, with the stirrups jingling against the heels of Cymon's boots, and Cymon's boots nearly scraping the ground.

'Way–way! Wo–o–o–o–!' cried Mr Cymon Tuggs as well as he could, in the midst of the jolting.

'Don't make it gallop!' screamed Mrs Captain Waters, behind.

'My donkey *will* go into the public-house!' shrieked Miss Tuggs, in the rear.

'Hi–hi–hi!' groaned both the boys together; and on went the donkeys as if nothing would ever stop them.

Every thing has an end, however; and even the galloping of donkeys will cease in time. The animal which Mr Cymon Tuggs bestrode, feeling sundry uncomfortable tuggs at the bit, the intent of which he could by no means divine, abruptly sidled against a brick wall, and expressed his uneasiness by grinding Mr Cymon Tuggs's leg on the rough surface. Mrs Captain Waters's donkey, apparently under the influence of some playfulness of spirit, rushed suddenly, head first, into a hedge, and declined to come out again: and the quadruped on which Miss Tuggs was mounted expressed his delight at this humorous proceeding by firmly planting his fore-feet against the ground, and kicking up his hind-legs in a very agile, but somewhat alarming manner.

This abrupt termination to the rapidity of the ride naturally occasioned some confusion. Both the ladies indulged in vehement screaming for several minutes; and Mr Cymon Tuggs, besides sustaining intense bodily pain, had the additional mental anguish of witnessing their distressing situation, without the power to rescue them, by reason of his leg being firmly screwed in between the animal and the wall. The efforts of the boys, however, assisted by the ingenious expedient of twisting the tail of the most rebellious donkey, restored order in a much shorter time than could have reasonably been expected, and the little party jogged slowly on together.

'Now let 'em walk,' said Mr Cymon Tuggs. 'It's cruel to over-drive 'em.'

'Werry well, sir,' replied the boy, with a grin at his companion, as if he understood Mr Cymon to mean that the cruelty applied less to the animals than to their riders.

'What a lovely day, dear!' said Charlotta.

'Charming; enchanting, dear!' responded Mrs Captain Waters. 'What a beautiful prospect, Mr Tuggs!'

Cymon looked full in Belinda's face, as he responded – 'Beautiful, indeed!' The lady cast down her eyes, and suffered the animal she was riding to fall a little back. Cymon Tuggs instinctively did the same.

There was a brief silence, broken only by a sigh from Mr Cymon Tuggs.

'Mr Cymon,' said the lady suddenly, in a low tone, 'Mr Cymon – I am another's.'

Mr Cymon expressed his perfect concurrence in a statement which it was quite impossible to controvert.

'If I had not been,' resumed Belinda; and there she stopped.

'What – what?' said Mr Cymon earnestly. 'Do not torture me. What would you say?'

'If I had not been' – continued Mrs Captain Waters – 'if in earlier life, it had been my fate to have known, and been beloved by a noble youth – a kindred soul – a congenial spirit – one capable of feeling and appreciating the sentiments which –'

'Heavens! what do I hear?' exclaimed Mr Cymon Tuggs. 'Is it possible! can I believe my – Come up!' (This last unsentimental parenthesis was addressed to the donkey, who with his head between his fore-legs, appeared to be examining the state of his shoes with great anxiety.)

'Hi–hi–hi,' said the boys behind. 'Come up,' expostulated Cymon Tuggs again. 'Hi–hi–hi,' repeated the boys: and whether it was that the animal felt indignant at the tone of Mr Tuggs's command, or alarmed by the noise of the deputy proprietor's boots running behind him, or whether he burned with a noble emulation to outstrip the other donkeys, certain it is that he no sooner heard the second series of 'hi—hi's,' than he started away with a celerity of pace which jerked Mr Cymon's hat off instantaneously, and carried him to the Pegwell Bay hotel in no time, where he deposited his rider without giving him the trouble of dismounting, by sagaciously pitching him over his head, into the very door of the tavern.

Great was the confusion of Mr Cymon Tuggs, when he was put right end uppermost by two waiters; considerable was the alarm of Mrs Tuggs in behalf of her son; and agonizing were the apprehensions of Mrs Captain Waters on his account. It was speedily discovered, however, that he had not sustained much more injury than the donkey – he was grazed, and the animal was grazing – and then it *was* a delightful party to be sure! Mr and Mrs Tuggs, and the captain, had ordered lunch in the little garden behind: – small saucers of large shrimps, dabs of butter, crusty loaves, and bottled ale. The sky was without a cloud; there were flower-pots and turf before them; the sea at the foot of the cliff, stretching away as far as the eye could discern any thing at all; and vessels in the distance with sails as white, and as small, as nicely-got-up cambric handkerchiefs. The shrimps were delightful, the ale better, and the captain even more pleasant than either. Mrs Captain Waters was in *such* spirits after lunch – chasing, first the captain across the turf, and among the flower-pots, and then Mr Cymon Tuggs, and then Miss Tuggs, and laughing too, quite boisterously. But as the captain said, it didn't matter; who knew what they were, there? For all the people of the house knew, they might be common people. To which Mr Joseph Tuggs responded, 'To be sure;' and then they went down the steep wooden steps a little further on, which lead to the bottom of the cliff, and looked at the crabs, and the seaweed, and the eels, till it was more than fully time to go back to Ramsgate again; and finally Mr Cymon Tuggs ascended the steps last, and Mrs Captain Waters last but one: and Mr Cymon Tuggs discovered that the foot and ankle of Mrs Captain Waters, were even more unexceptionable than he had at first supposed.

Taking a donkey towards his ordinary place of residence, is a very different thing, and a feat much more easily to be accomplished, than taking him from it. It requires a great deal of foresight and presence of mind in the one case, to anticipate the numerous flights of his discursive imagination; whereas in the other, all you have to do is to hold on, and place a blind confidence in the animal. Mr Cymon Tuggs adopted the latter expedient on his return; and his nerves were so little discomposed by the journey, that he distinctly understood they were all to meet again at the library in the evening.

The library was crowded. There were the same ladies and the same gentlemen who had been on the sands in the morning, and on the pier the day before. There were young ladies in maroon-coloured gowns and black velvet bracelets, dispensing fancy articles in the shop, and presiding over games of chance in the concert-room. There were marriageable daughters, and marriage-making mammas, gaming, and promenading, and turning over music, and flirting. There were some male beaux doing the sentimental in whispers, and others doing the ferocious in mustaches. There were Mrs Tuggs in amber, Miss Tuggs in sky-blue, and Mrs Captain Waters in pink. There was Captain Waters in a braided surtout; there was Mr Cymon Tuggs in pumps and a gilt waistcoat; and, moreover, there was Mr Joseph Tuggs in a blue coat, and a shirt-frill.

'Numbers three, eight, and eleven,' cried one of the young ladies in the maroon-coloured gowns.

'Numbers three, eight, and eleven,' echoed another young lady in the same uniform.

'Number three's gone,' said the first young lady. 'Numbers eight and eleven.'

'Numbers eight and eleven,' echoed the second young lady.

'Number eight's gone, Mary Ann,' said the first young lady.

'Number eleven,' screamed the second.

'The numbers are all taken now, ladies, if you please,' said the first. The representatives of numbers three, eight, and eleven, and the rest of the numbers, crowded round the table.

'Will you throw, ma'am?' said the presiding goddess, handing the dice-box to the eldest daughter of a stout lady, with four girls.

There was a profound silence among the lookers on.

'Throw, Jane, my dear,' said the stout lady. An interesting display of bashfulness – a little blushing in a cambric handkerchief – a whispering to a younger sister.

'Amelia, my dear, throw for your sister,' said the stout lady; and then she turned to a walking advertisement of Rowland's Macassar Oil,⁹ who stood next her, and said, 'Jane is so *very* modest and retiring; but I can't be angry with her for it. An artless and unsophisticated girl is *so* truly amiable, that I often wish Amelia was more like her sister.'

The gentleman with the whiskers, whispered his admiring approval; and the artless young lady glanced across, to observe the effect of her most unqualified simplicity.

'Now, my dear!' said the stout lady. Miss Amelia threw – eight for her sister, ten for herself.

'Nice figure, Amelia,' whispered the stout lady, to a thin youth beside her.

'Beautiful!'

'And *such* a spirit. I am like you in that respect. I can *not* help admiring that life and vivacity. Ah! (a sigh) I wish I could make poor Jane a little more like my dear Amelia!'

The young gentleman cordially acquiesced in the sentiment; and both he, and the individual first addressed, were perfectly contented.

'Who's this?' inquired Mr Cymon Tuggs of Mrs Captain Waters, as a short female, in a blue velvet hat and feathers, was led into the orchestra, by a fat man in black tights, and cloudy Berlins.¹⁰

'Mrs Tippin, of the London theatres,' replied Belinda, referring to the programme of the concert.

The talented Tippin having condescendingly acknowledged the clapping of hands, and shouts of 'bravo!' which greeted her appearance, proceeded to sing the popular cavitina of 'Bid me discourse,'¹¹ accompanied on the piano by Mr Tippin; after which Mr Tippin sang a comic song, accompanied on the piano by Mrs Tippin, the applause consequent upon which was only to be exceeded by the enthusiastic approbation bestowed upon an air with variations on the guitar, by Miss Tippin, accompanied on the chin by Master Tippin.

Thus passed the evening; and thus passed the days and evenings of the Tuggs's, and the Waters's, for six weeks afterwards. Sands in the morning – donkeys at noon – pier in the afternoon – library at night; and the same people every where.

On that very night six weeks, the moon was shining brightly over the calm sea, which dashed against the feet of the tall gaunt cliffs with just enough noise to lull the old fish to sleep, without disturbing the young ones, when two figures were discernible – or would have been, if any body had looked for them – seated on one of the wooden benches which are stationed near the verge of the western cliff. The moon had climbed higher into the heavens, by two hours' journeying, since those figures first sat down, and yet they had moved not. The crowd of loungers had thinned and dispersed, the noise of itinerant musicians had died away; light after light had appeared in the windows of the different houses in the distance, blockade-man[12] after blockade-man had passed the spot, wending his way towards his solitary post, and yet those figures had remained stationary. Some portions of the two forms were in deep shadow, but the light of the moon fell strongly on a puce-coloured boot and a glazed stock. Mr Cymon Tuggs, and Mrs Captain Waters, were seated on that bench. They spoke not, but were silently gazing on the sea.

'Walter will return to-morrow,' said Mrs Captain Waters, mournfully breaking silence.

Mr Cymon Tuggs sighed like a gust of wind through a forest of gooseberry-bushes, as he replied – 'Alas! he will.'

'Oh, Cymon!' resumed Belinda, 'the chaste delight, the calm happiness, of this one week of Platonic love, is too much for me.'

Cymon was about to suggest that it was too little for him, but he stopped himself, and murmured unintelligibly.

'And to think that even this glimpse of happiness, innocent as it is,' exclaimed Belinda, 'is now to be lost for ever!'

'Oh, do not say for ever, Belinda,' exclaimed the excitable Cymon, as two strongly-defined tears chased each other down his pale face – it was so long that there was plenty of room for a chase – 'Do not say for ever!'

'I must,' replied Belinda.

'Why?' urged Cymon, 'oh why? Such Platonic acquaintance as ours is so harmless, that even your husband can never object to it.'

'My husband!' exclaimed Belinda. 'You little know him. Jealous and revengeful; ferocious in his revenge – a maniac in his jealousy! Would you be assassinated before my eyes?' Mr Cymon Tuggs, in a voice broken by emotion, expressed his disinclination to undergo the process of assassination before the eyes of any body.

'Then leave me,' said Mrs Captain Waters. 'Leave me, this night, for ever. It is late; let us return.'

Mr Cymon Tuggs sadly offered the lady his arm, and escorted her to her lodgings. He paused at the door – he felt a Platonic pressure of his hand. 'Good night,' he said, hesitating.

'Good night,' sobbed the lady. Mr Cymon Tuggs paused again.

'Won't you walk in, sir?' said the servant. Mr Tuggs hesitated. Oh, that hesitation! He *did* walk in.

'Good night,' said Mr Cymon Tuggs again, when he reached the drawing-room.

'Good night!' replied Belinda; 'and, if at any period of my life, I – Hush!' The lady paused, and stared, with a steady gaze of horror, on the ashy countenance of Mr Cymon Tuggs. There was a double knock at the street-door.

'It is my husband!' said Belinda, as the captain's voice was heard below.

'And my family!' added Cymon Tuggs, as the voices of his relatives floated up the staircase.

'The curtain! the curtain!' gasped Mrs Captain Waters, pointing to the window, before which some chintz hangings were closely drawn.

'But I have done nothing wrong,' said the hesitating Cymon.

'The curtain!' reiterated the frantic lady; 'you will be murdered.' This last appeal to his feelings was irresistible. The dismayed Cymon concealed himself behind the curtain, with pantomimic suddenness.

Enter the captain, Joseph Tuggs, Mrs Tuggs, and Charlotta.

'My dear,' said the captain, 'Lieutenant Slaughter.' Two iron-shod boots and one gruff voice were heard by Mr Cymon to advance, and acknowledge the honour of the introduction. The sabre of the lieutenant rattled heavily upon the floor, as he seated himself at the table. Mr Cymon's fears almost overcame his reason.

'The brandy, my dear,' said the captain. Here was a situation! They were going to make a night of it: and Mr Cymon Tuggs was pent up behind the curtain, and afraid to breathe.

'Slaughter,' said the captain, 'a cigar?'

Now, Mr Cymon Tuggs never could smoke without feeling it indispensably necessary to retire immediately, and never could smell smoke without a strong disposition to cough. The cigars were introduced; the captain was a professed smoker, so was the lieutenant, so was Joseph Tuggs. The apartment was small, the door was closed, the smoke powerful: it hung in heavy wreaths over the room, and at length found its way behind the curtain. Cymon Tuggs held his nose, then his mouth, then his breath. It was all of no use – out came the cough.

'Bless my soul!' said the captain, 'I beg your pardon, Miss Tuggs. You dislike smoking?'

'Oh no; I don't indeed,' said Charlotta.

'It makes you cough.'

'Oh dear no.'

'You coughed just now.'

'Me, Captain Waters! Lor! how can you say so?'

'Somebody coughed,' said the captain.

'I certainly thought so,' said Slaughter. No; every body denied it.

'Fancy,' said the captain.

'Must be,' echoed Slaughter.

Cigars resumed – more smoke, another cough – smothered, but violent.

'Damned odd!' said the captain, staring about him.

'Sing'ler!' ejaculated the unconscious Mr Joseph Tuggs.

Lieutenant Slaughter looked first at one person mysteriously, then at another; then laid down his cigar; then approached the window on tiptoe, and pointed with his right thumb over his shoulder, in the direction of the curtain.

'Slaughter!' ejaculated the captain, rising from table, 'what do you mean?'

The lieutenant, in reply, drew back the curtain, and discovered Mr Cymon Tuggs behind it; pallid with apprehension, and blue with wanting to cough.

'Ah!' exclaimed the captain, furiously, 'What do I see? Slaughter, your sabre!'

'Cymon!' screamed the Tuggs's.

'Mercy,' said Belinda.

'Platonic,' gasped Cymon.

'Your sabre!' roared the captain: 'Slaughter – unhand me – the villain's life!'

'Murder!' screamed the Tuggs's.

'Hold him fast, sir!' faintly articulated Cymon.

'Water!' exclaimed Joseph Tuggs – and Mr Cymon Tuggs and all the ladies forthwith fainted away, and formed a tableau.

Most willingly would we conceal the disastrous termination of the six weeks' acquaintance. A troublesome form, and an arbitrary custom, however, prescribe that a story should have a conclusion in addition to a commencement; and we have therefore no alternative. Lieutenant Slaughter brought a message – the captain brought an action. Mr Joseph Tuggs interposed – the lieutenant negotiated. When Mr Cymon Tuggs recovered from the nervous disorder into which misplaced affection, and exciting circumstances had plunged him, he found that his family had lost their pleasant acquaintance; that his father was minus fifteen hundred pounds; and the captain plus the precise sum. The money was paid to hush the matter up, but it got abroad notwithstanding; and there are not wanting those who affirm that three designing impostors never found more easy dupes, than did Captain Waters, Mrs Waters, and Lieutenant Slaughter, in the Tuggs's at Ramsgate.

CHAPTER 5

Horatio Sparkins

'INDEED, my love, he paid Teresa very great attention on the last assembly night,' said Mrs Malderton, addressing her spouse, who, after the fatigues of the day in the City, was sitting with a silk handkerchief over his head, and his feet on the fender, drinking his port; — 'very great attention; and I say again, every possible encouragement ought to be given him. He positively must be asked down here to dine.'

'Who must?' inquired Mr Malderton.

'Why, you know whom I mean, my dear — the young man with the black whiskers and the white cravat, who has just come out at our assembly, and whom all the girls are talking about. Young — dear me! what's his name? — Marianne, what *is* his name?' continued Mrs Malderton, addressing her youngest daughter, who was engaged in netting[1] a purse, and endeavouring to look sentimental.

'Mr Horatio Sparkins, ma,' replied Miss Marianne, with a Juliet-like[2] sigh.

'Oh! yes, to be sure — Horatio Sparkins,' said Mrs Malderton. 'Decidedly the most gentleman-like young man I ever saw. I am sure, in the beautifully-made coat he wore the other night, he looked like — like —'

'Like Prince Leopold,[3] ma, — so noble, so full of sentiment!' suggested Miss Marianne, in a tone of enthusiastic admiration.

'You should recollect, my dear,' resumed Mrs Malderton, 'that Teresa is now eight-and-twenty; and that it really is very important that something should be done.'

Miss Teresa Malderton was a very little girl, rather fat, with vermilion cheeks, but good-humoured, and still disengaged, although, to do her justice, the misfortune arose from no lack of perseverance on her part. In vain had she flirted for ten years; in vain had Mr and Mrs Malderton assiduously kept up an extensive

Horatio Sparkins

acquaintance among the young eligible bachelors of Camberwell, and even of Wandsworth and Brixton;[4] to say nothing of those who 'dropped in' from town. Miss Malderton was as well known as the lion on the top of Northumberland House, and had an equal chance of 'going off.'[5]

'I am quite sure you'd like him,' continued Mrs Malderton; 'he is so gentlemanly!'

'So clever!' said Miss Marianne.

'And has such a flow of language!' added Miss Teresa.

'He has a great respect for you, my dear,' said Mrs Malderton to her husband, in a confident tone. Mr Malderton coughed, and looked at the fire.

'Yes, I'm sure he's very much attached to pa's society,' said Miss Marianne.

'No doubt of it,' echoed Miss Teresa.

'Indeed, he said as much to me in confidence,' observed Mrs Malderton.

'Well, well,' returned Mr Malderton, somewhat flattered; 'if I see him at the assembly to-morrow, perhaps I'll ask him down here. I hope he knows we live at Oak Lodge, Camberwell, my dear?'

'Of course – and that you keep a one-horse carriage.'

'I'll see about it,' said Mr Malderton, composing himself for a nap; 'I'll see about it.'

Mr Malderton was a man whose whole scope of ideas was limited to Lloyd's, the Exchange, the India House, and the Bank. A few successful speculations had raised him from a situation of obscurity and comparative poverty, to a state of affluence. As frequently happens in such cases, the ideas of himself and his family became elevated to an extraordinary pitch as their means increased; they affected fashion, taste, and many other fooleries, in imitation of their betters, and had a very decided and becoming horror of any thing which could by possibility be considered *low*. He was hospitable from ostentation, illiberal from ignorance, and prejudiced from conceit. Egotism and the love of display induced him to keep an excellent table: convenience, and a love of the good things of this life, ensured him plenty of guests. He liked to have clever men, or what he considered such, at his table, because it was a great thing to talk about; but he never could endure what he called 'sharp fellows.' Probably he cherished this feeling out of compliment to his two sons, who gave their respected parent no uneasiness in that particular. The family were ambitious of forming acquaintances and connexions in some sphere of society superior to that in which they themselves moved; and one of the necessary consequences of this desire, added to their utter ignorance of the world beyond their own small circle, was, that any one who could plausibly lay claim to an acquaintance with people of rank and title, had a sure passport to the table at Oak Lodge, Camberwell.

The appearance of Mr Horatio Sparkins at the assembly had excited no small degree of surprise and curiosity among its regular frequenters. Who could he be? He was evidently reserved, and apparently melancholy. Was he a clergyman? – He danced too well. A barrister? – he was not called. He used very fine words, and said a great deal. Could he be a distinguished foreigner[6] come to England for the purpose of describing the country, its manners and customs; and frequenting public balls and public dinners, with the view of becoming acquainted with high life, polished etiquette, and English refinement? – No, he had not a foreign accent. Was he a surgeon, a contributor to the magazines, a writer of fashionable novels, or an artist? – No; to each and all of these surmises there existed some valid objection. – 'Then,' said everybody, 'he must be *somebody*.' – 'I should think he must be,' reasoned Mr Malderton, with himself, 'because he perceives our superiority, and pays us so much attention.'

The night succeeding the conversation we have just recorded was 'assembly night.' The double-fly was ordered to be at the door of Oak Lodge at nine o'clock precisely. The Miss Maldertons were dressed in sky-blue satin trimmed with artificial flowers; and Mrs M. (who was a little fat woman), in ditto ditto, looked like her eldest daughter multiplied by two. Mr Frederick Malderton, the eldest son, in full-dress costume, was the very *beau idéal* of a smart waiter; and Mr Thomas Malderton, the youngest, with his white dress-stock, blue coat, bright buttons, and red watch-ribbon, strongly resembled the portrait of that interesting, though somewhat rash young gentleman, George Barnwell.[7] Every member of the party had made up his or her mind to cultivate the acquaintance of Mr Horatio Sparkins. Miss Teresa, of course, was to be as amiable and interesting as ladies of eight-and-twenty on the look-out for a husband usually are; Mrs Malderton would be all smiles and graces; Miss Marianne would request the favour of some verses for her album; Mr Malderton would patronise the great unknown by asking him to dinner; and Tom intended to ascertain the extent of his information on the interesting topics of snuff and cigars. Even Mr Frederick Malderton himself, the family authority on all points of taste, dress, and fashionable arrangement – who had lodgings of his own in town, who had a free admission to Covent-garden theatre, who always dressed according to the fashions of the months, who went up the water twice a week in the season, and who actually had an intimate friend who once knew a gentleman who formerly lived in the Albany,[8] – even he had determined that Mr Horatio Sparkins must be a devilish good fellow, and that he would do him the honour of challenging him to a game at billiards.

The first object that met the anxious eyes of the expectant family on their entrance into the ball-room, was the interesting Horatio, with his hair brushed off his forehead, and his eyes fixed on the ceiling, reclining in a contemplative attitude on one of the seats.

'There he is, my dear,' anxiously whispered Mrs Malderton to Mr Malderton.

'How like Lord Byron!'[9] murmured Miss Teresa.

'Or Montgomery!'[10] whispered Miss Marianne.

'Or the portraits of Captain Ross!'[11] suggested Tom.

'Tom – don't be an ass!' said his father, who checked him upon all occasions, probably with a view to prevent his becoming 'sharp' – which was very unnecessary.

The elegant Sparkins attitudinized with admirable effect until the family had crossed the room. He then started up with the most natural appearance of surprise and delight; accosted Mrs Malderton with the utmost cordiality, saluted the young ladies in the most enchanting manner; bowed to, and shook hands with Mr Malderton, with a degree of respect amounting almost to veneration, and returned the greetings of the two young men in a half-gratified, half-patronizing manner, which fully convinced them that he must be an important, and, at the same time, condescending personage.

'Miss Malderton,' said Horatio, after the ordinary salutations, and bowing very low, 'may I be permitted to presume to hope that you will allow me to have the pleasure —'

'I don't think I am engaged,' said Miss Teresa, with a dreadful affectation of indifference — 'but, really — so many —'

Horatio looked as handsomely miserable as a Hamlet sliding upon a bit of orange-peel.[12]

'I shall be most happy,' simpered the interesting Teresa, at last; and Horatio's countenance brightened up like an old hat in a shower of rain.

'A very genteel young man, certainly!' said the gratified Mr Malderton, as the obsequious Sparkins and his partner joined the quadrille which was just forming.

'He has a remarkably good address,' said Mr Frederick.

'Yes, he is a prime fellow,' interposed Tom, who always managed to put his foot in it — 'he talks just like an auctioneer.'

'Tom!' said his father solemnly, 'I think I desired you before not to be a fool.' — Tom looked as happy as a cock on a drizzly morning.

'How delightful!' said the interesting Horatio to his partner, as they promenaded the room at the conclusion of the set — 'how delightful, how refreshing it is, to retire from the cloudy storms, the vicissitudes, and the troubles of life, even if it be but for a few short, fleeting moments; and to spend those moments, fading and evanescent though they be, in the delightful, the blessed society of one individual — of her whose frowns would be death, whose coldness would be madness, whose falsehood would be ruin, whose constancy would be bliss; the possession of whose affection would be the brightest and best reward that Heaven could bestow on man.'

'What feeling! what sentiment!' thought Miss Teresa, as she leaned more heavily upon her companion's arm.

'But enough — enough!' resumed the elegant Sparkins, with a theatrical air. 'What have I said? what have I — I — to do with sentiments like these? Miss Malderton —' here he stopped short — 'may I hope to be permitted to offer the humble tribute of —'

'Really, Mr Sparkins,' returned the enraptured Teresa, blushing in the sweetest confusion, 'I must refer you to papa. I never can, without his consent, venture to — to —'

'Surely he cannot object —'

'Oh, yes. Indeed, indeed, you know him not,' interrupted Miss Teresa, well knowing there was nothing to fear, but wishing to make the interview resemble a scene in some romantic novel.

'He cannot object to my offering you a glass of negus,' returned the adorable Sparkins, with some surprise.

'Is that all?' said the disappointed Teresa to herself. 'What a fuss about nothing!'

'It will give me the greatest pleasure, sir, to see you to dinner at Oak Lodge, Camberwell, on Sunday next at five o'clock, if you have no better engagement,' said Mr Malderton, at the conclusion of the evening, as he and his sons were standing in conversation with Mr Horatio Sparkins.

Horatio bowed his acknowledgments, and accepted the flattering invitation.

'I must confess,' continued the manœuvering father, offering his snuff-box to his new acquaintance, 'that I don't enjoy these assemblies half so much as the comfort — I had almost said the luxury — of Oak Lodge: they have no great charms for an elderly man.'

'And after all, sir, what is man?' said the metaphysical Sparkins — 'I say, what is man?'

'Ah! very true,' said Mr Malderton — 'very true.'

'We know that we live and breathe,' continued Horatio; 'that we have wants and wishes, desires and appetites —'

'Certainly,' said Mr Frederick Malderton, looking very profound.

'I say, we know that we exist,' repeated Horatio, raising his voice, 'but there we stop; there is an end to our knowledge; there is the summit of our attainments; there is the termination of our ends. What more do we know?'

'Nothing,' replied Mr Frederick – than whom no one was more capable of answering for himself in that particular. Tom was about to hazard something, but, fortunately for his reputation, he caught his father's angry eye, and slunk off like a puppy convicted of petty larceny.

'Upon my word,' said Mr Malderton the elder, as they were returning home in the 'Fly,' 'that Mr Sparkins is a wonderful young man. Such surprising knowledge! such extraordinary information! and such a splendid mode of expressing himself!'

'I think he must be somebody in disguise,' said Miss Marianne. 'How charmingly romantic!'

'He talks very loud and nicely,' timidly observed Tom, 'but I don't exactly understand what he means.'

'I almost begin to despair of *your* understanding any thing, sir,' said his father, who, of course, had been much enlightened by Mr Horatio Sparkins' conversations.

'It strikes me, Tom,' said Miss Teresa, 'that you have made yourself very ridiculous this evening.'

'No doubt of it,' cried every body – and the unfortunate Tom reduced himself into the least possible space. That night Mr and Mrs Malderton had a long conversation respecting their daughter's prospects and future arrangements. Miss Teresa went to bed, considering whether, in the event of her marrying a title, she could conscientiously encourage the visits of her present associates; and dreamt all night of disguised noblemen, large routs, ostrich plumes, bridal favours, and Horatio Sparkins.

Various surmises were hazarded on the Sunday morning, as to the mode of conveyance which the anxiously-expected Horatio would adopt. Did he keep a gig? – was it possible he could come on horseback? – or would he patronize the stage? These, and various other conjectures of equal importance, engrossed the attention of Mrs Malderton and her daughters during the whole morning.[13]

'Upon my word, my dear, it's a most annoying thing that that vulgar brother of yours should have invited himself to dine here to-day,' said Mr Malderton to his wife. 'On account of Mr Sparkins's coming down, I purposely abstained from asking any one but Flamwell. And then to think of your brother — a tradesman — it's insufferable. I declare I wouldn't have him mention his shop before our new guests — no, not for a thousand pounds! I wouldn't care if he had the good sense to conceal the disgrace he is to the family; but he's so cursedly fond of his horrid business, that he *will* let people know what he is.'

Mr Jacob Barton the individual alluded to, was a large grocer; so vulgar, and so lost to all sense of feeling, that he actually never scrupled to avow that he wasn't above his business: 'he'd made his money by it, and he didn't care who know'd it.'

'Ah! Flamwell, my dear fellow, how d'ye do?' said Mr Malderton, as a little spoffish¹⁴ man, with green spectacles, entered the room. 'You got my note?'

'Yes, I did; and here I am in consequence.'

'You don't happen to know this Mr Sparkins by name? You know every body.'

Mr Flamwell was one of those gentlemen of remarkably extensive information whom one occasionally meets in society, who pretend to know every body, but in reality know nobody. At Malderton's, where any stories about great people were received with a greedy ear, he was an especial favourite; and knowing the kind of people he had to deal with, he carried his passion of claiming acquaintance with every body to the most immoderate length. He had rather a singular way of telling his greatest lies in a parenthesis, and with an air of self-denial, as if he feared being thought egotistical.

'Why, no, I don't know him by that name,' returned Flamwell, in a low tone, and with an air of immense importance. 'I have no doubt I know him though. Is he tall?'

'Middle sized,' said Miss Teresa.

'With black hair?' inquired Flamwell, hazarding a bold guess.

'Yes,' returned Miss Teresa, eagerly.

'Rather a snub nose?'

'No,' said the disappointed Teresa, 'he has a Roman nose.'

'I said a Roman nose, didn't I?' inquired Flamwell. 'He's an elegant young man?'

'Oh, certainly.'

'With remarkably prepossessing manners?'

'Oh, yes!' said all the family together. 'You must know him.'

'Yes, I thought you knew him, if he was any body,' triumphantly exclaimed Mr Malderton. 'Who d'ye think he is?'

'Why, from your description,' said Flamwell, ruminating, and sinking his voice almost to a whisper, 'he bears a strong resemblance to the Honourable Augustus Fitz-Edward Fitz-John Fitz-Osborne. He's a very talented young man, and rather eccentric. It's extremely probable he may have changed his name for some temporary purpose.'

Teresa's heart beat high. Could he be the Honourable Augustus Fitz-Edward Fitz-John Fitz-Osborne! What a name to be elegantly engraved upon two glazed cards, tied together with a piece of white satin ribbon! 'The Honourable Mrs Augustus Fitz-Edward Fitz-John Fitz-Osborne!' The thought was transport.

'It's five minutes to five,' said Mr Malderton, looking at his watch: 'I hope he's not going to disappoint us.'

'There he is!' exclaimed Miss Teresa, as a loud double-knock was heard at the door. Every body endeavoured to look – as people when they particularly expect a visitor always do – as if they were perfectly unsuspicious of the approach of any body.

The room-door opened – 'Mr Barton!' said the servant.

'Confound the man!' murmured Malderton. 'Ah! my dear sir, how d'ye do! Any news?'

'Why, no,' returned the grocer, in his usual honest, bluff manner. 'No, none partickler. None that I am much aware of. – How d'ye do, gals and boys? – Mr Flamwell, sir – glad to see you.'

'Here's Mr Sparkins,' said Tom, who had been looking out at the window, 'on *such* a black horse!' – There was Horatio, sure enough, on a large black horse, curvetting and prancing along like an Astley's[15] supernumerary. After a great deal of reining in and pulling up, with the usual accompaniments of snorting, rearing, and kicking, the animal consented to stop at about a hundred yards from the gate, where Mr Sparkins dismounted, and confided him to the care of Mr Malderton's groom. The ceremony of introduction was gone through in all due form. Mr Flamwell looked from behind his green spectacles at Horatio with an air of mysterious importance; and the gallant Horatio looked unutterable things at Teresa, who tried in her turn to appear uncommonly lackadaisical.

'Is he the Honourable Mr Augustus – what's his name?' whispered Mrs Malderton to Flamwell, as he was escorting her to the dining-room.

'Why, no – at least not exactly,' returned that great authority – 'not exactly.'

'Who *is* he then?'

'Hush!' said Flamwell, nodding his head with a grave air, importing that he knew very well; but was prevented by some grave reasons of state from disclosing the important secret. It might be one of the ministers making himself acquainted with the views of the people.

'Mr Sparkins,' said the delighted Mrs Malderton, 'pray divide the ladies. John, put a chair for the gentleman between Miss Teresa and Miss Marianne.' This was addressed to a man who on ordinary occasions acted as half-groom, half-gardener; but who, as it was most important to make an impression on Mr Sparkins, had been forced into a white neckerchief and shoes, and touched up and brushed to look like a second footman.

The dinner was excellent; Horatio was most attentive to Miss Teresa, and every one felt in high spirits, except Mr Malderton, who, knowing the propensity of his brother-in-law, Mr Barton, endured that sort of agony which the newspapers inform us is experienced by the surrounding neighbourhood when a pot-boy hangs himself in a hay-loft, and which is 'much easier to be imagined than described.'

'Have you seen your friend, Sir Thomas Noland, lately, Flamwell?' inquired Mr Malderton, casting a sidelong look at Horatio, to see what effect the mention of so great a man had upon him.

'Why, no — not very lately: I saw Lord Gubbleton the day before yesterday.'

'Ah! I hope his lordship is very well,' said Malderton, in a tone of the greatest interest. It is scarcely necessary to say that until that moment he had been quite innocent of the existence of such a person.

'Why, yes; he was very well — very well indeed. He's a devilish good fellow; I met him in the City, and had a long chat with him. Indeed, I'm rather intimate with him. I couldn't stop to talk to him as long as I could wish though, because I was on my way to a banker's, a very rich man, and a member of Parliament, with whom I am also rather, indeed I may say very, intimate.'

'I know whom you mean,' returned the host, consequentially, in reality knowing as much about the matter as Flamwell himself.

'He has a capital business.'

This was touching on a dangerous topic.

'Talking of business,' interposed Mr Barton, from the centre of the table. 'A gentleman that you knew very well, Malderton, before you made that first lucky spec of yours, called at our shop the other day, and —'

'Barton, may I trouble you for a potato,' interrupted the wretched master of the house, hoping to nip the story in the bud.

'Certainly,' returned the grocer, quite insensible of his brother-in-law's object — 'and he said in a very plain manner —'

'*Floury*, if you please,' interrupted Malderton again; dreading the termination of the anecdote, and fearing a repetition of the word 'shop.'

'He said, says he,' continued the culprit, after despatching the potato — 'says he, how goes on your business? So I said, jokingly — you know my way — says I, I'm never above my business, and I hope my business will never be above me. Ha, ha!'

'Mr Sparkins,' said the host, vainly endeavouring to conceal his dismay, 'a glass of wine?'

'With the utmost pleasure, sir.'

'Happy to see you.'

'Thank you.'

'We were talking the other evening,' resumed the host, addressing Horatio, partly with the view of displaying the conversational powers of his new acquaintance, and partly in the hope of drowning the grocer's stories — 'we were talking the other day about the nature of man. Your argument struck me very forcibly.'

'And me,' said Mr Frederick. Horatio made a graceful inclination of the head.

'Pray, what is your opinion of woman, Mr Sparkins?' inquired Mrs Malderton. The young ladies simpered.

'Man,' replied Horatio, 'man, whether he ranged the bright, gay, flowery plains of a second Eden, or the more sterile, barren, and, I may say, commonplace regions, to which we are compelled to accustom ourselves in times such as these; man, I say, under any circumstances, or in any place — whether he were bending beneath the withering blasts of the frigid zone, or scorching under the rays of a vertical sun — man, without woman, would be — alone.'

'I'm very happy to find you entertain such honourable opinions, Mr Sparkins,' said Mrs Malderton.

'And I,' added Miss Teresa. Horatio looked his delight, and the young lady blushed like a full-blown peony.

'Now it's my opinion,' said Mr Barton —.

'I know what you're going to say,' interposed Malderton, determined not to give his relation another opportunity, 'and I don't agree with you.'

'What?' inquired the astonished grocer.

'I am sorry to differ from you, Barton,' said the host, in as positive a manner as if he really were contradicting a position which the other had laid down, 'but I cannot give my assent to what I consider a very monstrous proposition.'

'But I meant to say —'

'You never can convince me,' said Malderton, with an air of obstinate determination. 'Never.'

'And I,' said Mr Frederick, following up his father's attack, 'cannot entirely agree in Mr Sparkins' argument.'

'What!' said Horatio, who became more metaphysical, and more argumentative, as he saw the female part of the family listening in wondering delight – 'what! is effect the consequence of cause? Is cause the precursor of effect?'

'That's the point,' said Flamwell.

'To be sure,' said Mr Malderton.

'Because, if effect is the consequence of cause, and if cause does precede effect, I apprehend you are decidedly wrong,' added Horatio.

'Decidedly,' said the toad-eating Flamwell.

'At least I apprehend that to be the just and logical deduction,' said Sparkins, in a tone of interrogation.

'No doubt of it,' chimed in Flamwell again. 'It settles the point.'

'Well, perhaps it does,' said Mr Frederick; 'I didn't see it before.'

'I don't exactly see it now,' thought the grocer; 'but I suppose it's all right.'

'How wonderfully clever he is!' whispered Mrs Malderton to her daughters, as they retired to the drawing-room.

'Oh, he's quite a love!' said both the young ladies together; 'he talks like an oracle. He must have seen a great deal of life.'

The gentlemen being left to themselves, a pause ensued, during which every body looked very grave, as if they were quite overcome by the profound nature of the previous discussion. Flamwell, who had made up his mind to find out who and what Mr Horatio Sparkins really was, first broke silence.

'Excuse me, sir,' said that distinguished personage – 'I presume you have studied for the bar? I thought of entering once myself – indeed I'm rather intimate with some of the highest ornaments of that distinguished profession.'

'No – no!' said Horatio, with a little hesitation; 'not exactly.'

'But you have been much among the silk gowns, or I mistake?' inquired Flamwell, deferentially.

'Nearly all my life,' returned Sparkins.

The question was thus pretty well settled in the mind of Mr Flamwell. – He was a young gentleman 'about to be called.'

'I shouldn't like to be a barrister,' said Tom, speaking for the first time, and looking round the table to find somebody who would notice the remark.

No one made any reply.

'I shouldn't like to wear a wig,' added Tom, hazarding another observation.

'Tom, I beg you'll not make yourself ridiculous,' said his father. 'Pray listen, and improve yourself by the conversation you hear, and don't be constantly making these absurd remarks.'

'Very well, father,' replied the unfortunate Tom, who had not spoken a word since he had asked for another slice of beef at a quarter past five o'clock, P.M., and it was then eight.

'Well, Tom,' observed his good-natured uncle, 'never mind; *I* think with you. *I* shouldn't like to wear a wig. I'd rather wear an apron.'

Mr Malderton coughed violently. Mr Barton resumed – 'For if a man's above his business —'

The cough returned with tenfold violence, and did not cease until the unfortunate cause of it, in his alarm, had quite forgotten what he intended to say.

'Mr Sparkins,' said Flamwell, returning to the charge, 'do you happen to know Mr Delafontaine, of Bedford-square?'[16]

'I have exchanged cards with him; since which, indeed, I have had an opportunity of serving him considerably,' replied Horatio, slightly colouring, no doubt, at having been betrayed into making the acknowledgment.

'You are very lucky, if you have had an opportunity of obliging that great man,' observed Flamwell, with an air of profound respect.

'I don't know who he is,' he whispered to Mr Malderton confidentially, as they followed Horatio up to the drawing-room. 'It's quite clear, however, that he belongs to the law, and that he is somebody of great importance, and very highly connected.'

'No doubt, no doubt,' returned his companion.

The remainder of the evening passed away most delightfully. Mr Malderton, relieved from his apprehensions by the circumstance of Mr Barton's falling into a profound sleep, was as affable and gracious as possible. Miss Teresa played the 'Fall of Paris,'[17] as Mr Sparkins declared, in a most masterly manner, and both of them, assisted by Mr Frederick, tried over glees and trios without number; they having made the pleasing discovery that their voices harmonized beautifully. To be sure, they all sang the first part; and Horatio, in addition to the slight drawback of having no ear, was perfectly innocent of knowing a note of music; still they passed the time away very agreeably, and it was past twelve o'clock before Mr Sparkins ordered the mourning-coach-looking steed to be brought out – an order which was only complied with, upon the distinct understanding that he was to repeat his visit on the following Sunday.

'But, perhaps, Mr Sparkins will form one of our party to-morrow evening?' suggested Mrs M. 'Mr Malderton intends taking the girls to see the pantomime.' – Mr Sparkins bowed, and promised to join the party in box 48, in the course of the evening.

'We will not tax you for the morning,' said Miss Teresa, bewitchingly; 'for ma is going to take us to all sorts of places, shopping. But I know that gentlemen have a great horror of that employment.' Mr Sparkins bowed again, and declared that he should be delighted, but business of importance occupied him in the morning. Flamwell looked at Malderton significantly. – 'It's term time!' he whispered.

At twelve o'clock on the following morning, the 'fly' was at the door of Oak Lodge, to convey Mrs Malderton and her daughters on their expedition for the day. They were to dine and dress for the play at a friend's house; first, driving thither with their band-boxes, they departed on their first errand to make some purchases at Messrs Jones, Spruggins, and Smith's, of Tottenham-court-road; after which they were to go to Redmayne's, in Bond-street;[18] and thence to innumerable places that no one ever heard of. The young ladies beguiled the tediousness of the ride by eulogizing Mr Horatio Sparkins, scolding their mamma for taking them so far to save a shilling, and wondering whether they should ever reach their destination. At length the vehicle stopped before a dirty-looking ticketed linen-draper's shop, with goods of all kinds, and labels of all sorts and sizes in the window. There were dropsical figures of a seven with a little three-farthings in the corner, something like the aquatic animalculæ disclosed by the gas microscope,[19] 'perfectly invisible to the naked eye;' three hundred and fifty thousand ladies boas, *from* one shilling and a penny halfpenny; real French kid shoes, at two and ninepence per pair; green parasols, with handles like carving-forks, at an equally cheap rate; and 'every description of goods,' as the proprietors said – and they must know best – 'fifty per cent under cost price.'

'La! ma, what a place you have brought us to!' said Miss Teresa; 'what *would* Mr Sparkins say if he could see us!'

'Ah! what, indeed!' said Miss Marianne, horrified at the idea.

'Pray be seated, ladies. What is the first article?' inquired the obsequious master of the ceremonies of the establishment, who, in his large white neckcloth and formal tie, looked like a bad 'portrait of a gentleman' in the Somerset-house exhibition.[20]

'I want to see some silks,' answered Mrs Malderton.

'Directly, ma'am. – Mr Smith! Where *is* Mr Smith?'

'Here, sir,' cried a voice at the back of the shop.

'Pray make haste, Mr Smith,' said the M.C. 'You never are to be found when you're wanted, sir.'

Mr Smith, thus enjoined to use all possible despatch, leaped over the counter with great agility, and placed himself before the newly-arrived customers. Mrs Malderton uttered a faint scream; Miss Teresa, who had been stooping down to talk to her sister, raised her head, and beheld – Horatio Sparkins!

'We will draw a veil,' as novel writers say, over the scene that ensued. The mysterious, philosophical, romantic, metaphysical Sparkins – he who, to the interesting Teresa, seemed like the imbodied idea of the young dukes and poetical exquisites in blue silk dressing-gowns, and ditto ditto slippers, of whom she had read and dreamt, but had never expected to behold – was suddenly converted into Mr Samuel Smith, the assistant at a 'cheap shop;' the junior partner in a slippery firm of some three weeks' existence. The dignified evanishment of the hero of Oak Lodge on this unexpected announcement, could only be equalled by that of a furtive dog with a considerable kettle at his tail. All the hopes of the Maldertons were destined at once to melt away, like the lemon ices at a Company's dinner; Almacks²¹ was still to them as distant as the North Pole; and Miss Teresa had about as much chance of a husband as Captain Ross had of the north-west passage.²²

Years have elapsed since the occurrence of this dreadful morning. The daisies have thrice bloomed on Camberwell-green – the sparrows have thrice repeated their vernal chirps in Camberwell-grove; but the Miss Maldertons are still unmated. Miss Teresa's case is more desperate than ever; but Flamwell is yet in the zenith of his reputation; and the family have the same predilection for aristocratic personages, with an increased aversion to any thing *low*.

CHAPTER 6

The Black Veil

ONE winter's evening towards the close of the year 1800, or within a year or two of that time, a young medical practitioner, recently established in business, was seated by a cheerful fire in his little parlour, listening to the wind which was beating the rain in pattering drops against the window, and rumbling dismally in the chimney. The night was wet and cold: he had been walking through mud and water the whole day, and was now comfortably reposing in his dressing-gown and slippers, more than half asleep and less than half awake, revolving a thousand matters in his wandering imagination. First he thought how hard the wind was blowing, and how the cold, sharp rain would be at that moment beating in his face if he were not comfortably housed at home. Then his mind reverted to his annual Christmas visit to his native place and dearest friends; he thought how glad they would all be to see him, and how happy it would make Rose if he could only tell her that he had got a patient at last, and hoped to have more, and to come down again in a few months' time and marry her, and take her home to gladden his lonely fireside, and stimulate him to fresh exertions. Then he began to wonder when his first patient would appear, or whether he was destined by a special dispensation of Providence never to have any patients at all; and then he thought about Rose again, and dropped to sleep and dreamed about her, till the very tones of her sweet merry voice sounded in his ears, and her soft tiny hand rested on his shoulder.

There *was* a hand upon his shoulder, but it was neither soft nor tiny; its owner being a corpulent round-headed boy, who, in consideration of the sum of one shilling per week and his food, was let out by the parish to carry medicine and messages. As there was no demand for the one, however, and no necessity for the other, he usually occupied his unemployed hours – averaging fourteen a day – in abstracting peppermint drops, taking animal nourishment, and going to sleep.

'A lady, sir – a lady!' whispered the boy, rousing his master with a shake.

'What lady?' cried our friend, starting up, not quite certain that his dream was an illusion, and half expecting that it might be Rose herself. – 'What lady? Where?'

'*There*, sir,' replied the boy, pointing to the glass-door leading into the surgery, with an expression of alarm which the very unusual apparition of a customer might have tended to excite.

The surgeon looked towards the door, and started himself, for an instant, on beholding the appearance of his unlooked-for visiter.

It was a singularly tall female, dressed in deep mourning, and standing so close to the door that her face almost touched the glass. The upper part of her person was carefully muffled in a black shawl, as if for the purpose of concealment, and her face was shrouded by a thick black veil. She stood perfectly erect; her figure was drawn up to its full height, and though the surgeon *felt* that the eyes beneath the veil were fixed on him, she stood perfectly motionless, and evinced, by no gesture whatever, the slightest consciousness of his having turned towards her.

'Do you wish to consult me?' he inquired, with some hesitation, holding open the door. It opened inwards, and therefore the action did not alter the position of the figure, which still remained motionless on the same spot.

The female slightly inclined her head, in token of acquiescence.

'Pray walk in,' said the surgeon.

The figure moved a step forward; and then turning its head in the direction of the boy – to his infinite horror – appeared to hesitate.

'Leave the room, Tom,' said the young man, addressing the boy, whose large round eyes had been extended to their utmost width during this brief interview. – 'Draw the curtain, and shut the door.'

The boy drew a green curtain across the glass part of the door, retired into the surgery, closed the door after him, and immediately applied one of his large eyes to the key-hole on the other side.

The surgeon drew a chair to the fire, and motioned the visiter to a seat. The mysterious figure slowly moved towards it, and as the blaze shone upon the black dress, the surgeon observed that the bottom of it was saturated with mud and rain.

'You are very wet,' he said.

'I am,' said the stranger, in a low deep voice.

'And you are ill?' added the surgeon, compassionately, for the tone was that of a person in severe pain.

'I am,' was the reply – 'very ill: not bodily, but mentally. It is not for myself, or on my own behalf,' continued the stranger, 'that I come to you. If I laboured under bodily disease, I should not be out alone at such an hour, or on such a night as this; and if I were afflicted with it twenty four hours hence, God knows how gladly I would lie down and pray to die. It is for another that I beseech your aid, sir. I may be mad to ask it for him – I think I am: but, night after night through the long dreary hours of watching and weeping, the thought has been ever present to my mind; and though even *I* see the hopelessness of human assistance availing him, the bare thought of laying him in his grave without it, makes my blood run cold!' And a shudder, such as the surgeon well knew art could not produce, trembled through the speaker's frame.

There was a desperate earnestness in this woman's manner that went to the young man's heart. He was young in his profession, and had not yet witnessed enough of the miseries which are daily presented before the eyes of its members, to have grown comparatively callous to human suffering.

'If,' he said, rising hastily, 'the person of whom you speak be in so hopeless a condition as you describe, not a moment is to be lost. I will go with you instantly. Why did you not obtain medical advice before?'

'Because it would have been useless before – because it is useless even now,' replied the woman, clasping her hands passionately.

The surgeon gazed for a moment on the black veil, as if to ascertain the expression of the features beneath it; its thickness, however, rendered such a result impossible.

'You *are* ill,' he said, gently, 'although you do not know it. The fever which has enabled you to bear without feeling the fatigue you have evidently undergone, is burning within you now. Put that to your lips,' he continued, pouring out a glass of water – 'compose yourself for a few moments, and then tell me, as calmly as you can, what the disease of the patient is, and how long he has been ill. The moment I know what it is necessary I should know, to render my visit serviceable to him, I am ready to accompany you.'

The stranger lifted the glass of water to her mouth without raising the veil, put it down again untasted, and burst into tears.

'I know,' she said, sobbing aloud, 'that what I say to you now, seems like the ravings of fever. I have been told so before, less kindly than by you. I am not a young woman, sir; and they do say, that as life steals on towards its final close, the last short remnant, worthless as it may seem to all beside, is dearer to its possessor than all the years that have gone before, connected though they be with the recollection of old friends long since dead, and young ones – children perhaps – who have fallen off from, and forgotten one as completely as if they had died too. My natural term of life cannot be many years longer, and should be dear on that account;

but I would lay it down without a sigh — with cheerfulness — with joy — if what I tell you now were only false, or imaginary. To-morrow morning he of whom I speak will be, I *know*, though I would fain think otherwise, beyond the reach of human aid; and yet, to-night, though he is in deadly peril, you must not see, and could not serve him.'

'I am unwilling to increase your distress,' said the surgeon, after a short pause, 'by making any comment on what you have just said, or appearing desirous to investigate a subject you seem so anxious to conceal; but there is an inconsistency in your statement which I cannot reconcile with probability. This person is dying to-night, and I cannot see him when my assistance might possibly avail; you apprehend it will be useless to-morrow, and yet you would have me see him then. If he be indeed as dear to you, as your words and manner would imply, why not try to save his life before delay and the progress of his disease render it impracticable?'

'God help me!' exclaimed the woman, weeping bitterly, 'how can I hope strangers will believe what appears incredible, even to myself? You will *not* see him then, sir?' she added, rising suddenly.

'I did not say that I declined to see him,' replied the surgeon; 'but I warn you, that if you persist in this extraordinary procrastination, and the individual dies, a fearful responsibility rests with you.'

'The responsibility will rest heavily somewhere,' replied the stranger bitterly. 'Whatever responsibility rests with me, I am content to bear and ready to answer.'

'As I incur none,' continued the surgeon, 'by acceding to your request, I will see him in the morning, if you leave me the address. At what hour can he be seen?'

'*Nine*,' replied the stranger.

'You must excuse my pressing these inquiries,' said the surgeon. 'But is he in your charge now?'

'He is not,' was the rejoinder.

'Then if I gave you instructions for his treatment through the night, you could not assist him?'

The woman wept bitterly, as she replied, 'I could not.'

Finding that there was but little prospect of obtaining further information by prolonging the interview; and anxious to spare the woman's feelings, which, subdued at first by a violent effort, were now irrepressible and most painful to witness, the surgeon repeated his promise of calling in the morning at the appointed hour; and his visiter, after giving him a direction to an obscure part of Walworth,[1] left the house in the same mysterious manner as she had entered it.

It will be readily believed that so extraordinary a visit produced a considerable impression on the mind of the young surgeon, and that he speculated a great deal and to very little purpose on the possible circumstances of the case. In common with the generality of people, he had often heard and read of singular instances, in which a presentiment of death at a particular day or even minute had been entertained and realized. At one moment he was inclined to think that the present might be such a case, but then it occurred to him that all the anecdotes of the kind he had ever heard, were of persons who had been troubled with a foreboding of their own death. This woman, however, spoke of another person – a man; and it was impossible to suppose that a mere dream or delusion of fancy would induce her to speak of his approaching dissolution with such terrible certainty as she had done. It could not be that the man was to be murdered in the morning, and that the woman, originally a consenting party and bound to secrecy by an oath, had relented, and, though unable to prevent the commission of some outrage on the victim, had determined to prevent his death if possible by the timely interposition of medical aid. The idea of such things happening within two miles of the metropolis appeared too wild and preposterous to be entertained beyond the instant. Then his original impression that the woman's intellects were disordered, recurred; and as it was the only mode of solving the difficulty with any degree of satisfaction, he obstinately made up his mind to believe she was mad. Certain misgivings upon this point, however, stole upon his thoughts at the time, and presented themselves again and again through the long dull course of a sleepless night, during which, despite of all his efforts to the contrary, he was unable to banish the black veil from his disturbed imagination.

The back part of Walworth, at its greatest distance from town, is a straggling, miserable place enough, even in these days; but five-and-thirty years ago the greater portion of it was little better than a dreary waste, inhabited by a few scattered people of most questionable character, whose poverty prevented their living in any better neighbourhood, or whose pursuits and mode of life rendered its solitude peculiarly desirable. Very many of the houses which have since sprung up on all sides, were not built until some years afterwards; and the great majority even of those which were sprinkled about at irregular intervals, were of the rudest and most miserable description.

The appearance of the place through which he walked in the morning was not calculated to raise the spirits of the young surgeon, or to dispel any feeling of anxiety or depression which the singular kind of visit he was about to make might have awakened. Striking off from the high road, his way lay across a marshy common, through irregular lanes, with here and there a ruinous and dismantled cottage fast falling to pieces with decay and neglect. A stunted tree, or pool of stagnant water, roused into a creeping sluggish action by the heavy rain of the preceding night, skirted the path occasionally; and now and then a miserable patch of garden-ground, with a few old boards knocked together for a summer-house, and old palings imperfectly mended with stakes pilfered from the neighbouring hedges, bore testimony at once to the poverty of the inhabitants, and the little scruple they entertained in appropriating the property of other people to their own use. Occasionally, a filthy-looking woman would make her appearance from the door of a dirty house, to empty the contents of some cooking utensil into the gutter in front, or to scream after a little slipshod girl, who had contrived to stagger a few yards from the door under the weight of a sallow infant almost as big as herself; but scarcely any thing was stirring around, and so much of the prospect as could be faintly traced through the cold damp mist which hung heavily over it, presented a lonely and dreary appearance perfectly in keeping with the objects we have described.

After plodding wearily through the mud and mire; making many inquiries for the place to which he had been directed; and receiving as many contradictory and unsatisfactory replies in return, the young man at length arrived before the house which had been pointed out to him as the object of his destination. It was a small low building, one story above the ground, with a more desolate and unpromising exterior than any he had yet passed. An old yellow curtain was closely drawn across the window up stairs, and the parlour shutters were closed, but not fastened. The house was detached from any other, and, as it stood at an angle of a narrow lane, there was no other habitation in sight.

When we say that the surgeon hesitated, and walked a few paces beyond the house before he could prevail upon himself to lift the knocker, we say nothing that need raise a smile upon the face of the boldest reader. The police of London were a very different body in that day to what they are now: the isolated position of the suburbs, when the rage for building and the progress of improvement had not yet begun to connect them with the main body of the city and its environs, rendered many of them (and this in particular) a place of resort for the worst and most depraved characters. Even the streets in the gayest parts of London were imperfectly lighted at that time, and such places as these were left entirely to the mercy of the moon and stars. The chances of detecting desperate characters, or of tracing them to their haunts, were thus rendered very few, and their offences naturally increased in boldness, as the consciousness of comparative security became the more impressed upon them by daily experience. Added to these considerations, it must be remembered that the young man had spent some time in the public hospitals of the metropolis; and although neither Burke nor Bishop[2] had then gained a horrible notoriety, still his own observation might have suggested to him how easily the atrocities to which the former has since given his name, might be committed. Be this as it may, whatever reflection made him hesitate, he *did* hesitate; but, being a young man of strong mind and great personal daring, it was only for an instant; – he stepped briskly back, and knocked gently at the door.

A low whispering was audible immediately afterwards, as if

some person at the end of the passage were conversing stealthily with another on the landing above. It was succeeded by the noise of a pair of heavy boots upon the bare floor. The door-chain was softly unfastened; the door opened, and a tall, ill-favoured man, with black hair, and a face, as the surgeon often declared afterwards, as pale and haggard, as the countenance of any dead man he ever saw, presented himself.

'Walk in, sir,' he said in a low tone.

The surgeon did so, and the man having secured the door again by the chain, led the way to a small back parlour at the extremity of the passage.

'Am I in time?'

'Too soon,' replied the man. The surgeon turned hastily round, with a gesture of astonishment not unmixed with alarm, which he found it impossible to repress, though he would gladly have recalled it.

'If you'll step in here, sir,' said the man, who had evidently noticed the action – 'if you'll step in here, sir, you won't be detained five minutes, I assure you!'

The surgeon at once walked into the room. The man closed the door, and left him alone.

It was a little cold room, with no other furniture than two deal chairs and a table of the same material. A handful of fire unguarded by any fender, was burning in the grate, which brought out the damp if it served no more comfortable purpose; for the unwholesome moisture was stealing down the walls in long, slug-like tracks. The window, which was broken and patched in many places, looked into a small enclosed piece of ground almost covered with water. Not a sound was to be heard, either within the house or without. The young surgeon sat down by the fireplace, to await the result of his first professional visit.

He had not remained in this position many minutes when the noise of some approaching vehicle struck his ear. It stopped; the street-door was opened: a low talking succeeded, accompanied with a shuffling noise of footsteps along the passage and on the stairs, as if two or three men were engaged in carrying some heavy body to the room above. The creaking of the stairs a few seconds afterwards, announced that the new comers having completed their task, whatever it was, were leaving the house. The door was again closed, and the former silence was restored.

Another five minutes elapsed, and the surgeon had just resolved to explore the house in search of some one to whom he might make his errand known, when the room-door opened, and his last night's visiter, dressed in exactly the same manner, with the veil lowered as before, motioned him to advance. The singular height of her form, coupled with the circumstance of her not speaking, caused the idea to pass across his brain for an instant that it might be a man disguised in woman's attire. The hysteric sobs which issued from beneath the veil, and the convulsive attitude of grief of the whole figure, however, at once exposed the absurdity of the suspicion, and he hastily followed.

The woman led the way up stairs to the front room, and paused at the door to let him enter first. It was scantily furnished with an old deal box, a few chairs, and a tent bedstead without hangings or cross-rails, which was covered with a patchwork counterpane. The dim light admitted through the curtain which he had noticed from the outside, rendered the objects in the room so indistinct, and communicated to all of them so uniform a hue, that he did not at first perceive the object on which his eye at once rested when the woman rushed frantically past him, and flung herself on her knees by the bedside.

Stretched upon the bed, closely enveloped in a linen wrapper, and covered with blankets, lay a human form, stiff and motionless. The head and face, which were those of a man, were uncovered, save by a bandage which passed over the head and under the chin. The eyes were closed. The left arm lay heavily across the bed, and the woman held the passive hand.

The surgeon gently pushed the woman aside, and took the hand in his.

'My God!' he exclaimed, letting it fall involuntarily — 'the man is dead!'

The woman started to her feet and beat her hands together. —

'Oh! don't say so, sir,' she exclaimed with a burst of passion, amounting almost to frenzy — 'Oh! don't say so, sir! I can't bear it — indeed I can't! Men have been brought to life before when unskilful people have given them up for lost; and men have died who might have been restored, if proper means had been resorted to. Don't let him lie here, sir, without one effort to save him. This very moment life may be passing away. Do try, sir, — do, for God's sake!' — And while speaking, she hurriedly chafed, first the forehead and then the breast of the senseless form before her, and then wildly beat the cold hands, which, when she ceased to hold them, fell listlessly and heavily back on the coverlet.

'It is of no use, my good woman,' said the surgeon, soothingly, as he withdrew his hand from the man's breast. 'Stay — undo that curtain.'

'Why?' said the woman, starting up.

'Undo that curtain,' repeated the surgeon, in an agitated tone.

'*I* darkened the room on purpose,' said the woman, throwing herself before him as he rose to undraw it. — 'Oh! sir, have pity on me! If it can be of no use, and he is really dead, do not — do not expose that corpse to other eyes than mine!'

'This man died no natural or easy death,' said the surgeon. 'I *must* see the body!' and with a motion so sudden, that the woman hardly knew that he had slipped from beside her, he tore open the curtain, admitted the full light of day, and returned to the bedside.

'There has been violence here,' he said, pointing towards the body, and gazing intently on the face, from which the black veil was now for the first time removed. In the excitement of a minute before, the female had dashed off the bonnet and veil, and now stood with her eyes fixed upon him. Her features were those of a woman of about fifty, who had once been handsome. Sorrow and weeping had left traces upon them which not time itself would ever have produced without their aid: her face was deadly pale, and there was a nervous contortion of the lip, and an unnatural fire in her eye, which showed too plainly that her bodily and mental powers had nearly sunk beneath an accumulation of misery.

'There has been violence here,' said the surgeon, preserving his searching glance.

'There has!' replied the woman.

'This man has been murdered.'

'That I call God to witness he has,' said the woman, passionately; 'pitilessly, inhumanly murdered!'

'By whom?' said the surgeon, seizing the woman by the arm.

'Look at the butchers' marks, and then ask me,' she replied.

The surgeon turned his face towards the bed, and bent over the body which lay full in the light of the window. The throat was swollen, and a blue livid mark, encircled it. The truth flashed suddenly upon him.

'This is one of the men who were hanged this morning!' he exclaimed, turning away with a shudder.

'It is,' replied the woman, with a cold, unmeaning stare.

'Who was he?' inquired the surgeon.

'*My son*,' rejoined the woman; and fell senseless at his feet.

It was true. A companion, equally guilty with himself, had been acquitted for want of evidence; and this man had been left for death, and executed. To recount the circumstances of the case at this distant period, must be unnecessary, and might give pain to some persons still alive. The history was an every-day one. The mother was a widow without friends or money, and had denied herself necessaries to bestow them on her orphan boy. That boy, unmindful of her prayers, and forgetful of the sufferings she had endured for him — incessant anxiety of mind, and voluntary starvation of body — had plunged into a career of dissipation and crime. And this was the result: his own death by the hangman's hands, and his mother's shame, and incurable insanity.

For many years after this occurrence, and when profitable and arduous avocations would have led many men to forget that such a miserable being existed, the young surgeon was a daily visiter at the side of the harmless mad woman; not only soothing her by his presence and kindness, but alleviating the rigour of her condition by pecuniary donations for her comfort and support, bestowed with no sparing hand. In the transient gleam of recollection and consciousness which preceded her death, a prayer for his welfare and protection as fervent as mortal ever breathed, rose from the lips of this poor friendless creature. That prayer flew to Heaven, and was heard. The blessings he was instrumental in conferring have been repaid to him a thousand fold; but, amid all the honours of rank and station which have since been heaped upon him, and which he has so well earned, he can have no one reminiscence more gratifying to his feelings than that connected with – The Black Veil.

CHAPTER 7

The Steam Excursion

MR PERCY NOAKES was a law-student, inhabiting a set of chambers on the fourth floor, in one of those houses in Gray's-inn-square[1] which command an extensive view of the gardens, and their usual adjuncts – flaunting nursery-maids, and town-made children, with parenthetical legs. Mr Percy Noakes was what is generally termed – 'a devilish good fellow.' He had a large circle of acquaintance, and seldom dined at his own expense. He used to talk politics to papas, flatter the vanity of mammas, do the amiable to their daughters, make pleasure engagements with their sons, and romp with the younger branches. Like those paragons of perfection, advertising footmen out of place, he was always 'willing to make himself generally useful.' If any old lady, whose son was in India, gave a ball, Mr Percy Noakes was master of the ceremonies; if any young lady made a stolen match, Mr Percy Noakes gave her away; if a juvenile wife presented her husband with a blooming cherub, Mr Percy Noakes was either godfather, or deputy-godfather; and if any member of a friend's family died, Mr Percy Noakes was invariably to be seen in the second mourning

Steam Excursion

Pl. 1

coach, with a white handkerchief to his eyes, sobbing – to use his own appropriate and expressive description – 'like winkin!'

It may readily be imagined that these numerous avocations were rather calculated to interfere with Mr Percy Noakes's professional studies. Mr Percy Noakes was perfectly aware of the fact, and he had, therefore, after mature reflection, made up his mind not to study at all – a laudable determination, to which he adhered in the most praiseworthy manner. His sitting-room presented a strange chaos of dress-gloves, boxing-gloves, caricatures, albums, invitation-cards, foils, cricket-bats, card-board drawings, paste, gum, and fifty other extraordinary articles heaped together in the strangest confusion. He was always making something for some-body, or planning some party of pleasure, which was his great *forte*. He invariably spoke with astonishing rapidity; was smart, spoffish,[2] and eight-and-twenty.

'Splendid idea, 'pon my life!' soliloquized Mr Percy Noakes, over his morning's coffee, as his mind reverted to a suggestion which had been thrown out the previous night, by a lady at whose house he had spent the evening. 'Glorious idea! – Mrs Stubbs,' cried the student, raising his voice.

'Yes, sir,' replied a dirty old woman with an inflamed coun-tenance, emerging from the bedroom, with a barrel of dirt and cinders. – This was the laundress. 'Did you call, sir?'

'Oh! Mrs Stubbs, I'm going out: if that tailor should call again, you'd better say – you'd better say, I'm out of town, and shan't be back for a fortnight; and if that bootmaker should come, tell him I've lost his address, or I'd have sent him that little amount. Mind he writes it down; and if Mr Hardy should call – you know Mr Hardy?'

'The funny gentleman, sir?'

'Ah! the funny gentleman. If Mr Hardy should call, say I've gone to Mrs Taunton's about that water-party.'

'Yes, sir.'

'And if any fellow calls, and says he's come about a steamer, tell him to be here at five o'clock this afternoon, Mrs Stubbs.'

'Very well, sir.'

Mr Percy Noakes brushed his hat, whisked the crumbs off his inexplicables[3] with a silk handkerchief, gave the ends of his hair a persuasive roll round his forefinger,[4] and sallied forth for Mrs Taunton's domicile in Great Marlborough-street,[5] where she and her daughters occupied the upper part of a house. She was a good-looking widow of fifty, with the form of a giantess and the mind of a child. The pursuit of pleasure, and some means of killing time, appeared the sole end of her existence. She doted on her daughters, who were as frivolous as herself.

A general exclamation of satisfaction hailed the arrival of Mr Percy Noakes, who went through the ordinary salutations and threw himself into an easy chair near the ladies' work-table, with all the ease of a regularly established friend of the family. Mrs Taunton was busily engaged in planting immense bright bows on every part of a smart cap on which it was possible to stick one; Miss Emily Taunton was making a watch-guard; and Miss Sophia was at the piano, practising a new song – poetry by the young officer, or the police officer, or the custom-house officer, or some equally interesting amateur.

'You good creature!' said Mrs Taunton, addressing the gallant Percy. 'You really are a good soul! You've come about the water-party, I know.'

'I should rather suspect I had,' replied Mr Noakes, triumphantly. 'Now come here, girls, and I'll tell you all about it.' Miss Emily and Miss Sophia advanced to the table, with that ballet sort of step which some young ladies seem to think so fascinating – something between a skip and a canter.

'Now,' continued Mr Percy Noakes, 'it seems to me that the best way will be to have a committee of ten, to make all the arrangements, and manage the whole set-out. Then I propose that the expenses shall be paid by these ten fellows jointly.'

'Excellent, indeed!' said Mrs Taunton, who highly approved of this part of the arrangements.

'Then my plan is, that each of these ten fellows shall have the power of asking five people. There must be a meeting of the committee at my chambers, to make all the arrangements, and these people shall be then named; every member of the committee shall have the power of black-balling any one who is proposed, and one black ball shall exclude that person. This will ensure our having a pleasant party, you know.'

'What a manager you are!' interrupted Mrs Taunton again.

'Charming!' said the lovely Emily.

'I never did!' ejaculated Sophia.

'Yes, I think it'll do,' replied Mr Percy Noakes, who was now quite in his element. 'I think it'll do. Then you know we shall go down to the Nore[6] and back, and have a regular capital cold dinner laid out in the cabin before we start, so that every thing may be ready without any confusion; and we shall have the lunch laid out on deck in those little tea-garden-looking concerns by the paddle-boxes − I don't know what you call 'em. Then we shall hire a steamer expressly for our party, and a band, and have the deck chalked, and we shall be able to dance quadrilles all day: and then whoever we know that's musical, you know, why they'll make themselves useful and agreeable; and − and − upon the whole, I really hope we shall have a glorious day, you know.'

The announcement of these arrangements was received with the utmost enthusiasm. Mrs Taunton, Emily, and Sophia, were loud in their praises.

'Well, but tell me, Percy,' said Mrs Taunton, 'who are the ten gentlemen to be?'

'Oh! I know plenty of fellows who'll be delighted with the scheme,' replied Mr Percy Noakes; 'of course, we shall have −'

'Mr Hardy,' interrupted the servant, announcing a visiter. Miss Sophia and Miss Emily hastily assumed the most interesting attitudes that could be adopted on so short a notice.

'How are you?' said a stout gentleman of about forty, pausing at the door in the attitude of an awkward harlequin. This was Mr Hardy, whom we have before described, on the authority of Mrs Stubbs, as 'the funny gentleman.' He was an Astley-Cooperish Joe Miller[7] − a practical joker, immensely popular with married ladies, and a general favourite with young men. He was always engaged in some pleasure excursion or other, and delighted in getting somebody into a scrape on such occasions. He could sing comic songs, imitate hackney-coachmen and fowls, play airs on his chin, and execute concertos on the Jews'-harp. He always eat and drank most immoderately, and was the bosom friend of Mr Percy Noakes. He had a red face, a somewhat husky voice, and a tremendously loud laugh.

'How are you?' said this worthy, laughing, as if it were the finest joke in the world to make a morning call, and shaking hands with the ladies with as much vehemence as if their arms were so many pump-handles.

'You're just the very man I wanted,' said Mr Percy Noakes, who proceeded to explain the cause of his being in requisition.

'Ha! ha! ha!' shouted Hardy, after hearing the statement, and receiving a detailed account of the proposed excursion. 'Oh, capital! glorious! What a day it will be! what fun! – But, I say, when are you going to begin making the arrangements?'

'No time like the present – at once, if you please.'

'Oh, charming!' cried the ladies. 'Pray, do.'

Writing materials were laid before Mr Percy Noakes, and the names of the different members of the committee were agreed on, after as much discussion between him and Mr Hardy as if at least the fate of nations had depended on their appointment. It was then agreed that a meeting should take place at Mr Percy Noakes's chambers on the ensuing Wednesday evening at eight o'clock, and the visiters departed.

Wednesday evening arrived, eight o'clock came, and eight members of the committee were punctual in their attendance. Mr Loggins, the solicitor, of Boswell-court,[8] sent an excuse, and Mr Samuel Briggs, the ditto of Furnival's Inn,[9] sent his brother, much to his (the brother's) satisfaction, and greatly to the discomfiture of Mr Percy Noakes. Between the Briggses and the Tauntons there existed a degree of implacable hatred, quite unprecedented. The animosity between the Montagues and Capulets[10] was nothing to that which prevailed between these two illustrious houses. Mrs Briggs was a widow, with three daughters and two sons; Mr Samuel, the eldest, was an attorney, and Mr Alexander, the youngest, was under articles to his brother. They resided in Portland-street,[11] Oxford-street, and moved in the same orbit as the Tauntons – hence their mutual dislike. If the Miss Briggs appeared in smart bonnets, the Miss Tauntons eclipsed them with smarter. If Mrs Taunton appeared in a cap of all the hues of the rainbow, Mrs Briggs forthwith mounted a toque, with all the patterns of a kaleidescope. If Miss Sophia Taunton learnt a new song, two of the Miss Briggses came out with a new duet. The Tauntons had once gained a temporary triumph with the assistance of a harp, but the Briggses brought three guitars into the field, and effectually routed the enemy. There was no end to the rivalry between them.

Now, as Mr Samuel Briggs was a mere machine, a sort of self-acting legal walking-stick; and as the party was known to have originated, however remotely, with Mrs Taunton, the female branches of the Briggs family had arranged that Mr Alexander should attend instead of his brother; and as the said Mr Alexander was deservedly celebrated for possessing all the pertinacity of a bankruptcy-court attorney, combined with the obstinacy of that pleasing animal which browses upon the thistle – he required but little tuition. He was especially enjoined to make himself as disagreeable as possible; and, above all, to black-ball the Tauntons at every hazard.

The proceedings of the evening were opened by Mr Percy Noakes. After successfully urging upon the gentlemen present the propriety of their mixing some brandy-and-water, he briefly stated the object of the meeting, and concluded by observing that the first step must be the selection of a chairman, necessarily possessing some arbitrary – he trusted not unconstitutional – powers, to whom the personal direction of the whole of the arrangements (subject to the approval of the committee) should be confided. A pale young gentleman in a green stock and spectacles of the same, a member of the honourable society of the Inner Temple,[12] immediately rose for the purpose of proposing Mr Percy Noakes. He had known him long, and this he would say, that a more honourable, a more excellent, or a better-hearted fellow, never existed – (hear, hear!) The young gentleman, who was a member of a debating society, took this opportunity of entering into an examination of the state of the English law, from the days of William the Conqueror down to the present period: he briefly adverted to the code established by the ancient Druids; slightly glanced at the principles laid down by the Athenian lawgivers; and concluded with a most glowing eulogium on pic-nics and constitutional rights.

Mr Alexander Briggs opposed the motion. He had the highest esteem for Mr Percy Noakes as an individual, but he did consider that he ought not to be intrusted with these immense powers – (oh, oh!) – He believed that in the proposed capacity Mr Percy Noakes would not act fairly, impartially, or honourably; but he begged it to be distinctly understood, that he said this without the slightest personal disrespect. Mr Hardy defended his honourable friend, in a voice rendered partially unintelligible by emotion and brandy-and-water. The proposition was put to the vote, and there appearing to be only one dissentient voice, Mr Percy Noakes was declared duly elected, and took the chair accordingly.

The business of the meeting now proceeded with great rapidity. The chairman delivered in his estimate of the probable expense of the excursion, and every one present subscribed his proportion thereof. The question was put that 'The Endeavour' be hired for the occasion; Mr Alexander Briggs moved as an amendment, that the word 'Fly' be substituted for the word 'Endeavour;' but after some debate consented to withdraw his opposition. The important ceremony of balloting then commenced. A tea-caddy was placed on a table in a dark corner of the apartment, and every one was provided with two backgammon men; one black and one white.

The chairman with great solemnity then read the following list of the guests whom he proposed to introduce: – Mrs Taunton and two daughters, Mr Wizzle, Mr Simson. The names were respectively balloted for, and Mrs Taunton and her daughters were declared to be black-balled. Mr Percy Noakes and Mr Hardy exchanged glances.

'Is your list prepared, Mr Briggs?' inquired the chairman.

'It is,' replied Alexander, delivering in the following: – 'Mrs

Briggs and three daughters, Mr Samuel Briggs.' The previous ceremony was repeated, and Mrs Briggs and three daughters were declared to be black-balled. Mr Alexander Briggs looked rather foolish, and the remainder of the company appeared somewhat overawed by the mysterious nature of the proceedings.

The balloting proceeded; but one little circumstance which Mr Percy Noakes had not originally foreseen, prevented the system working quite as well as he had anticipated — every body was black-balled. Mr Alexander Briggs, by way of retaliation, exercised his power of exclusion in every instance, and the result was, that after three hours had been consumed in incessant balloting, the names of only three gentlemen were found to have been agreed to. In this dilemma what was to be done? either the whole plan must fall to the ground, or a compromise must be effected. The latter alternative was preferable; and Mr Percy Noakes therefore proposed that the form of balloting should be dispensed with, and that every gentleman should merely be required to state whom he intended to bring. The proposal was readily acceded to; the Tauntons and the Briggses were reinstated, and the party was formed.

The next Wednesday was fixed for the eventful day, and it was unanimously resolved that every member of the committee should wear a piece of blue sarsenet ribbon round his left arm. It appeared from the statement of Mr Percy Noakes, that the boat belonged to the General Steam Navigation Company, and was then lying off the Custom-house;[13] and as he proposed that the dinner and wines should be provided by an eminent city purveyor, it was arranged that Mr Percy Noakes should be on board by seven o'clock to superintend the arrangements, and that the remaining members of the committee, together with the company generally, should be expected to join her by nine o'clock. More brandy-and-water was despatched; several speeches were made by the different law students present; thanks were voted to the chairman, and the meeting separated.

The weather had been beautiful up to this period, and beautiful it continued to be. Sunday passed over, and Mr Percy Noakes became unusually fidgety — rushing constantly to and from the

Steam Packet Wharf, to the astonishment of the clerks, and the great emolument of the Holborn cabmen. Tuesday arrived, and the anxiety of Mr Percy Noakes knew no bounds: he was every instant running to the window to look out for clouds; and Mr Hardy astonished the whole square by practising a new comic song for the occasion, in the chairman's chambers.

Uneasy were the slumbers of Mr Percy Noakes that night: he tossed and tumbled about, and had confused dreams of steamers starting off, and gigantic clocks with the hands pointing to a quarter past nine, and the ugly face of Mr Alexander Briggs looking over the boat's side, and grinning as if in derision of his fruitless attempts to move. He made a violent effort to get on board, and awoke. The bright sun was shining cheerfully into the bedroom, and Mr Percy Noakes started up for his watch, in the dreadful expectation of finding his worst dreams realized.

It was just five o'clock. He calculated the time – he should be a good half-hour dressing himself; and as it was a lovely morning, and the tide would be then running down, he would walk leisurely to Strand-lane,[14] and have a boat to the Custom-house.

He dressed himself, took a hasty apology for a breakfast, and sallied forth. The streets looked as lonely and deserted as if they had been crowded overnight for the last time. Here and there an early apprentice, with quenched-looking sleepy eyes, was taking down the shutters of a shop; and a policeman or milk-woman might occasionally be seen pacing slowly along; the servants had not yet begun to clean the doors, or light the fires, and London looked the picture of desolation. At the corner of a bye-street, near Temple-bar,[15] was stationed a 'street breakfast.' The coffee was boiling over a charcoal fire, and large slices of bread and butter were piled one upon the other, like deals in a timber-yard. The company were seated on a form, which, with a view both to security and comfort, was placed against a neighbouring wall. Two young men, whose uproarious mirth and disordered dress bespoke the conviviality of the preceding evening, were treating three 'ladies' and an Irish labourer. A little sweep was standing at a short distance, casting a longing eye at the tempting delicacies; and a policeman was watching the group from the opposite side of the street. The wan looks, and gaudy finery of the wretched thinly-clad females, contrasted as strangely with the gay sun-light, as did their forced merriment with the boisterous hilarity of the two young men, who now and then varied their amusements by 'bonneting'[16] the proprietor of this itinerant coffee-house.

Mr Percy Noakes walked briskly by, and when he turned down Strand-lane, and caught a glimpse of the glistening water, he thought he had never felt so important or so happy in his life.

'Boat, sir!' cried one of the three watermen who were mopping out their boats, and all whistling different tunes. 'Boat, sir!'

'No,' replied Mr Percy Noakes, rather sharply; for the inquiry was not made in a manner at all suitable to his dignity.

'Would you prefer a wessel, sir?' inquired another, to the infinite delight of the 'Jack-in-the-water.'[17]

Mr Percy Noakes replied with a look of the most supreme contempt.

'Did you want to be put on board a steamer, sir?' inquired an old fireman-waterman, very confidentially. He was dressed in a faded red suit, just the colour of the cover of a very old Court-guide.[18]

'Yes, make haste – the Endeavour – off the Custom-house.'

'Endeavour!' cried the man who had convulsed the 'Jack' before. 'Vy, I see the Endeavour go up half an hour ago.'

'So did I,' said another; 'and I should think she'd gone down by this time, for she's a precious sight too full of ladies and gen'lmen.'

Mr Percy Noakes affected to disregard these representations, and stepped into the boat, which the old man, by dint of scrambling, and shoving, and grating, had brought up to the causeway. 'Shove her off,' cried Mr Percy Noakes, and away the boat glided down the river, Mr Percy Noakes seated on the recently mopped seat, and the watermen at the stairs offering to bet him any reasonable sum that he'd never reach the 'Custum-us.'

'Here she is, by Jove!' said the delighted Percy, as they ran alongside the Endeavour.

'Hold hard!' cried the steward over the side, and Mr Percy Noakes jumped on board.

'Hope you'll find every thing as you wished, sir. She looks uncommon well this morning.'

'She does, indeed,' replied the manager, in a state of ecstasy which it is impossible to describe. The deck was scrubbed, and the seats were scrubbed, and there was a bench for the band, and a place for dancing, and a pile of camp-stools, and an awning; and then Mr Percy Noakes bustled down below, and there were the pastrycook's men, and the steward's wife laying out the dinner on two tables the whole length of the cabin; and then Mr Percy Noakes took off his coat, and rushed backwards and forwards, doing nothing, but quite convinced he was assisting every body; and the steward's wife laughed till she cried, and Mr Percy Noakes panted with the violence of his exertions. And then the bell at London-bridge wharf rang, and a Margate boat was just starting, and a Gravesend boat was just starting, and people shouted, and porters ran down the steps with luggage that would crush any men but porters; and sloping boards, with bits of wood nailed on them, were placed between the outside boat and the inside boat, and the passengers ran along them, and looked like so many fowls coming out of an area; and then the bell ceased, and the boards were taken away, and the boats started; and the whole scene was one of the most delightful bustle and confusion that can be imagined.

The time wore on; half-past eight o'clock arrived; the pastry-cook's men went ashore; the dinner was completely laid out, and Mr Percy Noakes locked the principal cabin, and put the key into his pocket, in order that it might be suddenly disclosed in all its magnificence to the eyes of the astonished company. The band came on board, and so did the wine.

Ten minutes to nine, and the committee embarked in a body. There was Mr Hardy in a blue jacket and waistcoat, white trousers, silk stockings, and pumps; habited in full aquatic costume, with a straw hat on his head, and an immense telescope under his arm; and there was the young gentleman with the green spectacles, in nankeen inexplicables, with a ditto waistcoat and bright buttons, like the pictures of Paul – not the saint, but he of Virginia notoriety.[19] The remainder of the committee, dressed in white hats, light jackets, waistcoats, and trousers, looked something between waiters and West India planters.

Nine o'clock struck, and the company arrived in shoals. Mr Samuel Briggs, Mrs Briggs, and the Misses Briggs made their appearance in a smart private wherry. The three guitars, in their respective dark green cases, were carefully stowed away in the bottom of the boat, accompanied by two immense portfolios of music, which it would take at least a week's incessant playing to get through. The Tauntons arrived at the same moment with more music, and a lion – a gentleman with a bass voice and an incipient red moustache. The colours of the Taunton party were pink; those of the Briggses a light blue. The Tauntons had artificial flowers in their bonnets; here the Briggses gained a decided advantage – they wore feathers.

'How d'ye do, dear?' said the Misses Briggs to the Misses Taunton. (The word 'dear' among girls is frequently synonymous with 'wretch.')

'Quite well, thank you, dear,' replied the Misses Taunton to the Misses Briggs; and then there was such a kissing, and congratulating, and shaking of hands, as would induce one to suppose that the two families were the best friends in the world, instead of each wishing the other overboard, as they most sincerely did.

Mr Percy Noakes received the visiters, and bowed to the strange gentleman, as if he should like to know who he was. This was just what Mrs Taunton wanted. Here was an opportunity to astonish the Briggses.

'Oh! I beg your pardon,' said the general of the Taunton party, with a careless air. – 'Captain Helves – Mr Percy Noakes – Mrs Briggs – Captain Helves.'

Mr Percy Noakes bowed very low; the gallant captain did the same with all due ferocity, and the Briggses were clearly overcome.

'Our friend, Mr Wizzle, being unfortunately prevented from coming,' resumed Mrs Taunton, 'I did myself the pleasure of bringing the captain, whose musical talents I knew would be a great acquisition.'

'In the name of the committee I have to thank you for doing so, and to offer you a most sincere welcome, sir,' replied Percy. (Here the scraping was renewed.) 'But pray be seated – won't you walk aft? Captain, will you conduct Miss Taunton? – Miss Briggs, will you allow me?'

'Where could they have picked up that military man?' inquired Mrs Briggs of Miss Kate Briggs, as they followed the little party.

'I can't imagine,' replied Miss Kate, bursting with vexation; for the very fierce air with which the gallant captain regarded the company, had impressed her with a high sense of his importance.

Boat after boat came alongside, and guest after guest arrived. The invites had been excellently arranged, Mr Percy Noakes having considered it as important that the number of young men should exactly tally with that of the young ladies, as that the quantity of knives on board should be in precise proportion to the forks.

'Now, is every one on board?' inquired Mr Percy Noakes. The committee (who, with their bits of blue ribbon, looked as if they were all going to be bled) bustled about to ascertain the fact, and reported that they might safely start.

'Go on,' cried the master of the boat from the top of one of the paddle-boxes.

'Go on,' echoed the boy, who was stationed over the hatchway to pass the directions down to the engineer; and away went the vessel with that agreeable noise which is peculiar to steamers, and which is composed of a pleasant mixture of creaking, gushing, clanging, and snorting.

'Hoi–oi–oi–oi–oi–oi–o–i–i–i!' shouted half-a-dozen voices from a boat about a quarter of a mile astern.

'Ease her!' cried the captain: 'do these people belong to us, sir?'

'Noakes,' exclaimed Hardy, who had been looking at every object, far and near, through the large telescope, 'it's the Fleetwoods and the Wakefields – and two children with them, by Jove!'

'What a shame to bring children!' said every body; 'how very inconsiderate!'

'I say, it would be a good joke to pretend not to see 'em, wouldn't it?' suggested Hardy, to the immense delight of the company generally. A council of war was hastily held, and it was resolved that the new comers should be taken on board, on Mr Hardy's solemnly pledging himself to tease the children during the whole of the day.

'Stop her!' cried the captain.

'Stop her!' repeated the boy; whizz went the steam, and all the young ladies, as in duty bound, screamed in concert. They were only appeased by the assurance of the martial Helves, that the escape of steam consequent on stopping a vessel was seldom attended with any great loss of human life.

Two men ran to the side, and after a good deal of shouting, and swearing, and angling for the wherry with a boat-hook, Mr Fleetwood, and Mrs Fleetwood, and Master Fleetwood, and Mr Wakefield, and Mrs Wakefield, and Miss Wakefield, were safely deposited on the deck. The girl was about six years old, the boy about four; the former was dressed in a white frock with a pink sash and a dog's-eared-looking little spencer, a straw bonnet and green veil, six inches by three and a half: the latter was attired for the occasion in a nankeen frock, between the bottom of which and the top of his plaid socks a considerable portion of two small mottled legs was discernible. He had a light blue cap with a gold band and tassel on his head, and a damp piece of gingerbread in his hand, with which he had slightly embossed his dear little countenance.

The boat once more started off; the band played 'Off she goes;'[20] the major part of the company conversed cheerfully in groups, and the old gentlemen walked up and down the deck in pairs, as perseveringly and gravely as if they were doing a match against time for an immense stake. They ran briskly down the Pool;[21] the gentlemen pointed out the Docks, the Thames Police-office, and other elegant public edifices; and the young ladies exhibited a proper display of horror and bashfulness at the appearance of the coal-whippers and ballast-heavers.[22] Mr Hardy told stories to the married ladies, at which they laughed very much in their pocket-handkerchiefs, and hit him on the knuckles with their fans, declaring him to be 'a naughty man – a shocking creature' – and so forth; and Captain Helves gave slight descriptions of battles and duels, with a most bloodthirsty air, which made him the admiration of the women, and the envy of the men. Quadrilling commenced; Captain Helves danced one set with Miss Emily Taunton, and another set with Miss Sophia Taunton. Mrs Taunton was in ecstasies. The victory appeared to be complete; but, alas! the inconstancy of man! Having performed this necessary duty, he attached himself solely to Miss Julia Briggs, with whom he danced no less than three sets consecutively, and from whose side he evinced no intention of stirring for the remainder of the day.

Mr Hardy having played one or two very brilliant fantasias on the Jews'-harp, and having frequently repeated the exquisitely amusing joke of slily chalking a large cross on the back of some member of the committee, Mr Percy Noakes expressed his hope that some of their musical friends would oblige the company by a display of their abilities.

'Perhaps,' he said in a very insinuating manner, 'Captain Helves will oblige us.' Mrs Taunton's countenance lighted up, for the captain only sang duets, and couldn't sing them with any body but one of her daughters.

'Really,' said that warlike individual, 'I should be very happy, but –'

'Oh! pray do,' cried all the young ladies.

'Miss Sophia, have you any objection to join in a duet?'

'Oh! not the slightest,' returned the young lady, in a tone which clearly showed she had the greatest possible objection.

'Shall I accompany you, dear?' inquired one of the Miss Briggses, with the bland intention of spoiling the effect.

'Very much obliged to you, Miss Briggs,' sharply retorted Mrs Taunton, who saw through the manœuvre; 'my daughters always sing without accompaniments.'

'And without voices,' tittered Mrs Briggs, in a low tone.

'Perhaps,' said Mrs Taunton, reddening, for she guessed the tenor of the observation, though she had not heard it clearly – 'Perhaps it would be as well for some people, if their voices were not quite so audible as they are to other people.'

'And perhaps, if gentlemen, who are kidnapped to pay attention to some persons' daughters, had not sufficient discernment to pay attention to other persons' daughters,' returned Mrs Briggs, 'some persons would not be so ready to display that ill-temper, which, thank God, distinguishes them from other persons.'

'Persons!' ejaculated Mrs Taunton.

'Yes; persons, ma'am,' replied Mrs Briggs.

'Insolence!'

'Creature!'

'Hush! hush!' interrupted Mr Percy Noakes, who was one of the very few by whom this dialogue had been overheard. 'Hush! – pray silence for the duet.'

After a great deal of preparatory crowing and humming, the captain began the following duet from the opera of 'Paul and Virginia,'[23] in that grunting tone in which a man gets down, Heaven knows where, without the remotest chance of ever getting up again. This, in private circles, is frequently designated 'a bass voice.'

> 'See (sung the captain) from o–ce–an ri–sing
> Bright flames the or–b of d–ay.
> From yon gro–ve, the varied so–ngs —'

Here the singer was interrupted by varied cries of the most dreadful description, proceeding from some grove in the immediate vicinity of the starboard paddle-box.

'My child!' screamed Mrs Fleetwood. 'My child! it is his voice – I know it.'

Mr Fleetwood, accompanied by several gentlemen, here rushed to the quarter from whence the noise proceeded, and an exclamation of horror burst from the company; the general impression being, that the little innocent had either got his head in the water, or his legs in the machinery.

'What is the matter?' shouted the agonized father, as he returned with the child in his arms.

'Oh! oh! oh!' screamed the small sufferer again.

'What is the matter, dear?' inquired the father once more – hastily stripping off the nankeen frock, for the purpose of ascertaining whether the child had one bone which was not smashed to pieces.

'Oh! oh! – I'm so frightened.'

'What at, dear? – what at?' said the mother, soothing the sweet infant.

'Oh! he's been making such dreadful faces at me,' cried the boy, relapsing into convulsions at the bare recollection.

'He! – who?' cried every body, crowding round him.

'Oh! – him,' replied the child, pointing at Hardy, who affected to be the most concerned of the whole group.

The real state of the case at once flashed upon the minds of all present, with the exception of the Fleetwoods and the Wakefields. The facetious Hardy, in fulfilment of his promise, had watched the child to a remote part of the vessel, and, suddenly appearing before him with the most awful contortions of visage, had produced his paroxysm of terror. Of course, he now observed that it was hardly necessary for him to deny the accusation; and the unfortunate little victim was accordingly led below, after receiving sundry thumps on the head from both his parents, for having the wickedness to tell a story.

This little interruption having been adjusted, the captain resumed and Miss Emily chimed in, in due course. The duet was loudly applauded, and, certainly, the perfect independence of the parties deserved great commendation. Miss Emily sung her part without the slightest reference to the captain, and the captain sang so loud that he had not the slightest idea of what was being done by his partner. After having gone through the last few eighteen or nineteen bars by himself, therefore, he acknowledged the plaudits of the circle with that air of self-denial which men always assume when they think they have done something to astonish the company, though they don't exactly know what.

'Now,' said Mr Percy Noakes, who had just ascended from the fore-cabin, where he had been busily engaged in decanting the wine, 'if the Misses Briggs will oblige us with something before dinner, I am sure we shall be very much delighted.'

One of those hums of admiration followed the suggestion, which one frequently hears in society, when nobody has the most distant notion of what he is expressing his approval of. The three Misses Briggs looked modestly at their mamma, and the mamma looked approvingly at her daughters, and Mrs Taunton looked scornfully at all of them. The Misses Briggs asked for their guitars, and several gentlemen seriously damaged the cases in their anxiety to present them. Then there was a very interesting production of three little keys for the aforesaid cases, and a melodramatic expression of horror at finding a string broken; and a vast deal of screwing and tightening, and winding and tuning, during which Mrs Briggs expatiated to those near her on the immense difficulty of playing a guitar, and hinted at the wondrous proficiency of her daughters in that mystic art. Mrs Taunton whispered to a neighbour that it was 'quite sickening!' and the Misses Taunton tried to look as if they knew how to play, but disdained to do so.

At length the Misses Briggs began in real earnest. It was a new Spanish composition, for three voices and three guitars. The effect was electrical. All eyes were turned upon the captain, who was reported to have once passed through Spain with his regiment, and who, of course, must be well acquainted with the national music. He was in raptures. This was sufficient; the trio was encored – the applause was universal, and never had the Tauntons suffered such a complete defeat.

'Bravo! bravo!' ejaculated the captain; – 'Bravo!'

'Pretty! isn't it, sir?' inquired Mr Samuel Briggs, with the air of a self-satisfied showman. By the by, these were the first words he had been heard to utter since he left Boswell-court the evening before.

'De–lightful!' returned the captain, with a flourish, and a military cough; – 'de–lightful!'

'Sweet instrument!' said an old gentleman with a bald head, who had been trying all the morning to look through a telescope, inside the glass of which Mr Hardy had fixed a large black wafer.

'Did you ever hear a Portuguese tambarine?' inquired that jocular individual.

'Did *you* ever hear a tom-tom, sir?' sternly inquired the captain, who lost no opportunity of showing off his travels, real or pretended.

'A what?' asked Hardy, rather taken aback.

'A tom-tom.'

'Never!'

'Nor a gum-gum?'

'Never!'

'What *is* a gum-gum?'[24] eagerly inquired several young ladies.

'When I was in the East Indies,' replied the captain, (here was a discovery — he had been in the East Indies!) — 'when I was in the East Indies, I was once stopping a few thousand miles up the country, on a visit at the house of a very particular friend of mine, Ram Chowdar Doss Azuph Al Bowlar[25] — a devilish pleasant fellow. As we were enjoying our hookahs one evening in the cool verandah in front of his villa, we were rather surprised by the sudden appearance of thirty-four of his Kit-ma-gars[26] (for he had rather a large establishment there), accompanied by an equal number of Consumars, approaching the house with a threatening aspect, and beating a tom-tom. The Ram started up —'

'The who?' inquired the bald gentleman, intensely interested.

'The Ram — Ram Chowdar —'

'Oh!' said the old gentleman, 'I beg your pardon; it really didn't occur to me; pray go on.'

'— Started up and drew a pistol. "Helves," said he, "my boy," — he always called me, my boy — "Helves," said he, "do you hear that tom-tom?" — "I do," said I. His countenance, which before was pale, assumed a most frightful appearance; his whole visage was distorted, and his frame shaken by violent emotions. "Do you see that gum-gum?" said he. "No," said I, staring about me. "You don't?" said he. "No, I'll be damned if I do", said I; "and what's more, I don't know what a gum-gum is," said I. I really thought the man would have dropped. He drew me aside, and, with an expression of agony I shall never forget, said in a low whisper —'

'Dinner's on the table, ladies,' interrupted the steward's wife.

'Will you allow me?' said the captain, immediately suiting the action to the word, and escorting Miss Julia Briggs to the cabin, with as much ease as if he had finished the story.

'What an extraordinary circumstance!' ejaculated the same old gentleman, preserving his listening attitude.

'What a traveller!' said the young ladies.

'What a singular name!' exclaimed the gentlemen, rather confused by the coolness of the whole affair.

'I wish he had finished the story,' said an old lady. 'I wonder what a gum-gum really is?'

'By Jove!' exclaimed Hardy, who until now had been lost in utter amazement, 'I don't know what it may be in India, but in England I think a gum-gum has very much the same meaning as a humbug.'

'How illiberal! how envious!' said every body, as they made for the cabin, fully impressed with a belief in the captain's amazing adventures. Helves was the sole lion for the remainder of the day — impudence and the marvellous are sure passports to any society.

The party had by this time reached their destination, and put about on their return home. The wind, which had been with them the whole day, was now directly in their teeth; the weather had become gradually more and more overcast; and the sky, water, and shore, were all of that dull, heavy, uniform lead-colour, which house-painters daub in the first instance over a street-door which is gradually approaching a state of convalescence. It had been 'spitting' with rain for the last half-hour, and now began to pour in good earnest. The wind was freshening very fast, and the waterman at the wheel had unequivocally expressed his opinion that there would shortly be a squall. A slight motion on the part of the vessel now and then, seemed to suggest the possibility of its pitching to a very uncomfortable extent in the event of its blowing harder; and every timber began to creak as if the boat were an overladen clothes-basket. Sea-sickness, however, is like a belief in ghosts — every one entertains some misgivings on the subject, but few will acknowledge them. The majority of the company, therefore, endeavoured to look peculiarly happy, feeling all the while especially miserable.

'Don't it rain?' inquired the old gentleman before noticed, when, by dint of squeezing and jamming, they were all seated at table.

'I think it does – a little,' replied Mr Percy Noakes, who could hardly hear himself speak, in consequence of the pattering on the deck.

'Don't it blow?' inquired some one else.

'No – I don't think it does,' responded Hardy, sincerely wishing that he could persuade himself it did not, for he sat near the door, and was almost blown off his seat.

'It'll soon clear up,' said Mr Percy Noakes, in a cheerful tone.

'Oh, certainly!' ejaculated the committee generally.

'No doubt of it,' said the remainder of the company, whose attention was now pretty well engrossed by the serious business of eating, carving, taking wine, and so forth.

The throbbing motion of the engine was but too perceptible. There was a large, substantial cold boiled leg of mutton at the bottom of the table, shaking like blanc-mange; a hearty sirloin of beef looked as if it had been suddenly seized with the palsy; and some tongues, which were placed on dishes rather too large for them, were going through the most surprising evolutions, darting from side to side, and from end to end, like a fly in an inverted wine-glass. Then the sweets shook and trembled till it was quite impossible to help them, and people gave up the attempt in despair; and the pigeon-pies looked as if the birds, whose legs were stuck outside, were trying to get them in. The table vibrated and started like a feverish pulse, and the very legs were slightly convulsed – every thing was shaking and jarring. The beams in the roof of the cabin seemed as if they were put there for the sole purpose of giving people headaches, and several elderly gentlemen became ill-tempered in consequence. As fast as the steward put the fire-irons up, they *would* fall down again; and the more the ladies and gentlemen tried to sit comfortably on their seats, the more the seats seemed to slide away from the ladies and gentlemen. Several ominous demands were made for small glasses of brandy; the countenances of the company gradually underwent the most extraordinary changes; and one gentleman was observed suddenly to rush from table without the slightest ostensible reason, and dart up the steps with incredible swiftness, thereby greatly damaging both himself and the steward, who happened to be coming down at the same moment.

The cloth was removed; the dessert was laid on the table, and the glasses were filled. The motion of the boat increased; several members of the party began to feel rather vague and misty, and looked as if they had only just got up. The young gentleman with the spectacles, who had been in a fluctuating state for some time – one moment bright, and another dismal, like a revolving light on the sea-coast – rashly announced his wish to propose a toast. After several ineffectual attempts to preserve his perpendicular, the young gentleman, having managed to hook himself to the centre leg of the table with his left hand, proceeded as follows:

'Ladies and gentlemen. – A gentleman is among us – I may say a stranger – (here some painful thought seemed to strike the orator; he paused, and looked extremely odd) whose talents, whose travels, whose cheerfulness –'

'I beg your pardon, Edkins,' hastily interrupted Mr Percy Noakes. – 'Hardy, what's the matter?'

'Nothing,' replied the 'funny gentleman', who had just life enough left to utter two consecutive syllables.

'Will you have some brandy?'

'No,' replied Hardy, in a tone of great indignation, and looking about as comfortable as Temple-bar in a Scotch mist; 'what should I want brandy for?'

'Will you go on deck?'

'No, I will not.' This was said with a most determined air, and in a voice which might have been taken for an imitation of any thing; it was quite as much like a guinea-pig as a bassoon.

'I beg your pardon, Edkins,' said the courteous Percy; 'I thought our friend was ill. Pray go on.'

A pause.

'Pray go on.'

'Mr Edkins *is* gone,' cried somebody.

'I beg your pardon, sir,' said the steward, running up to Mr

Steam Excursion

Pl. 2

Percy Noakes, 'I beg your pardon, sir, but the gentleman as just went on deck — him with the green spectacles — is uncommon bad, to be sure; and the young man as played the wiolin says, that unless he has some brandy he can't answer for the consequences. He says he has a wife and two children, whose werry subsistence depends on his breaking a wessel, and that he expects to do so every moment. The flageolet's been very ill, but he's better, only he's in such a dreadful prusperation.'

All disguise was now useless; the company staggered on deck, the gentlemen tried to see nothing but the clouds, and the ladies, muffled up in such shawls and cloaks as they had brought with them, lay about on the seats and under the seats, in the most wretched condition. Never was such a blowing, and raining, and pitching, and tossing, endured by any pleasure party before. Several remonstrances were sent down below on the subject of Master Fleetwood, but they were totally unheeded in consequence of the indisposition of his natural protectors. That interesting child screamed at the very top of his voice, until he had no voice left to scream with, and then Miss Wakefield began, and screamed for the remainder of the passage.

Mr Hardy was observed some hours afterwards in an attitude which induced his friends to suppose that he was busily engaged in contemplating the beauties of the deep; they only regretted that his taste for the picturesque should lead him to remain so long in a position, very injurious at all times, but especially so to an individual labouring under a tendency of blood to the head.

The party arrived off the Custom-house at about two o'clock on the Thursday morning — dispirited and worn out. The Tauntons were too ill to quarrel with the Briggses, and the Briggses were too wretched to annoy the Tauntons. One of the guitar-cases was lost on its passage to a hackney-coach, and Mrs Briggs has not scrupled to state that the Tauntons bribed a porter to throw it down an area. Mr Alexander Briggs opposes vote by ballot — he says from personal experience of its inefficacy; and Mr Samuel Briggs, whenever he is asked to express his sentiments on the point, says that he has no opinion on that or any other subject.

Mr Edkins — the young gentleman in the green spectacles — makes a speech on every occasion on which a speech can possibly be made, the eloquence of which can only be equalled by its length. In the event of his not being previously appointed to a judgeship, it is most probable that he will practise as a barrister in the New Central Criminal Court.[27]

Captain Helves continued his attention to Miss Julia Briggs, whom he might possibly have espoused, if it had not unfortunately happened that Mr Samuel arrested him in the way of business, pursuant to instructions received from Messrs Scroggins and Payne, whose town debts the gallant captain had condescended to collect, but whose accounts, with the indiscretion so peculiar to military minds, he had omitted to keep with that dull accuracy which custom has rendered necessary. Mrs Taunton complains that she has been much deceived in him. He introduced himself to the family on board a Gravesend steam-packet, and certainly, therefore, ought to have proved respectable.

Mr Percy Noakes is as light-hearted and careless as ever. We have described him as a general favourite in his private circle, and trust he may find a kindly-disposed friend or two in public.

CHAPTER 8

The Great Winglebury Duel

THE little town of Great Winglebury[1] is exactly forty-two miles and three quarters from Hyde Park corner. It has a long, straggling, quiet High-street, with a great black and white clock at a small red Town-hall, half-way up — a market-place — a cage — an assembly-room — a church — a bridge — a chapel — a theatre — a library — an inn — a pump — and a Post-office. Tradition tells of a 'Little Winglebury' down some cross-road about two miles off; and as a

The Winglebury Duel

square mass of dirty paper, supposed to have been originally intended for a letter, with certain tremulous characters inscribed thereon, in which a lively imagination might trace a remote resemblance to the word 'Little,' was once stuck up to be owned in the sunny window of the Great Winglebury Post-office, from which it only disappeared when it fell to pieces with dust and extreme old age, there would appear to be some foundation for the legend. Common belief is inclined to bestow the name upon a little hole at the end of a muddy lane about a couple of miles long, colonized by one wheelwright, four paupers, and a beer-shop; but even this authority, slight as it is, must be regarded with extreme suspicion, inasmuch as the inhabitants of the hole aforesaid concur in opining that it never had any name at all, from the earliest ages down to the present day.

The Winglebury Arms in the centre of the High-street, opposite the small building with the big clock, is the principal inn of Great Winglebury – the commercial inn, posting-house, and excise-office; the 'Blue' house at every election, and the Judges' house at every assizes. It is the head-quarters of the Gentlemen's Whist Club of Winglebury Blues (so called in opposition to the Gentlemen's Whist Club of Winglebury Buffs, held at the other house, a little further down); and whenever a juggler, or wax-work man, or concert-giver, takes Great Winglebury in his circuit, it is immediately placarded all over the town that Mr So-and-so, 'trusting to that liberal support which the inhabitants of Great Winglebury have long been so liberal in bestowing, has at a great expense engaged the elegant and commodious assembly-rooms, attached to the Winglebury Arms.' The house is a large one, with a red brick and stone front; a pretty spacious hall ornamented with evergreen plants, terminates in a perspective view of the bar, and a glass case, in which are displayed a choice variety of delicacies ready for dressing, to catch the eye of a new-comer the moment he enters, and excite his appetite to the highest possible pitch. Opposite doors lead to the 'coffee' and 'commercial' rooms; and a great wide, rambling staircase, – three stairs and a landing – four stairs and another landing – one step and another landing – half a dozen stairs and another landing – and so on – conducts to galleries of bedrooms, and labyrinths of sitting-rooms, denominated 'private,' where you may enjoy yourself as privately as you can in any place where some bewildered being or other walks into your room every five minutes by mistake, and then walks out again, to open all the doors along the gallery till he finds his own.

Such is the Winglebury Arms at this day, and such was the Winglebury Arms some time since – no matter when – two or three minutes before the arrival of the London stage. Four horses with cloths on – change for a coach – were standing quietly at the corner of the yard, surrounded by a listless group of post-boys in shiny hats and smock-frocks, engaged in discussing the merits of the cattle; half a dozen ragged boys were standing a little apart, listening with evident interest to the conversation of these worthies; and a few loungers were collected round the horse-trough, awaiting the arrival of the coach.

The day was hot and sunny, the town in the zenith of its dulness, and with the exception of these few idlers, not a living creature was to be seen. Suddenly the loud notes of a key-bugle broke the monotonous stillness of the street; in came the coach, rattling over the uneven paving with a noise startling enough to stop even the large-faced clock itself. Down got the outsides, up went the windows in all directions; out came the waiters, up started the ostlers, and the loungers, and the post-boys, and the ragged boys, as if they were electrified – unstrapping, and unchaining, and unbuckling, and dragging willing horses out, and forcing reluctant horses in, and making a most exhilarating bustle. 'Lady inside, here,' said the guard. 'Please to alight, ma'am,' said the waiter. 'Private sitting-room?' interrogated the lady. – 'Certainly, ma'am,' responded the chambermaid. 'Nothing but these 'ere trunks, ma'am?' inquired the guard. 'Nothing more,' replied the lady. Up got the outsides again, and the guard, and the coachman; off came the cloths, with a jerk – 'All right' was the cry; and away they went. The loungers lingered a minute or two in the road, watching the coach till it turned the corner, and then loitered away one by one. The street was clear again, and the town, by contrast, quieter than ever.

'Lady in number twenty-five,' screamed the landlady. — 'Thomas!'

'Yes, ma'am.'

'Letter just been left for the gentleman in number nineteen. — Boots at the Lion left it. — No answer.'

'Letter for you, sir,' said Thomas, depositing the letter on number nineteen's table.

'For me?' said number nineteen, turning from the window, out of which he had been surveying the scene we have just described.

'Yes, sir, — (waiters always speak in hints, and never utter complete sentences) — yes, sir, — Boots at the Lion, sir — Bar, sir — Missis said number nineteen, sir — Alexander Trott, Esq., sir? — Your card at the bar, sir, I think, sir?'

'My name *is* Trott,' replied number nineteen, breaking the seal. 'You may go, waiter.' The waiter pulled down the window-blind, and then pulled it up again — for a regular waiter must do something before he leaves the room — adjusted the glasses on the sideboard, brushed a place which was *not* dusty, rubbed his hands very hard, walked stealthily to the door, and evaporated.

There was evidently something in the contents of the letter of a nature, if not wholly unexpected, certainly extremely disagreeable. Mr Alexander Trott laid it down and took it up again, and walked about the room on particular squares of the carpet, and even attempted, though very unsuccessfully, to whistle an air. It wouldn't do. He threw himself into a chair and read the following epistle aloud:

'Blue Lion and Stomach-warmer,
Great Winglebury.

                                        '*Wednesday Morning.*

'SIR,

          'Immediately on discovering your intentions, I left our counting-house, and followed you. I know the purport of your journey; — that journey shall never be completed.

'I have no friend here just now, on whose secrecy I can rely. This shall be no obstacle to my revenge. Neither shall Emily Brown be exposed to the mercenary solicitations of a scoundrel, odious in her eyes, and contemptible in every body else's: nor will I tamely submit to the clandestine attacks of a base umbrella-maker.

'Sir, – from Great Winglebury Church, a footpath leads through four meadows to a retired spot known to the townspeople as Stiffun's Acre (Mr Trott shuddered). I shall be waiting there alone, at twenty minutes before six o'clock to-morrow morning. Should I be disappointed of seeing you there, I will do myself the pleasure of calling with a horsewhip.

'HORACE HUNTER.

'PS. There is a gunsmith's in the High-street; and they won't sell gunpowder after dark – you understand me.

'PPS. You had better not order your breakfast in the morning till you have seen me. It may be an unnecessary expense.'

'Desperate-minded villain! I knew how it would be!' ejaculated the terrified Trott. 'I always told father, that once start me on this expedition, and Hunter would pursue me like the wandering Jew.[2] It's bad enough as it is, to marry with the old people's commands, and without the girl's consent: but what will Emily think of me, if I go down there, breathless with running away from this infernal salamander? What *shall* I do? What *can* I do? If I go back to the city I'm disgraced for ever – lose the girl, and what's more lose the money too. Even if I did go on to the Brown's by the coach, Hunter would be after me in a post-chaise; and if I go to this place, this Stiffun's Acre, (another shudder) I'm as good as dead. I've seen him hit the man at the Pall-mall shooting gallery,[3] in the second button-hole of the waistcoat five times out of every six, and when he didn't hit him there, he hit him in the head.' And with this consolatory reminiscence, Mr Alexander Trott again ejaculated, 'What shall I do?'

Long and weary were his reflections as, burying his face in his hands, he sat ruminating on the best course to be pursued. His mental direction-post pointed to London. He thought of 'the governor's' anger, and the loss of the fortune which the paternal

Brown had promised the paternal Trott his daughter should contribute to the coffers of his son. Then the words 'To Brown's' were legibly inscribed on the said direction-post, but Horace Hunter's denunciation rung in his ears: — last of all it bore, in red letters, the words, 'To Stiffun's Acre;' and then Mr Alexander Trott decided on adopting a plan which he presently matured.

First and foremost he despatched the under-boots to the Blue Lion and Stomach-warmer, with a gentlemanly note to Mr Horace Hunter, intimating that he thirsted for his destruction and would do himself the pleasure of slaughtering him next morning without fail. He then wrote another letter, and requested the attendance of the other boots — for they kept a pair. A modest knock at the room-door was heard — 'Come in,' said Mr Trott. A man thrust in a red head with one eye in it, and being again desired to 'come in,' brought in the body and legs to which the head belonged and a fur cap which belonged to the head.

'You are the upper-boots, I think?' inquired Mr Trott.

'Yes, I am the upper-boots,' replied a voice from inside a velveteen case with mother-of-pearl buttons — 'that is, I'm the boots as b'longs to the house; the other man's my man, as goes errands and does odd jobs — top-boots and half-boots I calls us.'

'You're from London?' inquired Mr Trott.

'Driv a cab once,' was the laconic reply.

'Why don't you drive it now?' asked Mr Trott.

'Cos I over-driv the cab, and driv over a 'ooman,' replied the top-boots, with brevity.

'Do you know the mayor's house?' inquired Trott.

'Rather,' replied the boots, significantly, as if he had some good reason to remember it.

'Do you think you could manage to leave a letter there?' interrogated Trott.

'Shouldn't wonder,' responded boots.

'But this letter,' said Trott, holding a deformed note with a paralytic direction in one hand, and five shillings in the other — 'this letter is anonymous.'

'A — what?' interrupted the boots.

'Anonymous – he's not to know who it comes from.'

'Oh! I see,' responded the rig'lar,[4] with a knowing wink, but without evincing the slightest disinclination to undertake the charge – 'I see – bit o' sving,[5] eh?' and his one eye wandered round the room as if in quest of a dark lantern and phosphorous-box.[6] 'But I say,' he continued, recalling the eye from its search, and bringing it to bear on Mr Trott – 'I say, he's a lawyer, our mayor, and insured in the County.[7] If you've a spite agen him, you'd better not burn his house down – blessed if I don't think it would be the greatest favour you could do him.' And he chuckled inwardly.

If Mr Alexander Trott had been in any other situation, his first act would have been to kick the man down stairs by deputy; or, in other words, to ring the bell, and desire the landlord to take his boots off. He contented himself, however, with doubling the fee and explaining that the letter merely related to a breach of the peace. The top-boots retired, solemnly pledged to secrecy; and Mr Alexander Trott sat down to a fried sole, maintenon cutlet,[8] Madeira, and sundries, with much greater composure than he had experienced since the receipt of Horace Hunter's letter of defiance.

The lady who alighted from the London coach had no sooner been installed in number twenty-five, and made some alteration in her travelling-dress, than she endited a note to Joseph Overton, esquire, solicitor, and mayor of Great Winglebury, requesting his immediate attendance on private business of paramount importance – a summons which that worthy functionary lost no time in obeying; for after sundry openings of his eyes, divers ejaculations of 'Bless me!' and other manifestations of surprise, he took his broad-brimmed hat from its accustomed peg in his little front office, and walked briskly down the High-street to the Winglebury Arms; through the hall and up the staircase of which establishment he was ushered by the landlady, and a crowd of officious waiters, to the door of number twenty-five.

'Show the gentleman in,' said the stranger lady, in reply to the foremost waiter's announcement. The gentleman was shown in accordingly.

The lady rose from the sofa; the mayor advanced a step from the door, and there they both paused for a minute or two, looking at one another as if by mutual consent. The mayor saw before him a buxom richly-dressed female of about forty; and the lady looked upon a sleek man about ten years older, in drab shorts and continuations,⁹ black coat, neckcloth, and gloves.

'Miss Julia Manners!' exclaimed the mayor at length, 'you astonish me.'

'That's very unfair of you, Overton,' replied Miss Julia, 'for I have known you long enough not to be surprised at any thing you do, and you might extend equal courtesy to me.'

'But to run away – actually run away – with a young man!' remonstrated the mayor.

'You would not have me actually run away with an old one I presume?' was the cool rejoinder.

'And then to ask me – me – of all people in the world – a man of my age and appearance – mayor of the town – to promote such a scheme!' pettishly ejaculated Joseph Overton; throwing himself into an arm-chair, and producing Miss Julia's letter from his pocket, as if to corroborate the assertion that he had been asked.

'Now, Overton,' replied the lady, impatiently, 'I want your assistance in this matter, and I must have it. In the lifetime of that poor old dear, Mr Cornberry, who – who –'

'Who was to have married you, and didn't, because he died first; and who left you his property unencumbered with the addition of himself,' suggested the mayor, in a sarcastic tone.

'Well,' replied Miss Julia, reddening slightly, 'in the lifetime of the poor old dear, the property had the incumbrance of your management; and all I will say of that is, that I only wonder *it* didn't die of consumption instead of its master. You helped yourself then: – help me now.'

Mr Joseph Overton was a man of the world, and an attorney; and as certain indistinct recollections of an odd thousand pounds or two, appropriated by mistake, passed across his mind, he hemmed deprecatingly, smiled blandly, remained silent for a few seconds; and finally inquired, 'What do you wish me to do?'

'I'll tell you,' replied Miss Julia – 'I'll tell you in three words. Dear Lord Peter –'

'That's the young man, I suppose –' interrupted the mayor.

'That's the young nobleman,' replied the lady, with a great stress on the last word. 'Dear Lord Peter is considerably afraid of the resentment of his family; and we have therefore thought it better to make the match a stolen one. He left town to avoid suspicion, on a visit to his friend, the Honourable Augustus Flair, whose seat, as you know, is about thirty miles from this, accompanied only by his favourite tiger.[10] We arranged that I should come here alone in the London coach; and that he, leaving his tiger and cab behind him, should come on, and arrive here as soon as possible this afternoon.'

'Very well,' observed Joseph Overton, 'and then he can order the chaise, and you can go on to Gretna Green[11] together, without requiring the presence or interference of a third party, can't you?'

'No,' replied Miss Julia. 'We have every reason to believe – dear Lord Peter not being considered very prudent or sagacious by his friends, and they having discovered his attachment to me – that immediately on his absence being observed, pursuit will be made in this direction: to elude which, and to prevent our being traced, I wish it to be understood in this house, that dear Lord Peter is slightly deranged, though perfectly harmless; and that I am, un-known to him, waiting his arrival to convey him in a post-chaise to a private asylum – at Berwick,[12] say. If I don't show myself much, I dare say I can manage to pass for his mother.'

The thought occurred to the mayor's mind that the lady might show herself a good deal without fear of detection; seeing that she was about double the age of her intended husband. He said nothing, however, and the lady proceeded –

'With the whole of this arrangement, dear Lord Peter is acquainted: and all I want you to do is, to make the delusion more complete by giving it the sanction of your influence in this place, and assigning this as a reason to the people of the house for my taking the young gentleman away. As it would not be consistent with the story that I should see him until after he has entered the chaise, I also wish you to communicate with him, and inform him that it is all going on well.'

472

'Has he arrived?' inquired Overton.

'I don't know,' replied the lady.

'Then how am I to know?' inquired the mayor. 'Of course he will not give his own name at the bar.'

'I begged him, immediately on his arrival, to write you a note,' replied Miss Manners; 'and to prevent the possibility of our project being discovered through its means, I desired him to write anonymously, and in mysterious terms to acquaint you with the number of his room.'

'God bless me!' exclaimed the mayor, rising from his seat, and searching his pockets — 'most extraordinary circumstance — he *has* arrived — mysterious note left at my house in a most mysterious manner, just before yours — didn't know what to make of it before, and certainly shouldn't have attended to it. — Oh! here it is.' And Joseph Overton pulled out of an inner coat-pocket the identical letter penned by Alexander Trott. 'Is this his lordship's hand?'

'Oh yes,' replied Julia; 'good, punctual creature! I have not seen it more than once or twice, but I know he writes very badly and very large. These dear, wild young noblemen, you know, Overton —'

'Ay, ay, I see,' replied the mayor. — 'Horses and dogs, play and wine — grooms, actresses, and cigars, — the stable, the green-room, the brothel,[13] and the tavern; and the legislative assembly at last.'

'Here's what he says,' pursued the mayor; '"Sir, — A young gentleman in number nineteen at the Winglebury Arms, is bent on committing a rash act to-morrow morning at an early hour. (That's good — he means marrying.) If you have any regard for the peace of this town, or the preservation of one — it may be two — human lives" — What the deuce does he mean by that?'

'That he's so anxious for the ceremony, he will expire if it's put off, and that I may possibly do the same,' replied the lady with great complacency.

'Oh! I see — not much fear of that; — well — "two human lives, you will cause him to be removed to-night. — (He wants to start at once.) Fear not to do this on your responsibility: for to-morrow,

the absolute necessity of the proceeding will be but too aparent.
Remember: number nineteen. The name is Trott. No delay; for life
and death depend upon your promptitude." — Passionate language,
certainly. — Shall I see him?'

'Do,' replied Miss Julia; 'and entreat him to act his part well. I
am half afraid of him. Tell him to be cautious.'

'I will,' said the mayor.

'Settle all the arrangements.'

'I will,' said the mayor again.

'And say I think the chaise had better be ordered for one
o'clock.'

'Very well,' cried the mayor once more; and ruminating on the
absurdity of the situation in which fate and old acquaintance had
placed him, he desired a waiter to herald his approach to the
temporary representative of number nineteen.

The announcement — 'Gentleman to speak with you, sir,' induced
Mr Trott to pause half-way in the glass of port, the contents of
which he was in the act of imbibing at the moment; to rise from his
chair, and retreat a few paces towards the window, as if to secure a
retreat in the event of the visiter assuming the form and appearance
of Horace Hunter. One glance at Joseph Overton, however, quieted
his apprehensions. He courteously motioned the stranger to a seat.
The waiter after a little jingling with the decanter and glasses,
consented to leave the room; and Joseph Overton placing the
broad-brimmed hat on the chair next him, and bending his body
gently forward, opened the business by saying in a very low and
cautious tone,

'My lord —'

'Eh?' said Mr Alexander Trott in a very loud key, with the
vacant and mystified stare of a chilly somnambulist.

'Hush — hush!' said the cautious attorney: 'to be sure — quite
right — no titles here — my name is Overton, sir.'

'Overton!'

'Yes: the mayor of this place — you sent me a letter with
anonymous information, this afternoon.'

'I, sir?' exclaimed Trott with ill-dissembled surprise; for, coward as he was, he would willingly have repudiated the authorship of the letter in question. 'I, sir?'

'Yes, you, sir; did you not?' responded Overton, annoyed with what he supposed to be an extreme degree of unnecessary suspicion. 'Either this letter is yours, or it is not. If it be, we can converse securely upon the subject at once. If it be not, of course I have no more to say.'

'Stay, stay,' said Trott, 'it *is* mine; I *did* write it. What could I do, sir? I had no friend here.'

'To be sure – to be sure,' said the mayor, encouragingly, 'you could not have managed it better. Well, sir; it will be necessary for you to leave here to-night in a post-chaise and four. And the harder the boys drive the better. You are not safe from pursuit here.'

'Bless me!' exclaimed Trott, in an agony of apprehension, 'can such things happen in a country like this? Such unrelenting and cold-blooded hostility!' He wiped off the concentrated essence of cowardice that was oozing fast down his forehead, and looked aghast at Joseph Overton.

'It certainly is a very hard case,' replied the mayor with a smile, 'that, in a free country, people can't marry whom they like without being hunted down as if they were criminals. However, in the present instance the lady is willing, you know, and that's the main point, after all.'

'Lady willing!' repeated Trott, mechanically – 'How do you know the lady's willing?'

'Come, that's a good one,' said the mayor, benevolently tapping Mr Trott on the arm with his broad-brimmed hat, 'I have known her, well, for a long time, and if any body could entertain the remotest doubt on the subject, I assure you I have none, nor need you.'

'Dear me!' said Mr Trott, ruminating – 'Dear me! – this is very extraordinary!'

'Well, Lord Peter,' said the mayor, rising.

'Lord Peter?' repeated Mr Trott.

'Oh – ah, I forgot; well, Mr Trott, then – Trott – very good, ha! ha! – Well, sir, the chaise shall be ready at half-past twelve.'

'And what is to become of me till then?' inquired Mr Trott, anxiously. 'Wouldn't it save appearances if I were placed under some restraint?'

'Ah!' replied Overton, 'very good thought – capital idea indeed. I'll send somebody up directly. And if you make a little resistance when we put you in the chaise it wouldn't be amiss – look as if you didn't want to be taken away, you know.'

'To be sure,' said Trott – 'to be sure.'

'Well, my lord,' said Overton, in a low tone, 'till then, I wish your lordship a good evening.'

'Lord – lordship!' ejaculated Trott again, falling back a step or two, and gazing in unutterable wonder on the countenance of the mayor.

'Ha-ha! I see, my lord – practising the madman? – very good indeed – very vacant look – capital, my lord, capital – good evening, Mr Trott – ha! ha! ha!'

'That mayor's decidedly drunk,' soliloquised Mr Trott, throwing himself back in his chair, in an attitude of reflection.

'He is a much cleverer fellow than I thought him, that young nobleman – he carries it off uncommonly well,' thought Overton, as he wended his way to the bar, there to complete his arrangements. This was soon done: every word of the story was implicitly believed, and the one-eyed boots was immediately instructed to repair to number nineteen, to act as custodian of the person of the supposed lunatic until half-past twelve o'clock. In pursuance of this direction, that somewhat eccentric gentleman armed himself with a walking-stick of gigantic dimensions, and repaired with his usual equanimity of manner to Mr Trott's apartment, which he entered without any ceremony, and mounted guard in, by quietly depositing himself upon a chair near the door, where he proceeded to beguile the time by whistling a popular air with great apparent satisfaction.

'What do you want here, you scoundrel?' exclaimed Mr Alexander Trott, with a proper appearance of indignation at his detention.

The boots beat time with his head, as he looked gently round at Mr Trott with a smile of pity, and whistled an *adagio* movement.

'Do you attend in this room by Mr Overton's desire?' inquired Trott, rather astonished at the man's demeanour.

'Keep yourself to yourself, young feller,' calmly responded the boots, 'and don't say nothin' to nobody.' And he whistled again.

'Now mind,' ejaculated Mr Trott, anxious to keep up the farce of wishing with great earnestness to fight a duel if they'd let him, – 'I protest against being kept here. I deny that I have any intention of fighting with any body. But as it's useless contending with superior numbers, I shall sit quietly down.'

'You'd better,' observed the placid boots, shaking the large stick expressively.

'Under protest, however,' added Alexander Trott, seating himself, with indignation in his face but great content in his heart. 'Under protest.'

'Oh, certainly!' responded the boots; 'any thing you please. If you're happy, I'm transported; only don't talk too much – it'll make you worse.'

'Make me worse!' exclaimed Trott, in unfeigned astonishment: 'the man's drunk!'

'You'd better be quiet, young feller,' remarked the boots, going through a most threatening piece of pantomime with the stick.

'Or mad!' said Mr Trott, rather alarmed. 'Leave the room, sir, and tell them to send somebody else.'

'Won't do!' replied the boots.

'Leave the room!' shouted Trott, ringing the bell violently; for he began to be alarmed on a new score.

'Leave that 'ere bell alone, you wretched loo-nattic!' said the boots, suddenly forcing the unfortunate Trott back into his chair, and brandishing the stick aloft. 'Be quiet, you mis'rable object, and don't let every body know there's a madman in the house.'

'He *is* a madman! He *is* a madman!' exclaimed the terrified Mr Trott, gazing on the one eye of the red-headed boots with a look of abject horror.

'Madman!' replied the boots – 'dam'me, I think he *is* a madman with a vengeance! Listen to me, you unfort'nate. Ah! would you? –

[a slight tap on the head with the large stick, as Mr Trott made another move towards the bell-handle] I caught you there! did I?'

'Spare my life!' exclaimed Trott, raising his hands imploringly.

'I don't want your life,' replied the boots, disdainfully, 'though I think it 'ud be a charity if somebody took it.'

'No, no, it wouldn't,' interrupted poor Mr Trott, hurriedly; 'no, no, it wouldn't! I – I – 'd rather keep it!'

'O werry well,' said the boots; 'that's a mere matter of taste – ev'ry one to his liking. Hows'ever, all I've got to say is this here: You sit quietly down in that chair, and I'll sit hoppersite you here, and if you keep quiet and don't stir, I won't damage you; but if you move hand or foot till half-past twelve o'clock, I shall alter the expression of your countenance so completely, that the next time you look in the glass you'll ask vether you're gone out of town, and ven you're likely to come back again. So sit down.'

'I will – I will,' responded the victim of mistakes; and down sat Mr Trott and down sat the boots too, exactly opposite him, with the stick ready for immediate action in case of emergency.

Long and dreary were the hours that followed. The bell of Great Winglebury church had just struck ten, and two hours and a half would probably elapse before succour arrived. For half an hour the noise occasioned by shutting up the shops in the street beneath betokened something like life in the town, and rendered Mr Trott's situation a little less insupportable; but when even these ceased, and nothing was heard beyond the occasional rattling of a post-chaise as it drove up the yard to change horses, and then drove away again, or the clattering of horses' hoofs in the stables behind, it became almost unbearable. The boots occasionally moved an inch or two, to knock superfluous bits of wax off the candles, which were burning low, but instantaneously resumed his former position; and as he remembered to have heard somewhere or other that the human eye had an unfailing effect in controlling mad people, he kept his solitary organ of vision constantly fixed on Mr Alexander Trott. That unfortunate individual stared at his companion in his turn, until his features grew more and more indistinct – his hair gradually less red – and the room more misty and obscure. Mr

Alexander Trott fell into a sound sleep, from which he was awakened by a rumbling in the street, and a cry of – 'Chaise-and-four for number twenty-five!' A bustle on the stairs succeeded; the room-door was hastily thrown open; and Mr Joseph Overton entered, followed by four stout waiters, and Mrs Williamson, the stout landlady of the Winglebury Arms.

'Mr Overton!' exclaimed Mr Alexander Trott, jumping up in a frenzy of passionate excitement – 'Look at this man, sir; consider the situation in which I have been placed for three hours past – the person you sent to guard me, sir, was a madman – a madman – a raging, ravaging, furious madman.'

'Bravo!' whispered Overton.

'Poor dear!' said the compassionate Mrs Williamson, 'mad people always thinks other people's mad.'

'Poor dear!' ejaculated Mr Alexander Trott, 'What the devil do you mean by poor dear! are you the landlady of this house?'

'Yes, yes,' replied the stout old lady, 'don't exert yourself, there's a dear – consider your health, now; do.'

'Exert myself!' shouted Mr Alexander Trott, 'it's a mercy, ma'am, that I have any breath to exert myself with, I might have been assassinated three hours ago by that one-eyed monster with the oakum head. How dare you have a madman, ma'am – how dare you have a madman, to assault and terrify the visiters to your house?'

'I'll never have another,' said Mrs Williamson, casting a look of reproach at the mayor.

'Capital – capital,' whispered Overton again, as he enveloped Mr Alexander Trott in a thick travelling-cloak.

'Capital, sir!' exclaimed Trott, aloud, 'it's horrible. The very recollection makes me shudder. I'd rather fight four duels in three hours if I survived the first three, than I'd sit for that time face to face with a madman.'

'Keep it up, as you go down stairs,' whispered Overton, 'your bill is paid, and your portmanteau in the chaise.' And then he added aloud, 'Now, waiters, the gentleman's ready.'

At this signal the waiters crowded round Mr Alexander Trott.

One took one arm, another the other, a third walked before with a candle, the fourth behind with another candle; the boots and Mrs Williamson brought up the rear, and down stairs they went, Mr Alexander Trott expressing alternately at the very top of his voice either his feigned reluctance to go, or his unfeigned indignation at being shut up with a madman.

Mr Overton was waiting at the chaise-door, the boys were ready mounted, and a few ostlers and stable nondescripts were standing round to witness the departure of 'the mad gentleman.' Mr Alexander Trott's foot was on the step, when he observed (which the dim light had prevented his doing before) a human figure seated in the chaise, closely muffled up in a cloak like his own.

'Who's that?' he inquired of Overton, in a whisper.

'Hush, hush,' replied the mayor; 'the other party of course.'

'The other party!' exclaimed Trott, with an effort to retreat.

'Yes, yes; you'll soon find that out, before you go far, I should think – but make a noise, you'll excite suspicion if you whisper to me so much.'

'I won't go in this chaise,' shouted Mr Alexander Trott, all his original fears recurring with tenfold violence. 'I shall be assassinated – I shall be –'

'Bravo, bravo,' whispered Overton. 'I'll push you in.'

'But I won't go,' exclaimed Mr Trott. 'Help here, help! they're carrying me away against my will. This is a plot to murder me.'

'Poor dear!' said Mrs Williamson again.

'Now, boys, put 'em along,' cried the mayor, pushing Trott in and slamming the door. 'Off with you as quick as you can, and stop for nothing till you come to the next stage – all right.'

'Horses are paid, Tom,' screamed Mrs Williamson; and away went the chaise at the rate of fourteen miles an hour, with Mr Alexander Trott and Miss Julia Manners carefully shut up in the inside.

Mr Alexander Trott remained coiled up in one corner of the chaise, and his mysterious companion in the other, for the first two or three miles; Mr Trott edging more and more into his corner as he felt his companion gradually edging more and more from hers;

and vainly endeavouring in the darkness to catch a glimpse of the furious face of the supposed Horace Hunter.

'We may speak now,' said his fellow traveller, at length; 'the post-boys can neither see nor hear us.'

'That's not Hunter's voice!' – thought Alexander, astonished.

'Dear Lord Peter!' said Miss Julia, most winningly: putting her arm on Mr Trott's shoulder – 'Dear Lord Peter. Not a word?'

'Why, it's a woman!' exclaimed Mr Trott in a low tone of excessive wonder.

'Ah – whose voice is that?' said Julia – ''tis not Lord Peter's.'

'No, – it's mine,' replied Mr Trott.

'Yours!' ejaculated Miss Julia Manners, 'a strange man! Gracious Heaven – how came you here?'

'Whoever you are, you might have known that I came against my will, ma'am,' replied Alexander, 'For I made noise enough when I got in.'

'Do you come from Lord Peter?' inquired Miss Manners.

'Damn[14] Lord Peter,' replied Trott pettishly – 'I don't know any Lord Peter – I never heard of him before to-night, when I've been Lord Peter'd by one and Lord Peter'd by another, till I verily believe I'm mad, or dreaming –'

'Whither are we going?' inquired the lady tragically.

'How should *I* know, ma'am?' replied Trott with singular coolness; for the events of the evening had completely hardened him.

'Stop! stop!' cried the lady, letting down the front glasses of the chaise.

'Stay, my dear ma'am!' said Mr Trott, pulling the glasses up again with one hand, and gently squeezing Miss Julia's waist with the other. 'There is some mistake here; give me till the end of this stage to explain my share of it. We must go so far; you cannot be set down here alone, at this hour of the night.'

The lady consented; the mistake was mutually explained. Mr Trott was a young man, had highly promising whiskers, an undeniable tailor, and an insinuating address – he wanted nothing but valour, and who wants that with three thousand a-year? The lady had this, and more; she wanted a young husband, and the only course open to Mr Trott to retrieve his disgrace was a rich wife. So, they came to the conclusion that it would be a pity to have all this trouble and expense for nothing, and that as they were so far on the road already, they had better go to Gretna Green, and marry each other, and they did so. And the very next preceding entry in the Blacksmith's book was an entry of the marriage of Emily Brown with Horace Hunter. Mr Hunter took his wife home, and begged pardon, and *was* pardoned; and Mr Trott took *his* wife home, begged pardon too, and was pardoned also. And Lord Peter, who had been detained beyond his time by drinking champagne and riding a steeple-chase, went back to the Honourable Augustus Flair's, and drank more champagne, and rode another steeple-chase, and was thrown and killed. And Horace Hunter took great credit to himself for practising on the cowardice of Alexander Trott; and all these circumstances were discovered in time, and carefully noted down; and if ever you stop a week at the Winglebury Arms, they'll give you just this account of The Great Winglebury Duel.

CHAPTER 9

Mrs Joseph Porter

MOST extensive were the preparations at Rose Villa, Clapham Rise,[1] in the occupation of Mr Gattleton (a stockbroker in especially comfortable circumstances), and great was the anxiety of Mr Gattleton's interesting family, as the day fixed for the representation of the Private Play which had been 'many months in preparation,' approached. The whole family was infected with the mania for Private Theatricals; the house, usually so clean and tidy, was, to use Mr Gattleton's expressive description 'regularly turned out o' windows;' the large dining-room, dismantled of its furniture and

Mrs Joseph Porter

ornaments, presented a strange jumble of flats, flies, wings, lamps, bridges, clouds, thunder and lightning, festoons and flowers, daggers and foil, and all the other messes which in theatrical slang are included under the comprehensive name of 'properties.' The bedrooms were crowded with scenery, the kitchen was occupied by carpenters. Rehearsals took place every other night in the drawing-room, and every sofa in the house was more or less damaged by the perseverance and spirit with which Mr Sempronius Gattleton, and Miss Lucina, rehearsed the smothering scene in 'Othello'² – it having been determined that that tragedy should form the first portion of the evening's entertainments.

'When we're a *leetle* more perfect, I think it will go off admirably,' said Mr Sempronius, addressing his *corps dramatique*, at the conclusion of the hundred and fiftieth rehearsal. In consideration of his sustaining the trifling inconvenience of bearing all the expenses of the play, Mr Sempronius had been in the most handsome manner unanimously elected stage-manager. 'Evans,' continued Mr Gattleton, jun., addressing a tall, thin, pale young gentleman, with extensive whiskers – 'Evans, upon my word you play *Roderigo* beautifully.'

'Beautifully!' echoed the three Miss Gattletons; for Mr Evans was pronounced by all his lady friends to be 'quite a dear.' He looked so interesting, and had such lovely whiskers, to say nothing of his talent for writing verses in albums and playing the flute! The interesting *Roderigo* simpered and bowed.

'But I think,' added the manager, 'you are hardly perfect in the – fall – in the fencing-scene, where you are – you understand?'

'It's very difficult,' said Mr Evans, thoughtfully; 'I've fallen about a good deal in our counting-house lately for practice, only I find it hurts one so. Being obliged to fall backwards, you see, it bruises one's head a good deal.'

'But you must take care you don't knock a wing down,' said Mr Gattleton, sen., who had been appointed prompter, and who took as much interest in the play as the youngest of the company. 'The stage is very narrow, you know.'

'Oh! don't be afraid,' said Mr Evans, with a very self-satisfied air: 'I shall fall with my head "off," and then I can't do any harm.'

'But, egad!' said the manager, rubbing his hands, 'we shall make a decided hit in "Masaniello."[3] Harleigh[4] sings that music admirably.'

Every body echoed the sentiment. Mr Harleigh smiled, and looked foolish – not an unusual thing with him – hummed 'Behold how brightly breaks the morning,'[5] and blushed as red as the fisherman's nightcap he was trying on.

'Let's see,' resumed the manager, telling the number on his fingers, 'we shall have three dancing female peasants, besides *Fenella*, and four fishermen. Then there's our man Tom, he can have a pair of ducks of mine, and a check shirt of Bob's, and a red nightcap, and he'll do for another – that's five. In the choruses, of course, we can sing at the sides, and in the market-scene we can walk about in cloaks and things. When the revolt takes place, Tom must keep rushing in on one side and out on the other, with a pickaxe, as fast as he can. The effect will be electrical; 'twill look exactly as if there were a great number of 'em; and in the eruption scene we must burn the red fire, and upset the tea-trays, and hallo and make all sorts of noises – and it's sure to do.'

'Sure! sure!' cried all the performers *unâ voce*[6] – and away hurried Mr Sempronius Gattleton to wash the burnt cork off his face, and superintend the 'setting up' of some of the amateur-painted and never-sufficiently-to-be-admired scenery.

Mrs Gattleton was a kind, good-tempered, vulgar soul, exceedingly fond of her husband and children, and entertaining only three dislikes. In the first place, she had a natural antipathy to any body else's unmarried daughters; and in the second, she was in bodily fear of any thing in the shape of ridicule; and, lastly – almost a necessary consequence of this feeling – she regarded with feelings of the utmost horror one Mrs Joseph Porter over the way. However, the good folks of Clapham and its vicinity stood very much in awe of scandal and sarcasm; and thus Mrs Joseph Porter was courted, and flattered, and caressed, and invited, for very much the same reason that a poor author, without a farthing in his pocket, behaves with the most extraordinary civility to a twopenny-postman.

'Never mind, ma,' said Miss Emma Porter, in colloquy with her respected relative, and trying to look unconcerned; 'if they had invited me, you know that neither you nor pa would have allowed me to take part in such an exhibition.'

'Just what I should have thought from your high sense of propriety,' returned the mother. 'I am glad to see, Emma, you know how to designate the proceeding.' Miss P., by-the-by, had only the week before made 'an exhibition' of herself for four days, behind a counter at a fancy fair, to all and every of her Majesty's liege subjects who were disposed to pay a shilling each for the privilege of seeing some four dozen girls flirting with strangers, and playing at shop.

'There!' said Mrs Porter, looking out of window; 'there are two rounds of beef and a ham going in, clearly for sandwiches; and Thomas, the pastrycook, says there have been twelve dozen tarts ordered, besides blancmange and jellies. Upon my word! think of the Miss Gattletons in fancy dresses, too!'

'Oh, it's too ridiculous!' said Miss Porter, with a sort of hysterical chuckle.

'I'll manage to put them a little out of conceit with the business, however,' said Mrs Porter; and out she went on her charitable errand.

'Well, my dear Mrs Gattleton,' said Mrs Joseph Porter – after they had been closeted for some time, and when by dint of indefatigable pumping, she had managed to extract all the news about the play, – 'well, my dear, people may say what they please; indeed we know they will, for some folks are *so* ill-natured. Ah, my dear Miss Lucina, how d'ye do? – I was just telling your mamma that I have heard it said, that –'

'What?'

'Mrs Porter is alluding to the play, my dear,' said Mrs Gattleton; 'she was, I am sorry to say, just informing me that –'

'Oh, now pray don't mention it,' interrupted Mrs Porter; 'it's most absurd – quite as absurd as young What's-his-name saying he wondered how Miss Caroline with such a foot and ankle, could have the vanity to play *Fenella*.'

'Highly impertinent, whoever said it,' said Mrs Gattleton, bridling up.

'Certainly, my dear,' chimed in the delighted Mrs Porter; 'most undoubtedly. Because, as I said, if Miss Caroline *does* play *Fenella*, it doesn't follow, as a matter of course, that she should think she has a pretty foot; and then – such puppies as these young men are – he had the impudence to say, that —'

How far the amiable Mrs Porter might have succeeded in her pleasant purpose it is impossible to say, had not the entrance of Mr Thomas Balderstone, Mrs Gattleton's brother, familiarly called in the family 'Uncle Tom,' changed the course of conversation, and suggested to her mind an excellent plan of operation on the evening of the play.

Uncle Tom was very rich, and exceedingly fond of his nephews and nieces: as a matter of course, therefore, he was an object of great importance in his own family. He was one of the best hearted men in existence; always in a good temper, and always talking. It was his boast that he wore top-boots on all occasions, and had never worn a black silk neckerchief; and it was his pride that he remembered all the principal plays of Shakespeare from beginning to end – and so he did. The result of this parrot-like accomplishment was, that he was not only perpetually quoting himself, but that he could never sit by and hear a misquotation from 'The Swan of Avon,'[7] without setting the unfortunate delinquent right. He was also something of a wag; never missed an opportunity of saying what he considered a good thing, and invariably laughed till he cried at any thing that appeared to him mirth-moving or ridiculous.

'Well, girls!' said Uncle Tom, after the preparatory ceremony of kissing and how-d'ye-do-ing had been gone through – 'how d'ye get on? Know your parts, eh? – Lucina, my dear, act 2, scene 1 – place, left – cue – "Unknown fate," – What's next, ha? – Go on – "The heavens —"'

'Oh, yes,' said Miss Lucina, 'I recollect —'

'The heavens forbid
But that our loves and comforts should increase
Even as our days do grow.'[8]

'Make a pause here and there,' said the old gentleman, who was a great critic in his own estimation − '"But that our loves and comforts should increase" − emphasis on the last syllable, "crease," − loud "even," − one, two, three, four; then loud again, "as our days do grow;" emphasis on *days*. That's the way, my dear; trust to your uncle for emphasis. − Ah! Sem, my boy, how are you?'

'Very well, thankee uncle,' returned Mr Sempronius, who had just appeared, looking something like a ringdove, with a small circle round each eye, the result of his constant corking. 'Of course we see you on Thursday.'

'Of course, of course, my dear boy.'

'What a pity it is your nephew didn't think of making you prompter, Mr Balderstone,' whispered Mrs Joseph Porter; 'you would have been invaluable.'

'Well, I flatter myself, I *should* have been tolerably up to the thing,' responded Uncle Tom.

'I must bespeak sitting next you on the night,' resumed Mrs Porter; 'and then, if our dear young friends here, should be at all wrong, you will be able to enlighten me. I shall be *so* interested.'

'I am sure I shall be most happy to give you any assistance in my power.'

'Mind, it's a bargain.'

'Certainly.'

'I don't know how it is,' said Mrs Gattleton to her daughters, as they were sitting round the fire in the evening, looking over their parts, 'but I really very much wish Mrs Joseph Porter wasn't coming on Thursday. I am sure she's scheming something.'

'She can't make *us* ridiculous, however,' observed Mr Sempronius Gattleton, haughtily.

The long looked-for Thursday arrived in due course, and brought with it, as Mr Gattleton, senior, philosophically observed, 'no disappointments, to speak of.' True, it was yet a matter of doubt whether *Cassio* would be enabled to get into the dress which had been sent for him from the masquerade warehouse. It was equally uncertain whether the principal female singer would be sufficiently recovered from the influenza to make her appearance; Mr Harleigh, the Masaniello of the night, was hoarse, and rather unwell, in consequence of the great quantity of lemon and sugar-candy he had eaten to improve his voice; and two flutes and a violoncello had pleaded severe colds. What of that? the audience were all coming. Every body knew his part; the dresses were covered with tinsel and spangles; the white plumes looked beautiful; Mr Evans had practised falling, till he was bruised from head to foot and quite perfect; and *Iago* was perfectly sure that, in the stabbing-scene, he should make 'a decided hit.' A self-taught deaf gentleman, who had kindly offered to bring his flute, would be a most valuable addition to the orchestra; Miss Jenkins's talent for the piano was too well known to be doubted for an instant; Mr Cape had practised the violin accompaniment with her frequently, and Mr Brown, who had kindly undertaken at a few hours' notice, to bring his violoncello, would, no doubt, manage extremely well.

Seven o'clock came, and so did the audience; all the rank and fashion of Clapham and its vicinity was fast filling the theatre. There were the Smiths, the Gubbinses, the Nixons, the Dixons, the Hicksons, people with all sorts of names, two aldermen, a sheriff in perspective, Sir Thomas Glumper (who had been knighted in the last reign for carrying up an address on somebody's escaping from something); and last not least, there were Mrs Joseph Porter and Uncle Tom, seated in the centre of the third row from the stage; Mrs P. amusing Uncle Tom with all sorts of stories, and Uncle Tom amusing every one else by laughing most immoderately.

Ting, ting, ting! went the prompter's bell at eight o'clock precisely; and dash went the orchestra into the overture to 'The Men of Prometheus.'9 The pianoforte player hammered away with the most laudable perseverance; and the violoncello, which struck in at intervals, 'sounded very well, considering.' The unfortunate individual, however, who had undertaken to play the flute accompaniment 'at sight,' found, from fatal experience, the perfect truth of the old adage, 'out of sight, out of mind;' for being very near-sighted, and being placed at a considerable distance from his music-book, all he had an opportunity of doing was to play a bar now and then in the wrong place, and put the other performers out. It is, however, but justice to Mr Brown to say that he did this to admiration. The overture, in fact, was not unlike a race between the different instruments; the piano came in first by several bars, and the violoncello next, quite distancing the poor flute; for the deaf gentleman *too-too'd* away, quite unconscious that he was at all wrong, until apprized, by the applause of the audience, that the overture was concluded. A considerable bustle and shuffling of feet was then heard upon the stage, accompanied by whispers of 'Here's a pretty go! — what's to be done?' &c. The audience applauded again, by way of raising the spirits of the performers: and then Mr Sempronius desired the prompter, in a very audible voice, to 'clear the stage, and ring up.'

Ting, ting, ting! went the bell again. Every body sat down; the curtain shook, rose sufficiently high to display several pair of yellow boots paddling about, and there it remained.

Ting, ting, ting! went the bell again. The curtain was violently convulsed, but rose no higher; the audience tittered; Mrs Porter looked at Uncle Tom, and Uncle Tom looked at every body, rubbing his hands, and laughing with perfect rapture. After as much ringing with the little bell as a muffin-boy would make in going down a tolerably long street, and a vast deal of whispering, hammering, and calling for nails and cord, the curtain at length rose, and discovered Mr Sempronius Gattleton *solus*, and decked for *Othello*. After three distinct rounds of applause, during which Mr Sempronius applied his right hand to his left breast, and bowed in the most approved manner, the manager advanced, and said —

'Ladies and Gentlemen — I assure you it is with sincere regret, that I regret to be compelled to inform you, that *Iago* who was to have played Mr Wilson — I beg your pardon, Ladies and Gentlemen, but I am naturally somewhat agitated (applause) — I mean, Mr Wilson, who was to have played *Iago*, is — that is, has been — or, in other words, Ladies and Gentleman, the fact is, that I have just received a note, in which I am informed that *Iago* is unavoidably detained at the Post-office this evening. Under these circumstances, I trust — a — a — amateur performance — a — another gentleman undertaken to read the part — request indulgence for a short time — courtesy and kindness of a British audience' — (overwhelming applause). Exit Mr Sempronius Gattleton, and curtain falls.

The audience were, of course, exceedingly good-humoured; the whole business was a joke; and accordingly they waited for an hour with the utmost patience, being enlivened by an interlude of rout-cakes and lemonade. It appeared by Mr Sempronius's subsequent explanation, that the delay would not have been so great, had it not so happened that when the substitute *Iago* had finished dressing, and just as the play was on the point of commencing, the original *Iago* unexpectedly arrived. The former was therefore compelled to undress, and the latter to dress for his part; which, as he found some difficulty in getting into his clothes, occupied no inconsiderable time. At last the tragedy began in real earnest. It went off well enough, until the third scene of the first act, in which *Othello* addresses the Senate, the only remarkable circumstance being, that as *Iago* could not get on any of the stage boots, in consequence of his feet being violently swelled with the heat and excitement, he was under the necessity of playing the part in a pair of common hessians,[10] which contrasted rather oddly with his richly embroidered pantaloons. When *Othello* started with his address to the Senate (whose dignity was represented by, the *Duke*; a carpenter, two men engaged on the recommendation of the gardener, and a boy) Mrs Porter found the opportunity she so anxiously sought.

Mr Sempronius proceeded —

> 'Most potent, grave, and reverend signiors
> My very noble and approv'd good masters, —
> That I have ta'en away this old man's daughter,
> It is most true; — rude am I in my speech —'[11]

'Is that right?' whispered Mrs Porter to Uncle Tom.
'No.'

'Tell him so, then.'

'I will. – Sem!' called out Uncle Tom, 'that's wrong, my boy.'

'What's wrong, Uncle?' demanded *Othello*, quite forgetting the dignity of his situation.

'You've left out something. "True I have married –"'

'Oh, ah!' said Mr Sempronius, endeavouring to hide his confusion as much and as ineffectually as the audience attempted to conceal their half-suppressed tittering, by coughing with the most extraordinary violence –

> —— 'true I have married her; –
> The very head and front of my offending
> Hath this extent; no more.'

(*Aside*) 'Why don't you prompt, father?'

'Because I've mislaid my spectacles,' said poor Mr Gattleton, almost dead with the heat and bustle.

'There, now it's "rude am I,"' said Uncle Tom.

'Yes, I know it is,' returned the unfortunate manager, proceeding with his part.

It would be useless and tiresome to quote the number of instances in which Uncle Tom, now completely in his element, and instigated by the mischievous Mrs Porter, corrected the mistakes of the performers; suffice it to say, that having mounted his hobby, nothing could induce him to dismount; so, during the whole remainder of the play, he performed a kind of running accompaniment, by muttering every body's part as it was being delivered, in an undertone. The audience were highly amused, Mrs Porter delighted, the performers embarrassed; Uncle Tom never was better pleased in all his life; and Uncle Tom's nephews and nieces had never, although the declared heirs to his large property, so heartily wished him gathered to his fathers as on that memorable occasion.

Several other minor causes, too, united to damp the ardour of the *dramatis personæ*. None of the performers could walk in their tights, or move their arms in their jackets; the pantaloons were too small, the boots too large, and the swords of all shapes and sizes.

Mr Evans, naturally too tall for the scenery, wore a black velvet hat with immense white plumes, the glory of which was lost in 'the flies;' and the only other inconvenience of which was, that when it was off his head he could not put it on, and when it was on he could not take it off. Notwithstanding all his practice, too, he fell with his head and shoulders as neatly through one of the side scenes, as a harlequin would jump through a panel in a Christmas pantomime. The pianoforte player, overpowered by the extreme heat of the room, fainted away at the commencement of the entertainments, leaving the music of 'Masaniello' to the flute and violoncello. The orchestra complained that Mr Harleigh put them out, and Mr Harleigh declared that the orchestra prevented his singing at all. The fishermen, who were hired for the occasion, revolted to the very life, positively refusing to play without an increased allowance of spirits; and their demand being complied with, they got drunk in the eruption scene as naturally as possible. The red fire, which was burnt at the conclusion of the second act, not only nearly suffocated the audience, but nearly set the house on fire into the bargain; and, as it was, the remainder of the piece was acted in a thick fog.

In short, the whole affair was, as Mrs Joseph Porter triumphantly told every body, 'a complete failure.' The audience went home at four o'clock in the morning, exhausted with laughter, suffering from severe headachs, and smelling terribly of brimstone and gunpowder. The Messrs Gattleton, senior and junior, retired to rest with the vague idea of emigrating to Swan River[12] early in the ensuing week.

Rose Villa has once again resumed its wonted appearance: the dining-room furniture has been replaced; the tables are as nicely polished as formerly; the horsehair chairs are ranged against the wall as regularly as ever; Venetian blinds have been fitted to every window in the house to intercept the prying gaze of Mrs Joseph Porter. The subject of theatricals is now never mentioned in the Gattleton family, unless, indeed, by Uncle Tom, who cannot refrain from sometimes expressing his surprise and regret at finding that his nephews and nieces appear to have lost the relish they once possessed for the beauties of Shakspeare, and quotations from the works of the immortal bard.

CHAPTER 10

Passage in the Life of Mr Watkins Tottle

Chapter the First

MATRIMONY is proverbially a serious undertaking. Like an over-weening predilection for brandy-and-water, it is a misfortune into which a man easily falls, and from which he finds it remarkably difficult to extricate himself. It is no use telling a man who is timorous on these points that it is but one plunge, and all is over. They say the same thing at the Old Bailey, and the unfortunate victims derive about as much comfort from the assurance in the one case as in the other.

Mr Watkins Tottle was a rather uncommon compound of strong uxorious inclinations, and an unparalleled degree of anti-connubial timidity. He was about fifty years of age; stood four feet six inches and three-quarters in his socks – for he never stood in stocking at all – plump, clean, and rosy. He looked something like a vignette to one of Richardson's novels, and had a clean-cravatish formality of manner, and kitchen-pokerness of carriage, which Sir Charles Grandison[1] himself might have envied. He lived on an annuity, which was well adapted to the individual who received it, in one respect – it was rather small. He received it in periodical payments on every alternate Monday; but he ran himself out about a day after the expiration of the first week as regularly as an eight-day clock, and then, to make the comparison complete, his landlady wound him up, and he went on with a regular tick.

Mr Watkins Tottle had long lived in a state of single blessedness, as bachelors say, or single cursedness, as spinsters think; but the idea of matrimony had never ceased to haunt him. Wrapt in profound reveries on this never-failing theme, fancy transformed his small parlour in Cecil-street[2] into a neat house in the suburbs – the half-hundredweight of coals under the kitchen-stairs suddenly sprang up into three tons of the best Walls-end[3] – his small French bedstead[4] was converted into a regular matrimonial four-poster – and on the empty chair on the opposite side of the fireplace, imagination seated a beautiful young lady with a very little independence or will of her own, and a very large independence under a will of her father's.

'Who's there?' inquired Mr Watkins Tottle, as a gentle tap at his room-door disturbed these meditations one evening.

'Tottle, my dear fellow, how *do* you do?' said a short elderly gentleman with a gruffish voice, bursting into the room, and replying to the question by asking another; and then they shook hands with a great deal of solemnity.

'Told you I should drop in some evening,' said the short gentleman, as he delivered his hat into Tottle's hand, after a little struggling and dodging.

'Delighted to see you, I'm sure,' said Mr Watkins Tottle, wishing internally, that his visiter had 'dropped in' to the Thames at the bottom of the street, instead of dropping into his parlour. The fortnight was nearly up, and Watkins was hard up.

'How is Mrs Gabriel Parsons?' inquired Tottle.

'Quite well, thank you,' replied Mr Gabriel Parsons, for that was the name the short gentleman revelled in. Here there was a pause; the short gentleman looked at the left hob of the fireplace, and Mr Watkins Tottle stared vacancy out of countenance.

'Quite well,' repeated the short gentleman, when five minutes had expired. 'I may say remarkably well,' and he rubbed the palms of his hands together as hard as if he were going to strike a light by friction.

'What will you take?' inquired Tottle, with the desperate suddenness of a man who knew that unless the visiter took his leave he stood very little chance of taking any thing else.

'Oh, I don't know. – Have you any whiskey?'

'Why,' replied Tottle, very slowly, for all this was gaining time, 'I *had* some capital, and remarkably strong whiskey last week; but it's all gone – and therefore its strength —'

'Is much beyond proof; or, in other words, impossible to be proved,' said the short gentleman; and he laughed very heartily, and seemed quite glad the whiskey had been drunk. Mr Tottle smiled – but it was the smile of despair. When Mr Gabriel Parsons had done laughing, he delicately insinuated that, in the absence of whiskey he would not be averse to brandy. And Mr Watkins Tottle, lighting a flat candle[5] very ostentatiously, and displaying an immense key, which belonged to the street-door, but which for the sake of appearances, occasionally did duty in an imaginary wine-cellar, left the room to entreat his landlady to charge their glasses, and charge them in the bill. The application was successful – the spirits were speedily called; – not from 'the vasty deep,'[6] but the adjacent wine-vaults. The two short gentlemen mixed their grog; and then sat cosily down before the fire – a pair of shorts,[7] airing themselves.

'Tottle,' said Mr Gabriel Parsons, 'you know my way – off-hand, open, say what I mean, mean what I say, damn[8] reserve, and can't bear affectation. One is a bad domino which only hides what good, people have about 'em, without making the bad look better; and the other is much about the same thing as pinking a white cotton stocking to make it look like a silk one. – Now listen to what I'm going to say.'

Here the little gentleman paused, and took a long pull at his brandy-and-water. Mr Watkins Tottle took a sip of his, stirred the fire, and assumed an air of profound attention.

'It's no use humming and ha'ing about the matter,' resumed the short gentleman. – 'You want to get married – don't you?'

'Why,' – replied Mr Watkins Tottle, evasively; for he trembled violently, and felt a sudden tingling throughout his whole frame – 'why – I should certainly – at least, I *think* I should like it.'

'Won't do,' said the short gentleman. – 'Plain and free – or there's an end of the matter. Do you want money?'

'You know I do.'

'You admire the sex?'

'I do.'

'And you'd like to be married?'

'Certainly.'

'Then you shall be. — There's an end of that.' And thus saying, Mr Gabriel Parsons took a pinch of snuff, and mixed another glass.

'Let me entreat you to be more explanatory,' said Tottle. — 'Really, as the party principally interested, I cannot consent to be disposed of in this way.'

'I'll tell you,' replied Mr Gabriel Parsons, warming with the subject, and the brandy-and-water. — 'I know a lady — she's stopping with my wife now — who is just the thing for you. — Well educated; talks French; plays the piano; knows a good deal about flowers and shells, and all that sort of thing; and has five hundred a-year, with an uncontrolled power of disposing of it, by her last will and testament.'

'I'll pay my addresses to her,' said Mr Watkins Tottle. — 'She isn't *very* young — is she?'

'Not very; just the thing for you. — I've said that already.'

'What coloured hair has the lady?' inquired Mr Watkins Tottle.

'Egad! I hardly recollect,' replied Gabriel, with great coolness. 'Perhaps I ought to have observed, at first, she wears a front.'⁹

'A what!' ejaculated Tottle.

'One of those things with curls along here,' said Parsons drawing a straight line across his forehead, just over his eyes, in illustration of his meaning. — 'I know the front's black; I can't speak quite positively about her own hair; because, unless one walks behind her, and catches a glimpse of it under her bonnet one seldom sees it; but I should say, that it was *rather* lighter than the front — just a shade of a grayish tinge, perhaps.'

Mr Watkins Tottle looked as if he had certain misgivings of mind. Mr Gabriel Parsons perceived it, and thought it would be safe to begin the next attack without delay.

'Now, were you ever in love, Tottle?' he inquired.

Mr Watkins Tottle blushed up to the eyes, and down to the

chin, and exhibited a most extensive combination of colours as he confessed the soft impeachment.

'I suppose you popped the question more than once, when you were a young – I beg your pardon – a younger – man,' said Parsons.

'Never in my life,' replied his friend, apparently indignant at being suspected of such an act. 'Never! the fact is, that I entertain, as you know, peculiar opinions on these subjects. I am not afraid of ladies, young or old – far from it; but I think, that in compliance with the custom of the present day, they allow too much freedom of speech and manner to marriageable men. Now, the fact is, that any thing like this easy freedom, I never could acquire; and as I am always afraid of going too far, I am generally, I dare say, considered formal and cold.'

'I shouldn't wonder if you were,' replied Parsons, gravely; 'I shouldn't wonder. However, you'll be all right in this case; for the strictness and delicacy of this lady's ideas greatly exceed your own. Lord bless you, why when she came to our house, there was an old portrait of some man or other with two large black staring eyes hanging up in her bedroom; she positively refused to go to bed there till it was taken down, considering it decidedly improper.'

'I think so, too,' said Mr Watkins Tottle; 'certainly.'

'And then the other night – I never laughed so much in my life,' resumed Mr Gabriel Parsons; 'I had driven home in an easterly wind, and caught a devil of a face-ache. Well; as Fanny – that's Mrs Parsons, you know – and this friend of hers, and I, and Frank Ross, were playing a rubber, I said, jokingly, that when I went to bed I should wrap my head in Fanny's flannel petticoat. She instantly threw up her cards, and left the room.'

'Quite right,' said Mr Watkins Tottle, 'she could not possibly have behaved in a more dignified manner. What did you do?'

'Do? – Frank took dummy; and I won sixpence.'

'But didn't you apologize for hurting her feelings?'

'Devil a bit. Next morning at breakfast, we talked it over. She contended that any reference to a flannel petticoat was highly

Watkins Tottle

improper; – men ought not to be supposed to know that such things were. I pleaded my coverture; being a married man.'

'And what did the lady say to that?' inquired Tottle; deeply interested.

'Changed her ground, and said that Frank being a single man, its impropriety was obvious.'

'Noble-minded creature!' exclaimed the enraptured Tottle.

'Oh! both Fanny and I said at once, that she was regularly cut out for you.'

A gleam of placid satisfaction shone on the circular face of Mr Watkins Tottle, as he heard the prophecy.

'There's one thing I can't understand,' said Mr Gabriel Parsons, as he rose to depart, 'I cannot for the life and soul of me imagine how the deuce you'll ever manage to come together. The lady would certainly go into convulsions if the subject were mentioned.' And Mr Gabriel Parsons sat down again, and laughed till he was weak. Tottle owed him money, so he had a perfect right to laugh at his expense.

Mr Watkins Tottle feared in his own mind, that this was another characteristic which he had in common with this modern Lucretia.[10] He, however, accepted the invitation to dine with the Parsonses on the next day but one, with great firmness; and looked forward to the introduction, when again left alone, with tolerable composure.

The sun that rose on the next day but one had never beheld a sprucer personage on the outside of the Norwood[11] stage than Mr Watkins Tottle, and when the coach drew up before a card-board looking house with disguised chimneys, and a lawn like a large sheet of green letter-paper, he certainly had never lighted to his place of destination a gentleman who felt more awkward or uncomfortable.

The coach stopped, and Mr Watkins Tottle jumped – we beg his pardon – alighted with great dignity. 'All right!' said he, and away went the coach up the hill with that beautiful equanimity of pace for which 'short' stages are generally remarkable.

Mr Watkins Tottle gave a faltering jerk to the handle of the garden-gate bell. He essayed a more energetic tug, and his previous nervousness was not at all diminished by hearing the bell ringing like a fire alarum.

'Is Mr Parsons at home?' inquired Tottle of the man who opened the gate. He could hardly hear himself speak, for the bell had not yet done tolling.

'Here I am,' shouted a voice on the lawn, – and there was Mr Gabriel Parsons in a flannel jacket, running backwards and forwards from a wicket to two hats piled on each other, and then from the two hats to the wicket, in the most violent manner, while another gentleman with his coat off was getting down the area of the house, after a ball. When the gentleman without the coat had found it – which he did in less than ten minutes – he ran back to the hats, and Gabriel Parsons pulled up. Then the gentleman without the coat called out 'play' very loudly, and bowled: Mr Gabriel Parsons knocked the ball several yards, and took another run. Then the other gentleman aimed at the wicket, and didn't hit it; and Mr Gabriel Parsons, having finished running on his own account, laid down the bat and ran after the ball, which went into a neighbouring field. They called this cricket.

'Tottle, will you "go in?"' inquired Mr Gabriel Parsons, as he approached him, wiping the perspiration off his face.

Mr Watkins Tottle declined the offer, the bare idea of accepting which made him even warmer than his friend.

'Then we'll go into the house as it's past four, and I shall have to wash my hands before dinner,' said Mr Gabriel Parsons. 'Here, I hate ceremony, you know – Timson, that is Tottle – Tottle, that's Timson, bred for the church, which I fear will never be bread for him;' and he chuckled at the old joke. Mr Timson bowed carelessly. Mr Watkins Tottle bowed stiffly, and Mr Gabriel Parsons led the way to the house. He was a rich sugar-baker,[12] and mistook rudeness for honesty, and abrupt bluntness for an open and candid manner; many besides Gabriel mistake bluntness for sincerity.

Mrs Gabriel Parsons received the visiters most graciously on the steps, and preceded them to the drawing-room. On the sofa was seated a lady of very prim appearance, and remarkably inanimate. She was just one of those persons at whose age it is impossible to make any reasonable guess; her features might have been remarkably pretty when she was younger, and they might always have presented the same appearance. Her complexion – with a slight trace of powder here and there – was as clear as that of a well-made wax doll, and her face as expressive. She was handsomely dressed, and was winding up a gold watch for effect.

'Miss Lillerton, my dear, this is our friend Mr Watkins Tottle; a very old acquaintance I assure you,' said Mrs Parsons, presenting the Strephon[13] of Cecil-street, Strand. The lady rose, and made a deep courtesy; Mr Watkins Tottle made a serio-comic bow.

'Splendid, majestic creature!' thought Watkins Tottle. She was his *beau idéal* of a desirable female.

Mr Timson advanced, and Mr Watkins Tottle began to hate him. Men generally discover a rival instinctively, and Mr Watkins Tottle felt that his hate was deserved.

'May I beg,' said the reverend gentleman, – 'May I beg to call upon you, Miss Lillerton, for some trifling donation to my soup, coals, and blanket distribution society?'

'Put my name down for two sovereigns, if you please,' responded Miss Lillerton.

'You are truly charitable, madam,' said the Reverend Mr Timson, 'and we know that charity will cover a multitude of sins.[14] Let me beg you to understand that I do not say this from the supposition that you have many sins which require palliation: believe me when I say that I never yet met any one who had fewer to atone for than Miss Lillerton.'

Something like a bad imitation of animation lighted up the lady's face, as she acknowledged the compliment. Watkins Tottle incurred the sin of wishing that the ashes of the Rev. Charles Timson were quietly deposited in the churchyard of his curacy, wherever it might be.

'I'll tell you what,' interrupted Parsons, who had just appeared with clean hands, and a black coat, 'it's my private opinion, Timson, that your "distribution society" is rather a humbug.'

'You are so severe,' replied Timson, with a Christian smile; he disliked Parsons, but liked his dinners.

'So positively unjust,' said Miss Lillerton.

'Certainly,' observed Tottle. The lady looked up; her eyes met those of Mr Watkins Tottle. She withdrew them in a sweet confusion, and Watkins Tottle did the same – the confusion was mutual.

'Why,' urged Mr Parsons, pursuing his objections, 'what on earth is the use of giving a man coals who has nothing to cook, or giving him blankets when he hasn't a bed, or giving him soup, when he requires substantial food? – "like sending them ruffles when wanting a shirt."[15] Why not give 'em a trifle of money, as I do, when I think they deserve it, and let them purchase what they think best. Why? – because your subscribers wouldn't see their names flourishing in print on the church-door – that's the reason.'

'Really, Mr Parsons, I hope you don't mean to insinuate that I wish to see my name in print, on the church-door,' interrupted Miss Lillerton.

'I hope not,' said Mr Watkins Tottle, putting in another word, and getting another glance.

'Certainly not,' replied Parsons. 'I dare say you wouldn't mind seeing it in writing, though, in the church register – eh?'

'Register! What register?' inquired the lady, gravely.

'Why, the register of marriages, to be sure,' replied Parsons, chuckling at the sally, and glancing at Tottle. Mr Watkins Tottle thought he should have fainted for shame, and it is quite impossible to imagine what effect the joke would have had upon the lady, if dinner had not been that moment announced. Mr Watkins Tottle, with an unprecedented effort of gallantry, offered the tip of his little finger; Miss Lillerton accepted it gracefully, with maiden modesty; and they proceeded in due state to the dinner-table, where they were soon deposited side by side. The room was very snug, the dinner very good, and the little party in tolerable spirits. The conversation became pretty general, and when Mr Watkins Tottle had extracted one or two cold observations from his neighbour, and taken wine with her, he began to acquire confidence rapidly. The cloth was removed; Mrs Gabriel Parsons drank four glasses of port on the plea of her being a nurse just then, and Miss Lillerton took about the same number of sips, on the plea of her not wanting any at all. At length the ladies retired, to the great gratification of Mr Gabriel Parsons, who had been coughing and frowning at his wife, for half an hour previously – signals which Mrs Parsons never happened to observe, until she had been pressed to take her ordinary quantum, which, to avoid giving trouble, she generally did at once.

'What do you think of her?' inquired Mr Gabriel Parsons of Mr Watkins Tottle, in an under tone.

'I dote on her with enthusiasm already,' replied Mr Watkins Tottle.

'Gentlemen, pray let us drink "the ladies,"' said the Reverend Mr Timson.

'The ladies!' said Mr Watkins Tottle, emptying his glass. In the fulness of his confidence he felt as if he could make love to a dozen ladies, off hand.

'Ah!' said Mr Gabriel Parsons, 'I remember when I was a younger man – fill your glass, Timson.'

'I have this moment emptied it.'

'Then fill again.'

'I will,' said Timson, readily suiting the action to the word.

'I remember,' resumed Mr Gabriel Parsons, 'when I was a younger man, with what a strange compound of feelings I used to drink that toast, and how I used to think that every woman was an angel – quite a superior being.'

'Was that before you were married?' mildly inquired Mr Watkins Tottle.

'Oh! certainly,' replied Mr Gabriel Parsons, 'I have never thought so since; and a precious milksop I must have been, ever to have thought so at all. But, you know, I married Fanny under the oddest, and most ridiculous circumstances possible.'

'What were they, if one may inquire?' asked Timson, who had heard the story, on an average twice a week for the last six months. Mr Watkins Tottle listened attentively, in the hope of picking up some suggestion that might be useful to him in his new undertaking.

'I spent my wedding-night in a back-kitchen chimney,' said Parsons, by way of a beginning.

'In a back-kitchen chimney!' ejaculated Watkins Tottle. 'How dreadful!'

'Yes, it wasn't very pleasant,' replied the small host. 'The fact is, that Fanny's father and mother liked me well enough as an individual, but had a decided objection to my becoming a husband. You see I hadn't any money in those days, and they had; and so they wanted Fanny to pick up somebody else. However, we managed to discover the state of each other's affections somehow. I used to meet her at some mutual friends' parties; at first we danced together, and talked, and flirted, and all that sort of thing; then I used to like nothing so well as sitting by her side – we didn't talk so much then, but I remember I used to have a great notion of looking at her out of the extreme corner of my left eye, and then I got very miserable and sentimental, and began to write verses, and use Macassar.[16] At last I couldn't bear it any longer, and after I had walked up and down the sunny side of Oxford-street in tight boots for a week – and a devilish hot summer it was too – in the hope of meeting her, I sat down and wrote a letter, and begged her to manage to see me clandestinely, for I wanted to hear her decision from her own mouth. I said I had discovered, to my perfect satisfaction, that I couldn't live without her, and that if she didn't have me, I had made up my mind to take prussic acid, or take to drinking, or emigrate, so as to take myself off in some way or other. Well, I borrowed a pound, and bribed the housemaid to give her the note, which she did.'

'And what was the reply?' inquired Timson, who had found before, that encouraging the repetition of old stories is sure to end in a general invitation.

'Oh, the usual one, you know – Fanny expressed herself very miserable; hinted at the possibility of an early grave; said that nothing should induce her to swerve from the duty she owed her parents; and implored me to forget her, and find out somebody more deserving, and all that sort of thing. She said she could on no account think of meeting me unknown to her pa and ma; and entreated me, as she should be in a particular part of Kensington Gardens[17] at eleven o'clock next morning, not to attempt to meet her there.'

'You didn't go, of course?' said Watkins Tottle.

'Didn't I? – Of course I did. There she was, with the identical housemaid in perspective, in order that there might be no interruption. We walked about for a couple of hours; made ourselves delightfully miserable; and were regularly engaged. Then we began to "correspond" – that is to say, we used to exchange about four letters a day; what we used to say in 'em I can't imagine. And I used to have an interview in the kitchen, or in the cellar, or some such place, every evening. Well, things went on in this way for some time; and we got fonder of each other every day. At last, as our love was raised to such a pitch, and as my salary had been raised too, shortly before, we determined on a secret marriage. Fanny arranged to sleep at a friend's the previous night; we were to be married early in the morning, and then we were to return to her home and be pathetic. She was to fall at the old gentleman's feet, and bathe his boots with her tears; and I was to hug the old lady and call her "mother," and use my pocket-handkerchief as much as possible. Married we were the next morning; two girls – friends of Fanny's – acting as bridemaids, and a man, who was hired for five shillings and a pint of porter, officiating as father. Now, the old lady unfortunately put off her return from Ramsgate where she had been paying a visit, until the next morning; and as we placed great reliance upon her, we agreed to postpone our confession for four-and-twenty hours. My newly-made wife returned home and I spent my wedding-day in strolling about Hampstead-heath[18] and damning[19] my father-in-law. Of course I went to comfort my dear little wife at night as much as I could, with the assurance that our troubles would soon be over. I opened the garden-gate of which I had a key, and was shown by the servant to our old place of meeting – a back kitchen with a stone-floor and a dresser, upon which, in the absence of chairs, we used to sit and make love.'

'Make love upon a kitchen-dresser!' interrupted Mr Watkins Tottle, whose ideas of decorum were greatly outraged.

'Ah! – on a kitchen dresser!' replied Parsons. – 'And let me tell you, old fellow, that, if you were really over head-and-ears in love, and had no other place to make love in, you'd be devilish glad to avail yourself of such an opportunity. However, let me see; – where was I?'

'On the dresser,' suggested Timson.

'Oh – ah? Well, here I found poor Fanny, quite disconsolate and uncomfortable. The old boy had been very cross all day, which made her feel still more lonely; and she was quite out of spirits. So I put a good face on the matter, and laughed it off, and said we should enjoy the pleasures of a matrimonial life more by contrast; and, at length, poor Fanny brightened up a little. I stopped there till about eleven o'clock, and, just as I was taking my leave for the fourteenth time' the girl came running down stairs, without her shoes, in a great fright, to tell us that the old villain – God[20] forgive me for calling him so, for he is dead and gone now – prompted I suppose by the prince of darkness, was coming down to draw his own beer for supper – a thing he had not done before for six months, to my certain knowledge; for the cask stood in that very back kitchen. If he discovered me there, explanation would have been out of the question; for he was so outrageously violent, when at all excited, that he never would have listened to me. There was only one thing to be done. – The chimney was a very wide one: it had been originally built for an oven; went up perpendicularly for a few feet, and then shot backward and formed a sort of small cavern. My hopes and fortune – the means of our joint existence almost – were at stake. I scrambled in like a squirrel; coiled myself up in this recess; and, as Fanny and the girl replaced the deal chimney-board, I could see the light of the candle which my unconscious father-in-law carried in his hand. I heard him draw the beer; and I never heard beer run so slowly. He was just leaving the kitchen and I was preparing to descend, when down came the infernal chimney-board with a tremendous crash. He stopped, and put down the candle and the jug of beer on the dresser; he was a nervous old fellow; and any unexpected noise annoyed him. He coolly observed that the fireplace was never used, and sending the frightened servant into the next kitchen for hammer and nails, actually nailed up the board, and locked the door on the outside. So there was I on my wedding-night, in the light kerseymere[21] trousers, fancy waistcoat and blue coat that I had been married in in the morning, in a back-kitchen chimney, the bottom of which was nailed up, and the top of which had been formerly raised some fifteen feet, to prevent the smoke from annoying the neighbours. And there,' added Mr Gabriel Parsons, as he passed the bottle – 'there I remained till half-past seven the next morning, when the housemaid's sweetheart, who was a carpenter, unshelled me. The old dog had nailed me up so securely, that, to this very hour, I firmly believe that no one but a carpenter could ever have got me out.'

'And what did Mrs Parsons's father say, when he found you were married?' inquired Watkins Tottle, who, although he never saw a joke, was not satisfied until he heard a story to the very end.

'Why, the affair of the chimney so tickled his fancy that he pardoned us off-hand, and allowing us something to live upon till he went the way of all flesh. I spent the next night in his second-floor front much more comfortably than I had spent the preceding one; for, as you will probably guess —'

'Please sir, missis has made tea,' said a middle-aged female servant, bobbing into the room.

'That's the very housemaid that figures in my story,' said Mr Gabriel Parsons. – 'She went into Fanny's service when we were first married, and has been with us ever since; but I don't think she has felt one atom of respect for me since the morning she saw me released, when she went into violent hysterics, to which she has been subject ever since. Now, shall we join the ladies?'

'If you please,' said Mr Watkins Tottle.

'By all means,' added the obsequious Mr Timson; and the trio made for the drawing-room accordingly.

Tea being concluded, and the toast and cups having been duly handed, and occasionally upset, by Mr Watkins Tottle, a rubber was proposed. They cut for partners – Mr and Mrs Parsons; and Mr Watkins Tottle and Miss Lillerton. Mr Timson being a clergyman,[22] and having conscientious scruples on the subject of card-playing, drank brandy-and-water, and kept up a running spar with

Mr Watkins Tottle. The evening went off well; Mr Watkins Tottle was in high spirits, having some reason to be gratified with his reception by Miss Lillerton; and before he left, a small party was made up to visit the Beulah Spa[23] on the following Saturday.

'It's all right, I think,' said Mr Gabriel Parsons to Mr Watkins Tottle, as he opened the garden gate for him.

'I hope so,' he replied, squeezing his friend's hand.

'You'll be down by the first coach on Saturday,' said Mr Gabriel Parsons.

'Certainly,' replied Mr Watkins Tottle. 'Undoubtedly.'

But fortune had decreed that Mr Watkins Tottle should not be down by the first coach on Saturday. His adventures on that day however, and the success of his wooing, are subjects for another chapter.

Chapter the Second

'THE first coach has not come in yet, has it, Tom?' inquired Mr Gabriel Parsons, as he very complacently paced up and down the fourteen feet of gravel which bordered the 'lawn,' on the Saturday morning which had been fixed upon for the Beulah Spa jaunt.

'No, sir; I haven't seen it,' replied a gardener in a blue apron, who let himself out to do the ornamental for half-a-crown a day and his 'keep.'

'Time Tottle was down,' said Mr Gabriel Parsons, ruminating – 'Oh, here he is, no doubt,' added Gabriel, as a cab drove rapidly up the hill; and he buttoned his dressing-gown, and opened the gate to receive the expected visiter. The cab stopped, and out jumped a man in a coarse Petersham great-coat,[24] whity-brown neckerchief, faded black suit, gamboge-coloured top-boots, and one of those large-crowned hats, formerly seldom met with, but now very generally patronized by gentlemen and coster-mongers.

'Mr Parsons?' said the man, looking at the superscription of a note he held in his hand, and addressing Gabriel with an inquiring air.

'*My* name is Parsons,' responded the sugar-baker.

'I've brought this here note,' replied the individual in the painted tops,[25] in a hoarse whisper; 'I've brought this here note from a gen'lm'n as come to our house this mornin'.'

'I expected the gentleman at my house,' said Parsons, as he broke the seal, which bore the impression of her majesty's profile, as it is seen on a sixpence.

'I've no doubt the gen'lm'n would ha' been here,' replied the stranger, 'if he hadn't happened to call at our house first; but we never trusts no gen'lm'n furder nor we can see him – no mistake about that there' – added the unknown, with a facetious grin; 'beg yer pardon, sir, no offence meant, only – once in, and I wish you may[26] – catch the idea, sir?'

Mr Gabriel Parsons was not remarkable for catching any thing suddenly, but a cold. He therefore only bestowed a glance of profound astonishment on his mysterious companion, and proceeded to unfold the note of which he had been the bearer. Once opened and the idea was caught with very little difficulty. Mr Watkins Tottle had been suddenly arrested for 33*l*. 10*s*. 4*d*., and dated his communication from a lock-up house in the vicinity of Chancery-lane.[27]

'Unfortunate affair, this!' said Parsons refolding the note.

'Oh! nothin' ven you're used to it,' coolly observed the man in the Petersham.

'Tom!' exclaimed Parsons, after a few minutes' consideration, 'just put the horse in, will you? – Tell the gentleman that I shall be there almost as soon as you are,' he continued, addressing the sheriff-officer's Mercury.[28]

'Werry well,' replied that important functionary; adding, in a confidential manner, 'I'd adwise the gen'lm'n's friends to settle. You see it's a mere trifle, and, unless the gen'lm'n means to go up afore the court, it's hardly worth while waiting for detainers you know. Our governor's wide awake, he is. I'll never say nothin' agin him, nor no man; but he knows what's o'clock, he does, uncommon.' Having delivered this eloquent, and, to Parsons, particularly intelligible harangue, the meaning of which was eked out by divers nods and winks, the gentleman in the boots reseated himself in the cab which went rapidly off, and was soon out of sight. Mr Gabriel Parsons continued to pace up and down the pathway for some minutes, apparently absorbed in deep meditation. The result of his cogitations seemed to be perfectly satisfactory to himself, for he ran briskly into the house; said that business had suddenly summoned him to town; that he had desired the messenger to inform Mr Watkins Tottle of the fact; and that they would return together to dinner. He then hastily equipped himself for a drive, and mounting his gig was soon on his way to the establishment of Mr Solomon Jacobs, situate (as Mr Watkins Tottle had informed him) in Cursitor-street, Chancery-lane.

When a man is in a violent hurry to get on, and has a specific object in view, the attainment of which depends on the completion of his journey, the difficulties which interpose themselves in his way appear not only to be innumerable, but to have been called into existence especially for the occasion. The remark is by no means a new one, and Mr Gabriel Parsons had practical and painful experience of its justice in the course of his drive. There are three classes of animated objects which prevent your driving with any degree of comfort or celerity through streets which are but little frequented – they are pigs, children, and old women. On the occasion we are describing, the pigs were luxuriating on cabbage-stalks, and the shuttlecocks fluttered from the little deal battle-dores, and the children played in the road; and women, with a basket in one hand and the street-door key in the other, *would* cross just before the horse's head, until Mr Gabriel Parsons was perfectly savage with vexation, and quite hoarse with hoi-ing and imprecat-ing. Then, when he got into Fleet-street, there was 'a stoppage,' in which people in vehicles have the satisfaction of remaining stationary for half an hour, and envying the slowest pedestrians; and where policemen rush about, and seize hold of horses' bridles, and back them into shop-windows, by way of clearing the road and preventing confusion. At length Mr Gabriel Parsons turned into Chancery-lane, and having inquired for, and been directed to, Cursitor-street (for it was a locality of which he was quite ignorant), he soon found himself opposite the house of Mr Solomon Jacobs.

Confiding his horse and gig to the care of one of the fourteen boys who had followed him from the other side of Blackfriars-bridge on the chance of his requiring their services, Mr Gabriel Parsons crossed the road and knocked at an inner door, the upper part of which was of glass, grated like the windows of this inviting mansion with iron bars – painted white to look comfortable.

The knock was answered by a sallow-faced red-haired sulky boy, who, after surveying Mr Gabriel Parsons through the glass applied a large key to an immense wooden excrescence, which was in reality a lock, but which, taken in conjunction with the iron nails with which the panels were studded, gave the door the appearance of being subject to warts.

'I want to see Mr Watkins Tottle,' said Parsons.

'It's the gentleman that come in this morning, Jem,' screamed a voice from the top of the kitchen stairs, which belonged to a dirty woman who had just brought her chin to a level with the passage-floor. 'The gentleman's in the coffee-room.'

'Up stairs, sir,' said the boy, just opening the door wide enough to let Parsons in without squeezing him, and double-locking it the moment he had made his way through the aperture – 'First floor – door on the left.'

Mr Gabriel Parsons, thus instructed, ascended the uncarpeted and ill-lighted staircase, and after giving several subdued taps at the before-mentioned 'door on the left,' which were rendered inaudible by the hum of voices within the room, and the hissing noise attendant on some frying operations which were carrying on below stairs, turned the handle, and entered the apartment. Being informed that the unfortunate object of his visit had just gone up stairs to write a letter, he had leisure to sit down and observe the scene before him.

The room – which was a small, confined den – was partitioned off into boxes, like the common room of some inferior eating-house. The dirty floor had evidently been as long a stranger to the scrubbing-brush as to carpet or floor-cloth; and the ceiling was completely blackened by the flare of the oil-lamp by which the room was lighted at night. The gray ashes on the edges of the tables, and the cigar ends which were plentifully scattered about the dusty grate, fully accounted for the intolerable smell of tobacco which pervaded the place; and the empty glasses and half-saturated slices of lemon on the tables, together with the porter-pots beneath them, bore testimony to the frequent libations in which the individuals who honoured Mr Solomon Jacobs by a temporary residence in his house indulged. Over the mantel-shelf was a paltry looking-glass, extending about half the width of the chimney-piece; but, by way of counterpoise, the ashes were confined by a rusty fender about twice as long as the hearth.

From this cheerful room itself, the attention of Mr Gabriel Parsons' was naturally directed to its inmates. In one of the boxes two men were playing at cribbage with a very dirty pack of cards, some with blue, some with green, and some with red backs – selections from decayed packs. The cribbage-board had been long ago formed on the table by some ingenious visiter with the assistance of a pocket-knife and a two-pronged fork, with which the necessary number of holes had been made in the table at proper distances for the reception of the wooden pegs. In another box a stout, hearty-looking man, of about forty, was eating some dinner, which his wife – an equally comfortable-looking personage – had brought him in a basket; and in a third, a genteel-looking young man was talking earnestly, and in a low tone to a young female, whose face was concealed by a thick veil, but whom Mr Gabriel Parsons immediately set down in his own mind as the debtor's wife. A young fellow of vulgar manners, dressed in the very extreme of the prevailing fashion, was pacing up and down the room, with a lighted cigar in his mouth and his hands in his pockets, ever and anon puffing forth volumes of smoke, and occasionally applying, with much apparent relish, to a pint pot, the contents of which were 'chilling'[29] on the hob.

'Fourpence more, by gum!' exclaimed one of the cribbage-players, lighting a pipe, and addressing his adversary at the close of the game; 'one 'ud think you'd got luck in a pepper-cruet, and shook it out when you wanted it.'

'Well, that a'n't a bad un,' replied the other, who was a horse-dealer from Islington.[30]

'No; I'm blessed if it is,' interposed the jolly-looking fellow, who, having finished his dinner, was drinking out of the same glass as his wife, in truly conjugal harmony, some hot gin-and-water. The faithful partner of his cares had brought a plentiful supply of the anti-temperance fluid in a large flat stone bottle, which looked like a half-gallon jar that had been successfully tapped for the dropsy. 'You're a rum chap, you are, Mr Walker – will you dip your beak into this, sir?'

'Thank'ee, sir,' replied Mr Walker, leaving his box, and advancing to the other to accept the proffered glass. 'Here's your health, sir, and your good 'ooman's here. Gentlemen all – yours, and better luck still. Well, Mr Willis,' continued the facetious prisoner, addressing the young man with the cigar, 'you seem rather down to-day – floored, as one may say. What's the matter sir? Never say die, you know.'

'Oh! I'm all right,' replied the smoker. 'I shall be bailed out to-morrow.'

'Shall you, though?' inquired the other. 'Damme, I wish I could say the same. I am as regularly over head and ears as the Royal George, and stand about as much chance of being *bailed out*.[31] Ha! ha! ha!'

'Why,' said the young man, stopping short, and speaking in a very loud key, 'Look at me. What d'ye think I've stopped here two days for?'

''Cause you couldn't get out, I suppose,' interrupted Mr Walker, winking to the company. 'Not that you're exactly obliged to stop here, only you can't help it. No compulsion, you know, only you must – eh?'

'A'n't he a rum un?' inquired the delighted individual, who had offered the gin-and-water, of his wife.

'Oh, he just is!' replied the lady, who was quite overcome by these flashes of imagination.

'Why, my case,' frowned the victim, throwing the end of his cigar into the fire, and illustrating his argument by knocking the

The Lock-up house

bottom of the pot on the table, at intervals, – 'my case is a very singular one. My father's a man of large property, and I am his son.'

'That's a very strange circumstance!' interrupted the jocose Mr Walker, *en passant*.

'– I am his son, and have received a liberal education. I don't owe no man nothing – not the value of a farthing, but I was induced, you see, to put my name to some bills for a friend – bills to a large amount, I may say a very large amount, for which I didn't receive no consideration. What's the consequence?'

'Why, I suppose the bills went out, and you came in. The acceptances weren't taken up, and you were, eh?' inquired Walker.

'To be sure,' replied the liberally-educated young gentleman. 'To be sure; and so here I am, locked up for a matter of twelve hundred pound.'

'Why don't you ask your old governor to stump up?' inquired Walker, with a somewhat sceptical air.

'Oh! bless you, he'd never do it,' replied the other, in a tone of expostulation – 'Never!'

'Well, it is very odd to – be – sure,' interposed the owner of the flat bottle, mixing another glass, 'but I've been in difficulties, as one may say, now for thirty year. I went to pieces when I was in a milk-walk,[32] thirty year ago; arterwards, when I was a fruiterer, and kept a spring wan; and arter that again in the coal and 'tatur line[33] – but all that time I never see a youngish chap come into a place of this kind, who wasn't going out again directly, and who hadn't been arrested on bills which he'd given a friend and for which he'd received nothing whatsomever – not a fraction.'

'Oh! it's always the cry,' said Walker. 'I can't see the use on it; that's what makes me so wild. Why, I should have a much better opinion of an individual, if he'd say at once in an honourable and gentlemanly manner as he'd done every body he possible could.'

'Ay, to be sure,' interposed the horse-dealer, with whose notions of bargain and sale the axiom perfectly coincided, 'so should I.'

The young gentleman, who had given rise to these observations, was on the point of offering a rather angry reply to these sneers, but the rising of the young man before noticed, and of the female who had been sitting by him, to leave the room, interrupted the conversation. She had been weeping bitterly, and the noxious atmosphere of the room acting upon her excited feelings and delicate frame, rendered the support of her companion necessary as they quitted it together.

There was an air of superiority about them both, and something in their appearance so unusual in such a place, that a respectful silence was observed until the *whirr–r–bang* of the spring door announced that they were out of hearing. It was broken by the wife of the ex-fruiterer.

'Poor creetur!' said she, quenching a sigh in a rivulet of gin-and-water. 'She's very young.'

'She's a nice-looking 'ooman too,' added the horse-dealer.

'What's he in for, Ikey?' inquired Walker, of an individual who was spreading a cloth with numerous blotches of mustard upon it, on one of the tables, and whom Mr Gabriel Parsons had no difficulty in recognising as the man who had called upon him in the morning.

'Vy,' responded the factotum, 'it's one of the rummest rigs you ever heard on. He come in here last Vensday, which by the by he's a going over the water[34] to-night – hows'ever that's neither here nor there. You see I've been a going back'ards and for'ards about his business, and ha' managed to pick up some of his story from the servants and them; and so far as I can make it out, it seems to be summat to this here effect —'

'Cut it short, old fellow,' interrupted Walker, who knew from former experience that he of the top-boots was neither very concise nor intelligible in his narratives.

'Let me alone,' replied Ikey, 'and I'll ha' vound up, and made my lucky[35] in five seconds. This here young gen'lm'n's father so I'm told, mind ye – and the father o' the young voman, have always been on very bad, out-and-out, rig'lar knock-me-down sort o' terms; but somehow or another, when he was a wisitin' at some gentlefolk's house, as he knowed at college, he come into contract with the young lady. He seed her several times, and then he up and said he'd keep company with her, if so be as she vos agreeable. Vell, she vos as sweet upon him as he vos upon her, and so I s'pose they made it all right; for they got married 'bout six months arterwards, unbeknown, mind ye, to the two fathers – leastways so I'm told. When they heard on it – my eyes, there was such a combustion! Starvation vos the very least that vos to be done to 'em. The young gen'lm'n's father cut him off vith a bob, 'cos he'd cut himself off vith a wife; and the young lady's father he behaved even worser and more unnat'ral, for he not only blow'd her up dreadful, and swore he'd never see her again, but he employed a chap as I knows – and as you knows, Mr Valker, a precious sight too well – to go about and buy up the bills and them things on which the young husband, thinking his governor 'ud come round agin, had raised the vind[36] just to blow himself on vith for a time; besides vich, he made all the interest he could to set other people agin him. Consequence vos, that he paid as long as he could; but things he never expected to have to meet till he'd had time to turn himself round, come fast upon him, and he vos nabbed. He vos brought here, as I said afore, last Vensday, and I think there's about – ah, half-a-dozen detainers agin him down stairs now. I have been,' added Ikey, 'in the purfession these fifteen year, and I never met vith such windictiveness afore!'

'Poor creeturs!' exclaimed the coal-dealer's wife once more: again resorting to the same excellent prescription for nipping a sigh in the bud; 'Ah! when they've seen as much trouble as I and my old man here have, they'll be as comfortable under it as we are.'

'The young lady's a pretty creature,' said Walker, 'only she's a little too delicate for my taste – there ain't enough of her. As to the young cove, he may be very respectable and what not, but he's too down in the mouth for me – he ain't game.'

'Game!' exclaimed Ikey, who had been altering the position of a green-handled knife and fork at least a dozen times, in order that he might remain in the room under the pretext of having something to do. 'He's game enough ven there's any thing to be fierce about; but who could be game as you call it, Mr Walker, with a pale young creetur like that, hanging about him? – It's enough to drive any man's heart into his boots to see 'em together — and no mistake at all about it. I never shall forget her first comin' here; he wrote to her on the Thursday to come — I know he did, 'cos I took the letter. Uncommon fidgety he was all day to be sure, and in the evening he goes down into the office, and he says to Jacobs, says he, "Sir, can I have the loan of a private room for a few minutes this evening, without incurring any additional expense — just to see my wife in?" says he. Jacobs looked as much as to say — "Strike me bountiful if you ain't one of the modest sort!" but as the gen'lm'n who had been in the back parlour had just gone out, and had paid for it for that day, he says — werry grave — "Sir," says he, "it's agin our rules to let private rooms to our lodgers on gratis terms, but," says he, "for a gentleman, I don't mind breaking through them for once." So then he turns round to me, and says, "Ikey, put two mould candles[37] in the back parlour, and charge 'em to this gen'lm'n's account," vich I did. Vell, by-and-by a hackney-coach comes up to the door, and there, sure enough, was the young lady, wrapped up in a hopera-cloak, as it might be, and all alone. I opened the gate that night, so I went up when the coach come, and he vos a waitin' at the parlour-door — and wasn't he a tremblin', neither? The poor creetur see him, and could hardly walk to meet him. "Oh, Harry!" she says, "that it should have come to this! and all for my sake," says she, putting her hand upon his shoulder. So he puts his arm round her pretty little waist, and leading her gently a little way into the room, so that he might be able to shut the door, he says, so kind and soft-like — "Why, Kate," says he —'

'Here's the gentleman you want,' said Ikey, abruptly breaking off in his story, and introducing Mr Gabriel Parsons to the crestfallen Watkins Tottle, who at that moment entered the room. Watkins advanced with a wooden expression of passive endurance, and accepted the hand which Mr Gabriel Parsons held out.

'I want to speak to you,' said Gabriel, with a look strongly expressive of his dislike of the company.

'This way,' replied the imprisoned one, leading the way to the front drawing-room, where rich debtors did the luxurious at the rate of a couple of guineas a day.

'Well, here I am,' said Watkins, as he sat down on the sofa; and placing the palms of his hands on his knees, anxiously glanced at his friend's countenance.

'Yes; and here you're likely to be,' said Gabriel, coolly, as he rattled the money in his unmentionable[38] pockets, and looked out of the window.

'What's the amount with the costs?' inquired Parsons, after an awkward pause.

'37*l*. 3*s*. 10*d*.'[39]

'Have you any money?'

'Nine and sixpence halfpenny.'

Mr Gabriel Parsons walked up and down the room for a few seconds, before he could make up his mind to disclose the plan he had formed; he was accustomed to drive hard bargains, but was always most anxious to conceal his avarice. At length he stopped short, and said, – 'Tottle, you owe me fifty pounds.'

'I do.'

'And from all I see, I infer that you are likely to owe it me.'

'I fear I am.'

'Though you have every disposition to pay me if you could?'

'Certainly.'

'Then,' said Mr Gabriel Parsons, 'listen; here's my proposition. You know my way of old. Accept it – yes or no – I will or I won't. I'll pay the debt and costs, and I'll lend you 10*l*. more (which, added to your annuity, will enable you to carry on the war well), if you'll give me your note of hand to pay me one hundred and fifty pounds within six months after you are married to Miss Lillerton.'

'My dear —'

'Stop a minute – on one condition; and that is, that you propose to Miss Lillerton at once.'

'At once! My dear Parsons, consider.'

'It's for you to consider, not me. She knows you well from reputation, though she did not know you personally until lately. Notwithstanding all her maiden modesty, I think she'd be devilish glad to get married out of hand, with as little delay as possible. My wife has sounded her on the subject, and she has confessed.'

'What — what?' eagerly interrupted the enamoured Watkins.

'Why,' replied Parsons, 'to say exactly what she has confessed, would be rather difficult, because they only spoke in hints, and so forth; but my wife, who is no bad judge in these cases, declared to me that what she had confessed was as good as to say, that she was not insensible of your merits — in fact, that no other man should have her.'

Mr Watkins Tottle rose hastily from his seat, and rang the bell.

'What's that for?' inquired Parsons.

'I want to send the man for the bill stamp,' replied Mr Watkins Tottle.

'Then you've made up your mind?'

'I have,' — and they shook hands most cordially. The note of hand was given — the debt and costs were paid — Ikey was satisfied for his trouble, and the two friends soon found themselves on that side of Mr Solomon Jacobs's establishment, on which most of his visiters were very happy when they found themselves once again — to wit, the *out*side.

'Now,' said Mr Gabriel Parsons, as they drove to Norwood together — 'you shall have an opportunity to make the disclosure to-night, and mind you speak out, Tottle.'

'I will — I will!' replied Watkins, valorously.

'How I should like to see you together!' ejaculated Mr Gabriel Parsons. — 'What fun!' — and he laughed so long and so loudly, that he disconcerted Mr Watkins Tottle, and frightened the horse.

'There's Fanny and your intended, walking about on the lawn,' said Gabriel, as they approached the house — 'Mind your eye, Tottle.'

'Never fear,' replied Watkins, resolutely, as he made his way to the spot where the ladies were walking.

'Here's Mr Tottle, my dear,' said Mrs Parsons, addressing Miss Lillerton. The lady turned quickly round, and acknowledged his courteous salute with the same sort of confusion that Watkins had noticed on their first interview, but with something like a slight expression of disappointment or carelessness.

'Did you see how glad she was to see you?' whispered Parsons to his friend.

'Why I really thought she looked as if she would rather have seen somebody else,' replied Tottle.

'Pooh, nonsense!' whispered Parsons again — 'it's always the way with the women, young or old. They never show how delighted they are to see those whose presence makes their hearts beat. It's the way with the whole sex, and no man should have lived to your time of life without knowing it. Fanny confessed it to me, when we were first married over and over again — see what it is to have a wife.'

'Certainly,' whispered Tottle, whose courage was vanishing fast.

'Well now, you'd better begin to pave the way,' said Parsons, who, having invested some money in the speculation, assumed the office of director.

'Yes, yes, I will — presently,' replied Tottle, greatly flurried.

'Say something to her, man,' urged Parsons again. 'Confound it! pay her a compliment, can't you?'

'No! not till after dinner,' replied the bashful Tottle, anxious to postpone the evil moment.

'Well, gentlemen,' said Mrs Parsons, 'you are really very polite; you stay away the whole morning, after promising to take us out, and when you do come home, you stand whispering together and take no notice of us.'

'We were talking of the *business*, my dear, which detained us this morning,' replied Parsons, looking significantly at Tottle.

'Dear me! how very quickly the morning has gone,' said Miss Lillerton, referring to the gold watch, which was wound up on state occasions, whether it required it or not.

'*I* think it has passed very slowly,' mildly suggested Tottle.

('That's right — bravo!') whispered Parsons.

'Indeed!' said Miss Lillerton, with an air of majestic surprise.

'I can only impute it to my unavoidable absence from your society, madam,' said Watkins, 'and that of Mrs Parsons.'

During this short dialogue, the ladies had been leading the way to the house.

'What the deuce did you stick Fanny into that last compliment for?' inquired Parsons, as they followed together; 'it quite spoilt the effect.'

'Oh! it really would have been too broad without,' replied Watkins Tottle, 'much too broad!'

'He's mad!' Parsons whispered his wife, as they entered the drawing-room, 'mad from modesty.'

'Dear me!' ejaculated the lady, 'I never heard of such a thing.'

'You'll find we have quite a family dinner, Mr Tottle,' said Mrs Parsons, when they sat down to table: 'Miss Lillerton is one of us, and of course, we make no stranger of you.'

Mr Watkins Tottle expressed a hope that the Parsons family never would make a stranger of him; and wished internally that his bashfulness would allow him to feel a little less like a stranger himself.

'Take off the covers, Martha,' said Mrs Parsons, directing the shifting of the scenery with great anxiety. The order was obeyed, and a pair of boiled fowls, with tongue and et ceteras, were displayed at the top, and a fillet of veal at the bottom. On one side of the table two green sauce-tureens, with ladles of the same, were setting to each other in a green dish; and on the other was a curried rabbit, in a brown suit, turned up with lemon.

'Miss Lillerton, my dear,' said Mrs Parsons, 'shall I assist you?'

'Thank you, no; I think I'll trouble Mr Tottle.'

Watkins started – trembled – helped the rabbit – and broke a tumbler. The countenance of the lady of the house, which had been all smiles previously, underwent an awful change.

'Extremely sorry,' stammered Watkins, assisting himself to currie and parsley and butter, in the extremity of his confusion.

'Not the least consequence,' replied Mrs Parsons, in a tone which implied that it was of the greatest consequence possible, – directing aside the researches of the boy, who was groping under the table for the bits of broken glass.

'I presume,' said Miss Lillerton, 'that Mr Tottle is aware of the interest which bachelors usually pay in such cases; a dozen glasses for one is the lowest penalty.'

Mr Gabriel Parsons gave his friend an admonitory tread on the toe. Here was a clear hint that the sooner he ceased to be a bachelor and emancipated himself from such penalties, the better. Mr Watkins Tottle viewed the observation in the same light, and challenged Mrs Parsons to take wine, with a degree of presence of mind, which, under all the circumstances, was really extraordinary.

'Miss Lillerton,' said Gabriel, 'may I have the pleasure?'

'I shall be most happy.'

'Tottle will you assist Miss Lillerton, and pass the decanter. Thank you.' (The usual pantomimic ceremony of nodding and sipping gone through) –

'Tottle, were you ever in Suffolk?' inquired the master of the house, who was burning to tell one of his seven stock stories.

'No,' responded Watkins, adding, by way of a saving clause, 'but I've been in Devonshire.'

'Ah!' replied Gabriel, 'it was in Suffolk that a rather singular circumstance happened to me, many years ago. Did you ever happen to hear me mention it?'

Mr Watkins Tottle *had* happened to hear his friend mention it some four hundred times. Of course he expressed great curiosity, and evinced the utmost impatience to hear the story again. Mr Gabriel Parsons forthwith attempted to proceed, in spite of the interruptions to which, as our readers must frequently have observed, the master of the house is often exposed in such cases. We will attempt to give them an idea of our meaning.

'When I was in Suffolk,' said Mr Gabriel Parsons —

'Take off the fowls first, Martha,' said Mrs Parsons. 'I beg your pardon, my dear.'

'When I was in Suffolk,' resumed Mr Parsons, with an impatient glance at his wife, who pretended not to observe it, 'which is now some years ago, business led me to the town of Bury St Edmund's.[40] I had to stop at the principal places in my way, and therefore, for the sake of convenience, I travelled in a gig. I left Sudbury one dark night – it was winter time – about nine o'clock; the rain poured in torrents, the wind howled among the trees that skirted the road-side, and I was obliged to proceed at a foot-pace, for I could hardly see my hand before me, it was so dark —'

'John,' interrupted Mrs Parsons, in a low, hollow voice, 'don't spill that gravy.'

'Fanny,' said Parsons impatiently, 'I wish you'd defer these domestic reproofs to some more suitable time. Really, my dear, these constant interruptions are very annoying.'

'My dear, I didn't interrupt you,' said Mrs Parsons.

'But, my dear, you *did* interrupt me,' remonstrated Mr Parsons.

'How very absurd you are, my love! I must give directions to the servants; I am quite sure that if I sat here and allowed John to spill the gravy over the new carpet, you'd be the first to find fault when you saw the stain to-morrow morning.'

'Well,' continued Gabriel, with a resigned air, as if he knew there was no getting over the point about the carpet, 'I was just saying, it was so dark that I could hardly see my hand before me. The road was very lonely, and I assure you Tottle (this was a device to arrest the wandering attention of that individual, which was distracted by a confidential communication between Mrs Parsons and Martha, accompanied by the delivery of a large bunch of keys), I assure you, Tottle, I became somehow impressed with a sense of the loneliness of my situation —'

'Pie to your master,' interrupted Mrs Parsons, again directing the servant.

'Now, pray, my dear,' remonstrated Parsons once more, very pettishly. Mrs P. turned up her hands and eyebrows, and appealed in dumb show to Miss Lillerton. 'As I turned a corner of the road,' resumed Gabriel, 'the horse stopped short, and reared tremendously. I pulled up, jumped out, ran to his head, and found a man lying on his back in the middle of the road, with his eyes fixed on the sky. I thought he was dead; but no, he was alive, and there appeared to be nothing the matter with him. He jumped up, and putting his hand to his chest, and fixing upon me the most earnest gaze you can imagine, exclaimed —'

'Pudding here,' said Mrs Parsons.

'Oh! it's no use,' exclaimed the host, now rendered desperate.

'Here, Tottle; a glass of wine. It's useless to attempt relating any thing when Mrs Parsons is present.'

This attack was received in the usual way. Mrs Parsons talked *to* Miss Lillerton and *at* her better half; expatiated on the impatience of men generally; hinted that her husband was peculiarly vicious in this respect, and wound up by insinuating that she must be one of the best tempers that ever existed, or she never could put up with it. Really what she had to endure sometimes, was more than any one who saw her in every-day life could by possibility suppose. – The story was now a painful subject, and therefore Mr Parsons declined to enter into any details, and contented himself by stating that the man was a maniac, who had escaped from a neighbouring mad-house.

The cloth was removed; the ladies soon afterwards retired, and Miss Lillerton played the piano in the drawing-room overhead, very loudly, for the edification of the visiter. Mr Watkins Tottle and Mr Gabriel Parsons sat chatting comfortably enough, until the conclusion of the second bottle, when the latter, in proposing an adjournment to the drawing-room, informed Watkins that he had concerted a plan with his wife, for leaving him and Miss Lillerton alone, soon after tea.

'I say,' said Tottle, as they went up stairs, 'don't you think it would be better if we put it off till – till – to-morrow?'

'Don't *you* think it would have been much better if I had left you in that wretched hole I found you in this morning?' retorted Parsons, bluntly.

'Well – well – I only made a suggestion,' said poor Watkins Tottle, with a deep sigh.

Tea was soon concluded, and Miss Lillerton drawing a small work-table on one side of the fire, and placing a little wooden frame upon it, something like a miniature clay-mill without the horse, was soon busily engaged in making a watch-guard[41] with brown silk.

'God bless me!' exclaimed Parsons, starting up with well-feigned surprise, 'I've forgotten those confounded letters. Tottle, I know you'll excuse me.'

If Tottle had been a free agent, he would have allowed no one to leave the room on any pretence, except himself. As it was, however, he was obliged to look cheerful when Parsons quitted the apartment.

He had scarcely left, when Martha put her head into the room, with — 'Please ma'am you're wanted.'

Mrs Parsons left the room, shut the door carefully after her, and Mr Watkins Tottle was left alone with Miss Lillerton.

For the first five minutes there was a dead silence. — Mr Watkins Tottle was thinking how he should begin, and Miss Lillerton appeared to be thinking of nothing. The fire was burning low; Mr Watkins Tottle stirred it, and put some coals on.

'Hem!' coughed Miss Lillerton; Mr Watkins Tottle thought the fair creature had spoken. 'I beg your pardon,' said he.

'Eh?'

'I thought you spoke.'

'No.'

'Oh!'

'There are some books on the sofa, Mr Tottle, if you would like to look at them,' said Miss Lillerton, after the lapse of another five minutes.

'No, thank you,' returned Watkins: and then he added, with a courage which was perfectly astonishing, even to himself, 'Madam, that is Miss Lillerton, I wish to speak to you.'

'To me!' said Miss Lillerton, letting the silk drop from her hands, and sliding her chair back a few paces. — 'Speak — to me!'

'To you, madam — and on the subject of the state of your affections.' The lady hastily rose, and would have left the room; but Mr Watkins Tottle gently detained her by the hand, and holding it as far from him as the joint length of their arms would permit, he thus proceeded: 'Pray do not misunderstand me, or suppose that I am led to address you, after so short an acquaintance, by any feeling of my own merits — for merits I have none which could give me a claim to your hand. I hope you will acquit me of any presumption when I explain that I have been acquainted through Mrs Parsons, with the state — that is, that Mrs Parsons has

Mr Watkins Tottle and Miss Lillerton

told me – at least, not Mrs Parsons, but –' here Watkins began to wander, but Miss Lillerton relieved him.

'Am I to understand, Mr Tottle, that Mrs Parsons has acquainted you with my feeling – my affection – I mean my respect, for an individual of the opposite sex?'

'She has.'

'Then, what,' inquired Miss Lillerton, averting her face, with a girlish air, 'what could induce *you* to seek such an interview as this? What can your object be? How can I promote your happiness, Mr Tottle?'

Here was the time for a flourish – 'By allowing me,' replied Watkins, falling bump on his knees, and breaking two brace-buttons and a waistcoat-string, in the act – 'By allowing me to be your slave, your servant – in short, by unreservedly making me the confidant of your heart's feelings – may I say, for the promotion of your own happiness – may I say, in order that you may become the wife of a kind and affectionate husband?'

'Disinterested creature!' exclaimed Miss Lillerton, hiding her face in a white pocket-handkerchief with an eyelet-hole border.

Mr Watkins Tottle thought that if the lady knew all, she might possibly alter her opinion on this last point. He raised the tip of her middle finger ceremoniously to his lips, and got off his knees as gracefully as he could. 'My information was correct?' he tremulously inquired, when he was once more on his feet.

'It was.' Watkins elevated his hands, and looked up to the ornament in the centre of the ceiling, which had been made for a lamp, by way of expressing his rapture.

'Our situation, Mr Tottle,' resumed the lady, glancing at him through one of the eyelet-holes, 'is a most peculiar and delicate one.'

'It is,' said Mr Tottle.

'Our acquaintance has been of *so* short duration,' said Miss Lillerton.

'Only a week,' assented Watkins Tottle.

'Oh! more than that,' exclaimed the lady, in a tone of surprise.

'Indeed!' said Tottle.

'More than a month — more than two months!' said Miss Lillerton.

'Rather odd, this,' thought Watkins.

'Oh!' he said, recollecting Parsons's assurance that she had known him from report, 'I understand. But, my dear madam, pray consider. The longer this acquaintance has existed, the less reason is there for delay now. Why not at once fix a period for gratifying the hopes of your devoted admirer?'

'It has been represented to me again and again that this is the course I ought to pursue,' replied Miss Lillerton, 'but pardon my feelings of delicacy, Mr Tottle — pray excuse this embarrassment — I have peculiar ideas on such subjects, and I am quite sure that I never could summon up fortitude enough to name the day to my future husband.'

'Then allow *me* to name it,' said Tottle eagerly.

'I should like to fix it myself,' replied Miss Lillerton, bashfully, 'but I cannot do so without at once resorting to a third party.'

'A third party!' thought Watkins Tottle; 'who the deuce is that to be, I wonder?'

'Mr Tottle,' continued Miss Lillerton, 'you have made me a most disinterested and kind offer — that offer I accept. Will you, at once be the bearer of a note from me to — to Mr Timson?'

'Mr Timson!' said Watkins.

'After what has passed between us,' responded Miss Lillerton, still averting her head, 'you must understand whom I mean; Mr Timson, the — the — clergyman.'

'Mr Timson, the clergyman!' ejaculated Watkins Tottle, in a state of inexpressible beatitude, and positive wonder at his own success. 'Angel! Certainly — this moment!'

'I'll prepare it immediately,' said Miss Lillerton, making for the door; 'the events of this day have flurried me so much, Mr Tottle, that I shall not leave my room again this evening; I will send you the note by the servant.'

'Stay — stay,' cried Watkins Tottle, still keeping a most respectful distance from the lady; 'when shall we meet again?'

'Oh! Mr Tottle,' replied Miss Lillerton, coquettishly, 'when *we* are married, I can never see you too often, nor thank you too much;' and she left the room.

Mr Watkins Tottle flung himself into an arm-chair, and indulged in the most delicious reveries of future bliss, in which the idea of 'Five hundred pounds per annum, with an uncontrolled power of disposing of it by her last will and testament,' was somehow or other the foremost. He had gone through the interview so well, and it had terminated so admirably, that he almost began to wish he had expressly stipulated for the settlement of the annual five hundred on himself.

'May I come in?' said Mr Gabriel Parsons, peeping in at the door.

'You may,' replied Watkins.

'Well, have you done it?' anxiously inquired Gabriel.

'Have I done it!' said Watkins Tottle, 'Hush – I'm going to the clergyman.'

'No!' said Parsons. 'How well you have managed it!'

'Where does Timson live?' inquired Watkins.

'At his uncle's,' replied Gabriel, 'just round the lane. He's waiting for a living, and has been assisting his uncle here for the last two or three months. But how well you have done it – I didn't think you could have carried it off so!'

Mr Watkins Tottle was proceeding to demonstrate that the Richardsonian principle[42] was the best on which love could possibly be made, when he was interrupted by the entrance of Martha, with a little pink note folded like a fancy cocked-hat.[43]

'Miss Lillerton's compliments,' said Martha, as she delivered it into Tottle's hands, and vanished.

'Do you observe the delicacy?' said Tottle, appealing to Mr Gabriel Parsons. '*Compliments* not *love*, by the servant, eh?'

Mr Gabriel Parsons didn't exactly know what reply to make, so he poked the forefinger of his right hand between the third and fourth ribs of Mr Watkins Tottle.

'Come,' said Watkins, when the explosion of mirth, consequent on this practical jest, had subsided, 'we'll be off at once – let's lose no time.'

'Capital!' echoed Gabriel Parsons; and in five minutes they were at the garden-gate of the villa tenanted by the uncle of Mr Timson.

'Is Mr Charles Timson at home?' inquired Mr Watkins Tottle of Mr Charles Timson's uncle's man.

'Mr Charles *is* at home,' replied the man, stammering; 'but he desired me to say he couldn't be interrupted, sir, by any of the parishioners.'

'*I* am not a parishioner,' replied Watkins.

'Is Mr Charles writing a sermon, Tom?' inquired Parsons, thrusting himself forward.

'No, Mr Parsons, sir; he's not exactly writing a sermon, but he is practising the violoncello in his own bedroom, and gave strict orders not to be disturbed.'

'Say I'm here,' replied Gabriel, leading the way across the garden; 'Mr Parsons and Mr Tottle, on private and particular business.'

They were shown into the parlour, and the servant departed to deliver his message. The distant groaning of the violoncello ceased; footsteps were heard on the stairs; and Mr Timson presented himself, and shook hands with Parsons with the utmost cordiality.

'How do you do, sir?' said Watkins Tottle, with great solemnity.

'How do *you* do, sir?' replied Timson, with as much coldness as if it were a matter of perfect indifference to him how he did, as it very likely was.

'I beg to deliver this note to you,' said Watkins Tottle, producing the cocked hat.

'From Miss Lillerton!' said Timson, suddenly changing colour. 'Pray sit down.'

Mr Watkins Tottle sat down; and while Timson perused the note, fixed his eyes on an oyster-sauce-coloured portrait of the Archbishop of Canterbury, which hung over the fireplace.

Mr Timson rose from his seat when he had concluded the note, and looked dubiously at Parsons – 'May I ask,' he inquired, appealing to Watkins Tottle, 'whether our friend here is acquainted with the object of your visit?'

'Our friend is in *my* confidence,' replied Watkins, with consider-able importance.

'Then, sir,' said Timson, seizing both Tottle's hands, 'allow me in his presence to thank you, most unfeignedly and cordially, for the noble part you have acted in this affair.'

'He thinks I recommended him,' thought Tottle. 'Confound these fellows! they never think of any thing but their fees.'

'I deeply regret having misunderstood your intentions, my dear sir,' continued Timson. 'Disinterested and manly indeed! There are very few men who would have acted as you have done.'

Mr Watkins Tottle could not help thinking that this last remark was any thing but complimentary. He therefore inquired, rather hastily, 'When is it to be?'

'On Thursday,' replied Timson – 'on Thursday morning at half-past eight.'

'Uncommonly early,' observed Watkins Tottle, with an air of triumphant self-denial. 'I shall hardly be able to get down here by that hour.' (This was intended for a joke.)

'Never mind, my dear fellow,' replied Timson, all suavity, shaking hands with Tottle again most heartily, 'so long as we see you to breakfast, you know —'

'Eh!' said Parsons, with one of the most extraordinary expressions of countenance that ever appeared in a human face.

'What!' ejaculated Watkins Tottle, at the same moment.

'I say that so long as we see you to breakfast,' repeated Timson, 'we will excuse your being absent from the ceremony, though of course your presence at it would give us the utmost pleasure.'

Mr Watkins Tottle staggered against the wall, and fixed his eyes on Timson with appalling perseverance.

'Timson,' said Parsons, hurriedly brushing his hat with his left arm, 'when you say "us," whom do you mean?'

Mr Timson looked foolish in his turn, when he replied, 'Why – Mrs Timson that will be this day week: Miss Lillerton that is – '

'Now don't stare at that idiot in the corner,' angrily exclaimed Parsons, as the extraordinary convulsions of Watkins Tottle's countenance excited the wondering gaze of Timson, — 'but have the goodness to tell me in three words the contents of that note.'

'This note,' replied Timson, 'is from Miss Lillerton, to whom I have been for the last five weeks regularly engaged. Her singular scruples and strange feeling on some points have hitherto prevented my bringing the engagement to that termination which I so anxiously desire. She informs me here, that she sounded Mrs Parsons with the view of making her her confidant and go-between, that Mrs Parsons informed this elderly gentleman, Mr Tottle, of the circumstance, and that he, in the most kind and delicate terms, offered to assist us in any way, and even undertook to convey this note, which contains the promise I have long sought in vain — an act of kindness for which I can never be sufficiently grateful.'

'Good night, Timson,' said Parsons, hurrying off, and carrying the bewildered Tottle with him.

'Won't you stay — and have something?' said Timson.

'No, thank ye,' replied Parsons, 'I've had quite enough;' and away he went, followed by Watkins Tottle in a state of stupefaction.

Mr Gabriel Parsons whistled until they had walked some quarter of a mile past his own gate, when he suddenly stopped, and said —

'You are a clever fellow, Tottle, ain't you?'

'I don't know,' said the unfortunate Watkins.

'I suppose you'll say this is Fanny's fault, won't you?' inquired Gabriel.

'I don't know any thing about it,' replied the bewildered Tottle.

'Well,' said Parsons, turning on his heel to go home, 'the next time you make an offer, you had better speak plainly, and don't throw a chance away. And the next time you're locked up in a spunging-house, just wait there till I come and take you out, there's a good fellow.'

How, or at what hour, Mr Watkins Tottle returned to Cecil-street is unknown. His boots were seen outside his bedroom-door next morning, but we have the authority of his landlady for stating that he neither emerged therefrom, nor accepted sustenance for four-and-twenty hours. At the expiration of that period, and when a council of war was being held in the kitchen on the propriety of summoning the parochial beadle to break his door open, he rang his bell, and demanded a cup of milk-and-water. The next morning he went through the formalities of eating and drinking as usual, but a week afterwards he was seized with a relapse, while perusing the list of marriages in a morning paper, from which he never perfectly recovered.

A few weeks after the last-named occurrence, the body of a gentleman unknown, was found in the Regent's canal.[44] In the trousers-pockets were four shillings and threepence-halfpenny; a matrimonial advertisement from a lady, which appeared to have been cut out of a Sunday paper; a toothpick, and a card-case, which it is confidently believed would have led to the identification of the unfortunate gentleman, but for the circumstance of there being none but blank cards in it. Mr Watkins Tottle absented himself from his lodgings shortly before. A bill which has not been taken up was presented next morning; and a bill which has not been taken down was soon afterwards affixed in his parlour-window.

CHAPTER I I

The Bloomsbury Christening

[The Author may be permitted to observe that this sketch was published some time before the Farce entitled 'The Christening' was first represented.][1]

MR NICODEMUS DUMPS, or, as his acquaintance called him, 'long Dumps,' was a bachelor, six feet high, and fifty years old; cross, cadaverous, odd, and ill-natured. He was never happy but when he was miserable; and always miserable when he had the best reason to be happy. The only real comfort of his existence was to

Bloomsbury Christening

make every body about him wretched – then he might be truly said to enjoy life. He was afflicted with a situation in the Bank worth five hundred a-year, and he rented a 'first floor furnished,' at Pentonville,[2] which he originally took because it commanded a dismal prospect of an adjacent churchyard. He was familiar with the face of every tombstone, and the burial service seemed to excite his strongest sympathy. His friends said he was surly – he insisted he was nervous; they thought him a lucky dog, but he protested that he was 'the most unfortunate man in the world.' Cold as he was, and wretched as he declared himself to be, he was not wholly unsusceptible of attachments. He revered the memory of Hoyle,[3] as he was himself an admirable and imperturbable whist-player, and he chuckled with delight at a fretful and impatient adversary. He adored King Herod for his massacre of the innocents;[4] and if he hated one thing more than another, it was a child. However, he could hardly be said to hate any thing in particular, because he disliked every thing in general; but perhaps his greatest antipathies were cabs, old women, doors that would not shut, musical amateurs, and omnibus cads. He subscribed to the Society for the Suppression of Vice[5] for the pleasure of putting a stop to any harmless amusements; and he contributed largely towards the support of two itinerant methodist parsons,[6] in the amiable hope that if circumstances rendered any people happy in this world, they might perchance be rendered miserable by fears for the next.

Mr Dumps had a nephew who had been married about a year, and who was somewhat of a favourite with his uncle, because he was an admirable subject to exercise his misery-creating powers upon. Mr Charles Kitterbell was a small, sharp, spare man, with a very large head, and a broad, good-humoured countenance. He looked like a faded giant, with the head and face partially restored; and he had a cast in his eye which rendered it quite impossible for any one with whom he conversed to know where he was looking. His eyes appeared fixed on the wall, and he was staring you out of countenance; in short, there was no catching his eye, and perhaps it is a merciful dispensation of Providence that such eyes are not catching. In addition to these characteristics, it may be added that

Mr Charles Kitterbell was one of the most credulous and matter-of-fact little personages that ever took *to* himself a wife, and *for* himself a house in Great Russell-street, Bedford-square. (Uncle Dumps always dropped the 'Bedford-square,' and inserted in lieu thereof, the dreadful words 'Tottenham-court-road.'')

'No, but uncle, 'pon my life you must – you must promise to be godfather,' said Mr Kitterbell, as he sat in conversation with his respected relative one morning.

'I cannot, indeed I cannot,' returned Dumps.

'Well, but why not? Jemima will think it very unkind. It's very little trouble.'

'As to the trouble,' rejoined the most unhappy man in existence, 'I don't mind that; but my nerves are in that state – I cannot go through the ceremony. You know I don't like going out. – For God's sake, Charles, don't fidget with that stool so, you'll drive me mad.' Mr Kitterbell, quite regardless of his uncle's nerves, had occupied himself for some ten minutes in describing a circle on the floor with one leg of the office-stool on which he was seated, keeping the other three up in the air, and holding fast on by the desk.

'I beg your pardon, uncle,' said Kitterbell, quite abashed, suddenly releasing his hold of the desk, and bringing the three wandering legs back to the floor, with a force sufficient to drive them through it.

'But come, don't refuse. If it's a boy, you know, we must have two godfathers.'

'*If* it's a boy!' said Dumps, 'why can't you say at once whether it *is* a boy or not?'

'I should be very happy to tell you, but it's impossible I can undertake to say whether it's a girl or a boy, if the child isn't born yet.'

'Not born yet!' echoed Dumps, with a gleam of hope lighting up his lugubrious visage. 'Oh, well, it *may* be a girl, and then you won't want me, or if it is a boy, it *may* die before it is christened.'

'I hope not,' said the father that expected to be, looking very grave.

'I hope not,' acquiesced Dumps, evidently pleased with the subject. He was beginning to get happy. '*I* hope not, but distressing cases frequently occur during the first two or three days of a child's life: fits, I am told, are exceedingly common, and alarming convulsions are almost matters of course.'

'Lord, uncle!' ejaculated little Kitterbell, gasping for breath.

'Yes; my landlady was confined – let me see – last Tuesday: an uncommonly fine boy. On the Thursday night the nurse was sitting with him upon her knee before the fire, and he was as well as possible. Suddenly he became black in the face, and alarmingly spasmodic. The medical man was instantly sent for, and every remedy was tried, but –'

'How frightful!' interrupted the horror-stricken Kitterbell.

'The child died of course. However your child *may* not die, and if it should be a boy, and should *live* to be christened, why I suppose I must be one of the sponsors.' Dumps was evidently good-natured on the faith of his anticipations.

'Thank you, uncle,' said his agitated nephew, grasping his hand as warmly as if he had done him some essential service. 'Perhaps I had better not tell Mrs K. what you have mentioned.'

'Why, if she's low spirited, perhaps you had better not mention the melancholy case to her,' returned Dumps, who of course had invented the whole story, 'though perhaps it would be but doing your duty as a husband to prepare her for the *worst*.'

A day or two afterwards, as Dumps was perusing a morning paper at the chop-house which he regularly frequented, the following paragraph met his eye:

'*Births*. – On Saturday, the 18th inst., in Great Russell-street, the lady of Charles Kitterbell, Esq., of a son.'

'It *is* a boy!' he exclaimed, dashing down the paper to the astonishment of the waiters. 'It *is* a boy!' But he speedily regained his composure as his eye rested on a paragraph quoting the number of infant deaths from the bills of mortality.[8]

Six weeks passed away, and as no communication had been received from the Kitterbells, Dumps was beginning to flatter himself that the child was dead, when the following note painfully resolved his doubts:

'*Great Russell-street,*
'*Monday morning.*

'DEAR UNCLE,

'You will be delighted to hear that my dear Jemima has left her room, and that your future godson is getting on capitally. He was very thin at first, but he is getting much larger, and nurse says he is filling out every day. He cries a good deal, and is a very singular colour, which made Jemima and me rather uncomfortable; but as nurse says it's natural, and as of course we know nothing about these things yet, we are quite satisfied with what nurse says. We think he will be a sharp child; and nurse says she's sure he will, because he never goes to sleep. You will readily believe that we are all very happy, only we're a little worn out for want of rest, as he keeps us awake all night; but this we must expect, nurse says, for the first six or eight months. He has been vaccinated, but in consequence of the operation being rather awkwardly performed, some small particles of glass were introduced into the arm with the matter. Perhaps this may in some degree account for his being rather fractious; at least, so nurse says. We propose to have him christened at twelve o'clock on Friday, at Saint George's church, in Hart-street,[9] by the name of Frederick Charles William. Pray don't be later than a quarter before twelve. We shall have a very few friends in the evening, when of course we shall see you. I am sorry to say that the dear boy appears rather restless and uneasy to-day: the cause, I fear, is fever.

'Believe me, dear Uncle,
'Yours affectionately,
'CHARLES KITTERBELL.

'P.S. – I open this note to say that we have just discovered the cause of little Frederick's restlessness. It is not fever, as I apprehended, but a small pin, which nurse accidently stuck in his leg yesterday evening. We have taken it out, and he appears more composed, though he still sobs a good deal.'

It is almost unnecessary to say that the perusal of the above interesting statement was no great relief to the mind of the hypochondriacal Dumps. It was impossible to recede, however, and so he put the best face – that is to say, an uncommonly miserable one – upon the matter; and purchased a handsome silver mug for the infant Kitterbell, upon which he ordered the initials 'F.C.W.K.,' with the customary untrained grape-vine-looking flourishes, and a large full stop, to be engraved forthwith.

Monday was a fine day, Tuesday was delightful, Wednesday was equal to either, and Thursday was finer than ever; four successive fine days in London! Hackney-coachmen became revolutionary, and crossing-sweepers began to doubt the existence of a First Cause.[10] The *Morning Herald* informed its readers that an old woman in Camden Town had been heard to say that the fineness of the season was 'unprecedented in the memory of the oldest inhabitant;' and Islington clerks, with large families and small salaries, left off their black gaiters, disdained to carry their once green cotton umbrellas, and walked to town in the conscious pride of white stockings, and cleanly brushed Bluchers.[11] Dumps beheld all this with an eye of supreme contempt – his triumph was at hand. – He knew that if it had been fine for four weeks instead of four days, it would rain when he went out; he was lugubriously happy in the conviction that Friday would be a wretched day – and so it was. 'I knew how it would be,' said Dumps, as he turned round opposite the Mansion-house[12] at half-past eleven o'clock on the Friday morning. – 'I knew how it would be, *I* am concerned, and that's enough;' – and certainly the appearance of the day was sufficient to depress the spirits of a much more buoyant-hearted individual than himself. It had rained, without a moment's cessation, since eight o'clock; every body that passed up Cheapside,[13] and down Cheapside, looked wet, cold, and dirty. All sorts of forgotten and long-concealed umbrellas had been put into requisition. Cabs whisked about, with the 'fare' as carefully boxed up behind two glazed calico curtains as any mysterious picture in any one of Mrs Radcliffe's castles;[14] omnibus horses smoked like steam-engines; nobody thought of 'standing up' under doorways or arches; they were painfully convinced it was a hopeless case; and so every body went hastily along, jumbling and jostling, and swearing and perspiring, and slipping about, like amateur skaters behind wooden chairs on the Serpentine[15] on a frosty Sunday.

Dumps paused; he could not think of walking, being rather smart for the christening. If he took a cab he was sure to be spilt, and a hackney-coach was too expensive for his economical ideas. An omnibus was waiting at the opposite corner – it was a desperate case – he had never heard of an omnibus upsetting or running away, and if the cad did knock him down, he could 'pull him up' in return.

'Now, sir!' cried the young gentleman who officiated as 'cad' to the 'Lads of the Village,' which was the name of the machine just noticed. Dumps crossed.

'This vay, sir!' shouted the driver of the 'Hark-away,' pulling up his vehicle immediately across the door of the opposition – 'This vay, sir – he's full.' Dumps hesitated, whereupon the 'Lads of the Village' commenced pouring out a torrent of abuse against the 'Hark-away;' but the conductor of the 'Admiral Napier' settled the contest in a most satisfactory manner for all parties, by seizing Dumps round the waist, and thrusting him into the middle of his vehicle which had just come up and only wanted the sixteenth inside.

'All right,' said the 'Admiral,' and off the thing thundered, like a fire-engine at full gallop, with the kidnapped customer inside, standing in the position of a half doubled-up bootjack, and falling about with every jerk of the machine, first on the one side and then on the other, like a 'Jack-in-the-green,' on May-day,[16] setting to the lady with a brass ladle.

'For Heaven's sake, where am I to sit?' inquired the miserable man of an old gentleman, into whose stomach he had just fallen for the fourth time.

'Any where but on my *chest*, sir,' replied the old gentleman, in a surly tone.

'Perhaps the *box* would suit the gentleman better,' suggested a very damp lawyer's clerk, in a pink shirt, and a smirking countenance.

After a great deal of struggling and falling about, Dumps at last managed to squeeze himself into a seat, which, in addition to the slight disadvantage of being between a window that would not shut, and a door that must be open, placed him in close contact with a passenger, who had been walking about all the morning without an umbrella, and who looked as if he had spent the day in a full water-butt — only wetter.

'Don't bang the door so,' said Dumps to the conductor, as he shut it, after letting out four of the passengers; 'I am very nervous — it destroys me.'

'Did any gen'lm'n say any think?' replied the cad, thrusting in his head, and trying to look as if he didn't understand the request.

'I told you not to bang the door so!' repeated Dumps, with an expression of countenance like the knave of clubs in convulsions.

'Oh! vy, it's rather a sing'ler circumstance about this here door, sir, that it von't shut without banging,' replied the conductor; and he opened the door very wide, and shut it again with a terrific bang, in proof of the assertion.

'I beg your pardon, sir,' said a little prim, wheezing old gentleman, sitting opposite Dumps, 'I beg your pardon; but have you ever observed, when you have been in an omnibus on a wet day, that four people out of five always come in with large cotton umbrellas, without a handle at the top, or the brass spike at the bottom?'

'Why, sir,' returned Dumps, as he heard the clock strike twelve, 'it never struck me before; but now you mention it, I — Hollo! hollo!' — shouted the persecuted individual, as the omnibus dashed past Drury-lane, where he had directed to be set down. — 'Where is the cad?'

'I think he's on the box, sir,' said the young gentleman before noticed in the pink shirt, which looked like a white one ruled with red ink.

'I want to be set down!' said Dumps in a faint voice, overcome by his previous efforts.

'I think these cads want to be *set down*,' returned the attorney's clerk, chuckling at his sally.

'Hollo!' cried Dumps again.

'Hollo!' echoed the passengers. The omnibus passed St Giles's church.[17]

'Hold hard!' said the conductor; 'I'm blowed if we ha'n't forgot the gen'lm'n as vas to be set down at Doory-lane. − Now, sir, make haste, if you please,' he added, opening the door, and assisting Dumps out with as much coolness as if it was 'all right.' Dumps's indignation was for once getting the better of his cynical equanimity. 'Drury-lane!' he gasped, with the voice of a boy in a cold bath for the first time.

'Doory-lane, sir? − yes, sir, − third turning on the right-hand side, sir.'

Dumps's passion was paramount; he clutched his umbrella, and was striding off with the firm determination of not paying the fare. The cad, by a remarkable coincidence, happened to entertain a directly contrary opinion, and Heaven knows how far the altercation would have proceeded, if it had not been most ably and satisfactorily brought to a close by the driver.

'Hollo!' said that respectable person, standing up on the box, and leaning with one hand on the roof of the omnibus. 'Hollo, Tom! tell the gentleman if so be as he feels aggrieved, we will take him up to the Edge-er (Edgeware) Road[18] for nothing, and set him down at Doory-lane when we comes back. He can't reject that, anyhow.'

The argument was irresistible: Dumps paid the disputed six-pence, and in a quarter of an hour was on the staircase of No. 14, Great Russell-street.

Every thing indicated that preparations were making for the reception of 'a few friends' in the evening. Two dozen extra tumblers, and four ditto wine-glasses − looking any thing but transparent, with little bits of straw in them − were on the slab in the passage, just arrived. There was a great smell of nutmeg, port wine and almonds on the staircase; the covers were taken off the stair-carpet, and the figure of Venus on the first landing looked as if she were ashamed of the composition-candle in her right hand, which contrasted beautifully with the lamp-blacked drapery of the goddess of love. The female servant (who looked very warm and bustling) ushered Dumps into a front drawing-room, very prettily furnished, with a plentiful sprinkling of little baskets, paper table-mats, china watchmen, pink and gold albums, and rainbow-bound little books on the different tables.

'Ah, uncle!' said Mr Kitterbell, 'how d'ye do? Allow me – Jemima, my dear – my uncle. I think you've seen Jemima before, sir?'

'Have had the *pleasure*,' returned big Dumps, his tone and look making it doubtful whether in his life he had ever experienced the sensation.

'I'm sure,' said Mrs Kitterbell, with a languid smile, and a slight cough, 'I'm sure – hem – any friend – of Charles's – hem – much less a relation, is –'

'I knew you'd say so, my love,' said little Kitterbell, who, while he appeared to be gazing on the opposite houses, was looking at his wife with a most affectionate air; 'bless you!' The last two words were accompanied with a simper, and a squeeze of the hand, which stirred up all Uncle Dumps's bile.

'Jane, tell nurse to bring down baby,' said Mrs Kitterbell, addressing the servant. Mrs Kitterbell was a tall, thin young lady, with very light hair, and a particularly white face – one of those young women who almost invariably, though one hardly knows why, recal to one's mind the idea of a cold fillet of veal. Out went the servant, and in came the nurse, with a remarkably small parcel in her arms, packed up in a blue mantle trimmed with white fur. – This was the baby.

'Now, uncle,' said Mr Kitterbell, lifting up that part of the mantle which covered the infant's face, with an air of great triumph, '*Who* do you think he's like?'

'He! he! Yes, who?' said Mrs K. putting her arm through her husband's, and looking up into Dumps's face with an expression of as much interest as she was capable of displaying.

'Good God, how small he is!' cried the amiable uncle, starting back with well-feigned surprise; '*remarkably* small indeed.'

'Do you think so?' inquired poor little Kitterbell, rather alarmed. 'He's a monster to what he was – ain't he nurse?'

'He's a dear,' said the nurse, squeezing the child, and evading the question – not because she scrupled to disguise the fact, but because she couldn't afford to throw away the chance of Dumps's half-crown.

'Well, but who is he like?' inquired little Kitterbell.

Dumps looked at the little pink heap before him, and only thought at the moment of the best mode of mortifying the youthful parents.

'I really don't know *who* he's like,' he answered, very well knowing the reply expected of him.

'Don't you think he's like *me*?' inquired his nephew, with a knowing air.

'Oh, *decidedly* not!' returned Dumps, with an emphasis not to be misunderstood. 'Decidedly not like you. – Oh, certainly not.'

'Like Jemima?' asked Kitterbell, faintly.

'Oh dear, no; not in the least. I'm no judge, of course, in such cases; but I really think he's more like one of those little carved representations that one sometimes sees blowing a trumpet on a tombstone!' The nurse stooped down over the child, and with great difficulty prevented an explosion of mirth. Pa and ma looked almost as miserable as their amiable uncle.

'Well!' said the disappointed little father, 'you'll be better able to tell what he's like by and by. You shall see him this evening with his mantle off.'

'Thank you,' said Dumps, feeling particularly grateful.

'Now, my love,' said Kitterbell to his wife, 'it's time we were off. We're to meet the other godfather and the godmother at the church, uncle, – Mr and Mrs Wilson from over the way – uncommonly nice people. My love, are you well wrapped up?'

'Yes, dear.'

'Are you sure you won't have another shawl?' inquired the anxious husband.

'No, sweet,' returned the charming mother, accepting Dumps's proffered arm; and the little party entered the hackney-coach that was to take them to the church; Dumps amusing Mrs Kitterbell by expatiating largely on the danger of measles, thrush, teeth-cutting, and other interesting diseases to which children are subject.

The ceremony (which occupied about five minutes) passed off without any thing particular occurring. The clergyman had to dine some distance from town, and had two churchings, three christenings, and a funeral to perform in something less than an hour. The godfathers and godmother, therefore, promised to re-nounce the devil and all his works[19] – 'and all that sort of thing' – as little Kitterbell said – 'in less than no time;' and, with the exception of Dumps nearly letting the child fall into the font when he handed it to the clergyman, the whole affair went off in the usual business-like and matter-of-course manner, and Dumps re-entered the Bank-gates at two o'clock with a heavy heart, and the painful conviction that he was regularly booked for an evening party.

Evening came – and so did Dumps's pumps, black silk stockings, and white cravat which he had ordered to be forwarded, per boy, from Pentonville. The depressed godfather dressed himself at a friend's counting-house, from whence, with his spirits fifty degrees below proof, he sallied forth – as the weather had cleared up, and the evening was tolerably fine – to walk to Great Russell-street. Slowly he paced up Cheapside, Newgate-street, down Snow-hill, and up Holborn ditto,[20] looking as grim as the figure head of a man-of-war, and finding out fresh causes of misery at every step. As he was crossing the corner of Hatton-garden, a man apparently intoxicated, rushed against him, and would have knocked him down had he not been providentially caught by a very genteel young man who happened to be close to him at the time. The shock so disarranged Dumps's nerves, as well as his dress, that he could hardly stand. The gentleman took his arm, and in the kindest manner walked with him as far as Furnival's Inn. Dumps, for about the first time in his life, felt grateful and polite; and he and the gentlemanly-looking young man parted with mutual expressions of good will.

'There are at least some well-disposed men in the world,' ruminated the misanthropical Dumps, as he proceeded towards his destination.

Rat—tat—ta-ra-ra-ra-ra-rat — knocked a hackney-coachman at Kitterbell's door, in imitation of a gentleman's servant, just as Dumps reached it; and out came an old lady in a large toque,[21] and an old gentleman in a blue coat, and three female copies of the old lady in pink dresses, and shoes to match.

'It's a large party,' sighed the unhappy godfather, wiping the perspiration from his forehead, and leaning against the area-railings. It was some time before the miserable man could muster up courage to knock at the door, and when he did, the smart appearance of a neighbouring greengrocer (who had been hired to wait for seven and sixpence, and whose calves alone were worth double the money), the lamp in the passage, and the Venus on the landing, added to the hum of many voices, and the sound of a harp and two violins, painfully convinced him that his surmises were but too well founded.

'How are you?' said little Kitterbell, in a greater bustle than ever, bolting out of the little back parlour with a corkscrew in his hand, and various particles of sawdust, looking like so many inverted commas, on his inexpressibles.

'Good God!' said Dumps, turning into the aforesaid parlour to put his shoes on which he had brought in his coat-pocket, and still more appalled by the sight of seven fresh-drawn corks, and a corresponding number of decanters. 'How many people are there up stairs?'

'Oh, not above thirty-five. We've had the carpet taken up in the back drawing-room, and the piano and the card-tables are in the front. Jemima thought we'd better have a regular sit-down supper, in the front parlour, because of the speechifying, and all that. But, Lord! uncle, what's the matter?' continued the excited little man, as Dumps stood with one shoe on, rummaging his pockets with the most frightful distortion of visage. 'What have you lost? Your pocket-book?'

'No,' returned Dumps, diving first into one pocket and then into the other, and speaking in a voice like Desdemona with the pillow over her mouth.[22]

'Your card-case? snuff-box? the key of your lodgings?' continued Kitterbell, pouring question on question with the rapidity of lightning.

'No! no!' ejaculated Dumps, still diving eagerly into his empty pockets.

'Not – not – the *mug* you spoke of this morning?'

'Yes, the *mug*!' replied Dumps, sinking into a chair.

'How *could* you have done it?' inquired Kitterbell. 'Are you sure you brought it out?'

'Yes! yes! I see it all,' said Dumps, starting up as the idea flashed across his mind; 'miserable dog that I am – I was born to suffer. I see it all; it was the gentlemanly-looking young man!'

'Mr Dumps!' shouted the greengrocer in a stentorian voice, as he ushered the somewhat recovered godfather into the drawing-room half an hour after the above declaration. 'Mr Dumps!' – every body looked at the door, and in came Dumps, feeling about as much out of place as a salmon might be supposed to be on a gravel-walk.

'Happy to see you again,' said Mrs Kitterbell, quite unconscious of the unfortunate man's confusion and misery; 'you must allow me to introduce you to a few of our friends: – my mamma, Mr Dumps – my papa and sisters.' Dumps seized the hand of the mother as warmly as if she was his own parent, bowed *to* the young ladies, and *against* a gentleman behind him, and took no notice whatever of the father, who had been bowing incessantly for three minutes and a quarter.

'Uncle,' said little Kitterbell, after Dumps had been introduced to a select dozen or two, 'you must let me lead you to the other end of the room, to introduce you to my friend Danton. Such a splendid fellow! – I'm sure you'll like him – this way,' – Dumps followed as tractably as a tame bear.

Mr Danton was a young man of about five-and-twenty, with a considerable stock of impudence, and a very small share of ideas: he was a great favourite, especially with young ladies of from

sixteen to twenty-six years of age, both inclusive. He could imitate
the French-horn to admiration, sang comic songs most inimitably,
and had the most insinuating way of saying impertinent nothings
to his doting female admirers. He had acquired, somehow or other,
the reputation of being a great wit, and, accordingly, whenever he
opened his mouth, every body who knew him laughed very
heartily.

The introduction took place in due form. Mr Danton bowed and
twirled a lady's handkerchief, which he held in his hand, in a most
comic way. Every body smiled.

'Very warm,' said Dumps, feeling it necessary to say something.

'Yes. It was warmer yesterday,' returned the brilliant Mr Danton.
– A general laugh.

'I have great pleasure in congratulating you on your first
appearance in the character of a father, sir,' he continued, addressing
Dumps – 'godfather, I mean.' – The young ladies were convulsed,
and the gentlemen in ecstasies.

A general hum of admiration interrupted the conversation, and
announced the entrance of nurse with the baby. An universal rush
of the young ladies immediately took place. (Girls are always *so*
fond of babies in company.)

'Oh, you dear!' said one.

'How sweet!' cried another, in a low tone of the most enthusiastic
admiration.

'Heavenly!' added a third.

'Oh! what dear little arms!' said a fourth, holding up an arm
and fist about the size and shape of the leg of a fowl cleanly
picked.

'Did you ever' – said a little coquette with a large bustle, who
looked like a French lithograph, appealing to a gentleman in three
waistcoats – 'Did you ever!'

'Never, in my life,' returned her admirer, pulling up his collar.

'Oh! *do* let me take it, nurse,' cried another young lady. 'The
love!'

'Can it open its eyes, nurse?' inquired another, affecting the
utmost innocence. – Suffice it to say, that the single ladies unanim-

ously voted him an angel, and that the married ones, *nem. con.*,[23] agreed that he was decidedly the finest baby they had ever beheld – except their own.

The quadrilles were resumed with great spirit. Mr Danton was universally admitted to be beyond himself, several young ladies enchanted the company and gained admirers by singing 'We met'[24] – 'I saw her at the Fancy Fair'[25] – and other equally sentimental and interesting ballads. 'The young men,' as Mrs Kitterbell said, 'made themselves very agreeable;' the girls did not lose their opportunity; and the evening promised to go off excellently. Dumps didn't mind it: he had devised a plan for himself – a little bit of fun in his own way – and he was almost happy! He played a rubber and lost every point. Mr Danton said he could not have lost every point, because he made a point of losing: – every body laughed tremendously. Dumps retorted with a better joke, and nobody smiled, with the exception of the host, who seemed to consider it his duty to laugh till he was black in the face, at every thing. There was only one drawback – the musicians did not play with quite as much spirit as could have been wished. The cause, however was satisfactorily explained; for it appeared, on the testimony of a gentleman who had come up from Gravesend in the afternoon, that they had been engaged on board a steamer all day, and had played almost without cessation all the way to Gravesend, and all the way back again.

The 'sit-down supper' was excellent; there were four barley-sugar temples on the table, which would have looked beautiful if they had not melted away when the supper began; and a water-mill, whose only fault was that instead of going round, it ran over the table-cloth. Then there were fowls, and tongue, and trifle, and sweets, and lobster salad, and potted beef – and every thing. And little Kitterbell kept calling out for clean plates, and the clean plates did not come; and then the gentlemen who wanted the plates said they didn't mind they'd take a lady's; and then Mrs Kitterbell applauded their gallantry, and the greengrocer ran about till he thought his seven and sixpence was very hardly earned; and the young ladies didn't eat much for fear it shouldn't look romantic, and the married ladies eat as much as possible, for fear they shouldn't have enough; and a great deal of wine was drank, and every body talked and laughed considerably.

'Hush! hush!' said Mr Kitterbell, rising and looking very important. 'My love (this was addressed to his wife at the other end of the table), take care of Mrs Maxwell, and your mamma, and the rest of the married ladies; the gentlemen will persuade the young ladies to fill their glasses, I am sure.'

'Ladies and gentlemen,' said long Dumps, in a very sepulchral voice and rueful accent, rising from his chair like the ghost in Don Juan,[26] 'will you have the kindness to charge your glasses? I am desirous of proposing a toast.'

A dead silence ensued, and the glasses were filled – every body looked serious.

'Ladies and gentlemen,' slowly continued the ominous Dumps, 'I' – (here Mr Danton imitated two notes from the French-horn, in a very loud key, which electrified the nervous toast-proposer, and convulsed his audience).

'Order! order!' said little Kitterbell, endeavouring to suppress his laughter.

'Order!' said the gentlemen.

'Danton, be quiet,' said a particular friend on the opposite side of the table.

'Ladies and gentlemen,' resumed Dumps, somewhat recovered, and not much disconcerted, for he was always a pretty good hand at a speech – 'In accordance with what is, I believe, the established usage on these occasions, I, as one of the godfathers of Master Frederick Charles William Kitterbell – (here the speaker's voice faltered, for he remembered the mug) – venture to rise to propose a toast. I need hardly say that it is the health and prosperity of that young gentleman, the particular event of whose early life we are here met to celebrate – (applause). Ladies and gentlemen, it is impossible to suppose that our friends here, whose sincere well-wishers we all are, can pass through life without some trials, considerable suffering, severe affliction, and heavy losses!' – Here the arch-traitor paused, and slowly drew forth a long, white pocket-handkerchief – his example was followed by several ladies. 'That these trials may be long spared them, is my most earnest prayer, my most fervent wish (a distinct sob from the grand-mother). I hope and trust, ladies and gentlemen, that the infant whose christening we have this evening met to celebrate, may not be removed from the arms of his parents by premature decay (several cambrics were in requisition); that his young and now *apparently* healthy form, may not be wasted by lingering disease. (Here Dumps cast a sardonic glance around, for a great sensation was manifest among the married ladies.) You, I am sure, will concur with me in wishing that he may live to be a comfort and a blessing to his parents. ("Hear, hear!" and an audible sob from Mr Kitterbell.) But should he not be what we could wish – should he forget in after times, the duty which he owes to them – should they unhappily experience that distracting truth, "how sharper than a serpent's tooth it is to have a thankless child." '[27] – Here Mrs Kitterbell, with her handkerchief to her eyes, and accompanied by several ladies, rushed from the room, and went into violent hysterics in the passage, leaving her better half in almost as bad a condition, and a general impression in Dumps's favour; for people like sentiment, after all.

It need hardly be added, that this occurrence quite put a stop to the harmony of the evening. Vinegar, hartshorn, and cold water, were now as much in request as negus, rout-cakes, and *bon-bons* had been a short time before. Mrs Kitterbell was immediately conveyed to her apartment, the musicians were silenced, flirting ceased, and the company slowly departed. Dumps left the house at the commencement of the bustle, and walked home with a light step, and (for him) a cheerful heart. His landlady, who slept in the next room, has offered to make oath, that she heard him laugh in his peculiar manner, after he had locked his door. The assertion, however, is so improbable, and bears on the face of it such strong evidence of untruth, that it has never obtained credence to this hour.

The family of Mr Kitterbell has considerably increased since the period to which we have referred; he has now two sons and a daughter: and as he expects, at no distant period, to have another addition to his blooming progeny, he is anxious to secure an eligible godfather for the occasion. He is determined, however, to impose upon him two conditions. He must bind himself by a solemn obligation, not to make any speech after supper; and it is indispensable that he should be in no way connected with 'the most miserable man in the world.'

CHAPTER 12

The Drunkard's Death

WE will be bold to say, that there is scarcely a man in the constant habit of walking, day after day, through any of the crowded thoroughfares of London, who cannot recollect among the people whom he 'knows by sight,' to use a familiar phrase, some being of abject and wretched appearance whom he remembers to have seen in a very different condition, whom he has observed sinking lower and lower by almost imperceptible degrees, and the shabbiness and utter destitution of whose appearance, at last, strike forcibly and painfully upon him, as he passes by. Is there any man who has mixed much with society, or whose avocations have caused him to mingle, at one time or other, with a great number of people, who cannot call to mind the time when some shabby, miserable wretch, in rags and filth, who shuffles past him now in all the squalor of disease and poverty, was a respectable tradesman, or a clerk, or a man following some thriving pursuit, with good prospects, and decent means; – or cannot any of our readers call to mind from among the list of their *quondam* acquaintance, some fallen and degraded man, who lingers about the pavement in hungry misery – from whom every one turns coldly away, and who preserves himself from sheer starvation, nobody knows how? Alas! such cases are of too frequent occurrence to be rare items in any man's experience; and but too often arise from one cause — drunkenness, — that fierce rage for the slow, sure poison, that oversteps every other consideration: that casts aside wife, children, friends, happiness, and station; and hurries its victims madly on to degradation and death.

Some of these men have been impelled by misfortune and misery, to the vice that has degraded them. The ruin of worldly expectations, the death of those they loved, the sorrow that slowly consumes, but will not break the heart, has driven them wild; and they present the hideous spectacle of madmen, slowly dying by their own hands. But, by far the greater part have wilfully, and with open eyes, plunged into the gulf from which the man who once enters it never rises more, but into which he sinks deeper and deeper down, until recovery is hopeless.

Such a man as this, once stood by the bed-side of his dying wife, while his children knelt around, and mingled low bursts of grief with their innocent prayers. The room was scantily and meanly furnished; and it needed but a glance at the pale form from which the light of life was fast passing away, to know that grief, and want, and anxious care, had been busy at the heart for many a weary year. An elderly female with her face bathed in tears, was supporting the head of the dying woman — her daughter — on her arm. But it was not towards her that the wan face turned; it was not her hand that the cold and trembling fingers clasped; they pressed the husband's arm; the eyes so soon to be closed in death, rested on his face; and the man shook beneath their gaze. His dress was slovenly and disordered, his face inflamed, his eyes bloodshot and heavy. He had been summoned from some wild debauch to the bed of sorrow and death.

A shaded lamp by the bed-side cast a dim light on the figures around, and left the remainder of the room in thick, deep shadow. The silence of night prevailed without the house, and the stillness of death was in the chamber. A watch hung over the mantel-shelf; its low ticking was the only sound that broke the profound quiet, but it was a solemn one, for well they knew, who heard it, that before it had recorded the passing of another hour, it would beat the knell of a departed spirit.

It is a dreadful thing to wait and watch for the approach of death; to know that hope is gone, and recovery impossible; and to sit and count the dreary hours through long, long, nights – such nights as only watchers by the bed of sickness know. It chills the blood to hear the dearest secrets of the heart, the pent-up, hidden secrets of many years, poured forth by the unconscious helpless being before you; and to think how little the reserve, and cunning of a whole life will avail, when fever and delirium tear off the mask at last. Strange tales have been told in the wanderings of dying men; tales so full of guilt and crime, that those who stood by the sick person's couch have fled in horror and affright, lest they should be scared to madness by what they heard and saw; and many a wretch has died alone, raving of deeds, the very name of which, has driven the boldest man away.

But no such ravings were to be heard at the bed-side by which the children knelt. Their half-stifled sobs and moanings alone broke the silence of the lonely chamber. And when at last the mother's grasp relaxed; and turning one look from the children to their father, she vainly strove to speak, and fell backward on the pillow, all was so calm and tranquil that she seemed to sink to sleep. They leant over her; they called upon her name, softly at first, and then in the loud and piercing tones of desperation. But there was no reply. They listened for her breath, but no sound came. They felt for the palpitation of the heart, but no faint throb responded to the touch. That heart was broken, and she was dead!

The husband sunk into a chair by the bed-side, and clasped his hands upon his burning forehead. He gazed from child to child, but when a weeping eye met his, he quailed beneath its look. No word of comfort was whispered in his ear, no look of kindness lighted on his face. All shrunk from, and avoided him; and when at last he staggered from the room, no one sought to follow, or console the widower.

The time had been, when many a friend would have crowded round him in his affliction, and many a heartfelt condolence would have met him in his grief. Where were they now? One by one, friends, relations, the commonest acquaintance even, had fallen off from and deserted the drunkard. His wife alone had clung to him in good and evil, in sickness and poverty; and how had he rewarded her? He had reeled from the tavern to her bed-side, in time to see her die.

He rushed from the house, and walked swiftly through the streets. Remorse, fear, shame, all crowded on his mind. Stupified with drink, and bewildered with the scene he had just witnessed, he re-entered the tavern he had quitted shortly before. Glass succeeded glass. His blood mounted, and his brain whirled round. Death! Every one must die, and why not *she*. She was too good for him; her relations had often told him so. Curses on them! Had they not deserted her, and left her to whine away the time at home? Well; she was dead, and happy perhaps. It was better as it was. Another glass — one more! Hurrah! It was a merry life while it lasted; and he would make the most of it.

Time went on; the three children who were left to him, grew up, and were children no longer; — the father remained the same — poorer, shabbier, and more dissolute-looking, but the same confirmed and irreclaimable drunkard. The boys had, long ago, run wild in the streets, and left him; the girl alone remained, but she worked hard, and words or blows could always procure him something for the tavern. So he went on in the old course, and a merry life he led.

One night, as early as ten o'clock — for the girl had been sick for many days, and there was, consequently, little to spend at the public-house — he bent his steps homewards, bethinking himself that if he would have her able to earn money, it would be as well to apply to the parish surgeon, or, at all events, to take the trouble of inquiring what ailed her, which he had not yet thought it worth while to do. It was a wet December night; the wind blew piercing cold, and the rain poured heavily down. He begged a few half-pence from a passer by, and having bought a small loaf (for it was his interest to keep the girl alive, if he could) he shuffled onwards, as fast as the wind and rain would let him.

At the back of Fleet-street, and lying between it, and the waterside, are several mean and narrow courts, which form a portion of Whitefriars;[1] it was to one of these, that he directed his steps.

The alley into which he turned, might, for filth and misery, have competed with the darkest corner of this ancient sanctuary in its dirtiest and most lawless time. The houses, varying from two stories in height to four, were stained with every indescribable hue that long exposure to the weather, damp, and rottenness can impart to tenements composed originally of the roughest and coarsest materials. The windows were patched with paper, and stuffed with the foulest rags; the doors were falling from their hinges; poles with lines on which to dry clothes, projected from every casement, and sounds of quarrelling or drunkenness issued from every room.

The solitary oil lamp in the centre of the court had been blown out, either by the violence of the wind or the act of some inhabitant who had excellent reasons for objecting to his residence being rendered too conspicuous; and the only light which fell upon the broken and uneven pavement, was derived from the miserable candles that here and there twinkled in the rooms of such of the more fortunate residents as could afford to indulge in so expensive a luxury. A gutter ran down the centre of the alley – all the sluggish odours of which had been called forth by the rain; and as the wind whistled through the old houses, the doors and shutters creaked upon their hinges, and the windows shook in their frames, with a violence which every moment seemed to threaten the destruction of the whole place.

The man whom we have followed into this den, walked on in the darkness, sometimes stumbling into the main gutter, and at others into some branch repositories of garbage which had been formed by the rain, until he reached the last house in the court. The door, or rather what was left of it, stood ajar, for the convenience of the numerous lodgers; and he proceeded to grope his way up the old and broken stair, to the attic story.

He was within a step or two of his room door, when it opened, and a girl, whose miserable and emaciated appearance was only to be equalled by that of the candle which she shaded with her hand, peeped anxiously out.

'Is that you, father?' said the girl.

'Who else should it be?' replied the man gruffly. 'What are you trembling at? It's little enough that I've had to drink to-day, for there's no drink without money, and no money without work. What the devil's the matter with the girl?'

'I am not well father – not at all well,' said the girl, bursting into tears.

'Ah!' replied the man, in the tone of a person who is compelled to admit a very unpleasant fact, to which he would rather remain blind, if he could. 'You must get better somehow, for we must have money. You must go to the parish doctor, and make him give you some medicine. They're paid for it, damn 'em. What are you standing before the door, for? Let me come in, can't you?'

'Father,' whispered the girl, shutting the door behind her, and placing herself before it, 'William has come back.'

'Who!' said the man, with a start.

'Hush,' replied the girl, 'William; brother William.'

'And what does he want?' said the man, with an effort at composure – 'money? meat? drink? He's come to the wrong shop for that, if he does. Give me the candle – give me the candle, fool – I ain't going to hurt him.' He snatched the candle from her hand, and walked into the room.

Sitting on an old box, with his head resting on his hand, and his eyes fixed on a wretched cinder fire that was smouldering on the hearth, was a young man of about two-and-twenty, miserably clad in an old coarse jacket and trousers. He started up when his father entered.

'Fasten the door, Mary,' said the young man hastily – 'Fasten the door. You look as if you didn't know me, father. It's long enough, since you drove me from home; you may well forget me.'

'And what do you want here, now?' said the father, seating himself on a stool, on the other side of the fireplace. 'What do you want here, now?'

'Shelter,' replied the son, 'I'm in trouble; that's enough. If I'm caught I shall swing; that's certain. Caught I shall be, unless I stop here; that's *as* certain. And there's an end of it.'

'You mean to say, you've been robbing, or murdering, then?' said the father.

'Yes, I do,' replied the son. 'Does it surprise you, father?' He looked steadily in the man's face, but he withdrew his eyes, and bent them on the ground.

'Where's your brothers?' he said, after a long pause.

'Where they'll never trouble you,' replied his son: 'John's gone to America, and Henry's dead.'

'Dead!' said the father, with a shudder, which even he could not repress.

'Dead,' replied the young man. 'He died in my arms — shot like a dog, by a game-keeper. He staggered back, I caught him, and his blood trickled down my hands. It poured out from his side like water. He was weak, and it blinded him, but he threw himself down on his knees, on the grass, and prayed to God, that if his mother was in Heaven, He would hear her prayers for pardon for her youngest son. "I was her favourite boy, Will," he said, "and I am glad to think, now, that when she was dying, though I was a very young child then, and my little heart was almost bursting, I knelt down at the foot of the bed, and thanked God for having made me so fond of her as to have never once done any thing to bring the tears into her eyes. Oh, Will, why was she taken away, and father left!" There's his dying words, father,' said the young man; 'make the best you can of 'em. You struck him across the face, in a drunken fit, the morning we ran away; and here's the end of it.'

The girl wept aloud; and the father, sinking his head upon his knees, rocked himself to and fro.

'If I am taken,' said the young man, 'I shall be carried back into the country, and hung for that man's murder. They cannot trace me here, without your assistance, father. For aught I know, you may give me up to justice; but unless you do, here I stop, until I can venture to escape abroad.'

For two whole days, all three remained in the wretched room, without stirring out. On the third evening, however, the girl was worse than she had been yet, and the few scraps of food they had were gone. It was indispensably necessary that somebody should go out; and as the girl was too weak and ill, the father went, just at nightfall.

He got some medicine for the girl, and a trifle in the way of pecuniary assistance. On his way back, he earned sixpence by holding a horse; and he turned homewards with enough money to supply their most pressing wants for two or three days to come. He had to pass the public-house. He lingered for an instant, walked past it, turned back again, lingered once more, and finally slunk in. Two men whom he had not observed, were on the watch. They were on the point of giving up their search in despair, when his loitering attracted their attention; and when he entered the public-house, they followed him.

'You'll drink with me, master,' said one of them, proffering him a glass of liquor.

'And me too,' said the other, replenishing the glass as soon as it was drained of its contents.

The man thought of his hungry children, and his son's danger. But they were nothing to the drunkard. He *did* drink; and his reason left him.

'A wet night, Warden,' whispered one of the men in his ear, as he at length turned to go away, after spending in liquor one-half of the money on which, perhaps, his daughter's life depended.

'The right sort of night for our friends in hiding, Master Warden,' whispered the other.

'Sit down here,' said the one who had spoken first, drawing him into a corner. 'We have been looking arter the young un. We came to tell him, it's all right now, but we couldn't find him 'cause we hadn't got the precise direction. But that ain't strange, for I don't think he know'd it himself, when he come to London, did he?'

'No, he didn't,' replied the father.

The two men exchanged glances.

'There's a vessel down at the docks, to sail at midnight, when it's high water,' resumed the first speaker, 'and we'll put him on board. His passage is taken in another name, and what's better than that, it's paid for. It's lucky we met you.'

'Very,' said the second.

'Capital luck,' said the first, with a wink to his companion.

'Great,' replied the second, with a slight nod of intelligence.

'Another glass here; quick' – said the first speaker. And in five minutes more, the father had unconsciously yielded up his own son into the hangman's hands.

Slowly and heavily the time dragged along, as the brother and sister, in their miserable hiding-place, listened in anxious suspense to the slightest sound. At length, a heavy footstep was heard upon the stair; it approached nearer; it reached the landing; and the father staggered into the room.

The girl saw that he was intoxicated, and advanced with the candle in her hand to meet him; she stopped short, gave a loud scream, and fell senseless on the ground. She had caught sight of the shadow of a man, reflected on the floor. They both rushed in, and in another instant the young man was a prisoner, and handcuffed.

'Very quietly done,' said one of the men to his companion, 'thanks to the old man. Lift up the girl, Tom – come, come, it's no use crying, young woman. It's all over now, and can't be helped.'

The young man stooped for an instant over the girl, and then turned fiercely round upon his father, who had reeled against the wall, and was gazing on the group with drunken stupidity.

'Listen to me, father,' he said, in a tone that made the drunkard's flesh creep. 'My brother's blood, and mine, is on your head: I never had kind look, or word, or care, from you, and alive or dead, I never will forgive you. Die when you will, or how, I will be with you. I speak as a dead man now, and I warn you, father, that as surely as you must one day stand before your Maker so surely shall your children be there, hand in hand, to cry for judgment against you.' He raised his manacled hands in a threatening attitude, fixed his eyes on his shrinking parent, and slowly left the room; and neither father nor sister ever beheld him more, on this side of the grave.

When the dim and misty light of a winter's morning penetrated into the narrow court, and struggled through the begrimed window of the wretched room, Warden awoke from his heavy sleep, and found himself alone. He rose, and looked round him; the old flock mattress on the floor was undisturbed; every thing was just as he remembered to have seen it last: and there were no signs of any one, save himself, having occupied the room during the night. He inquired of the other lodgers, and of the neighbours; but his daughter had not been seen or heard of. He rambled through the streets, and scrutinized each wretched face among the crowds that thronged them, with anxious eyes. But his search was fruitless, and he returned to his garret when night came on, desolate and weary.

For many days he occupied himself in the same manner, but no trace of his daughter did he meet with, and no word of her reached his ears. At length he gave up the pursuit as hopeless. He had long thought of the probability of her leaving him, and endeavouring to gain her bread in quiet, elsewhere. She had left him at last to starve alone. He ground his teeth, and cursed her!

He begged his bread from door to door. Every halfpenny he could wring from the pity or credulity of those to whom he addressed himself, was spent in the old way. A year passed over his head; the roof of a jail was the only one that had sheltered him for many months. He slept under archways, and in brick-fields – any where, where there was some warmth or shelter from the cold and rain. But in the last stage of poverty, disease, and houseless want, he was a drunkard still.

At last, one bitter night, he sunk down on a door-step faint and ill. The premature decay of vice and profligacy had worn him to the bone. His cheeks were hollow and livid; his eyes were sunken, and their sight was dim. His legs trembled beneath his weight, and a cold shiver ran through every limb.

And now the long-forgotten scenes of a mispent life crowded thick and fast upon him. He thought of the time when he had a home – a happy, cheerful home – and of those who peopled it, and flocked about him then, until the forms of his elder children seemed to rise from the grave, and stand about him – so plain, so clear, and so distinct they were that he could touch and feel them. Looks that he had long forgotten were fixed upon him once more; voices long since hushed in death sounded in his ears like the music of village bells. But it was only for an instant. The rain beat heavily upon him; and cold and hunger were gnawing at his heart again.

He rose, and dragged his feeble limbs a few paces further. The street was silent and empty; the few passengers who passed by, at that late hour, hurried quickly on, and his tremulous voice was lost in the violence of the storm. Again that heavy chill struck through his frame, and his blood seemed to stagnate beneath it. He coiled himself up in a projecting doorway, and tried to sleep.

But sleep had fled from his dull and glazed eyes. His mind wandered strangely, but he was awake, and conscious. The well-known shout of drunken mirth sounded in his ear, the glass was at his lips, the board was covered with choice rich food – they were before him: he could see them all, he had but to reach out his hand, and take them – and, though the illusion was reality itself, he knew that he was sitting alone in the deserted street, watching the rain-drops as they pattered on the stones; that death was coming upon him by inches – and that there were none to care for or help him.

Suddenly, he started up, in the extremity of terror. He had heard his own voice shouting in the night air, he knew not what, or why. Hark! A groan! – another! His senses were leaving him: half-formed and incoherent words burst from his lips; and his hands sought to tear and lacerate his flesh. He was going mad, and he shrieked for help till his voice failed him.

He raised his head, and looked up the long dismal street. He recollected that outcasts like himself, condemned to wander day and night in those dreadful streets, had sometimes gone distracted with their own loneliness. He remembered to have heard many years before that a homeless wretch had once been found in a solitary corner, sharpening a rusty knife to plunge into his own heart, preferring death to that endless, weary, wandering to and fro. In an instant his resolve was taken, his limbs received new life; he ran quickly from the spot, and paused not for breath until he reached the river-side.

He crept softly down the steep stone stairs that lead from the commencement of Waterloo Bridge,[2] down to the water's level. He crouched into a corner, and held his breath, as the patrol passed. Never did prisoner's heart throb with the hope of liberty and life half so eagerly as did that of the wretched man at the prospect of death. The watch passed close to him, but he remained unobserved; and after waiting till the sound of footsteps had died away in the distance, he cautiously descended, and stood beneath the gloomy arch that forms the landing-place from the river.

The tide was in, and the water flowed at his feet. The rain had ceased, the wind was lulled, and all was, for the moment, still and quiet — so quiet that the slightest sound on the opposite bank, even the rippling of the water against the barges that were moored there, was distinctly audible to his ear. The stream stole languidly and sluggishly on. Strange and fantastic forms rose to the surface, and beckoned him to approach; dark gleaming eyes peered from the water, and seemed to mock his hesitation, while hollow murmurs from behind, urged him onwards. He retreated a few paces, took a short run, desperate leap, and plunged into the river.

Not five seconds had passed when he rose to the water's surface — but what a change had taken place in that short time, in all his thoughts and feelings! Life — life — in any form, poverty, misery, starvation — any thing but death. He fought and struggled with the water that closed over his head, and screamed in agonies of terror. The curse of his own son rang in his ears. The shore — but one foot of dry ground — he could almost touch the step. One hand's breadth nearer, and he was saved — but the tide bore him onward, under the dark arches of the bridge, and he sank to the bottom.

Again he rose, and struggled for life. For one instant — for one brief instant — the buildings on the river's banks, the lights on the bridge through which the current had borne him, the black water, and the fast flying clouds, were distinctly visible — once more he sunk, and once again he rose. Bright flames of fire shot up from earth to heaven, and reeled before his eyes, while the water thundered in his ears, and stunned him with its furious roar.

A week afterwards the body was washed ashore, some miles

down the river, a swollen and disfigured mass. Unrecognized and unpitied, it was borne to the grave; and there it has long since mouldered away!

THE END

APPENDIX A

The First Publication of the Sketches *in Periodical, Volume and Number Form*

A. Monthly Magazine *Tales*

1833	December	A Dinner at Poplar Walk
1834	January	Mrs Joseph Porter 'Over the Way'
	February	Horatio Sparkins
	April	The Bloomsbury Christening
	May	The Boarding-house
	August	The Boarding-house — No. 2 [the first sketch signed 'Boz']
	October	The Steam Excursion
1835	January	A Passage in the Life of Mr Watkins Tottle, Chapter the First
	February	A Passage in the Life of Mr Watkins Tottle, Chapter the Second

B. Bell's Weekly Magazine

1834	June 7	Sentiment! [unsigned]

C. Morning Chronicle *'Street Sketches'*

1834	September 26	Omnibuses
	October 10	Shops and Their Tenants
	23	The Old Bailey
	November 5	Shabby-genteel People
	December 15	Brokers' and Marine-store Shops

D. Evening Chronicle *'Sketches of London'*

1835	January 31	Hackney-coach Stands
	February 7	Gin-shops
	19	Early Coaches
	28	The Parish (The Beadle — The Parish Engine — The Schoolmaster)

E. Bell's Life in London *'Scenes and Characters' (by 'Tibbs')*

F. Sketches by Boz *(8 February 1836)*

A Visit to Newgate
London Recreations
The Boarding-house (2 chapters)
Hackney-coach Stands
Brokers' and Marine-store Shops
The Bloomsbury Christening
Gin Shops
Public Dinners
Astley's
Greenwich Fair
The Prisoners' Van
A Christmas Dinner

Horatio Sparkins
The Pawnbroker's Shop
The Dancing Academy
Early Coaches
The River
Private Theatres
The Great Winglebury Duel
Omnibuses
Mrs Joseph Porter
The Steam Excursion
Sentiment

G. Morning Chronicle

1836.   March 18   Our Next-door Neighbours

H. The Library of Fiction, or Family Story-teller

1836   · March 31   The Tuggs's at Ramsgate
             May 31   A Little Talk about Spring, and the Sweeps

I. Carlton Chronicle

1836   August   6   The Hospital Patient
            September 17   Hackney-cabs, and Their Drivers

J. Morning Chronicle 'Sketches by Boz, New Series

1836   September 24   Meditations in Monmouth-street
            October   4   Scotland-yard
                     11   Doctors' Commons
                     26   Vauxhall-Gardens by Day

K. Sketches by Boz: Second Series [1837]

1836   December 17   The Streets by Morning
                          The Streets by Night
                          Making a Night of It
                          Criminal Courts

Scotland-Yard
The New Year
Meditations in Monmouth-Street
Our Next-door Neighbours
The Hospital Patient
Seven Dials
The Mistaken Milliner
Doctors' Commons
Misplaced Attachment of Mr John Dounce
Vauxhall-Gardens by Day
A Parliamentary Sketch — with a few Portraits
Mr Minns and his Cousin
The Last Cab-driver, and the First Omnibus Cad
The Parlour Orator
The First of May
The Drunkard's Death

L. *The Periodical Numbers of* Sketches by Boz

Part 1

1837	November	The Beadle — The Parish Engine — The Schoolmaster
		The Curate — The Old Lady — The Half-pay Captain
		The Four Sisters
		The Election for Beadle

Part 2

	December	The Election for Beadle (concluded)
		The Broker's Man
		Our Next-door Neighbours

Part 3

1838	January	Our Next-door Neighbours (concluded)
		The Streets — Morning
		The Streets — Night
		Shops and Their Tenants
		Scotland-yard

Part 17

March   Horatio Sparkins (concluded)
The Black Veil
The Steam Excursion

Part 18

April   The Steam Excursion (concluded)
The Great Winglebury Duel

Part 19

May   The Great Winglebury Duel (concluded)
Mrs Joseph Porter
Passage in the Life of Mr Watkins Tottle

Part 20

June   Passage in the Life of Mr Watkins Tottle
(concluded)
The Bloomsbury Christening
The Drunkard's Death

M. Sketches by Boz *(1839)*

Complete in one volume, contents arranged as in monthly parts above, in four sections: Seven Sketches from Our Parish, Scenes, Characters and Tales.

Running headlines on the right-hand leaf of each page were added for this edition. They are indicated here by the opening and closing words of each passage they refer to.

OUR PARISH

CHAPTER 1 *,The Beadle – The Parish Engine – The Schoolmaster*

holder next day, for . . . he had never *The Schoolmaster.*

CHAPTER 2 *The Curate – The Old Lady – The Half-pay Captain*

gruel and a quarter . . . the glass and picture- *The Curate.*
A very different personage . . . [Chapter 3] once without further preface *The Captain.*

CHAPTER 3 *The Four Sisters*

the other, that the . . . to speak with a *A Quadrilateral Marriage.*

CHAPTER 4 *The Election for Beadle*

asperity and determination with . . . his capacity of director *Party Politics.*
in rusty black, with . . . years of age. Spruggins *Nomination.*

CHAPTER 5 *The Broker's Man*

his fluctuations have been . . . as if they wished it *Mr Bung's Materials.*
and the gentleman laughed . . . who sat rocking herself *Mr Bung's best Job.*
crying, letting the warrant . . . wife he has lost.' *Another kind of Execution.*

APPENDIX B

CHAPTER 6 *The Ladies' Societies*

the mother of seven . . . of age, respectively, *The Three Miss Browns.*
At length, a very . . . [Chapter 7] and never say *do. Knockers of the Past.*

CHAPTER 7 *Our Next-door Neighbour*

ing songs with half-a-dozen . . . and Sunday papers. *The Single Gentleman
  next door.*
her hastily towards him . . . The boy was dead. *The Dying Request.*

SCENES

CHAPTER 1 *The Streets — Morning*

women (principally the . . . whether the friends and *An Hour after Daybreak.*
their aid, and they . . . [Chapter 2] and Mrs Macklin *Beginning Business.*

CHAPTER 2 *The Streets — Night*

in her arms, round . . . patronizing manner possible *A Cave of Harmony.*

CHAPTER 3 *Shops and Their Tenants*

fall – of particular shops . . . females who interfere with *A Doomed Shop.*

CHAPTER 4 *Scotland-yard*

SCOTLAND-YARD is a small – . . . bring vague rumours *The public-house at
  the Corner.*
dow the pattern of . . . [Chapter 5] a pure mixture of *The Spirit of Change.*

CHAPTER 5 *Seven Dials*

posts. We never saw . . . summer's evening, and *The Dials in General.*

CHAPTER 6 *Meditations in Monmouth-street*

nary wearers; lines of . . . meant to be *Old Clothes.*
regard; and we had got . . . a shrill, and *A Jolly Pair of Boots.*

CHAPTER 7 *Hackney-coach Stands*

were not blind. We . . . at a standstill. *Our Knowledge of our Subject.*

CHAPTER 8 *Doctors' Commons*

names, we no sooner . . . though – perhaps with *The Arches Court.*
over large volumes . . . Doctors' Commons! *Wills.*

CHAPTER 9 *London Recreations*

maintaining it. This . . . and periwinkles – tea *The Light of Life.*

CHAPTER 10 *The River*

Chapter X . . . defunct oyster-swallower *No successful Water-party*
  possible.
have been waiting at . . . 'Passenger to Gravesend' *The Stout Father.*

CHAPTER 11 *Astley's*

We never see . . . eye, with a look *Family Party at the Play.*
uniform with a . . . has to boast night *The Ring.*

CHAPTER 12 *Greenwich Fair*

If the Parks . . . consequence of having *The Road down.*
Five minutes' walking . . . heir, who loves *Richardson's.*
himself up like a . . . [Chapter 13] gentleman's dressing-room *The Shows*
  and the Ball-room.

CHAPTER 13 *Private Theatres*

inferior performances as . . . his father's, coal and *Stage-struck.*
ment. The black-eyed . . . [Chapter 14] great deal in the *'Ring-up!'*

CHAPTER 14 *Vauxhall-gardens by Day*

similar manner; then . . . little man. 'If he *Disenchantment.*

CHAPTER 15 *Early Coaches*

before the one . . . all night, be- *New Torture of the Wheel.*
for aught you can . . . conclusion of our paper. *The Start.*

CHAPTER 16 *Omnibuses*

can chuck an old . . . opened to receive *Cads and Regulars.*

CHAPTER 17 *The Last Cab-driver, and the First Omnibus Cad*

have performed such . . . with merriment. The *The Red Cab.*
A story is nothing . . . A want of appli- *Mr William Barker.*
scrunched children, and . . . men to which *A Rival Genius.*

CHAPTER 18 *A Parliamentary Sketch*

two young fellows . . . to the Strangers' *M.P.*
You are curious . . . wine-inspired fancies, in *The Potent Two-and-Sixpence.*
wonder he ever . . . from some cause *Jane.*

CHAPTER 19 *Public Dinners*

ALL public dinners . . . screwing tremendously – *The Indigent Orphans.*
as if it were . . . twenty pound' [protracted *Silence for the Chair!*

CHAPTER 20 *The First of May*

In former times . . . question is settled *Spring Recollections.*
expressed himself in . . . of cinders, and *Mr Sluffen's Oration.*

CHAPTER 21 *Brokers' and Marine-store Shops*

WHEN we affirm . . . equalled by our *Odds and Ends.*
backs of the . . . [Chapter 22] and he either *The Surrey Side.*

CHAPTER 22 *Gin-shops*

which divide it . . . such cases, abruptly *Company at the Bar.*

CHAPTER 23 *The Pawnbroker's Shop*

OF the numerous . . . cheap silver pen- *From Without.*
ankecher, as . . . till you're sober *A Lord of Creation.*
There are strange . . . [Chapter 24] look like multiplica- *Just let out.*

CHAPTER 24 *Criminal Courts*

his face when . . . trouble as possible *Juvenile Offenders.*

CHAPTER 25 *A Visit to Newgate*

but for his . . . into an irrepres- *Its Internal Arrangement.*
shelf above. At . . . at all. We *Its Women and Boys.*
with all their . . . some mitigatory cir- *Its Chapel and Press-yard.*
can know. He . . . speed and lightness, *Its condemned Prisoner.*

CHARACTERS

CHAPTER 1 *Thoughts about People*

It is strange . . . lasts the year *A monotonous Existence.*
members of them . . . dotage anywhere. *Second-hand Airs.*

CHAPTER 2 *A Christmas Dinner*

things, and grandpapa . . . room to welcome *Under the Mistletoe.*

CHAPTER 3 *The New Year*

NEXT to Christmas-day . . . politics and *The House with the Green Blinds.*
year to them!' . . . within us now. *Speech of Mr Tupple.*

CHAPTER 4 *Miss Evans and the Eagle*

after a great blushing . . . in inverse proportion. *Dazzling Excitement.*

CHAPTER 5 *The Parlour Orator*

'You had much . . . *them*,' says I. *The Parlour itself.*
'What is a . . . [Chapter 6] and desolation *The Red-faced Man waxes warm.*

CHAPTER 6 *The Hospital Patient*

two long rows . . . covered a corpse. *At the Bedside.*

CHAPTER 7 *Misplaced Attachment of Mr John Dounce*

and did when . . . Dounce's red *Concerning Old Boys.*
that the three . . . [Chapter 8] complaint, Miss *Miss Amelia Martin.*

CHAPTER 8 *The Mistaken Milliner*

Ruffian, retire!' . . . Drummond-street, George- *Miss Martin resolves to come out.*

CHAPTER 9 *The Dancing Academy*

OF all the . . . nice man – and *A Pupil attracted.*
should pay for . . . Billsmethi betrayed *Mr Augustus Cooper gets on.*

CHAPTER 10 *Shabby-genteel People*

We will endeavour . . . meditation on *Haunted by a Shabby-gentleman.*

CHAPTER 11 *Making a Night of It*

DAMON and Pythias . . . with a dinner; *Messrs Potter and Smithers.*
'Give that dog . . . of the specta- *A disastrous end.*

CHAPTER 12 *The Prisoners' Van*

gentlemen under the . . . as men of fifty — *Reaping the whirlwind.*

TALES

CHAPTER 1 *The Boarding-house*

Chapter the First

MRS TIBBS was . . . with all the com- *Mr Tibbs.*
another of the boarders . . . failure, for no *The Boarders.*
of those *chef-d'œuvres* . . . parenthesis in *Dinner and Dinner Talk.*
Juan — it was . . . in full operation. *Six Months After.*
'Will you have . . . all three laughed. *Mr Calton in an unpleasant situation.*
geration, cant, and . . . [Chapter the Second] Saint something *T.I. to I.T.*

Chapter the Second

'No what?' . . . added to the *Mrs Bloss.*
and exceedingly short . . . bottling up his *New set of Boarders.*
'On his arrival . . . Sunday evenings.' *General Conversation.*
repeat, I fear . . . 'Excellent!' said Tomkins. *Assistance for Mrs Tibbs.*
'This way . . . was Wisbottle. *General Bewilderment.*
'The devil you . . . inverted commas *Retirement of Mrs Tibbs.*

CHAPTER 2 *Mr Minns and His Cousin*

'Budden!' . . . galvanic battery. *Mr Budden.*
rendered desperate . . . ensued, during which *Mr Budden's Guests.*
'Hear! hear!' . . . the boy in *Toasts.*

CHAPTER 3 *Sentiment*

'Cornelius Brook . . . Alfred Muggs. *Mr Cornelius Brook Dingwall.*
Preparations, to make . . . in her face. *The Ball.*
paid to Miss Lavinia's . . . Dingwall, Esq., M.P., *Theodosius Butler.*
Some time has . . . [Chapter 4] and a blue bag. *Tidings from the Temple.*

CHAPTER 4 *The Tuggs's at Ramsgate*

'We must leave . . . said the young lady. *Captain (and Mrs Captain)*
  Waters.
with a pressure of . . . placid Mrs Tuggs. *Sea-side Lodgings.*
bed, and the . . . Mary Golding, too.' *Wonders of the Sea-shore.*
This abrupt termination . . . without a cloud; *Towards Parnassus, on a*
  Donkey.
'Amelia, my dear . . . murmured unintelligibly. *Platonic love.*
'Oh, no; I . . . [Chapter 5] say again, every *A Frightful Tableau.*

CHAPTER 5 *Horatio Sparkins*

to his two . . . was very unnecessary. *The Conquering Hero comes.*
Horatio bowed his . . . vulgar, and *Tom.*
'Here's Mr Sparkins!' . . . plain manner –' *Mr Flamwell referred to.*
'I don't exactly . . . to the slight *'The point' gained.*
Mr Samuel Smith . . . [Chapter 6] lady? Where?' *A patient for a young*
  doctor.

CHAPTER 6 *The Black Veil*

expression of the . . . information by *An appointment made.*
yards from the . . . fender, was *In a strange position.*
him as he rose . . . The Black Veil. *Past recovery.*

CHAPTER 7 *The Steam Excursion*

with a silk . . . short a notice. *Modern Council of Ten.*
thistle, he . . . Briggs, by *Vote by Ballot.*
sweep was . . . pastrycook's men went *On Board.*
'Now, is every . . . Briggs, with whom *Off!*
'What is the . . . complete defeat. *The Briggses and Tauntons.*
'How illiberal! . . . the same moment. *Wind getting up.*
scrupled to state . . . [Chapter 8] the elegant and *The Captain a Failure.*

CHAPTER 8 *The Great Winglebury Duel*

adjusted the glasses . . . Stiffun's Acre;' *Alarming Missive.*
other manifestations . . . can't you?' *Miss Julia Manners.*

'I will,' said the mayor . . . *very* extraordinary!' *Mr Trott acknowledges it.*
'Won't do!' . . . furious madman.' *A Madman in the House.*
more and more . . . Winglebury Duel. *Drive to Gretna Green.*

CHAPTER 9 *Mrs Joseph Porter*

of course, we . . . to say, that −' *Private Theatricals.*
into the dress . . . rounds of applause, *Uncle Tom and Shakspeare.*
'Yes, I know . . . immortal bard. *Uncle Tom obligingly prompts.*

CHAPTER 10 *Passage in the Life of Mr Watkins Tottle*

Chapter the First
may say remarkably . . . − is she?' *Mr Gabriel Parsons.*
A gleam of . . . of very prim *Timson and Tottle arrive.*
for shame, and . . . had walked *Mr Parsons describes his Courtship.*
laughed it off . . . card-playing, drank *Cutting for Partners.*

Chapter the Second
'Werry well,' . . . to let Parsons *Mr Solomon Jacobs's.*
'ooman's here . . . bitterly, and the *A liberally educated young gentleman.*
be very respectable . . . fifty pounds.' *Ikey.*
'Pooh, nonsense!' . . . awful change. *Mr Tottle makes a bold start.*
could hardly see . . . you're wanted.' *Clearing the way.*
'It is,' . . . it off so!' *Enchanting avowal.*
Mr Watkins Tottle . . . therefrom nor *Slightly mistaken.*

CHAPTER 11 *The Bloomsbury Christening*

sharp, spare man . . . as warmly *Dumps and Nephew.*
Monday was . . . disadvantage of being *On the way to the Christening.*
and almonds . . . mantle off.' *Uncle Dumps sees a likeness.*
'Good God!' . . . general laugh. *Where is the Mug?*
rueful accent . . . in the world.' *Uncle Dumps does his duty.*

CHAPTER 12 *The Drunkard's Death*

it had recorded . . . many days, *The last link broken.*
'Hush,' replied . . . for two or *His Children.*
He raised his . . . words burst *The memory of the past.*

NOTES

I have not normally glossed words or phrases to be found in current dictionaries of English. Some entries indicate textual variants. Brief details of the initial publication of each item are given at the head of their respective notes. Like all other commentators on Dickens's work, I am indebted to the painstaking labours of T.W. Hill, whose notes on *Sketches by Boz* are in the *Dickensian*, vols. 46–8 (1950–52). I have also found Arthur Hayward, *The Dickens Encyclopaedia* (London: Routledge & Sons, 1924), William Kent, *An Encyclopaedia of London* (London: J.M. Dent & Sons, 1951 revised edn.), and Nicholas Bentley, Michael Slater and Nina Burgis, *The Dickens Index* (Oxford: Oxford University Press, 1988) useful.

I have referred to John Butt and Kathleen Tillotson, *Dickens at Work*, first published 1957 (London: Methuen, 1968 edn.), as *Dickens at Work*; Charles Dickens, *The Uncommercial Traveller and Reprinted Pieces*, New Oxford Illustrated Dickens (London: Oxford University Press, 1968), as *Uncommercial Traveller*; and *The Letters of Charles Dickens*, eds. Madeline House and Graham Storey, The Pilgrim Edition (Oxford: Clarendon Press, 1965–?), as Pilgrim *Letters*.

PREFACE TO THE FIRST EDITION OF THE FIRST SERIES

1. (p. 7) *GEORGE CRUIKSHANK* Cruikshank (1792–1878), largely self-taught artist and caricaturist, and the leading illustrator of the time, went on to collaborate with Dickens on *Oliver Twist* and some minor pieces. His tendency towards the fantastic and grotesque, however suitable for *Oliver*, subsequently led the author to cast about for alternatives. But Cruikshank's knowledge of London life and scenery made him an ideal partner for Dickens's first venture, as the publisher who proposed him (John Macrone) must have realized. Cruikshank came to believe he had inspired or originated some of Dickens's novels, and many others by contemporaries. But he and Dickens had already parted over the artist's conversion to the temperance movement.

2. (p. 7) *FURNIVAL'S INN* Former Inn of Chancery, Holborn, rebuilt in 1817 when it ceased to exist as a legal community. Dickens lived in chambers here from 1834 to 1837, and wrote most of the *Sketches* here. Demolished in 1895, now the site of the Prudential Assurance Company head office.

PREFACE TO THE SECOND SERIES

1. (p. 9) *brevity be the soul of wit*   See *Hamlet*, II.2.90.
2. (p. 9) *Christmas Piece*   Although the Second Series was published by John Macrone in 1837, it came out in time for Christmas 1836: the first instance of Dickens looking to that festival as an opportunity to sell his work.

PREFACE TO THE FIRST CHEAP EDITION

1. (p. 11) *FIRST CHEAP EDITION*   This Preface to the 1850 edition was reprinted unchanged in all later editions.
2. (p. 11) *beyond a few words and phrases here and there*   A 'misleading, if not disingenuous' remark, according to *Dickens at Work*, p. 39. Dickens continued to revise the *Sketches* in successive editions. See A Note on the Text and Illustrations (pp. xl–xlii) for the choice of the 1839 edition as the basis of this text, rather than the 1850 or later editions.

SEVEN SKETCHES FROM OUR PARISH

The first six sketches under this title were originally published as part of the series of twenty 'Sketches of London' in the *Evening Chronicle*. They were collected for volume 1 of *Sketches by Boz* (1836), where they were placed at the beginning; and then, with a seventh chapter ('Our Next-door Neighbour') from the *Morning Chronicle*, were similarly included for the 1839 edition. See Appendix A and individual headnotes for further details.

CHAPTER 1 *The Beadle − The Parish Engine − The Schoolmaster*

First published in the *Evening Chronicle* (28 February 1835).

1. (p. 17) *'The Parish!'*   The basic administrative division of local government, originally an area having its own church and clergyman; governed until the Local Government Act of 1894 by a body known as the vestry, from the vestry-room attached to a church or chapel, where ratepayers elected the parish officers, that is, the vestry-clerk, churchwardens and overseers − the latter being in charge of relieving the poor in the parish. The New Poor Law of 1834 transferred responsibility for dealing with the local poor from vestries to newly constituted Boards of Guardians; parishes were grouped together into 'poor law unions', and new workhouses built for the reception of the destitute under deliberately austere conditions. See also *Oliver Twist*, Chapters 1−3; and 'Our Vestry' (1852), in *Uncommercial Traveller*, pp. 574−80.

2. (p. 17) *The parish beadle*   This minor functionary was to be the object of Dickens's scorn throughout his career, although the classic depiction is Mr Bumble in *Oliver Twist*. Mediating between the authorities and the poor, the beadle was a figure likely to be trusted by those above him, and feared by those below.

3. (p. 18) *order into the House*   That is, into the workhouse, for food and shelter on the rates.

4. (p. 18) *one of Mr Hobler's*   Francis Hobler, solicitor and principal clerk at the Mansion House (Lord Mayor of London's) Police Court, well known as a cracker of jokes.

5. (p. 20) *his legal reward*   That is, his fee for the fire engine (a manual pump on a four-wheeled carriage).

6. (p. 21) *national school*   Anglican day school. The National Society for Promoting the Education of the Poor in the Principles of the Established Church was founded in 1809, and by 1831 there were 13,000 national schools. The British and Foreign Society administered schools for Nonconformists.

CHAPTER 2 *The Curate — The Old Lady — The Half-pay Captain*

First published in the *Evening Chronicle* (19 May 1835).

1. (p. 24) *the three Miss Browns* They reappear in Chapter 6, below, as Sunday School organizers and teachers.

2. (p. 24) *free seats* For those who could not afford to hire a pew in church. See also Chapter 6, note 2 below.

3. (p. 24) *half-baptize* Children not yet received into the Church could be 'half-baptized', that is, at home, when the full service was inconvenient or impossible, for instance because of illness or impending death. The new curate's willingness to go to the poor, his preaching extempore, his support for the anti-slavery movement, and his personal vanity, suggest an Evangelical type. See also Chapter 6, below. Oliver Twist was half-baptized (Chapter 2).

4. (p. 24) *watch-box on wheels* A movable contrivance used by workmen or night-watchmen.

5. (p. 25) *bosom friends* Slang: chest-protectors.

6. (p. 25) *the antipodes of the curate* The forerunner of many satirical portraits of Methodist, Low Church, Evangelical or Nonconformist clergymen or ministers in Dickens, from Stiggins in *Pickwick Papers* to Boanerges Boiler in 'City of London Churches' (1860), in *Uncommercial Traveller*, pp. 83–93. See also Chapter 6, note 3, below.

7. (p. 26) *old lady . . . list of baptisms* Mrs Mary Newnham (?1754–1843), a neighbour of the Dickens family when they lived in Chatham (1817–22).

8. (p. 26) *little picture of the Princess Charlotte and Prince Leopold . . . Drury-lane Theatre* Dates the old lady: the Princess Charlotte (1796–1817) was the only daughter of the Prince Regent (later George IV), who married Leopold (1790–1865: son of the Duke of Saxe-Coburg) in 1816, but died the year after. Drury Lane Theatre, established in the 1660s, is at the corner of Catherine and Russell Streets, Covent Garden. The present building was opened in 1812.

9. (p. 26) *cheerful, but rather more serious* 'Serious' implied more religious, and was commonly used of and by Evangelicals; hence the open Bible. See also Chapter 7, below, and the 'serious' new neighbour.

10. (p. 27) *Pope Joan board* Card game for three or more players, on a circular painted board or table with counters; so named after legendary female pope who reigned as John VIII in the ninth century. 'Pope Joan' is the nine of diamonds.

11. (p. 27) *pew-opener* In the days of pews with doors, usually a woman (like Mrs Miff in *Dombey and Son*, Chapter 31).

12. (p. 28) *naval officer on half-pay* Named in Chapter 4, below, as Captain Purday. Naval or military officers were placed on half-pay when they retired from active service.

13. (p. 28) *'A regular Robinson Crusoe'* Hero of one of Dickens's favourite books, Daniel Defoe's *The Life and Strange Adventures of Robinson Crusoe of York, Mariner* (1719).

CHAPTER 3 *The Four Sisters*

First published in the *Evening Chronicle* (18 June 1835).

1. (p. 30) *'time and tide wait for no man'* Originally 'Time and tide stayeth for no man,' Richard Brathwaite, *The English Gentleman* (1630).

2. (p. 30) *register-stoves* Stoves with a movable flap in the hole leading to the chimney-flue, by which to regulate the draught and so control the heat of the room.

3. (p. 30) *three long graces . . . the three fates . . . Siamese twins multiplied by two* Dickens draws first on the mythical three daughters of Zeus who embodied beauty, charm and grace (a favourite marble ornament in Victorian households), then on the three cruel sister Fates, and to make the comparison more complicated (and perhaps muddled) still, brings in a contemporary allusion; to the twins born in Thailand in 1811 joined at the breastbone, and exhibited in London in 1829.

4. (p. 31) *of Eastern descent* Facetious: that is, he was a Muslim and permitted to marry several wives at once.

5. (p. 32) *glass-coaches* Coaches with glazed panels all round. Ordinary coaches had no windows, and sliding wooden shutters in the doors.

6. (p. 32) *kersey* Woollen material formerly manufactured in Kersey, Suffolk.

7. (p. 33) *in the best regulated families* Toned down for family readership from the *Evening Chronicle* version by omitting '— indeed the best regulated are usually supposed to be the most subject to such occurrences'.

8. (p. 34) *long white roller . . . conjecture* Fuller details of Victorian babyclothes, including the 'roller' in which they were bandaged, can be found in Dickens's 'Births. Mrs Meek, of a Son' (1851), in *Uncommercial Traveller*, pp. 426–30.

9. (p. 34) *in propriá personá* Latin: in person, personally. The use of such tags is unusual in Dickens, and he avoided them in his later writings.

CHAPTER 4 *The Election for Beadle*

First published in the *Evening Chronicle* (14 July 1835).

1. (p. 35) *Watching-rates* Tax levied for the upkeep of the watchmen who were later superseded by the police. All the rates/taxes here listed were later incorporated into a single general rate.
2. (p. 35) *stamp duty on newspapers* The tax on newspapers was reduced in 1836, but not repealed until 1855.
3. (p. 36) *paupers' soup* A regular topic of attack, famously repeated in *Oliver Twist*, Chapter 2.
4. (p. 38) *'high-lows'* Popular term for ankle-boots − not as far up the leg as top-boots, nor as low cut as shoes.
5. (p. 39) *'taking a double sight'* 'Taking a sight' is putting the thumb to the nose and spreading the fingers out: a vulgar expression of defiance or contempt.
6. (p. 39) *envy . . . and all uncharitableness* From the Litany, Book of Common Prayer. The full petition runs 'Good Lord, deliver us. From all blindness of heart; from pride, vain-glory, and hypocrisy; from envy, hatred, and malice, and all uncharitableness.'
7. (p. 40) *anti-slavery petition* Slavery was abolished in 1833.

CHAPTER 5 *The Broker's Man*

First published in the *Evening Chronicle* (28 July 1835).

1. (p. 43) *a broker* Employed by the courts to value debtors' effects for rent or other unpaid debt. Dickens knew about all this at first hand, as a result of his impecunious father's activities.
2. (p. 44) *levying a distress* Distraint, or legal warrant for the seizure of possessions to settle a debt.
3. (p. 44) *an old Dutch clock* That is, German (*Deutsch*) clock, originally from the Black Forest and made of wood, with brass works.
4. (p. 45) *as a kitten in a wash-house copper with the lid on* An early

example of a 'Wellerism', the comic working-class figurative speech tags developed in Sam Weller, *Pickwick Papers, passim.*

5. (p. 45) *as a cheap cowcumber* Cockney rendering of 'cucumber', later used by Mrs Gamp in *Martin Chuzzlewit,* Chapter 26. The broker's man's monologue is a good example of Dickens's early interest in rendering working-class speech.

6. (p. 46) *sheriff's poundage* Fee based on the value (one shilling in the pound up to £100, and sixpence thereafter) on goods distrained by a broker, payable to a sheriff's officer for his services in court (obsolete).

7. (p. 49) *all in the house* The workhouse.

8. (p. 50) *an execution* Forcible possession of a debtor's house and goods to be sold to pay the debt.

CHAPTER 6 *The Ladies' Societies*

First published in the *Evening Chronicle* (20 August 1835).

1. (p. 53) *A little learning is a dangerous thing* From Pope, *An Essay on Criticism* (1711), line 215.

2. (p. 54) *in the free seats* See also Chapter 2, note 2, above. One East End curate of the time observed that the 'steady poor' who 'occupied the free seats in his church practised the highest standard of Christianity that he had ever known' (quoted in Owen Chadwick, *The Victorian Church* (London: A. & C. Black, 1970), Part I, p. 332.

3. (p. 54) *A missionary returned from the West Indies* Highly topical, and characteristic of Dickens to present the missionary in a satiric light. After the 1833 abolition of slavery, many Evangelicals, within and outside the Church of England, were even more eager to encourage the conversion of black people. It is worth noting that some missionaries so roused the wrath of the white planters in the West Indies that their chapels were burnt down. See *Pickwick Papers*, Chapter 27; and Norris Pope, *Dickens and Charity* (London and Basingstoke: Macmillan, 1978), pp. 96–8. See also Chapter 2, note 6, above.

4. (p. 57) *'Exeter Hall'* Built in the Strand in 1830–31 for concerts and undenominational religious meetings, long since pulled down. Dickens later remarked that 'It might be laid down as a very good general rule of social and political guidance, that whatever Exeter Hall champions, is the thing by no means to be done.' 'The Niger Expedition', *Examiner* (19 August 1848),

reprinted in *Miscellaneous Papers*, ed. B.W. Matz (London: Chapman and Hall, 1914), p. 108.

5. (p. 57) *the orator (an Irishman) came*   Presented to first readers of the *Chronicle* as 'Mr Somebody O'Something, a celebrated Catholic renegade and Protestant bigot' and in the first edition as 'Mr Mortimer O'Silly-one', a reference to the Reverend Mortimer O'Sullivan, who had described the conditions of the Irish Protestant clergy at meetings in Exeter Hall in June and July 1835: see *Dickens at Work*, p. 47.

CHAPTER 7 *Our Next-door Neighbour*

First published in both the *Morning Chronicle* and the *Evening Chronicle* as 'Our Next-door Neighbours' (18 March 1836).

1. (p. 61) *Eaton Square, then just building*   In Belgravia, south-west London. A fine flowering of late Georgian London, Eaton Square was begun in 1827 as part of the development of the area, by the great building speculator Thomas Cubitt.
2. (p. 63) *surtout . . . with frogs behind*   Overcoat with ornamental looped cords at the back, as on a uniform, hence 'rather a military appearance'.

SCENES

Five of these sketches were originally published as 'Street Sketches' in the *Morning Chronicle*, thirteen as 'Sketches of London' in the *Evening Chronicle*, one under the heading 'Scenes and Characters' in *Bell's Life in London*, and one in *The Library of Fiction, or Family Story-teller*. Four original sketches were combined into two. The last was written specially for the First Series of 1836. See Appendix A and individual headnotes for details.

CHAPTER 1 *The Streets — Morning*

First published in the *Evening Chronicle* (21 July 1835).

1. (p. 69) *water-butt, then on the dust-hole*   'Dust' covered all kinds of street dirt and refuse. This, and the water-butt, reflect London streets before the arrival of sanitation reform and proper drainage, from the 1840s onwards.

2. (p. 70) *Covent Garden* Area north of the Strand, and until the early 1970s site of London's main wholesale fruit, vegetable and flower market. One of Dickens's favourite districts, described in several places in his fiction and non-fiction.

3. (p. 71) *the Hummums* The Hummums (from *hammam*, or Turkish bath, according to Hill) Hotel was at the corner of Russell Street, Covent Garden. See also *Great Expectations*, Chapter 45.

4. (p. 71) *spontaneous combustion* Better known as the process whereby Krook in *Bleak House*, Chapter 32, turns into a greasy liquor. There are numerous sources for this (pseudo-scientific) idea, including *The Terrific Register* (1824–5), a penny weekly devoured by Dickens as a youth. See Trevor Blount, 'Dickens and Mr Krook's Spontaneous Combustion', *Dickens Studies Annual*, vol. 1, ed. Robert B. Partlow Jr. (London and Amsterdam, Carbondale and Edwardsville: Southern Illinois University, 1970), pp. 183–6. See also Characters, Chapter 8.

5. (p. 73) *Somers and Camden towns, Islington, and Pentonville* Residential districts of north-west and north London, long since absorbed into the metropolis. Dickens's family lived for a year (1823) in Bayham Street, Camden. Pentonville was the more prosperous and fashionable area of the four at the time.

6. (p. 73) *stale tarts . . . at the pastry-cooks' doors* A detail from Dickens's own boyhood: see *David Copperfield*, Chapter 1.

CHAPTER 2 *The Streets — Night*

First published in *Bell's Life in London* (17 January 1836).

1. (p. 75) *nine o'clock 'beer'* A boy sent round the streets at supper-time with pint measures of beer.

2. (p. 75) *'Yesterday's 'Tiser'* The *Morning Advertiser* (established 1794), the organ of the Licensed Victuallers.

3. (p. 76) *Marsh-gate and Victoria Theatre* Formerly squalid area of Lambeth, close to Waterloo Bridge, on the south bank of the Thames. Built in 1817 as the Coburg Theatre, Waterloo Road, the Royal Victoria as it became in 1833 was famous for its melodramas, and is now known as the Old Vic.

4. (p. 76) *weekly Dorset* Butter from Dorset, usually arriving once a week.

5. (p. 76) *cloudy rolls of 'best fresh'*   The cloudiness of the fresh butter arose from its being wrapped in muslin.

6. (p. 76) *'come the double monkey'*   Slang: a double somersault.

7. (p. 78) *large brass plates*   Licence badges for the man who watered the coach horses at their stands.

8. (p. 78) *purl*   Warm beer laced with gin and spices.

9. (p. 78) *harmonic meeting*   A singsong held in the upper room of a public house; forerunner of the music hall.

10. (p. 78) *'My 'art's in the 'ighlands'*   Cockney version of popular song, 'My Heart's in the Highlands', by Robert Burns (1759–96).

11. (p. 78) *'The brave old Hoak'*   Cockney version of popular song, 'The Brave Old Oak', words by H.F. Chorley (1808–72) and music by E.J. Loder (1813–65).

12. (p. 79) *'Fly, fly from the world, my Bessy with me'*   Song by Thomas Moore (1779–1852).

13. (p. 79) *glasses off their legs*   Before being ousted by tumblers, glasses often had stems with a bulge half-way up.

CHAPTER 3 *Shops and Their Tenants*

First published in the *Morning Chronicle* (10 October 1834).

1. (p. 80) *Sterne ... travel from Dan to Beersheba, and say that all was barren*   Alluding to Sterne's *A Sentimental Journey* (1768), which in turn referred to Judges 20: 1. Dan was at the extreme north of the land of Canaan; Beersheba the extreme south. Hence, pitying the man who can travel so far, and find nothing of interest.

CHAPTER 4 *Scotland-yard*

First published in the *Morning Chronicle* (4 October 1836).

1. (p. 84) *Scotland-yard*   In 1829 Peel's newly founded Metropolitan Police Force was established on the site described by Dickens at 4 Whitehall Place, where once stood the palace of the kings of Scotland. In 1890 'the Yard' moved to Cannon Row, near Westminster Bridge, and in 1967 to its present location in Victoria Street.

2. (p. 85) *Barclay's best*   From Barclay and Perkins, famous London brewers.

3. (p. 87) *Patent Shot Manufactory* A London landmark, the tower erected by Messrs Watts in 1789, south-east of Waterloo Bridge.

4. (p. 87) *Waterloo-bridge* Between Blackfriars and Westminster Bridges, built in 1811–17, with nine arches. Demolished in 1936 to be replaced by the present bridge.

5. (p. 87) *old London-bridge* This bridge, which had stood for many centuries, was finally demolished in 1832, when a new bridge opened across the Thames from the City of London (this was replaced finally in the 1960s). There are numerous references in Dickens, for example, *David Copperfield*, Chapters 5 and 11.

6. (p. 87) *best Wallsend* Coal from Wallsend near Newcastle.

7. (p. 88) *done by a Duke – the King's brother* According to Hill, by the Lord Mayor, with Frederick, the Duke of York (1763–1827) in attendance.

8. (p. 88) *Pedlar's Acre* A riverside district north of the Thames between Waterloo and Westminster Bridges, said to have been bequeathed to the parish of Lambeth by a pedlar.

9. (p. 88) *new market sprung up at Hungerford* The original seventeenth-century market was closed in 1815, and reopened in new buildings in 1833; to disappear when Charing Cross Station was built on the site in 1862.

CHAPTER 5 *Seven Dials*

First published in *Bell's Life in London* (27 September 1835).

1. (p. 90) *Tom King and the Frenchman* Tom King (1730–1804), actor who persecuted a French resident of Seven Dials by asking for a mythical Mr Thompson, pronounced 'Tonson', the name used for *Monsieur Tonson* (1821), a farce based on the episode by W.T. Moncrieff (William Thomas, 1794–1857).

2. (p. 90) *Seven Dials* District of central London so named after seven streets converging on a point once marked by a Doric column with six dials (as two of the streets open into one angle at the centre) or faces, removed in 1773. This area was one of the worst slums in London during the early nineteenth century, and remained a synonym for poverty throughout the century, although it was also known for its ballad-singers and -sellers.

3. (p. 90) *Catnach and of Pitts* James Catnach (1792–1841) and John Pitts (1768–1844), rival printers of street literature whose shops were in Seven Dials.

4. (p. 90) *penny yards of song*   Songs printed in three columns on sheets a yard long and sold for a penny.

5. (p. 90) *gordian knot*   Difficult to unravel. From the story of Gordius, a poor peasant who became King of Phrygia, and who fastened the yoke of his wagon to the beam by a knot so ingenious and secure no one could untie it, until Alexander cut it through with his sword.

6. (p. 90) *maze of Hampton Court*   Maze at the palace near Richmond upon Thames, built by Cardinal Wolsey in 1515.

7. (p. 90) *maze at the Beulah Spa*   Once fashionable health resort that opened in Norwood, south-east London, in 1831.

8. (p. 92) *Belzoni-like*   Giovanni Battista Belzoni (1778–1823), Italian explorer who found fame for his discoveries among the ancient tombs of Egypt.

9. (p. 92) *'three-outs'*   Slang: a glass holding three-pennyworths.

10. (p. 93) *put the kye-bosk on her*   Slang: put the kibosh on, stop, crush her.

11. (p. 93) *St Giles's*   Adjoining slum area, equally notorious.

12. (p. 94) *Blucher boots*   Sturdy half-boots, named after Prussian field marshal, Gerhart von Blücher (1742–1819), commander against Napoleon at Waterloo.

13. (p. 95) *'increase and multiply'*   From Genesis 1: 28: 'Be fruitful and multiply, and replenish the earth.'

14. (p. 95) *'jemmy'*   Slang: a sheep's head.

15. (p. 95) *Mr Warren*   Proprietor of the blacking warehouse where the young Dickens toiled for some months as a boy. Tony Weller in *Pickwick Papers*, Chapter 33, pokes fun at the use of 'poetry' by 'Warren's blackin', or Rowland's oil, or some o' them low fellows'.

CHAPTER 6 *Meditations in Monmouth-street*

First published in the *Morning Chronicle* (24 September 1836).

1. (p. 96) *Monmouth-street*   Continuation of St Martin's Lane, absorbed into Shaftesbury Avenue in 1885. Headquarters of second-hand clothing shops in London in Dickens's day.

2. (p. 96) *Holywell-street*   Ran parallel to the Strand on the north side, demolished with the widening of the Strand and making of Aldwych, 1899–1905. Centre of the second-hand book trade, with clothing shops as well.

3. (p. 98) *half-boots*   That is, extending half-way up the leg to the knee.

4. (p. 102) *pair of tops*   High boots with tops of a contrasting colour.

5. (p. 102) *knee-cords*   Corduroy trousers extending to just below the knee.

6. (p. 102) *Denmark satin*   Smooth-surfaced worsted material used for women's shoes.

7. (p. 102) *Hammersmith suspension-bridge*   Completed in 1827, and replaced by present bridge in 1883, linking Hammersmith on the north side of the Thames with Barnes on the south.

8. (p. 103) *imperence!*   Slang: impudence!

CHAPTER 7 *Hackney-coach Stands*

First published in the *Evening Chronicle* (31 January 1835).

1. (p. 106) *wisdom of Parliament*   The London Hackney Carriage Act of 1831 fixed coach fares; drivers could charge by distance or time.

2. (p. 106) *swamped by cabs and omnibuses*   Increasingly popular, cabs and omnibuses (first introduced in 1829) were to drive the ancient hackney-coaches out of business. See also Chapters 16 and 17, below.

3. (p. 106) *watermen*   Licensed attendants who watered the horses.

4. (p. 106) *Mr Martin, of costermonger notoriety*   Richard Martin (1754–1834), Irish MP and co-founder of the Royal Society for the Prevention of Cruelty to Animals, introduced the Act for Protecting the Rights of Animals in 1822, and brought many cases before the magistrates, including many costermongers (street-traders).

5. (p. 106) *under the very window at which we are writing*   At the time Dickens was living at Furnival's Inn, Holborn.

6. (p. 107) *faded coat of arms*   Many of the early hackney-coaches were disused carriages of the nobility; Dickens develops this at the end of the sketch.

7. (p. 108) *Golden-cross, Charing-cross*   Coaches ran from the Golden Cross Hotel (built 1831–2 to replace the old coaching inn whence Mr Pickwick started his travels on 13 May 1827, *Pickwick Papers*, Chapter 2). It faced Charing Cross Station, central London.

8. (p. 108) *Tottenham-court-road*   Runs north from St Giles Circus, Oxford Street, to Euston Road.

9. (p. 108) *Berlin gloves*   Knitted from Berlin wool, a fine, dyed yarn, fashionable during the nineteenth century.

CHAPTER 8 *Doctors' Commons*

First published in the *Morning Chronicle* (11 October 1836).

1. (p. 109) *'Paul's-chain'*   Street named after the site of a chain across the carriageway of St Paul's Churchyard to ensure quiet during services. Formerly connected the churchyard and Doctors' Commons.

2. (p. 109) *Doctors' Commons*   College of lawyers founded in the thirteenth century for the study and practice of civil and canon law, and which purchased in 1567 a site near St Paul's for the residences of the judges and advocates, and buildings for holding the courts. In 1768 a royal charter established a College of Doctors of Law, consisting of elected advocates having taken that degree; also attached were the proctors, whose duties were analogous to that of solicitors. There were five courts, namely the Court of Arches; the Prerogative Court; the Court of Faculties and Dispensations; the Consistory Court of the Bishop of London; and the High Court of Admiralty. Dickens shared an office at 5 Bell Yard, Paul's Chain, leading into the Commons, during his time (1829–31) as a shorthand writer for the proctors in the Consistory Court. The buildings, which were extensive and included a large court room, were demolished in 1867 to make way for Queen Victoria Street. The Commons' occupation had gone ten years before, partly through the reforms introduced by the Probate Act of 1857. Doctors' Commons appears in several of Dickens's books, for example, in *David Copperfield* young David is articled to Mr Spenlow, a proctor. William J. Carlton, *Charles Dickens: Shorthand Writer* (1926), pp. 57–67, identifies the originals of the cases described in the following sketch, some details of which were edited out when Dickens revised it for book publication.

3. (p.110) *apparitor*   Usher.

4. (p.111) *Arches Court*   Provincial court of the Archbishop of Canterbury, formerly held under the arches of Bow Church.

5. (p. 111) *brazen Colossus*   After the giant bronze statue of Apollo built on Rhodes, thought to have straddled the harbour, one of the Seven Wonders of the World, destroyed by earthquake in 225 BC.

6. (p. 113) *'Prerogative-Office'*   Court dealing with testamentary matters in certain dioceses, transferred in 1857 to the Court of Probate.

CHAPTER 9 *London Recreations*

First published in the *Evening Chronicle* (17 March 1835).

1. (p. 115) *Almack's*   Exclusive and expensive Assembly Rooms in King Street, St James's, opened by William Almack in 1765. A weekly ball and supper was held during the London season.
2. (p. 117) *fancy fair*   Charitable event.
3. (p. 117) *Hackney, Clapton, Stamford-hill*   Districts all since absorbed within the metropolis, but sufficiently far at the time to be considered comfortable residences for City men and their families.
4. (p. 117) *paroquet*   The original French term: parakeet.
5. (p. 118) *Hampstead-road . . . Kilburn-road*   In north London.
6. (p. 121) *'gin-and-water warm with'*   That is, with sugar, which had to be asked for.
7. (p. 121) *hand-chaises*   Small chairs on wheels, forerunner of prams.

CHAPTER 10 *The River*

First published in the *Evening Chronicle* (6 June 1835).

1. (p. 122) *'Red-us'*   The Red House, riverside public house in Battersea, popular winning-post for boat races, long since demolished.
2. (p. 122) *The Penitentiary*   Early name of Millbank Prison, completed in 1821, pulled down in 1893 to make a site for the Tate Gallery.
3. (p. 123) *Searle's yard*   Boat-building yard by Westminster Bridge, on the shore now covered by the Albert Embankment (1866–9).
4. (p. 123) *Guernsey shirts*   Seamen's woollen sweaters.
5. (p. 123) *'jack'*   Riverside odd-job man.
6. (p. 123) *Dando*   John Dando, whose name became a byword for running up bills at restaurants and leaving without paying. On one occasion, according to *The Times* (30 August 1830) he was summoned for eating eleven dozen oysters at a stall and leaving without paying. Died in Clerkenwell Prison.
7. (p. 124) *the Reverend Mr Dilworth*   Thomas Dilworth wrote *A New Guide to the English Tongue* (1812), on the title-page of which he was depicted in a head-dress resembling a nightcap.
8. (p. 124) *when the Royal George went down*   On 29 August 1782 in Portsmouth Harbour, when 1,000 men, women and children drowned.

9. (p. 125) *Two pots to a pint*   A pot was a quart, so the odds were four to one.

10. (p. 125) *St Katharine's Dock Company*   Whose wharf near Tower Bridge in east London was a terminus for steamboats to and from towns on the Thames estuary.

11. (p. 126) *Corporation Bill*   Of 1835: governing the administration of the Thames, under the authority of the City of London Corporation; superseded in 1909 by the Port of London Authority.

12. (p. 127) *Blackwall*   District on the north bank of the Thames; an important point of arrival and departure on the river.

13. (p. 127) *'Dumbledum-deary'*   A refrain; possibly to a song of the same name; here, a dance.

CHAPTER 11 *Astley's*

First published in the *Evening Chronicle* (9 May 1835).

1. (p. 129) *Astley's*   Astley's Equestrian Amphitheatre, one of the most popular places of entertainment in London, was founded in 1769 by cavalry officer Philip Astley in Westminster Bridge Road. It specialized in melodramatic spectacles into which horses were introduced. See also *The Old Curiosity Shop*, Chapter 39, and *Hard Times*, Book III, Chapter 7. A favourite of Dickens, it burnt down several times but did not close until 1893.

2. (p. 129) *a 'Royal Amphitheatre'*   Originally, the Royal Saloon or Astley's Amphitheatre, it subsequently became Astley's Royal Equestrian Amphitheatre.

3. (p. 129) *Ducrow*   Andrew Ducrow (1793–1848), famous equestrian performer and tightrope walker, joined Astley's in 1808, becoming manager in the 1830s. Dickens as narrator here pretends to an age he could not claim, as he was born in 1812.

4. (p. 130) *Drury-lane*   Drury Lane Theatre, established by royal patent in Charles II's reign, rebuilt in 1812.

5. (p. 132) *frogs*   Decorative fastenings or loops.

6. (p. 133) *Berlin gloves*   See Chapter 7, note 9, above.

7. (p. 134) *the New Cut*   Then New, now the Cut, near the Old Vic Theatre and Waterloo Station.

8. (p. 135) *'dirty swell'*   Slang: a type of vulgar, flashily dressed person.

CHAPTER 12 *Greenwich Fair*

First published in the *Evening Chronicle* (16 April 1835); the Thursday before the Easter holiday that year, hence timely.

1. (p. 135) *'the lungs of London'*   A saying of William Pitt, Earl of Chatham (1708–78), quoted in a parliamentary debate of 1808 about maintaining Hyde Park free of building.

2. (p. 135) *Greenwich Fair*   A favourite resort of Londoners, the fair at Greenwich, a suburb on the south bank, down-river from the City, was held annually at Easter and Whitsun until abolished in 1857.

3. (p. 138) *a bender*   Slang: a sixpenny piece, so called because of its thinness.

4. (p. 138) *the observatory*   The Royal Observatory, begun in 1675 from the designs of Wren, still stands on its hill, an extension of the National Maritime Museum.

5. (p. 139) *Lucretian ejaculations*   Exclamations of the kind uttered by Lucretia, Roman woman of legend who killed herself after being raped.

6. (p. 139) *puzzle a Solomon*   Biblical King of Israel, renowned for wisdom: see 1 Kings: 3–4.

7. (p. 139) *Mr Horner . . . of Colosseum notoriety*   That is, not little Jack Horner of the nursery rhyme, but Thomas Horner (d. 1844), projector of the Colosseum, a place of amusement that stood at the south-east corner of Regent's Park and which contained his famous panorama of London, exhibited from 1829 until 1854. The Colosseum was demolished in 1875.

8. (p. 139) *majestic building*   Greenwich Hospital, on the site of the Palace of Placentia, where Henry VIII and Elizabeth I were born, replaced by a hospital for aged or disabled seamen of the fleet, designed by Wren in 1694, though many others worked on it. Today the building contains the Royal Naval College.

9. (p. 140) *the voices of the boys*   Choristers of the Naval College Chapel.

10. (p. 140) wilks   That is, whelks; and a play on the name of T.E. Wilks (1815–54), well-known journalist and playwright.

11. (p. 141) *'Richardson's'*   John Richardson (1761–1837) called himself 'The Penny Showman', lived in a caravan, and offered many cheap and popular shows, including *Dr Faustus, or the Devil will have his Own*, at Bartholomew and Greenwich Fairs. Dickens's enjoyment of the absurdities of melodrama recurs, for example, in *Nicholas Nickleby*; 'The Amusements of the People' (1850), reprinted in *Miscellaneous Papers*, ed. B.W. Matz (London: Chapman and Hall, 1914), pp. 171–83; and *Great Expectations*, Chapter 31.

12. (p. 141) *harlequin and columbine* Characters from the Italian *commedia dell'arte* transplanted into pantomime, usually wearing typically decorated costumes: Harlequin was a silent, acrobatic figure, in love with Columbine, Pantaloon's daughter.

13. (p. 142) *'Oft in the stilly night'* By Thomas Moore (1779–1852), from *Irish Melodies* (1807–34).

14. (p. 144) *indescribables* Jocular euphemism: trousers.

CHAPTER 13 *Private Theatres*

First published in the *Evening Chronicle* (11 August 1835).

1. (p. 145) *'RICHARD THE THIRD ... LORD MAYOR OF LONDON'* The figures quoted are graded according to the relative importance of the characters in Shakespeare's *Richard III*.

2. (p. 145) *private theatre* After the licensed theatres (Covent Garden, Drury Lane and the Haymarket), and many unlicensed (such as Astley's, which evaded the rules), these small, cheaper theatres allowed stage-struck young amateurs for a fee to play the major roles. Dickens probably attended them with his fellow clerk Thomas Potter in the early 1830s, when he was a lawyer's clerk himself. According to F.G. Kitton, *Charles Dickens by Pen and Pencil* (1890), he may even have acted in them.

3. (p. 147) *'So much for Bu-u-u-uckingham!'* Not in Shakespeare's original play, but Colley Cibber's adaptation.

4. (p. 147) *Astley's and Sadler's Wells* For Astley's, see Chapter 11, above. Sadler's Wells Theatre in Islington, north London, took its name from medicinal springs (discovered in 1683) in the grounds of the Music House belonging to Thomas Sadler. Water dramas and equestrian performances were in vogue from 1804 to 1844, when Samuel Phelps took over and introduced Shakespearian productions. A cinema when it closed in 1916, it has since become a theatre specializing in opera and ballet.

5. (p. 148) *Count D'Orsay* Artist and fashionable man-about-town, Alfred, Count D'Orsay (1801–52) was the leader of London dandies such as Bulwer Lytton. Dickens is supposed to have modelled himself on D'Orsay after meeting him in 1836. See also Chapter 18, note 6, below.

6. (p. 148) Richards, Shylocks . . . Charles Surfaces   Of the non-Shakespearian favourite characters, Beverley is from Edward Moore's tragedy *The Gamester* (1753), Young Dornton from Thomas Holcroft's *The Road to Ruin* (1792), Rover from John O'Keefe's *Wild Oats* (1791), Captain Absolute from Sheridan's *The Rivals* (1775) and Charles Surface from his *The School for Scandal* (1777).

7. (p. 150) *O.P. side*   The opposite prompt side of the stage, that is, stage right.

8. (p. 151) *Mrs Siddons*   Sarah Siddons (1755–1831), great tragedy actress, famous for her Lady Macbeth and other Shakespearian characters.

9. (p. 152) *first P.S. wing*   First or front wing on the prompt side of the stage, that is, stage left.

CHAPTER 14 *Vauxhall-gardens by Day*

First published in the *Morning Chronicle* (26 October 1836).

1. (p. 153) *Vauxhall-gardens*   These once popular and famous pleasure gardens were just across Vauxhall Bridge on a site now covered with small streets. The original New Spring Gardens of 1660 were improved and reopened in 1732 by Jonathan Tyers, with a pavilion, tree-lined walks and a semi-circular arcade; and at night, hundreds of small lamps. Earlier novelists introduced the gardens as a resort visited by every Londoner and his or her country cousin, and Victorian writers followed suit. Musical entertainments, fireworks, rope-dancing and balloons became attractions, but it was not until 1836 that they were open to the public by day – an experiment to boost profits duly seized upon by Dickens for this sketch. The gardens were closed in 1859, partly because of increasing rowdyism.

2. (p. 153) *cosmoramas*   Peep-shows for viewing magnified pictures of large-scale human or natural phenomena.

3. (p. 155) *the late Mr Simpson*   C.H. Simpson was the popular Master of Ceremonies at the gardens for thirty-seven years.

4. (p. 155) *Mr Blackmore*   American acrobat who performed at Vauxhall Gardens from 1823.

5. (p. 155) *Madame Somebody*   Probably Madame Saqui, tightrope performer who preceded Blackmore.

6. (p. 155) Tancredi   Opera by Gioacchino Rossini (1792–1868), popular Italian composer. The overture remains a favourite in the repertory of orchestras and military bands.

7. (p. 156) *name of one of the English counties* This was Paul Bedford (?1792–1871), a popular comic vocalist, who could have sung many songs on the traditional subject of the Seven Ages of Man.

8. (p. 157) *Mr Green* Charles Green (1785–1870), well-known aeronaut, the first to ascend in a gas balloon, who made many ascents from Vauxhall Gardens, in 1838 reaching over 27,000 feet.

9. (p. 158) *pochayses* Post-chaises: Hill says a 'concertina' version of a post-chaise.

CHAPTER 15 *Early Coaches*

First published in the *Evening Chronicle* (19 February 1835).

1. (p. 159) *constant travelling . . . mortal could endure* This and other sketches on travelling reflect Dickens's early reporting days on the *Morning Chronicle*, which coincided with the earliest sketches, when he was frequently obliged to dash about the countryside (1834–6).

2. (p. 159) *Ixion* Thessalian king of legend, punished by Zeus for his love of Hera by being bound to a perpetually revolving wheel of fire. Referring to the times when tortures such as being broken on the wheel were used by Christians to enforce their faith.

3. (p. 161) *in the sacred cause of religion* Dickens's readiness to attack religious intolerance was to become a common theme in his comments upon religion, past and present. See my *Dickens and Religion* (London: George Allen & Unwin, 1981), Chapter 4.

4. (p. 161) *large posting-bills* Announcements of the routes, times and fares, often headed with an illustration of a loaded coach.

5. (p. 161) *so many Atlases* In Greek mythology, Atlas was a giant condemned to support the sky on his shoulders.

6. (p. 162) *unmentionables* Jocular euphemism: trousers.

7. (p. 162) à la *Ducrow* See Chapter 11, note 3, above.

8. (p. 163) *Petersham great-coat* Heavy overcoat named after Viscount Petersham (d. 1851), fashionable sportsman.

9. (p. 164) *Golden-cross* See Chapter 7, note 7, above.

10. (p. 165) *St Martin's* St Martin-in-the-Fields, in Trafalgar Square, central London: the present building dates from 1721–6.

11. (p. 165) *Times . . . Chron . . . Herald* Major newspapers of the period, *The Times* (founded 1788), the *Morning Chronicle* (1769) and the *Morning Herald* (1780).

12. (p. 165) *Pan's pipes* Named after Pan, the Greek god of wood and field; a number of reeds or whistles of graduated lengths bound together to form a musical wind instrument.

CHAPTER 16 *Omnibuses*

First published in the *Morning Chronicle* (26 September 1834).

1. (p. 166) *omnibus* First introduced into London in 1829, by George Shillibeer. Passengers sat facing each other on two long benches.
2. (p. 166) *Cross Keys* Coaching-inn in Wood Street, Cheapside; starting-place for Kent coaches. This may be a memory of Dickens's own journey at the age of eleven when he came up from Chatham to the Cross Keys, referred to in 1860 in 'Dullborough Town', *Uncommercial Traveller*, p. 116.
3. (p. 167) *glass-coach* See Our Parish, Chapter 3, note 5.
4. (p. 167) *'buss'* Soon contracted to the modern abbreviated form 'bus'.
5. (p. 167) *cad* Omnibus conductor.
6. (p. 169) *Ba—nk. —Ty* Phonetic rendering of omnibus cad's cry, 'Bank, City,' as he announces his route – which is carefully outlined in the street names Dickens mentions.
7. (p. 170) *Shoe-lane . . . Farringdon-street* Shoe Lane in east London was partially demolished to make way for Holborn Viaduct. Until the late 1840s Farringdon Street did not extend as far as what is now the Farringdon Road, but just to Holborn Hill.

CHAPTER 17 *The Last Cab-driver, and the First Omnibus Cad*

First published in this form in the Second Series (December 1836). The first part is a revised version of 'Hackney-cabs, and Their Drivers', originally published in the *Carlton Chronicle* (17 September 1836); the second, a revised version of 'Some Account of an Omnibus Cad', was first published in *Bell's Life in London* (1 November 1835).

1. (p. 171) *knee-smalls* Breeches that reached only to the knees, fastened with a strap or ribbon.
2. (p. 171) *Paddington or Holloway* Paddington Green in west London

was the terminus for the first (1829) omnibus route from the City; now dominated by Paddington Station. Holloway is a north London suburb.

3. (p. 171) *Astley's*   See Chapter 11, above.

4. (p. 172) *offer of eightpence* . . . *save the fourpence*   Eightpence a mile was the legal fare until 1831, when it became one shilling (see Chapter 7, above), so fourpence was the change out of a shilling, which the cabman might look for as a tip.

5. (p. 172) *Fleet-street*   Major thoroughfare connecting the Strand with Ludgate Hill in the City.

6. (p. 172) *chemist's shop*   Street casualties would be hurried into a chemist's shop for first aid, since they often had a surgery attached.

7. (p. 173) *Mr Hobler's*   See Our Parish, Chapter 1, note 4.

8. (p. 175) *House of Correction* . . . *silent system*   The so-called Silent System was introduced into the Metropolitan House of Correction, Coldbath Fields, Clerkenwell, by the prison's reformist governor George Chesterton in 1834. Under this system prisoners could work together but were strictly forbidden to communicate with one another. Dickens paid several visits, becoming a friend of the governor, and contemplated writing a sketch on the place; but decided the paper on Newgate would suffice, and be more interesting (see Pilgrim *Letters*, vol. 1, pp. 101–3; also Chapter 25, below; and Characters, Chapter 12). The prison was closed in 1877.

9. (p. 175) *'wheels'*   That is, the tread-wheel or treadmill, a form of punishment common in the nineteenth century, abolished by the Prisons Act of 1898.

10. (p. 175) *'All round my hat'*   Popular and derisive Cockney ballad.

11. (p. 177) *Lucinian mysteries*   Lucina is the name given to Juno as goddess of childbirth.

12. (p. 177) *Fatima-like*   Bluebeard's wife Fatima risked her life to penetrate the mysteries of the Blue Room, in the children's story.

13. (p. 178) *Bow-street, Newgate, and Millbank*   The Bow Street Police Court in Covent Garden, Newgate Prison in the City, and Millbank Penitentiary on the Thames.

14. (p. 178) *quitted his ungrateful country* . . . *at the expense, of its Government*   Transportation, as it was known, was a common punishment, involving deportation to a penal colony for a set number of years.

15. (p. 178) *like another Cincinnatus*   After the Roman statesman and model of virtue, twice called from retirement on his farm to defend his country, each time returning successfully to his plough.

16. (p. 178) *the first omnibus*   Introduced in 1829: see Chapter 16, above.

17. (p. 179) *'Royal William'*   Old omnibuses carried on the tradition of the coaches that preceded them of bearing names.

18. (p. 180) *Newgate Calendar*   Famous publication that first appeared in 1773, containing potted biographies of notorious criminals, frequently revised.

CHAPTER 18 *A Parliamentary Sketch*

First published as two sketches, 'The House' and 'Bellamy's' (7 March and 11 April 1835), in the *Evening Chronicle*, before inclusion in the Second Series as 'A Parliamentary Sketch – with a Few Portraits' (December 1836). Dickens edited out a number of topical political allusions, the 'Portraits' alluded to in the Second Series title. W.J. Carlton, 'Portraits in "A Parliamentary Sketch"', *Dickensian*, vol. 50 (June 1954), pp. 100–109, quotes some of the omitted matter and identifies several of the portraits. Much of it would be libellous today, since the originals of the characters were easily recognizable. Dickens knew them through his career as a parliamentary reporter 1832–6, an experience that left him disillusioned.

1. (p. 181) *'the House'*   The old Houses of Parliament burnt down in October 1834 and the new, present Palace of Westminster was not opened until 1847; during the interval the two houses assembled in a temporary building on the site.

2. (p. 181) *Serjeant-at-Arms*   Official responsible for maintaining discipline in the House.

3. (p. 184) *ferocious-looking gentleman*   Easily identifiable at the time as Colonel Charles Sibthorp (1783–1855), an ultra-Tory who represented Lincoln (1826–33, 1834–55), and who 'conscientiously opposed' the Reform Bill of 1832; the most extended portrait in the sketch.

4. (p. 184) *Dutch clock*   See Our Parish, Chapter 5, note 2.

5. (p. 184) *Bellamy's . . . a refreshment-room*   Beside the old House of Commons and popular with members because of the good food and because the division bell rang on the premises. Opened in 1773 by John Bellamy; shut down on the opening of the dining rooms in the present building.

6. (p. 185) D'Orsay *hat*   Named after Count Alfred D'Orsay (see Chapter 13, note 5, above), this had an extra-tall crown and wide brim.

7. (p. 185) *'Honest Tom,' a metropolitan representative*   Thomas Duncombe (1796–1861) became MP for the newly created borough of Finsbury in 1834.

8. (p. 185) *a very well-known character*   John Gully (1783–1863), a former prizefighter, and MP for Pontefract (1832–7).

9. (p. 185) *The old hard-featured man*   George Byng (1790–1847), MP for Middlesex.

10. (p. 185) *the memory of man is not to the contrary*   Alluding to a familiar phrase in Blackstone's *Commentaries on the Laws of England* (1765–9), meaning from time immemorial.

11. (p. 185) *Fox, Pitt, Sheridan, and Canning*   All eminent statesmen and parliamentarians of the previous generation: Charles James Fox (1749–1806), William Pitt (1759–1806), Richard Brinsley Sheridan (1751–1816) and George Canning (1770–1827).

12. (p. 185) *'that young Macaulay'*   Thomas Babington Macaulay (1800–1859), an MP by 1830, already known as an historian, essayist and statesman.

13. (p. 185) *Lord Stanley*   Edward, later 14th Earl of Derby (1799–1869) went on to become Conservative prime minister in 1852, 1858–9 and 1866–8. Dickens was one of those who took down Stanley's famous speech on the Suppression of Disturbances (Ireland) Bill in 1833.

14. (p. 186) *whipper-in*   Nowadays known as a whip, that is, organizer of the members of a political party, especially to attend for voting. Originally a hunting term.

15. (p. 186) *Exquisites*   Dandies.

16. (p. 186) *'hereditary bondsman'*   From Byron, *Childe Harold's Pilgrimage* (1812), Canto II, stanza 76:

> Hereditary bondsmen! know ye not
> Who would be free themselves must strike the blow . . .

17. (p. 186) *forty-second frank*   Until 1840 and the penny post, MPs could send letters free by signing and so 'franking' them. The Irish journalist has taken full advantage of the privilege.

18. (p. 187) *would rival Babel*   See Genesis 11: 1–9. A tower, the builders of which all spoke different languages – hence, a confusion of voices.

19. (p. 187) *Smithfield on a market-day*   The wholesale meat market, near Holborn Viaduct, just north-east of the City.

20. (p. 189) *Sheridan, and Perceval, and Castlereagh*   Eminent parliamentarians: Sheridan (see note 11 above); Spencer Perceval (1762–1812), prime minister (1809–12), assassinated; Robert Stewart, Viscount Castlereagh (1769–1822), foreign secretary (1812–22).

21. (p. 189) *Reform Bill*   Passed in June 1832, 'to amend the representation of the people in England and Wales', by an increase (less than 50 per cent) of the franchise, and a redistribution of seats.

22. (p. 189) *Manchester-buildings, or Millbank-street*   Where provincial MPs had temporary lodgings during parliamentary sessions. The former were pulled down in the 1860s and Westminster underground station built on part of the site. Millbank Street is now known as Millbank Road.

23. (p. 190) *St Margaret's church*   Since 1614 the parish church of the House of Commons, alongside Westminster Abbey.

24. (p. 191) *Lord's-Day-Bill Baronet*   Sir Andrew Agnew (1793–1849), who had introduced a bill for the Better Observance of Sunday for the third time in May 1836. The bill finally passed on a second reading in 1837, when Parliament was dissolved (on the death of William IV) and, with Agnew not re-elected, his bill was not re-introduced, and so lapsed. Dickens mounted a fierce attack in his pamphlet, *Sunday under Three Heads*, published under the pseudonym 'Timothy Sparks' in 1836 and ironically dedicated to the Bishop of London. The novelist opposed Sabbatarianism throughout his career.

25. (p. 191) *the Hebe*   Daughter of Zeus and cupbearer, hence, waitress.

26. (p. 191) *Jane's only recreations*   'and they are very innocent too' was added for the 1850 edition, and kept thereafter.

27. (p. 192) *shared Yorick's fate*   Died. See *Hamlet*, V.1, where Hamlet picks up the King's jester's skull.

28. (p. oo) *Falstaff!*   Jovial glutton of Shakespeare's *Henry IV*, Parts I and II.

CHAPTER 19 *Public Dinners*

First published in the *Evening Chronicle* (7 April 1835). Cruikshank's illustration shows Dickens and himself behind the leading stewards, thought to be Chapman and Hall.

1. (p. 193) *White Conduit House*   Tavern in Penton Street, Islington, north London, with pleasure garden (demolished in 1849).

2. (p. 195) *Great Queen-street . . . Freemasons'*   In Holborn, site of the Freemasons' Hall, popular venue for public dinners; rebuilt in 1863.

3. (p. 195) *accession of George the First*   In 1714. The Freemasons' Tavern was first built in 1786, so an obvious exaggeration.

4. (p. 197) *Auber's music*   Daniel Auber (1782–1871), popular French composer of light opera. See also Tales, Chapter 9, note 3.

5. (p. 197) *the ladies' gallery*   Women were only admitted to the dinners in time to hear the speeches, and then were confined to a gallery overlooking the event.

6. (p. 197) Non nobis   That is, 'Non nobis, Domine' ('Not unto us, Lord'), opening words of Psalm 115, and a famous vocal canon traditionally attributed to William Byrd (1538–1623), formerly a common grace or thanksgiving at public banquets.

CHAPTER 20 *The First of May*

First published as 'A Little Talk about Spring, and the Sweeps' in Chapman and Hall's *The Library of Fiction, or Family Story-teller*, No. 3 (31 May 1836).

1. (p. 200) *'Now ladies   ... BRASS LADLE'.* A woman carrying a ladle or other implement would solicit contributions with some such cry; a 'sky-parlour' is colloquial for a garret.

2. (p. 200) *ILLEGAL WATCHWORD*   Refers to recent legislation prohibiting sweeps from advertising their presence by calling out in the street. See also Scenes, Chapter 1.

3. (p. 200) *The first of May!*   Long celebrated to mark the revival of growth after winter, a traditional, popular and pagan festival (like Christmas), which Dickens would always support against puritan condemnation or 'sabbath enthusiasts' as he calls them. Among the surviving processions, the chimney-sweeps were conspicuous with their 'Jack-in-the-Green', who was hidden (as in the illustration) within a portable framework of leaves and branches.

4. (p. 202) *colours ... after-life!*   Deleted from the 1850 and later editions.

5. (p. 202) *Duke of York's column in Carlton-terrace*   Erected in 1831–4 to the memory of Frederick, Duke of York, son of George III, and commander-in-chief of the British army.

6. (p. 202) poussette   Figure in country dancing.

7. (p. 202) *Alderman Waithman's monument in Fleet-street*   Robert Waithman (1764–1833), Lord Mayor of London (1823) and MP. The monument no longer exists.

8. (p. 202) *hands-four-round ... ten-pound householders*   In 1832 the Reform Act extended the franchise to some of the urban middle class by including the owners or tenants of property worth an annual rent of ten pounds or more. A 'hands-four-round' is a figure in country dancing.

9. (p. 202) *Obelisk in St George's-fields* One of the landmarks of south London, erected in 1771 in the centre of what is now St George's Circus, later removed to the Bethlehem Hospital grounds. It was 'more generally' called 'the Obstacle' according to 'Somebody's Luggage' (1862), reprinted in *Christmas Stories*, New Oxford Illustrated Dickens (London: Oxford University Press, 1968), p. 349.

10. (p. 204) *Grosvenor-square* Fashionable square in London's West End.

11. (p. 204) *Battle Bridge* The old name for King's Cross, after a bridge over the Fleet river where a battle took place between the Romans and the Britons under Boadicea. Since 1830 called King's Cross in honour of George IV, of whom a statue was erected there (later demolished). Dickens refers to the area, well-known as a criminal haunt and for its dust-heaps, again in *Our Mutual Friend*.

12. (p. 204) *Somers Town and Camden Town* See Scenes, Chapter 1, note 5.

13. (p. 205) *Paul Pry to Caleb Williams* An inquisitive busybody in the eponymous farce *Paul Pry* (1825) by John Poole (?1786–1872); contrasted with the faithful servant of *The Adventures of Caleb Williams* (1794) by William Godwin (1756–1836).

14. (p. 205) *a 'green'* That is, a 'Jack-in-the-Green', or Green Man: see note 3, above.

15. (p. 205) *a set of Pan-pipes . . . 'mouth-organ'* For Pan-pipes, see Chapter 15, note 12, above; the mouth-organ, a small musical instrument, was invented in 1829.

16. (p. 205) *White Conduit House* Tavern: see Chapter 19, note 1, above.

17. (p. 206) *Adam-and-Eve-court* Formerly disreputable street between Oxford Circus and Tottenham Court Road.

18. (p. 206) *a chummy* Slang: a chimney-sweep's boy.

19. (p. 207) *register-stoves* See Our Parish, Chapter 3, note 2.

20. (p. 207) *the second* Because 1 May 1836 fell on a Sunday.

21. (p. 207) *Copenhagen House* Well-known tea garden and place of entertainment in Islington, north London; replaced by the clock tower of the Caledonian Market set up on the adjacent Copenhagen Fields in the 1850s.

22. (p. 207) *Maiden-lane* Now known as York Way, in Holloway, north London (not to be confused with the better known Maiden Lane in Covent Garden).

23. (p. 207) *Love tenanted when he was a young man* Alluding to a song in Thomas Moore's comic opera *MP, or the Blue Stocking*, 'Young Love lived once in a humble shed'.

24. (p. 208) *Belcher handkerchief*   Dark blue neckerchief with white spots, so named after the famous pugilist Jem Belcher (1781–1811).

25. (p. 208) *bed-furniture*   Bed draperies, or other hangings over a four-poster or 'tent' bed.

26. (p. 208) *tape sandals*   Straps passing over the instep or around the ankle, to keep the shoes on.

27. (p. 209) *How has May-day decayed!*   The rest of this paragraph was deleted from the 1850 and succeeding editions, presumably on the grounds of its tone.

CHAPTER 21 *Brokers' and Marine-store Shops*

First published in the *Morning Chronicle* (15 December 1834).

1. (p. 209) *Long-acre*   Street running east to west, just north of Covent Garden.

2. (p. 211) *marine stores*   Originally sold goods required on board ship; later miscellaneous second-hand items. The black doll swinging over the door was a trade sign.

3. (p. 212) *Royal Coburg Theatre ... Tongo the Denounced*   In 1833 the Royal Coburg Theatre, Waterloo, became the Victoria, in honour of the future queen. It is now the Old Vic. 'Tongo the Denounced' is a fictitious melodrama.

4. (p. 212) *Sun Fire-office*   Insurance Company, which affixed its own plate to the premises covered by its policies.

5. (p. 212) *Ratcliff-highway*   Notoriously rough East End riverside district, replaced by St George's Street.

6. (p. 213) *King's Bench prison ... 'the Rules'*   Debtors' prison in the Borough Road, 'the Rules' was the adjoining district within which prisoners might reside on giving payment and security that they would not abscond. Mr Micawber in *David Copperfield* was incarcerated there. The last prisoner left in 1860.

CHAPTER 22 *Gin-shops*

First published in the *Evening Chronicle* (7 February 1835).

1. (p. 216) *Commissioners of Bankrupts ... of Lunacy*   The Commissioners of Bankruptcy were officials appointed by law to administer bankrupts' estates; the Commissioners of Lunacy were appointed to supervise conditions in lunatic asylums.

2. (p. 217) *Clare-market* Street market near Lincoln's Inn Fields, which became a slum and was demolished to make way for the Kingsway, 1899–1905.

3. (p. 218) *'kervorten and a three-out glass'* Cockney slang: a quartern measure (a quarter of a pound, or four ounces); for 'three-out glass' see Scenes, Chapter 5, note 9.

4. (p. 219) *rum srub* Mixture of lemon juice, sugar and a little rum, mildly alcoholic and considered a ladies' drink.

CHAPTER 23 *The Pawnbroker's Shop*

First published in the *Evening Chronicle* (30 June 1835).

1. (p. 220) *of vice and poverty* Deleted from 1850 and later editions.

2. (p. 222) *Belcher neckerchief* See Chapter 20, note 24, above.

3. (p. 223) *Ferguson's first* Alluding to the astronomer and early watch-maker, James Ferguson (1710–76).

4. (p. 224) *regularly round my hat* See Chapter 17, note 10, above.

5. (p. 225) *up the spout* Colloquial: in pawn. From: up the pawnbroker's shoot, a kind of chimney by which pawned objects were removed from the shop to a store room above.

CHAPTER 24 *Criminal Courts*

First published as 'The Old Bailey' in the *Morning Chronicle* (23 October 1834).

1. (p. 229) *fetters over the debtors' door* An architectural device, not real fetters. For a fuller account of Newgate Prison, see Chapter 25, below, which this evidently anticipates.

2. (p. 229) *half-and-half* A drink of equal quantities of mild ale and bitter beer, or ale and porter.

3. (p. 230) *'Mr Ketch'* Public hangman active from 1663 to 1686, whose name became generic by the eighteenth century. Referred to several times in Dickens's works, for example, *Oliver Twist*, Chapter 26.

4. (p. 230) *Mrs Fry . . . Mrs Radcliffe* Elizabeth Fry (1780–1845) was a prison reformer whose revelations of conditions therein were more shocking than the popular 'romances' of Ann Radcliffe (1764–1823).

5. (p. 230) *Old Bailey* Central Criminal Court of England in London, formerly the Sessions House, in Old Bailey, a street running from Ludgate Hill to Newgate. Burnt down by the Gordon rioters in 1780, rebuilt and enlarged in 1809, it was demolished with Newgate Prison, which it adjoined, in 1904–5, before being reconstructed twice more.

6. (p. 231) bouquet The flowers were originally to counteract the smell in the courtroom.

7. (p. 232) *herbs . . . before him* Again, to counteract the smell and also as a precaution against gaol fever. This scene memorably anticipates that of Fagin in the dock, in *Oliver Twist*, Chapter 52.

8. (p. 233) *a conspiracy 'again' him* Anticipating the Artful Dodger in *Oliver Twist*, Chapter 43.

9. (p. 233) *prigging* Slang: petty thieving.

CHAPTER 25 *A Visit to Newgate*

Specially written for the first collection of *Sketches* in volume form, the First Series (February 1836).

1. (p. 234) *Bedlam . . . Aladdin's palace* Bedlam was the common name for Bethlehem Hospital, the famous lunatic asylum transferred to Lambeth in 1812–15 and today the Imperial War Museum. 'The Story of Aladdin, or the Wonderful Lamp' in *The Arabian Nights* has the genie of the lamp build a splendid palace, which is later removed to Africa on the command of a wicked magician who steals the lamp.

2. (p. 234) *Newgate* London's main prison during the eighteenth century, built in the twelfth century, destroyed by the Gordon rioters in 1780 (see *Barnaby Rudge*, Chapter 36), rebuilt 1782, and demolished with the Old Bailey in 1903 to make way for an extension of the Courts.

3. (p. 234) *Old Bailey* The street: see Chapter 24, note 5, above.

4. (p. 235) *visit . . . Newgate* Dickens's visit (with his publisher Macrone and an American journalist) took place on 5 November 1835: see Pilgrim *Letters* vol. 1, pp. 83, 97–8, 103 and 115; and Philip Collins, *Dickens and Crime*, 2nd edn. (London: Macmillan, 1965), pp. 27–41, for an account of its importance in his career. *Oliver Twist* culminates, as does this sketch, in the condemned cell at Newgate, imagining the condemned man's last thoughts and feelings. Many readers thought this the most impressive piece in the *Sketches* at the time of its appearance.

5. (p. 236) *Bishop and Williams*   Two body-snatchers, John Bishop and Thomas Head, alias Williams, hanged before a huge crowd in front of Newgate on 5 December 1831 for the murder of a young boy. See also Tales, Chapter 6, note 2.

6. (p. 236) *Jack Sheppard . . . Dick Turpin*   Sheppard (1702–24) and Turpin (1705–39) were notorious thieves and highwaymen, both hanged – the former at Tyburn, the latter at York – and made the subject of popular novels by Dickens's friend William Harrison Ainsworth (1805–82).

7. (p. 236) *Sessions-house*   Former court, and part of Newgate Prison.

8. (p. 240) *stump bedstead*   That is, without posts.

9. (p. 241) *hopeless and irreclaimable wretches*   Altered to 'hopeless creatures of neglect' for 1850 and later editions.

10. (p. 241) *Scotch cap*   Woollen cap with tails.

11. (p. 242) *'turn, and flee from the wrath to come!'*   Adapted from Matthew 3: 7; Luke 3: 7: 'O generation of vipers, who hath warned you to flee from the wrath to come?'

12. (p. 243) *ordinary's*   Prison chaplain's.

13. (p. 244) *recorder's report*   Appraisal by the recorder (or main presiding judge) at the old Sessions House, upon the circumstances of a crime, possibly leading to mitigation of sentence.

14. (p. 244) *three men*   Identified by W.J. Carlton as Robert Swan, a guardsman convicted of robbery with menaces; John Smith; and John Pratt, convicted of a homosexual offence. See *Review of English Studies*, New Series, vol. 8 (1957), pp. 402–7. Swan was reprieved by the King, as stated by Dickens's footnote.

CHARACTERS

Nine of these sketches were originally published under the heading 'Scenes and Characters' in *Bell's Life in London*, one in the *Morning Chronicle*, one in the *Evening Chronicle*, and one in the *Carlton Chronicle*. See Appendix A and individual headnotes for further details.

CHAPTER 1 *Thoughts about People*

First published in the *Evening Chronicle* (23 April 1835).

1. (p. 251) *St James's Park* One of the Royal Parks of London; south of the Mall, near Buckingham Palace.
2. (p. 252) *Bucklersbury* Street in the City, formerly the site of taverns and coffee-houses.
3. (p. 253) *Russell-square* In the prosperous central district of Bloomsbury.
4. (p. 253) *Hessian boots* High boots with tassels at the front on top; popular with military men; name derived from Hesse, in Germany.
5. (p. 254) *New Police* The Metropolitan Police, founded by Sir Robert Peel in 1829.
6. (p. 255) *Ribstone pippin* Kind of apple, from Ribston Park, Yorkshire.
7. (p. 255) *St Clement's . . . Horse Guards* Following a clearly defined route westwards along the Strand: St Clement's is St Clement Dane's, the famous seventeenth-century church in the Strand; the New Church was St Mary-le-Strand, so called because it replaced an earlier church (1714–17); Exeter' Change was on the north side of the Strand, with shops on the ground floor and an exhibition hall above; St Martin-in-the-Fields is in Trafalgar Square; the Horse Guards (1763) in Whitehall now houses the Ministry of Defence.
8. (p. 255) *Brookes's . . . Bagnigge Wells* Brooks's is a fashionable West End club founded in 1674; Snooks's means nobody's; Crockford's was a gaming club in St James's, established in 1827 and closed down in 1848; Bagnigge Wells, Islington, was a popular place of resort for the less fashionable from 1760 until its closure in 1841.
9. (p. 255) *the Quadrant* Curve in Regent Street between Piccadilly Circus and Vigo Street, formerly with arcades on either side (demolished in 1848).

CHAPTER 2 *A Christmas Dinner*

First published as 'Christmas Festivities' in *Bell's Life in London* (27 December 1835), and the first instance of Dickens's enthusiasm for the festival, anticipating the Christmas chapter (28) of *Pickwick Papers*, and his later Christmas Books and Stories.

1. (p. 260) *Burton ale*   A pale ale from Burton upon Trent, Staffordshire.
2. (p. 261) *all the homilies ... by all the Divines*   Revised to 'half the homilies ... by half the Divines' for the 1850 and later editions.

CHAPTER 3 *The New Year*

First published in *Bell's Life in London* (3 January 1836).

1. (p. 261) *thirty-six*   An error for thirty-five.
2. (p. 262) *rout-furniture-warehouse-carts*   Rout-furniture is furniture hired for 'routs' or parties: cane chairs, potted plants, etc.
3. (p. 262) *French lamps*   An improved kind of oil lamp.
4. (p. 262) *quadrille party*   Party with square dancing involving four or more couples.
5. (p. 262) *Somerset-House*   In the Strand, government office employing numerous clerks.

CHAPTER 4 *Miss Evans and the Eagle*

First published in *Bell's Life in London* (4 October 1835).

1. (p. 268) *He came, and conquered*   From Caesar's 'Veni, vidi, vici.' – 'I came, I saw, I conquered.'
2. (p. 268) *seven-and-sixpenny green ... best fresh*   Green tea was an expensive luxury, the 'best fresh' less so.
3. (p. 268) *the Eagle*   Famous tavern and pleasure garden in the City Road, with a Grecian Saloon for dancing and sideshows, attracting crowds of up to 6,000 customers a night. Demolished in 1901 and rebuilt as a public house, which still stands. Said to have gained a wide reputation through being introduced into the popular song:

> Up and down the City Road
> In and out the Eagle,
> That's the way the money goes
> Pop goes the weasel.

To 'pop' is to pawn; a 'weasel' is an iron. This verse was later modified as the well-known nursery rhyme 'Half a pound of tuppeny rice', etc. See James T. Lightwood, *Charles Dickens and Music* (London: Charles Kelly, 1912), p. 48.

4. (p. 269) *Pancras road*   In Camden, north-west London.

5. (p. 269) *the rotunda*   The large concert hall at the Eagle.

6. (p. 270) *'The soldier tired', Miss Somebody in white satin*   Popular song for soprano composed by Thomas Arne (1710–78), being his own translation of an aria from Metastasio's *Artaserse*: 'The soldier, tired of war's alarms,/ Forswears the clang of hostile arms.' Hill suggests the Miss Somebody was Miss Fraser James, whose portrait appears in Wroth's *Cremorne and the Later London Gardens* (1907).

CHAPTER 5 *The Parlour Orator*

First published as 'The Parlour' in *Bell's Life in London* (13 December 1835).

1. (p. 272) *the New-road*   Renamed Euston Road in about 1838. The lounge described takes in some seven miles from Furnival's Inn (see Preface to the First Edition, note 2), where Dickens was living at the time.

2. (p. 275) *the twenty million that was paid for 'mancipation*   The British taxpayer bore the burden of £20 million compensation paid to slave-owners as a result of the Emancipation Bill of 1833, which abolished slavery throughout the British colonies.

3. (p. 276) *what's o'clock by an eight-day*   By a clock that goes for eight days without winding up.

4. (p. 276) *window-tax*   Tax payable according to the number of windows in a house, repealed in 1851.

5. (p. 276) *beer-chiller*   Funnel-shaped vessel, actually for taking the chill off the beer.

CHAPTER 6 *The Hospital Patient*

First published in the *Carlton Chronicle* (6 August 1836).

CHAPTER 7 *Misplaced Attachment of Mr John Dounce*

First published as 'Love and Oysters' in *Bell's Life in London* (25 October 1835).

1. (p. 284) *Offley's* Well-known tavern in Henrietta Street, Covent Garden.

2. (p. 284) *Rainbow Tavern in Fleet-street* Originally a famous coffee-house dating from the seventeenth century, now demolished. In 1835 referred to simply as 'the Rainbow' by Dickens.

3. (p. 284) *Cursitor-street* Named after the cursitors or clerks who made out writs issued in the Court of Chancery. Mr Snagsby in *Bleak House*, Chapter 10, lives here. See also Tales, Chapter 10, note 27.

4. (p. 285) *Master Betty* William H. Betty (1791–1874), celebrated child actor who played most of the Shakespearian roles, retiring from the stage in 1824 – an indication of when Mr Dounce was 'a young man'.

5. (p. 288) *and the young lady said 'Ha' done, sir,' very often* Omitted from 1850 and later editions.

6. (p. 289) *'whether he was to have any gloves?'* Refers to the custom of supplying wedding guests with gloves.

CHAPTER 8 *The Mistaken Milliner*

First published as 'The Vocal Dress-maker' in *Bell's Life in London* (22 November 1835).

1. (p. 290) *Euston-square* In north Bloomsbury, near Euston Station.

2. (p. 291) *Somers-town* See Scenes, Chapter 1, note 5.

3. (p. 292) *Kidderminster carpet* From the Worcestershire town famous for its carpets.

4. (p. 292) *White Conduit* Tavern: see Scenes, Chapter 19, note 1.

5. (p. 292) *'Red Ruffian, retire!'* Unknown, probably invented to suggest popular melodrama.

6. (p. 292) *patent theatres* Having a licence under royal patent to present regular plays: Drury Lane, Covent Garden and (in summer) the Haymarket. Other theatres were subject to the Lord Chamberlain's authority.

7. (p. 293) *Signora Marro Boni* Fictitious rendering of 'marrowbone', perhaps inspired by the marrowbones and cleavers of butchers' wedding celebrations.

8. (p. 295) *'I am a Friar'* Popular song by John O'Keeffe (1747–1833), 'I am a Friar of Orders Gray'.

9. (p. 295) *'The Time of Day'* Comic duet, very popular at the Vauxhall Gardens in about 1820.

CHAPTER 9 *The Dancing Academy*

First published in *Bell's Life in London* (11 October 1835).

1. (p. 296) *'King's Theatre'* Formerly at the corner of Tottenham Street and Charlotte Street, Tottenham Court Road. Became the Queen's Theatre on Victoria's accession.

2. (p. 298) *unstamped advertisement* Until 1833 public advertisements were subject to duty, indicated by a stamp to show payment. A private placard or poster, such as that carried here, required no such stamp.

3. (p. 298) *Bethel Chapel* Dissenting or Nonconformist chapels were commonly so named (after *Bethel*, Hebrew for House of God).

4. (p. 300) *Columbine* See Scenes, Chapter 12, note 12.

5. (p. 301) *Turnstile* Passageway in central London, leading from Holborn to Newman's Row, thence to Lincoln's Inn Fields, formerly popular with tailors.

6. (p. 302) *oxalic acid* Highly poisonous, sour acid.

7. (p. 303) *Serpentine* Artificial lake in central London, between Hyde Park and Kensington Gardens.

CHAPTER 10 *Shabby-genteel People*

First published in the *Morning Chronicle* (5 November 1834).

1. (p. 304) *the statue at Charing-cross, or the pump at Aldgate* London landmarks: bronze equestrian statue of Charles I cast in 1633 and placed on its present site, facing down Whitehall, in mid eighteenth century; pump over a well near the junction of Leadenhall and Fenchurch Streets in the City of London.

2. (p. 305) *neither a philosopher, nor a political economist* Alluding to the Utilitarians, followers of Jeremy Bentham (1748–1832), who held that human conduct was motivated by self-interest. Satirized in *Oliver Twist* (for example, Chapter 43) and, most notably, *Hard Times*.

3. (p. 305) *Scott speaks in his Demonology* In the first volume of the *Letters on Demonology and Witchcraft* (1830) by Sir Walter Scott (1771–1832), a man is persecuted by the apparition of a 'gentleman-usher' in 'court dress', succeeded by that of a skeleton.

4. (p. 305) *reading-room at the British Museum* Montague House, Great Russell Street, opened in 1759, rebuilt 1823–47. The famous domed reading room was not opened until 1857. Dickens took out a reader's ticket the day after his eighteenth birthday.

5. (p. 307) *on 'Change* The Royal Exchange in the City, a trading centre from 1570 to 1939. The present building dates from 1844.

CHAPTER 11 *Making a Night of It*

First published in *Bell's Life in London* (18 October 1835).

1. (p. 308) *DAMON and Pythias* Inseparable friends: when Dionysius (405–367 BC) the Syracusan tyrant condemned Pythias to death, Damon stood surety for him, and when Pythias arrived just in time to redeem his friend, they were both spared.

2. (p. 308) *Thomas Potter* The name of a colleague of Dickens when he was a young lawyer's clerk at Ellis and Blackmore.

3. (p. 308) *slap-bang* Slang: cheap eating-house.

4. (p. 310) *the Albion* Former public house in Little Russell Street, Bloomsbury.

5. (p. 311) *the slips at the City Theatre* The seats at the sides of the gallery; the City Theatre, in a converted chapel in Milton Street, Finsbury, closed in 1835.

6. (p. 313) *patent Bramahs* After a type of lock invented by Joseph Bramah (1748–1814) and patented in 1784.

CHAPTER 12 *The Prisoners' Van*

First published in *Bell's Life in London* (29 November 1835).

1. (p. 316) *stone jug*   Slang: gaol.
2. (p. 316) *the mill's* ... *Sessions*   The treadmill (to which a magistrate would have sentenced the prisoner) is better than the Quarter Sessions at the Old Bailey, which would have handed down a longer and more serious sentence.
3. (p. 316) *Cold Bath Fields*   Prison: Metropolitan House of Correction, Coldbath Fields, Clerkenwell. See Scenes, Chapter 17, note 8.

TALES

Seven of these tales first appeared in the *Monthly Magazine*; one in *Bell's Weekly Magazine*; one in Chapman and Hall's *The Library of Fiction, or Family Story-teller*; 'The Black Veil' was written specially for the First Series; and 'The Drunkard's Death' for the Second Series. See Appendix A and individual headnotes for details.

CHAPTER I *The Boarding-house*

First published as 'The Boarding-house' and 'The Boarding-house No. 2', in the *Monthly Magazine* (May and August 1834). The latter was the first of Dickens's sketches to be signed 'Boz'. The name 'Tibbs' in this tale was used for his signature under the twelve sketches published in *Bell's Life in London* (see Appendix A).

Chapter the First

1. (p. 321) *Great Coram-street*   Bloomsbury: now Coram Street.
2. (p. 321) *stair-wires*   Stair-rods.
3. (p. 322) *the wandering Jew of Joe Millerism*   According to legend the Wandering Jew knew no rest; Joe Miller (1684–1738) was a celebrated wit whose name was appropriated for the popular collection *Joe Miller's Jests* (1739), hence a stock joke.

4. (p. 322) *French bed*   Bedstead without posts, but with scrolled ends.

5. (p. 324) *'Much linen . . . leave them neat'*   From Byron's *Don Juan* (1819–24), Canto I, stanza 143.

6. (p. 327) *the 'swell' . . . at 'Richardson's Show'*   The dandy at one of showman John Richardson's pantomimes. See also Scenes, Chapter 12, note 11.

7. (p. 327) *Bartellot's window*   Bartellot was a fashionable hairdresser at 254 Regent Street, in the West End of London.

8. (p. 329) *bucellas*   Portuguese white wine resembling hock.

9. (p. 329) *'But beef is rare . . . spits they put on'*   From Byron's *Don Juan*, Canto II, stanza 154.

10. (p. 329) *Tom Moore*   Thomas Moore (1779–1852): Irish poet whose popularity in the early nineteenth century rivalled Byron's.

11. (p. 320) *'Julia's letter'*   From Byron's *Don Juan*, Canto I, stanzas 192–7.

12. (p. 330) *the Fire Worshippers*   One of the few verse romances making up Thomas Moore's longest and best-known work, *Lalla Rookh* (1817), an Oriental fantasy.

13. (p. 330) *Paradise and the Peri*   Another of the verse romances in *Lalla Rookh*. A Peri is a spirit of the air, offspring of fallen angels.

14. (p. 330) *London University now stands*   The original site was where University College now stands, at the northern end of Gower Street, Bloomsbury.

15. (p. 330) *Lord Chesterfield's Letters*   The 4th Earl of Chesterfield (1694–1773) is best remembered as the author of *Letters* (1774), instructions to his natural son, emphasizing the importance of good breeding.

16. (p. 332) *Punch*   Hero of traditional puppet play performed in the streets by itinerant showmen. Frequently referred to in Dickens's works.

17. (p. 332) *Hamlet's . . . father's ghost*   See *Hamlet*, I.4.

18. (p. 333) *'Good God!'*   Softened to 'Good Heaven' in 1850 and later editions.

19. (p. 334) *'Oh Powers . . . upon the pair'*   From Byron's *Don Juan*, Canto IV, stanza 35.

20. (p. 334) *familiars of the Inquisition*   Veiled figures who interrogated suspects under the authority of a court set up by the Roman Catholic Church in the thirteenth century to detect and punish heresy.

21. (p. 336) *the pencil of Hogarth*   William Hogarth (1697–1764), English painter and graphic artist, much admired by Dickens for his satire.

22. (p. 337) *mantua-maker's*   Ladies' dressmaker's. The Fleet Prison, Farringdon Lane, west of the City, was a debtors' prison rebuilt in 1780 after being burnt down in the Gordon Riots. Mr Pickwick gets sent there, *Pickwick Papers*, Chapters 41–7.

Chapter the Second

23. (p. 338) *the twopenny postman*   Before the introduction of the penny post in 1840 the charge for local post in London was twopence.

24. (p. 340) *wafer*   Thin adhesive disc of flour-and-water paste for sealing letters, before the arrival of envelopes generally.

25. (p. 340) *New Saint Pancras Church*   Built in 1819–22 in the New (now Euston) Road.

26. (p. 340) *the Foundling*   The Foundling Hospital was established by Thomas Coram (?1668–1751), a retired sea-captain, for the care of unwanted children in 1741. In 1745 it moved to a site north of Guilford Street, Bloomsbury, now known as Coram's Fields.

27. (p. 341) *Pan's pipes*   See Scenes, Chapter 15, note 12.

28. (p. 341) *unitarian*   A malapropism for 'valetudinarian'.

29. (p. 344) *Columbine*   See Scenes, Chapter 12, note 12.

30. (p. 344) *installation of the Duke of Wellington ... Oxford*   In January 1834.

31. (p. 345) *journeyman Giovanni*   That is, an apprentice Don Giovanni or Don Juan.

32. (p. 346) *'The Light Guitar'*   Song by H.S. van Dyke, with music by John Barnett (1802–90).

33. (p. 346) *Woods and Forests Office*   Later merged into the Commissioners of Crown Lands.

34. (p. 347) *franks for every body in the house*   See Scenes, Chapter 18, note 17.

35. (p. 347) *Orson*   A wild man of the woods, from the popular children's story *Valentine and Orson*, based on an old French romance, in which one of a pair of twins is brought up in court, the other carried off by a bear. A favourite of Dickens, frequently alluded to, for example, *A Christmas Carol*, stave 2.

36. (p. 347) *'Di piacer'*   Popular air from Rossini's opera *The Thieving Magpie* (1817).

37. (p. 347) *like a second Nebuchadnezzar*   Daniel 4: 32: King Nebuchadnezzar in his madness 'did eat grass as oxen'.

38. (p. 348) *mandarins in a grocer's shop*   Porcelain models used by China tea merchants.

39. (p. 348) *Lindley Murray* Murray (1745–1826) was author of the standard *English Grammar* (1795).

40. (p. 349) *Lord Lieutenant's levees* Receptions held by the British sovereign's representative in Ireland.

41. (p. 350) *'Flow on, thou shining river'* From Thomas Moore's (1799–1852) *National Airs* (1815), where it appears as 'Portuguese Air'. Set to music by J.A. Stevenson (1760–1833).

42. (p. 352) *Horace* Roman poet (65–8 BC), famous for his Odes and Satires.

43. (p. 354) *Captain Ross's set-out* Spectacle entitled 'The Polar Regions' staged at Vauxhall Gardens (see Scenes, Chapter 14) in 1834 by popular Arctic explorer Sir John Ross (1777–1856).

44. (p. 354) *omnibus cads* Conductors. See Scenes, Chapter 17.

45. (p. 355) *smoke-jack* Turns a spit rotated by air rising in chimney.

46. (p. 356) *Queen Anne in the tent scene in Richard* In Shakespeare's *Richard III*, V.3, the ghost of Richard's queen appears to him before the Battle of Bosworth.

47. (p. 357) *the Phœnix* Insurance company (est. 1782), which maintained its own fire brigade and merged with the Sun and others in 1832 to form the London Fire Engine Establishment.

48. (p. 358) *register stove* Which had a movable flap preventing any such idea. See Our Parish, Chapter 3, note 2.

49. (p. 359) *tapping . . . woodpeckers* Alluding to the song 'The Woodpecker' by Thomas Moore (1779–1852), music by M. Kelly: 'Every leaf was at rest, and I heard not a sound,/But the woodpecker tapping the hollow beech tree.'

50. (p. 359) *the dragon at Astley's* Doubtless part of one of the equestrian dramas. See Scenes, Chapter 11.

51. (p. 360) *Newington Butts* Area of London south of Elephant and Castle in Lambeth.

52. (p. 360) *Walworth* Formerly a village south of London, now part of Southwark. Wemmick in *Great Expectations*, Chapter 24, lives here.

53. (p. 361) *Mr Robins* George Henry Robins (1778–1847), London auctioneer famous for his wit and eloquence.

CHAPTER 2 *Mr Minns and His Cousin*

First published as 'A Dinner at Poplar Walk' in the *Monthly Magazine* (December 1833); Dickens's first appearance as an author. Retitled for inclusion in the Second Series (see Appendix A). A facsimile of the original may be found in the *Dickensian*, vol. 30 (Summer, 1934), pp. 3–10

1. (p. 361) *inexplicables*   Euphemism for trousers.

2. (p. 361) *Somerset-house*   In the Strand; see Characters, Chapter 3, note 5.

3. (p. 361) *invested in the funds*   The national debt: investment securities.

4. (p. 363) *Stamford-hill*   Now a north London suburb.

5. (p. 364) *the deuce*   Mild oath deleted from 1850 and later editions.

6. (p. 366) *the Flowerpot*   Well-known inn in Bishopsgate, City of London, from which short-stage coaches started. Demolished in 1866.

7. (p. 366) *the Swan*   Inn at Stamford Hill in north London, stopping-place for coaches, since disappeared.

8. (p. 368) *high-lows*   See Our Parish, Chapter 4, note 4.

9. (p. 370) *Sheridan*   The dramatist and MP, about whom many lively stories survived. See Scenes, Chapter 18, note 11.

10. (p. 370) *to be, to do, or to suffer*   From Lindley Murray's *English Grammar*: see Chapter 1, note 39, above.

CHAPTER 3 *Sentiment*

First published in *Bell's Weekly Magazine* (7 June 1834).

1. (p. 373) *Hammersmith*   Riverside district of south-west London.

2. (p. 376) *the Adelphi*   Area of imposing streets south of the Strand, between Waterloo and Hungerford Bridges; built from 1768 onwards, by the brothers Robert (1728–92) and James (1730–94) Adam (Greek *adelphoi*: brothers).

3. (p. 380) *practising* l'été   The second figure in quadrilles.

4. (p. 382) *'The Recollections of Ireland'*   Unidentified compilation of songs strung loosely together under the generic title.

5. (p. 382) *Moschelles*   Ignaz Moscheles (1794–1870), Bohemian pianist and composer, who settled in England in 1826, and later taught Dickens's sister Fanny at the Royal Academy of Music.

6. (p. 386) *Ball's-pond*   District of north London near Stoke Newington; named after a pond, long disappeared, near a house kept by a John Ball.

7. (p. 386) *marriage contracted in haste, and repented at leisure*   In Congreve's *The Old Bachelor* (1693), V.8, a character remarks 'Thus grief still treads upon the heels of pleasure:/Marry'd in haste, we may repent at leisure.'

8. (p. 386) *in* statu quo   Latin: in the same state.

CHAPTER 4 *The Tuggs's at Ramsgate*

First published in Chapman and Hall's *The Library of Fiction, or Family Story-teller*, No. 1 (31 March 1836), coinciding with the first number of the same publishers' *Pickwick Papers*.

1. (p. 386) *old London Bridge*   See Scenes, Chapter 4, note 5.

2. (p. 388) *weekly Dorset*   See Scenes, Chapter 2, note 4.

3. (p. 389) *from the Temple*   Legal London: extending from the Strand to the Thames, this area of Inns of Court and chambers features frequently in Dickens's works. Originally the property of the Knights Templar, hence the name.

4. (p. 391) *Gravesend ... Margate ... Brighton ... Ramsgate*   Seaside resort towns. Brighton is on the Sussex coast, the rest are in Kent.

5. (p. 391) *the grand tour*   Tour of principal cities and sites of interest in Europe, since the eighteenth century, considered an essential part of the education of a young gentleman of good birth or fortune.

6. (p. 394) *'Fly sir?'*   A fly was originally a light, one-horse, double-seated carriage let out to hire; the term came to apply to any vehicle for hire.

7. (p. 399) *a patent Mackintosh*   The waterproofing of cloth by covering it with rubber was patented by Charles Macintosh (1766–1843).

8. (p. 399) *Pegwell?*   Pegwell Bay, a popular beach adjacent to Ramsgate.

9. (p. 404) *Rowland's Macassar Oil*   Men's hair-oil from a district in the Celebes Islands, popularized by A. Rowland of Hatton Garden, London, whose successful sales campaign drove out bear's-grease preparations.

10. (p. 404) *cloudy Berlins*   Less than clean gloves made from Berlin wool; see Scenes, Chapter 7, note 9.

11. (p. 404) *popular cavitina of 'Bid me discourse'*   Popular aria composed by Sir Henry Bishop (1786–1855) to words adapted from Shakespeare's *Venus and Adonis*, and a favourite with coloratura sopranos.

12. (p. 405) *blockade-man*   Coastguard.

CHAPTER 5 *Horatio Sparkins*

First published in the *Monthly Magazine* (February 1834).

1. (p. 409) *netting* A kind of fancy needlework.
2. (p. 409) *Juliet-like* An allusion to Shakespeare's *Romeo and Juliet* omitted from the 1850 and later editions.
3. (p. 409) *Prince Leopold* See Our Parish, Chapter 2, note 8.
4. (p. 411) *Camberwell . . . Wandsworth and Brixton* South London suburbs aspiring towards middle-class respectability.
5. (p. 411) *lion on the top of Northumberland House . . . 'going off'* In 1749 a bronze statue of a lion, crest of the Percy family, was installed over the entrance of their residence, Northumberland House, Northumberland Avenue, Charing Cross. According to Hill, there was a popular tradition that if the lion was gazed at long enough its tail would wag. The house was demolished in 1874.
6. (p. 412) *a distinguished foreigner* Possibly alluding to Hermann, Prince of Pückler-Muskau (1785–1871), who visited England in 1830, publishing his memoirs on the country and its manners shortly afterwards; also satirized as Count Smorltork in *Pickwick Papers*, Chapter 15.
7. (p. 413) *George Barnwell* Central character of George Lillo's popular domestic melodrama, *The History of George Barnwell, or The London Merchant* (1731): a London apprentice who robs his employer and murders his uncle and is eventually hanged, having maintained an air of high-minded virtue throughout. Frequently alluded to in Dickens (for example, *Great Expectations*, Chapter 15).
8. (p. 413) *the Albany* Select residential chambers adjoining Burlington House, Piccadilly, named after Frederick, Duke of York and Albany, from whose former house (built 1771–5) the chambers were adapted in 1802.
9. (p. 413) *Lord Byron* George Gordon, 6th Baron Byron of Rochdale (1788–1824), immensely popular and influential poet whose moral satire and romantic character made him both widely praised and criticized. See Chapter 1, above, for Septimus Hicks's enthusiasm for *Don Juan*.
10. (p. 413) *Montgomery* Probably the Reverend Robert Montgomery (1807–55), author of a poem entitled 'Woman, the Angel of Life' (1833).
11. (p. 413) *Captain Ross* The Arctic explorer: see Chapter 1, note 43, above. For 1850 and later editions, altered to Captain Cook, that is, James Cook (1728–79), perhaps a better known explorer.

12. (p. 414) *as a Hamlet sliding upon a bit of orange-peel* Omitted from succeeding editions.

13. (p. 416) *the whole morning* Dickens added in 1850 'after church'.

14. (p. 417) *spoffish* Slang: fussy, bustling, officious.

15. (p. 418) *Astley's* See Scenes, Chapter 11, above.

16. (p. 423) *Bedford-square* In Bloomsbury, a residence of judges. It was formed in 1775–80 as part of the Duke of Bedford's estate.

17. (p. 424) *'Fall of Paris'* 'The Surrender of Paris, a Descriptive Fantasia for the Pianoforte' (1816) by L. Jensen.

18. (p. 424) *Redmayne's, in Bond-street* West End milliner, since demolished.

19. (p. 425) *gas microscope* The oxy-hydrogen-powered microscope was patented in 1824. It is also referred to in *Pickwick Papers*, Chapter 34.

20. (p. 425) *Somerset-house exhibition* See Characters, Chapter 3, note 5; From 1780 to 1838 the Royal Academy's annual exhibitions were held here.

21. (p. 426) *Almacks* See Scenes, Chapter 9, note 1.

22. (p. 426) *north-west passage* From the Atlantic to the Pacific. Ross the Arctic explorer tried twice to navigate this passage. See note 11, above.

CHAPTER 6 *The Black Veil*

Specially written for *Sketches by Boz*, vol. 2 (February 1836), later called the First Series.

1. (p. 431) *Walworth* See Chapter 1, note 52, above.

2. (p. 433) *Burke ... Bishop* William Burke (1792–1829), Irish criminal executed in Edinburgh for conspiring with William Hare to murder people whose bodies they then sold for dissection. John Bishop was another body-snatcher who was executed in 1831 – see also Scenes, Chapter 25, note 5.

CHAPTER 7 *The Steam Excursion*

First published in the *Monthly Magazine* (October 1834). A source for the story has been proposed by Kathleen Tillotson in 'Dickens and a Story by John Poole', *Dickensian*, vol. 52 (March 1956), pp. 69–70.

1. (p. 438) *Gray's-inn-square* Named after Gray's Inn, one of the four Inns of Court in London, situated to the north of Holborn and west of

Gray's Inn Road. Dickens was a clerk in the offices of Ellis and Blackmore, 1 Raymond Building, originally off Gray's Inn Square. Mr Perker the lawyer in *Pickwick Papers* (Chapter 10) has his office there.

2. (p. 440) *spoffish*   see Chapter 5, note 14, above.

3. (p. 441) *inexplicables*   Euphemism for trousers.

4. (p. 441) *roll round his forefinger*   When men's hair was worn long and dressed with bear's grease, the ends were rolled round the forefinger to prevent a ragged appearance.

5. (p. 441) *Great Marlborough-street*   Runs east to Soho from the upper end of Regent Street in the West End; at the time, largely consisted of substantial residential houses.

6. (p. 442) *the Nore*   Thames estuary sandbank, midway between the Essex and Kent coasts, about forty-five miles below London Bridge and marked by a lightship.

7. (p. 442) *Astley-Cooperish Joe Miller*   Sir Astley Cooper (1768–1841), surgeon, noted for his humour, Joe Miller was a byword for jokes (see Chapter 1, note 3, above).

8. (p. 443) *Boswell-court*   On the north side of the Strand; swept away by the New Law Courts in 1874–82.

9. (p. 443) *Furnival's Inn*   See Preface to the First Edition, note 2.

10. (p. 443) *Montagues and Capulets*   The rival families in Shakespeare's *Romeo and Juliet*.

11. (p. 444) *Portland-street*   Like Great Marlborough Street near by, prosperous West End residential area; runs north of Oxford Circus towards Marylebone Road.

12. (p. 444) *honourable society of the Inner Temple*   One of the four legal societies (including Gray's Inn, Lincoln's Inn, and Middle Temple) with the exclusive right of calling persons to the bar (enabling them to qualify as barristers).

13. (p. 446) *the Custom-house*   In Lower Thames Street, on the north bank of the Thames, between London Bridge and the Tower of London, originating in 1385, frequently rebuilt. Peepy Jellyby gets work here in *Bleak House*, Chapter 67.

14. (p. 447) *Strand-lane*   Beside Somerset House, running from the Strand to the river bank and a pier. There was no Embankment at the time.

15. (p. 447) *Temple-bar*   Ancient gate of the City, dividing the Strand from Fleet Street. Removed in 1878. Site now marked by a Griffin, erected in 1880.

16. (p. 448) *'bonneting'*   Slang: crushing hat down over the wearer's eyes with a blow.

17. (p. 448) *'Jack-in-the-water'*　See Scenes, Chapter 10, note 5.

18. (p. 448) *Court-guide*　Directory containing names and addresses of the nobility and gentry.

19. (p. 450) *Paul — not the saint . . . Virginia notoriety. Paul et Virginie* (1788) was a sentimental prose romance by Jacques Bernardin de Saint-Pierre (1737–1814), immensely popular in the original and as translated.

20. (p. 452) *'Off she goes'*　Popular dance tune in the repertory of street musicians.

21. (p. 452) *the Pool*　Stretch of the Thames between Tower Bridge and Limehouse Reach.

22. (p. 452) *coal-whippers and ballast-heavers*　Dockers who hoist cargoes of coal on to and from ships and barges, using a pulley; a ballast of gravel or sand was used in sailing-ships with a light cargo.

23. (p. 454) *the opera of 'Paul and Virginia'*　A ballad opera based on the book (words by J. Cobb, music by W. Reeve and J. Mazzinghi) was produced in 1800. The captain sings the opening number.

24. (p. 457) *gum-gum*　Hollow iron bowl, struck with a wooden stick (probably Malay).

25. (p. 457) *Ram Chowdar Doss Azuph Al Bowlar*　Largely fanciful Oriental name, the first two names perhaps an echo of Ramachandra, hero of the *Ramayana* and a character in the *Mahabharata*, an incarnation of the Hindu god Vishnu.

26. (p. 457) *Kit-ma-gars*　Fanciful name, derived perhaps from the Magars, a people of Nepal and Sikkim.

27. (p. 463) *New Central Criminal Court*　The Old Bailey. See Scenes, Chapter 24 note 5.

CHAPTER 8 *The Great Winglebury Duel*

First published in *Sketches by Boz*, vol. 2 (February 1836) (later called the First Series) and dramatized as *The Strange Gentleman*, a comic burletta in two acts by Dickens under the pseudonym 'Boz', and first produced at the St James's Theatre (29 September 1836), where it ran for over fifty performances.

1. (p. 463) *Great Winglebury*　A fictitious town, perhaps based on Rochester.

2. (p. 468) *the wandering Jew*　See Chapter 1, note 3, above.

3. (p. 468) *Pall-mall shooting gallery*   A public gymnasium (now defunct) in this fashionable area of west (central) London.

4. (p. 469) *rig'lar*   Colloquial: a 'regular' tradesman was one who thoroughly knew his job.

5. (p. 470) *bit o' sving*   Alluding to the letters, signed 'Captain Swing', sent to farmers who introduced machinery during 1830–32, threatening to burn their ricks.

6. (p. 470) *phosphorous-box*   Supplied with a splinter of wood, forerunner of the lucifer-match of 1827, which had the phosphorous attached to its head for striking a light.

7. (p. 470) *insured in the County*   The County Fire Office was one of the earliest fire insurance firms in London.

8. (p. 470) *maintenon cutlet*   From the Marquise de Maintenon, secretly married to Louis XIV; a cutlet served with onion sauce and mushrooms.

9. (p. 471) *continuations*   Slang: stockings worn with 'shorts' or knee-breeches.

10. (p. 472) *tiger*   Young groom, so called from the black-and-yellow striped waistcoats favoured by these servants.

11. (p. 472) *Gretna Green*   Just across the Scottish border in Dumfriesshire: formerly eloping couples could marry here by simply declaring to a blacksmith, toll-keeper, etc., their willingness to do so.

12. (p. 472) *Berwick*   Berwick upon Tweed, town in the north of England, near the Scottish border.

13. (p. 473) *the brothel*   Omitted from 1850 and later editions.

14. (p. 481) *Damn*   Modified to 'Confound' in 1850 and later editions.

CHAPTER 9 *Mrs Joseph Porter*

First published as 'Mrs Joseph Porter "Over the Way"' in the *Monthly Magazine* (January 1834).

1. (p. 482) *Clapham Rise*   Probably fictitious street in residential district of Clapham, south London.

2. (p. 484) *smothering scene in 'Othello'. Othello*, V.2.

3. (p. 485) *'Masaniello'*   Hugely popular adaptation by James Kenny (1780–1849) of *La Muette de Portici* (1829: *The Dumb Girl of Portici*), an opera by Auber (see Scenes, Chapter 19, note 4), about the Neapolitan fisherman, Tommaso Aniello, who led a brief revolt against Spanish rule in 1647 before being betrayed and murdered.

4. (p. 485) *Harleigh* Probably an in-joke: John Pritt Harley (1786–1858), singer and leading comedian, was the stage-manager and principal actor at the St James's Theatre where Dickens's *The Strange Gentleman* was staged with Harley in the title-role (see headnote to Chapter 8, above).

5. (p. 485) *'Behold how brightly breaks the morning'* Aria from *Masaniello*; see note 3, above.

6. (p. 485) unâ voce Latin: with one voice, unanimously.

7. (p. 487) *'The Swan of Avon'* As Ben Jonson (1573–1637) famously referred to Shakespeare.

8. (p. 488) *'The heavens forbid . . . days do grow'* Desdemona in *Othello*, II.1.187–9.

9. (p. 489) *'The Men of Prometheus'* From the German ballet *Die Geschöpfe von Prometheus* (1801) for which Beethoven (1770–1827) wrote the music, including the overture.

10. (p. 491) *hessians* see Characters, Chapter 1, note 4.

11. (p. 491) *'Most potent, grave, and reverend . . . rude am I in my speech'* *Othello*, I.3.76–81. The missing lines are provided in the next extract.

12. (p. 493) *Swan River* In Western Australia.

CHAPTER 10 *Passage in the Life of Mr Watkins Tottle*

First published in the *Monthly Magazine* in two chapters (January–February 1835).

Chapter the First

1. (p. 494) *Richardson's novels . . . Charles Grandison* Eponymous hero of Samuel Richardson's novel (1753–4), and a model of virtue.

2. (p. 495) *Cecil-street* Formerly south of the Strand, one of a number of small streets with lodgings, turning off the main thoroughfare.

3. (p. 495) *best Walls-end·* Coal: from a famous colliery district in Northumberland.

4. (p. 495) *French bedstead* Lika a sofa, with scrolled ends.

5. (p. 496) *flat candle* In a flat candle-holder (as opposed to a candlestick).

6. (p. 496) *'the vasty deep'* Alluding to Shakespeare, *I Henry IV*, III.1.50: 'I can call spirits from the vasty deep.'

7. (p. 496) *a pair of shorts* Also knee-breeches, to make the pun.

8. (p. 496) *damn*   Replaced by 'hate' for 1850 and later editions.

9. (p. 497) *front*   Band of false hair, often curls, worn by women across the forehead.

10. (p. 500) *Lucretia*   Model of chastity. See Scenes, Chapter 12, note 5.

11. (p. 500) *Norwood*   Prosperous south-east London suburb.

12. (p. 501) *sugar-baker*   Sugar refiner or confectioner.

13. (p. 502) *Strephon*   Devoted love, from the character of that name in Sir Philip Sidney's pastoral romance *Arcadia* (1590).

14. (p. 502) *charity . . . multitude of sins*   1 Peter 4: 8.

15. (p. 503) *'like sending them ruffles when wanting a shirt'*   From *The Haunch of Venison* (1770), a poetical epistle by the Irish poet, dramatist and novelist, Oliver Goldsmith (?1730–74), whose works Dickens knew from boyhood, and to which he often refers.

16. (p. 505) *Macassar*   Hair-oil. See Chapter 4, note 9, above.

17. (p. 506) *Kensington Gardens*   Adjoining Hyde Park, and attached to Kensington Palace, London: gardens laid out in the reign of William III (1650–1702), subsequently extended and opened to the public.

18. (p. 506) *Hampstead-heath*   Large open area of heath and woodland in north London, between Hampstead and Highgate villages (as they then were).

19. (p. 506) *damning*   Modified to 'execrating' in 1850 and later editions.

20. (p. 507) *God*   Modified to 'Heaven' in 1850 and later editions.

21. (p. 508) *kerseymere*   Fine woollen cloth, from 'cassimere', another form of cashmere, by association with the rougher 'kersey' wool (see Our Parish, Chapter 3, note 6).

22. (p. 508) *being a clergyman*   Omitted from 1850 and later editions, perhaps to modify the implied criticism of the Church: Dickens preferred to attack dissenters for their strictness.

23. (p. 509) *Beulah Spa*   See Scenes, Chapter 5, note 7.

Chapter the Second

24. (p. 509) *Petersham great-coat*   . See Scenes, Chapter 15, note 8.

25. (p. 510) *painted tops*   See Scenes, Chapter 6, note 4.

26. (p. 510) *and I wish you may*   Popular catch-phrase: 'I wish you may have luck.' Here, in discharging your debts.

27. (p. 510) *lock-up house in . . . Chancery-lane*   House kept by a sheriff's officer for the preliminary confinement of debtors. If they were unable to raise money to discharge their debts, they were then transferred to a debtors' prison, as happened to Dickens's father after three days' detention in 1824.

The lock-up here is confirmed a few sentences on to be in Cursitor Street (see Characters, Chapter 7, note 3), which runs off Chancery Lane. In November 1834, Dickens had to bail out his father at Abraham Soloman's 'sponging-house' at 4 Cursitor Street: clearly the model for Solomon Jacobs's lock-up. See Pilgrim *Letters*, vol. 1, pp. 44ff.

28. (p. 510) *Mercury*   Ironic reference to classical deity who was the messenger of the gods.

29. (p. 513) *'chilling'*   Warming, having the chill taken off.

30. (p. 514) *Islington*   District of north London.

31. (p. 514) *Royal George . . . bailed out*   See Scenes, Chapter 10, note 8. Repeated attempts were made to salvage the ship up until 1840.

32. (p. 516) *milk-walk*   Delivering milk to private homes.

33. (p. 516) *coal and 'tatur line*   Cockney slang: delivering coal and potatoes.

34. (p. 517) *going over the water*   To one of the debtors' prisons.

35. (p. 517) *made my lucky*   Thieves' slang: escaped.

36. (p. 518) *raised the vind*   Slang: obtained the money.

37. (p. 519) *mould candles*   Made by pouring wax into the mould (and not by dipping the wick).

38. (p. 520) *unmentionable*   Euphemism for trouser.

39. (p. 520) *37l. 3s. 10d.*   Since the original debt was £33 10s 4d, Tottle has accumulated a further £3 13s 6d for a few hours' stay in the lock-up house.

40. (p. 524) *Bury St Edmund's*   Ancient market town in west Suffolk. Dickens stayed there in 1835 while reporting a parliamentary election. Nearby Sudbury was the basis of Eatanswill in *Pickwick Papers*, Chapters 13 and 15.

41. (p. 526) *watch-guard*   Used for securing a watch worn on the person; often a ribbon or small chain.

42. (p. 531) *Richardsonian principle*   That is, according to the epistolary method; alluding to the novels of Samuel Richardson (1689–1761).

43. (p. 531) *like a fancy cocked-hat*   Folded three times instead of being put into an envelope.

44. (p. 535) *Regent's canal*   Opened in 1820, it runs between Paddington in west London, and Limehouse in the east, where it joins the Thames.

CHAPTER 11 *The Bloomsbury Christening*

First published in the *Monthly Magazine* (April 1834).

1. (p. 535) *'The Christening' was first represented*   Referring to a popular dramatization of Dickens's story by the playwright and comedian John Buckstone (1802–79), first performed on 13 October 1834 at the Adelphi Theatre and later published without acknowledgement. Dickens took the piracy in good humour.

2. (p. 537) *Pentonville*   One of the earliest planned suburbs of London, lying north of the City, and named after Henry Penton, MP, whose estate was developed in 1773.

3. (p. 537) *Hoyle*   Edmund Hoyle (1672–1769), an authority on whist, the rules of which he standardized.

4. (p. 537) *massacre of the innocents*   See Matthew 2: 2–16. Herod ordered the slaughter of the children of Bethlehem so as to destroy his rival, the 'king of the Jews'.

5. (p. 537) *Society for the Suppression of Vice*   Originally the Proclamation Society, founded in 1787 by William Wilberforce (1759–1833), as one of a number of lay and clerical organizations aimed at transforming the morals of the nation.

6. (p. 537) *two itinerant methodist parsons*   The term 'methodist' was loosely used to attack extremes of Evangelical fervour. Nicodemus' name refers to the 'new birth' doctrine favoured by the Evangelicals (see John 3: 3–5).

7. (p. 538) *'Bedford-square'* ... *'Tottenham-court-road'*   Bedford Square was a select Bloomsbury address (see Chapter 5, note 16, above), superior to nearby Tottenham Court Road.

8. (p. 539) *bills of mortality*   Official returns of deaths in the district.

9. (p. 540) *Saint George's church, in Hart-street*   St George's Bloomsbury, as it is known, was designed by Nicholas Hawksmoor in 1720–30, and stands in what is now called Bloomsbury Way.

10. (p. 541) *First Cause*   That is, God the Creator.

11. (p. 541) *Bluchers*   See Scenes, Chapter 5, note 12.

12. (p. 541) *Mansion-house*   In the City: official residence of the Lord Mayor of London, built in 1739–53.

13. (p. 541) *Cheapside*   Street in the City, near St Paul's Cathedral. Former market site.

14. (p. 541) *mysterious picture* ... *Mrs Radcliffe's castles*   Refers to the picture behind 'a veil of black silk' in the castle that so frightens the heroine of *The Mysteries of Udolpho* (1794) by Ann Radcliffe (1764–1823).

15. (p. 542) *Serpentine*　See Characters, Chapter 9, note 7.

16. (p. 542) *'Jack-in-the-green', on May-day*　See Scenes, Chapter 20, note 3.

17. (p. 544) *St Giles's church*　West of Drury Lane and still standing between Shaftesbury Avenue, Charing Cross Road, and St Giles High Street, built in 1731–3.

18. (p. 544) *(Edgeware) Road*　The Edgware Road runs north from Oxford Street.

19. (p. 547) *renounce the devil and all his works*　From the Book of Common Prayer: Service for Baptism.

20. (p. 547) *down Snow-hill, and up Holborn ditto*　A steep walk, before Holborn Viaduct spanned the valley of the river Fleet, in 1869.

21. (p. 548) *toque*　Woman's round brimless hat, often quite elaborate.

22. (p. 549) *Desdemona with the pillow over her mouth*　See *Othello*, V. 2.

23. (p. 551) nem. con.　Latin: *nemine contradicente*: no one contradicting.

24. (p. 551) *'We met'*　From the well-known ballad by Nathaniel Thomas Haynes Bayly (1797–1839), 'We met – 'twas in a Crowd'.

25. (p. 551) *'I saw her at the Fancy Fair'*　Inaccurate rendition of humorous ballad by Bayly, 'I saw her as I fancied, fair'.

26. (p. 552) *like the ghost in Don Juan*　Alluding to the frightening final scene of Mozart's opera *Don Giovanni* (1787) in which the dead Commendatore's statue arrives to supper.

27. (p. 553) *to have a thankless child*　See *King Lear*, I.4.285–6.

CHAPTER 12 *The Drunkard's Death*

Specially written as the last of the Second Series (December 1836) [1837], 'to finish the volume with *eclat*', said Dickens: Pilgrim *Letters*, vol. 1, p. 208 (7 December 1836).

1. (p. 558) *Whitefriars*　Slum district between Fleet Street and the Thames, so named after the Carmelite friary that once stood on the site. Cleared and rebuilt during the nineteenth century.

2. (p. 565) *Waterloo Bridge*　See Scenes, Chapter 4, note 4.